Ahearn leaned away ... "They're heading back th...

Nolus and Druadaen tu...ed, eyes tracking along the direction set by the swordsman's finger.

The other ship had tacked across the wind but, being close-hauled as she angled back northward, she was struggling to make headway.

In the next instant, the waters swirled and rose in a fitful black surge a dozen yards to the port side of the struggling boat—and then subsided.

"All hands to deck! Arms at the ready!" Captain Nolus shouted.

—Just as a sinuous shape slid up out of the water on the other side of the fleeing vessel, like a tapered snake of immense proportions. It reared back, poised like a cobra.

The towering black tentacle crashed down athwart the shallop's keel. Planking and strakes flew up in a shower of gleaming fragments. The hull snapped in two with a crack like thunder and less resistance than a toy caught beneath a wagon wheel. With a gurgling rush, dark water surged into the two halves of the ship, bow and stern rising as it did. Figures struggled in the distempered swells between them, screaming.

Ahearn uttered an oath and reached for the hilt of his sword. His hand stopped halfway; assessment had apparently overridden instinct, showing him the futility of that reflex.

From the other side of the sinking wreck, another tentacle jetted up out of the water, but rose to twice the height and steadily widened as it did. Druadaen swallowed; the still-unrevealed creature was many times larger than its first attack had suggested...

BAEN BOOKS by CHARLES E. GANNON

THE VORTEX OF WORLDS SERIES
This Broken World • *Into the Vortex*
Toward the Maw. forthcoming

THE TERRAN REPUBLIC SERIES
Fire with Fire • *Trial by Fire* • *Raising Caine*
Caine's Mutiny • *Marque of Caine*
Endangered Species • *Protected Species*
Killer Species, forthcoming
Misbegotten (with David Weber), forthcoming

OTHER BOOKS IN THE TERRAN REPUBLIC SERIES
Murphy's Lawless (with Griffin Barber, Kacey Ezell,
Kevin Ikenberry, Chris Kennedy,
Mike Massa & Mark Wandrey)
Watch the Skies (with Kacey Ezell,
Kevin Ikenberry & William Ian Webb)
Mission Critical (with Griffin Barber,
Chris Kennedy, and Mike Massa; forthcoming)
Admiral and Commander (with Chris Kennedy)

THE RING OF FIRE SERIES (WITH ERIC FLINT)
1635: The Papal Stakes
1636: Commander Cantrell in the West Indies
1636: The Vatican Sanction
1637: No Peace Beyond the Line
1636: Calabar's War (with Robert Waters)

JOHN RINGO'S BLACK TIDE RISING SERIES
At the End of the World
At the End of the Journey

THE STARFIRE SERIES (WITH STEVE WHITE)
Extremis • *Imperative* • *Oblivion*

To purchase any of these titles in e-book form,
please go to www.baen.com.

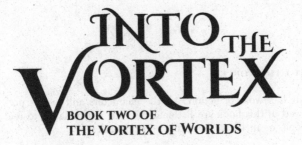

INTO THE VORTEX

BOOK TWO OF
THE VORTEX OF WORLDS

CHARLES E. GANNON

INTO THE VORTEX

This is a work of fiction. All the characters and events portrayed in this book are fictional, and any resemblance to real people or incidents is purely coincidental.

Copyright © 2023 by Charles E. Gannon

All rights reserved, including the right to reproduce this book or portions thereof in any form.

A Baen Books Original

Baen Publishing Enterprises
P.O. Box 1403
Riverdale, NY 10471
www.baen.com

ISBN: 978-1-9821-9346-1

Cover art by Kurt Miller
Maps by Rhys Davies

First printing, March 2023
First mass market printing, June 2024

Distributed by Simon & Schuster
1230 Avenue of the Americas
New York, NY 10020

Library of Congress Control Number: 2022056097

Printed in the United States of America
10 9 8 7 6 5 4 3 2 1

This book is dedicated to my dear friend
and mentor-colleague Eric Flint, who
passed on as I was completing this book.
Words cannot begin to compass the depth of
his compassion, the breadth of his intellect, the
unalloyed integrity at his core or, especially,
the staggering generosity—particularly to new
writers or friends in need. I miss you every
day, Eric . . . and those who do are legion.

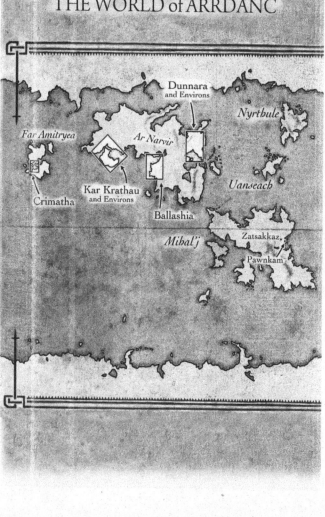

THE WORLD of ARRDANC

(POST CATACLYSM)

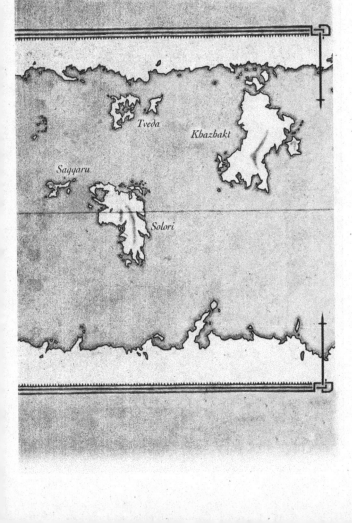

Tveda

Khazhakt

Saqqaru

Solori

BALLASHIA and MIRROSKYE

MEDVIR BIGHT

DAVYARA-NADIA

Porsyolti

Esléntecrë

THE MIRROSKYE

F'Shéssa

MIRROSKYE

Kœsdri'yrm

THE WILDS

RETTARISHA

TARUILDOR

SHAPNAPA
DESERT

VARDA

Olthrafarg

Yu'Serda

T'ORIDREA

to ANATHA
DAMIANNA
↓

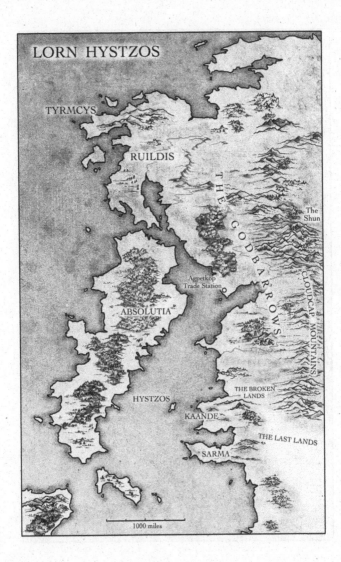

LORN HYSTZOS

TYRMCYS

RUILDIS

THE GODBARROWS

The Shun

Agpetkop
Trade Station

ABSOLUTIA

CLOUDCAP MOUNTAINS

HYSTZOS

THE BROKEN
LANDS

KAANDE

THE LAST LANDS

SARMA

1000 miles

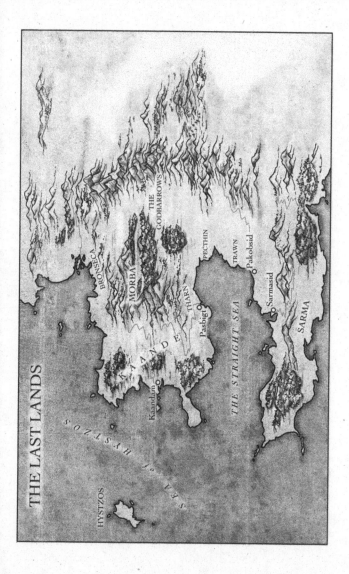

PART ONE
SHADOWMERE

CHAPTER ONE

"Hey-o, Philosopher, your relief is here!"

Druadaen turned at the sound of Ahearn's voice, rising up from the aft companionway that descended into the *Atremoënse*'s darkened sterncastle. The ship's Corrovani captain glanced over the forward rail of the quarterdeck, frowning down upon the unwonted loudness. "Outrider Druadaen," he muttered loudly, "I trust you shall better marshal your companions. We run dark and quiet when navigating the Passwater at night."

Ahearn's head popped up from the companionway. "What's that now, Captain? Are my good spirits an annoyance?"

"Your good spirits are your own business." The captain's tone was grim, even for a Corrovani. "But to shout about them is against the orders I gave earlier. And insofar as you travel free of fare, I expect not merely adequate, but grateful, compliance."

Ahearn's broad face, lit only by the dim glow of

the two moons sinking toward the dove-gray predawn horizon, conveyed his response: one raised eyebrow.

The captain glared at the swordsman, then Druadaen. "I require that your companions make their intent to comply explicit, Master Outrider!"

"I shall urge them to do so," Druadaen answered with a shallow nod, "but as you say, they are my *companions*, not my servitors."

The Corrovani snorted. "Whatever your arrangement, they follow you readily enough. Despite your casual exercise of authority."

Ahearn glanced up at the much older man. "Aye, an' that's no small part of *why* we follow him."

The captain stiffened, raised his chin—

"Captain Nolus," Druadaen interjected before that worthy could speak, "I'm sure Ahearn's, er, outburst was an oversight caused by eagerness to stand on dry land once again. The last hours are the hardest to wait through, and I suspect that all of us shore-lovers are a bit distracted."

"Aye," Ahearn mumbled with his back to the Corrovani and a grin on his face, "very distracted."

"Well, then, Master Ahearn, I trust you will henceforth follow the orders I gave last night."

"That I will, sahr. No lights, no loud voices, no clumping about the decks or down below." He looked back up at the captain. "Ye've my word on it, Captain."

Nolus nodded curtly and returned to the con, where the pilot was busy keeping them to the northern edge of the strait known as the Passwater.

"*Teeesht*, but his codpiece must chafe," Ahearn hissed at Druadaen. "And I didn't take him for the superstitious type."

Druadaen leaned on the gunwale, looked at the southern landmass coming into view. "I'm not sure he is."

Ahearn's head cocked back in surprise. "Here, now: surely the Dunarran Philosopher doesn't pay any never-mind to sailor's tales!"

Druadaen shrugged. "If tales they are. The waters around Shadowmere have a grim reputation."

"Aye, as well as the island on which it sits. And the moat around it. And the buildings in it. And the great majority of its inhabitants. No doubt its lapdogs and housecats are equally fearsome."

Druadaen couldn't keep from grinning. "No doubt. But you heard Tharêdæath's warning before he doubled back to Dunarra. 'In Shadowmere—'"

"'—nothing is as it seems.'" Ahearn crossed his thick arms. "I was surprised that he'd spout such superstitions, but it seems that even an Uulamantre can't resist speaking darkly about the city. And making warding signs as they do."

"Tharêdæath made no warding signs."

"And you criticize *me* for being too literal? Shame on yer lofty self!"

Druadaen nodded at the dark coast. "Still, when anyone of Tharêdæath's years and experience gives a warning, I don't disregard it out of hand." The lights dotting the black inland reaches were far back from its shore's most dramatic feature: a steep promontory that plunged down into the equally black waters the captain insisted on skirting. "Besides, there are dozens of accounts in the Archive Recondite which make it quite clear that—"

"Tell me you're *not* about to quote the same scholars

who you've proven to be wrong about almost everything?" Ahearn's incredulity was loud enough to draw a sharp glance from Nolus.

Druadaen shook his head, but grinned, too. "When scholars draw upon ships' logs and incidents reported by multiple observers, I don't dismiss them out of hand."

"Fine for you, but I'll put my faith in the locals," Ahearn countered, nodding toward the low-sided shallop that had drawn abeam, crowding sail it sheered off toward the southern landmass.

Druadaen didn't point out that there was no way to know if the ship in question was truly "local." The *Atremoënse* had been passing such boats ever since they'd entered the long strait that cut through the continent of Far Amitryea from east to west: the Earthrift Channel. A natural artery for trade and schools of migrating fish, its fickle winds and narrow stretches favored small hulls rigged to catch the wind from all angles.

Nolus had overheard. "That boat is not 'local,' but from back Dorzhena-way," he asserted. "Unlikely they're in these waters much. Pilot!" he growled to the man at the wheel. "Give me another point to starboard."

"Aye, Captain. With respect, sir, that puts us at the edge of the shallows."

Nolus shook his head. "We've a mile and more before they're a worry. Besides, better risking the shallows than the deeps around Dasgal's Mantle."

Ahearn squinted up at him. "Around what?"

Nolus pointed south at the sheer-sided promontory. "That headland."

"Aye, but . . . 'Mantle'?"

"Do you not see the shape? Like the body of a squid?"

Ahearn peered at it, shook his head. "Don't see it."

Nolus' smile was mirthless. "You might, yet."

Druadaen turned to him. "I've seen the name on charts, but who or what is Dasgal?"

The captain glanced down. "You've not heard of Dasgal's Kraken?"

Ahearn rolled his eyes, shook his head by way of response.

Nolus answered with a shake of his own. "I'm surprised Dunarra would send an Outrider to Far Amitryea without knowing that."

Druadaen did not point out that his first official assignment to Far Amitryea had simply been an ill-disguised excuse to send him away from his homeland. This second journey, while entirely voluntary, was also far more needful. The same incident that resulted in his being driven from Dunarra by the proverbial stick of official displeasure had also precipitated an equally proverbial carrot: his present invitation to Shadowmere, tendered by its enigmatic Lady of the Mirror.

But Druadaen had boarded the *Atremoënse* determined not to share these tangled details with Nolus or his crew, and he had no reason to revisit that decision now. He simply shook his head, reaffirming, "I have never heard of Dasgal's Kraken."

The captain didn't respond, however. He was staring at the shallop. It was marked by two stern lights that guttered sharply in the breeze as it heeled harder southward. Nolus strangled what should have been a shout into a loud, hoarse growl: "Those idiots! They'll get us all killed!"

"Perhaps they haven't heard of Dasgal's Kraken, either," Ahearn speculated, following the boat's speedy progress. His voice was innocent; his averted face wore a mischievous grin.

"Make sport at your peril, Swordsman," Nolus snapped. "Outrider Druadaen, you'd do better by having better friends. Now, about Dasgal," he muttered, not seeing Ahearn's hard, resentful glance. "He was a figure of some importance in one of Amitryea's many wars. Some accounts say he made an ally of the Kraken. Others say that he was its enemy and found a way to bind it forever in the Mere-Moat that surrounds Shadowmere.

"Whatever the details might be, the Kraken that Dasgal put in this place"—he waved at the black land beyond the receding shallop—"dwells there still, over a thousand years later."

Coming to stand beside Druadaen, Ahearn had to duck his head so that the quaking of his neck and shoulders might not betray his muffled laughter.

"And what of the Kraken now?" prompted Druadaen, trying to keep Nolus' focus upon him. "Is it still seen?"

The Corrovani captain shrugged. "Rarely, and there's no knowing if it's the original or its malicious progeny. It's rarer still that any live to tell of it; the waters around Dasgal's Mantle remain as dangerous as they ever were. At night or in the mist—but especially when both render mariners blind—ships go missing without a trace. Sometimes driftwood washes up on the island's northern shores. Sometimes a crewman's body rises to the inky surface of the Mere-Moat. And I ask you, how would it get there unless dragged into the black trenches that wind beneath the island?" He shook his head. "You'll find few sailors in Shadowmere who think it something other than the Kraken's handiwork."

"Or maybe some other creature?" Druadaen wondered aloud.

"Mayhap, mayhap," Nolus agreed with a glum nod. "But if the Kraken—"

Ahearn leaned away from the gunwale, pointing. "They're heading back this way."

Nolus and Druadaen turned, eyes tracking along the direction set by the swordsman's finger.

The shallop had tacked across the wind but, being close-hauled as she angled back northward, she was struggling to make headway.

Nolus advanced to the quarterdeck's rail like a sleepwalker. "By the Helpers, no..." Druadaen could not tell whether the captain's entreaty was profane or genuine.

In the next instant, the question became moot; the water swirled and rose in a fitful black surge a dozen yards to the port side of the struggling boat—and then subsided.

"Is that the—?" the pilot began.

"All hands to deck! Arms at the ready!" Nolus interrupted.

—Just as a sinuous shape slid up out of the water on the other side of the fleeing vessel, like a tapered snake of immense proportions. It reared back, poised like a cobra.

The quarterdeck's alarm gong sounded; rather than quietly going below to rouse the crew, the pilot had resorted to the fastest but much louder means.

Nolus shouted for him to stop.

The towering black tentacle crashed down athwart the shallop's keel. Planking and strakes flew up in a shower of gleaming fragments. The hull snapped in two with a crack like thunder and less resistance than a toy caught beneath a wagon wheel. With a gurgling rush, dark water surged into the two halves of the ship, bow and stern rising as it did. Figures struggled in the distempered swells between them, screaming and reaching out toward the distant *Atremoënse*.

Ahearn uttered an oath and reached for the hilt of his sword. His hand stopped halfway; assessment had apparently overridden instinct, showing him the futility of that reflex.

From the other side of the sinking wreck, another tentacle jetted up out of the water, but rose to twice the height and steadily widened as it did. Druadaen swallowed; the still-unrevealed creature was many times larger than its first attack had suggested. The slick black appendage passed appraisingly over the debris in the water then swept across it, rather than down.

As it grazed the surface, the tentacle's underside turned sideways. It was not furnished with suckers, but questing radial clusters of hooks and barbs that snapped like bear traps upon whatever they touched. They caught up a good amount of shattered wood, but mostly pincered or impaled the boat's struggling crewmen before pulling them down under the low swells.

Feet thudded on the deck behind Druadaen. Familiar voices cursed, gasped, or managed to do both simultaneously.

"First Bole," S'ythreni's voice hissed at his ear, "is that Dasgal's Kraken?"

Leave it to an Iava to know ancient lore, Druadaen thought. But his reply was, "Possibly."

Umkhira drew up to the gunwale on his other side. "Elweyr," she said hoarsely over her shoulder, "can your mancery protect us from that?"

"I wouldn't know where to begin," the thaumantic muttered through chattering teeth.

Druadaen heard Nolus muttering to a crewman at the base of the quarterdeck stairs. "Shorten sail by half, Master."

"But sir, we'll be near dead in the water!" The pilot managed to make his exclamation a loud whisper.

"I'll ask for your advice when and if I want it. Tend to your wheel. Prepare to give me two more points starboard. And gently! Leave a wake and I'll feed your fingers to sharks."

"I'm with the pilot," Ahearn grumbled. "The faster we move away from that beast, the better."

Druadaen shook his head. "Nolus knows what he's about."

Ahearn's Adam's apple worked rapidly. "Which is?"

"Trying not to attract the beast's attention." Druadaen shot a glance upward at the furling mainsails. "Even at this hour, with the moons still up, that square-rigged canvas is like a bright flag and a strong gust will set it flapping loudly. Best to bear away into a gradual turn and leave a small wake."

Despite having little knowledge of ships, Umkhira nodded her understanding. "I have hunted many creatures that are not easily distracted from a kill, but once they are, that distraction becomes their new quarry."

As if to underscore the creature's fixation upon its present prey, three tentacles breached the surface with a blast of foam and spray, curled around the rapidly sinking halves of the boat and drew them—and the howling men clinging to them—under the risers so abruptly that twin geysers shot up.

A few paddling survivors waved to the *Atremoënse*, their distant cries so faint that Druadaen could not make out the words, only that they were desperate, weeping entreaties.

A tentacle slipped up to sweep the surface and, almost as a lazy afterthought, gathered them down into the lightless depths.

Only then did Druadaen realize that the innocuous mirror-steel bracer around his wrist had unfurled into its true form: the small metallic dragon shape that the Uulamantre called a velene. Its neck was fully extended, its long snout questing until the last ripples of the creature had subsided and the sea was calm again.

"Now can we go a little faster?" Ahearn muttered as if he hoped for the captain to overhear.

"No need," Druadaen answered, nodding toward the enigmatic velene as it transitioned back to a bracer in the blink of an eye. "The danger is past."

CHAPTER TWO

The rising sun chased the moons out of the sky, sending bronze and gold glitters skipping along the risers of the Passwater as they rubbed gently against the *Atremoënse*'s transom. For the third time, Captain Nolus measured the distance to the town-crowded northern coast. Nodding to himself, he finally let some of the crew go back to their hammocks. All accounts agreed that once the black swells around Dasgal's Mantle dropped out of sight, a ship was once again in waters that had never been frequented by the Kraken or any other reputed cryptigants. The other measure of reaching safety was being able to spy the tower-tops of Shadowmere. Glittering in the dawn, they had just begun to peek over the low bluffs that were the city's wind-brake.

When he was done sorting out the revised watches, the captain turned toward Druadaen and his companions. "You were wise not to flee," he observed soberly.

"Flee?" Druadaen asked. "Where would we have fled?"

Nolus shrugged. "After spying the Kraken, there's many that have taken their chances in small boats when their ships slowed."

"Hard to believe there are such foolish people in the world," Elweyr sighed.

"I'll grant you this," the captain rejoined, "nothing brings out more panic and stupidity in land-lovers than trouble a-sea. So maybe I've seen them at their worst."

"Still," Umkhira asserted, "we would not have fled. You agreed to carry us if we swore to help protect your ship from any dangers that might arise during the journey. We are our word...or we are nothing."

"Speak for yourself," S'ythreni muttered, looking away.

Umkhira glanced at her; in earlier times, she would have frowned at such a comment, but now she merely smiled ruefully. "You have never once failed to stand with us in the face of death. Not *once*."

S'ythreni shrugged diffidently. "All that proves is that I'm too stupid to learn from my mistakes."

But Nolus was shaking his head. "I agree with your *ur zhog* companion, Mistress Iava. I've seen cowards aplenty in my time. You are not cut from that cloth." He glanced around the group. "None of you are. Although some of you are damnably loud at times." He did not look at Ahearn, but he hardly needed to.

The swordsman rolled his eyes, but this time with a smile. "Aye, I tend not to be a retiring sort, Captain."

Now Nolus looked at him. "I have noticed that." It might have been serious or it might have been ironic; there was no telling with the Corrovani mariner.

Ahearn elected to interpret it congenially. "Well, then, Captain, you'll not be surprised that I've a question: When do we get to the docks and debark?"

"Those are two different questions, Master Swordsman. And both are subject to considerable uncertainty."

"Such as?" S'ythreni's murmur had a discernible edge. The Corrovani tendencies toward both seriousness and literalism rarely failed to chaff her.

The captain shrugged. "If word reaches the harbor mistress that the Kraken's been sighted, she might close the gates. No way of knowing how long until she reopens them. Or how many hulls will be in the queue before us, either. And I'm not going to tie up at the north slips."

"The what?" asked Umkhira.

"Berths outside the city walls. Well, outside the moat."

Umkhira squinted at his correction. "This city has a moat, but no walls?"

"Shadowmere doesn't need walls, Mistress Light-strider," he said, using the common name for her people, who lived above- rather than below-ground. "Not given what lives in its moat."

"And what would that be?" S'ythreni asked through what might have been a real—or feigned—yawn.

"Very likely the Kraken itself. And its brood."

"What?" Umkhira said with a start. "It swims out so far as we saw? And how does it get past the harbor gates?"

S'ythreni was grinning at her friend's gullibility until Elweyr shook his head. "It doesn't have to. As the captain mentioned, it's rumored that parts of the Passwater connect to passages under the island. Some are said to run all the way out to the ocean on the far side."

When incredulous eyes turned toward Nolus, he simply shrugged. "So say those who've sailed these waters all their lives."

Ahearn was tapping his toe impatiently. "Good captain, I shall rephrase my original question: Can we hope to feel land under our feet by sunset?"

Nolus thought, then nodded. "I can think of no reason why that should not be the case. Well before, in fact. But I reiterate my warning: it is unlikely that I shall be able to tie up near the tower that the Lady of the Mirror calls home."

S'ythreni shrugged. "No matter. I should like to stretch my legs a bit before climbing the stairs of any tower."

The captain's brow furrowed. "Just so you're aware, Mistress Iava: its actual name is not the Lady's Tower, but Moorax Tower."

She looked at Druadaen, then Elweyr. "Is nothing straightforward in this accursed city?"

Druadaen smiled. "Perhaps," he said to Nolus, "you would be so kind as to tell us why it is not named for the Lady who presides over it?"

"Because the tower is defined not by any one of the Ladies—or occasionally, Lords—who've overseen it, but the Mirror for which it's famous."

"Then why isn't it called the Tower of the Mirror?" An edge of exasperation was growing in Ahearn's voice.

"Well, in fact, some do."

Druadaen frowned. "But you just told us it was called Moorax Tower. Why?"

S'ythreni stared at him. "You had to ask." She tapped

her forehead with her forefinger. "Wait, of course you did, because you can't ignore a mystery—or shorten the tedium as we wait for you to solve it."

If Nolus noticed the half-serious asperity in S'ythreni's voice, he elected not to show it. "The legend is that long ago, when the city's defenders were on the verge of being overthrown by a powerful mantic, the leader of the Galspearrean Guild—a fellow named Dakon—was mortally wounded. He asked his honor guard to prop him up and he hurled his axe into the bay and instructed that wheresoever it fell, they should build a great tower."

"Wait." Elweyr, who was typically quiet and even cautious, sounded impatient. "Are you telling us that Moorax Tower got its name because ... well, because it's moored to an axe?"

Nolus frowned, as if the question was too obvious to warrant asking. "Aye. Of course. Well, maybe not *literally* moored to it."

"Oh, well," S'ythreni exclaimed with a painfully bright smile, "that makes *much* more sense." Anyone who knew her well would have known that her reasonable tone indicated she was being savagely facetious.

Druadaen hoped to fill in the silence before the captain detected that undercurrent. "Thank you. We shall bear those distinctions in mind when we go in search of it."

"Well, it's not hard to find. It's at the north end of the protected docks. It is the highest tower in the city but also one of the most slender. Now, I've a ship to run and a pilot to chasten." With a nod, he marched up the stairs to the quarterdeck.

Druadaen meant to follow the captain's upward

progress, but his gaze lingered on the glittering waters
behind them, as it so often did. While the others
wandered away from the gunwale, Druadaen scanned
aft; no silhouettes marred the shining, swell-ripped
expanse or troubled the perfect line of the horizon.

"No sign of them astern," Ahearn murmured from
behind; he'd not kept up with the rest of their company.

"I know," Druadaen murmured back.

"You should. That's at least the fifth time you've
checked since the start of the afternoon watch yesterday." Ahearn glanced down at the bracer-shaped
velene on his friend's arm. "And nothing from the
silver beastie? No dreams or visions of where they
might be?"

Druadaen shook his head. "Nothing. Not since
Tharêdæath left us at Ereolant."

Ahearn sucked his teeth. "Convenient how that Iavan
ship just happened to be waiting there, bound back
north to Dunarra." He stared sideways at Druadaen.

Druadaen shrugged. "The Iavarain—but particularly
the Uulamantre—have a sense for where others of
their kind are located. That's how S'ythreni led us to
Tharêdæath in the first place."

Ahearn raised an eyebrow. "Even so, that ship being
in just the right port at just the right time? 'Twas too
lucky for it to be 'luck.'"

Druadaen shook his head. "Maybe so, maybe not.
Ereolant has a large population of Iavarain, mostly
aeostu. And it's home to more Uulamantrene hulls
than anywhere else on Arrdanc, save Mirroskye."

Ahearn stared aft, his chin out. "Say what you will,
Philosopher, but where Uulamantre go, mancery seems
to follow—or is already there waiting for them."

Druadaen smiled. "Well, we're in agreement on that, at least."

Ahearn nodded, glanced sideways. "So, are you finally going to attend to that scribbling you've been putting off?"

Druadaen felt his stomach knotting. "What do you mean, 'putting off'?"

"Now, don't play the innocent Dunarran schoolboy with me, mate. Until we left the wharf at Tlulanxu, you were ever and again scribbling in that journal of yours. But since then, you've been holding off, waiting until you saw some sign that your uncle had caught up to us."

Druadaen opened his mouth to deny it, but he shut it again. Beyond avoiding lies, it was foolish to deny what had become so obvious over the many weeks that had passed. When he finally spoke, he did so quietly. "We should have heard something. I am worried that Varcaxtan got caught up in the politics I narrowly escaped."

"You mean, that led to your banishment." The swordsman turned to look him in the eyes. "See here, Druadaen, it's not as though Dunarra's priests wield enough power to put a noose around your uncle's neck, particularly when he's given them no reason."

Druadaen elected not to correct Ahearn's presumptions regarding the nature of punishment meted out by temples in the Consentium. "I am not worried about a noose, Ahearn. I am worried that he is going to remain a 'guest' at the Waiting House, just like poor Shaananca."

"Poor Shaananca!" Ahearn exclaimed. "The only way your magic auntie can be held is if she consents to it!" He grew more serious. "But I suppose she might feel duty-bound to cooperate, lest she make matters worse between the priests and your Propretoriate."

The swordsman glanced astern. "You know," he mused, "even if there's a ship right over the horizon, we won't see it before the harbor gates close behind us. We've a following wind and a square rig to catch it. And once we're ashore, who knows what will happen, and how quickly?" He paused. "It is Shadowmere, after all." Druadaen could feel the assessment lurking behind the swordsman's seemingly casual gaze.

Druadaen managed not to smile. *Trying to get me to scribble, again, eh? To finally commit the last six moonphases to paper and posterity?* He frowned. And unfortunately, Ahearn was right. Once they set foot on the streets of Shadowmere, there was no telling what might happen. If their travels had taught them anything, it was that when you travel on behalf of—or with—people of power or repute, you get caught up in their affairs, for good or bad. It was more often the latter, it seemed.

Druadaen pushed away from the gunwale and squared his shoulders. "I don't suppose there's any good to putting it off. Besides, if I don't, it makes it just that much harder for someone else to pick it up."

"And why would anyone want to do that?"

"Well . . . if something happened to me."

Ahearn looked horrified, but apparently not at the notion of something happening to Druadaen. "'Pick it up'? Chum, your journal is . . . well, it's *your* journal."

Druadaen nodded. "Yes, but if I'm dead, *then* whose is it? It's become *our* story, not just mine." He smiled. "If you didn't feel a bit the same way, I don't imagine you'd be encouraging me to return to it."

Ahearn looked away with an almost spasmic shrug. "Ah, well: your journal, your business. If we don't remember every little detail of our journeys, it's no never-mind to me. So if you decide to let our voyage from Tlulanxu be but a footnote—or not even that—so be it."

Druadaen shook his head. "No, I should. Every time I've felt the urge to leave out a detail, the odds are good that's the one we'll have most want of later on." He turned to go below, thought, turned back. "Of course, if something *should* happen to me, maybe one of you should pick it up. For posterity's sake."

Ahearn made a warding sign. "I'll carry that suggestion to the others, but that's all I'll have to do with it."

Druadaen shrugged. "As you wish," and he headed to their cabin to end the longest lapse between journal entries since he'd started keeping it at age nine.

As Druadaen's broad shoulders turned slightly sideways to more easily navigate the companionway down into the stern, Ahearn smiled shrewdly—and fondly. *A true son of Dunarra; appeal to his conscience and he'll follow it whether he wants to or not.* Ahearn felt his smile fade. *Can't really blame him for wanting to avoid this entry, though.* He'd have to start by recounting why the bright hopes with which they'd begun their journey to Shadowmere hadn't lasted twelve hours.

As he sought out the others, Ahearn also had to admit that Druadaen might have a point about one of them picking up the tale of their travels if he no longer could. But who? Only one way to find out; propose it to the group.

The instant Ahearn did, Umkhira literally took a

step back, shaking her heavy head. Hardly a surprise; she had repeatedly made it clear that she considered all things involving reading or writing a chore.

When his eyes came to rest upon Elweyr, his friend's neutral expression transformed into one of aggrieved alarm. "I spend too much of my time with books and formulas as it is. I haven't the time or inclination to agree to more!"

Before Ahearn's eyes could even shift to S'ythreni, she shook her head sharply. "There's an old saying that in recording the lives of others, writers reveal the most about themselves. So, no." She drifted off to follow the other two.

"Well, this is a fine turn of events!" Ahearn almost shouted at their collective backs. "Do you seriously think *I* should be left with such a task? Me? Are you all mad?"

"You seem to be the one who feels it should be done," Umkhira observed matter-of-factly.

Elweyr smiled back at him. "It's like you've always said, Ahearn; when you get close enough to a fellow for your ways to rub off on him, his are just as likely to rub off on you."

S'ythreni laughed and the three of them continued making their way to the bow.

"Well, I'll be curst for a cretin, if you think that just because I've befriended a naive Dunarran book-worm, I'm about to take up his scribbler's ways!" he shouted after them.

But for some reason, those words rang hollow even in his own ears.

Journal entry 214
5th of Sun, 1799 S.C.
Approaching Shadowmere

Since leaving Tlulanxu, I have avoided this journal.

Well, not entirely. I kept track of the ports we passed through, and the notable events and weather that occasioned our passage. But that is merely a dry chronicle of our voyage, during which there was little worthy of remark.

But still, Ahearn is correct; I was reluctant to sit down and make a more detailed report. The simple truth is that I did not want to spend even more time dwelling upon the endless refrain that has dominated my thoughts since leaving Tlulanxu: Where is my adoptive uncle, Varcaxtan? And where is Tharêdæath's ship?

That ship, a hired Uershaeli brigantine, was the one that was supposed to have carried us to Shadowmere. But unforeseen events in Tlulanxu, the city of my youth, made nonsense of those plans.

Tharêdæath told us that the ship would cast off at dawn, but in the middle of the night, we were awakened by the sound of hasty yet stealthy feet thumping about on the deck. Going above, we discovered that the lines were already away even though it was the darkest hour of the night. The pilot was calling hoarse orders for the sail-handlers to reset the fore-and-aft rigged mizzenmast to bring us sharply away from our berth in the foreigner's quarter.

Rereading that last sentence, I can hardly believe having written the words "foreigner's quarter." For as long as I lived in Tlulanxu, it was simply known as the "trade quarter." But the change of nomenclature is just one dire sign of the changing times that I encountered upon my final return.

And those are still more words that I can hardly believe I wrote: "my final return." Because it is. Concerns that would not have merited mention five years ago became grounds for a protest by the temples which forced the Propretoriate to consent to my exile. My worst fear when I entered that closed hearing was that I might lose my status as one of Dunarra's Outriders; I never dreamed I would lose my citizenship.

My guardians of old were caught up in the same net of suspicion and xenophobia. Indeed, Shaananca was already under the equivalent of house arrest when I arrived. And Varcaxtan himself was concerned that he might soon be sought to answer questions, since my responses had left several temples' hierarchies unsettled and anxious.

How word of the latter reached Tharêdæath I never did discover. I sought him out to ask that he wait for my uncle, but he cut off my entreaties with a raised hand. "We act now that we may have the leisure to discuss it later." He spoke with that strange blend of abruptness and regret that I have come to associate with Uulamantre embarked upon urgent—or perilous—business.

We later learned that Tharêdæath had no choice but to leave before dawn. Whatever message he received included a warning that the authorities would soon close the harbor: an almost unprecedented event that was yet another sad sign of the times. I doubt they would have taken such action had we been on an Iavarain hull; that would have been so provocative a step that I doubt the Propretorium would have relented to the pressure from the temples. However, since their action would only indirectly concern the freedom of a single Uulamantre on a leased Uershaeli hull, the secular authorities were apparently unwilling to risk an incident and yet again relented to the pressure exerted by their sacrist counterparts. Actually, given their dismal treatment of him when he appeared at my hearing, I am quite convinced that the hieroxi would have been happy to have Tharêdæath depart with all haste had they not also known or suspected that Varcaxtan meant to be aboard when he left.

Should the reader of these pages be unfamiliar with the traditional relationship between the secular and sacred authorities in Dunarra, it bears mention that such friction and differences are several orders of magnitude greater than any others recorded across twenty centuries (or more, depending upon the date one accepts as the "beginning" of Dunarra). The most orthodox of the hieroxi attributed the strife to my discoveries. Their more moderate peers, along with the propretors and the Uulamantre, all opined differently. Some obliquely suggested that I was simply a convenient casus belli for other, emerging divisions between them. Those observations did not improve the relations between the parties.

So, after we fled (rather than merely departed) Dunarra, we made swift progress down the southeastern coast of Ar Navir. Upon reaching Cape Joshad, we bent slightly east and seaward, thereby giving Caottalura a wide berth; as earlier entries in this journal recount, we became targets of that nation's Sanslovan mantics and assassins. The reasons for that enmity remain unclear.

Once beyond those hostile shores, we turned west to parallel the southern coast of Ar Navir as we neared Alriadex. This was when Tharêdæath informed us of his intent to part ways. He was determined to swing back north to Dunarra in the hope that he could assist Varcaxtan—and possibly Shaananca—should they wish to leave their homeland.

Surprisingly, we found berthing at Ereolant, the busiest port along the continent's southeastern coast. This was either the result of great good fortune or the silent influence of friendly parties. Lest that sound unduly mysterious, it is worth noting that Alriadex is the only nation which is a codominium between humans and Iavarain. Unlike countries such as Irrylain (where aeostu such as S'ythreni inhabit an autonomous border region), they have an equal share in governing—and supporting—the state. As such, it is the site of a large population of every kind of Iavarain, second only to Mirroskye itself. Naturally, we presumed that Tharêdæath's presence aboard had something to do with the "serendipity" of immediately finding a spot along Ereolant's main wharf. However, we never asked him and he never spoke of it.

He enjoyed an equally suspicious measure of fortuity when, within hours, he engaged an Alriadexan ship departing for Dunarra on the very next day. He transferred his contract with the Uershaeli ship to us, making us its de facto lessees. However, I had several pressing questions, held in abeyance since we'd sailed from Tlulanxu. He'd spent most of that time closeted with his Iavarain entourage, considering contingency plans for whatever situation they might discover upon returning. But now, with time running out, I pressed him for a few minutes in private.

He was as gracious as always. Before I could get the first ritual honorific past my lips, he waved me to a seat. "We are beyond that, Druadaen. We have travelled and faced challenges together. As I said at the outset, you remind me of Dunarrans as they used to be; there shall be no formalities between us." When he'd found his own seat, he fixed me with a steady gaze. "You wish to know what I hope to achieve by returning to Tlulanxu."

I simply nodded.

He frowned. "There are times when one does not know enough to formulate a clear plan, yet can foresee a place where their help may be needed in the near future. This is such a time." He released the first sigh I ever heard from him. "You know my life and memories reach back past the beginning of the Consentium. Bear that in mind as I tell you this: I have seen Dunarra evolve and transform itself in various ways. Some were beneficial, some detrimental, and most—as is true of most things—proved to be a mixture of both. But I have never witnessed the internecine tensions nor the suspicious bigotry that suffused several of the hieroxi during your hearing.

"I hoped that it was an aberration of individual personalities, that my withdrawal from contact—along

with Mirroskye's—would start a current in the opposite
direction, lead toward rapprochement." He shook his
head. "Instead, it emboldened the most antagonistic
of the hieroxi."

"So, do you think that the temples intend to—?"

Tharêdæath held up a taper-fingered hand. "No. You
and I must keep our speculations separate, which is
why I refrained from contact during our journey here.
You are well aware that if questioned, our veracity—or
lack thereof—can be established." He allowed himself
a small smile. "Of course, you may constitute an exception. You might prove no more susceptible to truth-
checking mancery than other kinds." He nodded in
response to my surprised blink. "Your companions are
neither subtle nor silent people. In recounting tales of
your travels, they have made it quite clear that *manas*
finds no purchase upon you. Indeed, surmising from
what has been overheard, mantic constructs unravel
when they come into contact with your person."

I simply nodded and did not expand on the sometimes alarming extent to which that was true. "So you
are returning to render help to help my mentors?"

"Among others. If they need it." Tharêdæath may
have suppressed a second sigh. "Alas, my worry reaches
beyond individuals in this situation. It is such a profound departure from what I have seen and experienced in Dunarra, that I am unable to distinguish
which developments are trivial from those which are
portentous—and dire." He frowned. "One of the oldest
Uulamantrene axioms is this: Only when one beholds
the novel, may further illumination occur. But at that
same moment, one could also be teetering on the edge
of chaos because, being unfamiliar, mortal threats

may not be discerned soon enough to ameliorate—or avoid—them."

I discovered I was nodding. "So, all you may do is keep moving: to stay near enough to help, yet far enough to dodge an unexpected blow."

Tharêdæath's smile was pleased. "I shall miss traveling with you. And since we must part, I would offer you one word of advice."

I sat forward on my chair.

"You must keep moving, as well." He saw my puzzlement. "I am not speaking of keeping distance from Dunarra. Such concerns are properly behind you. I am speaking of your lengthy detours to archives or libraries. You should put those behind you, also. At least for the present."

I smiled. "That is very like what the dragon said to me, just before we parted."

Tharêdæath shook his head slightly. "The words are the same, but my meaning is different. The dragon was counseling you not to put too great a measure of trust in the writings of antiquity, that they are often every bit as suspect as modern ones." He leaned toward me. "I mean: do not stop moving *at all*. Be always in motion—because it is harder to hit a moving target."

My entire body felt like it was coated in fine snow. "You believe I am a...a target?"

"I believe it is possible. Given the questions you feel compelled to ask, you will come to the attention of those who do not wish such inquiries to be made. Some may warn you to desist, but others may adopt the simpler expedient of silencing you before you can ask them in a public forum." He leaned back. "I am afraid that, at least for now, you must concentrate on being a survivor rather than a scholar."

"With respect, I mean to be both."

"For the nonce, I fear that could be the end of you and your journeys after the truth of the world."

There it was again; that crushing term both he and the dragon had used to refer to my investigations. I opened my mouth to object—

Tharêdæath jabbed a finger at me. "Even if you were not at risk, answer me this: Do you mean to punctuate every new discovery by shackling yourself to some ancient desk in some equally ancient reading room? Do you believe that by meticulously research-ing and recording its every detail, it will somehow be remembered a day longer than you? Is that how your discoveries will most benefit your Consentium, perhaps all your kindred species? Or will it be by following each new revelation to the next, until you may return with knowledge and truths that shall, by their nature, be both the catalysts and agents of long-needed change?"

I struggled to separate those weighty words from the ones I heard echoing behind them: among the last my father ever uttered. "How can anyone, even Uulamantre, assert outcomes with such certainty? Do you presume I am some creature of fate?"

He smiled. "No. None of us are. But like every drop in the sea, our lives are borne upon the currents and confluences of prior events." His smile seemed to sadden. "And I have sailed upon those seas for a very long time." He rose. "Which is not only a metaphor but a reminder; I must transfer to the waiting ship." He took me by the shoulders. I was too startled to react; I was not even aware that Uulamantre touched humans. "Do not doubt the voice that urges you onward, because wherever you find yourself—"

"There should you be," I murmured, completing the best-known Uulamantrene aphorism.

He smiled again. "I do indeed regret that our currents carry us to different destinations. Travel in safety, young Druadaen u'Tarthenex."

That was a bit over five moonphases ago. Our ship left Ereolant two days later, keeping to its westerly course until it arrived at its home port: Ruros, first city of Uershael. We had been resigned to biding our time there as she was refitted for passage across the Great Western Ocean to Far Amitryea and Shadowmere, but the first mate sought us at our lodgings on the second day, charged to deliver news that was sure to disappoint: "refitting" had become "repair." In plying the warmer waters off the southern coast of Ar Navir, the hull had become infested with tropical rotworms; dozens of strakes needed replacing, a task that required several weeks of labor while the ship was careened.

It seemed that our already long journey was sure to become longer and more costly. Which might seem a quibble, given how fortune had shone upon us in the year leading up to our journey. But like any prudent travelers, we had put the great balance of that wealth in trustworthy hands, safe from the vicissitudes of travel and mishap. In my case, those hands were in Dunarra and might well have been (and still be) in shackles. It is a strange pass of events, to have adequate resources elsewhere but to be on the brink of penury in one's current location.

However, just as fate sees fit to close one door, it often opens another. Two days later, a familiar ship hove into Ruros: the *Atremoënse*, fresh from having copper hull plates replaced in Marshakerra. She was the Corrovani ship we had encountered just prior to debarking at Treve, the endpoint of our first voyage to Far Amitryea. It happened that she was bound there again, after completing a circuit of the ports that line Pelfarras Bay. Captain Nolus received us with the solemn grace typical of his people and was kind enough to offer us passage in exchange for protecting his ship.

While this may sound like yet more serendipity, it is not so implausible as one might think. Contrary to the common fancy which imagines ships roving boldly about the waves from one exotic destination to the next, the reality is that most follow a largely consistent (not to say monotonously repetitive) circuit between a limited number of ports. In this way, not only is there some predictability of service between different centers of commerce, but captains and crews become intimately familiar with hazards particular to those waters: shallows, reefs, and the seasonal caprice of their winds and weather.

So with little delay we were on our way once again and experienced another largely dull crossing. We dined with the captain on several occasions and apprised him of the fate of the fellow Corrovani that had traveled with us last year: Padrajisse, a congenial (if occasionally cantankerous) sacrist who was treacherously poisoned during an ambush upriver from Marshakerra. He knew her name—and reputation—and nodded sadly, wishing her troubled soul more peace wandering the creedlands of her deity Thyeru than she had known walking and sailing upon the surface of Arrdanc.

During our five moonphases a-sea, we occupied ourselves according to our interests and merits, training with our weapons, lending a hand with (or learning) the daily operations of the ship, and trading knowledge of languages we know. Elweyr was often absent from our impromptu forays into different tongues; he dedicated himself to poring over the seminal treatises on thaumancy we unearthed from the lost library in the isles of Imvish'al.

I kept myself busy with our many activities, but try as I might, I could not keep my thoughts from wandering back across the ocean to Tlulanxu and the "family" I had left there: Shaananca and Varcaxtan. I frequently found myself staring at the velene-as-bracer on my wrist, wondering (and irritated) at its dormancy. Visions such as the ones it formerly shared of far-off conversations were as absent from my chaotic dreams as was its toy-dragon manifestations in the waking world. And so I passed much of the voyage in worried distraction.

Five days ago, we neared the end of the Earthrift Channel and so, neared the end of our journey. All that remained was to traverse the Sea of Marthanlar. The maintopwoman cried down that it was shrouded in mist. None of us considered that particularly newsworthy. Marthanlar is known for such weather and we'd experienced it on our first trip to Far Amitryea, so we were quite sure it held no surprises or novelty for us.

As it often does, the natural world demonstrated that human surety is close kin to delusion.

This time, the Sea of Marthanlar was not merely

misty; it was blanketed by a fog so thick that it was easy to imagine we had sailed out of the world and into a gray limbo. Whatever might have been of interest on either coast was blocked from view. The water itself—renowned for a surface so still that it perfectly mirrored the sky above—was only occasionally visible when we peered over the gunwale. A fine, intermittent rain persisted for almost the entirety of that seventy-league journey. Consequently, when we sailed out of that weather, the sudden change amplified the sensation of emerging into another realm of existence.

The coastlines both to the north and the south began to pinch closer to us, those to the north checkered with farmlands. At night, the lights of small fishing hamlets marked the contours of the shores of Sazzax first, and then A'Querlaan. To the south were rolling woodlands which were far more sparsely inhabited, judging from the paucity of lights: the northern shore of Crimatha, which was nowhere near so well developed as the southern parts through which we had traveled.

Another day brought us to a fork in the narrowing channel. One arm continued west, the other bent sharply to the south. Each was speckled with white sails of ships of all sizes. The northern branch, the Passwater, is used by almost all maritime commerce to and from Far Amitryea due to the two cities that sit astride it: Moonfleet, capital of A'Querlaan on the northern coast and Shadowmere on the south.

Captain Nolus took it upon himself to characterize Shadowmere for us first-time visitors, sententiously explaining that while it was not the largest city on Arrdanc, nor the most grand, nor even the most powerful, it was unquestionably the most famous. It had

had many names over the millennia, and it had risen and fallen so many times that no two scholars could agree on a complete list of them, nor even a tally.

Looking out the porthole before me, I can see its towers of varied design and age. And although the captain's remarks were self-consciously portentous, they were in no way exaggerations. As one of the few cities which existed before the Cataclysm, Shadowmere is indeed steeped in the legend, lore, and enigmatic legacies that have accumulated over centuries of constant tumult and intrigue. Small wonder that so many of the great figures in Arrdanc's history have learned, lived, and repeated the enduring truth of the place: that all great journeys will eventually pass through Shadowmere.

As we stand off its northern slips, barely a mile out, I tell myself—for the twentieth time—that I will not romanticize the city. I have seen many ports over the course of my years as a Courier. Many rise higher, spread wider, are more humming hubs of commerce and power. And yet, here I sit, either feeling or imagining that Shadowmere simultaneously broods and beckons. Or maybe that is just one more trick being played by the back of my brain, the part that also wonders, and worries:

What has become of Shaananca? And where is Varcaxtan?

CHAPTER THREE

Druadaen craned his neck as they neared the gates that flanked the entry to Shadowmere's protected docks. Each was an immense sheet of solid stone, controlled by machinery presumably housed in one of the two looming bastions that flanked the harbor mouth. They reminded Druadaen of treble-sized versions of the towers and gates that operated the locks of Dunarra's canals. A similarly gargantuan arrangement protected the anchorage of the naval base at Galasmyrn, but there, the titanic mechanisms were housed in windowless edifices built into the high, thick walls that not only protected the fleet from attack, but from the weather that came straight off the ocean.

Here, well in the lee of a headland and away from the path of storms that came off the ocean some ten leagues to the west, Shadowmere's harbor gates appeared decidedly anomalous, given the lack of similarly impressive walls to either side. There were walls, in fact, but they were barely more than what Druadaen associated with a frontier outpost: twenty-foot-high double-coursed stone without any sign of improvement other than crenellation and the implied promise of a wallwalk just behind it.

However, as Nolus had suggested, perhaps the city did not need walls after all. Rather than huddling behind it, the perimeter towers straddled the black water of the Mere-moat, which spilled into the bay just beyond the gates, spreading like twin runoffs of ink.

"Gives me shivers just looking at it," Ahearn grumbled.

Umkhira frowned. "Still, that is a strange defense. The towers would be more formidable if one had to cross the moat to reach them."

"That presumes," S'ythreni said mildly, "that it's easier to cross the water inside the tower...where no great weapons may bear on the behemoths that wait beneath its surface."

Umkhira's eyes widened and she may have paled slightly.

As Nolus had predicted, it was impossible to find a berth near the needlelike Moorax Tower, which was at the northern end of the docks; in the end, *Atremoënse* tied up over two hundred yards to the south. By the time her hawsers were around the bollards and cordage fenders were hung between her side and the pier's stonework, Druadaen and the others were making for the gangplank, eager to be on their way.

"Hoi, you!" called Nolus. "Aren't you forgetting something?"

Druadaen waved and smiled. "Many thanks for the passage, Captain!" Which they'd said already, but perhaps the captain had been distracted and so, had forgotten.

But Nolus shook his head. "This is Shadowmere."

Druadaen looked around at the others, who appeared as baffled as he was.

Nolus shook his head again. "In this city, your armor and weapons aren't part of your luggage. You wear them in the street."

Druadaen wondered if his expression was as dumfounded as the ones around him.

"Why?" Ahearn called up to the captain, who was leaning on the forward rail of the quarterdeck. "Thieves?"

"Gangs?" added Elweyr.

"Bigots?" asked Umkhira with a glower.

"Idiots?" sighed S'ythreni.

Nolus shrugged. "Take your pick." He may have smiled. "As I said, it's Shadowmere."

Druadaen had, in the course of his years as a Courier, visited over three dozen port cities, excluding those of Dunarra and its closest allies. That did not include the smaller towns and even waterside hamlets where those ships had stopped to take on fresh water, provisions, chandlery, timber, or shelter from approaching storms. Since traveling with his present companions, that number had undergone further increase. But for all of that, he had never yet been in a place with so many strange sights and strange customs.

It seemed that there were at least three separate militias, all of which claimed to be the one in charge of the city. Messengers or factotums ran back and forth, wearing different combinations of colored ribbons, their meaning a complete mystery. Within the first five minutes they spotted or heard humans from at least twenty different nations, several pair of aeostu, two patrols—or possibly gangs—of mixed urzhen, and two beings that might have been related to the dog-legged hyek. Food vendors pushed through the throngs with trays trailing as many novel aromas as familiar ones. And while most of the crowd was neither armed nor armored, anyone who was not dressed for work in a trade or on the docks was either adequately equipped, adequately guarded, or noticeably wary.

Druadaen and the other four had, by instinct rather than plan, retracted into a tight group, S'ythreni following a step behind, as if daring cutpurses to try their luck. But so far as Druadaen could tell, they were not attracting any particular notice. If anything, other armed parties simply gave them a slightly wider berth. They returned the favor.

However, they soon found their northward progress blocked. Numerous ships were offloading newly arrived cargos to the warehouses on the other side of the wharf-following thoroughfare, resulting in a series of de facto roadblocks. The only answer seemed to be to push into the streets that led away from the docks, and once there, find an unobstructed route north.

A fine concept, Druadaen conceded shortly after, but not so successful in practice...because everyone else had the same idea. And if the crowds diminished somewhat, so did the width of the streets, rendering their progress only marginally better and far less direct.

Their detours revealed the eclectic mixture of buildings that seemed characteristic of Shadowmere. Old stone houses hemmed in recent wood structures, some little more than shacks. Former palaces that had partially succumbed to time or strife had been rebuilt into perversely ornate manors. Winding in between were streets of eye-gouging diversity. Frame-and-mortar facades with overhanging second stories sported weathered wood intarsia. Brick balconies vied with sandstone cupolas and ancient porticoes. Gables protruded from steep roofs, drooping as if frozen in weary frowns.

The deeper into these off-wharf streets they pushed, the more the crowds around them changed. People of means became fewer and were equipped not only with guards but almost overpowering pomanders—whether to ward off infections or the growing stink of the narrow lanes was unclear. The rest were a mix of sailors between voyages, traveling merchants, mercenaries, indigent scholars, and itinerant artisans.

But for every person with a clear livelihood, there were at least two others hoping to find a job, a purpose, or both. Minstrels, second sons of impoverished gentry, scions of fallen houses, and self-styled "adventurers" rubbed elbows—and on two occasions, were preparing to cross swords—with cutpurses, assassins, thieves, and fugitives, several of whom were drunkenly proclaiming their innocence to any who would listen. Druadaen speculated that some might even have been telling the truth. And finally, in every alley and on every corner, stranded refugees, escaped slaves, and émigrés without local friends, family or sponsors, begged for enough work or alms to survive just one more day.

From behind, S'ythreni's voice was impossibly sweet. "Does anyone actually know where we are?"

"I think about sixty yards east of the wharf and seventy yards further north than we started," Druadaen guessed.

Umkhira nodded. "That is approximately correct, but I mistrust such precise numbers."

Druadaen smiled; he did too.

"Well," Ahearn mused, "about now, I'm wishing we brought field gear."

"Why?" Elweyr asked.

"Because at this rate, we'll be camping on these pestiferous streets tonight!"

Druadaen saw a wide patch of sky to the left, headed that way in the hope that they could catch sight of Moorax Tower over the roofs there.

They emerged into a small square built around a cistern—or rather, what remained of it. S'ythreni pointed just above the opposite rooftops. "There's the tower. We haven't come as far as you two thought."

Druadaen sighed. "I agree. Well, we'd better—"

The low growl of a dog came out of an alley that opened on the square. Two more emerged from a twisting lane opposite it.

The few people who had been crossing the square quickened their pace to exit it.

"You know," Elweyr observed with a sigh, "half of the structures around us are ruined or abandoned."

"Weapons," Druadaen said, as calmly as he could.

The sound of metal clearing scabbards and sheaths rode over the top of more growling, this time from the gaping doorway of a particularly dilapidated building. A group of gulls—flying as a tight flock, like crows—appeared over a much-boarded manse behind them. They veered, swept low, and disappeared behind the roof of an adjacent building.

Ahearn hissed a question at Elweyr: "Faunamancer?"

Druadaen didn't hear the answer; he was suddenly nine years old again, watching his family's suddenly blank-eyed farm animals turn on them, their movements as spasmodic as marionettes manipulated by a palsied puppeteer. Then there were the birds: diving at them, clawing, pecking—

Druadaen bumped into something: Umkhira's broad, solid back. She shot a perplexed glance at him; although he had not been aware of being part of the maneuver, they had all formed a tight, outward-facing ring.

Men in armor emerged from doorways in the side streets.

Druadaen shook his head, trying to dislodge images of the animal attack that only he had survived.

"I count four on my side," Ahearn muttered.

"Six here," S'ythreni answered. "And they're looking to the roofs."

"Waiting to let the birds start in on us?"

"No," mumbled Elweyr, whose eyes were closed in concentration. "They're watching for signals from whatever mantic is up there." His voice became low, regretful. "Druadaen, you're going to have to step out."

Druadaen blinked: "What?" Fighting through the last memories of his parents, he understood what the thaumantic was referring to: the way that all mancery inexplicably unraveled when it came close to Druadaen. So if Elweyr was to bring his own powers to bear, he needed more space. Druadaen raised his sword and heavy parrying dagger into a guard position that favored defense over attack and moved forward.

Across the square, dogs leaped through the ruin's doorway. Flying low, gulls gushed out of a narrow, flanking lane, crying madly. The armored men drew their own weapons and started toward the group at a measured pace—then halted.

The gulls' cries became alarmed; they scattered upward. The dogs skidded to dusty stops, eyes blinking as they stared around, disoriented.

Unseen, two men behind the peak of the highest roof to the north began an accusatory exchange in heavily accented Commerce.

Their voices stilled as a single figure sauntered out of the western, and widest, lane. Armored in what looked like striated mail, the fellow's hair was the salt-and-pepper that came with the onset of middle age. His world-weary tone was a match for it: "I think there must be some misunderstanding, here," he called up to the persons on the roof.

"This is not your affair!" a voice cried down. "Begone! Now!"

As the last dog slunk out of the square, the man scratched his ill-shaven chin. "I'm sorry, but are you the militia?"

The voice that answered from the roof was equal parts sarcastic and contemptuous. "Why, yes: we *are* the militia."

The man in the square sighed. "Ironic or not, you're a poor liar." He ignored angry mutters from the armed men poised at the mouths of three different alleys. "Let's stop this nonsense. I think it's about time for you to return to your barracks. Or ship. If that's how you got here from Azanzral."

A different voice from the roof challenged, "And what makes you so sure we are from that city?"

"Even if I were deaf, my ears would still be stinging from that bark-chewing accent you Sazzaxan's bring from your capital. Come now, off you go."

One of the men in the street stepped forward aggressively. "And who are you, to give orders to soldiers of Sazzax?"

"Oh, so you're here in an *official* capacity? Well, that's sure to be of interest to the city guard."

The first voice from the rooftop was a sustained sneer. "*The* city guard? This is Shadowmere; there are at least half a dozen rabbles vying for that role. So pray tell, which ones do you mean to tell?"

"All of them," the increasingly disgruntled man shot back irritably. "Unless, of course, you are here at the behest of one or more of them? Because the others would be quite interested to learn which of their number had broken the accord against foreign interference."

The other voice did not respond to that challenge. "And why should we leave?" The men in the alleys stepped into the square, grinning. "What have we done? We are free persons in an open city."

"Well, firstly," the middle-aged man replied wearily, "it was quite obvious what you were *about* to do. Besides that, you should leave because I've asked you to. Nicely." His voice was suddenly as gray and pitiless as his assessing eyes. "So far."

The Sazzaxans looked at each other and stopped again.

Druadaen felt several of his companions about to move; he gestured for them to be still.

"You give bold orders for a single man," retorted one of the rooftop voices.

"Firstly, I have *asked*, not ordered. Secondly, do I look like a mancer to you?"

The other rooftop voice cracked as it asked, "What does that have to do with anything?"

"Well, aren't you wondering what happened to your own mancer's little tricks?" Hissed, mutual imprecations arose from behind the roof. "Because if I didn't put a stop to them, aren't you the slightest bit curious—and concerned—about who did? And you haven't even bothered to ask my name."

"Not interested," the deeper voice barked. He shouted a single, unfamiliar word. The men surrounding the square began moving again—but this time, toward the group's would-be intercessor. "This is your last chance to leave."

"Sadly, I can't do that. And my own friends won't be pleased if you try cases with me."

The largest of the men approaching him chuckled. "Assuming any are here, they'll soon be as likely to hit you as the men approaching."

Umkhira cocked her axe; Druadaen rose a hand to still her, watching their intercessor carefully.

Who shook his head. "You think I haven't planned for that? Well, come at me then—and learn your lessons."

The men continued to close. A figure on the roof rose from concealment—

"This is over," asserted a new voice from the smallest lane, which wound into the square from the north. When the Sazzaxan's advance did not stop but only slowed, a hooded figure emerged from the shadows of the flanking buildings and the same voice added, "These five, the ones you meant to ambush, are under the Lady's protection."

Struck motionless by that phrase, the Sazzaxans seemed to be suspended between a surge of angry resentment and slowly growing worry.

"And who are *you*?" asked the man standing cross-armed on the roof. By way of answer, the figure slowly, deliberately, drew back its hood.

The weapons in Druadaen's hands sagged momentarily—because the man's appearance catapulted him back into yet another memory from his ninth year.

The man's straight-features and high cheekbones were striking, but it was the hair that transported Druadaen back in time—to when the Lady of the Mirror visited Dunarra with an entourage led by just such a man.

This man, like that one, had severely straight, silver-white hair, evenly cut. But what made it unique was the dark tips which formed a fringe of night-black so straight that it would have been easy to believe it was painted there. It was the most distinctive natural hair coloration on all of Arrdanc, and marked those who bore it as persons from the reclusive nation known as Tualar.

Druadaen had encountered a few others from that land during his years as a Courier, enough to discern that there were individual distinctions in the general pattern. Which in this case signified that the Tualaran who had served as the commander of the Lady's body-guard when he was nine was either standing before him now, or had a near twin.

The Sazzaxans read something different, but equally profound, in the coloration of the man's hair. The one on the roof disappeared; sounds of a scrambled retreat rose up from over its peak. The armed men in the square backed away slowly, but, once in the alleys, began to run.

When they were gone, the Tualaran walked over to the man who'd interceded on the group's behalf. "I am in your debt, my friend."

"Ah, think nothing of it. Just put in a good word for me and mine with the Lady." As he said it, four other individuals stood up on separate roofs slightly farther back from the square. Their armor and equipment was every bit as varied as that worn by Druadaen and his companions.

The Tualaran nodded up at them. "They are already very high in her regard, but I shall not fail to acquaint her with this further proof of your quick wits and valor."

They exchanged nods and as the middle-aged man swung about, he tossed a parting comment over his shoulder toward Druadaen and his companions. "You lot! You were wise to stay ready even as you stayed out of the parley. If you wish, seek me out before you journey on. Buy my bunch a drink, and we just might share a hint or two about avoiding Shadowmere's pitfalls."

The Tualaran glanced over at Druadaen as the other exited the square. "You could do worse than accept that offer." He raised an eyebrow. "You seem to be staring at me."

Druadaen nodded. "I think I may have, er, seen you before."

His answer came along with the slightest hint of a smile. "I suppose that is possible."

Ahearn was still looking down the alleys where the Sazzaxans had disappeared. "So do those bully-boys often come here to make trouble?"

The Tualaran nodded. "Often enough, but today, their main intent was to send a message."

Umkhira huffed. "Messages usually involve words, not weapons."

The Tualaran shrugged as he waved a lean fellow out of the shadows from which he'd emerged. "Shadowmere is a loud city, so loud that even shouting is no guarantee that a message will be heard. On the other hand, deeds—and particularly injury—cannot be so easily ignored."

"So then who were the Sazzaxans trying to injure?" Elweyr wondered aloud. "Certainly not us. We are nothing to them."

Druadaen frowned. "However, if they were aware that the Lady summoned us—"

The Tualaran sighed. "Striking at her through you might have been a factor here, but Sazzaxans' motives are typically more layered, more complex."

"Which seems typical of the trouble attracted by Dunarrans...or at least this one," S'ythreni muttered, even as she bent a rueful smile toward Druadaen.

The Tualaran turned back toward the lane from which he'd appeared. "Suffice it to say that the sovereign of Sazzax feels himself at pains to remind the powers of Shadowmere that though they tend to prefer their immediate neighbors in A'Querlaan, they would be ill advised to let that affinity evolve into overt favoritism."

Druadaen nodded. "And you have our deep gratitude for interceding when you did, but we do not know who you are."

"I am the Warder of the Tower of the Mirror." He smiled at Druadaen's politely persistent gaze. "My name is Corum Torshaenyx."

Ahearn was still intermittently glancing back toward the square. "And that fellow who showed up first, how should we call him and his lot?"

The Tualaran waved for the tall young fellow he'd summoned from the shadows to lead the way north. "If they wished you to have their names at this point, I am sure they would have shared them."

"Well, how in the bloody hells are we to stand them a round if we don't know how to ask after them? Does he have something against sharing his name?"

"I am sure he will make it easy to locate him. As for his name, he uses an alias."

Umkhira frowned. "He refuses to connect his name to his deeds?" Her tone clearly expressed what her words only intimated: that such an act was devoid of honor or dignity.

Corum shook his head as they emerged on a wider street that paralleled the wharf. "In Shadowmere, it is not uncommon for real names to be kept secret. Aliases prevail, often to keep families and friends safe from vengeful visits by defeated adversaries."

Umkhira emitted a revolted grunt as Ahearn leaned in. "Well, then, what does this fellow call himself?"

The Tualaran did not break his stride as he looked straight ahead and said, "Stormhawk."

Druadaen stared. "You are joking."

"I am not."

Druadaen perceived a pause, as if Corum had suppressed a sigh at the last possible instant.

"Actually, 'Stormhawk' has a ring to it," Ahearn muttered.

"Yes, *you'd* think so," sighed S'ythreni, rolling her eyes.

"The human warrior has taken a proud battle-name," Umkhira snapped. "What of it? Great Lightstrider warriors of similar age have often done no less." She darted a look at her Iavan friend, as if daring her to utter another snide quip.

Elweyr's voice was carefully neutral as he turned toward the Tualaran. "Is anonymity the only reason persons follow this, er, practice?"

Corum shook his head. "It is how the convention arose, but not why it has persisted. Now it is merely a means for recently arrived fortune-seekers to attempt to draw—usually unwarranted—attention to themselves. And then there are those who adopt an alias because . . . well, because their given names do not inspire confidence."

Umkhira frowned again. "Why would one take up a new name rather than adorning their own by performing worthy deeds?"

"Sometimes, even the worthiest deeds are not up to such a task, Mistress Warrior."

She shook her head in perplexity. "What do you mean?"

Corum shrugged. "There was a hero—renowned across all of Arrdanc—who might have been forgotten by now, had he not changed his name."

Ahearn stared sidelong at him. "I mean no disrespect, but that sounds, well, unlikely."

"Indeed!" Umkhira agreed fiercely. "I would hear this forgotten name, that I might judge for myself!"

The Tualaran met her eyes ruefully. "Derb Piggles."

As the rest of the group glanced away or lowered their eyes, Ahearn's mouth became a round, soundless "Oh." But he was also the first to recover, leaning toward their second rescuer with a knowing grin. "So now I'm wondering if the hero-name by which we know him might be something as musical and memorable as Corum Torshaenyx, eh?" He punctuated his jocular speculation with a nudge to that worthy's ribs.

The only reply was a dead-eyed stare.

Elweyr muttered at Ahearn before Druadaen could. "Tualarans frown on bragging and noms de guerre. And their names indicate their origins even more clearly than their hair."

"Well, it's easy to understand what you mean about the hair—I never saw the like—but I've no idea what you mean by their names."

Corum inclined his head toward the thaumancer. "Tualaran family names all begin with a T. Additionally, each new generational cohort's given names begin with the same letter, one that is distinct to their sex. In my generation, all the males were given names beginning with the letter *c*. For females, their given names begin with *n*."

Ahearn stared in surprise. "Why?"

For the first time, Corum smiled; his teeth were very broad and very bright. "I have no idea how that tradition began. Whatever utility or significance this naming convention had has long since passed from memory. However, you should also become acquainted with the name of your *actual* savior"—he jutted a square chin at the young fellow leading them—"Cerven Ux Reeve."

They looked curiously at the young man in light armor, who glanced back at them with a small smile.

S'ythreni almost whispered, "And he is our savior... how?"

"By alerting me to your arrival."

"Really?" Ahearn exclaimed. "Given what we've heard about your Lady, I thought it might have been mancery at work." He glanced at Cerven's back. "Assuming the mancery wasn't his, of course."

The young fellow looked over his shoulder with a smile. "Well, keeping up with changes to the docking rota *has* been likened to a mantic art." Smiles answered him.

"But to the first matter," Ahearn pressed before Elweyr or Druadaen could stop him, "since the Lady certainly seems to have such abilities, why wasn't she aware even before this admirably skilled lad?"

Torshaenyx nodded with the slow, deliberate tempo of someone determined to remain patient. "Such abilities are used only when the need is truly pressing."

"And what defines that level of need?" Ahearn asked it so quickly that Druadaen never had the chance to anticipate that the swordsman might be so blunt. "What would prompt the Lady to use her powers, then?"

The Tualaran raised an eyebrow. "Keeping the peace. And not just on these docks."

"Or even on all the docks on Arrdanc, yeh?"

Corum glanced quickly at Ahearn and then, just as quickly, smiled. "Aye, you almost caught me with that. Come, enough clever questions. We must quicken our pace."

As they lengthened their strides to match the

Tualaran's, Druadaen subtly dropped back with Ahearn. "You took quite a risk, there."

Ahearn suppressed a snort. "No, I didn't—not so long as he thought me a buffoon. But he caught me out."

"And you almost caught him off guard, which I suspect is no small feat."

Ahearn shook his head. "Ah, but still, I didn't get an answer out of him."

Druadaen smiled. "Didn't you? Now, let's not lag."

CHAPTER FOUR

The Tower of the Mirror did not seem so narrow when they approached. It was at least seventy feet in girth with smooth basalt sides that seemed to run straight up into the clouds: an illusion caused by what master builders called the vanishing point effect, enhanced by the lack of any other tower close enough to provide perspective.

Its single, recessed door was built to accommodate a small portcullis which was currently raised. There was one guard standing within its shadows.

About ten paces away, Corum halted, nodded at Druadaen, then turned to the others. "This is as far as the rest of you may go."

Umkhira stepped forward. "I shall not allow him to proceed alone."

Druadaen smiled, but held up a hand to stop her further progress. "My friend, you must. Those were the terms upon which we journeyed here."

She frowned. "Not so. We were invited—"

"Actually," Elweyr corrected softly, "*he* was invited, not us."

Ahearn sounded cross. "See here, when the dragon's human puppet conveyed the Lady's message, it included a direct request that we accompany him here!"

"Yes," Elweyr persisted, "but as his *protectors*: to make sure he arrived safely."

S'ythreni shrugged in the direction of the thaumantic. "He's right. I remember because it annoyed me. To travel all that way, just as bodyguards? Hmph."

Ahearn was frowning. "Well, damned if I don't remember feeling the same thing, now that you mention it." He glanced at Corum. "I wonder if the lot of us could have a few moments alone, Warder Torshaenyx?"

Corum nodded, waved Cerven into the shadows of the tower's entry and followed a step behind.

Ahearn turned to Druadaen. "So we agreed to this. Doesn't mean I like it, though."

Umkhira nodded. "We survive by staying together."

Druadaen put a hand on each of their shoulders. "I agree, and I could not ask for faster, or finer, friends. But as you say, this is what we agreed to. Most importantly, I have met the Lady before and I do not fear her." *What she might have to tell or show me—well, that's a different matter.*

"You were but a boy," Umkhira muttered. "And a trusting one. Are you so very sure what you perceived then was, in fact, correct?"

Druadaen just smiled. If he started refuting every rejection, or enumerating the many reasons why he felt the tower was more likely to be a safe haven than a danger, they might still be in the street talking when the sun started to set. So he held up both hands, halting the entire conversation. "Reflect back on the powers that counseled us to journey to this place. Even before the Lady sent her own message, the dragon suggested this as our destination. It evinced such respect for her that it almost seemed awestruck. And remember how I first met the Lady: through the intercession of Shaananca, my mentor."

"Ah, we always come back to your magic auntie," Ahearn added.

Druadaen pushed on. "So there are two logical reasons why I have nothing to fear. Firstly, the Lady has been commended to me by persons—and beings—who have amply shown they have my best interests at heart. But no less compelling is the simple fact that, given what they have intimated and we have witnessed of her power, she could have already killed me any time she wanted. For the past fifteen years."

His logic quieted their misgivings except S'ythreni's, who—*of all people!*—cocked her head dubiously. "And what if you, and all of them, are wrong?"

He couldn't tell if her question was out of concern for his well-being, the group's, or her own, but that didn't alter the only answer he could give her: "In that event, you must save yourselves." He glanced toward Corum. "And given the capabilities of our escort, if you truly fear such an outcome, then I suggest waiting at an even greater distance than this." Not as though that would do much good, but it was the only advice he could think of and he had to say *something* in order to bring the discussion to a close. "Now, I must go. I doubt I shall be very long."

Elweyr stared at him. "Those are famous last words, you know."

Druadaen just smiled and began unbuckling his sword as he turned toward Ahearn.

The swordsman saw his intent, shook his head. "No. You keep that right where it is. It's been too helpful for you to leave it behind, and it's too eerie for me to even think of taking up."

Druadaen shrugged, reattached the scabbard, and shook his head when Umkhira stood ready to follow him back to the tower. "No, you—all of you—remain here. If it gets late, find a comfortable place and leave word with Warder Torshaenyx so I know where to find you." Without waiting for a reply, he turned and walked briskly toward the entrance. Cerven was nowhere to be seen, but the Tualaran was still waiting in the shadows.

When Druadaen reached the doorway, Corum smiled tightly, pushed back the iron-bound timbers before them, and stood aside so Druadaen could enter the blackness beyond.

It took Druadaen's eyes several seconds to adapt to the dim light piping in from two overhead ducts. Two humans were flanking a further door, slightly offset from the one that had just closed behind him. There was some medium-sized animal beside the larger one: a dog, perhaps? He did hear a faint sniffing from its general vicinity. From the other side of that door was a clacking sound, as if someone was opening and closing a small box.

"I believe I am expec—"

"You are," said the slightly smaller one. The accent was distinctly Corrovani. "Wait a moment." The clacking continued, then stopped. "You might want to shield your eyes."

Druadaen had barely brought up a hand before he heard overhead shutters snap open; even through his fingers, he could tell there was a great deal more illumination in the room. Squinting preemptively, he uncovered his eyes.

The larger human was thickly muscled and wearing the livery of Teurodn, a realm Druadaen had visited several times in the course of his duties as an Outrider. The other was wearing Corrovani colors, but the uniform was unfamiliar: certainly not that of its army. A second, narrower squint settled the uncertainty; the urn-and-sword symbol on his tabard indicated that he was a Grayblade, a member of his country's most elite martial order.

Hearing the dog sniffing and snorting again, Druadaen glanced down—and discovered a creature that resembled a lean, long-legged sloth with a body about the size of a small dog. Its vaguely canine head ended in a snout which was turned in his direction, the end of which was a widening and contracting array of writhing leathery folds. Druadaen blinked in stunned recognition: "A snufflecur!"

The man in the Teurodn livery was startled. "You are familiar with them?"

"Familiar enough to know that most are kept by the borderers of Eld Shire." He didn't add that they were typically used by the realm's bounty hunters, who genocidally targeted all the Bent races even when they were not a-hordeing.

The Teurond was smiling. "My family was originally from Eld Shire. Three generations back, now. You know it?"

Druadaen smiled apologetically. "Only through the

stories of others." He nodded at the livery. "But I'm passably well acquainted with Teurodn."

"How so?"

The Corrovani looked sideways at him. "He is Dunarran." When that didn't kindle understanding in the others' eyes, he added, "He's an Outrider." The Grayblade paused, casually inspected Druadaen's gear. "Or he was. Still has some of that kit, though."

"'S that so?" The younger, larger guard looked for but did not appear to detect what the other had, then glanced at his thoroughly disinterested snufflecur. He shrugged amiably. "Well, in you go, then."

Cerven was waiting on the other side of the door, the steady light of oil lamps illuminating a round chamber at the base of a broad, upward-spiraling stairway. "We have a walk," he said, glancing at the steps, which radiated out from a single column of dark, glassy basalt that was almost three yards across and rose up through the tower like a spine.

Druadaen nodded. "No reason to keep the Lady waiting. Lead on."

No longer distracted by the enigmatic Tualaran and winding streets that had been his two points of focus during the walk to the tower, Druadaen considered the young man leading him up the stairs. Probably not out of his teens, he wore a shortsword at his hip and light leather armor, but was not otherwise outfitted as a warrior. Careful to listen for an accent, he asked, "How many times a day do you make this trip?"

Cerven slowed until he was just half a step ahead, turned, and smiled. "Too often, however much the actual number may vary." Druadaen smiled back.

As they approached the first story landing, two

more guards—one a Taruildorean in a kilt, the other a Saqqari in the oddly angled armor of their warrior caste—made a casual challenge to confirm that Cerven was indeed escorting a visitor to the Lady. Their questions were laughably quotidian—except to anyone who might have enough skill or mancery to mimic the young Ux Reeve. During the exchange, Druadaen's initial impressions of him were confirmed: extremely well spoken, calm, and amiable without any hint of servility.

As they ascended, every rise of twenty feet showed them the underside of another story overhead, the stonework held up by a combination of buttresses and groined vaulting. At the third there was a landing that extended outward into a corridor that surrounded the staircase. Doors and dark archways on the far wall indicated that there was at least one more concentric ring of rooms between them and the outside world.

At the next landing, Druadaen was surprised to discover that the spine of basalt was, in fact, hollow. A weathered ogee arch of markedly different workmanship opened unto a round chamber not quite five feet across. In the center of its floor was a hole so lightless that it might have led down to the core of Arrdanc. Anchored in those stygian depths was a narrow, free-standing slab of flat, pitted stone. It continued up through a matching aperture overhead. Druadaen tarried to listen; far below, he heard intermittent burblings...but with cadences that reminded him of conversation.

As they went higher, they passed two people descending the stairs. One was apparently of Solari extraction. His woven hide tunic and kirtle suggested he might well be one of that continent's hermit-nativists. The other was a woman cased in the light steel chainmail of Uanseach's best armorers, but the baldrics of her two shamshirs and the sheath of her wide-bladed jambiya were emblazoned with the fiery script of Lajantpur. Her eyes flashed as they played across each man's upturned face, then refocused on the descending stairs.

But it was the eighth landing that presented the strangest surprise of all: yet another opening into the tower's basalt spine. However, this one was simply a rough cleft and so narrow that Druadaen had to turn sideways to enter it.

He discovered a small alcove lit by a dim but steady glow that had no discernible source: almost certainly mantic illumination. A single occupant—spare, bald and seated upon a thick gabbeh rug—was gazing into the darkness as her fingers flew swiftly over something on her lap. As Druadaen stepped closer, she turned, smiled, and nodded, revealing that she was not just bald but hairless, right down to her lack of eyelashes. Her empty, off-center stare indicated that she was also quite blind. Neither her dress nor appearance suggested any particular land of origin.

Or maybe, Druadaen reconsidered, it was that she seemed oddly universal. Her face struck him as an amalgam of what he had seen in the many lands he'd visited upon every one of Arrdanc's continents, and so, called to mind all the ports he had visited but no one of them in particular.

She turned back toward the darkness at the core of the tower, flowing into a meditative pose favored by the Baskayan mountain mystics as her fingers resumed their nimble dance upon a device that Druadaen initially mistook for an abacus. A moment of study showed that it was not structured for a base-ten number system; indeed, he began to doubt it was a counting mechanism at all.

But when Druadaen followed her gaze into the hollow core of the basalt spine, he forgot the device, her, and every other feature of this strange alcove. Before him, the same stone tablet he had seen earlier descended from the dark above and vanished into the darkness below . . . but this time, he realized it actually *was* vanishing into the lower darkness. By sinking very, very slowly.

Druadaen stared, squinted and discovered that its surface was not pitted as he'd originally thought, but engraved in impossibly fine patterns that followed a linear scheme. He was about to abandon his attempt to further scrutinize the carvings when he saw that it was extending—*growing*—further along the horizontal axis, as if an invisible scalpel was incising additional enigmatic markings into it as he watched.

He turned, leaned back out into the staircase, his mouth open to ask the first of many questions. But Cerven simply shook his head and motioned that they should resume their upward journey.

Druadaen glanced back at the woman and the strange chamber. "I don't suppose you can share anything you might know about that."

Cerven smiled slightly. "I don't know any more than you do." He shrugged. "As the Warder said, I'm new here." He glanced up the stairs. "We should continue."

Ten stories later, they reached a landing which did

not open on to another landing and perimeter corridor. In place of that expected feature was a black, steel-banded door. Druadaen peered at the silken sheen of the timbers. "Is that ironwood?"

Cerven smiled. "I believe so. You have a keen eye." He waited. When Druadaen showed no sign of continuing, he explained, "From here, you go on alone."

"Why?"

"Because from here, *everyone* goes on alone." Cerven smiled faintly, nodded, and started down the stairs.

After climbing two more stories, Druadaen found himself mounting a final riser to stand on a small landing which offered only one way forward: a door of plain construction, the wood dark with age and held together by even older iron fittings. As he reached toward it, he heard the sound of a latch falling aside; the handle retreated from his hand, revealing a sliver of the jamb.

Well, I see I'm expected. He once again reached for the crudely fashioned handle—

And halted, but not out of trepidation or awe. Rather, he abruptly realized that he'd failed to prepare himself in one important way: to be ready for how time might have changed the Lady.

To Druadaen, she was timeless in the way that persons met in childhood become firmly fixed in memory, like a butterfly in glass. He had seen her only one other time, almost a decade later and at a considerable distance as she prepared to depart Tlulanxu. Less than an hour later, his comatose father had finally passed, which had left an infinitely greater imprint upon his recollections of that day.

So Druadaen's strongest memories of her were those of a bedazzled nine-year-old on his first visit to a city with his parents. Which, he realized, might have left him with a reflexively positive impression of her, might incline him to be disposed to trust her uncritically, particularly since her features and her long black hair had recalled his own mother's.

But that was where the similarity ended. Whereas his mother had possessed effortless social graces and unfailing tact, the Lady of the Mirror had been . . . well, not exactly awkward, but decidedly unusual. She had been determined to acknowledge each of the hundreds of well-wishers who came to see her that day, pausing to make some response, no matter how fleeting, to every bow or word of welcome. And when she encountered a gesture of greeting she did not recognize—persons from many distant lands came to her Conferral—she tarried longer still, her brows knitted in concentration even as she smiled.

It was as though on the one hand, the Lady's speech, manners, and wit indicated that she was a learned woman who moved among persons of importance with the ease and surety of a peer. But, on the other hand, she seemed wholly unschooled in the practicalities and practice of how to behave at an affair of state. Indeed, her insistence upon treating every person, regardless of station, in precisely the same fashion had attracted private comment—not all of it positive.

Druadaen wondered how much the Lady had changed since then, schooled himself to as much preemptive aplomb he could muster, pushed the door inward, and strode into whatever chamber or fate lay beyond. Even so, he was not fully prepared for what he encountered.

The Lady of the Mirror stood before him, hands folded, a small, serene smile on her face. "Welcome, Druadaen u'Tarthenex."

And in that instant, he discovered he'd failed to anticipate the way that time had, in fact, changed her:

Not at all.

She was still the same woman of early middle age that moved energetically through his childhood memories, like a vibrant dancer always trying to outrun her own skirts. The crow's feet at the corners of her eyes were merely creases left upon a face that was always animated and poised to change expression. And as Druadaen had both hoped and feared, her tresses were as shiny and long as he recalled—just like his mother's.

He remembered to bow before the delay became noticeable. "Lady of the Mirror, I thank you for your invitation."

"I am glad that you accepted it. Please, enter." The Lady stepped away from the door, half turning as she did.

Whatever Druadaen meant to say next evaporated like mist in a desert. Behind her, an immense freestanding mirror stood revealed. Speechless, he didn't realize its full size until he had moved to face it directly.

It was a perfect circle, approximately ten feet in diameter. Its reflection of the chamber was extraordinarily crisp, but seemed to curve inward, as if, although unmoving, the image was perpetually falling into the center of the glass.

If it is *glass, that is,* Druadaen revised a moment later. The mirror had no frame, and if it was suspended in midair by wires, they were too thin for his eyes to see. Instead, its utter stillness reminded him of a mantic effect: motionless in the exact spot of its creation until it faded.

He nodded at it and, throat dry, croaked, "The Mirror."

"So it is called," the Lady said after a pause that suggested her agreement was reluctant.

"What do *you* call it?" Druadaen asked, curiosity expelling the words before tact could hold them back.

She smiled. "It has many names in many languages. I prefer 'the Shimmer.'"

Druadaen frowned and, emboldened by her willingness to talk about the object, observed, "Shimmer often implies radiance, rather than mere reflection."

The Lady nodded. "And so it does here." In response to his dubious glance at their unaltered images in the Mirror, she added. "This chamber is also a Refractorium. It allows the Shimmer to influence how and where radiance is expressed."

Druadaen had spent a decade and a half working in Tlulanxu's Archive Recondite, reading widely among texts enigmatic and arcane, but not once had he encountered the puzzling term she had used. "What is a Refractorium?"

The Lady smiled again. "You shall find out soon enough, I suspect. But why don't we start with something simpler?"

"Such as?"

Her eyes held his. "The questions you came to ask."

"But...I am here at *your* invitation."

"So that you might ask the questions that are the next waypoint on your journey."

"You mean, the answer to the truth of the world?"

She shook her head. "No. We only discover that answer by living the question as a perpetual quest, moment to moment."

Druadaen felt lost. "Then, what questions do you mean?"

She shrugged. "The ones about yourself. Of course."

CHAPTER FIVE

Druadaen stared at her and was surprised by his own reaction: he chortled.

"Having your questions answered amuses you?" Despite her frown, she sounded bemused, not annoyed.

"No. I was just thinking how much I could have used such answers ten or fifteen years ago."

Her eyes fell. "I understand. I hope it is not too late for them to be of some use. Or comfort."

Druadaen stared into the Mirror. Or Shimmer. Or whatever it was. "Perhaps, but now my questions are very different. And very pressing."

She nodded. "That is why I invited you."

"For which I am also very grateful." Druadaen didn't add that he and his companions had been both mystified and startled at her means of conveying that invitation. A factotum of the Lady had occupied the body of a mindless invalid a continent away, who then sought out a similarly possessed proxy of a dragon—all in the space of two hours. Druadaen labored to produce a rueful grin. "It was a timely offer, too. Had I remained in Dunarra, I doubt I'd have found any place where I was still welcome."

"I am not so sure," the Lady countered gently. "The temples remain silent regarding your exile. I suspect they wish to avoid being asked—and put to task—about it."

Druadaen paused. Any ship which had already brought news to Shadowmere would have set sail *after* his own, so... "My Lady, you seem extraordinarily well informed for someone at such great remove from Dunarra."

"Shaananca keeps me apprised," she said simply.

"How...thoughtful," Druadaen replied as he digested the significance of her words. *You make it sound like you're a pair of cottagers chatting across a garden fence...instead of an ocean.*

She shook her head. "Not thoughtful: necessary. You may now find there is rarely enough time to seek answers to past questions—answers that could be crucial to your further journeys." When he frowned uncertainly, she added, "One should not push forward into uncharted regions without an adequate map of those already traversed."

Druadaen lifted one eyebrow. "Are my questions already known to you?"

She held his eyes. "I only know that you *have* questions. I do not know what they are nor will I be the one to answer them."

Druadaen resisted the impulse to shake his head. "Then how—?"

The Lady held up a hand and approached the Shimmer. "In the oldest extant records, the Mirror's name is rendered in a slightly different fashion. It is called the 'Looking Glass.'" She stared into its center, where the image of the two of them seemed to eternally fall inward. "In those days, that term was not only used to signify regular mirrors, but those that were able to show observers what they most needed to see."

"You mean, anywhere in the world?"

"Yes." She turned to him. "Or in themselves." She held his eyes. "What have you most wanted to see?"

Druadaen's forehead suddenly grew hot and then turned clammy. "My parents' relatives."

She nodded. "Because after your parents died, none could be located." Her tone was a statement, not a question.

He nodded, wondered: *another of Shaananca's apprisals?* "So do I just...look into the Mirror?"

The Lady was already doing so. "Yes."

For a moment, Druadaen kept his gaze away from the shining surface. After the fateful attack on his parents' farm, he'd wondered if the Consentium's failure to discover any relatives had been a merciful pretense, a means of concealing forebears who had been caught up in a singular disaster—or disgrace. He steeled himself for whatever might be revealed after all these years, then glanced at the mirror.

Nothing.

He looked more closely: still nothing. "So, it is true that I have no relatives?"

The Lady's wave was a negation. "If the Mirror is unchanged, it does not necessarily mean there is nothing to show. Rather, it may mean it lacks information or that the inquiry is not pertinent."

"And who decides that?" Druadaen said, controlling a surge of irritation.

The Lady shook her head. "If there is a consciousness that determines what the Mirror shows, no one has ever discerned what it is or why it operates as it does."

"So: it is still possible that members of my family were accursed."

The Lady frowned. "Why do you even suspect such a thing?"

"Well, if they angered a god, that could certainly explain their absence." Druadaen looked away. "That might explain why not one deity of the Helper pantheon would accept me into its creedland." He pushed down a resurgent pulse of old rage and helplessness. "The one time I was called to an epiphanium—Amarseker's—was so that I might be *personally* rejected."

The Lady folded her hands. "The deities of the Helper pantheon only visit vengeance upon those who have earned it by their *own* deeds."

"But I may have: my petitions were false. I only sought to adopt a creed because I thought I might then be able to speak to my parents again. How could a god fail to detect that?"

The Lady's eyebrows arched as she studied him. "Neither Shaananca nor I ever learned why you were turned away from so many temples, nor why Amarseker allowed you to become an epiphane. But I am certain of this: it was not to torment you."

"Yet he rejected me just like the rest."

"No," the Lady contradicted forcefully, "not *at all* like the rest. Amarseker brought you to the epiphanium, to the very edge of its creedland, so that you would know that his decision was neither disinterested nor capricious, but *unavoidable*."

Druadaen started. "And what would make my rejection 'unavoidable'? What could restrain a god's freedom of choice?"

The Lady's eyes sharpened as she leaned forward. "Now, *that* is a worthy question indeed." Her eyes grew softer as a small ironic smile bent one corner of her mouth. "It is a question that few sacrists would welcome."

"But it is not theirs to answer," Druadaen objected. "It was Amarseker himself who turned me away, not his sacrists."

The Lady looked positively sly. "An entity of great foresight might anticipate that a particularly clever mortal might eventually ask the troubling questions *you* have. If so, such an entity would be doing you a great favor by *not* accepting your petitions."

Perplexed, Druadaen matched her unwavering gaze—until it jarred loose a realization. "You mean—if I'd been accepted into Amarseker's Creedland and had asked such questions, I would have been guilty of *heresy*."

She nodded. "Once consecrated in a Helper creed, your questions about the truth of the world would have been a temple matter...with far more serious consequences."

Even as he started nodding, Druadaen realized that her answer begged a more confounding question. "But if the gods were protecting me, then Shaananca was right: that it was they who kept my father alive but inert. For years."

"That is logical," agreed the Lady.

"So how were you able to supersede their will?"

Her eyes opened wide. "Why do you say that?"

He kept his eyes steady on hers. "Because when last you visited Tlulanxu, Shaananca bade me ask you these very questions. But it was your final day and you were returning to your ship. I only saw you from afar, heading away from my father's patientium. So I ran there and found it empty. Except for what you left behind in his place."

"And what did I leave there?"

"A silver leaf that crumbled to dust the instant I saw it. As if it had been waiting for me to arrive." When the Lady did not respond, he asked pointedly, "Whatever power maintained my father was gone, and so was his body. Are you saying that *wasn't* your doing?"

"My doing?" Her frown was not one of trying to find a memory, but the right words. "My will precipitated what you saw, but I neither invoked nor witnessed the change."

Druadaen tried to keep his voice level. "I am not even sure what that means."

Her nod was sympathetic. "I am an ear to voices—and a monitor of certain forces—that are not of this world yet influence what passes within it. I traveled to Tlulanxu so that what my eyes and heart beheld became part of their awareness as well, that they might be moved to withdraw their intercession. When I sensed that my perception had been conveyed unto theirs, I left. And as for the silver leaf"—she smiled ironically—"though I may brush against forces which influence our destiny, I am not privy to their intents nor a witness of their manifestations. I am but an observer and a channel; neither the craft nor the doing is mine." The Lady considered him for a long moment. "What troubles you the most: how your father left this world or what he left in *you*?"

Druadaen was surprised by a sudden chill that ran the length of his body. "What do you mean?"

She shrugged. "I am aware that you greatly desire to honor him by realizing what he envisioned for you."

Druadaen shook his head, glanced away. "I reconciled myself to a very different path. Long ago."

"Have you?"

"When I was not assigned to the Legion—"

"I am not referring to the way in which your youthful hopes and plans were thwarted. What I am asking is this: Are you so very sure your present path is not actually the one your father foresaw?" She turned and looked at the mirror. He followed her gaze, wondering what drew her attention there . . .

. . . And saw himself at nine years of age, following his father down to the deck of one of the barges that plied the canals paralleling Dunarra's immense wallways.

Druadaen knew exactly what day he was seeing, down to the very minute. His family was preparing to depart Aedmurun for the voyage back to their farm in Connæar. He watched his young self scramble down the steep stairs, saw his father's vigilant eyes. They became thoughtful when his son was safely on the deck. "Well," he asked, leaning forward, "what did you think of Dunarra?"

As Druadaen saw himself turn to answer, he was suddenly as much in that moment as the one he was living atop Moorax Tower. Joy rose and flowered inside him—but was abruptly coated with salt-tipped thorns. Because that other moment, that brief sliver of the past, was one in which the world was so much simpler, in which both his mother and father were still alive, in which there was far more joy than sadness: where grief was still a stranger.

The Druadaen of that world frowned as he replied, "Well...I thought there would be more mancery in a big, Dunarran city."

His father nodded somberly. "Many have said the same thing."

Encouraged by learning that others shared his opinion, Druadaen added, "I also didn't expect so many machines. But they're so clever that I'll bet some people *think* they are magic."

His father nodded seriously as he tried to hide a smile behind his hand. "So, Dunarra was a disappointment?"

Druadaen reflected. "Well, not exactly a disappointment. But...well, it wasn't as grand as I imagined." He frowned again. "If the empire really does have all the power that people say, why not show more of it?"

His father shrugged. "Because Dunarra is *not* an empire, regardless of what 'people say.' If it was, it would rarely miss an opportunity to display its power. But that is not the Consentium's way."

"Why?" Druadaen asked.

"Because needless shows of power can make peoples who have less very envious. That envy can lead to hate, even war."

"And that is why we always have legions at the ready!" Druadaen offered as a triumphant conclusion.

But his father shook his head. "No, son. The Legion is not our first response to envy or even violence. It is our last."

"But our legions are what others fear," Druadaen answered, puzzled.

His father nodded. "Which is why they are our last step. A nation that holds its power through fear is hastening its fall almost as surely as if it appears weak. That is why when dealing with other nations, the Consentium works toward agreements that please everyone, but far more important is that they preserve everyone's pride."

"And if that fails? And they attack us?"

His father shook his head. "Then—and only then—are we justified in calling upon the Legion." His eyes were warm as he regarded Druadaen before adding. "Of course, I am not so sure that the Legion will still interest you when you are old enough to join it."

Druadaen started. "What do you mean?"

"Tell me, my son: why do you wish to become part of the Legion?"

Druadaen recalled thinking that question was very strange, particularly since he had explained his reasons many times before. "To defend the empi—eh, Consentium. To become a great and noble leader. Maybe one day, to become the Propretor Principles myself!"

"I think you mean Propretor Princeps," his father corrected with a soft smile. "But being a great general does not necessarily make one a great leader for the Consentium."

Druadaen frowned. "I guess that makes sense. Besides, leading a nation might be, well, boring. Even if it is *very* important!" he hastened to add, worried that his father might be disappointed that he considered it "boring."

But his father simply shook his head. "Not all

leaders become pretors. Or propretors, or emperors, or kings, either."

Druadaen had struggled to think about what other kind of leaders there might be. "Do...do you mean leaders like the ones in the old stories and legends? The kind that people followed because it just seemed like the right thing to do?"

At the time, he'd missed the subtle rue in his father's grin. "Yes, something like that. Although leaders do not always have followers, either."

Druadaen remembered being very confused by that. A leader without followers sounded a bit like a bird without wings. But before he could ask how such a thing was possible, his mother appeared at the top of the stairs. As they hurried to assist her, she rolled her eyes and reminded them that she was merely pregnant, not an invalid. However, they were not deterred and she did not insist that they relent...

The image in the Mirror faded. As it did, thin, glistening ripples played briefly across its surface... and Druadaen understood where its other name had come from. It had indeed shimmered, if only for a fraction of a second. Exhaling, he realized he'd been holding his breath. "Thank you," he murmured.

The Lady shook her head. "I did nothing. The doing is the Mirror's. And it only reacts to a small fraction of those who stand before it."

"So you must have known it would react to me."

The Lady pursed her lips. "Let us just say I had a strong suspicion that it would."

"Why?"

She gestured toward their reflections. "Just as it showed your past unbidden, so it showed me images of you." She nodded at his surprise. "That usually means that the Mirror has something to reveal to that person. And your images began appearing the day you were exiled. So I suspect they were prompted by that and the course upon which it has put you."

"The course upon which—?"

"Despite official disinterest and then disapproval, you investigated conundrums posed by the Bent, the giants, the dragons, and even the history of Arrdanc itself. It makes little sense, therefore, that you would now ignore the deeper, cosmological quandaries which those raised—and which led to your exile."

Druadaen tried to keep the disbelief from his face. "So you suspect that the Mirror will show me where I should go next?"

The Lady shook her head. "Many believe that the terms Shimmer and Mirror are synonyms. They are not. A Shimmer is not just a way to see another place, but to travel there."

Druadaen felt his scalp tug back sharply. He had seen mentions of such things in a few older, eccentric tomes, but had dismissed them as the fabulations of overly imaginative—or gullible—minds. "So this Mirror—this Shimmer—is a ... a portal, of some kind?"

"In the scant, ancient sources that refer to such objects, they are typically called *osmotia*. But a Shimmer"—she gestured behind her—"is different from other portals. And this one has a special name; it is known as the gateway to the Domain of the Dead. Or possibly, the Domain of the Deities. Translations differ."

Druadaen swallowed. "They sound equally ominous."

She smiled. "They do, don't they? I suspect the

scholar who coined them had a flair for the dramatic. However, the Shimmer does have three unique properties. Firstly, those who pass through it cannot return through it—those few who return to Arrdanc at all. Secondly, persons on the other side of it have been able to reach out to the mind of the Lady or Lord of the Mirror. Some speculate that these are the voices of those who have died, others conjecture them to belong to those who passed through yet remain marginally connected to this world. Lastly, there are other, unknown voices that occasionally send whispers through the Shimmer. Many of them use ancient tongues to convey cryptic messages. Some scholars assert those to be messages from the gods themselves."

Druadaen was beyond being surprised. "Are you suggesting that I pass through this portal—eh, this Shimmer? To find out about what? The gods? And learn the truth of the world from them?"

The Lady folded her hands. "I suggest nothing. If you are meant to go through, you shall." She saw his perplexity. "The annals kept by the prior Lords and Ladies of the Mirror claim that those who step through the Shimmer feel a compulsion to do so, as if they are completing a journey upon which they are already embarked."

"Couldn't that also be a euphemism for suicide?"

"Again, I cannot say." She gazed sadly at him. "Perhaps you would have been happy simply to receive answers to the vexing questions of your youth."

He swallowed. "Possibly. But at various points along the winding path that brought me here, several others have mentioned this tower . . . and you . . . as the next step toward—well, toward wherever I am bound." He glanced at the suddenly terrifying mirror. "I did not anticipate that it would require a leap of faith into what might be oblivion."

As the word "oblivion" left Druadaen's lips, the surface of the Shimmer ceased to reflect the room; it became a glimmering disk with faint currents moving back and forth upon it.

The Lady nodded. "Ah." Turning to meet his inquiring stare, she explained: "It is calling to you."

CHAPTER SIX

Ahearn happened to be stealing glances at Corum Torshaenyx's striking hair when the Tualaran looked up, as if hearing a sound that was inaudible to the rest of them. He pushed off the wall against which he'd been leaning. "Come with me," he murmured.

"Here, now," Ahearn began, but found himself following even as he was preparing to object, "we're not about to leave our mate without a word from or about him!"

But Corum was already approaching two lithe figures that had emerged from a homely building not much larger than a shed, set slightly back from the edge of the street. Before Ahearn could continue forward to press his point, a thin but very strong hand clamped down upon his bicep.

S'ythreni was staring at the figures as they left the shadows: Iavu in their customary—and much-coveted—sheathe armor. "Don't follow him," she hissed, but her tone said, *don't intrude.*

Ahearn was as startled by her actions as her words; she had never before touched him. "What's got into you, High Ears?"

"Don't call me that! Not here."

"But—?"

Elweyr interrupted. "Not around them." He tilted his head slightly toward the two Iavarain now in quiet council with the Tualaran.

Ahearn frowned. "I'll not be tethering my tongue for the likes of—"

"Please," she muttered, her voice as desperate as it was angry. "They are not just Iavarain. They are Uulamantre."

"What? How do you know?"

"Because I could not"—she fought for a word—"'sense' them."

Ahearn sighed. "I'm sure I'll regret asking what you mean by that, but—?"

Elweyr stepped in front of Ahearn, as if trying to block the open space between him and the Uulamantre. "You've seen that Iavarain are often aware of each other at considerable distances."

Ahearn considered. "Aye. After our time with the dragon, S'ythreni was sure we'd meet Tharêdæath in—"

Elweyr waved away the details. "Well, only Uulamantre can elect to make themselves undetectable to others of their kind."

Ahearn frowned, glanced at S'ythreni. "Would those...gentlemen...think less of you simply because I used your nickname?"

She looked both annoyed and grateful. "Firstly, I don't like that nickname and you know it. Secondly, they're not both gentlemen. Well, not presently."

Ahearn squinted, then realized he was about to bump his nose into more of the unfathomable sex and gender changeability that often made dealings with both Iavarain and aeostu so bloody exasperating. He managed to suppress an annoyed oath. "Well, then . . . S'ythreni . . . I shall not make trouble," he vowed somberly . . . just as he felt Elweyr poke him in the ribs.

He rounded on his friend with an impatient "What now?" . . . and found himself looking over the mantic's shoulder and into Corum's startlingly blue eyes. "Didn't hear you return," the swordsman mumbled.

The Tualaran merely nodded and held out a small black leather folio, not much larger than a wallet. Ahearn stared at it as the other explained, "The Lady's invitation assured you recompense for the costs of your journey here. This should prove sufficient."

Ahearn managed to resist the temptation of snatching the strange purse before anyone—including himself—could reflexively point out that they'd spent almost no coin getting to Shadowmere. Their travel with Tharêdæath had been gratis, and their voyage aboard Nolus' *Atremoënse* had been working passage. But the inner voice of parental care and prudence hurried to remind him: *yeh must put by as much as you can for your little tad—*

He cut off that tempting thought with a sharp shake of his head. "Nay, we spent no coin reaching these shores." He felt the others' eyes on him, couldn't tell if they were aghast or amazed. *Likely both.*

One of Corum's eyebrows might have elevated slightly. He withdrew the folio . . . but only to add one more small gold ingot to the others that peeked briefly beyond the open leather flap. Once secured, he proffered it again. "Then this is in consideration for your troubles"—one side of his mouth crinkled upwards—"and your honesty."

Ahearn had to keep himself from calculating the approximate value of the wallet's contents based on its heft and what he had glimpsed. Instead, he handed it off to Umkhira whose role as group purser had been, in retrospect, inevitable; her attitude toward coin ranged from distaste to disdain. "We are very much obliged," the swordsman answered. "I do hope we will have the opportunity to thank the Lady for her kindness and generosity." He had to take long strides to complete his courtesies; Corum was already setting a brisk pace away from the tower and the one Uulamantre who had taken his place near its entrance. "The opportunity to thank her *in person*, is what I mean to say," Ahearn added fretfully, glancing back at the iron-bound door.

Corum nodded. "We shall learn that soon enough."

Ahearn exchanged glances with the others, whose surprised frowns were probably matches for the one he'd felt pulling down his own brow. "Eh, just *how* soon d'yeh think that might be?"

With the second Uulamantre following at a distance, Corum slowed to an unhurried walk. "I cannot say. But this axiom was old before I was born: the only thing predictable about a visit to the Lady's Tower is that the outcome is never predictable."

They continued westward in silence until, leaving the shop-lined street, they merged into the foot traffic of the broad wharfside boulevard. Although less congested than before, navigating it as a group remained frustrating.

Ahearn glanced around, noticing how far back their Uulamantre rearguard had dropped. "With all due respect, is it prudent that you escort us alone?"

Corum's dimples twitched. "I suspect I am ready for any challenges we might encounter."

From the direction of the Uulamantre, Ahearn heard a smothered exclamation of "*Mahu!*" He had heard S'ythreni utter a similar reaction to a quip or a gaffe—usually his; it was the Iavarain equivalent of an amused scoff.

Corum pretended not to have heard it. "More importantly, where I go, the Lady's will and eye is known to follow. Twenty more like me could not make us so safe as that."

Elweyr still sounded slightly anxious. "And where, exactly, are you leading us?"

"To a safe place overseen by a friend: Talshane, the Outrider station chief who I believe assisted you in Treve last year."

Ahearn nodded gratefully, but thought, *You seem a fine fellow, Corum, but you know entirely too much about us.*

"But he was only visiting Treve, as I recall," Umkhira said. "His actual post was here in Shadowmere."

Corum nodded. "You recall correctly. He is the officer in charge of the Consentium's primary base in Far Amitryea."

Umkhira looked and sounded even more interested. "A military base?"

Corum shook his head. "The Outrider Expeditionary Cohort's premises are primarily diplomatic, having limited exequatur granted by A'Querlaan and this city."

Ahearn was so focused on the exchange about

Talshane that he almost missed S'ythreni's mumbled "I shall slow for a moment, then catch up."

As she turned in the direction of their Uulamantre rearguard, Ahearn frowned, puzzled. "Why?"

"I was asked to."

Ahearn shook his head. "I didn't hear anything." S'ythreni stared at him; understanding dawned. "Ah, you can sense him now?"

"Her. Yes. I won't be long."

Corum glanced briefly at Ahearn before setting a slightly faster pace. The swordsman understood the signal, gestured for the others to hang back. When he had caught up, the Tualaran asked, "Your Iavan companion seems reluctant to meet her own kind. May I ask why?"

Ahearn shrugged as they made their way through a line of waiting stevedores. "I don't know and I don't ask. It's part of how we all manage to get along."

Corum was silent for a moment. Then: "Are you aware how Iavarain normally travel?"

"You mean 'not amongst humans'? Yes, I'm quite familiar. She mentions it regularly."

Corum tactfully refocused the topic. "I was alluding to the fact that they almost never travel *alone*. That is very unusual. Especially when traveling among humans."

Ahearn shrugged. "I suppose she has her reasons. She's very private."

"Clearly," the Tualaran answered. Another pause. "You would do well to be prepared for...surprises."

Ahearn stared at him. "What kind of surprises?"

Corum sounded faintly apologetic. "If I knew, I'd tell you." He pointed to a squat, walled compound that was far more reminiscent of a citadel than a consulate. "Our destination."

Umkhira snorted. "And what manner of diplomats staff such a sturdy place?"

"Those who are also Couriers and Outriders."

"So," S'ythreni's voice called from behind as she returned, "they're mostly scouts, trackers, observers, rescuers, and prospectors for anything of interest to the Consentium. I'll warrant they're as polite as any other Dunarrans, but don't scruple to use force when they deem it necessary."

"You are quite correct, *Sahn* S'ythreni," Corum said, pronouncing the formal ungendered title with a surprisingly good accent. "That is why both groups are deemed to be elite; their duties are for more complex than those performed by legiars."

Umkhira nodded. "Not all who can wield a weapon are equally skilled at restraining the urge to do so."

Corum nodded. "Or to seek other means to achieve their ends."

"They still seem to do a lot of fighting," S'ythreni muttered darkly.

"Their duties often take them to places where they are given no alternatives," Corum agreed. "But unwarranted violence results in dismissal—particularly when it is a first reaction to an unknown species."

As if reciting from memory, Elweyr said, "'All too easily, the different becomes the excluded, which becomes the feared, which becomes the hated, and so, becomes a soulless foe to be slain.'" They all stared at him, including Corum. He shrugged. "If you live in a city on Dunarra's border, you meet Outriders."

"And learn their axioms?" Umkhira wondered.

He shrugged. "The basic ones. I'm told there are others that we don't hear."

S'ythreni frowned. "Why not?"

It was Corum who answered. "Because most long-service Outriders who'd know those less common axioms spend less and less time in or near Dunarra. Most live out their lives elsewhere."

Ahearn smiled sideways at the Tualaran. "So they go a bit native, do they?"

"Many do," he replied somberly. "Those without families often do not come back at all. Fewer still participate in the public life of the Consentium." Turning a corner, he gestured to the fortlike structure that had been only partially visible over the roofs. He gestured toward its portcullised entry.

"What?" Ahearn exclaimed. "Yer not coming with us?"

"I am not. Please bear this to Talshane personally." He held out a leather advice pouch. "Tell him it comes from Cerven. Do not give it to intermediaries; it must go directly into Talshane's hands. I shall wait without, that you may converse freely with him."

Ahearn scratched one ear. "We've naught private to discuss with the man."

Corum's answer came with a small smile. "Such expectations can prove erroneous—and are often awkward to discover in the presence of others. Besides, I instructed Cerven to rejoin me here, and he will be along presently."

Umkhira nodded her understanding: as she had at Treve, she admired the portcullis as she passed beneath it. S'ythreni followed with a rueful shake of her head, as if the fortified entrance confirmed her opinion that Dunarrans suffered from linked manias of anxiety and precaution. Ahearn brought up the rear with Elweyr.

Although it took a while to reach Talshane himself—stopping to announce themselves to numerous sentries—he reacted to their appearance at his office with a broad grin, one palm swept toward waiting chairs, the other held up against formal greetings. Ahearn admired the deft social skills which made it feel as though they had seen him in Treve just yesterday, instead of nineteen moonphases ago.

When Ahearn approached Talshane's desk, the other's grin turned crafty. "So you've got the advice pouch from Cerven, then."

Ahearn handed it over and took a seat as Talshane thumbed hastily through the contents. "You're just off the *Atremoënse*, yes?"

Ahearn managed not to start. *Another bloke who knows way too much about us.* "As well informed as ever, I see."

The station chief's only reply was a rueful bend to his grin. "In my experience, 'just off a ship' means 'just escaped from ship's food,' so how about a meal?"

"Please," breathed S'ythreni.

Ahearn nodded as he probed, "And yeh even have lunch waiting for us. Well, well: it seems we were expected."

Talshane nodded as he sat. "The news came a few hours ago." He sat back and steepled his hands. "And I take it Druadaen is closeted with the Lady."

"That is a very astute guess...*if* it's a guess," Elweyr commented.

Talshane's tone was wry. "He's the only one of

you who's missing and the only one with an obvious reason to go there."

S'ythreni sighed. "So you've heard about what happened in Tlulanxu, then."

"Nothing specific, but we meet regularly with Helper sacrists. They mentioned a closed hearing in the Propretorium that sent a ripple through all their temples some moonphases ago. Now the Lady is chatting with Druadaen, and I get a request from her factotums to, er, entertain you for a while."

"I do not see why you would so readily connect the events in Tlulanxu to our arrival here," Umkhira muttered, frowning.

Talshane's grin brightened. "Even from Far Amitryea, I can read the political weather in Tlulanxu. Besides, when I met you last year, Druadaen's researches had already unnerved some powers there, but the first thing he asked me was how to find the giants south of Treve." He shook his head. "Anyone who stays a course so costly is likely to keep steering by whatever star guides them, come what may." He spread his hands to indicate the group. "And here you are. Now, what exactly did he do this time?"

Ahearn smiled crookedly. "He asked more questions that weren't supposed to be asked. Got exiled for his troubles."

Talshane started. "Exiled? Do you mean to say they took away his citizenship?"

Ahearn's slow, somber nod was a match for the others'.

S'ythreni's addition was arch. "Worse yet, not even the highest and mightiest of them could answer his questions. Or resolve the apparent contradictions."

Talshane sighed. "Yes, if one wants to be banished, that will do it every time." He rubbed his chin. "In one way, though, I suppose his exile was fortuitous."

Umkhira frowned mightily. "How so?"

"Well, so long as he remained in the service of Dunarra, the parties he made nervous would not have been likely to believe that an invitation from the Lady was anything other than a sign that she was taking sides. Against them."

Ahearn nodded, managed not to point out that none of them had mentioned the Lady's invitation to their exceedingly affable host.

Elweyr frowned. "Everything I hear that connects the Mirror to the affairs of kings and countries is, well . . ."

"Perplexing?"

"And enigmatic," he amended. "Even perverse."

Talshane emitted a sound that was half grunt and half chortle. "Quite true. But compared to the perversities that pass for normal affairs in Tlulanxu right now?" He shook his head. "I'm much happier here, half a world away. There's little joy in walking those streets if you have to keep your elbows tucked in and your chin tucked down. If you take my meaning."

Umkhira huffed in sympathetic fellowship. "By which you mean, all the rules of that place? They are like its walls: to keep people in their place. And to keep everyone else outside."

Talshane squinted at her summation. "I view it a bit differently, Mistress Warrior. I don't see the walls as the disease, but the symptom. Long ago, they protected us in dangerous times. The problem is that they became old, comfortable friends and, as you say, walls don't just keep things out; they hem you in. So the cost of our safety has been ignorance of the wider world."

"And fear of outsiders?" Elweyr ventured.

"Not so much." He smiled ruefully. "Except, of course when it's one of our own who's been *changed* by that wider world. Now *that* is worrisome."

S'ythreni's face was impassive, but her voice scornful. "So, Couriers—the only Dunarrans who routinely *do* interact with the rest of the world—now encounter distrust and suspicion in their own land because it makes them 'different'?"

Talshane frowned. "Well, I wouldn't put it as baldly as that."

S'ythreni's mouth didn't smile, but her eyes did. "I'm waiting to hear you say you disagree."

Talshane's rueful grin was back. "Well, I didn't say that either, did I, *Alva* S'ythreni?"

Ahearn couldn't suppress a chortle. "I hope you won't mind me saying that you're...well, you're not like most of the Dunarrans I've met."

Talshane almost laughed himself. "Well, I suppose most of us Outriders are a bit atypical to start out with. One of the first things we're asked is if we're 'willing to be washed by the waters of other peoples and places.'" He shrugged. "Not many people like that in any culture. Mine included."

Elweyr looked over folded hands. "Many people think Dunarrans are actually much *worse* at that than other nations."

Talshane nodded. "I can see how it seems so, but I think that would be mistaking an effect for a cause."

"Eh?" grunted Ahearn.

S'ythreni nodded slowly. "It goes back to the walls. Dunarrans don't have a greater instinct to avoid new cultures, but they have few neighbors and no reason to go beyond their well-patrolled borders."

"Ah, so it's just as if you don't exercise a muscle. It weakens, atrophies." Ahearn tried not to be offended when S'ythreni reacted to his use of the word "atrophy" with a sharply raised eyebrow and look of surprise.

Talshane grimaced. "And that weakness has grown ever since we retracted at the end of the First Consentium." He glanced over their heads and, relieved, jumped to his feet. "But now, lunch is served! And not a moment too soon!"

CHAPTER SEVEN

Druadaen discovered he was still staring into the Shimmer, simultaneously terrified and fascinated. His question came out as a dry croak. "My Lady, you said that those who enter this, er, special *osmotium*, are unable to return through it?"

"'Unable'? That is not known one way or the other. I said that so far as we know, no one who used it to exit Arrdanc has used it to return."

Well, that's certainly a significant difference, but it doesn't help me decide whether I should risk stepping into what could be infinity, oblivion, or both. "Is there any speculation as to why the Shimmer doesn't allow anyone to come back?"

The Lady laughed ruefully. "There is *always* speculation. But the simple fact is that no one knows how it works, or when it was made, or by whom. It is not even known if it was built into this tower or if this tower was built around it. We only know that it is very, very old, since it is mentioned in the earliest records."

Druadaen nodded, discovered he was staring into the Shimmer again. Studying it more closely, he noticed that the fine, glimmering ripples followed a pattern similar to the one he'd detected in the reflection: a slow inward collapse toward the center. It imparted the impression that he was always on the verge of falling into it ...

He started, stepped back: *why am I even considering this? It's madness! Is it really worth risking my life just to find out what is on the other side—even assuming it's not a void?* But a quieter voice kept reminding him of the unlikely combination of meetings and discoveries that had led him to the Shimmer, and that it might just lead to a place where he could learn the truth of the world.

Behind him, fabric rustled; the Lady had taken a seat to one side of the Shimmer.

"I am sorry, my Lady. I am ... conflicted."

She smiled, waved away his concern. "I am in no hurry." She frowned. "I cannot speak for the Shimmer, though."

Druadaen straightened. "How long does it remain in this state?"

She shrugged. "The duration varies, but how much and why—?" She raised a single resigned palm toward the ceiling. "If there is a pattern, the occurrences are so infrequent and the circumstances so different that speculation is pointless."

Druadaen shook his head. "This is madness," he muttered. *And yet, yet ...* "My Lady, are you *sure* this is the best way to see the truth of the world?"

Her smile was sad and apologetic. "I wish I was. But my affinity with the Shimmer only confers impressions and a sense of the rhythms which may govern events. It helps me feel and see pieces of reality as they move around me, forming and evolving patterns. But I have no idea how I come to that awareness."

Druadaen returned a sad smile of his own. "I wish I could see those patterns the way you do, for just one moment. But I can't. I can't even be sure they exist."

Before the Lady could answer, Druadaen felt sudden movement on his wrist. In the blink of an eye, the velene had spun out of its bracer form and wrapped around his forearm, staring at him. Then it turned toward the Shimmer for several seconds—long enough that Druadaen could not possibly mistake its focus—and then back toward him. As he overcame his surprise, the small deep-silver dragonette leaned toward the portal, tilting almost comically.

Druadaen raised an eyebrow at it. "So what's your intent this time: saving my life or sending me to my doom?"

"It will not mislead you," the Lady said, standing as if meeting a newly arrived visitor.

Druadaen looked dubiously from her to the velene. "About half of the time, it's led me into danger."

She smiled. "I did not say it would always steer you toward safety. Sometimes, taking the most promising path is also the most hazardous."

He glanced at the Shimmer, then the velene. "And which is it this time?"

"I have no way to know...and yet, I am sure it is not malign."

Druadaen swallowed, could hardly believe he was starting to consider walking through the—"Wait: the others! I have to discuss this with them. We travel as a company, so any decision here—"

The Lady shook her head. "The Shimmer did not show images of them. Nor is it calling to them."

Druadaen wondered how she could be certain of the last, but her tone was the same she used when making her other preternaturally certain assertions. "Well, at least I have to tell them what I might be doing. They deserve to know."

"They do, but if you leave, it is unlikely the Shimmer will call you again."

"*How* unlikely?"

She considered the glimmering circle. "It has never opened more than once for any person. Those who only meant to defer its invitation returned to find it unresponsive." She stepped to one side of the Shimmer. "It has decided. Now, so must you."

Druadaen rubbed his forehead. "I must at least write my friends a letter," he muttered—but then realized: *And what should I write? That I'm stepping into a maelstrom of infinite possibilities, including ignominious death? That I don't know when or if I will ever return?*

The Lady had come to stand alongside him. "I have some experience explaining such matters to those who are left behind."

"You will tell them?"

"I will craft the message. It will be borne to them by an intermediary whom they trust. And whose understanding of the Shimmer's nature will afford them answers to more questions than I may anticipate and touch upon in a mere letter."

Druadaen nodded his thanks, glanced toward the

shutters that separated them from the strange skyline of Shadowmere. "But if I leave them here, what will become of the hopes they vested in further journeys together, of making a better—?"

The Lady shook her head sharply. "They shall remain under my protection as long as they choose, and I can offer them employment that will be both useful to me and quite beneficial to them."

Druadaen couldn't be sure whether the Lady was being kind, was pushing him toward the Shimmer, or both. But a deeper reluctance was rising. "I owe my life to each of them. In some cases, more than once."

She nodded. "Yes. And they to you."

"That doesn't mean I won't worry about them."

"Just as you will worry about them if you stay," she nodded.

"What do you mean?"

She folded her hands. "Let us say that you turn away from this portal to whatever lies beyond. You will still persist in your quest, and so, continue to arouse the ire—and attacks—of those who wish you not to." Her brows lowered into a severe line. "The more questions you ask, the more risky it becomes to travel with you."

Druadaen nodded, stared at the Shimmer. Put that way, it was difficult to see which path might bring his friends greater safety, just as it was impossible to know—*know*!—the best path to find the answers he sought.

The velene unwrapped slowly from his forearm and bent downward. He glanced at it just as the tiny paws pulled up his sword by its baldric, brushing its pommel against his hand.

Light exploded somewhere behind Druadaen's eyes as a shock moved through his body. Not painful, but very intense. He gripped the hilt—and felt the sword stir in its scabbard, as if it were tugging his hand.

Toward the Shimmer.

The Lady smiled. "Evidently, both your sai'niin companions have very strong opinions on your best course of action."

Companions? Is the sword some kind of entity, too? He glanced at the Lady, then at the sword. "Trying to get me killed again, are you?"

Where Druadaen's voice had been wry, even playful, the Lady's was solemn. "Sai'niin has never been known to intentionally lead anyone to death. That is never its purpose."

"It has a 'purpose'?"

"Surely you have seen signs of that."

Druadaen had, and had tried to discern what that purpose might be, but both the velene and the sword had been obdurately unresponsive. "Unfortunately, they do not deign to become active until a situation threatens to take a fatal turn."

The Lady studied him. "Do they respond to events that might prove fatal—or, rather, *fateful*?"

Druadaen stared at her. "I will have to think on that." His eyes slipped sideways to the glimmering circle in the room. "I have one last reservation."

She nodded. "That your friends might try to follow you, and so, meet their deaths."

He started. "Is it that obvious?" He considered. "Or that common?"

"Both. Although we know relatively little about those who pass through the Shimmer, the reactions of those left behind are well recorded. Among those groups where the personal bonds are strong, the instinct to 'rescue' the one who has departed is often equally strong."

"If my companions decide to do so, could you, well, persuade them otherwise?"

The Lady frowned. "There is a more fundamental question: *Should* I persuade them otherwise? What if it is their path to follow you, just as it is yours to pass through the Shimmer?"

Druadaen sought an answer, found none. He wasn't eager to take that step, or even compelled. But the responses of the velene and the sword seemed to echo a deeper voice within: that the ultimate consequence of all his travels, all his discoveries, had been to bring him to this place and point in time. That his next step was not the end of his journey, but the beginning.

He sighed. "I am decided." The velene re-curled around his wrist and became a bracer. Druadaen smiled. "I guess all three of us are. So, how do I prepare to pass through?"

The Lady crossed her arms. "There is little to be done. But I must share one last thing that could have influenced your reaction when the Shimmer called you."

Druadaen nodded for her to continue. "I am intrigued."

"It involves the Hidden Archivist."

He stood straighter. The kidnapping of the Hidden Archivist from his sanctuary in Tlulanxu—and Druadaen's wildly circumstantial connections to its probable perpetrators—had been the pretext under which Dunarra's authorities had called him to appear before them.

Druadaen nodded. "So they had to, er, maintain the effect until the Archivist had gone through. Which means they were unable to go through themselves."

The Lady's hands were clenched and white. "And we hadn't the time to worry over that person's fate."

Druadaen nodded, even as he wondered, *And who is "we"?*

"As the Archivist stumbled through, he shouted that he was being pursued. For all we knew, his captors could have arrived in the next moment and overwhelmed us."

"So you destroyed the osmotium you made on this end?"

The Lady seemed to collect herself for a moment. "No, we employed a more...aggressive alternative. We had foreseen that, if the Archivist had to be brought through the Nidus' osmotium, the person controlling it would have to remain behind—and close at hand. So if any of the forces pursuing the Archivist could not follow him, they were likely to turn on that person. So we used the osmotium here to eliminate those pursuers."

"How?"

"By repositioning our osmotium in this chamber before the pursuers came through."

Druadaen shook his head. "I do not understand."

The Lady pointed at the Shimmer.

Druadaen's spine grew suddenly cold. "You moved it closer to the Mirror. So that when the pursuers emerged here, they went through?"

She nodded. "I am told it has only been used that way three times before."

"What happens to those who enter that way?"

She closed her eyes. "A few seem to survive. Most are never seen again." She opened her eyes. "Understand: this outcome only occurs when the person entering the Shimmer has *not* been called by it."

Druadaen, slightly relieved, could not tell if this made the idea of entering the Shimmer more terrifying, more compelling, or both. "How many of the enemy were...well..." He gestured at the silent portal.

"At least half a dozen, but they were just a blur. The osmotium was only two feet from the Shimmer and they came at a run. But I would not be surprised if several survived. At least three of those who came into contact with it did not simply disappear, but dwindled into the surface of the Shimmer—just like those whom it has called."

"And the others?"

She shook her head. "They simply passed into the Shimmer. I saw no shrinking, no transition at all."

Druadaen nodded. "Only one other question. It has been almost nine moonphases since the Hidden Archivist was rescued, yet it seems you believe that some of the pursuers might have survived on the other side of the Shimmer."

"Yes."

"So do you have reason to suspect that they will still be near the other end of the Shimmer? After all this time?"

"Not particularly. But then again, they are among the least predictable of opponents." She measured his uncomprehending stare. "They were Tsost-Dyxoi, of course."

"Of course," Druadaen croaked. Dunarra's foes since the end of the First Consentium. The ones who'd probably killed his parents and had come quite close to killing him just before he'd been inducted into the Couriers.

The Lady was studying his face closely. "Are you still resolved to go?"

"I am," Druadaen heard himself say. Instead of pushing him away from the Shimmer, the possibility that the Tsost-Dyxoi might be involved was drawing him toward it. "I will trust to your wisdom and discretion concerning a message to my friends." He smiled ruefully, expecting he already knew the answer. "I would prefer to go with my full kit, but I suspect there isn't time for that, either."

The Lady smiled back. "Almost certainly not. However, we have adequate gear here." She gestured to a low, wide trunk at the other end of the room.

He discovered a small, efficiently packed backpack and first-rate equipment. It was all, however, of wildly different manufactures and origins. "I can see you have done this before."

"And even so, we usually neglect to include something important. Do you anticipate any other needs?"

He considered. "A parka."

"You shall have it. But...why that?"

"Because as a Courier I visited climes that were intemperate due to heat and to cold. One learns quickly enough that in a hot region, you may strip off whatever layers you must. But in a cold region, if you cannot add a thick layer to retain heat, death can come very, very quickly."

Before long, a prefatory knock on the door barely preceded the entry of the Solorin nativist that he had passed on the stairs. The fellow was carrying a very well-made coat. It wasn't exactly a parka, but it was more than adequate and probably less bulky.

The Lady, who'd watched Druadaen's preparations, observed, "I suspect that you already are better prepared than most who step through the Shimmer."

Druadaen felt slightly more optimistic about the outcome of his impending mad adventure. "You refer to the velene and the sword, I presume?"

"They will no doubt be helpful, but I was reflecting upon something the dragon communicated to me: that you have a dragon mind."

"A dragon's mind?"

"No: that you have a *dragon-mind*."

Unsure how those things could be different, Druadaen murmured, "That's a rather strange thing to say."

"Yet that is specifically what was conveyed."

Druadaen shrugged his shoulders into the rucksack's straps. "I imagine a dragon-mind is one that can't be read." The dragon had certainly been surprised, and somewhat rattled, by that discovery.

But the Lady was shaking her head. "As you point out, a dragon's mind is inviolate: their thoughts cannot be influenced nor can their memories be read. But also like you, a dragon's dreams are neither predetermined nor orderly. Nor has there ever been contact between them and the gods. They deem all this to mean that theirs is 'a mind beyond reach.'" Her eyes grave, she held his for a moment before adding, "If you do indeed have a dragon-mind, you are singularly well suited to investigate mysteries that others might wish to hide."

"That would make me singularly threatening to their interests, as well."

The Lady, eyes unchanged, nodded slowly, somberly. "You seem to be ready."

Druadaen made sure the bow's string was both secure and came easy to hand. "It seems I am." He walked back toward the Shimmer. "Is there *anything* else you can tell me about the other side? Factual or fanciful: it doesn't matter."

"I am not sure 'the other side' is a single place. The few stories we have are so different in every regard that some speculate that it may lead to several different destinations. That may be why it is also called the Vortex of Worlds."

"And it is called that by whom?"

"The name is as old as the Shimmer itself. But that, too, could be truth, rumor, or a bit of both." She nodded at his readiness. "I wish you good luck, Druadaen u'Tarthenex." She waited as if expecting him to say something.

Druadaen almost laughed. Such a pivotal moment—stepping through a portal into another world or reality or both—and he had no words to share. He didn't even have any thought in his head, other than to be alert and yet not too hasty in reacting to—well, whatever he first saw on the other side.

Then he thought about Ahearn and he did laugh.

The Lady's eyebrows arched in surprise. "I am not sure anyone has ever laughed on the threshold of the Shimmer."

He chuckled. "That may be because they did not have such a confounding companion as my friend Ahearn who would, this second, be making merry at my expense."

"How so?"

"Why, for being a needlessly voluble Dunarran, who—at the worst possible moment—had nothing to say!"

She laughed with him. "He sounds a good friend."

"He is." *And maybe, having no grand parting words is a virtue akin to simplicity.* "Just wish them well for me."

He stepped through the silvery ripples of the Shimmer, wondering what would happen next.

CHAPTER EIGHT

The empty lunch trenchers had just been removed and Ahearn was about to wax both poetic and prolific upon the virtues of common food excellently prepared when S'ythreni started as though she'd been stuck with a very long pin.

Alarmed, expecting to see her choking on the pit of a just-finished peach, Ahearn exclaimed, "Some't went down sideways?" He rose to help—but she angrily waved him into his seat. But her face was pale with shock, not fury. "What is it, High Ears? What has—?"

"He's gone." Her whisper was almost a gasp.

"What?" said Ahearn, utterly confused.

"Who?" Umkhira asked, frowning. But Elweyr was simply nodding.

"Who do you think?" S'ythreni snapped.

"Druadaen?" Ahearn asked, knowing that's what she meant, but too stunned to fully accept it.

S'ythreni plainly understood his question as disbelief rather than confusion: she nodded, jaw rigid.

Talshane had been watching her carefully, quietly. "So: you skeined him, at some point."

Her eyebrows raised as the strange term came out of his mouth, but she nodded.

"Skeined?" repeated Ahearn helplessly. "Please: in a language I speak! And *now!*"

It was Elweyr who answered. "All Iavarain sense each other in what they call the Great Weave. However, they can pick out another strand—usually a being from another race—and so bring it into the awareness of the others."

"And you did this to the Dunarran?" Umkhira asked in a tone both surprised and affronted. "Did he know? Did you ask him?"

"Neither was necessary," S'ythreni hissed through nearly clenched teeth.

"How dare—!"

Ahearn interrupted, as much to prevent a fight as resolve what, to him, seemed a certain contradiction. "What I want to know is how you did it, High Ears. After all, it's settled fact that the Dunarran's mind can't even be touched or tickled by a dragon."

She rolled her eyes. "The Great Weave has no need of 'touching' or 'tickling' a mind to be aware of it."

Ahearn had risen to his feet without even realizing it, was itching to be out the door, through the portcullis, and on the streets of Shadowmere in order to— Well, what the bloody blazes could he do, anyway, if the daft Dunarran's meeting with the Lady resulted in his being swept out of existence? "I realize that I am not a vaulting intellect, S'ythreni, but I didn't ask what skeining *isn't*; I asked what it *is*. And if you can't or won't do me the simple courtesy of—"

Talshane leaned forward slowly, calmly. "One of her people explained it this way to me: Think of yourself among thousands of people, all lying half-asleep in an endless field, on the edge of dreaming the same dream."

Ahearn frowned. "Eh...very well."

"One of them rouses, gets up, notices a butterfly perched on your arm, points it out, lies down again—and in that moment, your awareness of it becomes part of everyone's shared almost-dream."

Ahearn's awareness was, however, fixed upon making sure his frown did not become a scowl. "I'd hoped for an explanation rather than a long string of metaphors. But if I've the right of your meaning, ye're saying that the dream is the Great Weave and if someone that's part of it draws attention to something outside it, everyone becomes aware of that 'something.'"

Talshane was nodding agreeably. "Yes, but without any knowledge of its particulars. Just that it exists."

Ahearn looked around the room. "Am I truly the only one here who's never heard of this"—he avoided the word "foolishness" at the last second—"this phenomenon?"

Only Umkhira shook her head. But quite vigorously. *Wonderful: my educational compass matches that of a wilderness-reared Lightstrider.* "So when did you, er, 'skein' Druadaen?" *Sounds vaguely risqué, that.*

"Just before we entered the Under of Gur Grehar. Same time I skeined the rest of you."

"What?" Ahearn exclaimed in a chorus with the other two.

S'ythreni stared at them out of eyes akin to those of a cornered and very irate cat. "If we were separated in those trackless warrens, what plans did *you* have for finding each other?" She nodded at their silence, looked away. "You are all very welcome, I'm sure."

Umkhira crossed her considerable arms. "How reliable is the direction you receive from this awareness?"

"With other Iavarain, we know roughly the direction and distance."

Ahearn leaned on the back of his chair. "And with us?"

S'ythreni shrugged. "The connection of the skeining is much weaker. At best, it's like a crude compass, but at least we know if the being is still present."

Elweyr frowned. "And by 'present' you mean . . . ?"

"Anywhere on the face of Arrdanc."

Ahearn tried to ignore what felt like an icicle piercing his skull from the rear. "You're saying Druadaen is dead?"

She shook her head. "Death causes a different sensation, like a winnowing of the person's being, even if the passing is very swift." She shuddered. "This was abrupt. Here one instant, gone the next."

Elweyr nodded, said, "It could be some manner of portal"—and glanced quickly at Talshane.

Who raised an eyebrow, setting off an expression that Ahearn read as *You'll not see any tells so easily on me, my friend.* Not too proud to publicly admit and add another measure of ignorance to his already ample supply, Ahearn appealed to the Dunarran with an outstretched hand. "Are tales of such portals included in the whisperings about the Lady's Tower?"

Talshane nodded but held up a hand against Ahearn's eager, relieved smile. "And to answer the question I'd surely ask in your place, no, I cannot help you in this matter."

Umkhira's frown was grave rather than angry. "Why not?"

Elweyr sighed. "Because of who he works for... and why Druadaen is here at all."

S'ythreni's low mutter was almost a hiss. "What I think you mean to say is, 'because Druadaen is not just an exile, but a pariah.'" She turned wide, questioning eyes upon Talshane.

Whose answer began with a sigh. "Well, that's part of it. But I also have very specific rules about any actions or discussions with Moorax Tower."

Umkhira crossed again. "Which are?"

Talshane sighed. "Would you care to guess what the first and most important rule is?"

Elweyr looked like he was trying to smile while sipping vinegar. "The first rule is that you must never discuss or reveal the other rules."

Talshane nodded sadly.

Ahearn leaned in. "But there's another reason ye're tossing water on our hopes. It's because *we're* not part of your precious empi—er, Consentium, either. You already know that no appeal from us will budge your superiors."

"I'd contradict you if I could," Talshane muttered. "Unfortunately, the only assistance I can provide is unofficial."

"Such as?"

"To believe me when I say that Corum Torshaenyx has both the freedom and knowledge to help you."

"And you think he will? The Lady's lapdog? Smiling to our faces while our friend is either evaporated or whisked off to gods know where?"

Elweyr put a restraining hand on Ahearn's forearm.

"Hear him out. This is not Talshane's doing. And he'd be unworthy of this post if he couldn't follow its special rules."

S'ythreni glared at the mantic. "By the Bole, whose side are you on?"

Elweyr's eyes closed as he drew in a measured breath. "There aren't any 'sides,' here. Talshane is trying to help us within the limited scope of his permissions. Besides, the Lady has no reason to bring Druadaen all this way just to send him to his doom." He turned to Ahearn. "And if you really believe that Torshaenyx is anyone's lapdog, just don't tell him."

"Why?"

"Because despite his patience, he might decide to show you just how wrong you are."

Ahearn grumbled. "Well, I suppose that's wisdom, right enough ... but d'yeh think he'd help us against the will of the Lady?"

Talshane shook his head. "I strongly suspect that helping you is exactly what the Lady will want him to do." He called out to his orderly, who appeared in the doorway, hand on hilt. "Ureth, please summon Cerven."

"Here to your office, sir?"

"Yes. Promptly."

Ahearn leaned toward Elweyr, whispered, "And what the devils does that lad have to do with any o' this?"

Elweyr shushed him just as quick, light footsteps approached.

Cerven appeared in the doorway. "Yes, Captain Talshane?"

The Dunarran waved him in, faced the others. "Cerven is a very skilled fellow and, as it happens, is free to accompany you. In fact, the sooner he leaves, the better."

Before Ahearn could object to such a scheme, Umkhira frowned. "Shadowmere is unsafe for him?"

Talshane's expression was so unchanged it might have been painted on. "*Far Amitryea* is unsafe for him. Which is why his next assignment is on Ar Navir."

Ahearn clicked his tongue against his teeth. "Well, not to be difficult, but there's no certainty that our next port o' call will be on Ar Navir."

"No, but I strongly suspect it will be." Before Ahearn or the others could probe the certainty of Talshane's assertion, he stood. "I hope your travels are safe. If they bring you back to Shadowmere, you're always welcome in this place. Now, Cerven will bring you to Corum, who I suspect will be happy—and ready—to help you find your next steps."

Even before the portcullis was fully closed behind them, Ahearn was striding toward Corum Torshaenyx. "So, Station Master Talshane told us to seek you out. Something about being likely to help us?"

Ahearn had hoped to see some hint of surprise in the other. All he got was a calm nod as they gathered around him. "The Lady would be happy to retain your services as free agents, taking only those assignments which you wish. She is a generous employer."

S'ythreni stared at his words. "So, you know, already. About Druadaen. That he is . . . gone."

He nodded. "I do. He has passed through the Lady's Mirror." He answered their stares with a shrug. "It was not unexpected."

"By which you are suggesting it was voluntary?" Ahearn pressed.

Corum's patience seemed to wear a bit thin. "The

Lady invites no one to their deaths. And she leaves no one adrift whose lives are touched by the Mirror. Hence, her offer of employment."

"We have no doubt that she is a kind and generous patron," Elweyr replied, "but our goal is to be reunited with our friend, and I suspect that will not be accomplished by waiting for him here."

Corum put one hand in a pocket and nodded somberly. "That is almost certainly correct. What do you intend to do, then?"

"Too soon to say," Ahearn grumbled. "B'damn, we need to figure out the questions we should be asking before we can start coming up with answers. I don't suppose the Lady would deign to give us a few minutes of counsel?"

"As I understand it, she is drafting a letter that will convey the events concerning your friend and share what she may about the nature of his probable travels beyond the Mirror. You are correct in presuming that waiting here for him will be fruitless. None who leave by way of the Mirror return through it."

"Why is that?" Umkhira almost snarled.

The Tualaran shook his head. "None know. Should Cerven deliver the Lady's letter to the *Atremoënse*?"

"If she means to send it tonight, then yes; all our kit is there. But while we're on the topic of ships, Talshane said something about this young chap"—he gestured toward Cerven—"heading to Ar Navir. But we don't know where we're headed yet. And we don't even know whose service he's sworn to: your Lady's, the Dunarrans, or—?"

"He is not sworn to anyone's service. However, his *mentors* are friendly with the Lady and the

Dunarrans. And as for his destination, trust me in this: he will be a worthy companion and your paths are likely to steer by the same stars, at least for a while." He seemed about to add something but became distracted, as if by a distant sound. He smiled, returned his attention to the faces around him. "Now, before I leave, there is one last matter to be settled."

S'ythreni sounded suspicious. "Which is?"

By way of answer, Corum drew his hand from his pocket and opened it: a silver ring lay upon his palm. They stared at it.

S'ythreni leaned over to study it even more closely. "Is that...sai'niin?" she murmured.

Torshaenyx nodded.

"What is it for?"

"To aid you in your search."

As they stared at him, Umkhira stared at the ring. "It knows to look for Druadaen?"

He frowned. "Well, it might...but it most assuredly can detect the velene. And the sword. Here." He held it out to her.

Umkhira almost flinched back, then extended a thumb and a forefinger to gingerly grasp it.

The Tualaran shook his head. "No, just allow it to rest on your palm."

She did, stared at it, shrugged. "And now?"

"And now, pass it to the next person."

The ring made its way around the circle, Ahearn being the last and very bored by the whole process. *Just what are we supposed to divine from this silly bit of—?* "Hey-o! Gets a little warm, now and again, eh?"

Torshaenyx smiled and shook his head. The others

did the same, but without the smile. S'ythreni looked a bit disappointed.

Ahearn blinked at the faces hemming him in. "What? *I'm* to wear it? Is the thing daft? No one could be less a mantic or miracle-weaver than my own poor self!"

S'ythreni glanced at Corum. "Why him?"

But it was Umkhira who answered with an impatient shake of her head. "Because he loves Druadaen best."

Ahearn started. "Here now, that's not—!"

Umkhira might not even have heard him. "Though they may seem like filings from different castings of iron, the pull is strongest between them."

"But—" S'ythreni began.

"Do you truly think you can know better than *it* does?" Umkhira interrupted, nodding at the ring that sent another warm pulse into Ahearn's palm. "Besides, what does it matter? It has chosen Ahearn. It needs give no reason. Its actions are determined by its nature. Only creatures that think feel the need to have reasons—usually to create the illusion of order among those parts of the universe which we cannot understand."

Ahearn was not sure which left him more astounded: that the ring had chosen him, or that Umkhira had so thoroughly bested S'ythreni in an argument. He leaned toward the Tualaran. "So how...how does it work?"

Corum smiled. "All you have to do is wear it. Once Druadaen has returned to Arrdanc, it will urge you to find him."

Ahearn raised an eyebrow. "It's a passably big world, y'know."

"True, but it is attracted to other 'metal filings' like itself," he said, with an appreciative nod to Umkhira for

her metaphor. "And now I must truly take my leave."
He started off, Cerven right behind him.

"Was it something we said?" S'ythreni called after
him facetiously.

He ignored the jibe. "Once again, were I to stay
longer, that might turn out to be an intrusion."

"Upon whom?" Ahearn asked.

Torshaenyx's only answer was a glance down an
empty alley.

Umkhira frowned. "There's no one there."

"Not yet. I bid you safe travels and, truly, good
fortune."

The somber emphasis he put on the last phrase
made Ahearn wince. "Sounds like we'll need it."

"All of us do, all the time," Corum answered as
he began walking toward a narrow lane opposite the
alley he'd glanced at. "But some have more urgent
need of good fortune than others."

"That's not a comfort!" S'ythreni called after him.

The Tualaran turned, smiled ruefully, shrugged and
slipped behind a passing wain sagging beneath a high
load of crates. By the time it had moved on, neither
he nor Cerven were to be seen.

CHAPTER NINE

"Ahearn!" a voice cried from behind.

The swordsman turned, saw two figures emerging from the alley down which the Tualaran had glanced—and started as he recognized the one in the lead. "Varcaxtan? What the devils are you doing here?" Even as he smiled to see Druadaen's adoptive uncle approaching, he wondered at the Dunarran's almost gaunt female companion. Watching her nonresponsive state as the older man towed her gently behind him, Ahearn whispered, "Your friend: is she well?"

"Sadly, no," the woman answered firmly, but with no change to her expression.

Along with the others, Ahearn was startled by the juxtaposition between her ready answer and almost lifeless affect—until he remembered the last time he had seen such a peculiar contrast: "Dragon? You've come along, too?"

"Well, I would have thought that self-evident. Does it look like this poor woman would even be conscious, otherwise?" The voice was a reedy wheeze, but the snappish hauteur was unmistakably that of the great wyrm they'd come to know in the foothills of Kar Krathau.

"Well," Ahearn exclaimed, hands on hips, "for all your airs and crankiness, I am happy to see you! We are very well met, indeed!"

"The pleasure is all yours, I'm sure," the dragon sniffed. "Although despite your oafish greeting, I find it tolerable to be in your presence once again." The sunken-eyed woman surveyed them all. "Some more than others," he added with a hint of warmth as his gaze swept over S'ythreni and Umkhira:

"Oh, you are a beastly old wyrm," Varcaxtan scolded. "For the better part of this moonphase, he's been wondering why Tharêdæath's ship couldn't go any faster."

"I am used to wings, you know. It is incomprehensible, how your various species can endure creeping along by foot or by ship. Oh, wait, no, I *can* comprehend it after all: the dull pace of that travel is nicely matched to the pace at which you cogitate." He turned toward Ahearn. "That word means 'think,' by the way."

Ahearn crossed his arms, frowning and smiling at the same time. "Yes, my cogitation keeps pace with your barbs quite nicely, 'old wyrm.'"

"You are not allowed such liberties!"

Ahearn smiled. "Seems I am, actually."

The woman's blank eyes fixed on his. "If I were back in my body—"

"Ah, but yer not." Turning to Varcaxtan before the dragon could react, Ahearn asked, "How'd you lot manage to catch up to us? Gods, Druadaen was near certain that the jackals who nearly snared him might have put you in the same lazarette as his magic auntie!"

"And I very well might have been." Varcaxtan's genial smile took on an edge of shrewdness. "But as it so happens, I have a great many friends throughout Dunarra. Especially in the river port of Aedmurun."

S'ythreni smiled. "And I'm sure some of those friends have ocean-faring boats."

"Why, so they do! And one in particular was just about to set out downriver to do a bit of fishing on the Sea of Kedlak."

Elweyr nodded. "Probably 'needed' to make port over the border in Menara, to repair some damage to the hull."

Varcaxtan's smile broadened. "In fact, she did, though it's the Helpers' own guess how such sturdy strakes came to be roughed up in such calm, nighttime seas."

Ahearn smiled and leaned his arm knowingly against the Dunarran's. "And I suppose Tharêdæath's ship just happened to make port there at the same time."

"Now, how did you guess? As it turns out, I would have been obligated to appear at a hearing akin to the one where Druadaen was ambushed—oh, I misspoke: where he was 'interviewed.' But I never did receive such a summons."

"A shame that you were traveling faster than the couriers who didn't know where to find you." S'ythreni's words were sly, but her eyes were gentle and even warm upon the older Dunarran.

"I suppose it was, *Alva* S'ythreni," he agreed with a respectful nod and a small wink.

Throughout the recounting of Varcaxtan's departure from Dunarra, the dragon had been staring up into the mostly cloudless skies. Ahearn leaned toward its terribly pale female avatar. "Cogitating, are you?"

The head shook, sweat-oiled locks swaying like ragged vines. "No." The eyes opened. "We have come too late. He is gone."

"He?" echoed Varcaxtan. "You mean, Druadaen?"

"How do you know?" Elweyr asked carefully.

"I marked him. Just after I decided not to eat you all for invading my home."

Ahearn crossed his arms. "I thought you don't eat our breed."

A sideways glance. "I may reconsider that. Noxious though you are."

Elweyr poked Ahearn in the ribs before he could reply, then leaned toward the dragon. "Did you only mark Druadaen?"

A shrewd look. "Hmm. Your understanding of the world has grown, thaumancer."

"I hope so. But you didn't answer the question."

"Apparently your understanding hasn't grown enough to refrain from annoying a dragon. But yes, I marked all of you." It glanced at Ahearn. "Odd. I had expected you to take semi-eloquent umbrage at my not having asked your permission."

Ahearn sighed. "Rather like scolding a torturer after you've been racked, don't you think?"

Before the dragon could respond, Umkhira crossed her arms. "So, this marking: is it like S'ythreni's skeining?"

The dragon shrugged. "Different method, but the same result." He glanced sideways at his now crest-fallen companion. "What is it, Varcaxtan?"

"What do you think? I'm too late to petition the Lady alongside Druadaen."

The dragon's voice was milder than his words.

"Which I told you was unlikely to occur, but when have you ever listened?"

Elweyr's gaze flickered between them, came to rest on Varcaxtan. "What do you mean by 'petitioning her' alongside Druadaen?"

"Well, it's as I said the eve of what should have been our departure from Tlulanxu: my Indryllis never left the Nidus. And if anyone can find out what became of her, it would be the Lady of the Mirror."

Ahearn nodded hesitantly. "Well, that seems sensible enough, but doesn't Dunarra have persons with the required, er, gifts?"

"It does, but they're few in number and their skills are reserved for matters involving the Consentium's collective safety. But even if the fate of my Indryllis was deemed a matter of national interest, the request was sure to be denied once the temples decided that I, too, should be 'interviewed.'"

"Happily," the dragon offered in a tone of conclusion, "we needn't rely on their help or good graces."

Elweyr frowned. "How so?"

"Unless I miss my guess—and I never do—whatever aid the Lady provides will offer a pathway to make progress on both searches: the one for Druadaen and the one for Indryllis." The ring of diverse faces was unified in total perplexity. The dragon raised his chin and one didactic finger. "Consider how Druadaen's disappearance is bound up with Varcaxtan's quandary, so that in addressing one, we address the other."

Varcaxtan stared at the shriveled woman that was the dragon. "What do you mean?"

It shrugged. "Where did you last see your wife?"

"In the Nidus," he said thickly. "Leaving her behind. I should never have—"

"You were obeying orders," the dragon interrupted. "But to return: why was she ordered to remain behind?"

As Varcaxtan gasped in surprise, Elweyr blurted out, "Osmotia . . . er, 'portals.'" His eyes measured the dragon. "So, they're not just rumors, are they?"

"No."

"Portals!" Varcaxtan almost wept. "So . . . so if the Lady's 'Mirror' is what took off my dear lad and how we have to find him, then we can combine that with a search for Indryllis!"

The dragon had leaned slightly away from the Dunarran's sudden rush of enthusiasm. "Hoping to achieve both those ends through a single course of action is, well . . . improbably optimistic. Let us rather say this, old friend: that our concerns are clustered about the entries and exits of what was once called the Vortex of Worlds."

Elweyr grew very pale at the dragon's last three words.

Ahearn saw the reaction from the corner of his eye, followed up with "A vortex, eh? From what my lost love told me of the sea, a vortex is usually a one-way trip to a deep and briny death."

The dragon considered the swordsman. "Though revoltingly quaint, I cannot dismiss the wisdom of that warning nor deny that it may be an apt metaphor for the path before us. Such a journey precludes foresee-ing either waypoints or outcomes. We may only be sure that to undertake it is far more perilous than to choose not to. So none among you should be ashamed or hesitant to step back from it, if this is the course we decide upon."

Ahearn didn't have to think about his response, but even so, he was not the first to step forward. He'd expected Umkhira might match him, but—against all logic and reason—S'ythreni beat them both.

She stared down the surprised glances. "A young idealistic Dunarran on his own, diving headfirst into an abyss of uncertainty?" She snorted. "Not to go is like unto letting him die by the side of the road." Their stares became dubious smiles. She looked down and finally murmured, "Besides, he never let us down. Not once. Tried to push us off when he thought the danger was too great. Not sure I could live with myself if I turned away now."

The arms that caught her up in a sudden hug—and were probably the only ones she hadn't the temerity or heart to bat away—were Varcaxtan's. "Light love you, *Alva* S'ythreni, as a wish from me as well as for him. By the moons, that lad has made fine friends!"

She slipped out of the Dunarran's embrace, but held both his hands in hers. "I do this as much for me as for either of you."

He nodded. "Be that as it may, I'm grateful. These past ten or so years—losing the lad's parents, then Indryllis, and now perhaps him as well—well, you'd think living a long life prepares you for loss. But not for so much, and not all in the space of a decade."

Umkhira put a hand on the man's muscular shoulder. "I think there must be much pain in living so many years as Dunarrans do."

Varcaxtan's eyes were sad, even as he regarded the Lightstrider warmly. "Aye, but do you know one of the *best* things about living so long? You spend more time with the one you love. Not all Dunarran couples are so lucky, but Indryllis and I have been together for many, many decades." He stopped, his mouth smiling but his eyes set in a brittle squint. "Now, shall I tell you one of the *worst* things about living so long?"

S'ythreni shook her head and clasped his hands tightly; her eyes were wet. "That when you have spent so much time with the one you love, you wish you could die with them. That this life is too empty to endure when they are gone." She looked up, her eyes fierce and filled with defiance at life itself. "If there is any chance your Indryllis is alive, then I am going on with you. No matter how long or how far."

"Bole-blessed friend, this path could be the death of me...and any who follow to its end."

"I don't care." She raised her chin in response to the puzzled look on his face. "No, don't ask: I have my reasons. It is settled."

Umkhira looked gruffly pleased. "So, where do we start?"

"Now there's a practical lass after my own heart," Ahearn agreed loudly. "Maybe this will help us." He slipped the sai'niin ring on his finger. It jammed halfway down—too small—but before he could twist it past his knuckle, it loosened of its own accord and eased past the joint. *Well, now that's odd*, Ahearn thought—right before he felt a sensation in the back of his head, as if a vague memory of something he'd lost had manifested physically and was now prodding him to go in search of it.

"Damn, but if it doesn't seem to be guiding me now!" he blurted out. He glanced at the dragon and then S'ythreni. "The two of you seem to have the best instincts for mystic bits of eld. Is it possible that Druadaen is still somewhere on Arrdanc, and that it's trying to physically push me toward him?"

"No," S'ythreni said sharply. "He's beyond the Great Weave."

The dragon nodded agreement.

"Then why in the worlds is it trying to turn me back around toward the bay? Is it trying to get us to return to the *Atremoënse*?"

"Or maybe," the dragon added in a droll tone, "it is because Tharêdæath's ship is there waiting for us."

"Which is preferable in what way?" Umkhira asked frankly.

"I am not implying that the *ship* is preferable—although it is. Rather, I suspect the ring is signaling that its *destination* is more amenable to our purposes."

Elweyr nodded. "However else they may differ, all accounts of osmotia—and other kinds of portals—agree on one point: that they are very old objects. So perhaps it's urging us to seek out the persons with oldest memories."

"Iavarain," Umkhira breathed with a measure of trepidation.

"Specifically, Uulamantre, who are best reached by sailing to Tharêdæath's home port in Mirroskye."

"Eslêntecrë," murmured S'ythreni. To Ahearn's ear, her tone was not one of fondness, but reluctance and regret.

Umkhira's response was far more blunt. "So we travel toward Mirroskye? We hope to be welcomed in the place that has made a reputation for welcoming no one?"

The dragon smiled with one side of its gray-lipped mouth. "I suspect our experience shall be different."

"Well, let's hope so," Ahearn exclaimed loudly. "Now, before we take even one step on the path to becomin' mates, Uncle Varcaxtan, I must begin by telling you how happy I am to have you with us." He frowned, reflecting. "Well, for the most part."

"Oh? And what part gives you pause?"

"Well, you take this conversation, for instance. Here we are, setting out on an adventure as strange as it is sure to be wondrous. But rather than a happy embrace of the road ahead and of the novelties we might encounter—or slip into our packs—it's all gloom and doom. In two shakes, you and the old wyrm here have us on the verge of sitting chin on fist, contemplating the great seriousness of the many 'implications' of our choices."

He reared back. "Now that won't do at all. A Dunarran and a dragon are more than twice as much seriousness as I can handle. And see how you've infected poor High Ears with a similar tendency? Even the green lass is already so somber that she only smiles to sharpen her teeth. And Elweyr—forgive the truth, my old friend—has never been renowned for his ready congeniality and lively banter. So there's naught but me to keep you all from cryin' in your beers. And that prospect makes even *me* sad. So there'll be no joy among us. None at all," he finished in a morose voice. "Not even from the beers."

Varcaxtan glanced sideways at Elweyr. "He's quite the performer. Tell me: how long can he keep it up?"

"How long do you have to watch?" Elweyr shot back.

"Cut to the quick I am by such hard-hearted opinions of me!" Ahearn protested. "I've half a mind to send you both packing. But I'm willing to *cogitate* upon the alternatives...if it's done over a few full tankards for us to cry in."

The dragon sighed, exchanged glances with Varcaxtan. "And I presume those tankards are to be filled from what remains in *our* pockets?"

Ahearn beamed. "See? You're not so bad at cogitatin' yourself. Now let's find a generous hand on an open tap before I die of thirst."

PART TWO
LORN HYSTZOS

CHAPTER TEN

The sun—morning bright—was in Druadaen's eyes as he completed his step through the Shimmer.

And toppled forward.

Even as he put his hands out to break his fall, he knew it wasn't the kind that happens when you step wrong descending dark stairs. This was because his own weight had suddenly shifted, just as when a heavy load or pack slips unexpectedly off one's back.

As he turned his head—not a good time for a broken nose—his hands hit dirt: soft, uneven, faintly wet. It clung lightly to his palms and the rest of his body.

He started: it was not sticking to his clothes, but his *naked* body.

Druadaen pushed partially up from the ground. Despite a wave of intense curiosity and rising fear, he followed his Outrider training. If one awakes in an unknown place, scan surroundings to locate cover and potential enemies.

But there was only wiry grass and clusters of

unfamiliar foliage. He spied a small building across a country lane to his front. The Shimmer was behind him, and although it was the same dimensions and in the same upright position, it wasn't shimmering. Here, it was akin to a desert heat haze, distorting the objects behind it but without imparting watery waver typical of mirages.

Druadaen's rehearsed instincts pushed him to seek cover, but in this instance, he had an even more urgent task: to discover what, if anything, had come through the Shimmer with him. He rolled to his knees rapidly, ready to scan for his sword, but before he could, the velene—the only thing left on his body—swirled off his wrist into a dragon shape. It flew straight upward, faster than he had ever seen.

He was not surprised to find his sword close alongside him, but it, too, was naked; neither sheath nor baldric was present. He took it up gratefully, wondered if it had known it would make it through the Shimmer...

Druadaen frowned: *if it had* known *it would make it through? So you really believe it's conscious?* But then again, the Lady had suggested as much...

Unbidden, a memory pushed through that thought; he saw the Lady's serious eyes and voice as she said, "Evidently, both your sai'niin companions have very strong opinions on your best course of action." He started at the abrupt intrusion of the recollection—because it actually felt that it had somehow come from some part of his mind that was acting on its own accord. *Or maybe—?*

Druadaen looked at the sword in his hand. "Was that you, talking to me through my own memories?"

His formless hope that there might be some response from the sword was disappointed; the mirror-silver blade remained inert.

Rising, he noted the velene had not returned, which was actually a relief. Prior experience indicated that, if he was in immediate danger, the sai'niin dragonette would be nearby to do something useful. So these might be the safest moments in which to pause and study his surroundings before deciding where and how to move.

The dirt into which he had fallen was part of a shallow ditch that ringed the Shimmer. Both within and beyond that ring, the unruly—and utterly unfamiliar—grass spread in all directions like a rough carpet. It straggled its way down a gentle slope to the road, which ran away to the right and the left.

On the right, the lane dwindled into little more than a cart track. It showed few signs of use, mottled by weeds as it wound up a modest incline that culminated in a hill a mile to the northeast. On the left, the lane cut a straight line toward the western horizon. It was less overgrown and widened into a proper, stone-laid road just before it topped and disappeared behind a distant rise. That certainly looked like the more promising route to an inhabited area, but the hilltop in the other direction offered a vantage point which would help to confirm or disprove that conjecture.

The small building was set back thirty yards from the road, with a stone foundation and narrow lancet windows: a shelter or watch post of some kind. High weeds intruded upon the narrow dirt path that led to it, and at a few points, it was partially obstructed by naked corpses mostly concealed by the undergrowth.

The velene returned to his wrist and became a bracer again, all in the same instant. Druadaen used that hand to wipe his moist brow. The sun wasn't far above the hill to the northeast, but it was already warm and growing humid. Had he been on Arrdanc, he would have guessed himself to be in the southernmost parts of Ar Navir during a hot spell, or the shores of equatorial Mihal'j.

A quick inspection of the plants didn't reveal any definitive clues as to how close or far a coast might be. The soil was as much sand as loam, and both the grasses and bushes were crabbed and low, with waxy, spatulate leaves: all traits frequently encountered close to the sea. But the rest of the foliage could have been from any temperate region. Crossing the road to both examine and hide behind a small copse, Druadaen discovered that what he had believed were trees was a single large bush with upward shoots resembling saplings. However, they did not evince the single-sided weathering or distinctive lean consistent with strong prevailing winds off a sea or ocean.

But by the time he finished studying the local growth, Druadaen had learned something far more useful—and arresting—than if he were close to a coast; he had never seen any of these plants before, and in his years as a Courier, he'd visited every continent on Arrdanc. So it seemed as if this might indeed be a different world. As the magnitude of that thought struck him, he noticed that even the sun itself seemed different. It was more sharply white, yet smaller in the sky.

Druadaen suppressed a shiver, not of fear so much as profound isolation. The Lady's explanation of where the Shimmer might lead included such a possibility, but knowing that one might emerge in a "different world" was just words—until it happened. Besides, from childhood, that phrase had signified a metaphysical domain, such as the creedland of a deity or one of many legendary lands of the dead: a void in which physical form was gone and where spirits conversed, contended, or both.

But this was, in the most literal sense, a wholly different world, and it was that utterly mundane tangibility that made it so profoundly unnerving, more so than the place he'd tried to envision: a place that was not physically recognizable, yet had been foreshadowed in legend. Instead, he found himself in a world which, if he were to regard it through a fogged lens, would appear quite similar to his own, but when seen more clearly and closely, announced its arresting differences in every detail.

Advancing to the small building, Druadaen was only mildly surprised that the five bodies to either side of the path were human. He noted their positions, then took a quick peek inside; one additional corpse was sprawled amidst wrecked furnishings. He ducked back out and circled the building twice, first at a distance of ten yards, then thirty. Using his nose as well as his eyes, he found one more body in that final orbit, after which he reentered what had obviously been a watchhouse. Despite the close air of the interior, the shade made it easier to focus on what he had seen and smelled.

Seven bodies in all. All but one lay along the path or in the building. Everything of obvious value had been removed from them, including their clothes. The interior of the watchhouse had been similarly stripped, after which someone had made a hasty attempt to set it afire. The only sign of recent movement were tracks left by whatever small scavengers were still visiting the bodies outside the shelter. Judging from the smell and the state of decay, the bodies were a week old at most. Maybe two. At most.

Druadaen's thoughts abruptly left this world, and returned to Arrdanc: specifically, to his conversation with the Lady less than an hour earlier. She had explicitly confirmed that almost nine moonphases had passed since the Hidden Archivist's rescue and, therefore, since the pursuers from the Nidus were diverted through the Shimmer. *But if that's true*...

Druadaen glanced at the body lying a yard away from him. The stink of rotting flesh was already fading. Even disregarding how the local heat should have increased the speed at which it decayed and then began to dry out, it was still not more than one moonphase old.

Druadaen frowned. Whatever had killed the seven men had done so *long* after the Tsost-Dyxoi had passed through the Shimmer. But then why had these men been here? Had the S'Dyxoi killed an earlier set of guards, or perpetrated crimes nearby? Had the locals who had built this structure sent the now-dead men here to watch for the intruders' return or to pursue them? If so, perhaps the S'Dyxoi discovered or anticipated that and stealthily circled back to ambush this second set of watchmen. But why? Perhaps this locale was the only part of the world with which they had become familiar? Or perhaps there was no connection between the S'Dyxoi and these corpses. Perhaps the small garrison had run afoul of something entirely different.

Correction, he thought. *Some* one *entirely different.* Whatever killed the watchmen had also valued their goods. Only a few pieces of well-gnawed clothing remained; almost all their garments had been removed, as well as any tools or weapons. Several were missing one or more of the three middle fingers on one or both hands; typical of how bandits harvested rings from their victims.

Then there was the matter of why the watchhouse was at this location in the first place. Presumably because of the Shimmer, but that only spawned more questions. Perhaps some foolish wayfarers had touched or tried walking through it, and this station had been established to warn them of the consequences of doing so—whatever those might be. But did that really require seven men? Perhaps if the area was dangerous, but then why risk any watchers at all?

Besides, with a regularly trafficked road running through it, the area was unlikely to be very wild. And if a Shimmer could have its connection altered like other osmotia, then the one here might have the traffic of two, twenty, or two hundred other osmotia pouring out of it. But, no: if *that* were true, there would be more than a small watch post across a small lane, just as the grass around the Shimmer itself would be trampled into bare dirt, not overgrown.

Druadaen stood and shook his head as if that might shake loose some of the burgeoning imponderables roosting there. Maybe it was called the Vortex of Worlds not because of its shape, but because it spawned a whirlpool of uncertainties and mysteries that could easily pull one down into despair, enervated by endlessly swirling questions without answer.

Druadaen stretched to reawaken his muscles. In general, the antidote to enervation was activity, and right now, he had plenty to do, beginning with finding anything that he might salvage. He smiled, thinking how he'd come late to the skill that Ahearn called "scrounging"...

Without warning, the faces of Druadaen's friends flitted through his mind, and with them, an approaching tide of regret...

He shook his head again, harder, and walked quickly out past the sundered door of the watch post.

When the sun was almost directly overhead, Druadaen returned and sat to survey the fruits of his grim harvest.

Clothing had been a challenge. He'd found rags in the watch post; they'd do for patches or even a head cover if the sun proved unexpectedly strong. What meager coverings he now wore had come from the still-clothed body behind the shelter. Druadaen wondered at the decision to leave the body unstripped, concluded that they had deemed his garments too bloody and torn to be worth taking. Due to the rent shirt, scavengers had no trouble getting directly at the remains, and insects and worms had only recently infested what was left. The pants were mostly intact and the blouse was somewhat serviceable, but anyone seeing Druadaen wearing them would surely presume him to be a pauper—and a desperate one, at that. His greatest—and most worrisome—disappointment was the lack of shoes. Not surprising, really—even shabby sandals had value—but proceeding in bare feet did not bode well for either swift or safe movement.

The attackers' indifferent attempt at arson had spared a stout table with an intact leg; it was now a reasonable club. With patient labor and the aid of a nail, Druadaen also removed the door's crude iron hinges: flat and thin, they could be used as anything from small prybars to scrapers. He had just concluded that tedious process, however, when the most serious insufficiency of all announced itself with a low animal growl. That was his stomach's reminder that while gathering tools was all well and good, their usefulness would be short-lived if he didn't find food and water.

Unfortunately, foraging—always questionable in unfamiliar regions—was an incalculable risk in an unknown world; he had no way to distinguish what he could eat from that which would kill him. But first, he had to find something—anything—that looked like food. That need propelled him to the roof for a better look at his surroundings.

The results were not promising; there were no signs of farmlands. Worse still, the Shimmer appeared to be at the center of a shallow declivity; in almost every direction, a low-rise blocked his view of what lay beyond. The one direction in which that lip was not present was where the northeast road followed a low slope that rose toward the hill he'd seen earlier and which he now studied in earnest.

That careful survey kindled the first spark of hope he'd felt since coming through the Shimmer: halfway up the slope, the road briefly disappeared into a ragged array of trees that was probably a long-untended orchard. Further study revealed a small but decidedly polyglot cluster of ruins on the crest of the hill. Druadaen could make out squat—or half-tumbled—towers and low, angled surfaces that might be small pyramids. The road ran directly past it, only slightly downhill. Although he could see no sign that it was occupied, it was so distant that Druadaen doubted he could have spotted the presence of a modest camp, much less individuals.

Which left him with an unpleasant choice: prudence suggested that the road to the west would be the one most likely to lead to a settled area. But there was no guessing how far might that journey be, and therefore, if his present lack of water, food, and footwear would prevent him from completing it.

On the other hand, the old orchard and hilltop ruins held out the promise of food and, possibly, more productive scavenging for needful items such as clothes, weapons, and tools. But if such potential resources were there, they would also be likely to attract both two-legged and four-legged dangers. He might have a sai'niir sword in one hand and a club in the other, but with no armor for protection, and no shoes to ensure swift movement upon the rough hill, choosing that destination was a desperate gamble in the face of unquantifiable risks. After all, what if that's where the murderers of the watchmen were hiding, lurking in wait for unsuspecting arrivals from the Shimmer?

Such as himself.

Druadaen glanced through the empty doorway at the corpse he'd dragged outside. Whoever had murdered the fellow had tortured him first. It hadn't been the simple pummeling of soldiers or the crushed bones and split joints often used by brutish bandits. They had teased apart nerves without severing the arteries or veins that nourished them, had used a knife-point on gums and other sensitive areas, and ended with unspeakable yet precise removals of body parts. Whoever had perpetrated these horrors was well versed in the malign arts of inflicting a maximum amount of pain for a maximum amount of time. A skill possessed by far too many S'Dyxoi.

Druadaen frowned: it made no sense that the S'Dyxoi would still be in the area—if they ever had been. Assuming that several of them had come through the Shimmer, they would have had even more mouths to feed, which would have necessitated moving to find a much larger food source, much more quickly. The only reason they might have been willing to remain in such a remote region would be to return through the Shimmer—but even if that were possible, doing so would have put them back in the Lady's Tower, surrounded by mortal enemies.

No, it made no sense that the S'Dyxoi were nearby, or even behind what happened at the watch post. His only nagging worry was the lack of any other reasonable explanation.

Druadaen stood. Either way, there was no benefit in waiting. He was still well slept, but he'd only get water by seeking it, and finding food was likely to be even more challenging. So every minute he waited was a minute during which he became weaker.

He walked out the yawning doorway, careful to give the corpse a wide berth as he started for the distant hilltop.

CHAPTER ELEVEN

Druadaen finished the first tamaril he'd picked and looked around the tree's twisted trunk. Still no movement up in the ruins, and there were no signs that they attracted visitors.

The hike to the hill had been easy, except for his feet; he'd remained several yards to the side of the road. Traveling directly upon it as an individual in desperate circumstances was an invitation to ambushers, particularly in a sparsely populated area such as this one.

In hindsight, it had been an unnecessary precaution. The further up the slope the road wound, the less wear it showed until it had become little more than a half-grassed path. There were sandal and boot prints in what had recently been mud, but they were all heading back the way he had come. Some other marks might have been the edges of hooves, but no sign of the ruts left by wagons or even carts. By the time he arrived at the foot of the orchard,

Druadaen was convinced that settled lands lay in the other direction.

The fruit trees had grown wild and intermingled with others, all protected by ample skirts of bushes and brambles. But only after walking among them, and seeing how uneven the rows were, did Druadaen realize he was looking at new growth. The original trees had long since become mulch for these offspring. He also discovered that it had been a mixed orchard, but the alternating rows had become ragged ranks. However, upon spotting the first ripe fruit, his mouth began to water.

It also stopped him in mid-stride; peeking through the branches about twelve feet off the ground was a yellow spiny apple. It was a fruit he knew from Arrdanc, mostly cultivated near the coasts of Othaericus and along rivers in the southern drylands of Mihal'j. Two happy realizations rushed in upon him simultaneously: eating no longer meant risking his life; and, the chances were good that he would find other familiar flora and fauna.

Within minutes, it was no longer a matter of chance; peering into the shadowy canopies of the other species of tree, he spotted clusters of purplish, plum-sized fruits: tamarils. They were typically grown on mountain slopes back home.

By the time he returned to the ground with a half dozen of each, he was crisscrossed by cuts from brambles and thorny vines. He paid no mind to them, nor to the infamous tartness of both fruits. After all, he'd found food, and better still, while in the higher branches, he heard a chuckle of water over rocks from further up the slope.

He could have easily eaten more than one of each fruit, but ignored his stomach's appeals. In addition to husbanding his food, he could not afford the lethargy that might follow a larger meal. Since he had no way to carry his bounty, he hid what remained before making his way to the uphill edge of the orchard, courting the sparse shadows as he did.

What had sounded like a stream was actually water tumbling through the remains of an open, stone, irrigation system. The sections had long since cracked apart and split in many places. It had once carried water to croplands hugging the eastward slope of the hill; they were now lush, lightly wooded meadows due to the diffuse trickles that ran down from the ruined half-pipes.

Druadaen's throat seemed to get a bit more dry every time liquid sparkles jumped up from the higher reaches of the irrigation system, marking where the flow hit a gap or break in the broken stonework. He surveyed the broken towers that peeked over the crest of the hill. Thirsty or not, if he didn't inspect the source of the water first, drinking it could mean imbibing an awful dose of harmful minerals, diseases, and even animal wastes—or otherwise, if the ruins were home to unseen inhabitants. That resolve to inspect the source of the water, to survey the region from a tower, and to comb the ruins for salvage all pointed him toward the same destination: the hilltop.

He considered the three possible routes to approach. The road was too open and obvious; if the ruins had occupants, they would keep it under observation. Following the ruined irrigation system meant moving uphill in an open field. The final alternative was hug tight against the downhill edge of the orchard until he came upon the shortest, or best concealed, path up to the crest.

Druadaen wished he could wash his hands—it was unwise to handle weapons with sticky palms—but turned and jogged down toward the lower tree line that overlooked the road and would shield him from any eyes that might be watching from the hilltop.

At the point where the brush stretching up beyond the orchards began to dwindle, Druadaen came to an even more overgrown lane that branched off from the main road and ran uphill at a steep angle. It was only thirty yards to the crest. At one time, the lane had given defenders in the now-ruined towers a clear field of fire upon any ascending attackers. But that approach was hemmed by overarching trees. The lane itself was still mostly intact, dotted by the cobbles that still stuck through the grass here and there. And halfway between the main road and the crest, there was a crumpled figure, lying at a strange angle.

Druadaen slowed, reversed, crouched, and took a longer, careful look.

The dark, awkward angles that stuck up from the side-slumped corpse were familiar; it was wearing armor too stiff to flatten against the ground. Also, unless Druadaen's eyes were being too hopeful, the outline of its feet were squared off: boots or heavy shoe. There were no weapons nearby nor the thrashed undergrowth typical of a recent melee. However, near the center of the path, an irregular track of crushed weeds and grass extended five yards upslope from the body.

Druadaen, feet aching from cuts and moving over rocks, crept forward again until he reached the fly-covered body. He pushed it over on its back and dragged it—again, slowly—into the higher weeds at the side of the road. A quick scan behind showed no movement along the crest or in the ruins. Promising. However, until reaching this point, there had been intermittent birdsong. Here, there was only silence. *Not* promising.

Once under cover, he took stock of the corpse as the flies returned—along with a thick carrion stench. The dead man's face was cut and bruised, but there were no signs of a killing blow. Not until Druadaen undid the heavy leather armor's straps.

A putrid mass of half-rotted organs and bone chips poured out. The consistency was almost like heavy porridge, and much of it was just as gray. Druadaen covered his nose before he could arrest the reflex; then, swallowing and reminding himself of things that had smelled worse, he finished free-ing the armor.

Something massive and blunt had crushed the man's lower left abdomen, fraying and scarring the cured leather without penetrating it. However, despite the smell, armor was armor and whereas Druadaen could easily wash off a stink, he couldn't shrug off a blade.

Once he'd wiped it clean with rags from the watch-house, Druadaen shouldered into the hardened leather and looked for a weapon. All he found was a still-sheathed dagger, but there was also a wide, well-worn loop on the opposite side of the weapon belt: probably for a heavy, single-handed axe. There might have been more to learn from a closer study of the dead warrior's kit, but ever since emerging from the upslope limit of the orchard, Druadaen presumed an attack could come at any moment. No time to waste, therefore. Staying to the side of the lane, he moved up toward the crest.

Peering over that grassy lip, Druadaen surveyed the level hilltop. The remains of three towers brooded over the scattered ruins, even as they pointed overhead at the post-noon sun. One of them rose up from within a small, mostly collapsed keep that was the largest structure. The pyramids were lower and smaller, apparently fortified underground entrances, but two of the three were clogged with stones from their own inward collapse. And just beyond the furthest of them, he heard what he'd been listening for: the smooth rush of free-flowing water.

Druadaen almost started in that direction, but reined in his thirst and reconsidered the two closest towers. The taller one was merely a hollow shell; fire or age having swept away its floors, it appeared more like the cross section of an improbably large chimney. However, either time or squat sturdiness had favored the second tower, which was largely intact up to the third story. Beyond that, attackers or force majeure had sheared off the higher floors.

Druadaen studied its structure with the eyes of his roof-running youth. He saw the signs of treacherous footing and loose masonry but also a promising, if zigzag, climb to the top. Passing his sword through the wide loop on his belt, he made for its black-shadowed entrance.

❖   ❖   ❖

Druadaen hauled himself over the broken edge of the second tower's highest floor. Climbing up from beneath had allowed him to determine that the carved tenon corbels supporting were still firm and not unduly weathered. Even the remaining part of this top floor looked sturdy, but around ruins one could never tell. Druadaen walked slowly and carefully to the closest exterior wall; usually the best-supported part of any upper level. He followed along until he reached a point where he could see beyond the shattered and saw-toothed rim of it in almost all directions.

Again, his Courier training proved invaluable. Guessing the hilltop to be no more than three hundred feet above the surrounding terrain, and the tower beneath him adding another thirty-five, the horizon would be roughly twenty miles away. But that presumed a perfectly clear day rather than the present humidity. So he was surprised to spot terrain features far beyond the presumed limit of his vision.

To the east, a high, distant mountain range ran from north to south: a single, mist-shrouded wall of sharp, forbidding peaks. However, whatever existed between those mountaintops and the moisture-grayed horizon was a complete mystery.

A similar view presented itself to the south. There, he descried the end of a different and less imposing mountain chain barely rising above the horizon. However, rather than presenting him with its broad side, he seemed to be viewing it end-on. The north was not mountainous but hilly and rolling, building into a series of ridges that were increasingly uneven and forested. However, what the terrain lacked in majesty it made up for in mystery.

Sprinkled across that rugged landscape were structures at once imposing and enigmatic. Lines of great
stone rings—some broken, some tilting—staggered away
into the distance. Other strange shapes appeared singly
or in clusters, some fully visible, others barely rising
up through the low-lying haze. Their details blurred,
he only had impressions of what the structures might
be: snapped obelisks, half-domes, tilting remains of
slab-sided citadels, all ghostlike in the water-heavy
air as they faded into the distance.

Finally, Druadaen turned west. He had purposely
left that facing for last, anticipating that what he
saw there might be far more absorbing, and so, dis-
tract him from careful study of the other directions.
Shielding his eyes from the sun, he reflected that,
until this moment, he had never fully appreciated the
extraordinary advantages conferred by the Consentium's
much-coveted telescopes.

But naked eyes told him everything he needed to
know. At the edge of his vision, small gray tendrils
climbed toward the clouds: fires. Here and there were
hints of lines in the surrounding sward; cart-tracks.
As he shifted his attention to where the road from
the watch post threatened to disappear into the west,
he caught a glimpse of angular green expanses: farms.
And at two points, a tiny, dun-colored patch sat astride
the highway: towns.

Druadaen released a sigh and resisted an impulse
to rest back against the weathered wall of the scarred
tower. Relief didn't allow him to rest, not yet. He
had another urgent area to survey in detail from this
vantage point: the layout of the ruins below.

He found the source of the water as much by

sound as sight: a small, spring-fed catch basin. At one time, it had fed a number of smaller reservoirs with regulated outlets to release water into the segmented stone pipes that ran downhill. However, the passing centuries had split or broken most of the reservoirs and the water now followed the winding path of least resistance through the debris. Most of it gathered behind the one remaining sluice-head at the crest of the hill. From there, it streamed downward as Druadaen had seen and heard, spreading quickly as it did.

Unfortunately, there was also spoor scattered liberally among the ruined reservoirs and the cisterns among them. It was difficult to make out details, but Druadaen had seen similar patterns outside the lairs of large predators: bones and mostly stripped carcasses scattered in a wide arc, dried by the sun and worn by the weather. It might also indicate that predators visited the ruins to ambush animals that drank from the spring. Either way, determining the cause of the spoor—and its location—was Druadaen's first order of business when he descended.

His survey yielded several other interesting results. The nearby tower that wasn't much more than a shell still had a small, relatively intact building attached to it. The un-collapsed pyramid boasted a black, triangular entrance at the bottom of a down-sloping ramp. And while the base of the third tower looked somewhat promising, it was also still partially hidden behind one of the ruined pyramids. Determining its condition would require a visit.

Druadaen took one last look at the farms to the west and then lowered himself over the side of the half-missing floor with a small sigh. He wasn't looking forward to creeping around the ruins as if he were playing hide-and-seek with Old Man Death.

But damn it all, he was getting very, very thirsty.

Crouching, Druadaen stared at free-flowing water just beyond his feet, shining as it wound around broken stone half-pipes and skipped down the sides of stepped reservoirs like it was running over a terraced spillway. He wiped his lips, looked up at the sun and gauged the amount of time he had left: four hours of full light, two more in which it would still be safe to move. But after that, he'd better be in a safe place to spend the night.

He'd been alert for such a spot as he had explored the rest of the ruins. The hollowed tower's attached workshop proved profitless; the fallen stonework had broken through the smaller building's wall and filled it. The tower that had been partially hidden was ruined above the first story, and while there appeared to be a cellar, its stairway had watermarks that nearly reached the ground floor: anything down there had long since been ruined.

Now, finally, he stood staring at the one intact pyramid. It sat with such timeless, sunbaked solidity that it was easy to imagine it had ever been thus, from the day of its creation down to this very moment. And from here, Druadaen could see that descending entry ramp levelled off and rose beyond ground level before access to the dark interior beyond. So, not much chance of water damage. But there was still one small problem with the pyramid.

Well, maybe not so small.

Even had he not had the training and experience

of an Outrider, Druadaen could not have missed that the gruesome remains scattered about the ruined irrigation system were arrayed in the shape of a fan—one with its head centered squarely upon the pyramid's entrance. Furthermore, judging from the condition of the bones, whatever creature denned there was either one of great size, or one that took great pleasure in breaking apart and crushing its kills.

Some of which had been human.

Druadaen sighed. His next step should have been an easy decision, after seeing that. He had water, armor, food, weapons, and a direction to travel. The day was already much, much better than it was after stepping through the Shimmer. But there was a confounding factor: there was no sign of whatever the humans had been carrying, and even the oldest of their closely-gnawed remains hadn't been fully bleached by the sun.

Which meant that, somewhere beyond the triangle of stygian darkness that led into the pyramid, he was likely to find canteens or skins to hold water, packs in which to store food, and all manner of useful gear that would improve his chances of surviving long enough to reach the closest town.

He knew what Ahearn would have done: unsheathed his sword and charged into the darkness, hoping for riches but ready for a battle either way. He knew that Umkhira would have been alongside him, even as Elweyr and S'ythreni would have been trying to pull them in the opposite direction.

But just as he had learned to do in the Under of Gur Grehar, Druadaen was pondering the odds of survival. Which was wiser? Turning away to ensure present safety, or taking an unmeasurable risk to be better prepared for the further challenges of this mad quest? *Of course,* he realized after a moment, *there might be another way to determine which path is best.*

As he began walking toward the pyramid, he glanced at the sai'niin bracer. *Well, come on then; give me a sign, will you?*

But it didn't, even after he had come to the edge of the entry ramp.

He drew the sword, shook it faintly.

Again, nothing.

"Well," he said aloud, "unless you both want to spent gods know how many years as junk in a creature's den, you'd best warn me off now."

Both bracer and sword remained inert.

Druadaen sighed and walked into the darkness.

CHAPTER TWELVE

The level section at the bottom of the ramp—just enough to create a flood-trap—rose into a more steep walkway to the entrance. Two strides into that blackness confirmed Druadaen's first misgiving: that waiting a few minutes in the shadows at the bottom of the ramp was not sufficient to accustom his eyes to the darkness. A torch would have helped, but without any ready means of starting a fire or a supply of suitable wood, fashioning one was likely to take almost as many hours as he had left. But pressing on blindly was tantamount to suicide.

He prepared to retrace his steps . . . and the bracer on his wrist abruptly became the velene.

About time, he thought at it.

As if answering, the velene began to glow: fainter than the animalcules that dimly mark the wakes of ships, but enough to make out his immediate surroundings. Certainly not enough to fight by, but maybe he wouldn't have to—at least, not in the dark. If he took pains to closely observe his path in, he might be able to run back into daylight faster than whatever creature he might lure out.

The less optimistic part of his mind pointed out that if it *was* nocturnal, then it might not be willing to follow him out into the light. And why should it bother? Even if it was not as swift as Druadaen, it would see and pursue him with the same ease as its nighttime prey. On the other hand, if it wasn't nocturnal, and it returned while Druadaen was blundering about in the dark...well, that wouldn't end well at all. Velene or no, retreat still seemed to be the only sane option...

Except that it was looking at him with its metallic eyes. They were featureless, but the silver dragonette's posture spoke in their place; it was expectant and ready.

It would be so much easier if you could talk...

The velene turned away...until its snout pointed straight ahead into the darkness.

Well, that *is a clear recommendation,* Druadaen allowed. But it was still reckless.

The velene simply kept staring into the dark.

"I hope you know what you're getting us into," Druadaen muttered as he eased forward, watching the floor for debris that make noise underfoot.

It was a prudent decision; within a few more steps, the corridor became a veritable junk heap of weapons, tools, shields, helmets, shoes, packs, and everything else one might expect to find in the kit of a person traveling wild lands. Most of it was broken, rusted, or moldy, and he had no time to watch for exceptions. That could wait until—well, *if*—he survived.

The debris did impart some useful, albeit daunt-ing, information. The shattered bones outside could indicate either of two possibilities: that the creature was very large or so ferocious that it dismembered its prey. Now, judging from the remains within its lair, the answer was obvious; it was probably both. A surprising number of shields still had desiccated arms attached, the limb having been struck from the torso by a single, joint-shattering blow.

Just as the density of detritus began thinning, Druadaen caught sight of a bend ahead. It was only half as acute as a right angle, and was immediately followed by yet another in reverse: a defensive dogleg.

And beyond it, he heard restless movement.

Druadaen held his breath, stepped back, was sur-prised the velene did not stop glowing. Not even when he wished—very hard—that it would.

And just as Druadaen feared, the intermittent sounds beyond the dog-leg changed into the fast, purposeful thuds of very large feet.

Druadaen started to pivot on his back foot, ready to run for the exit, not sure which he hoped more: that the creature would follow or that it would not—

The velene unwrapped itself before he finished turning and flew toward the approaching footfalls. As it exited the second part of the dogleg, its illu-mination changed. Less dim, it also began flashing arrhythmically, like a large metallic firefly stricken by the paroxysms of a seizure.

The creature beyond the dogleg evidently saw it instantly: a loud bellow—more human or ape than animal—and the sound of its movement shifted toward the intermittent flashes.

Druadaen held back; this was madness. Following that bloody velene would mean—

The hilt of the sword began to vibrate like a clothesline in a high wind. *No: not vibrating: pulsing.* The grip sent rapidly successive waves along his palm, running from the pommel to the quillons, urging him to move toward whatever creature was in the next chamber, rather than away from it.

Insanity, Druadaen told himself as he dodged around the corner of the first dogleg, careful to remain in the lee of the farther one. He glanced around that final barrier separating him from whatever creature was raging after the velene in the space just beyond.

Manic flickers from beyond the corner illuminated the near part of a large chamber, the floor peeking through between piles of rubbish. His nose pricked; even if there was a corpse smell, he wondered if he'd detect it through the thick nesting reek.

The light brightened rapidly as the velene appeared near the far wall, flying more like a hummingbird than a small dragon. The unseen creature pounded toward it, and just as Druadaen saw a hint of movement beyond the corner sheltering him, the velene stopped in midair, hovering—and became black, just as an immense, two-legged silhouette appeared, closing on it.

Druadaen blinked. No, the velene was not simply black; its outline had abruptly become a volume of space where there was no light at all, neither emitted nor reflected. Which made him suddenly aware that there was now a faint blue sheen on the far wall and the creature's hulking back. *Another light? But where—?*

Druadaen looked down. The sword was glowing, the hilt-pulse still coursing relentlessly toward the

point: toward the creature. Druadaen took a breath,
leaned forward to charge—

The insistent vibrations in his palm waned; he
paused.

From a new location along the far wall, the velene
flashed, now quite brightly. The creature came around
with a roar, leaped toward the airborne annoyance—
and so, was facing directly away from Druadaen. He
saw the ploy and charged, even as the velene's second
flare revealed his opponent.

It was at least nine feet tall, and at least as massive
as the blugners he'd faced in the Under of Gur Grehar. But whereas those creatures had been corpulent,
this monstrosity was top-heavy with muscle. Biceps
bulging, both arms swatted the air where the velene
had been; another, thinner arm raking the same space
an instant after the gleaming miniature dragon once
again disappeared into the darkness around it.

As Druadaen closed with his target, he almost
started: *a* third *arm?* It had been long and almost
skeletally thin, with three talons instead of fingers. As
Druadaen came within leaping range, the monster's
head was cocked to the side; perhaps it was hoping
that a new angle might reveal the velene?

Except, no, its head was not cocked; the strange
posture was because it had no neck on that side.
Just below the jaw, the head was directly attached
to the bunched muscles of its shoulder. The creature
turned—either at the sound of Druadaen's charge or
the faint, constant light of the sword—and revealed
the full extent of its deformity: head misshapen as if
its chin had started melting into one clavicle, eyes
askew, teeth buckled and uneven in a jaw that was half

again too large. But it was alarmingly swift, spinning sharply to face the new threat.

Too late: Druadaen slipped sideways, finding the flank opposite the one that the creature was turning toward him. He drove the sword deep into the torso, then sprang away—

Or tried to. The blade briefly hooked against a rib, was pinched in place by another that the creature's turn twisted into it. The moment Druadaen meant to have been sprinting past the monster, he was just pulling the sword free and leaping back desperately.

The creature roared. The third arm raked at him. Only as Druadaen ducked under it did he realize the attack's actual purpose: to force him to dodge rather than retreat. One of the creature's massive arms swept at Druadaen before he could fully recover, the bucket-sized fist coming around at him in what was certain to be a lethal blow.

Druadaen snapped his sword up into a quick two-handed block, his own arms braced to resist as much of the blow as possible.

In the instant before the arm struck it, the sword flared brightly, raising a sharp chemical smell akin to the kind after a close lightning strike. The blade hissed as if being quenched—and the forearm was severed at the point of contact.

Druadaen, prepared for a bone-breaking blow, was stunned—but mentally, not physically. There was no perceptible impact, as if the muscle and bone of the creature had simply parted as it encountered the edge of the sword. The only physical shock came just after, as the sheared flesh dragged against both sides of the blade. That still sent him sprawling across the floor, bouncing into objects he could not see—and about which he did not care—as he focused on only one thing: *hold on to the sword!*

But as he staggered to his feet, the weapon's glow was no longer steady. Dimming, it tried to re-brighten but faltered. Could even swords become exhausted?

No time to wonder or worry. The monstrosity's roar of pain and rage sprang back from the stolid walls as it came around, eyes seeking Druadaen. Who took that moment to watch how it began its inevitable charge.

Its thick right leg rushed forward, planted, tensed as the left started rising; the creature was too enraged and its movement too forceful to be preparing a feint.

Druadaen gauged. The monstrosity only needed two steps to reach him. The first was nearly complete; the right leg relaxed and its heel was starting to come off the floor. As it did, the left leg planted, ready to propel the creature into contact with Druadaen.

Who waited for its right foot to leave the ground before springing forward.

The creature's expression of eager bloodlust became surprise at the vermin's stupidity: that it was charging rather than dodging. But a hint of misgiving crept into those melted features as it realized the vermin was veering toward its already wounded side—

As Druadaen dodged to the creature's left—the flank opposite its narrow third arm—he stooped and took his left hand off the hilt, thereby breaking almost every cardinal rule of swordcraft. The monstrosity flailed with its left arm, trying to intercept him... but without the lower half of its forearm, it no longer had enough reach. The third arm made to slash at him, but the creature's own broad torso blocked it as

Druadaen arrived on its opposite flank. Howling in frustration, the monstrosity began to come around, pivoting on its left foot—

—Just as Druadaen, ducking as he went past, hacked down at the left ankle. He had to twist at the waist to land the blow: an extremely awkward maneuver that almost tumbled him. But he stumbled past the creature and opened the distance just enough to be out of reach. Regaining his balance, he knew it hadn't been a finishing blow, but halfway in, the blade had slowed abruptly; at the very least, it had cut to the bone.

This time, the creature's howl was different; the previous fury was now mixed with pain and distress: Trying to complete its turn on the wounded foot, it staggered heavily before falling to that knee, groaning.

Druadaen recovered while it was still trying to stand and, charging its left once again, kept tracking with the creature's turn in order to get behind it. It turned to match his movement, trying to protect that critical flank, but its speed and agility were now markedly inferior to that of its smaller foe.

Druadaen reached a clear flank angle again and rushed in, bringing the sword up in a two-handed grip that put the blade level with his shoulders—just as he discovered the third arm was now reaching backwards at him, its elbow joint contorting grotesquely. One meaty pop, and the grotesque appendage was now flexing behind the creature, slashing at him. Druadaen resisted the instinct to dodge the unexpected attack; it was hasty and improvised, whereas his thrust was already set.

Druadaen did not break his momentum, but turned

his last step into a long stride as he reached the rear of the behemoth's ribcage and drove the sword's point toward it—in the same moment that the long, ragged talons of the third arm raked across his chest and flung him away.

For a moment, Druadaen was unable to think clearly; it was instinct that brought him back to his feet. He was still dazed but could feel the sword still in his hand. He raised it, but as his vision cleared, he realized it was not necessary to do so.

The creature was struggling to get to its feet, even as it was weeping through its rage. Its cries had become high-pitched, childlike.

Appalled—even more by its sudden emotional transformation than its appearance—Druadaen backed away from it. The two wounds to its left flank had opened further; it now appeared to have been ripped open by a single, savage bite. A constant stream of blood was pouring out of the ragged gashes, spattering loudly on the stone floor where the melee had cleared it of debris.

Moaning and crying like a monstrous, misshapen toddler, the creature made a desperate charge, but between its wounded ankle and ebbing vitality, Druadaen avoided it with two swift sidesteps at the last moment.

After three more successively weaker attempts to close with its enemy, the creature collapsed, tried to rise, but could not. It fell and began to weep and yowl in a tantrum of terror, the volume of its piteous sounds ebbing as the mounting flow of blood spread into a widening puddle around it. But Druadaen continued to hold his sword at the ready until all sound and movement had stilled.

A moment later, the velene returned to Druadaen's wrist and, after turning its metal face toward his for a moment, became a bracer once again. He leaned back against the wall, sighed, and noticed that the sword's gleam was beginning to fade. *Guess I'm not the only one that's tired—or relieved.* But at this rate he wouldn't have light for very long. So it was time to see if he could find a flint striker and tinderbox among the debris that was mute testimony to the outcome of the many prior battles that had been fought in this chamber.

After sorting out and rifling through the intact rucksacks, Druadaen found the needed flint, masses of dried cordage that proved eager to burn, and a single taper with which he then located enough torches to light the room. At which point, he discovered just how daunting a task was ahead of him.

The greatest single source of labor—and tedium—was the challenge of sorting items of value from the rubbish. This was because many objects that appeared to be promising had been rendered worthless by brutish impacts, repeated trampling, and a fair amount of scat. However, none of the damage appeared to be intentional; apparently, the creature's abuses were byproducts of the eagerness with which it sated its ravenous appetite and the consequently violent impatience with which it removed any obstructions to that end.

Time had been similarly indifferent and destructive. Anything fashioned from wood now only good for kindling. This included every bow, spear, and axe, even though many of their blades and points were still useful. What little armor he discovered was rusted, brittle, or broken. And whereas metal objects were more rugged, the ores used to create them were of low quality, although the actual workmanship evinced the typical range from crude to accomplished.

Still, Druadaen found more than enough serviceable rucksacks and waterskins amongst the dross, and was able to piece together a set of cured leather armor less battered than what he had. He augmented it with a set of admirably wrought bronze greaves which he found along with an equally fine shortsword of the same metal. The only other weapon of any value was an ornate steel broadsword that had been protected by its scabbard and was probably worth more than all the currency Druadaen had found: copper coins, amber beads, jade tokens, and rough garnets.

He also discovered what had inflicted the mortal wound upon the fellow whose remains he'd found on the lane up to the hilltop: a gigantic mattock, set aside in a small alcove and caked in dried blood. And having now seen the size and strength of the monstrosity which had wielded that weapon, it was quite clear how the corpse came to be halfway down the hill: the creature had simply flung it there. That in itself was a curiosity, given its avidity for meat, but Druadaen had neither the interest nor need to solve that mystery.

On the other hand, a more worthy mystery was posed by some of the broken armor, weapons, and tools he had come across: they were not made from metal, but rather, what appeared to be a cured hide or shell. They reminded Druadaen of the equipment created by a secretive guild on the metal-poor continent of Mihal'j, as well as the much-coveted sheath armor fashioned by the Uulamantre. The actual material and designs were different, but still, the parallels begged the question: had the knowledge of such a process come through the Shimmer—or some other osmotium—in the past, just like the fruit trees he'd found? Even if the answer remained obscure, searching for it might lead him to other portals that connected to Arrdanc, and possibly, a better understanding of both worlds.

But the strangest find of all was a door handle made from a yellowish alloy, possibly electrum. Druadaen's initial attention had been drawn by its ornamental scrollwork. However, on closer inspection, he was far more impressed by its perfect symmetry in every dimension. Indeed, the extreme precision of the grooves that separated the grip from the mounting disks at either end made it appear to be comprised of several parts, rather than a single casting. Clearly, it had been cast and trued by a master.

But whereas most handles have holes for the nails or screws to affix them to a surface, this had none. Instead, the mounting plates at either end of the grip had apparently been glued to—of all things—a simple jute sack, now dried and fraying. Shaking his head at whoever had used such a fine piece for such a quotidian purpose, Druadaen resolved to free it by twisting the crudely woven cloth one way and the grip, the other.

The handle tore off the bag with a sound like ripping paper, but left a thick thatch of threads on the "underside" of the mounting disks. Druadaen frowned, worked at the clods of jute and was surprised that he couldn't get them to budge. He had easily picked away those threads that were not in contact with the mounting disks, but the fibers that were directly affixed to them were immovable; he couldn't even pry up their ends.

He considered simply tossing the handle into a rucksack with other odds and ends, but decided— more out of annoyance than prudence—to see if the threads could be sliced away with a knife. He drew his dagger, working to get the edge under the jute. When that didn't work, he resorted to counter-twisting the handle to maximize the cutting or grinding force of the knife.

The jute did not budge . . . but the handle's grip moved slightly.

Druadaen stopped; perhaps it *was* made from separate parts, after all. He turned the object over in his hands, studying its lines before gently attempting to turn the grip again. After a moment of resistance, it rotated until its slightly darker underside faced him, and the "normal" side faced in the same direction as the mounting disks—where it stopped with an audible click.

The remaining pieces of ruined sack fell away. There was no residue of glue on them and the place where they'd been attached was as pristine as the rest of the handle.

Druadaen leaned back, considering. He touched the bottom of one of the disks to one of clods of jute and lifted; it did not re-adhere. Frowning, Druadaen twisted the grip back to its original position before once again touching the disk to the jute; again, it did not reattach. *But what if—?* Keeping the disks in contact with the ruined fabric, he twisted the grip back into the underside-out position.

The fraying material was held fast. As before, any strands protruding beyond the rim of the mounting disk were easy to pluck away. But anything in actual contact with it remained fixed there.

So, clearly not glue. Druadaen went through the process again, touching it to a different part of the sack, observed the same effects.

Is it possible that—? Hardly daring to breathe, he tested it upon a rusted bronze cuirass—and lifted it off the ground; the handle was as firmly attached as if it had been part of the armor. He repeated the procedure, laying the handle flush against the wall. It not only remained in place, but held his entire weight. Druadaen wished he had Elweyr's encyclopedic knowledge of artifacture, both mantic and sacred, to learn if either mentioned such a peculiar device.

Druadaen's thoughts stumbled as it touched upon the word mantic: *but, if this is mancery or miracle, then how is it that I'm able to use it? Am I not subject to the mancery in this world?* Another question he could not answer. At least, not yet.

He half-rotated the grip to release it and put the handle in the rucksack he'd filled with salvage. The last torches were starting to gutter. If he meant to make it back to the shelter before dark, he would have to move quickly.

CHAPTER THIRTEEN

The second time that Druadaen watched this world's slightly whiter sun touch the horizon, he was far beyond the watchhouse near the Shimmer.

He had not slept much after his foray into the ruins, but instead, watched the night sky to see if any moons would present themselves. Instead of the three, stately large ones he knew from home, two small, bright ones fairly raced across the sky. When he finally did sleep, it was with his bracered wrist to one side, and the sai'niin sword on the other. It wasn't as if they were companions, but with them on either flank, he didn't feel quite so alone, either.

He woke shortly after dawn, hoping to reach the first town he had seen from the tower by day's end. But, as on his ascent to the ruins, he considered travel on the road itself imprudent. Besides, there were long stretches where its surface was little better than the land through which it ran, which was often as rough and difficult to traverse as wilderness.

As the day neared its end, the terrain ahead became more even, which meant swifter travel but also less concealment. He decided it was better to stop where he was, move further away from the road, and find shelter among the copses and brush that still predominated in the rough ground to either side.

Druadaen's search did not last very long. Between two sizable stands of trees, he discovered a large, solitary rock surrounded by brushes and fronds which hid its windward overhang. Taking care to step on stones wherever possible, he tucked his goods into the crevice at the rear of the low, natural alcove before clambering up above it to eat his meal. He began with the radishes and carrots he'd found in the overgrown fields of one of the abandoned farms he'd passed: more happy, if puzzling, examples of crops that seemed as common here as they were on Arrdanc.

Those desolate tracts predominated during his first few hours following the road, but had eventually given way to occasional houses. They were all set back from the road and surrounded by rude palisades that were also nighttime paddocks. On the one occasion when he was forced to remain on the road as he passed, several people came out to watch him. Wary, they moved their goats and sheep further away, their staffs held defensively despite being separated by almost a hundred yards of meadow that had once been cropland.

Druadaen finished with a tamaril and hurled it, along with the other remains of his dinner, in the direction opposite the one from which he'd approached the rock. He would need to vary his diet soon, but the closest of the towns he'd seen was only a day or two further along. With any luck, he would trade some of his heavier salvage for meat, bread, and a sleeping roll, and in so doing, start learning the local language. Towns meant trade, trade meant merchants, and merchants meant visitors from distant places, so most shopkeepers learned to build bridges of communication across mutually unfamiliar tongues.

Crawling down from his perch atop the rock, his stomach growled loudly. By the time he slipped beneath the overhang, the sound had become a shrill gurgling. Experience had taught him that a body could survive for weeks on raw fruits and vegetables, but it was not a pleasant experience. He lay back, his kit an unfortunate excuse for a pillow, but better than the stony ground.

Between the rock overhead and the top of the bushes, he saw only a narrow band of sky, the first of the unfamiliar stars beginning to glimmer faintly through the gloaming. Whether the two small moons would traverse the visible slice of the heavens was as unknowable as whether they appeared every night or not. But once he reached civilization, he could find answers to all these questions and many, many more.

Druadaen had slept in more precarious circumstances, but never in a land where he had no idea what species might be nearby, let alone any idea of their habits. He unsheathed the shortsword—if something got under the overhang, he'd need a compact weapon—and laid it on the side opposite the sai'niin blade. Beyond those precautions, all he could do was get some sleep.

And hope that he lived to see the sun again.

Druadaen started awake at the sound of rustling so casual and so close that it meant one of two things:

either the creature passing had no better sense of smell than a human, or it had no interest in him.

The rustling stopped... but not all at once.

Very well: more than one creature. He shifted so that he was clear of the overhang and reached a hand toward his sword.

A few yards back in the bushes, a low growl arose. Druadaen stopped moving his hand but did not withdraw it... and was surprised by a sudden dim glow.

From the sword.

More growls.

The sword's glow became a surly blue violet—and in a blink, the velene was off Druadaen's wrist. It soared overhead into the night and vanished.

All but one of the growls ceased, the last becoming more akin to the stony grumble of a disciplined dog—because, that's what it was, more or less. *Wolves,* Druadaen realized, *several of them. And they don't mean to attack—at least, not yet. But why—?*

A woman's voice called from the dark beyond the bushes, using words that were meaningless to him.

Druadaen put out his hands and, folding his legs under him, pushed straight up into a standing position, the sword still within a leaping reach. But the words from the dark, a surly sword, and a—presumably—watchful velene led him to believe that so far, he had little to fear. But without any words, he could not communicate. *Unless...*

He began to sing, just as he and his companions had done to announce their peaceable intents to the giantess Heela, a whole year and a whole world ago.

Rustling resumed in the bushes, but did not approach or withdraw. It was the sound of creatures repositioning themselves. *Probably to get a better look at the human who is so pitiably insane that when accosted by wolves, he chooses to sing instead of fight or flee.*

After a few seconds of the simple lullaby he'd chosen, the woman called out a longer string of words, but the tone had changed from "Who goes there?" to "That will be enough, thank you."

Druadaen stopped singing, and an instant later the velene returned—but to his shoulder, not his wrist. Its face was aimed in the general direction of the woman's voice. A moment later, the bushes began parting at that point, but more expansively than any woman or man would logically require. Or could achieve.

An accurate assessment, Druadaen silently affirmed as a very large brown bear shouldered casually through growth that would have tested the strength and resolve of ten strong warriors. The last thing he wanted to do was stand his ground, but fighting or fleeing was pointless, and at least he could demonstrate that he was not easily frightened.

It was unclear if that mattered to the woman who walked out of the brush behind the bear, which promptly sat to one side of the gap and began scratching itself. Behind them, at least six pairs of eyes reflected the sword's glow. Knowing the tactics instinctual to wolves, there would be at least half as many again where Druadaen could not see them, but from which they could either cut off a retreat or attack his flanks.

The other thing that arrived was a strong, but not overpowering, animal scent. It was musky and mostly doglike: not unpleasant, if one liked the scents of animals. Which Druadaen largely did. Except goats. And chickens. Especially their coops.

But the young woman who approached to within arm's length did not smell like that. Her scent was more a mix of woods and wet hair. Her garments, which were scant, were fashioned from tightly corded vines that possessed a satiny finish and unusual flexibility. She looked him up and down, the corner of her mouth quirking as she did. That mild amusement departed as her eyes drifted past the now dim sword on the ground, and was replaced by wonder when they settled on the velene.

Which returned her regard with its featureless statue eyes before flowing down Druadaen's arm to arrive at his wrist in the form of a bracer.

Her eyes widened slightly. Then, as if annoyed at showing her surprise, she crossed her arms and nodded at Druadaen, uttering three words, very slowly.

Now that his demise did not seem imminent, Druadaen noticed several phonemes clustered in familiar groups. It was as if, in listening to wholly alien music, one discovered a few scattered notes that resembled phrases in a traditional ballad. And now that she had signaled her desire to converse, he fell back upon his Courier training.

He tapped his chest twice. "Druadaen," he said, and nothing else. At this point, it was imperative to utter one sound and indicate one object. Anything else was a pathway to confusion. He reversed the order: he uttered his name before tapping his chest twice.

Frowning, the young woman tapped her chest and said, "Aleasha," paused a moment, then repeated the process in reverse, just as he had: first the name, then the taps. In the silence that followed, the bear looked from one to the other, then uttered a groan that sounded very like a human realizing that an interval of profound boredom was about to commence.

Looking back from the bear, their eyes met again and, unexpectedly, they shared a smile.

Perhaps, Druadaen speculated as she gestured for them to sit beneath the overhang, he might survive the night after all.

Druadaen's experience as both a Courier and an Outrider proved very valuable over the hours that followed.

They began by trading the most basic of words: nouns with which to identify objects that they could hold up and tap. The progress was comparatively rapid; in addition to finding almost thirty shared words in as many minutes, Aleasha proved not only extremely clever but also relatively familiar with the process of building up a shared language.

Once each had a sense of how the other thought and learned, they added the touchstone for all inquiries and discussions: "yes" and "no." That prepared them for determining what Druadaen had been taught was the foundation of exchanging ideas: fifty terms which all known human languages needed to function. Fortunately, a Senior Outrider had taught him how to accelerate the process: sharing the relevant term in every tongue they knew.

However, since this was an entirely different world, Druadaen almost disregarded that shortcut; there was no reason to assume it would reveal any linguistic overlap. But a whiff of ripening tamarils from his food pouch made him reconsider; given the many species of plants and animals that existed on both sides of the

Shimmer, perhaps people—and their languages—had also propagated from one world to the other.

Aleasha not only understood the shortcut but had obviously used it before. During their seventh attempt to find a shared word—"woman"—she cocked her head when he uttered it in Commerce. Frowning, she echoed with a word that was similar but not a match.

Druadaen wondered if the difference, which was mostly at the end of the word, might be a qualifier of some kind—possibly a diminutive? If so, then maybe she was using a word for . . . "Girl?" he said in Commerce.

She appeared frustrated, simultaneously encouraging further attempts but still not understanding.

Druadaen stood, invited her to do the same. Once she had, he held his hands out, level with the top of her head. "Woman," he said in Commerce. She shook her head. Then he lowered it to a point just above her midriff. "Girl," he repeated in the same language.

Aleasha nodded, smiled brightly: at some point, two different languages had grabbed hold of the same basic word and went different ways with it. After that, their shared vocabulary began expanding rapidly. Commerce was the source of almost all their words in common. It was also a language for which she had a visible measure of contempt. He was not surprised: Commerce had been accumulated from over a dozen languages and was simple and brutishly literal. Writing poetry in it would have been comparable to crafting delicate earrings with a sledgehammer.

However, one other surprising source of shared words emerged. Druadaen had been including equivalent terms from several ancient languages and was surprised when she knew several words in archaic Tualaran, but did not know what the language itself was called. Still, it was an interesting piece of information. Many of Corum Torshaenyx's people were not only long-lived but renowned as adventurous travelers. Perhaps, Druadaen wondered, that included other worlds?

Turning words into phrases came much more slowly. But like Druadaen, Aleasha's prior experience had disabused her of any great expectations. They both anticipated and accepted that the many mangled meanings and mistaken contexts were part of the process, and that the aim was not to attain eloquence, merely understanding.

They kept at it until, shortly after sunrise, Aleasha's eyes began to droop. She shook her head sharply, reached into a belt pouch and produced what looked like a handful of thin, dried roots. Biting into one, she held a second out toward him. "Eat. No sleep," she explained, widening her eyes almost comically to make her point.

Druadaen almost paused—accepting local foods at a first meeting was rarely wise—but in this case, if she had meant him harm, her various furred companions would have decisively completed that grim work before he could have emerged from the overhang. Besides, from the moment Aleasha had appeared, there had been nothing in her demeanor suggesting deception or malign intent. She was reserved and cautious, but he found that reassuring. A Courier learned quickly enough that easy amiability in an initial encounter was often a harbinger of deceit and a prelude to ambush or betrayal. So after a moment's thoughtful hesitation, Druadaen accepted one of the roots—and in so doing, they discovered common words for "thank you" and "you are welcome."

When the sun had climbed halfway to its zenith, she stood, passed the back of her hand over her glistening brow, and gestured that he should follow her to the larger of the two copses flanking the rock. "You come with. Yes?" she asked, head tilting slightly.

He rose, nodding. "Yes. I do happy."

There was a cold spring that bubbled up near the center of the trees which grew close around it, their shade and the cool spray a welcome respite from the growing heat of the day. Before settling in, Aleasha made the rounds of the animals that followed her, touching noses, rubbing ears, making noises that sounded quite like the ones with which they greeted her. They became increasingly relaxed, after that. Different ones would rise at various intervals, always touching noses with her before they trotted off. The impetus for their departure was never obvious. They might have left to patrol, hunt, relieve themselves, or simply rid their ears of the incessant, arrhythmic chatter of humans cobbling together a common language.

But those who were nearby had changed their postures. They were still moderately vigilant, but their attention was now directed outward, not at Druadaen. *So, I'm not a member of the pack, but considered a friend. Or harmless,* was the other, chastening possibility. Either way, it was a welcome change.

After half an hour of further language-building, his stomach growled so suddenly and loudly that several of the wolves looked over. Aleasha simply smiled and raised a hand. "We stop. Now food. Then words more." Druadaen nodded gratefully.

She rustled around in the only hide item she carried—a heavy, shaggy haversack—and produced two flat-pressed cakes. They were a mix of nuts and berries held together by a hard, odorless cheese. "You eat," she said, passing one over. They rehearsed their respective courtesies once again, and savored the food in companionable silence. When they resumed their labors, the shadows had begun to shorten, and Druadaen realized that what had started out as a task crucial to his survival had begun to feel like play.

The shadows had almost disappeared in the noon-day glare and Druadaen was just beginning to feel hungry again, when Aleasha leaned back with a long sigh. "Sleep short then more talk, yes?"

Druadaen nodded, closed his eyes, but unlike his body, his mind would not relax. First he had to review the sizable vocabulary they had amassed. Then consider the implications of all the common words they'd discovered. Then assess what phrases they should work through next.

He sighed. He probably wouldn't get any rest at all. There was still so much to do.

If only I was tired enough to fall aslee—

CHAPTER FOURTEEN

Druadaen awoke with a start. The shadows were half as long as the objects casting them. Aleasha, apparently awakened by his sudden movement, rose, stretched, and glanced in his general direction. "Before sun, you had bad dream."

Druadaen suppressed the urge to deflect the inquiry. No doubt Aleasha's intent was simple solicitousness. But if this world had even stronger reactions against those who were rejected by the gods and dreamed the chaotic dreams of the Wildscape, his time here might not merely become difficult, but fatal. "Dream not bad. I make loud?" Both statements were technically true, but avoided touching on his exclusion from the creedlands of the gods.

Aleasha looked at him quizzically. "No worry. I hear worse."

So . . . are Wildscape dreamers more common here? "Many worse?"

She shrugged. "Yes." Considered, tapped her chest. "Me."

So does she, too, wander the Wildscape when she sleeps? "You dream worse?"

"Some times. Not many." She considered him. "You are, eh, surprise? At bad dreams?"

Druadaen really didn't know how to answer, in part because he needed to be careful what he revealed, but also because he'd run into the limits of their shared vocabulary. He shook his head. "No have good words to talk dreams."

She nodded, the gesture conveying both understanding and agreement. "Then, we learn more words, yes?" she asked, settling into a relaxed cross-legged posture that Druadaen had noticed among many peoples whose lives made chairs and other furniture largely unnecessary.

The trees' shadows were longer than they were tall when they arrived at a point where they not only understood each other, but were even able to trade simple quips. Druadaen was not sure what language they were actually speaking; it was as if they had made their own.

"So, now we talk on dreams," Aleasha said, a hand on either knee.

Druadaen had hoped she might forget. "Yes."

"You seem worried to share words on dreams."

"Such words are not shared, where I from."

"Why?"

Druadaen glanced at her animal entourage. "You dream of, eh, wild place?"

She frowned. "Your words not clear."

"Do you dream of a god place, or place where mountains and fields and trees go, eh, forever?"

She stared at him and laughed. "I dream many things, but I do not dream of talking with gods, if your words mean that. Who would want that?"

He frowned, asked in a cautious tone, "None your people dream of lands kept by gods?"

Her answering frown was deeper than his. "What are these words? Not even priests dream of gods much. But you do?"

"No. *I* do not."

She heard his emphasis on "I." "But people in your home dream of gods?"

"And their lands. Every night."

Aleasha did not simply sit back; it was more as if she recoiled from the idea. "Then you have big luck, not having those dreams!"

Druadaen shook his head. "My people think I sick."

"You are sick because you do not dream of gods?" She snorted out a derisive laugh. "I think people who *do* are sick! Or those dreams make them sick." She frowned. "Your people like the god dreams?"

Druadaen nodded. "Yes. They are good dreams. In 'creedlands,' no fears. Sometimes they see family who is dead."

Her eyes opened wide. "I have never heard this." She shook her head. "Here, no one dreams of god land." She reflected. "Maybe mad priests. I do not know."

Even though Aleasha's comments had prepared Druadaen to expect her denial of the gods and their creedlands, her frank, unabashed statement of it still felt like a physical blow. For a moment he could not think—and then he was awash in more questions and speculations than he could sort through. But rising above them all were two realizations:

Creedlands are not known in this world... because Arrdanc's gods are not here.

He did not anticipate his reaction or the feeling it sent coursing through him: freedom, absolute and complete. Whatever else the people here might think of him, his dreams would not make him a pariah. But on the other hand, this revelation begged several questions about the temples and priests Aleasha *had* alluded to. Why would either be in this place, if the gods themselves were not? What was the basis of their power, their authority?

Fragments of his conversation with the Lady of the Mirror rose up, suddenly seemed part of a greater whole, all converging upon the central question—and quandary—she'd put to him: "And what if it is your path to pass through the Shimmer?"

His throat was dry. He may have blinked. He didn't know. His world had shrunk to one question: *So, did she suspect... or did she* know... *that my questions cannot be answered on Arrdanc, but only on a world where its gods are absent?*

He blinked again, discovered that Aleasha was staring at him. "You are well, yes?"

He nodded. "I am. But it is strange, to be in a world without gods. Or the god-houses we name 'temples.'"

She frowned. "There are no gods here. But there are many who build temples. Too many." She looked ready to spit.

He was ready to match her disdain with his own, but an unbidden memory leavened that impulse. Padrajisse, a sacrist who had traveled with his group until slain by an assassin, had been adamant that his exclusion from the creedlands was not a sign of the gods' rejection. So perhaps the Lady was right: that by turning him away at the last moment, Amarseker had not been tormenting him, but foresightedly helping him. Not only because it had ultimately saved him from being labeled a heretic, but because it had freed him to turn everything he knew on its head. Because if the Wildscape was the normal state of human dreams, then why had the gods created the creedlands? And why did those deities—or at least their hieroxi—claim to be omnipresent when they were not even known on this world?

Druadaen shielded his eyes with his hand and leaned back—mentally as well as physically—to keep from plunging headlong into the further questions rising up out of the abyss of what his world had taught him.

Aleasha had leaned back, watching him carefully. When his silence persisted, she gamely tossed out a question to change the topic, perhaps rescue him from it. "I am be curious. Your clothes and war-tools are much strange, much confusing."

Druadaen shook his head, as if recovering from a blow. "In what way?"

Her gaze played across the odd amalgam of garments, armor, and equipment that he had gathered from the pyramid. "I wonder: are you a noble in beggar clothes, or a beggar who found a noble-sword?" Her eyes went to the velene. "And whether you are noble or beggar, you *do* have intra . . . um, intesring . . . eh, strange friends."

"Strange and *interesting*," Druadaen replied, providing the word she could not recall.

She nodded gratefully. "Interesting. Yes, that word."

She leaned closer, almost near enough to touch the velene. "It is alive, even though it is metal."

Druadaen shrugged obligingly. "Well, it moves like an animal. But it is not."

She shook her head. "How it moves is not why I say it lives. It *thinks* before it moves. Like you and me." She shrugged. "Not creatures such as us, but I would, er, promise my best bowstring that it is alive, not a...eh, wyrdcraft. It is itself."

Druadaen had thought no less on many occasions. "Wyrdcraft," he repeated. "Is that your word for a thing made from mantic power?"

She nodded. "What some call magic." She nodded toward the velene. "Does it protect you from wyrding?"

"I think so. At least a little."

She leaned away, met his eyes. "Just before I walked out from bushes, I tried to—eh, reach your thinkings." She shrugged. "But there were none."

Druadaen smiled. "Some of my teachers said the same."

She chortled. "That is the first lie you tell." She became serious again. "When I sat with you, I tried again, but with, with..." She frowned, not finding a word. "I did not try from here"—she tapped her forehead—"but from here," she finished tapping her heart.

Druadaen nodded. "I think my home's mantics call that 'affining.' But when you try, you found empty."

Aleasha shook her head hesitantly. "No. That is not the feel. And it did not feel like a wall." She thought. "It was like sounds wolves hear, but I do not. Something is there, but I cannot reach it."

Druadaen leaned forward. "So, you work magic?"

She shook her head, perplexed at his question. "*Not* magic." She gestured at the animals around them. "I am a wyldwyrd. Do you not have them in your home?"

Druadaen thought that over for a moment. "I think we name them naturalists. Or gritches—green witches," he expanded, seeing her perplexity at the first term.

She shrugged. "Same thing, different name." She frowned. "We need *more* names, and words, if we want speak more clearly. Let us learn while walk, yes?"

Druadaen nodded and rose. "Where should we start?"

Several hours later, Aleasha sent two of the wolves ahead. "We near a crossroad, the last before a big town." She hesitated. "I do not want to meet anyone else." A more awkward pause. "This is where we part. But we shall share another meal, and there is a good, hidden place for you to make camp three, four miles up the north road."

Druadaen simply nodded. There were several unspoken assumptions—or suggestions—in her words, but her halting speech told him that it was better not to inquire after them. Either she'd unfold them in her own time or not.

They walked half a mile before she confirmed his instincts. "You are patient. Most people from towns and even farms are quick to ask questions when they meet a new person. And are quick to tell about themselves, even when not asked." She glanced at him, uncertain.

He smiled, hearing the request she refused to utter. "You are free to ask anything you wish."

She returned his smile but her brow was furrowed,

as if asking personal questions was unfamiliar or even unpleasant. "I cannot decide whether you are from a town or not. At first I saw your dress, your weapons, the way you walk. I thought, 'surely, from a town.'"

Druadaen heard the hanging tone. "And then?"

Aleasha shrugged. "And then I see that you do not walk on the road; you follow it at a distance. I thought, 'ah, he has been a soldier moving through dangerous lands.' But then you made camp. You moved from rock to rock. You threw food-waste as far as you could. You slept beneath the chin of the rock. And without a fire." She shook her head. "Not even farmers do that. And not all shepherds."

He shrugged. "I have spent enough time in the wild to know that fire attracts attention from far away. And it cannot always be used to chase off what it attracts."

"Huh," she answered. Her tone was reminiscent of a teacher discovering that an unwashed and presumably untutored youngster could actually count, add, and subtract.

"But even without a fire, sometimes you are still found," he added with a rueful grin at the animals flanking her.

She smiled sharply. "This is true. But then, we"—she gestured to her companions—"knew where to find you." Seeing the surprise he failed to keep off his face, she added, "We saw and watched you from middle of the day."

He nodded. "But why follow?"

"You look different. And not many people come from that way." She gestured eastward. "Mostly wanderers come from Trawn or Pecthin." She studied his gear more closely. "Much of that is Trawnish. Most of it has seen more years than you have. Did you get it in Trawn? Or do you have relatives there?"

Even if he hadn't heard the leading tone—the bait to see if he would lie—he would have given the same answer: "No. I do not know Trawn."

She smiled. "I did not think so." She tilted her head slightly, looking at his mouth.

He raised an eyebrow. "What are you—?"

"I am trying to see where you come from." She leaned back. "And I still do not know. Your teeth say the country; they have not been rotted by soft breads and rich food. But your hair and skin says a city, or at least much time under a roof. You do not act like a princeling, lost without retainers. But your speech is that of books. Many books." Her eyes wandered back to his clothes and kit. "But more strange is what you wear and carry. None of it matches. Most does not fit."

He nodded. "I have not had it long. It is still unfamiliar."

"Hmmmm...except for that sword and that 'bracer.'"

He smiled. "Yes, except for them."

"So: Trawnish and Pecthini gear, but not from there. From much farther away, from a place where people visit the lands of their god in their dreams. Much, *much* further away than Trawn."

Druadaen simply smiled and waited.

"You could talk a little more!" she exclaimed, frustrated. And what he heard behind it was, "Must I ask you *directly*? Really?" When he still did not speak, she crossed her arms and muttered crossly, "You're from the Fickle."

When Druadaen frowned at the odd word, she

seemed ready to clap her hands in delight at his perplexity. "What is the Fickle?"

Her smile lessened as she nodded, gestured back along the road. "It is a very old Haze. Those few who know it call it the Sometimes Door. Of old, it was called a Shimmer. Most folk just think it a cursed place." She recrossed her arms in triumph. "You are from there."

"I am," he admitted. "But why do you call it the Fickle?"

"Because it is not always there . . . so it is a Sometimes Door. It is said that those who come out of it are not always from this world. Or at least, they do not seem to be." Speaking of it, her voice had become solemn. Her eyes fell away from his. "Let us eat."

Druadaen wondered what was troubling her as she silently produced several unleavened disks of bread and gave each of them two. Next came a small corked pot that contained a piquant mash of apples, citrus, and very hot peppers. She gestured and they ate.

She finished one of the breads, looked at the other, pushed it away, and sat so that she could wrap her arms around her knees. When he stopped eating, she murmured, "You know you cannot return, through the Sometimes Door, yes?"

He nodded.

She frowned. "So you tried to return and could not?"

Druadaen realized why it was considered cursed. "No. I knew, before I came, that I could not go back through it. I was also told that those who tried might be sent to dangerous places. Maybe scattered in space like the stars. No one knows."

"They told you that . . . and still you came? You are very strange. Or you are very mad. Or maybe both."

"Probably the last," said Druadaen with a rueful smile.

She answered with a surprised grin, but persisted. "I would know what made a person start a journey from which they cannot return."

"Well, that is not what I was told. I was warned I cannot return *the way I came*. But it likely there are other ways to do so."

"That is a slim thread on which to place the weight of so great a step."

Druadaen sighed. "I agree, but I cannot quickly explain why I took it."

"For such a tale, I will make more time." She quirked a smile from one side of her mouth. "It is amusing when sane people try to explain their mad plans."

They had long finished the rest of their meal when Aleasha finally leaned back and stared at him. "So, you came to this world to ask questions about your own."

"Yes. But now, I must determine if others from my world have done anything to harm this one."

She frowned. "But how will you learn where they are, what they've done, or even if they are here at all?"

He shrugged. "I must start by traveling to a large city." Seeing her frown deepen, he added, "They hear more news, and faster."

"And will you find such cities, and hear this news?"

"By following the road"—he gestured over his shoulder—"I presumed I would come to a town where I might learn of the nearest city. Once there, I hoped to find news of those who came through the Fickle before me . . . as soon as I learned how to understand what I heard, that is." He smiled. "Which I can do now. Thanks to you, Aleasha."

His smile seemed to further deepen her frown. She did not appear to be disappointed or angry at him, but rather, that she was having an argument with herself. Finally, she said, "I do not like cities. Too much filth. Filth in streets. Filth in water. Filth in hearts." She sighed. "But I agree: a city is where you must go. So I shall show you a road to one. Walk three days and you will be there."

"A city is so close?"

"A small one. But it has ships that go to the greatest city of Sarma; that is the nation which claims these lands. That is where you should go to listen for news. But be careful when you talk. Bigger cities mean smaller hearts. And keep walking beside, but not on, the road as you travel to the first city. I do no less. And it has saved me much trouble."

Druadaen scanned her furred followers, whose numbers had swelled. They now included one brown bear, one black bear, a weasel, seven wolves, two owls, a hawk, and—impossibly, given all those predators—a stag and an indeterminate number of doves. Obviously, she did not consider the local wildlife dangerous. So logically, that meant—"Bandits are common along the road?"

She nodded. "Bandits . . . and worse."

"Worse?"

"Servants of a power to the east."

"A rival of Sarma?"

Aleasha seemed about to reply in the negative, but then shrugged. "Only in the nature of greed and ambition. It is not a nation. It is a . . . a cult."

"Of priests?"

"So they claim. In the past, they remained hidden.

Now, they range farther and are bolder. Some think they work miracles."

Druadaen frowned at the word "miracles." "Are you *sure* there is not some deity conferring bestowals in response to their entreaties?"

"I have told you, there are no gods here."

"Yes. But, while these cultists were hidden, could they have *discovered* a god?" *Or could it be that* they *were discovered by a god?* "I have seen the works of deities in my world. Perhaps they were once here, too, but slumbered. Or were forgotten." *Or recently arrived?*

"I have seen these 'priests.'" Aleasha's reply was both grumpy and sardonic. "Their powers are much like mine. But they tell simple folk that those are miracles from the god they worship. That is how they spread fear. And attract followers who want power like theirs." She shook her head. "So many people kneel to mute gods. They pray for a safe life. They long for an end of fear. And others pray for the power to cause it." She shook her head. "I do not understand this."

"What is this cult called?"

She glanced up at him sharply. "They go by many names, but who knows if there is a true one or what it might be?" She rose. "Let us go to the crossroads where we shall part."

CHAPTER FIFTEEN

The meeting of the roads was without grass or weeds, so it was well trafficked. But Druadaen would never have guessed that the humble lane that wound northward led to a city, even a small one.

At the edge of the forest through which they'd approached, Aleasha put out a hand and gestured him to sit. "First, Druadaen, if you were preparing to offer payment for the food and knowledge I have shared, do not. It is what beings should do for each other without thought of gain. I tell people, 'help another as I have helped you.' But your words and your eyes tell me you know this already. So you do not need that lesson from me.

"Instead, you must learn where you are and what is around you. So attend.

"This world—strange to think of it that way!—is called Hystzos by those who dwell around the sea of that same name. The name of the sea itself comes from the largest island, whose people built an empire that reached far in all directions. What other peoples from other places call this world, I do not know.

"The Haze—Shimmer—through which you came is at the south edge of a vast land called the Godbarrows. You saw the many strange ruins and strongholds? They were already old when the Hystzossi came to rule there and for hundreds of leagues all around. After several thousand years, they were overthrown by an even mightier invader: the Annihilators. I know little about them except that they arrived without warning and, after several generations, departed even more suddenly than they came.

"The Annihilators did not take the Hystzossian empire for their own; they destroyed it, starting with the Godbarrows. The lands we are in now were the empire's most distant part: small states that paid tribute to it, and were safe and wealthy under its protection. Pecthin and Trawn were two such colonies, valuable only because they had ports at the eastern end of the Straight Sea, which reaches in to them from the Sea of Hystzos.

"It was the cities along the south shore of the Straight Sea that became truly wealthy, because they were crafty merchants and even better liars. And that was also why they did not suffer as much when the Annihilators arrived, because under the empire, its princes had learned to bow down to stronger powers. So they excelled at being the Annihilators' *djheb'wasi*." When Druadaen frowned at the unfamiliar word, she stopped, considered. "Lickers of rectums," she supplied.

"Across the Straight Sea to the north, there were two other realms that the Annihilators did not completely destroy: Morba and Kaande. Morba is called the Shield because no invaders can reach Kaande without conquering it first, and that has never happened because of its many mountains. And so Kaande was not much touched by the hand of the Annihilators.

"Because these three countries and the lands around them survived the coming of the Annihilators and the chaos that followed after they left, they became known as the Last Lands. The smaller countries beyond them—Trawn, Tharn, Pecthin, Bronseca, more—were not so fortunate and so are still called the Broken Lands.

"Across the Sea of Hystzos are scattered towns and cities, and two lands large enough to be called nations: the horse-people of Ruildis, and the sea-people of Tyrmeys. But, large or small, that far coast had fewer people and less metal when the Annihilators arrived and so were of little import to them. Together, these western and northern lands are known as Absolutia: a strange name with strange stories to explain it. Some say it is because their distance from the empire ensured that their deliverance from the Annihilators was near-absolute. Others insist it was because their 'gods' were pleased by their entreaties and, as a sign that their sins had been absolved, spared them that fate. I do not know which of those, or other stories, is correct. Nor do I care."

"And what of the island of Hystzos itself?"

Aleasha shrugged. "Not much is said of it. It still has a city, I am told, but mostly deserted. A strange place. After birthing an empire, it fell into a . . . a waking sleep. I do not know your word."

"I think you mean a coma."

"If that is a waking sleep, then yes. But it still gives

its name to all these lands: Lorn Hystzos. Beyond them, you enter the Godbarrows, which stretch all the way to the Cloudcap Mountains: the ones you say you saw beyond the eastern horizon."

"And beyond them?"

Aleasha cast a sideways glance at him. "I see why the priests chased you away from your homeland. Beyond those mountains is the Shun, about which very little is known. Mariners know more, but not a great deal, I think. Most of those lands are wild. Tribes roam them."

"Is it called the Shun because it is forbidden to go there?"

She shrugged. "No, it is just unknown and feared. Those who go there rarely return. Legend has it that long before the Annihilators and even before Great Hystzos itself, the people of those lands were the first in learning and power. But they were proud and polluted by their own greed and arrogance. That is why the first abominations were bred among them."

Druadaen tried to keep his voice casual but failed. "Abomination?"

"Dangerous creatures. Monsters, really. They are mostly found in Death Lands: the only places that *are* forbidden."

"And where are the Death Lands?"

"Where are they *not*? The largest of them are in the Godbarrows, but there are even small ones in Absolutia. Many say they are unhealthy to inhabit. Whether or not that is true, criminals, outcasts, lepers—and yes, abominations—hide there."

She waved away Druadaen's queries before the first could leave his lips. "I do not know more about these places. I know little enough of what happens in the Godbarrows, and I was born there. Live there, too." She sighed. "There is nothing much to know about the Godbarrows. Creatures live and creatures die. People pass through or settle, then disappear or depart."

"Why did you leave?" *And how do you know about the road to the city, if you are rarely here?*

"I left because there are strange disturbances. I do not mean the bandits and tribes that are always at war over some forgotten or imagined insult. This is different. Many of the bandits and tribes are gone, now. Those that remain work together. Creatures from the Death Lands destroy farms and hamlets. And it is thought that the cause of these changes came from down here, in the south. Possibly from the Broken Lands, or maybe from the coast." Druadaen watched as her eyes became less focused on her surroundings, began seeing something beyond: assessing, measuring, projecting.

As if she were aware—and annoyed—that she had done so, she stood quickly. "You will need to move quickly to reach the hidden spot in which you can make camp. Look for two tall pine trees on the right side of the road. Walk between them. Walk another ten paces. You will find a small glen with a place that is easy to defend and safe for sleeping. There is a spring close by. If you start before the sun is up tomorrow, you might arrive in the city—Pakobsid—just before dark on the second day." Her various animal followers had risen, sensing—or having been informed?—that the other human would not be traveling with her; the way they formed around her left no room for a companion.

Druadaen rose. "If I could ask one last, practical question?"

Her almost worried impatience relented slightly. "Ask."

"Where should I say I am from?"

Her sharp nod signaled both approval at his inquiry and her certainty answering it. "Say you come from a steading in the northern Godbarrows. Your accent is not unlike one that exists up there. It is a wilderness with few hamlets, and even fewer towns, so will not meet anyone who has been there."

"Still, anyone who has heard of it might also expect me to know the regions that border it, or with which it trades."

She sighed. "There is little trade that far north, but yes, they will expect you to know the places from which settlers have come and to which others may travel. I have already mentioned two: Ruildis and Tyrmcys. They are where Absolutia touches the Godbarrows."

"Which of the two is closer?"

"Ruildis, but the ships of Tyrmcys range farther and may have small trading settlements along the rivers or the coast." She thought for a moment. "Tyrmcys is actually the best place to mention. You have some of that accent. You even know some of its words."

Druadaen started. "I do?"

"Of course. Some of the words in that ancient tongue you tried—Tualaran, I think?—were ones that I understood because I know a bit of Tyrmcysan. Now, stop asking questions! You must get to that camp before the sun sets. These lands were never safe, but they are less so now."

Dusk was starting to tip into night as Druadaen began to unpack. Having just finished filling his largest skin with fresh water, he considered taking a bite of one of the cheese-nut-berry cakes that Aleasha had gifted him.

A distant whinny. In the direction of the road, but closer. So perhaps Aleasha wasn't the only one who knew of this campsite.

Druadaen didn't rise but began hastily reloading his goods into his rucksack. By the time he was finished, he could hear voices. Not enough time to get into the brush, let alone hide. *And if I'm caught wearing this damnable pack during a fight...* He stood, checked the angle and placement of his weapons, and called in the local dialect, "Who goes?"

"Ho, the camp!" came a reply from just beyond the two pines. The speed of the response and the lack of surprised, whispered debate indicated that he had probably been detected beforehand. And if so, why hadn't they called out earlier? Druadaen measured his distance from the path to the spring, from his back to the sheer stone shelf behind him, from the various low bushes and large rocks between him and the direction of those approaching. But his primary attention was not upon what his eyes saw in front of him, but what his ears might detect behind.

"I say again, ho, the camp!"

Druadaen had no reason to expect it would have any effect, but he glanced down at the bracer. "You would be most effective as a surprise."

Faster than Druadaen could blink, his wrist was obscured by a flash of uncoiling silver that became a mad flutter of wings. But as it arrowed into the darkening sky, the velene blackened...and disappeared.

Well, there's a first time for everything, Druadaen

told himself, feeling that the odds had tipped in his favor as he prepared to confront . . . well, whatever was out beyond the two trees. "You may advance." He was pretty sure he got the local word for advance wrong.

A responding guffaw confirmed that suspicion. "Ah, a traveler from far parts, then!" The speaker appeared between the trees. A modestly tall man of average build, he led a horse into the small dell, still chuckling. He was followed closely by a slightly shorter and very lean younger man in a full-length cloak, hand near the bit of his rather shaggy palfrey. He glanced at Druadaen with the barest hint of a nod and he drew his increasingly skittish mount behind him, clearing the gap between the trees. In which appeared the third, and very strange, member of this group.

He was a big man, almost as tall as Druadaen and easily half again as heavy. He was bulky in the way of wrestlers for whom victory depends as much upon weight as strength, the kind he'd seen when visiting Z'datien as a young Courier. The fellow was wearing only a kirtle, sandals, and a harness. Its shoulder straps were each fitted with a loop, and each loop held a hatchet. The load upon the harness's frame was so large that it would have been a reasonable load for the two horses. However, despite the punishing burden, the man was smiling. And blinking rapidly.

Without any words of introduction, the other two tied off their horses on a half-fallen tree and approached, the older one lighting a pipe as he came. He stared around, as if surprised. "What? No fire, yet?"

"I mean to keep to myself," Druadaen replied,

watching to see how they'd respond to that extremely broad hint.

If they realized he was indicating that he meant to camp alone, none of them gave evidence of it. Rather, the oldest of them sat on a stump and rummaged in his pocket. "Fancy a pipe?"

Druadaen shook his head.

"Ah, that's a shame...but more for me!" he said merrily. He studied Druadaen soberly. "I must say, I've seldom seen a man less happy for company while camping alone on the edge of wilderness."

"I'm used to it."

"I suppose you are," the younger man murmured, staring more fixedly at his gear. "A nice sword, judging from that hilt. But the rest looks Trawnish."

Druadaen wondered at his ability to understand the man—understand him far too well, in fact. Although there were a few stumbles and hesitations, it was as if the newcomer already knew which words Aleasha had taught him from which local languages. Which was not possible—unless Druadaen was *not* proof against this world's mancery or wyrding, contrary to what he'd experienced thus far.

The middle-aged man stroked a neat beard as he waited for a response that did not come. "Quite the dialect you speak," he commented finally. "Where are you from?"

"The far north."

"Tyrmcys, maybe, judging by that accent?"

Druadaen shook his head. "Beyond that. North and inland." *And thank you, Aleasha.*

"That's far indeed!" He waved the broad bearer to approach the camp as he stared at Druadaen's clothes and gear. He waved at the whole ensemble with a circular gesture. "Your kit: is all of it, er, your local wares?"

"Not all. I had to replace some."

The fellow nodded sagely. "Trouble along the road?"

"So to speak."

"What from?"

Druadaen shrugged. "Bent."

The other one scowled in confusion.. "Bent? What's that?"

Damn me for a fool! Of course there might not be any urzh here. Wait: maybe . . . Druadaen managed to keep his voice and face unchanged as he offered, "You might call them urzh, here."

"Hah! Yes, urzh," the older one agreed, motioning that the bearer was free to shrug out of his harness and sit down. "Although Bent is a right enough name for them. So, you have trouble with them, up north?"

"More than here, from what I've seen."

"What makes you say that?" asked the thin one, who had opened a sachet and was scattering lightly scented dust in ritual motions.

Druadaen shrugged. "Where I'm from, every steading has to have a wall. *Has* to. Here, some do, some don't."

"That's because some farmers are smart and some aren't," explained the lean one.

"Aye, 'cause there's trouble enough here, too," the garrulous one agreed in a more congenial tone than his partner. "But the threat isn't from urzh. None around these climes, and they're far more likely to avoid than attack."

Druadaen nodded, but did not take the bait to

find out what, rather than the Bent, was the source of the local danger.

The leader's brow curved in annoyance—but straightened just as quickly. "So, then," he restarted, "judging from your gear and your readiness to travel alone, I presume you're a sell-swor—er, soldier of fortune. Am I right?"

Druadaen shrugged. "I have been called that, from time to time." Which was technically true.

"Maybe you'd be looking for work, then? Is that why you're bound north for the big city?"

Another shrug. "That's one possibility. But I'm told there's more work in Sarmasid."

The other emitted a bark of surprised laughter. "Work? You think that folk with coin will use it to hire someone who—well, who looks like *that*?" He pointed at Druadaen's mismatched and much-battered gear.

The human pack mule laughed maniacally, eyes still wide and staring. But they no longer blinked.

The quiet one barely smiled. "Why would you wish to go to Sarmasid? It does not look like your purse could support lodging there ... unless you mean to sleep in the fields. Which are half a day's walk from the walls."

Druadaen sighed. "I've slept in worse places."

The leader of the three waited for him to expand upon that answer. When none came and the silence grew long enough to be uncomfortable, he scratched an ear and made a great show of looking crestfallen. "You don't talk much, but you say even less. Why is that, friend?"

Druadaen had intended to make a slower, casual exit, but the leader's carefully controlled tone and intrusive question told him: *it's time to go. Now.* "I keep to myself, mostly," Druadaen answered, fastening the flap of his rucksack as he rose. *Can't put it on, but carrying it in my hand makes me look eager to leave. Well, nothing for it.* He picked up his kit.

"Here now, where are you going? I didn't mean to insult you."

"I'm not insulted. But I'm in want of quiet."

Before he'd finished, the big, staring fellow had risen and stepped in his way. His eyes widened along with his grin. "Quiet," he giggled. "Yes, quiet."

Druadaen dropped his pack.

"Now, this won't do!" said the taller one as the lean one rose and backed away . . . but moved out toward Druadaen's flank as he did. "There's room for us all, here. And see: you've upset Mawnk." He indicated the staring bearer.

"Is that what I've done?"

The fellow smoking on the stump studied Druadaen, gaze suddenly canny. "Ah, so yer *not* interested in a job. Well, it was worth trying." He made a rapid gesture with both hands that ended with them focused on Druadaen.

Who, in the instant before it occurred, knew—did not conjecture, but *knew*—two things: he could ignore the older fellow's wyrding, but *not* that which might come from the lean one on his flank.

As he drew his sword and turned to face that threat, the pipe-smoker grunted in surprise, then snarled orders at Mawnk in a completely unfamiliar tongue.

The lean fellow had thrown open his cloak, hands raising much as did Elweyr's just before finishing a readied thaumate. The space separating them emitted a snap like shattering slate and the hair on Druadaen's arms rose abruptly, along with the smell of lightning-burnt air. He started forward, saw his enemy's hands moving into the position of completion, feared he would not close the distance in time. But at the same instant, Druadaen again knew—*knew*—the correct counter: to stand fast and extend the tip of his sword toward his opponent. *Madness!* he thought—and thrust the sai'niin blade outward as far as he could.

An instant later, a roiling mass of sparks appeared between, rushing toward Druadaen. But the point of the sword seemed to suck them out of the air, brightening the whole blade—from which they immediately shot back across the space, leaving blue after-images on Druadaen's eyes.

The coruscating discharge hit the summoner in his hands and chest, blowing him off his feet and backwards into the brush. His fluttering robes trailed smoke as he fell.

Running feet—heavy, thudding—closed from the other side: the bearer. Druadaen started to spin back in that direction, but heard the rush of small wings: the velene, coming down just beyond the sound of the footfalls. Druadaen ended his turn at the midpoint, turning it into a long step toward the pipe-smoking mantic.

That ambusher was just getting his feet under him, reaching for a small bag on his belt. Mancery or not, Druadaen had no immunity to alchemical compounds; he ran the blade through his enemy's chest. As he turned away from the falling man's gargling shriek, he discovered the ogrish bearer just a few feet away, clawing at his ears. The velene hovered just out of

reach, projecting a thin, almost undetectable sound
that was the apparent cause of the hatchet wielder's
desperate agony. A hand clamped to one side of his
head, he pulled a hatchet and hacked at the dragonette. It fluttered back and sideways. The howling ogre
turned to follow.

Druadaen stared as the fellow's broad back finished
rotating, his bullish spine facing the tip of the sai'niin
blade. For a moment he couldn't move. *All battles are
slaughter, but this*—? On the other hand, Hystzos
might be a world where combatants never gave nor
asked for quarter. Besides, the bearer's mad eyes held
no promise of scruples: just unbridled mayhem.

But Druadaen was a creature of a different world
and the Consentium's values. "Stop!" he shouted at the
man's back, stepping beyond leaping range.

The meaty fellow turned quickly, an instant of
puzzlement burned away by a howling blast of sheer,
animal rage. He raised his hatchet, bounded forward—

"*Stop!*" Druadaen shouted more urgently.

The man yowled a single word in reply as he closed,
bringing the hatchet back for a cut.

A feint wasn't necessary. He was too slow to shift
with Druadaen's sidestep or counter the quick cut
behind his left knee.

The man went down heavily, his yowls becoming
one long bellow of pain.

Druadaen raised his sword meaningfully. "Stop.
Now."

The man's face contorted, darkened until it was
almost purple, and he screamed the same word at
Druadaen. Again and again. Then he rose to one knee,
right hand cocking the hatchet to throw—

Druadaen leaped to the man's left, cutting at the level of his neck as he went past. The man threw up a vantbrassed forearm to block the blow...

The sword's edge shone, crackling faintly as it sliced through vantbrass, arm, and neck as easily as if they had been half-melted butter. Then:

Silence. Except for the high-tempered palfrey, which was whinnying and rolling its eyes.

Druadaen felt a strange surge of emotion. Not guilt, exactly: more akin to regret, and not just for the three lives he had taken. Somehow, without ever intending it, his existence had become one in which killing was not merely frequent, but almost routine. He had certainly aspired to a life in the military, as legiar of the Consentium—ironic, since few who served in the Legion ever drew a sword in anything larger than a skirmish. But still, those were *battles*, whereas this...

He surveyed the three bodies. When he killed, it was not part of a battle. It was close, brutal murder. You didn't just see your enemy's eyes as you fought; you watched as the light in them went dark, left them as lusterless and inert as old beads.

Druadaen started, then stepped sharply away from the bodies and his thoughts. First task: determine if the melee had attracted any attention. He clambered up the striated stone spur at his back and scanned the open woodlands around him. Half an army could have been hidden in the scattering of trees and brush, but if anything was out there, it was not moving in his direction.

Still, it was not safe to remain in this camp. The sounds of the fight might not have been heard, but the smell of fresh kills were almost sure to attract predators, scavengers, or even more dangerous visitors.

He hopped back down, already planning the best way to choose the salvage, load, and leave in the shortest amount of time. As he began the grisly work, it occurred to him that without the sword, it might have been him who wound up like the still-smoking corpse in the bushes. And not just because of the way it had reflected the lightning. How else had he known exactly what he needed to do at every step, even when he did not know his enemies' powers?

As the velene swept back toward him, he asked it, "I don't suppose you had something to do with that, too?"

The velene simply curled back into a smooth bracelet on his arm.

"No, of course not," Druadaen sighed. "You're a great friend, but poor company."

The velene's head reappeared, emerging far enough from the bracelet to regard him balefully. But only for a moment; before Druadaen could respond, it flowed back into the featureless bracelet.

Walking toward the horses, he stepped around the body of the dead axeman, his severed forearm, then his head. *Well, since the velene is listening now…* Druadaen shook the sword. "I am not complaining, but if many others see you are *this* sharp, tales will be told. Soon, we will not be fighting off a few chance-met highwaymen, but legions of sword-stealers. We wouldn't want that, now, would we?"

After a moment, the blade became a little less like a perfect mirror seen through the waters of a pure mountain lake. It resembled steel.

Surprised at the response, Druadaen managed to mumble, "Well...that's a bit better," and got on with the unpleasant job of salvaging what he could and hiding the bodies.

Druadaen did not stop to equip himself with the much better gear of his attackers; he simply packed it for travel. Besides, he spent too much time contemplating two mysterious discoveries.

Beneath the lean mantic's traveling cloak was a full-length gray robe with a faint hint of purple in its weave. It did not feel or look like a garment made for personal use, but rather had the appearance and simplicity of an item distributed to the members of an army or a temple. He was tempted to take it, but he was already carrying too much on the two horses. It might prove to be an item of interest, but it might just as easily invite pointed questions from the servitors of a great power. But more interest was a torc worn by the middle-aged mantic whose effect had failed to exert any influence over Druadaen.

Firstly, it had a pronounced, musky scent: not unpleasant, but not particularly appealing either. It might simply indicate that some fluid or growth had leaked into its presumably hollow interior, but Druadaen did not dismiss the possibility that it was built around, or to house, something that was alive. Secondly, where it had rested against its owner's neck, the flesh was as pristine as an infant princess's. The torc's purpose was as mysterious as its origins; it had no characters or pictograms which might indicate who had fashioned it or to what end.

But all such concerns were secondary to the

challenges of Druadaen's current circumstances: to travel alone, at night, mounted on an unfamiliar horse while leading a second, skittish one. The only way he could have made it worse was by attaching bells to them all and blowing a coronet every ten minutes. Which he would have been sorely tempted to do, had he been carrying such frivolous objects.

After all, if one was going to tempt fate, one might as well do so boldly.

Journal Entry
Tenth day on Hystzos

I am finally on land again, and—furnished with paper and a quill pen that is spongy rather than hollow—may resume this journal. It is urgent that I put down what I learned between finding a ship in Pakobsid and arriving here in the Sarmese capital, not only because I wish to record the events while they are still fresh in my mind, but because it is prudent to review them one more time before my unexpected meeting with the Vizierate of Sarmasid.

Having the use of my ambushers' two mounts, I was passing villages and even two sizable towns as my first day of travel came to an end. And pass them I did; I had no way of knowing if the horses, or my newly salvaged gear, was identified either by subtle physical marks or some wyrdcrafted tag. Until I was farther from the site of the attack, and until I had greater facility in the local language, I preferred the known risks of sleeping in one of the now-ubiquitous meadows or orchards. Furthermore, I wanted solitude when I made a detailed assessment of the salvage; it is not wise to undertake such a task where eyes at peepholes might see and wonder at unusual and still-bloodstained gear.

As I spread the salvage out on the dusty margin of a long-neglected vineyard, I was struck by the same sad realization that had first struck me in the wake of another, more costly, ambush that my friends and I repelled on the frontier of Kar Krathau. The rumors of riches lost in the ruins of long-dead civilizations or in the lairs of great beasts are not only chimerical but ironic: such riches are usually realized by vanquishing other self-seeking fortune-hunters.

The kit spread out before me certainly supported that sad observation. There were many philters and powders and vials. I suspected some were mundane compounds, others the creation of alchemists, or the local equivalent. The weapons—shortswords and daggers—were of respectable quality and all coated with a clinging, viscous paste: no doubt poisons to kill or incapacitate. Oddly, they had not possessed any armor, but unless I am much mistaken, their traveling cloaks have been treated by a compound that resists flame.

They had coins of various kinds and alloys (what I would give for a proofing kit!), few of which bore any resemblance to some of the ones I'd found in the hilltop ruins. However, they each had well-cut gems, all with lacquer characters on one facet; an appraisal, perhaps? They also possessed several tomes, many papers, and even a map, albeit for a location of which I had no knowledge; profitless in the present, but perhaps of great value later. Of immediate use was their basic kit: well-made sleeping rolls, ample dry rations, and an unusually compact compass.

By the time I had gone through the lot of it, there was little I was determined to keep from the hilltop ruin, other than the armor and the mantic handle. The excess I decided to sell or trade, as circumstances and opportunities allowed.

The next day's travel was unique in my short experience of Hystzos; it was blissfully uneventful. The skies were hazy and the air was wet and warm, but the road was dry and the palfrey was slightly calmer. Much of the grass—or what passed for it—had patches that the horses seemed keen to graze in. I trusted that, being native to the place, they knew far better than I which were safe. But just in case some of the ground cover was the local equivalent of sour grass, I did not allow them to eat much or for very long in any one place and remained alert for signs of colic or sourgut.

But none arose and as the sun began its descent, I caught sight of Pakobsid—or so I conjectured, given the tan and gilt domes that peeped over its smooth, thick walls and the amber-gold glitter of the sun on the sea beyond them.

As I approached, I was glad to see many of the region's typical mud-brick buildings cluttering the approaches to the city's various gates, albeit always half a bow shot from the walls. Until I learned—either through observation or conversation—a bit more about the tolls, taxes, and prices inside the city, it was always more economical to remain outside, where lodging was usually less dear. Or, failing that, fields provided cover for a few hours' sleep.

From Aleasha's remarks on Sarma, I was not surprised to discover that Pakobsid's most noticeable, and arresting, features were the stark distinctions of wealth and the ill treatment of persons beneath one's own station. It brought to mind some of the harshest caste-based realms I had encountered on Arrdanc. However, here there were no theological or even inherited bases for the obvious distinctions. The only factor that determined one's social status was affluence—or the appearance of it.

Leading both horses through the cramped streets, the sights and smells of unwashed and abject poverty rose along with the dust. From the distance, the mudbrick structures had appeared to be predominant, but once among them, I discovered that margins separating them were often packed tight with crudely built houses and shacks. Even tents became permanent features, some sporting waist-high walls built from loose stones and fragments of adobe. In some cases, these were also the stalls of the poorest class of merchants, who were beginning to store their wares and dismantle their tables: usually just discarded doors thrown across the tops of empty crates and barrels. Yet it was in the midst of this unpromising jumble that I came across my first true treasure: a door through which I was able to enter into the language and history of Sarma.

Its physical manifestation was a wide pair of folding doors. They took up almost the entire front of a shop that had begun as a narrow wooden house, one side of which now leaned against a moneychanger's squat adobe establishment. The doors were folded back to display an intriguing mélange of odds, ends, and artifacts which burgeoned out over their threshold and spread down to the very edge of the parched lane. I could not discern what its trade might be and so ventured within.

There I discovered a fingerless grandfather, moving

various objects from one perfectly good place to another, carrying them between his seamed and leathery palms. His first response to my entry was brief annoyance; it reminded me of the reaction of the Archive Recondite's head facilitator whenever I had the temerity to ask a question.

But then the Sarmese grandfather threw a second glance my way, shrewd eyes reading my garb and gear as if it too were a book. His words of invitation were meaningless, but his hand-stumps communicated clearly; I was bidden to come fully within his shop. I did so, explaining and apologizing with my polyglot patois of local languages that I spoke no Sarmese.

His eyes widened—whether in surprise or aroused avarice, I could not tell—and he answered me in a similar mix, inviting me to examine his wares.

"Which are?" I asked.

His voice was injured; his eyes remained shrewd. "Why, antiquities, far traveler. All artifacts of great rarity and historic importance."

I nodded, guessing that as many as one in ten might indeed warrant that description. The rest were a bit worse for wear, and would more accurately have been described as "junk."

He surely noticed my assessment of his dubious wares—how could I conceal it?—but he was also canny enough to see where my eyes lingered: several objects that were given more space and which, by their style and means of manufacture, distinguished themselves not only from the other wares, but anything I had ever seen before.

He smiled, sat, and invited me to do the same. As he did, his look changed from a narrow and disdainful assessment of my penury to one of hunger for conversation with a visitor who not only had an eye for true antiquities but who hailed from parts unknown.

In the course of his descriptions of the various items, he moved us from the initial combination of tongues to an increasing amount of Sarmese. But it was evident that he knew many more languages still. When I did not prove interested in any of his priceless objects, he seemed genuinely crestfallen, and indicated that he regretted being uncourteous, but he had to begin closing his shop. I smiled and passed him two silver coins across the tabletop. "For your trouble," I said, "and to trouble you a little further."

As I withdrew my arm, a pouch on my harness gapped—and his quick eyes caught on the torc which I had decided to store there. The antiquarian's carefully casual inquiry to inspect it told me that my suspicion was indeed correct: "That is an interesting curio," he almost drawled, nodding in the direction of the exposed end of the torc.

I shrugged.

His persistence told me that it was valuable indeed. "If you wish, I could examine it to determine if it possesses any value."

Again I shrugged . . . but handed it over.

He took it a little too quickly, his fingerless palms surprisingly deft. He studied it closely, sniffing at it. I was left with the strong impression that he had seen its like before. "Interesting," he admitted, laying it back on the table. "I might be persuaded to buy it as a native bauble."

I smiled. "I am not selling it."

His demeanor became less casual. "Perhaps you

would be interested in knowing what I would pay for such a bauble."

"Perhaps I would...if you stop calling it a 'bauble.'" I allowed my smile to widen.

He stared, then smiled back—again, genuinely. It told me that, whatever else he might deem me, "fool" was no longer among the descriptors. He quoted me a very handsome sum.

I shook my head, and instead, pushed two more coins across the table toward him.

He looked at them and sighed. "I cannot persuade you?"

"That depends upon what you tell me about it."

I watched as a mental abacus worked rapidly just behind his eyes, calculating the odds of misleading me just enough to get me to be willing to sell it for an even higher price. But something he saw in my own eyes made him sigh again. He palmed the two additional coins to his side of the table and commenced to explain that the torc was not exactly arcane, but it belonged to a very old, and now very rare, form of artifacture that required the skills of both an alchemist and a wyrdcrafter.

This particular torc was designed to assist the wearer in the learning of unfamiliar languages. An improbably lucky find, I thought for a moment, then realized that the man who had been in possession of it was clearly a traveler also, and very possibly one who needed to remain comparatively innocuous and capable of blending into new places.

My host did not fully understand how the torc worked, but it apparently did not confer understanding of a foreign language through wyrding. Rather, it accelerated normal learning by alerting the wearer to when their understanding of words were accurate or in error and could create mental impressions that suggested more correct understandings. He refrained from calling it a device, implying instead that it altered its behavior in response to each new wearer, becoming more effective the more frequently that person used it.

"Has it ever visited any harm upon its wearers?" I asked.

He shrugged. "If so, I have never heard of it."

"Well," I said, "then let us see if it works." And despite my lighthearted tone, I had two great misgivings as I put it around my neck. Firstly, that what the Lady called my dragon-mind would make this object useless to me. And secondly, whether I would sense any deleterious effects in time to tear it off.

Happily, it worked and in just the way he'd foretold. He nodded, glad or at least gratified that I had not collapsed after placing it around my neck, but also sad; I could well imagine how much he might have been able to charge for such an artifact. I offered a small smile of commiseration and pushed one of the larger garnets across to him. "Again, for your troubles." He stared at it, at me, smiled broadly enough to show that he still retained about half of his teeth, rose, and returned with tea, after which we chatted amiably for two hours.

On reflection, I suppose I should say that it was he who chatted—more animated than amiable—insofar as I interrupted him only to ask for increasingly subtle corrections to my rapidly growing mastery of Sarmese. For he was in his glory as he unwound the tale of his land's strange and ill-starred history.

If there has ever been another realm so ruled and obsessed by coin and prestige, I have yet to hear of it. Sarma's origins are obscured by the many tides of history that have washed through, and occasionally over, it, but when reached by Great Hsytzos' expansion, it was a motley collection of city-states ruled by self-styled kings. After a few years of obedient groveling toward their new masters, they once again fell to fighting among themselves, which disrupted the commerce that made them marginally valuable as a province of the empire. Rather than sending an army, the autocrat of Great Hystzos sent a decree. It required that the Sarmese accept one of two alternatives. Either the petty kings would find a way to end their incessant internecine wars, or they would be stripped of their titles, lands, and very likely, their limbs. My host pointed out that the Hystzarchy did not make threats; it made promises, and was renowned, respected, and resented for always making good on those oaths.

That one decree accomplished what generations of bickering had not: a settlement that all parties could live with. The many petty kings became the Princes of Sarma, who nominated one of their number to be the King-Father (who later became more commonly known as the Father of Princes). His possessions were shielded within an inviolable trust and guaranteed handsome rents in perpetuity. In exchange, he and his family withdrew from the affairs of the nation with one crucial exception; he was not merely Sarma's titular head, but became the foundation of the blood brotherhood of all the Princes by adopting them all as his sons. However, shortly after, this initially symbolic linkage was replaced by a tradition of ensuring universal consanguinity amongst the offspring of all the Princes—or at least the legitimate possibility of it.

More specifically, it became the duty of all King-Fathers and their sons to have conjugal relations with the First Wife of any Prince that was desirous of fathering a child in line for the succession of that Principality. A monthly assignation was arranged until the First Wife was announced to be with child, thereby making the actual parentage of the offspring uncertain. That uncertainty allowed the King-Father to legitimately claim progenitorship, which in turn conferred the legal imprimatur for that child to be an inheritor of the Prince in question. Trade flourished, as did scheming and mercenary opportunism. As one mordant moralist favored by my host had written, "Greed became Sarma's only civic virtue."

The depredations of the Annihilators brought disarray and confusion to the agreements, partnerships, and even bloodlines that had grown as thick and entangled as a nest of adders. By the time that blood-tide receded, the intricate arabesque of relationships upon which Sarma was founded had been riddled by fire, disease, death, and the destruction of most of its immense repositories of records, deeds, and contracts. Loud claims and counterclaims to Principalities and the bloodline of the King-Father filled the streets of Sarmasid even before it had finished burning.

Ultimately, a group of families—including many of the most duplicitous and ruthless—came to dominate the coastal trading cities that lined the Straight Sea. They quickly put a new King-Father on the Quartz Divan, who was chosen not only for the comparatively reliable pedigree of his claim to it, but also his family's extreme depletion. And so Sarma's new aristocrats—the self-styled Merchant Princes—got exactly the leader they wanted: one so weak that he was little more than a figurehead embodiment of what was now called Old Sarma.

The antiquarian smirked sadly as he congratulated those architects of modern Sarma on their cunning and shrewd decision to appeal to tradition, but averred that its success also dissolved whatever modest national spirit had existed beforehand. He held up his hand as if it still possessed an index finger to raise in didactic remonstrance. "Base meretricious opportunism," he pronounced, "has become the defining trait of Sarma. Those who pursue wealth and position no longer bother to wrap themselves and their deeds in appeals to strengthening the nation; they announce their ambitions without excuse or apology."

The sun had almost sunk beneath the horizon as he concluded this declamation of his own country and, realizing the time, commenced to pepper me with questions. Did I have lodgings yet? Was I planning to take ship to Sarmasid after all? Had I considered the problem of doing so with my horses? And would I be amenable to showing him any other curios I might have picked up in my travels?

While he inspected my "curios" (which were certain to mysteriously transmogrify into "priceless antiquities" the moment they touched his shelves), he gave me valuable guidance on the concerns he had raised about my travel. He commended me to the services of a small caravansary just beyond Sarmasid's docks yet still outside its walls. It was slightly more expensive, but in all probability, would be an excellent place to liquidate any of my excess goods and even trade away my horses. Also, since it served no small number of captains and pursers, it was likely to provide me with news of the best rates for taking ship to Sarma. And lastly, he felt that among other non-native speakers, my limited aptitude in Sarmese—which he charitably dubbed "promising"—meant I was less likely to become a target for the confidence men who roamed the docks and merchant's quarter, looking to "assist" foreigners with the local bureaucracy and line their pockets in the process.

However, his voluble stream of advice ended abruptly when he came across the strange hide or shell fragments of armor and weapons that I had found in the hilltop ruins, and which had reminded me of similar Mihal'ji implements. "Where did you find these?" he breathed with a quaver in his voice. At first I thought it was from a surge of avarice, but by the time he'd finished, I'd discerned the actual cause: terror.

"Near the southern limit of the Godbarrows, east of Trawn."

He folded their wrappings over them, averting his eyes as he did. "These are the remains of Annihilator artifacture. You must report this to the Princes in Sarmasid. And tell no one else—especially me!—how you came by them. I want no part of this." He handed them back, even as he eyed them covetously. "I have enjoyed our discussion. It is rare to meet someone, especially of your age and origins, whose interest and learning makes them . . . well, interesting to one of *my* age." His eyes crinkled in a painful smile. "But now, you must go. Quickly. Please."

❖   ❖   ❖

I did not ask any questions about the Annihilators until I was safely off the boat in Sarmasid, a city of such scope and grandeur—and desperate poverty— that by comparison, it made Pakobsid seem a sleepy little town.

Domes of many shapes, colors, and metallic finishes towered bright and high over the broad urban skirts that spread out from the steeply sloped walls of its center: the restricted precincts known as the Princely City. The Merchant's District ringed that aristocratic core of gold leaf and filigree with spired palaces and broad, palm-lined avenues, all of which announced that this was where the commercial magnates dwelled. The Trade Quarter was wedged between its walls and those which comprised Sarmasid's defenses. It was a place of impressive stone buildings and cobbled streets, where elephants and purpose-bred supragants (called gigasenes) bore passengers and dragged loads to and fro, albeit much more slowly than the bustling tempo of commerce through which they moved. As the out-ermost of Sarmasid's concentrically-walled sub-cities, it fronted on an immense harbor which was in turn shielded from foul weather by serried ranks of cays which trailed from a long spit of land like ellipses.

Beyond its outer defenses, Sarmasid underwent abrupt changes. A higher, wall-hugging arc of stone and mud-brick buildings defined the reasonably prosperous Peddler's Crescent, its narrow streets dotted with cis-terns and spanned by brightly-colored awnings: poor refuges from the heat and sun compared to cooling effects of the walled districts' many fountains.

But beyond the outer bulwark of the Crescent's solid buildings, the streets narrowed and writhed outwards

like the tightly clustered roots of a distempered swamp
bush. There, Sarmasid became a trackless, chaotic
tangle that began with houses and suqs, descended
into shacks and flimsy stalls, and finally devolved into
a welter of tents, huts, and hovels built from cast-off
ships' sides and wagon beds. And as unbearable as
the heat was, the stench was even more so.

Had I not heeded the antiquarian's advice about
the caravansary, and thereby acquired a great deal
more of both the language and coin of the realm, I
would have been fortunate to find, and lodge within,
Peddler's Crescent. However, the lessons learned
in Pakobsid about the layout and administration of
Sarmese cities now paid excellent dividends. In Sarmasid, most foreigners were shown scant patience
and charged inflated prices. But I now knew enough
of their ways and tongue that neither my purse nor
trust were presumed to be easily had and so found
a room in an inn normally reserved for merchants.
I was able to claim that status simply by posting a
sale price from my palfrey: a loophole that the ship's
captain passed along while laying an index finger
alongside his aquiline nose.

After my conversation with the antiquarian, I was
mindful not to speak of my origins. The larger the city
and the more powerful the persons I might encounter, the more likely that they would have either the
breadth of experience or depth of means to investigate
any story's veracity—or lack thereof.

So on my first day in Sarmasid, because I was already
present in the Trade Quarter it was relatively simple to
enter the Merchant's District. After presenting a not
entirely untrue explanation that I had business with the

powers within, and a few coins to demonstrate that I understood how business was done, I was through the gates and on my way to the citadel of the city's most accessible yet formidable bureaucrat: the Hazdrabar.

While I knew no personal details of the current holder of that post, I did not really need to. I chose the Hazdrabar simply because his is an office that must deal with the public in his role of overseeing security for and access to the council of viziers known as the Vizierate. It may seem strange that viziers have their own council, but among the prestige-conscious Princes, a negotiation between their highest respective functionaries is a prerequisite to any royal meeting, let alone contemplation of joint endeavor.

However, because of their prestige, the viziers dwelt in the Princely City and were loath to emerge from its high, alabaster walls. So they had long ago created the position of the Hazdrabar, whose job was to assess and then recommend or reject the petitions of supplicants. Not surprisingly, the Hazdrabar's place of work was a citadel that was both a garrison for his security forces and intelligencers and housing for the considerable bureaucracy that supported his service to the viziers and Princes.

I did not dress as anything other than what I was: a traveler, now of reasonable means, who was clearly accustomed to providing for his own needs and safety while making his way through the world. The guards manning the postern gate in the citadel walls would almost surely have turned me away as a lost, imbecilic outlander except that I had reasonable facility with their language, knew the proper way to address them and state my business, and whom to ask for.

Such knowledge was common among the silk-robed foreign merchants who waited at the main gate with their attendants. But it was uncommon at the postern gate, where I approached them alone and in armor. As soon as I saw their uncertainty and hesitation, I played the card I had held for that very moment.

"Here," I said, holding out the smallest of the Annihilator shards. "If you would be kind enough to bring this to the attention of your master's master, I would be grateful." They took the object and studied it in mute perplexity . . . which doubled when I turned to leave.

"Will you not await an answer?" one asked.

I shook my head. "I have business to attend to. In two hours, I will return to hear whatever answer has come down from the Hazdrabar's second assistant, and also, to tangibly express my appreciation to you both. I presume you shall still be here?" Their eager nods told me that they would not miss the opportunity to pocket a gratuity, even if they had to remain beyond the duration of their watch.

Sure enough, two hours later, they were not only still at the postern gate, but with a senior guardsman present. He asked what my business was. I responded that I was putting myself at the disposal of anyone who desired information regarding where I had found the shard—as well as many others—and the circumstances under which I took possession of it. The guardsman instructed me to tell him these things; I demurred, saying that I would not wish the weight of so delicate and confidential a matter to fall on anyone other than myself. Annoyed, he instructed me to wait. Shortly after, I was ushered within the walls of the Citadel of the Hazdrabar.

Over the rest of the day, I went through four more almost identical bureaucratic rituals, although each was in a more grand and imposing space than the one before. At each step, the officer or bureaucrat in question attempted to inveigle me to share more information and more of the shards I claimed to have. In every instance, I demurred for the same reasons. Twice we reached an impasse. Twice I was on my feet to leave. Twice I was called back with greater deference than I had been shown before, and asked to wait—before being shown to the next, more senior interviewer.

The last one was less fixated upon where I had found the shards and what I had seen there. Instead, his inquiries focused on my origins, my business in the Last Lands, and ultimately, how I earned a living.

My answer to the last question led to deceptively casual remarks about my armor, my gear, and the unusual sword that I refused to be parted from but had allowed to be peace-bonded. In fact, each one of those conversational gambits were means of determining if the equipment of my apparent profession was part of a sham. Eventually, he was satisfied that I was what I appeared to be, and soon I was following him to a location deep within the citadel.

After a great many twists and turns, we emerged into a training yard. He called over a waiting warrior—the Sarmese term for "soldier" is actually quite degrading—and proposed a quick sparring match with wooden training swords. They were well weighted, quite accurate to the real blade in every regard, but the weapon itself was not to my liking. It was a stolid, point-heavy cleaver, something between a broadsword and a tulwar.

Instead, I scanned the racks of ready weapons, and chose two shortswords with long quillons. The warrior and my interviewer exchanged glances. The former shrugged, the latter raised an eyebrow, and we squared off.

Two passes later, both of the warrior's eyebrows were lowered in consternation. After the fifth pass, they were curved down in ferocious chagrin. My interlocutor waved away any further exercise, asked me where I dwelt, and bade me be alert to receive a message before nightfall.

He evidently knew the minds of his masters (for so one's employers are called in Sarma). A young runner arrived just before the sun set. I could not read the message, of course, but that had been anticipated. The boy told me what was written, reciting it from memory, no less. I was peremptorily instructed—not requested—to report to the West Gate of the Princely City just after dawn, where the First Guardsman of the Hazdrabar would be waiting for me with an escort.

I thanked the young fellow, asked why his "masters" had bothered with a letter at all since he knew the message word for word. He told me that, if I had misgivings, I might thus take the letter to one who could read it for a fee (because everything in Sarma requires a fee) and so be satisfied that he had accurately conveyed the contents. I nodded my thanks and extended a small silver coin toward him. He shook his head, almost in fear. Reflecting upon what I had seen of Sarma, understood; in this money-conscious—or -crazed—society, so precious a metal was likely to quicken suspicions. Where could one such as he have come by such a coin? Surely, not by honest means.

I changed my token of gratitude to a small piece of what I conjectured was base billon. His eyes shone—because they watered—and with a deep bow, he stepped closer. He reached his hand toward mine, a question in his eyes. I nodded. He took the coin, stepped back, bowed even more deeply than the first time, and ran out of the room as if hordes of red urzh were hot on his heels.

And now I lay the quill aside and will hope to sleep rather than restlessly count the gonged watches of the night, eager to see what tomorrow brings.

CHAPTER SIXTEEN

Since entering the Vizierate—a squat, ancient ziggurat—Druadaen had lost his sense of direction. This was no doubt an intentional consequence of its design. Some corridors were straight, others were curved. Its various rooms and halls and chambers were arrayed in a maze of clusters, each separated from the others by long, empty stretches of corridor.

Besides, it was difficult to see much, walking at the center of a square of the Hazdrabar's own guard. All but one of the men was at least as tall as Druadaen, and their plumed helmets made it impossible to get more than fleeting glimpses of the featureless walls. They did not so much walk as march, every one of them more heavily built and broader in the body than he was. More daunting, they all moved lightly, surely: no heavy-plodding brawlers in this handpicked unit.

So Druadaen had no idea where he was when the contingent turned abruptly left, took three long strides and entered a room shaped like an arena, narrow skylights illuminating the center of it.

The back half of the arena was raised, a narrow aisle for scribes at the bottom, behind whom a much higher tier rose up. Eleven seats were perched atop it in an even arc, as well as a twelfth, well off to the left-hand side. Seven of the heavy wooden chairs were currently occupied by men of considerable years. The man in the twelfth, and less stately, side chair was only middle-aged.

Behind each of the eleven viziers, a veritable squad of advisors, scholars, assistants, and guards waited, and beyond them a motionless group of what Druadaen presumed were runners. A pair of guards also stood before each one down on the floor of the arena itself, in the center of which stood an empty table. The Hazdrabar's lieutenant motioned Druadaen toward it, holding out a hand for his sword.

Druadaen removed the scabbard from its baldric, but did so as he walked toward the table.

Most of the guards started toward him, but as Druadaen held the sword to his side, hand firmly around the center of its scabbard, two of the older viziers motioned them to stillness.

Druadaen placed the sword on the table and then walked around to stand in front of it, stopping two paces closer to the viziers.

"You stand *behind* the table, brute," muttered one of the guards who'd started forward.

Druadaen glanced over his shoulder. "The weapon is to my rear, and if by some feat of acrobatics I could reach it before you stop me, I would be *further* away from the august gentlemen of this council. So you tell me: all things considered, am I not in the place where I present the *least* threat?"

"Filth, you shouldn't have your sword at all," another guard growled, leaning forward.

"Stop your growling, dog," the leftmost vizier muttered irritably. "He refused to appear before us without the sword. He agreed to lay it aside as he came before us. So, if his respect for our rules and our authority is wanting, his attention to our insistence upon safety is apt." The vizier turned his almost black eyes upon Druadaen. "Still, you are willful, Outlander."

Druadaen nodded at the mixed messages in that comment. It verged on rebuke, but the vizier had used "outlander," which was marginally more respectful than "foreigner," which was in turn better than "barbarian" or "savage." "I apologize for seeming defiant, Respected Vizier. But I gave an oath not to be parted from that blade. And if the cost of that oath had been to forfeit the honor of appearing before you, then I would have had to pay that cost."

The grumbles among the viziers combined grudging respect, impatience, and scorn for such childish trifles as "oaths." The same vizier rapped his signet ring on his onyx side table. "Outlander, you give your name as Druadaen. This name is unknown to us. What is its root?"

Druadaen was grateful that the first question was simple to answer truthfully without conveying any meaningful information. "I do not know the exact origins of my name, Respected Vizier. Its sound is similar to some words in old Tyrmcysan legends, but beyond that . . ." He concluded with a shrug but remained alert to any sign of a short report being made to any of the viziers. If there was a wyrdward—or mantic, or master of some other mystic art—who could discern not merely untruths but any intent to deceive, they now had reason to alert their masters.

However, most of the viziers were occupied with appearing bored, sipping wine, or rolling their eyes at the impossibly unrefined provincial who had come before them. Druadaen made note of the three who were not indulging in such distractions: the speaker, the very old one at the center of the arc of viziers, and the middle-aged one occupying the twelfth chair set apart from the rest.

The speaker frowned. "So you are from the lands near Tyrmcys?"

Druadaen shook his head. "No. I have merely heard of it. It is actually quite far to the west."

Another of the viziers, a very thin one, leaned forward abruptly. "So you are from the Godbarrows, then?"

"Beyond that. It is a very far land, farther than the mountains on the edges of your maps." Again, all true... strictly speaking.

One of the eye-rolling viziers frowned and pointed a chubby finger at Druadaen. "No one has asked you about the quality of our maps. We are asking for the name of your town."

Druadaen shrugged again. "I am not from a town."

"So you told the Hazdrabar's numerous, witless seneschals. Then give us the name of the *closest* town, foreigner!"

He chose the village closest to where he'd grown up in Connæar. "Houênne."

"Never heard of it!"

Druadaen shrugged. "It would have been very strange if you had." Again, entirely true.

The one who had spoken initially laid his hands flat upon the arms of his chair. "You requested this meeting. It is unprecedented."

"So was my means of making the request," Druadaen deadpanned.

"You know the significance of those fragments?"

"I know what others told me."

"To whom did you show it?"

"A merchant, chance-met on my travels."

"And what was *his* name? And city of origin?"

"Again, I did not share mine and so did not learn his." Druadaen saw and responded to irritated stares. "It is not an unreasonable precaution, for a traveler about to enter an unknown land." *Or who wishes to protect a fingerless antiquarian who wants to stay well clear of the affairs of captains and kings.*

"Very well," said the vizier who was the apparent spokesperson for the group, "just tell us where and how you came by these shards you presume to be important to us."

As if I'd be here if they weren't. But he answered, "Certainly," with a deep nod and then launched into the complete tale of his encounter at the hilltop ruins. He added the aftermath he had seen at the watchhouse, but by putting it second, led them to believe—without ever claiming—that it took place *after* his battle with the abomination. He naturally left out any mention of Aleasha.

Then came the part of his tale he was most hesitant to include: the encounter with the three men who'd ambushed him at the camp. Initially, there had been as many reasons to leave it out as include it, but given the unexpected alacrity with which the viziers had convened, the three reasons to share it became decisively compelling.

Firstly, having tested his martial experience, Druadaen suspected that beyond the exchange of information, the Vizierate might have further employment in mind. If so, the outcome of the campsite ambush might prove useful in securing the coin needed for daily life and his attempts to answer an ever-expanding list of questions. Of course, the actions of the velene and the sword would have to remain unmentioned.

Secondly, the episode at the camp might help correct the rest of his tale's one possible flaw: a strange lack of complications and spurious details. As it stood now, the interval between his encounter at the ruins and his arrival in Sarmasid left so great a silence that some vizier, acting on either suspicion or spite, might decide to ask questions that required Druadaen to either lie or demur. However, if he included the story of the ambush, that vacuum was filled and his tale became convincingly detailed and messy.

Lastly, sharing the story might ultimately gather as much information as it gave. If, as Aleasha had suggested, Sarma had worries about that region, the viziers might reveal much through their comments or questions. If so, this council was an ideal place to play dumb and learn more.

As soon as he began to unfold the tale of the ambush, their reactions confirmed his hunch about their concern with the region or the powers that might be abroad there. Significant looks were exchanged in the chamber.

By the time he concluded, several of those glances became accusatory glares. The thin vizier who'd asked

Druadaen if he was from the Godbarrows jabbed a finger at his colleague who had called the Hazdrabar's lieutenants "seneschals" and deemed them "witless." "Did I not say the watch post at the Haze needed funding? Did I not foretell that the Sentinels were too weak to man it?"

The accused vizier waved a dismissive hand. "They are of no consequence and their order was an expense we could ill afford. And for what? If they were so thoroughly dispatched as this barbar—er, foreigner claims, then a few more of them with slightly better equipment would not have changed the outcome. As it is, our investment in them was perfectly balanced."

"They died, to a one!"

"And in doing so, warned us of the probable use of the Haze." His voice became evasive. "And so, suggests a connection to other recent concerns." He shot a glance at Druadaen. "Are you sure you found nothing else at the watch post? No tracks leading away? No documents? No strange writings or rubbish?"

"No tracks or strange rubbish. And I would not know strange writing if I saw it, Respected Vizier, not being familiar with the scripts of these lands. About which: if those men were an order of sentinels, what were they guarding?" He knew the answer—the reference to the Haze had established that—but if he was to learn more of their concerns and to conceal his own connection to it, it was necessary to feign ignorance.

The vizier who'd put the questions to him frowned, affronted as if a cockroach had spoken to him. However, his accuser provided the answer. "Those men are—well, *were*—the Sentinels of the Lorn: an order that watches for . . . for intrusions into the lands of Lorn Hystzos.

They are from many lands, and this was their largest watch post." He glared at his disinterested colleague. "It is doubtful that they shall recover from the loss of so many senior members of their order."

Druadaen affected an uncertain frown. "Were they there to keep watch over the ruins atop the hill?"

"No," snapped the disinterested one without looking at him, "and you are here to answer questions, not ask them."

The main spokesman on the far right leaned forward. "Let us turn to that part of your account, Outlander. The abomination: did you know in advance that it laired in those ruins?"

The inquisition that followed was not exactly brusque, but it was certainly brisk. Druadaen was somewhat surprised by the often painstaking nature of their queries about the monster's anatomy and behavior. They ended by asking if he tried to communicate with it before attacking. Druadaen answered that, given several score of well-gnawed human remains and the creature's violent response as he approached, its intent was clearly to consume visitors, not converse with them.

If they heard his sardonic quip, they ignored it in favor of debating among themselves about the creature's particulars. Their primary concern was whether this was of the same breed that had been reported in the various Broken Lands, some of which were rumored to possess rude speech. But in discussing their depredations, they did not speak of them making an incursion, but rather of being "introduced."

Druadaen risked further disapproval by echoing, "Introduced?"

The speaker preemptively held up a hand to still his more arrogant peer. "Yes, introduced. Why? Do abominations with the power of thought occur naturally in your land?"

Druadaen shrugged and told the pure truth: "In my land, abominations do not occur at all."

This generated a buzz of surprise and consternation among all the viziers. The man in the smaller seat to the far left did not join in the discussion, but glanced at Druadaen as if just noticing him.

The speaker for the council turned back toward Druadaen. "But you know the name we use for them—abominations—so surely you have heard tales?"

"Well," Druadaen said, thinking of the strange patchwork beast he and his companions had encountered in the subterranean library of Imvish'al, "I have heard tales, and I may have seen ancient examples of them"—*which happened to be alive*—"but I did not know that they were a species. Nor did I know your name for them until I shared my story with other travelers."

"They are not a 'species,'" the man in the smaller side chair stated sharply.

The speaker nodded. "It is our understanding that they do not breed naturally and that compared to smaller ones, larger and more capable varieties are less stable."

Less stable?

"They were known to our distant forefathers, and many now still believe them to be mere legend. But it seems they are being reintroduced to our lands, either from the Cloudcap Mountains or the Shun beyond them." He surveyed his fellows. "It is all the more ominous that it was found with this." He held up the Annihilator shard with which Druadaen had set the present meeting in motion. "Tell us: what do you know of the Annihilators?"

"Beyond the name, very little."

"How little?" snapped the perpetually annoyed vizier.

"That those who bore the name destroyed the great kingdoms of these lands and very possibly others beyond. But I am uncertain how much to believe."

"But have you not seen their aftermath all around you?" the thin one asked. "Do you not have ruins in your land?"

Careful, now. "We do," he said, remembering the First Consentium ruins he had seen on Arrdanc. "However, where I am from, they are less plentiful than those which I saw at the eastern edges of the Broken Lands."

"You say you are uncertain of what you have been told about the Annihilators," mused the spokesman. "Who did you ask and what did they tell you?"

There was no need to hide any part of the truth. "I did not broach the topic with chance-met fellow travelers. Rather, I waited until I reached Sarma proper, where I was resolved to find persons of higher station and education to ask about them. However, they did not deign to speak to me, except to command me to make way for their palanquins.

"So I sought out scribes, merchants, junior administrators: people who are accustomed to gathering and assessing information. But without fail, they made warding signs and fled at the mere mention of the Annihilators. Ultimately, I hit upon speaking to older persons without family, particularly those who had fallen on hard times."

"Ah, so you relied upon beggars in their dotage. A singularly reliable source of information, I must say."

Druadaen faced the dismissive vizier with a cool smile. "The primary impediment I encountered was a lack of willingness, Respected Vizier, so that was the first barrier to be overcome. About which: I have observed that age often makes solitary people garrulous for want of company. And those who have little coin feel the lack of it more keenly as infirmity takes a greater toll on their vitality. Only then did I spend the additional time required to determine if literacy had figured in their work and if their wits remained keen. So, if I gained information on the Annihilators, and I helped fill the pockets of a person in need, it was a beneficial exchange for both of us."

The snide fellow adjusted his robes. "And what pearls of wisdom did your softheaded charity buy you?"

Druadaen let his smile become wider. "There were many. That the Annihilators were wanton killers from northern empires, and were ultimately struck down by the gods for their pride. That they were not of this world at all. That they were great wizards who despised and sought to exterminate all rivals to their power. That they were a scourge sent by the gods themselves, after which those deities became mute: a final punishment for the hubris of the peoples of that time. Quite a collection of pearls, is it not?" He turned to the spokesman. "But you began by saying that it was particularly worrisome that this abomination had these shards in its lair. Why? Are they creatures of the Annihilators? Does it portend their return?"

Several of the viziers sat straight at those words. "We have said too much," the arrogant one huffed.

"For once I agree with Vizier Bapalkas," the man in the side chair snapped. "You have *all* said too much. But now that you have, it would be foolish not to aim our inquiries directly at what we wish to ascertain, even if that requires sharing a bit more to get it."

"Such as?" the thin one asked.

"Details of the ambush he recounts. Specifically, the nature of the wyrding the attackers used."

Druadaen nodded. "I will share everything I remember."

"And I will surely die of boredom where I sit."

"Be silent," hissed the man in the side chair. "I am the Vizier of Prince Zetya—!"

"You are an over-padded, arrogant burden to this council...Respected Vizier. Now, Vizier Manakon, will you commence questioning the foreigner, or must I?"

The spokesman regarded the other man down a long, patrician nose. "Do not take airs with *me*, Circline Fasurem. My Prince—and his faction—will hear of such behavior with great displeasure."

"I crave your pardon," Fasurem lied in a monotone.

But Manakon had already turned toward Druadaen, as if the other man had evaporated. "Outlander, tell us every detail you recall of the ambush. Nothing is too small."

Druadaen complied, leaving out the actions of the velene and sword. When he finished a quarter of an hour later, most of the viziers were leaning forward in their chairs. After a long moment of silence, they began jabbering without any regard for order:

"You heard the barbarian's descriptions; that is magic of the old school. Those two were not wyrdwards or hedge-wizards."

"Come now: you truly believe the sorcerers of the northern hills endure? After all this time?"

"Just because they have not moved openly upon the land, do you conclude that they remained in their hiding places until they were slain by old age?"

"No: by each other! That is their way!"

"His tale is nonsense. Every bit of it. Why would masters of the old art have a porter that repeatedly cries out that he is death-vowed? Insipid."

"Well, is it impossible that they were Nightfall cultists?"

"Which you conclude just because one of their number cried out the mantra of their martyrs?"

"You mean, 'their berserkers'—and you are conveniently ignoring that the one who worked an effect wore a purple-tinted robe."

"You are saying a sorcerer wears the robe of a cultist? Absurd. They can't be working together!"

"Unless they are one in the same, or have been united under the banner of this new warlord, Ancrushav. Which I've been speculating for—"

"It cannot all be chance. An abomination, agents of the Nightfall cult, the old arts, and the strange adventuress—all in the same time and place?"

"Perhaps those ruins are where she encountered the abominations first, drew others with her. Perhaps the one killed by the foreigner simply remained—or was left—behind."

"And the group that ambushed the outlander: could they have been searching for her?"

"To what end?"

"Who can say? But her arts and theirs are more similar than different."

"Which signifies what?"

"That she could be a threat, an ally, or a tutor."

"Or that she misled them as completely as she later misled us, here in this very chamber."

It wasn't until the last one mentioned that the "adventuress" had been where he stood now that Druadaen was *certain* that the "she" of whom they were speaking was someone other than Aleasha. He had doubted it from the outset simply because he could not imagine her entering so decadent a place as Sarmasid—or being so convincing a dissembler. But if she wasn't the adventuress, then he needed to know:

"Who is this woman of which you speak?"

CHAPTER SEVENTEEN

The viziers turned to stare at Druadaen as though they'd forgotten he was in the chamber.

Bapalkas lifted his chins. "That is none of your conce—"

"Hold," said Fasurem. "He may have something to tell us about her, too."

"Him? About her? Surely you are—"

"Fasurem is right," Manakon interrupted. "Clearly, the outlander was in the same place she was, shortly after her arrival there."

"What place do you refer to?" Druadaen asked. "The ruins on the hill?"

Manakon studied him carefully. "Outlander, do you know what a haze is?"

"If so, my people must call it by another name." Technically true, and if something involving this adventuress had happened near the Shimmer, then perhaps—

"A haze," Fasurem said quietly, "is a doorway

between different worlds. Do you know of such things?"

"There are legends of them," he answered truthfully. "Most hold them to be nothing more than stories." More truth, still.

"They are real. And you passed very close to one."

"Opposite the watch post," Manakon supplied when Druadaen affected perplexity. "The Sentinels were not there to guard a border; they were there to watch the Haze. And we believe that a person who misrepresented themselves to us here was responsible for the butchery you discovered there."

Druadaen did not have to summon a frown; it formed of its own accord. "Do you mean to imply that—?"

"That the woman in question, and her compatriots, arrived through the Haze. Which we call the Fickle Haze. Some hazes are predictable; that one is not."

"It is not a typical haze at all," added the side-seated man almost testily. "Some are constant, some are periodic, some function only if you know how to properly propitiate whatever being—er, deity—is the master of it. But the Fickle Haze is just that; it obeys no master, follows no pattern."

"And if there truly *is* an otherworldly group abroad in our land—" began Bapalkas.

"Let us not rush to conclusions," interrupted Fasurem.

"Is it 'rushing' to be mindful that this is what it might look like if the Annihilators were returning, O Great Circline?"

Fasurem frowned: perhaps at the title, perhaps at the facetious tone. "There is much we do not know about the priestess who deceived us. Or about this foreigner's account."

"Well, according to your Circline powers, has he lied?"

Fasurem glanced at Druadaen. "Not that I can tell."

Druadaen wondered if that was simply his way of saying "no" or whether he was telling his own partial truth: that he could not determine the truth of what they'd heard because he could not reach the mind of the one who had spoken. And if the latter was true, then the one named Fasurem was not eager to share that information: a fact worth remembering. "You call her a priestess. Did she name her deity?"

"She did not." Manakon stared at him. "You ask after her deity but are unsurprised to learn that our adversary is a woman."

Druadaen shrugged. "I have traveled in places where differences between men and women are small. Or nonexistent."

"Well, we were stunned when she came before us," grumbled the thin vizier. "And with a retinue of men, no less! Not only deferring to, but taking orders from her!"

As the other viziers added their own expressions of outrage and shock, Druadaen paid only enough attention to detect when they might return to matters of import. In the meantime, he needed every second possible to puzzle through how the timing of the woman's arrival compared with his own and its possible implications.

The Sentinels' deaths agreed with his estimate of how long the corpses had lain there: but a few weeks. That, in turn, meant that they could not have been slaughtered by the S'Dyxoi, who had plunged through the Lady's Shimmer almost ten moonphases ago.

That did not entirely eliminate the possibility that the S'Dyxoi, arriving as naked as he, had fled the area at once, returning only after they had gathered knowledge of the world and the means to attack the watch post. But that course of action made even less sense now than when he had first contemplated it. Why would it have taken them twenty weeks to return, and why bother, at that point? It was far more likely that the Shimmer had sent the S'Dyxoi to some other world—or oblivion—and that it was an entirely different group which had slain the Sentinels and appeared at the Vizierate. Whether it had arrived from the Godbarrows or the Shimmer was not of immediate import and was unknowable, besides.

As he finished reconciling the probable timing and cause of the events at the watchhouse, the tone and volume of the viziers' exchanges shifted. The general furor over having accorded equal respect to a woman was winding down and evolving into dismay and anger over how she had manipulated them. Manakon used that to refocus them on the more practical concern of what to do next, in part by gesturing toward Druadaen and asking, "Did you hear anything of such a woman on your travels here? You must have passed through many of the same places but two weeks after she did."

Druadaen shook his head. "If she did, her passage did not attract enough attention to prompt remarks from common folk. Admittedly, as I was traveling alone, I avoided the roads as much as possible. And want of coin led me to avoid towns, since there was nothing there I could afford. But perhaps if you told me what you have heard about her travels, I may realize that what I deemed casual chatter about local events might in fact be related to her actions, even though she herself was not mentioned. Possibly because she was not known to have caused the events."

The viziers agreed and the resulting description of her progress to Sarmasid was not conveyed without some heated contradictions among them. But they had become so accustomed to sharing information with him—or the need to do so—that the relevant chronicle unfolded fairly quickly.

The so-called priestess had represented her group as being travelers from a far country, well beyond where the Cloudcap Mountains bent slightly west: not too far from the region that Druadaen had claimed as his own place of origin. The viziers had little reason to either believe or doubt her; beyond those peaks was the Shun, their knowledge of which was centuries old and largely anecdotal. More recent information came from the imprecise maps sketched by bold trading vessels which had risked sailing to the other side of the landmass of which Lorn Hystzos was merely the northwestern quarter.

However, unlike Druadaen, the woman not only arrived before the vizierate with extensive knowledge of the abominations, but a proposal to undertake a journey to learn more about their recent spread and the appearance of new and dangerous types. They noted that by distinguishing new variants from new species, she had not only demonstrated familiarity with the current resurgence of the monsters, but was well versed in subtle details of their nature. So they accepted her proposal, and provided her with additional equipment, funds, and passage on one of their own ships. And that was the last they had heard from her.

But in the days that followed, they heard a great deal more *about* her—or more specifically, the path of destruction that marked her path from the Fickle Haze. Shortly after the approximate date of the massacre there, she appeared on the outskirts of a town more than halfway to Sarmasid. She and her companions were in possession of two wild supragants that were as notoriously difficult to domesticate as they were rare. They approached an ostler who traded in beasts of burden and exchanged the animals for swift horses and a reasonable balance of coin, leaving without entering the town itself.

Shortly after, though, the supragants became unmanageable and then ferocious, killing one handler and laming another. A later report indicated that while the stablemaster presumed she had kept the beasts tractable with alchemical compounds, farm folk were convinced it was the result of witchcraft or "wyrding." Fasurem had agreed with the farmers, as did several viziers. However, they differed on one point: that this was not mere wyrding, but more akin to the powers attributed to the sorcerers of old.

Further evidence supporting that speculation accrued in the days that followed. The woman had inadvertently marked her route by leaving another pair of supragants behind her, but these had died from exhaustion. Shortly after, several recently missing persons who were involved in the capture and training of such creatures turned up as corpses, victims of extended and inhuman torture.

None of this came to light during her time in

Sarmasid, where she found a way to completely circumvent the many-tiered vetting process that Druadaen had navigated. In an event so serendipitous that the viziers now damned themselves for having doubted it could be anything but a design, she met the son of a powerful Prince in a house of drink and pleasure. Revealing herself to be a priestess of high rank, she so impressed him with her knowledge and bold proposals that, a day later, she was standing where Druadaen was now. She was authoritative in all her responses and questions, particularly regarding abominations.

But in retrospect, many of her clever questions also seemed improbably well informed. Had she been a man, such piercing insight might have aroused suspicions, might have led the viziers to be alert for hidden intents. But they were so outraged (and yet captivated) by her decisiveness, and so unwilling to admit the full measure of their surprise and discomfiture, that she was gone before they realized that their failure to dispassionately question her motivations was not merely unfortunate. Shocking and flustering them had just been one more piece in pursuit of her greater plan—whatever that was.

The crimes she had committed to accrue such profound and pertinent knowledge was not discovered until after she had departed. The thin vizier's frustration was palpable as he explained. "The most significant of those infractions was without logical connection to her," explained the thin vizier, "and seemed nothing more than perverse hooliganism, at the time. Indeed, we did not realize its full significance until she left—"

"You mean, 'until you called upon the Circle,'" snapped Fasurem.

"—at which point," the thin vizier continued without acknowledging the other's correction, "it came to our attention that the premises of the Principate Repository had been violated in the early-morning hours, just two days after she arrived in Sarmasid. It was an odd case, in that while quite a few references were misfiled, none had been stolen. We did not think to involve the Mystic Circle until we learned that the misfiled tomes and scrolls all discoursed upon one common theme: lands *adjoining*, rather than *within*, the region for which she sailed."

"And what have you heard of her since then?"

"The ship has not been seen since it bore north, just beyond Barrasid's lighthouse at Cape Hegralep. Its return to these southern waters is long overdue. Nor has the 'priestess' contacted us as she promised."

Druadaen frowned. "How did she mean to report from so great a distance? And how did she master your language, having arrived so recently?" *Not that I lack my own hypothesis on that point.*

"Communication was effected through her translator."

"Her mouthpiece," the Circline corrected glumly.

Druadaen raised an eyebrow. "What do you mean?"

"She possesses the old art. She is a sorcerer or something like it. She addressed us in an unknown tongue, but the one who conveyed her meaning in Sarmese was not translating. He uttered the words in our language the same instant she spoke them in hers."

"Was he entranced, then?"

"No. That would have been detected beforehand, and they would have been forbidden to enter this chamber. Ensorcelled individuals are more likely to be assassins than spokespersons. Rather, I believe she was in his mind, telling him what to say."

Druadaen managed to transmogrify his sudden foreboding into an expression of wondrous awe. "That must take great power."

"It does. Which is why we felt she and her followers were excellent choices for the task we set her."

"Which was?"

Manakon leaned forward to answer. "The same one we mean to set you. But let us set that aside a moment longer. The coda to this tale is that many places she would have logically passed on her voyage tell of increased attacks by abominations. Almost all our coastal trade stations, from the east shore of the Sea of Hystzos to its furthest northern reaches, have made such reports. Some even insist that the monsters are acting under the direction of one of their own kind."

Druadaen did not have to feign surprise, this time. "Could that be coincidence? It seems to follow behind her with improbable speed, does it not?"

"We were mindful of that. But since then, the agent we sent with her has not been heard from. And shortly after he accompanied her inland, the overseer he was to keep apprised—the one at Agpetkop, our northernmost trade station—fell silent, too." Seeing Druadaen's curious glance, Manakon answered the mystery of why the Vizierate had expected such prompt reporting. "Both our agent and the overseer have—or *had*—means of sending messages that were as swift as those she demonstrated to us."

So either those two factotums were wyrdwards or given appropriate creations of wyrdcraftery. "Do you conclude, then, that this priestess has gone to seek her fortune with the power controlling the abominations, instead of working to unseat it?"

Fasurem sounded more interested than impatient. "You have an alternate hypothesis?"

Druadaen shook his head. "I would tell you if I did." He turned to face the Circline directly. "Also, I must apologize for not knowing your role here, nor knowing the proper honorific for one of your order or creed. May I know what title you prefer?"

"No, you may not. 'Master' is what you shall call me, just as you should call all others above your station. Whatever that might be. And as for my creed"—a mirthless smile played at the corners of his mouth— "the Circle does not concern itself with the rites and matters of chanters and gizzard-readers. We are concerned with actions, not theology, and so, in the truest sense of the word, we are agnostic. We must be, for we represent all temples equally."

Druadaen let the man's arrogant disdain roll off him; his only object had been to learn more about his order. Which was baffling: no nation on Arrdanc had a comparable arrangement between mantics and temples. He turned back to the Vizierate's speaker. "So what is her actual goal, do you think?"

Manakon nodded. "We hope you will discover that for us, that we may prevent it." Seeing the doubtful look on the "outlander's" face, he held up his hand. "Understand: we are not so foolish to believe that her ploys may be stopped by one man"—Druadaen noted that the word he'd used specifically meant a male, was not the equivalent of the gender-neutral "person"—"but we must learn where she is and what she means to do. Additionally, we wish you to complete the mission she took under false pretenses."

"Which is?"

"Bringing back one of the abominations that have been attacking our trading stations."

"Alive," added Fasurem. Seeing Druadaen's pause, he leaned forward. "One of the reasons we are still speaking with you is that you obviously have some familiarity with the various physical and even wyrding arts whereby altering breeds is effected. You will therefore appreciate that a long-dead corpse will be of little use to us. We need pristine and living samples for examination and observation."

"And be cautious," Manakon added. "Although we do not require that you bring one of the large varieties of abomination, even the smallest ones often have unexpected, concealed, or disguised traits that make them difficult to control."

"Traits such as?"

Druadaen was not prepared for the staggering and almost encyclopedic list of known deformities of anatomical features, as well as strange amalgams of them, including some from entirely incompatible species. The latter, Fasurem explained, were, along with greater size, the two features that predicted an abomination to be much less stable.

Druadaen frowned; *there's that phrase again.* "What do you mean by 'less stable'?"

Fasurem stared at him balefully. "I do not mean it as a euphemism. They are all unstable, mentally and physically. As time goes on, abominations lose the ability to govern their behavior, just as various parts of their bodies evince increasing disunity and decay." His smile was feral and unfriendly. "Are you still sure you wish to undertake this task, foreigner?"

"I am, but only because you intend observation of the abomination, not vivisection."

After a moment of surprised silence, various viziers assured him that a live specimen was too valuable to kill and that they'd already had ample opportunity to study corpses. "So," Fasurem repeated when the viziers had finished, "I ask again: are you willing to undertake this task?"

Druadaen let his requirements be his answer. "I shall need a horse and a mule, both accustomed to combat. I also require my choice of equipment, both for the journey and that which I will need to bind and sedate the abomination." *All of which will prove useful if my own search takes me in a different direction before I return.*

Bapalkas sputtered indignance. "You have a horse of your own!"

"Which I have already contracted to sell, once you began assessing my ability to fight. That horse is not suited for this work. I need a steed already trained for war and accustomed to transport aboard ship."

Bapalkas' irritation became perplexity. "Why that?"

"Not all horses adapt to the motion of the sea, Respected Vizier. Some go off their feed and need weeks to recover. Given your urgency, I doubt you wish me to be delayed if my mount sickens. Or in the worst case, be forced to turn back because it dies."

"Turn back? Are you so irresolute?"

Druadaen shrugged. "Proceeding by foot would take much longer and be far less likely to result in success."

The vizier's voice was smug and sadistic. "We are willing to accept that risk."

"Are you? After you have paid a third of my fee in advance?"

Bapalkas had returned to full indignation, now amplified by outrage. "Extortion and insolence! Why, I've half a mind to—!"

"Half a mind is indeed all you have," muttered a new voice. The chamber fell silent. All the viziers turned to look at their oldest member, the one who sat silently at the center of their arc. "The laborer is worth his wages," he resumed. "And the outlander's insistence that we risk treasure to secure his services—and thereby, are doubly interested in the outcome because we have invested in it—shows he is both experienced and not wanting in wits. Two of the most important criteria to seek in one who is charged with so delicate and unusual a task." He looked at Druadaen. "You shall have what you need, that you may bring us what we need."

Despite the layered wrinkles that almost hid his eyes, Druadaen saw them narrow and focus upon him more intently. "But I am perplexed by one thing, Outlander. Your singular accent tells what your words did at the outset: that you are from a very far land indeed. Yet you come before us on a matter of little import to your own interests, and become more focused upon it the more you hear. I wonder: why is that?"

Druadaen had encountered other oligarchs who, oldest among their peers, demonstrated the same shrewd discernment. Long experience and patience allowed them to focus on factors that younger ones missed while busied with the details and political implications of an unfolding debate. In this case, the oldest vizier had detected a disjuncture between Druadaen's aptitudes and intentions. Specifically, the same abilities which made the newly met outlander a promising agent also made it unlikely that he went wherever the winds of opportunity and fate happened to blow him. Rather, people such as he usually tacked across those breezes in pursuit of their own ends. And now, Druadaen—for both practical and ethical reasons—had to answer the oligarch's question without lying.

"Respected and sage vizier, the more I have heard this council speak, the more I realized that my interests may not be so different from your own. Some months ago, friends of mine contended with attackers who were not native to our region. They did not speak our language, and for no apparent reason, killed many of our people and kidnapped one whose wisdom we depend upon. Then they disappeared."

All true; they just don't know it refers to the Hidden Archivist.

"I resolved to follow the intruders. I do not know if the destruction I have seen in the course of my pursuit is their doing, but it is by following their path that I came here. And now, given what I have heard, I must wonder: could they, too, have come through a... a haze?" *And now, a true question, as well:* "Could the intruders you seek and killers that I pursue be one and the same?"

"It is possible," Manakon muttered, glancing at Fasurem. Who shrugged.

"Besides," Druadaen added, "my pursuit has left me alone and destitute. Most of what I now possess was taken from the bodies of those who sought to take what little I still had...including my life. So, yes, I also came before you hoping that it might lead to some manner of assignment. But now, I cannot shake the impression that my quest and your needs are linked by what feels like fate."

The oligarch's flesh-hidden eyes remained fixed on him a moment more. "My success lies in one thing above all others: knowing men. You do not reveal everything about yourself. But no clever man does, particularly when he is but new in a strange land." He glanced at the Circline, who shrugged. "However, what you have said are not lies, and that is good enough for me."

With a single gesture, he waved Druadaen to leave and for the Hazdrabar's lieutenant to go with him. "Get him whatever he needs for his labors and a third of the measure we discussed. Make it silver talents. He should not be burdened by the weight of an equivalent value in lesser metals."

The sky above Sarmasid's main pier was an aerial list where graceful gulls and rakish crows jousted for scraps and dominance. Or so it seemed to Druadaen as he led an unfamiliar charger along the waterfront. He paused to glance down the length of each jetty, hoping for a glimpse of the ship he'd been told to seek. It was a mixed rig—a square mainmast and a fore-and-aft mizzen—which meant it should have been easy to find among the low-hulled xebecs, dhows, and occasional galleys jockeying for berths and room to turn. But with so many sails being furled and unfurled, and winches loading and unloading cargo, he was almost upon the object of his search before spying its pronounced quarterdeck.

As he approached, he heard a cry in heavily accented Sarmese: an accent not unlike his own, in fact. "Are you the landlubber we're waiting to load? Well, come aboard smartly, then! We're to leave with the last tide—unless you want to pay for the extra day's berthing fees." A figure at the base of the mainmast had come to the gunwale to stare down at him.

Druadaen waved his understanding and led the horse up the livestock ramp; it was calm, if a bit stubborn. Better than a high-blooded steed, though—particularly for a sea voyage. He was about to guide the charger aft when the same voice turned him around. "Here, now, let one of the hands earn their pay."

Seen at only a few yards distance, the speaker was early middle age, lanky, a bit weatherworn, and with hair that was streaked black and silver, as if some child had set about it with a narrow paintbrush. "Welcome aboard the *Oath*, stranger. I hear you're headed out to the Sea of Hystzos and up northeast to Agpetkop."

"You have heard a-right," Druadaen answered with a smile. Stepping on deck and getting a bluff mariner's welcome felt . . . well, in many ways, it felt more like home than anything else, now.

The older man ambled closer—a strange gait for such long legs—shaking his head as he came. "Since your passage is paid for by the powers that be"—he cocked his head in the direction of the Princely City—"I'm wondering if you're already familiar with that bit of coast?" His voice was lively but his eyes were grave.

"I'm familiar with its reputation. So I'm not going there lightly."

The fellow nodded, looked up at the hands who were shaking out the top-main's reef. "Aye, aye, that's well said." He grinned slightly. "Just wanted to make sure you aren't as naive as you look."

"Oh, I probably am," Druadaen drawled. "But I always try to make a good first impression."

The mariner's smile widened. "A passenger who'll take the piss out of himself: that's a rarity and right welcome. I'm Lorgan R'Mura." He put out a hand. After Druadaen had introduced himself, the older man started aft, nodding for Druadaen to join him. "So, youngster, what are you about, then?"

Druadaen considered how best to answer . . . and realized that despite all the agreements and seals and signatures that his Sarmese employers had insisted upon, they hadn't sworn him to secrecy. So, with a few omissions for sake of privacy, a few more for brevity, and one or two to ensure his own safety, he shared his tale.

In the process of doing so, he discovered that Lorgan was an excellent listener, that they'd ascended to the quarterdeck, and had been leaning against the taffrail for some time.

After a long silence, Lorgan looked north. "I've seen icebergs. Sailed around them. Funny thing; there's far more below the water than above." He winked. "Like unto you and that tale. No, no, I'm not asking to know more! Just an observation."

Druadaen's awareness caught on his pronunciation of the word for "observation," and he remembered how he and Aleasha had discovered that word. "You're from Tyrmcys, aren't you?"

"I am. They didn't tell you? That's home to the *Oath* and no small number of us aboard her. It's why we're headed toward Agpetkop at all: bound for home the long way, touching our own trade stations as we get close." He paused. "That's after we set you on land again; no stops on the way. By order of the Vizierate." He shrugged. "Cost them a pretty penny. But then again, they've got more 'pennies' than they know what to do with, eh?"

Druadaen answered with a shrug of his own. "It's a job."

Lorgan glanced sideways at him. "Is it? Hmmm. From that tone, you know they've other purposes in mind."

"I do, but I am too ignorant in the ways of these lands to conjecture what those purposes might be."

Lorgan smiled sideways at the unlikely claim to complete ignorance. "Well, we've almost two weeks to touch on that."

"Two weeks? But it's a journey of some—"

"It's long in miles, but short in time. We've the help of two coastal currents, one after the other—and some old friends who'll speed us on our way."

Druadaen wondered what kind of friends those might be, but before he could find a way to ask such a ticklish question. Lorgan was descending the stairs to the weather deck. "For now, let's see to getting your gear stored." Halfway down, he turned and looked appraisingly at the younger man. "You've a cabin to yourself, by the by. Your masters paid for it in—"

"My *employers* paid for it."

"—Or," Lorgan resumed, "you could bunk with us. Two to a cabin that's half the size. Common space and a common cookpot. And I have a sneaking suspicion I could get the captain to return half the difference.

He's been known to carry a passenger or two among the crew." He smiled. "It's up to you."

"I'd be honored...and you can keep the difference in coin. Besides, I've found a common cookpot is usually where the uncommon food is to be found."

Lorgan smiled. "Rather expected you'd say that. I'll talk to the purser, make sure there's no problem splitting the difference with you." He glanced at the way Druadaen was standing. "But the captain; he's an old tightwad. But it might be possible to squeeze a bit more coin out of him if you can stand watch, do the easier bits of a working passage. You ever sailed as crew before?"

Druadaen couldn't keep the grin off his face, remembering the years he'd spent as a Courier. "Yes, you could fairly say that." Lorgan nodded approval, was about to head below but Druadaen stopped him. "I suppose there are two points I ought to square away before anything else. First, where do I stow my kit?"

"That's where I'm taking you now. Second point?"

"I should pay my respects to the captain."

Lorgan laughed. "You just did, you gullible sod! Now, let's get below and get you acquainted with your bunk—and watch the coaming!"

PART THREE
AR NAVIR

JOURNAL Entry Three
South of Uershael, entering the Medvir Bight

I enjoy reading well enough, but I am not much for writing. I remember my Da saying that taking pen in hand was "too much like work." *Like* work? I don't know what the hells he was talking about; it *is* work. And thankless, too.

But blast that Druadaen if he wasn't right to point out that someone needs to record the tale of our travels, if for no other reason than to keep the days from all running into one another the way memories do. So I suppose I'd best repent my jibes about his incessant scribbling, particularly inasmuch as I was one of those who flatly refused to lend him a hand. Because now that I'm the keeper of our story, I see that it helps keep the lot of us from becoming just so many pieces of flotsam and jetsam bouncing around the world and against each other. We are a company only because we have a story. Strange to think that I always presumed it was the other way around.

Another thing I have discovered is that the true labor of the writing is not recording the dangers and deeds but the dull dross of daily life. Because there's been little else since we weighed anchor and left

Shadowmere almost five moonphases ago. At the outset, there wasn't even any interesting scenery. After all, we'd already seen the length of the Earthrift Channel three times, so our passage back to the Great Western Ocean seemed that much longer.

Of course, that's where the real boredom set in. Waves and swells and risers; again and again and again. It's a puzzlement that mariners do not lose their minds from the boredom of it. When a few sea gulls trailed us in hope of scraps it became a bloody event that drew an audience. And not one sea monster—not even a tiny one—had the common decency of troubling our ship. And the sai'niin ring remained as lively as a stone at the bottom of a sinkhole. So I had little to do but observe and learn a little bit more about our newest companions.

Varcaxtan is quite amiable and, for a Dunarran of his age and experience, surprisingly chummy—but never reveals much. Early on, I meant to nudge him toward a more serious chat, but then I saw his eyes when even the banter of the crew set him to thinking on the fate of his lady-wife. So I held my peace, watching and waiting for a moment when there was no possibility any words of mine would quicken that pain. And I'm still waiting.

Lacking his sage advice about this mad journey, I turned to the other member of our company who seems versed in the hidden ways of this old world: the dragon. He certainly has the knowing of many strange things. Unfortunately, what's stranger still are his explanations of them. By whatever soul I might have, I swear that his rhetoric and reasoning is even more brain-breaking than Druadaen's—so much so that the Dunarran now seems to have been a model of clarity. And brevity.

I do wish I conned more of the damn wyrm's recitations about the cosmic madness that are osmotiums—or osmotia, or Shimmers, or whatever the bleeding things are called. I suspect he takes secret pleasure in making the whole sodding mess just that much more confusing by insisting that they are not just different words for the same thing, but they are, in fact, different things. At my wits ends, I've objected that, since they're all gateways into different worlds, what could be more similar? That's the moment when the old serpent rolls his dying avatar's yellowing eyes, blows out a long suffering sigh, and explains the distinctions yet again. And with words even more confounding than the ones with which he began. I tell you true: they say that a dragon is most deadly because of the flame it spews from its mouth, or the eyes that can read your mind, but this one's got a more fatal weapon than either of those. It's his unending gush of highfalutin palaver that can do you in, certain to bore any and all listeners until they're as stiff as stone.

A week ago, a bit of interest finally returned to our lives. Tharêdæath appeared in our quarters with word that our return to Ar Navir would not follow the course we had taken last time. Instead of rounding the south edge of Corrovane, we would slip north of that land and make for the Tashqend Straits. They separate the mainland from the canal-severed Corro Peninsula.

Entering them a day later, we had the grace of fair winds and still seas. Never more than twelve leagues in width yet never less than eight, the Straits are a deepwater passage that ends in a southeast bend which carried us into the oddly named Channel of Glass. That canal—or so it appeared—took us past the Channel Cities—Rhuutun and Asak-Cor. They're said to be hotbeds of strife and intrigue between the proxies and agents of Corrovane and Kar Krathau, so I suppose it was best that we didn't port in either one. Our business with the shore was carried out by cargo lighters and advice skiffs, after which we carried on into the body of water known as Onel's Pool.

There, captains prefer to stay in easy reach of land, but the Iavarain crew steered as if meaning to draw a line across the widest part of that strange, still circle of water which separated Corro from the mainland. Whispers say the tall, ragged ruins we could see on the north coast—Ladsomar—are dangerous, even deadly, to approach. Never have been able to find a body that could tell me why. Or perhaps those with the knowing of it are not at ease with the sharing of it.

We emerged from Onel's Pool heading due south and hugging close by the mainland where we watched the familiar coastlines of Vallishar and Tavnolithar roll past as we made for the southern headland of Uershael.

Or rather, that's how our journey should have unfolded. We were laying over at Tavnolithar's capital—Herres—when Tharêdæath got word that a messenger was waiting at his house. He hadn't intended on debarking; it was a near surety that if he so much as put foot on land, he'd get snared in the affairs of the place. So when we watched him stride down the gangway, we were busy making bets on how long it would be before we'd see him again: a day, a week, a moonphase, or more.

To our surprise (and the ruination of all our bets!) he was back within the hour, but with troublesome news. Just a day earlier, a packet from Rhuutun had put in with word that several Iavu had gone missing there. Tempers were high between the two Channel Cities, which had already been rubbed raw by the threat of a tariff war by Kar Krathau. Not to put too fine a point on it, the region was on edge and the Iavu might have stuck their fine, straight noses where they didn't belong. So Tharêdæath was duty bound to find them, hopefully with their noses still attached. Because his name and influence are known thereabouts, he could count on polite cooperation where others would have had doors shut in their faces. Even so, it was by no means a certainty that he'd be told the truth once behind those doors. From the tone of his voice, I'd say he doubted it.

Without missing a beat, he gave us to understand that it wasn't he who would be leaving the ship, but us. Frankly, none of us expected any different; this hull is fast and strong and her crew are not only accomplished as mariners but also as armsfolk. Just what might be wanted if his business in the Channel Cities become lively. Happily, he'd already arranged new passage for the last leg of our journey: a small merchant brig with which he'd had prior dealings and that mostly plied the seas between Herres and the Ballashan lands south of the Medvir Bight.

He finished by asking Cerven to find several hands who would move our kit to the other ship. As soon as the young fellow was gone, he handed me a letter that Talshane had put in his trust before leaving Shadowmere. Tharêdæath had meant to keep it until we all reached Eslêntecrë, but since we'd get there ahead of him, he felt obliged to put it in our hands now. He advised us not to make hasty judgments based on its contents and bid us farewell.

I waited until his footsteps faded, then cocked my head toward S'ythreni. Her ears shifted a bit before she nodded; since she couldn't hear him, he was well and gone. Keeping my voice low, I pointed out that since our new ship might have fewer—or no—places where we might read the letter in private, we'd best do so now.

The only answer was S'ythreni's testy retort that I should have already been reading the letter aloud.

Talshane began with courtesies celebrating our second meeting and gratitudes for our willingness to take Cerven along with us. The lot of us exchanged stares after those words came out of my mouth. "Perhaps," I wondered aloud, "Talshane didn't notice that we weren't turning happy handsprings over becoming the warders of his wayward pup of an adjutant."

"More like he didn't *want* to notice," S'ythreni groused.

Varcaxtan's brow rose slightly; none of us could meet his "patient uncle" gaze. Talshane had never been aught but a friend to us, and the lad, while callow, had proven a fine shipmate, hard worker, and capable in every task to which he'd put a hand. I raised the letter to my eyes—if only to avoid Varcaxtan's.

Alas, but Talshane's next line was not only just as dubious, but even more audacious: "In the person of Cerven, you have the best assistance I can render for your journey in search of Druadaen."

I looked up again. The faces around me reflected

the doubt that was surely on my own. "I can't wit how this lad might help us," was the most charitable comment I could offer. I also suspect they, too, were thinking what I'd not added: "Unless the lad has been in few scrapes of his own, he's more likely to be a millstone 'round our necks."

I continued reading. "Cerven has been trained by powers that are among the Consentium's oldest and truest friends on Far Amitryea. He is their trusted intermediary to the Outrider Expeditionary Cohort, the Lady of the Mirror, as well as several concealed communities which share ancient roots with Dunarra itself."

All eyes turned toward Varcaxtan. I tapped the line on the sheet I was holding. "Now what do you suppose he meant by *that*?"

"I can't be sure."

S'ythreni leaned forward, a bit testy. "Then how about a guess?"

When his only answer was a smile and a shrug, I glanced at the old wyrm. "How about you, then? You were around in ancient times."

"Yes, and in the course of those long years, I have become wise enough not to speculate upon or reveal other beings' business. You might take a page from that book."

"And so I might, if this was a casual matter. But as it so happens, knowing as much as we can about this lad, and those who reared him, could bear upon our survival as well as his."

But it was Elweyr who piped up loud at my elbow. "I think I've heard of those concealed communities."

"*You?* How?"

His look of halfhearted disdain suggested I wasn't worth a full measure of it. "Tell me, Ahearn: how much do you really know about me?"

"More than enough, after all these years!" But even as I said it, I knew that was more codswallop than cleverness. Elweyr was not given to idle chatter and I—well, being orphaned at a young age, I presumed that since his parents still lived, he'd grown up happy, or at least safe. But now, something in his eyes told me otherwise.

"I suspect Talshane is referring to the Old Amitryeans," Elweyr murmured.

"A dead race, by all accounts."

Elweyr's smile was more mockery than humor. "'By all accounts'? If that phrase was worth the air it takes to say, Druadaen wouldn't have any reason to go seeking 'the truth of the world,' would he?"

I cast about for a retort—not because I disagreed with the damned mantic, but because I hate giving up without a fight. All I could muster was, "So how is it that these Old Amitryeans are related to Dunarrans?"

Elweyr glanced at Varcaxtan, who showed no willingness to join the discussion. "As Talshane said, they share ancestors. Or so it is said."

The dragon stirred, but settled back immediately.

"Nothing to add, wyrm?"

"No, merely an aside."

"Which is?"

"Which is, if you keep addressing me as 'worm,' what's left of you shall be referred to as 'worm-meat.'"

I laughed, looking at his ghoulish avatar. "I think you'll need to return to your actual body to make good on that threat."

"I am nothing if not patient. After all, I have endured your 'witticisms' for weeks on end, now. But enough of this talk of ancient times and peoples; what else did Talshane reveal about the youth?"

I read out the rest of the letter. Shortly before we arrived in Shadowmere, Cerven had been in the nearby city of Moonfleet, finishing an apprenticeship. He'd also been tending to his mysterious mentors' interests, which was noticed by their equally mysterious enemies. There was no account of what had attracted their ire, or what nastiness might have followed, but those charged with his safety bundled him over the Passwater to Talshane's little fort. There, and possibly in the Lady's Tower, able hands were able to finish Cerven's tutelage. Talshane closed by assuring us that his skills and learning would no doubt "be quite useful to you."

When it dawned on the others that my silence marked the end of the letter, Umkhira shook her head and let fly an exasperated cry that got the rest of them nodding: "Well, can Cerven help us find Druadaen or not?"

We never got the chance to suss that out. A rumble of feet coming down the companionway heralded the return of Cerven and the moving crew—each of whom looked younger than me but were probably older and more capable than any of us. Except the bloody damned dragon, of course.

An hour later, we were on the new ship. There, life did what it seems to do best: toss out one bothersome bit of business after another. It's ever thus settling in on a new hull: learning your way around her decks, meeting the captain and crew, repacking stores, and making oneself useful however one might.

And now, here we are, crossing the wide mouth of the Medvír Bight. Once we're in sight of its southern coast, we'll follow it east to Eslêntecrë. So if we mean to learn why Talshane is so impressed with Cerven's skills, we'd best do it before we have need of them. Which could be very soon. There's heavy weather coming down on us from the northwest: a coast-following storm from Pelfarras Bay. Like as not, by dinner it will be all hands busy manning the pumps, hauling the lines, and keeping down dinner. Which means we might have just enough time to sit the lad down and find out what's what.

CHAPTER EIGHTEEN

If Cerven found the slow, noiseless approach of Ahearn and the others ominous, he gave no sign of it. As they came down the companionway, he set aside the foresail sheet he was unknotting and stood to face them respectfully. "Yes, gentles?"

Ahearn managed not to roll his eyes. *Back to calling us "gentles," now? Creeds, that's like addressing a sow as "your Ladyship."* "It's time we had a chat, young Cerven."

"Ah! About how I may be of service as we travel together?"

Ahearn exchanged looks with the others, tried to smile. "Well, if you can always read minds so easily, that would certainly be a help." Ahearn found he was half hoping it to be true. "But yes, Master Cerven, that's what we mean to establish. Talshane wrote a letter that came into our hands just before we sailed from Herres. It sings your praises, but the lyrics are, well, a bit vague."

Cerven nodded with a hint of hesitation. "So this

is in the nature of a formal inquiry regarding my capabilities and background."

Ahearn managed not to shrug. There might actually be some benefit to hearing the stripling make an official report of himself. And by making it at Ahearn's behest certainly reinforced who was in charge of the group. "You may consider it so, Master Cerven."

The young man stood very straight. "Very well. Firstly, Sir Ahearn"—but he was unable to continue because of the general outburst of laughter...at which Cerven's eyebrows rose.

Ahearn's were descending as S'ythreni waved a hand at the young man. "Once you've wandered about with us," she gasped through fading paroxysms, "you'll understand how impossibly funny it is to picture Ahearn as a...a *noble*!" She fell back into speech-defeating chortles.

"I apologize for the churlish interruption," Ahearn said with a warning frown at his companions. "Pray continue, Master Cerven."

"If I may, Si—er, Ahearn—it might help to hear Station Chief Talshane's letter, assuming it does not touch upon confidential matters."

By way of answer, Ahearn read it out.

Cerven nodded when he reached the end. "I shall endeavor to clarify the most oblique statements first. The allies of whom Captain Talshane speaks educated me in the history, languages, and, er, conditions of several ancient groups that are largely presumed to have wholly diffused into contemporary populations. This is not the case, but most of them live incognito in various amenable nations or establish communities in remote locales."

Before Ahearn could stop himself, he blurted out, "Fish teats, he speaks just like a Dunarran!" Then, with an abashed and apologetic glance at Varcaxtan: "Well, at least like *some* Dunarrans."

Cerven watched the exchange with faint anxiety. "Is my speech a matter of concern?"

Ahearn almost stuttered as he sought a suitable reply. "Well, let's just say it's a mixed blessing."

Elweyr leaned toward the youth. "He means no offense."

"I took none, Magister Elweyr."

The mantic closed his eyes in supreme patience. "Just Elweyr, if you please. What skills do you have beyond that of being a scholar of the history and languages of hidden peoples?"

"Well, I have similar knowledge pertaining to cultures that have truly vanished from the surface of Arrdanc."

The dragon sighed. "I believe they wish to know about your less esoteric abilities."

"Ah!" And Cerven rattled off an impressive list of skills he had acquired from his mentors and then honed while an apprentice in the wider world.

When he was done, Varcaxtan leaned back. "If I didn't know better, I'd say that your, er, mentors, were training you to be a Courier for the Archive Recondite. Just like Druadaen."

The young man nodded. "Captain Talshane said something quite similar. Which reminds me; I must reemphasize that while I have been taught how to fight from horseback, I have not been trained in the charge."

"At least you know the difference," murmured Varcaxtan.

Ahearn avoided S'ythreni's amused glance. One time

on Aswyth Plain, he'd made it embarrassingly clear that he *hadn't* known the difference. "Well, then, Cerven, welcome to the company. Officially, I suppose. You've all the kit you need for all your talents?"

"I do . . . more or less."

Hmmm . . . "I'm not a man who rests easy with a hanging tone like that one."

"Apologies. My saddle and tack remained behind in Moonfleet, as did my bow. My departure did not include any gear or preparations that might have alerted enemies to my intent."

"Well," Ahearn said agreeably, "I'm sure we can see to correcting those lacks. And perhaps Elweyr can take time to acquaint you with the scribblings of mantics, teach you how to comb through the various sources he's not had time to fully decipher. He's always complaining that—"

"He already knows," Elweyr said in a low voice, studying Cerven narrowly. "At least some of the scripts. Don't you?"

The young man had turned slightly pale. He nodded hesitantly. "I would not call myself accomplished in the deciphering of such writings, but—"

Umkhira had straightened. "Hold: does this mean the man-boy is a mantic, himself?"

Cerven shook his head vigorously, but could not answer before Elweyr said, "No. But it's unusual. Hardly anyone but mantics learn the scripts."

"How did you suss he had the knowing of them?" asked Ahearn.

"He didn't goggle like a fool when he learned I was a mantic. And he's inquired after my books during the journey. Several times."

The dragon cleared its avatar's now perpetually phlegmy throat. "Familiarity with those scripts was not always as uncommon as it is now. What you call mancery was once but a single part of a larger array of disciplines which had knowledge as its first object, not power."

"Knowledge?" Umkhira repeated. "What manner of knowledge?"

"Cosmology. Ontology. The synergies between them."

"So, more or less what Druadaen went in search of: the truth of the world."

The dragon answered Ahearn with a wintry smile. "In a manner of speaking." It lifted its chin. "The weather has turned. Sharply."

Ahearn glanced out a porthole. The sky had darkened, and what had been port quarter breeze had spun about into a headwind out of the east that painted frothy ruffles atop the risers of the following seas. "We'd best leave off until there are fewer clouds on the horizon. And when our bowsprit isn't pointing straight at 'em. Let's check on our crates. Wouldn't do for them to be poorly fit to the dunnage. Then we'll go above."

"On deck?" Umkhira said hoarsely. "Even as a storm is coming?"

"It's where we're likely to be needed," Ahearn replied. "Come on; the weather won't wait on us, y'know."

"You're sure we're only a few leagues from the coast?" Ahearn shouted over the rain hammering down on the ship's small poop deck.

"I will be once your boy comes back with those charts!" the captain replied with a hint of reproach.

Why, you—! "If you had enough crew, you wouldn't have needed me to send him—"

A hand came to rest on his shoulder. Varcaxtan used the swordsman's surprised silence to lean over it and into the captain's thin, leathery face. "I'm sure he'll be along soon enou—why, here he is, now!" Although the Dunarran's mouth was alongside his ear, Ahearn could barely hear the last words over the sudden squall that howled down the length of the ship, drenching it from bow to stern and pushing it slightly to starboard.

"Mind the rudder!" the captain yelled at his pilot. "Half a point to port!"

Cerven made his way quickly but carefully up the stairs. He'd rarely been on a ship before they'd sailed from Shadowmere, but had readily adapted to the rhythms and routines of life a-sea. "I have the charts, Captain," he articulated sharply, the crisp sounds cutting through the drumming sheets of rain better than shouting would have. "I took the liberty of finding an oilskin in which to—"

"Give them here, boy," growled the captain. And it really did sound like a growl. Swaying side to side with the deck, he unfolded the oilskin and then the map, scanning quickly. He looked up, studying the seas over the starboard bow. "Can't see it anymore, but I caught sight of a headland there before the clouds opened up. I'd bet my life on it."

Sure'n you're betting everyone's *life on it*. But Ahearn only said, "And how far to safe harbor?"

"Can't say, but that headland means it's the stretch of coast we want. Now, leave me to getting us there... unless there be one amongst you who'd do a better job?"

He'd ended on a sarcastic tone and an annoyed glare that raked across the faces of the gathered company. But Ahearn held his peace, careful not to allow his expression to betray his true reaction: that by all accounts, Varcaxtan was at least as skilled a mariner as he.

Indeed, as the weather had worsened, so had the company's opinion of the ship and crew. It had been mostly clear sailing from Herres, down the coast of Uershael and across the wide mouth of the Medvir Bight that curved its way into the very center of the mainland.

But that crossing had taken them out of the sight of land for two days, and when the skies darkened, and then the rain arrived, Ahearn and the others saw worry edge into the deck crew and the sailhands' tense faces. Now, with the wind rising sharply, their eyes were widening into barely suppressed panic.

Ahearn started at a sudden overhead wailing; contending gusts were tearing into each other. "Banshees in the rigging," he muttered, glancing up at the distended mainsail. It was strained taut against its tyes, all along the yard. "Damn, but that canvas might not hold."

Varcaxtan sighed. "Not as though we have much choice but to crowd sail. If we don't make port at F'Shëssa, or at least run safe aground, this weather is like to tear us apart."

Umkhira, who had either been distracted by the fearsome weather or repeated attempts to hold down her supper, looked up with widened eyes of her own. "Is this ship so weak?"

Varcaxtan's smile was avuncular. "Peace now, Lightstrider. It's a matter of the weather more than the ship."

"How so?" asked Elweyr.

Varcaxtan jerked his head toward the stern. "We have strong following seas: always do, when you're eastward bound along the southern edge of Medvir Bight. But now the storm has turned and we're moving into a westerly headwind that's growing stronger by the minute."

Ahearn nodded, remembering what his one and only love had told him not long before she'd died. "Aye. I'm told the fishermen in these parts call that the 'spinwind.' You can't keep way because you're always being jostled from both fore and aft. Or from port and starboard, if you're set athwart both the current from the stern and the breeze over the bow." He *tsk*ed his tongue against the back of his teeth. "Wish we were a smaller hull."

"Why?" gulped Umkhira.

Varcaxtan answered as he wiped the rain out of his face. "Small boats, like those used by fishermen, are rigged fore-n-aft. Tacking is easier for them. So's dropping your canvas or smartly hoisting it aloft." He glanced at the wind-quivering mainmast just forward of the waist. "But on this bigger ship, we've no choice but to hope all that square-rigged canvas will last long enough to push us to safety."

"You make it sound as though we're in a race for our lives," S'ythreni muttered.

Varcaxtan shrugged. "Well, we just might be. Particularly if—"

Exasperated shouting from back at the wheel rose over the growing cacophony of contrary and combative gusts. Ahearn ascended the stairs to better hear the increasingly heated debate between the captain and the pilot.

Unfortunately, as the two saw the approaching "special passengers," they shifted into a language Ahearn did not understand. All he could tell is that they were pointing to slightly different headings to the south, which, with the onset of evening and the stars, had become as black as night. When they'd concluded, the captain smiled in their direction; it was more a satisfied smirk at having frustrated their attempts at eavesdropping.

"Well, that's more'n a mite aggravatin'," Ahearn muttered.

"It is," Varcaxtan agreed. "Frankly, I think the captain is just hoping that the pilot is right about our position."

"Wait: you understand that gabble?"

Varcaxtan nodded. "It's Davyaran."

Ahearn frowned. "As in Davyara-Nadia? At the other end of the Bight, yeh?"

"The same."

"Well, then you'd think he'd know his own seas, wouldn't you?"

"You might," S'ythreni muttered, just loud enough to be heard over the shrill creaks of the wet rigging. "But his people haven't sailed close to our coast for decades." Seeing Ahearn's perplexity, she added, "A kinslaying. It left bad blood between us."

Elweyr shouted, possibly to be heard over the wind, possibly out of impatience. "But what were they *saying*, damn it?"

The ship pitched heavily to port; beneath their feet, a groan ran the length of the keel. Varcaxtan waited for the hull to right itself. "The captain hasn't full knowledge of this stretch of coast. Like most of the crew, he's from up near the Channel Cities. The pilot is Davyaran. Sounds like he claimed he was familiar with these waters."

"You don't think he is?"

Varcaxtan shook his head. "Possibly less than the captain."

"Why?"

"Because I've sailed these waters a few times." When Umkhira stared at him, Varcaxtan shrugged. "Thirty years as an Outrider and you see a lot of Ar Navir. At any rate, the pilot never refers to specific landmarks. He just talks about 'the coast down here.'"

"Even so," Umkhira pronounced, crossing her considerable arms, "the captain is just as much at fault for not knowing his crew better."

"Neither of which will matter if we're dead," S'ythreni snapped, rolling with a swell that almost tumbled Umkhira against, and almost over, the gunwale.

Ahearn steadied himself. "Now, it hasn't come to that—"

"Yet!"

Ahearn cut a sharp glance at S'ythreni. "But just in case, let's be prepared for"—he was suddenly and intensely aware that Cerven was hanging on his every word—"for any outcome. High Ears, you stand by the conn—"

"And keep my eyes out for the coast. About time." She was off.

"Umkhira, get below, hook the marked ballast to our crates, and for the sake of any god you care to name, get rid of your greaves and vantbrasses." When she opened her mouth to protest, he shook his head.

"Doesn't matter that they're leather. Right now, you're more likely to be swimming than fighting. Now, go!"

She nodded, turned to descend the stairs ... which left her looking along the weather deck and over the bow. Even in the dim light, Ahearn saw her blanch as she faced the mounting risers. But after swallowing mightily, she kept moving.

Ahearn turned to Elweyr. "No arguments, now. You find the safest place up here on the poop and stay put until we see how these bones roll."

"Uh ... why?"

"Because this is the safest place to jump off the boat. If you're in its wake, it can't very well wind up on top of you. Dragon—well, where the devils is that cranky old wyrm?"

"I'm right here. And if you call me a wyrm again, I shall surely eat you."

Startled by the proximity of the voice, Ahearn scanned for the dragon's avatar ... and discovered her, curled into the quarterdeck's portside privy partition, half descended into the head itself. "Gods, Dragon, why are you there?"

"Because I fit, O paragon of human insight. If the ship founders, I shall surely reach the water close to its stern." Despite the prickly reply, its voice was thin and ragged.

Ahearn stared, stepped toward it. "Dragon, are you—?"

"Desist, idiot! I am quite well and have no need of your solicitous mewling! But, this body is—well, it will not function much longer, nor does it retain enough strength to survive a long swim or be useful on deck. This spot, if cramped, is not only secure but requires little strength to hold fast while the ship pitches about. Now, go tend your other charges."

Ahearn turned, looked at Varcaxtan, who'd overheard. Without a word, each knew what was to be done, and that they'd both agreed to it. Varcaxtan would stay close to the irascible creature and see to its avatar's survival—about which the dragon itself seemed singularly cavalier. Yes, that would simply cause it to reawaken in its own body, but that posed problems of its own—none which Ahearn had the time to consider.

He turned to see who might need his help—and found just such a person standing next to him: Cerven. *Ah, crabs in a codpiece, just what I feared: relegated to a nursemaid.* Careful to keep his impatience out of his voice, he began, "Now, Cerven—"

He stopped when the young fellow held out an object it took him a moment to identify: an inflated cow's bladder. "Wha—what's this?"

"For the, er, invalid. It—er, *she* may have need of this to stay afloat. She looks quite poorly."

Ahearn took it from him, managed not to shake his head as he handed it off to Varcaxtan. "This is—blast, just *where* did you get this?"

"Brought it with me, Si—um, Ahearn. Told it was prudent."

"Well...well, yes, it seems to be." *Too damn like Druadaen; all that fool planning...and then, worst of all, it turns out to be useful!* "And are you ready for—?"

"You've no need to worry about me. I've not been in high seas, but I swam often enough in the river Sunderflow and have no fear of the water."

Whether that was all true or not, Cerven said it with such surety and aplomb that Ahearn had neither the inclination nor time to contest it. "Very well, then stay here with the others."

Before he could resume scanning for a place where his strength or knowledge might be put to best use, he heard another dispute arising back at the conn. This time, S'ythreni's voice was in the mix: "So you actually know where you're going?"

Oh, fer the love of— Ahearn swayed along with the deck as he made his way back to the group clustered about the wheel.

But before he could speak, the pilot was shouting an answer over a new set of howling gusts. "Of course I do!" His accent was as thick as his theatrical umbrage at the question.

"What's this about?" Ahearn asked, fairly sure he already knew.

"This . . . lady," began the captain, "does not believe we know our jobs!"

S'ythreni shook her head. "I did not say that. I am questioning whether you know these waters. And you have yet to tell me," she added, turning to the pilot, staring over the white-knuckled hands with which he was gripping the wheel, "what you should be looking for on the coast."

"We looking for the lighthouse at F'Shëssa."

"Of course, but specifically, what will guide you to it?"

The pilot was either confused or panicked. "Well, er, a light, of course." At which the captain rolled his eyes before he could stop himself.

S'ythreni leaned in. "We know that; I mean, in the

absence of the light. What features are you watching for to steer you toward it? What about the foam of the reefs on the way? How best to approach?"

The man's face grew as pale as his hands. "Can't see in this dark and rain."

"But if you could—?"

Ahearn drew her away, back toward Varcaxtan. "You've trapped the rat in its corner, High Ears. Nothing more to be done."

"And you are satisfied being in his hands?" she asked of both of them.

Varcaxtan smiled sadly. "We're in the hands of whatever gods care to hold us, because this much is certain:"—he nodded toward the pilot—"we were never in *his*."

S'ythreni stared at them, then angrily began removing her boots.

Ahearn shouted at her. "Have ye gone daft, now?"

"No, I'm being sensible."

"How's that?"

"Because it's better not to be wearing boots if you have to swim."

Ahearn swallowed, saw Elweyr wince at her words and then turn his attention to his own footwear. *Might not be a bad idea, that . . .*

"A light!" the pilot shouted. "Up ahead!"

All of them followed his eyes over the bow: nothing but darkness.

"Where?" Elweyr shouted back.

"There . . . wait for us to climb the riser so that we—there! There!"

"I see it!" shouted the captain. "Make for it! Bo'sun, let out the canvas! All speed!"

S'ythreni's urgent and very shrill question—"The light: is it steady or flickering?"—was lost in the babble of voices issuing orders and cursing the sea. Ahearn wondered at her odd question, but kept his focus on remaining watchful and ready to either help the ship or save themselves.

As the captain finished screaming his orders, the wind answered by rising into a sustained, rageful howl. The square-rigged mainsail snapped taut with an explosive crack. Before anyone could so much as loosen a sheet, a corner of the canvas tore free of the yard with a fateful pop.

With a sound like an immense leather hide being ripped in two, the sail surrendered to the gale all at once. Its lower half slapped downward like a pale, sodden palm. It caught the sailmaster full on, launching him over the gunwale into the darkness and lashing rain.

The ship lost way, flung about by the wind and angry risers as the captain fought to keep the pilot's rudder work matched to the mizzen's handlers as they fought with the yard. If the ship was to reach safety, they had to both keep the only remaining sail set to the wind and the prow pointed toward the intermittent light.

A set of loud thumps arose from the companionway. Ahearn partly ran, partly skittered across the quarterdeck to investigate and saw Umkhira's hands scrabbling at the coaming, trying to mount the slippery steps. He moved toward the stairs, ready to lend her a hand.

Cursing, she finally came level with the deck—just as the risers shoved hard against the stern and gusts pivoted sharply. The yard handlers struggled to keep the wind in the sail, but as they did, the poop rose so high that the rudder lost purchase with the sea. The ship spun like a wild spindle and struck a submerged rock—hard.

The world did not just tilt; it became complete nonsense. For a moment, Ahearn couldn't tell which way he was facing or even if he was still standing with his head pointed upward—

Then he was in the air. But only for a moment: he slammed down on the deck, bounced off it, started falling back—except the deck jerked up and hit him again. The air went out of him in a hooting rush and pain shot hot along a rib, but the pitching of the deck began to slow. He followed that motion and managed to roll up to his feet, more surprised than pleased.

Along the length of the weather deck, soaked silhouettes were struggling to stand but fewer than had been there before. Umkhira crawled back up out of the companionway, her head now half-black with dim-lit blood. Ahearn staggered down the poop deck's stairs and hauled her upright—just as her eyes lost focus. Her head lolled and she vomited, half of the acrid mess hitting him, half spiraling off into the swirling rain.

Ahearn got an arm around her and, lodging that hand in her armpit, half-helped, half-dragged her back up to the poop. The captain was now berating rather than arguing with the pilot. For one terrified moment, Ahearn thought Elweyr had disappeared—but then saw that he had followed the dragon's example and was crouching in the starboard head.

"I don't understand," the pilot was saying as Ahearn propped up Umkhira so she could hold herself to the

side of the head's partition. "The light at F'Shëssa—
that's a clear run to the port. No rocks! I can't—"

"That's because it's *not* the light at F'Shëssa,"
S'ythreni almost spat from where she was clinging
to the rail.

"But I—!"

"You know nothing. That's a Yylm trick. To wreck
ships trying to reach Mirroskye."

"Yylm?" echoed the puzzled captain, his voice
strangely loud in the sudden calm. "What's that?"

From the opposite rail, Varcaxtan's voice was quiet
but sharp. "There's no time for talk."

S'ythreni was too angry to have heard. "The Yylmyr
are fallen Iavarain. Did Tharêdæath not tell you?"

"You mean, did he tell me the lands around you
deathless tree spirits are filled with your own ghosts?
Aye, he may've mentioned it."

Ahearn was stunned at the disdain in the captain's
voice. "And you paid no mind to his words?"

From behind, Varcaxtan's voice was as grim as
Ahearn had ever heard. "Wind also comes in waves;
they're just longer. Be ready for—"

But the captain was heedless, too busy flinging his
embarrassed resentment into Ahearn's face. "I paid as
much mind to your patron—or is it patroness?—as I
would to anyone who walks on to my ship, claiming
to be a legend."

S'ythreni gaped, objected. "But it *was* Tharêdæath.
He's Uulamantre. He's *different*."

The captain retorted through a sneer. "He was
different in only one way that mattered, lady sprite:
he paid top fees in silver ingots."

Sudden as lightning, the wild gusts returned. One

moment, they were scudding along through rough but almost manageable seas: the next, they were blinded by a mix of rain and wind-risen spray. The ship heeled to leeward, the sail filling and luffing as if possessed by spirits locked in a tug-of-war. And close alongside, a brace of slick rocks pushed through the Bight's eager, watery gums before receding from sight once again.

"Witch quim!" the pilot swore, cheating the ship in the other direction. "The gods saved us that time!"

"What saved you," S'ythreni told him, "is that the river pushing out against us swung the bow a point southward. That's why we missed the outer reefs."

The captain stepped hastily between them. "Can you talk us to safety, then? You know these waters so well?"

S'ythreni's chin came up. "Better than you, it seems."

"Not what I asked. So if you can steer us in, take the wheel. If not, take a seat."

"Come, S'ythreni," Ahearn muttered, putting a light hand on her arm. "We haven't time for this." When she turned on him, he glanced at the dragon's avatar and then Umkhira. She blinked, then nodded and went back to the rail, tying her boots to her belt as Ahearn removed his own.

For the next several minutes, they dodged the rocks—for the most part. The bumps and scrapes were modest, but between those and the first, heavy impact, the ship was taking on water. Worse yet, each dodge required a last-second haul at the wheel that took them farther and farther south—and no closer to shore.

"How long until you get around the reefs?" Elweyr shouted from the open-air head.

The captain glanced at the pilot who pointedly did not meet his eyes. "As long as it takes," he yelled back, holding on to the binnacle for dear life as the wind shoved them away from the shoals even as the waves tried pushing them directly onto its fangs.

When the wind shifted so that it was directly over the beam, Varcaxtan stood straight, watching the captain carefully. Ahearn was about to ask what he meant to do when the Dunarran spoke, his voice very loud although he did not shout. "Angle this ship in closer. Now."

The captain swallowed. "But the reef will tear it open like shark's teeth, gut it beyond saving!"

"Y'fool: this ship is already dead! But the wind's come 'round, enough that you needn't fight it—for now. So drive her in as far as you can. That, or the outer rocks will cut us to chum before you can find us a way between them and over the bar."

A rough shattering of wood seemed to cackle in response to Varcaxtan's exhortation: the hull had been torn by more submerged stones. Two planks caught the weak light as they flew up from the port side and then disappeared into the black of the storm.

"We're in the shoals!" the pilot screamed.

"I know that!" howled the captain. "Hard a'port!"

Varcaxtan's eyes widened at the brash maneuver, even as S'ythreni's head jerked back in alarm. "No! The rocks—!"

But the pilot, eyes distended in a double terror of steering blind in a storm and ignorant of the waters before him, had obeyed the captain too abruptly. The ship heeled over to the left—and straight into the tail-end of the reef.

Ahearn saw the black, glistening stones rise into the trough of a receding swell like suddenly drawn obsidian knives. He reacted before he could think. Racing across the poop toward Umkhira, he yelled "Jump!"

He caught up the startled Lightstrider in one arm and, holding her as tightly as he could, flung himself over the taffrail at an angle. He saw the dark, angry seas off the starboard quarter reaching up for him—

Just before the storm-dimmed dusk gave way to utter blackness.

CHAPTER NINETEEN

Coughing, Ahearn spat out seawater, waited for the dizziness to fade enough that he could orient himself. He was just a bit beyond a clutter of foam-flecked rocks. The current seemed to be drawing him away from them, but a moment later, it reversed and threatened to push him amongst them. *Odd, unless...*

He turned, saw the silhouette of the coast behind him. *So, not a shifting current, but undertow.* He shook his head in an attempt to clear it—he'd hit the water hard—gathered a breath for the long swim, and—

Bollocks! Umkhira!

He shouted her name, treading water, scanning in all directions. He couldn't remember what had happened after landing among the swells with a *smack!* Like a stunning blow, he didn't have a memory of the impact or losing his hold on his ur zhog friend. And with night coming on and the storm still driving rain into his face, he couldn't see well or far, and she might not have long to—

"Here." It was Umkhira's voice, but groggy.

He swam in the direction of the sound. Two strokes and his mind sharpened a bit—enough for him to realize that the noise of the surf among the rocks was tricking his ears. But he had to do something, even if that meant swimming in circles. Except now, damn it all, he'd injured his hand. Or maybe it was just one finger that was throbbing—?

No, not throbbing: pulsing.

It was the ring, sending an urgent surge halfway up his arm whenever he faced the shore to the right. He started swimming in that direction, arms digging deep into the swells.

Umkhira wasn't far off, but being almost inert in the water, little of her broke the surface to mark her location. He closed the distance rapidly, felt clear thought returning as he reached her. She was still moving sluggishly—the blood from her head wound was flowing again—but she wasn't so much swimming as pawing the water. Not uncommon among the urzh, most of whom had an aversion to water, but in her case—"I thought you told me you knew how to swim!"

"May have," she murmured. She sounded both dazed and evasive.

"Ah. I see. Too proud to admit otherwise to a thinskin?"

"I do . . . do swim," she insisted crossly, evincing no ability to coordinate the motion of her legs and arms.

"Ah, sure you do, my brave green lass, sure you do. Come now, I'll just give you a hand—" But as Ahearn slipped an arm around her waist, he discovered another problem: "Gods and sods, woman; do you have coin in all your pockets? Ye're heavy as a millstone."

"Tha's me." She retched but nothing came up. "Not easy swimming."

Which made a kind of sense Ahearn had never considered before: urzh had heavier frames, but they did not tend toward fat. So like as not they didn't float, even with their lungs full of air. "Well, I see why you're not fond of boat rides. C'mon; lend a hand. And a leg. With me, now. Follow what I do. That's right. Better."

And she *was* doing better, he admitted, but at this rate, they'd be lucky to make the shore by dawn.

Or possibly, next week.

Happily, as Umkhira's head began to clear, her ability to swim improved, although at first he couldn't figure out why she moved like a frog; her kicks scissored the water and she swept with her arms right at the surface or just beneath it.

"We learn to swim underwater," she explained as they neared the shore: a patchwork of faint illumination wherever the two moons found gaps in the clouds. "Easy for us to stay there. Good for hiding," she added between strokes. "You humans are very messy swimmers."

"Aye," Ahearn muttered, "must annoy you no end, being saved by one."

She was silent. "I repent my remark. It was unkind. And petty. Because although you *do* splash a great deal, you swim faster and further."

Ahearn was so surprised that he got a mouthful of water. "Well, now...I'm not sure I've ever heard you apologize before."

"That is because I have not done anything which warrants an apology."

Which, Ahearn had to admit, was the simple truth.

It was also true that despite her extraordinary endurance on foot, her awkward efforts at keeping her
head above water taxed what little strength she had
left. Once they crested through the rippling froth of
the bar, he saw another row of black rocks, arrayed
before them like a line of broken crocodile teeth. He
scanned them, located the largest, and made for it.

As he hoped, once in the lee of that half-submerged
boulder, they were able to rest a moment. The undertow
was not strong enough to sweep them around its sides,
so all they had to do was keep their backs against it.
In the intervals when the water had ebbed out past
them, it didn't quite reach their waists.

"Wait here," he told her after a minute.

She caught his arm as he turned to swim in the
rest of the way. "Where are you going?"

"To find the others. You stay here. I'll come back
out as soon as I can."

"You need not do so. My head has cleared. And I
can surely make the shore from here."

Ahearn raised an uncertain eyebrow.

"I can!"

"I don't doubt it, but at night and on a strange
coast—with more squalls, possibly—there's no reason
to prove that right now, is there?"

"Well, I—"

"Now see here: if you set out on your own, and
then if I come looking, I could miss you in the dark.
And then it might be me who's so weary that I go
under and stay there. You wouldn't want to be the
cause of that, now, would you?"

She stared sullenly at him. "Do you think me a
child, trying to 'reason' with me that way? If you wish

me to stay here, I shall—at least until the weather clears and the light is better. Does that satisfy you?"

In fact, it did, but Ahearn frowned and grudgingly conceded, "Well, I suppose it must."

Umkhira rolled her eyes. "Please. Swim away. Now. Before you try to 'convince' me of something else."

Ahearn shrugged and slid back into the surf. A moment later, the ring started to lead him again, but more gently this time.

The rest of the swim to the shore took less than ten minutes, and the storm seemed to be passing. Rain spat at him once or twice but had given up and gone elsewhere by the time he staggered out of the water in a small inlet. The footing was still treacherous, though: it was a scree-and-sand beach, framed by high sea-sharpened rocks that reached far out into the waves. And it was empty, except for him. *Well, damn you, ring; what good are you if you lead me wrong?*

But above the crash of the waves against the rocks, he heard what sounded like angry cries: definitely frustrated, possibly desperate. Following the sound led him back out into the water, wading and then swimming around the steep rocks to the right.

There the ring throbbed once as he discovered a narrow-mouthed notch: a round pool that had been scoured from the stone by the pinched inflows of the waves. A vicious circular current bashed about inside the funnel in pulses of foaming fury.

S'ythreni was caught against its back wall, flailing as much as swimming to keep her head above the wild, irregular swells and surges.

Ahearn started toward her.

She saw him, screamed words he couldn't make

out, but her waving arm made her meaning clear; she wanted him to turn around. Whether she was too proud to accept his help or concerned that it might kill both of them was unclear, but either way he was not about to comply; he tried to keep tight to one wall of the notch as he made his way around its periphery.

But to no avail: about halfway to her, a savage current pushed between him and the wall, rolled him away from it, and slammed him down against sharp, submerged rocks. Their presence further explained why the water's movement was so unpredictable; as it ebbed and flowed between the debris at the bottom of the pool, it created a host of smaller currents that hit and split the waves hammering into it.

After two more attempts, which left Ahearn's clothing shredded and his limbs marked by many cuts, he began to wonder if the notch was the creation of some malign ocean deity, a watery oubliette designed to drown all who had the temerity—or misfortune—to enter it.

"Begone!" S'ythreni shouted at him the third time he struggled back to a comparatively smooth part of the wall. "You're distracting me!"

"From what? Dying?"

Despite her rage-contorted face, she threw her head back and laughed. "Well, at least I shall die with a smile on my face."

"I don't think you'll die at all," said a new voice from above.

They both looked up.

Cerven was smiling down at S'ythreni from a narrow crag in the rocks, a belt in his hand. "When last I saw you aboard ship, you were wearing a belt or sash. Is it still on your person?"

She nodded, had the belt off in a moment. He motioned for her to throw it; he caught it and linked it to his own. As he lowered the much longer lifeline down to her, he glanced at Ahearn. "Do you require assistance?"

Ahearn could only shake his head at the young fellow's calm competence. "No, I'm not trapped here yet." *Well, I don't think I am.*

Just to be safe, he waited until S'ythreni had climbed up the sheer wall, using the line as a handhold where necessary. Cerven smiled at her as she clambered to safety. She glared at him and snarled gratitude in her own language: "*Uuth.*"

His smiled widened. "*As'aa,*" he responded in excellently accented Iavarain.

She started. "Where did you learn that?"

"Iavarain?" he asked. "It was my second—"

"No, *that* accent."

"Ah. From a neighbor. Now, I shall seek Varcaxtan, Elweyr, and our fellow traveler." With a nod, he disappeared back into the crag from which he'd appeared.

S'ythreni glanced over her shoulder at Ahearn; their raised eyebrows were a match for each other.

"I think," Ahearn began slowly, "that we need to find out where that lad grew up. And whom with."

"*H'ai*, he had some 'neighbors,'" she muttered back, almost drowned out by the fuming vortex in the notch. "He doesn't just speak classical Iavarain instead of aeostun. He uses archaic idioms and pronunciations that you only hear when you're around, well..."

"Around Tharêdæath?"

"I was going to say 'around Uulamantre,' but those are just two ways of saying the same thing." She shook her head and disappeared where Cerven had moments before.

Great, Ahearn thought, as he began edging back along the curving wall of the notch toward the surf beyond, *just what this group needs: another walking, talking mystery.*

By the time Ahearn had struggled back to the small inlet where he'd come ashore, Elweyr was already there. Less than a minute later, Varcaxtan mounted the dunes at its rear, a wholly unexpected person following behind him: the captain.

"Well," said Ahearn, trying to sound convincing, "I'm certainly glad to see you survived, Captain. Now, Varcaxtan, about our, er, sickly friend—"

The captain sighed. "Are you truly so dense?"

Ahearn started. "Dragon? *Another* change? This is getting entirely too confusing!"

"Dragon?" breathed Cerven quietly. "Well, yes—it all makes sense now."

"Oh, well done, steel-waver," the "captain" drawled archly. "A capital job, keeping that secret. Perhaps we should tarry here and etch it into the rocks, just so that no one who passes by will be left in ignorance."

Ahearn, who couldn't decide whether the heat in his face was from anger or embarrassment, shot back, "Well, how was I supposed to know that—well, damn it all, you miserable wyrm: how the hells did you do whatever it is you've done to be inside the captain?"

Varcaxtan cleared his throat. "It's more a matter of being inside what's *left* of the captain, Ahearn."

Ahearn frowned; the mood of arch banter evaporated. "I'm not sure what that means."

The captain avatar sighed. "It means that I may have killed the poor creature."

Varcaxtan shook his head. "Now, that's just not how it was."

"Wasn't it?" The dragon sat on the sand; if Ahearn hadn't known the self-centered and egotistical being better, he would say that he looked and sounded crestfallen, even remorseful. "You see," he said, gaze moving slowly about the group, "I knew the other avatar would not survive the ordeal of being flung into wild seas in the middle of the night. She had barely enough strength left to breathe."

"You said as much," Elweyr nodded.

"Yes, so I knew I would have to occupy one of the others nearby." He shrugged. "The captain was the logical choice. He would be recognized as the leader by any survivors, and I meant to get to the bottom of his resentment for Tharêdæath—a rather nasty surprise, that. And I am no longer easily surprised.

"However, he had a stronger will than I expected. What should have been the work of a second became the work of three—and that was the moment the ship capsized. So as he fell toward the water, he was not entirely aware of his surroundings—and was dashed against one of the rocks, in consequence. A blow to the head. When I awakened within him, he was no longer breathing, let alone thinking."

The dragon sighed, looked out to sea. "I was able to put life back into his heart and lungs, and his brain is not significantly damaged, but it is no longer capable of independent thought. When I leave this body, it will collapse as would a puppet deprived of its strings. So I have killed yet another of your kind."

"Well, you hardly *killed* the captain—" began Ahearn.

"Had I not been subjugating his mind at that moment, he would have had his wits about him. And lived."

Elweyr folded his arms. "You cannot know that."

The dragon regarded the mantic. "Never before have you made such a blunt asseveration when addressing me. Good for you—and I understand that you are trying to be kind. But these were my deeds; the deaths are justly weights upon my wings." He sighed. "Assuming I ever have my wings, again."

Elweyr folded his arms against the sharp wind. "I had no idea that dragons were so..."

"Philosophical?" the body of the captain supplied.

"Principled," the thaumancer clarified.

The dragon snorted. "If you should ever meet another of my breed, do not generalize from my behavior in forming your expectations. In that regard, we are as varied as your own species. Probably more so, in that there is little we respect or fear enough to compel us toward moderation in our feelings or convictions."

"So," S'ythreni smirked, "you're saying you're all self-centered and selfish."

The dragon could not help but smile. "I wonder what aeostu taste like," he mock-threatened.

"A discussion for another time," Ahearn announced, standing and feeling sand rubbing into the cuts inflicted by the whirlpool. "Let's see what's behind those dunes: hopefully a windbreak to sleep behind. Because we have our work cut out for us tomorrow."

"Work?" Cerven said wonderingly. "What kind of work? Searching for more survivors?"

"And salvage," Elweyr muttered. "We hope."

CHAPTER TWENTY

Well, mused Ahearn, as he collapsed on the shore in exhausted abandon, *that could have gone better, and it could have gone worse.*

The best outcome of the day's salvage efforts was also the most important. The possessions for which they'd built special protection—a steel box, all seams tin-welded, coated in dried tar, and protected within three sleeved crates with padding between—had survived. Being heavy to begin with, and further ballasted, it had sunk straight down where the ship sank.

Which yielded a pleasant surprise: although the reef had gutted the hull like a fish, her speed and the inrushing tide had pushed her a few hundred yards closer to shore before she finally foundered. The outer two crates had been mauled, but the third was mostly intact and the steel box wholly spared. It was in only four fathoms, so they might have found it even if Elweyr had not put a mantic marker in each of its layers of protection. And, because the markers in the broken layers had been deposited along the course the ship had taken before succumbing to the waves, they showed the most likely path where other salvage or even survivors might be found.

But those high hopes were quickly dashed. Ahearn had chosen the right moment to leap from the fated hull; fifty yards further on, the stony teeth of the reef crowded closer and had not only chewed the ship to bits, but created treacherous crosscurrents from which none of the crew had escaped. In consequence, there was little salvage except that which washed up along with storm-slain fish: sheets and other rigging, a few shattered spars, a broken barrel, and the invariable flotsam and jetsam.

The rigging turned out to be not merely useful, but invaluable. The box was too heavy for a handful of swimmers to bring to the surface, but Elweyr and Cerven hit upon the expedient of fashioning the rat-lines into a cradle for it, and splicing the sheets into a towline for dragging it closer. But the work of doing so proved slow, mostly because the box had to be guided over and around obstacles by the three who had any skill at diving: Varcaxtan, S'ythreni, and Ahearn himself.

Once affixed to the cradle, they ran the line so that it rested within a groove atop a submerged rock; a serviceable guide channel for the sheets, but one which needed watching lest its rough edges strip away one of the splices. From thence, they ran the tail of the line back to an anchor rock on shore with which they took up the slack as they drew the strong-box closer. But the arrangement had two significant drawbacks: it wasn't safe for the divers or the sheets when the tide was running out; and even when the tide was running in, the divers became so exhausted that they had to work in shifts.

Ironically, their most arduous labors were not so much caused by the box, but the makeshift line. Every few minutes, the divers had to guide its play so that rocks did not snag or sever it. Or they had to repair a fraying sheet by tying off the weak section with a new splice, which often required untying the box while they did so.

All the while, the others were either hastily winding new slack around the anchor rock or hauling the box closer to the shore, often a few agonizing inches at a time. In the end, they recovered the box but their labors proved so long and draining that, even if other salvage had been available, they no longer had the time or energy to find—let alone recover—it.

Varcaxtan and Umkhira staggered over to where Ahearn lay, still panting. In many ways, the Lightstrider had contributed more muscle-power than anyone else; with Varcaxtan and Ahearn diving, it was mostly her considerable strength which had brought the box ashore.

"So," Ahearn asked through a long, wracking pull of air, "is everything in one piece?"

Varcaxtan nodded. "Contents of the box are intact. Just the odd scratch."

Ahearn almost laughed for joy. Or maybe relief. Or maybe simply because the universe hadn't played the joke on them that they'd most feared: that, after the punishing labor, they'd open the damn thing up and find that everything except for the metal objects had been ruined by seawater, anyhow.

S'ythreni staggered toward them. "What, after a day like this, could possibly be amusing?" she grumbled.

Ahearn smiled, thought he might giggle. "I'm not really sure."

"Well, I hope it keeps you warm tonight," she groused, picking at what was left of her clothes. "And fed."

Umkhira grunted. "At least we shall be well armed." Among other things, the box held their best weapons and the sheath armor that Tharêdæath had pressed upon S'ythreni.

"And Cerven and the dragon have found old driftwood well back from the dunes," added Varcaxtan. "Blown in by a monsoon, they guess. Good for both tinder and kindling, and Elweyr has the means of setting it ablaze."

Ahearn glanced at the fish Elweyr had piled up in the shadows to keep them from spoiling in the heat of the day. "And see, dinner awaits! So, leave off the long face, High Ears. We have what we need and recovered what we can't replace. Not half bad, for a first day."

S'ythreni glanced to the northeast, where a river ran out into the sea and beyond which ruins were murky outlines in the spray-laden air. "The day isn't over yet," she muttered and made for a higher dune from which to survey the land around them.

"So," asked Ahearn as he picked the last bits of a roasted fish off its bones, "just how far are we from F'Shëssa, then?"

As sparks from the cookfire rose into the dusk, the dragon snorted. "You travel to a new region and do not trouble yourself to acquire a better knowledge of it. You are an embarrassment to your already pitiable species."

"See," sighed Ahearn, "now there's your *real* reason for choosing to enter the captain. His foul temper shaped him into a ready vessel for your own." He continued before the dragon could find a retort. "But in point of fact, no one—including you—knew we'd wind up so far from our destination." When the dragon did not answer, Ahearn counted it a victory—despite the avatar's single snicker and rolled eyes.

S'ythreni hesitated, glanced at Varcaxtan. "F'Shëssa is seventy leagues to the east."

"Seventy leagues!" exclaimed Umkhira. "That storm was strong, but how could it blow us so far in half a day?"

Varcaxtan smiled. "It didn't, Lightstrider. The captain was making for a headland at the very opening of the Medvir Bight. From there, they meant to follow the coast eastward for the twenty-five leagues to F'Shëssa." He shrugged. "But they must have drifted west while heading south from Uershael. So when they caught sight of this coast and followed it east, they never realized they weren't even in the Bight. The headland they saw before the wreck"—he gestured at the promontory just beyond the river to the north—"is smaller than F'Shëssa's and still forty leagues south of the Medvir's waters. We might have closed the distance by five leagues while tacking northeast during the storm, but no further."

"Well, there's your seventy leagues, then," Ahearn muttered, tossing the well-cleaned skeleton of the fish away. "So come the morrow, we'll need to find—" Ahearn stopped, leaped to his feet, hand going to his sword hilt. "What's that?" he hissed, pointing and squinting toward the crumbling buildings on the other side of the river. Even as he watched and the dusk faded toward night, a light seemed to be brightening at the top of the tallest ruin.

"That's what's left of the city of Kœsdri'yrm," S'ythreni said, nibbling at her own fish.

"I mean the bloody light!"

S'ythreni waved him back toward the last fish on his slab of driftwood. "It's always there, dim but constant. It just *seems* to appear as it gets darker."

Elweyr had also stood, but his tone was speculative rather than urgent. "So when the crew spotted the light, that's why you asked if it was steady or flickering."

S'ythreni nodded, licking the tips of her fingers; she made it look like the height of fine etiquette. "It was put there a long time ago, a blinking light that warned ships that they were not approaching F'Shëssa's larger headland, but steering toward deadly reefs." Seeing their wondering stares, she explained, "In those days, the light had wind vanes which rotated a screen around it. Then as now, any ship that strayed a bit off course while sailing down from Uershael or Pelfarras Bay was likely to make the same mistake the captain did."

"And so now ships can't tell the difference and think they're close to safe harbor—just before they founder on the rocks. Like us."

"Worse, usually. If we had headed straight for the light, we'd have been impaled on the larger, outer reefs: the Teeth of Zhnal'ë."

Umkhira crossed her arms. "And how would that be any worse?"

"Well, if the tales are true, most ships caught in them can't even sink. The rocks are so thick and sharp that they remain propped above the swells."

"Would that not have been better?"

"Not if the other legends are equally true. The Yylmyr of Kœsdri'yrm are said to sustain themselves by waiting for the cover of night to board the trapped hulls, slay the crews, and remove whatever they wish."

Ahearn frowned. "And how do the, ah, Eh-yulm avoid becoming well-chewed chum themselves?"

"Because the *Yylm* supposedly know safe passages that only they could navigate because they approached in small boats, knew where to look, and how best to steer. At any rate, it was far better to run aground where we did."

Cerven sat up very straight. "So, since we came much closer than the Teeth of Zhnal'ë, wouldn't they have detected us?"

Varcaxtan shook his head. "By then, all the ship's lights had been doused by the storm. And although the sound of her being gutted in the rocks was loud to our ears, I doubt it reached the ruins above the roar of the wind and waves."

"So what exactly are these, eh, Yylmyr?" Ahearn asked, S'ythreni nodding at his more careful pronunciation.

"They are fallen Iavarain," Umkhira replied darkly.

Ahearn didn't even try to conceal his surprise. "There are such things?" S'ythreni nodded again. He glanced back across the river. "And they live among those ruins?"

"They dwell beneath, not among, many of our old ruins," S'ythreni corrected. "Or at least they did. Most say they're just legend, now."

It was Umkhira's turn to show frank surprise. "So the fallen Iavarain are like urzhen? They live in an Under?"

The aeosti shook her head. "Not exactly. Unders are

natural caverns, sometimes abandoned mineshafts. The Yylm retreated to parts of our cities that had sunk, or been buried, underground. Like many others, Kœsdri'yrm was built—and rebuilt—many times. Floods, wars, plagues: it saw and was emptied by them all, over the millennia preceding the Cataclysm. Sometimes it was lost for so long that only its basements and hidden temples remained."

Cerven nodded. "So it is like Shadowmere. It has extensive subterranean ruins, those of each epoch stacked atop the ones that preceded it."

Ahearn and his original companions all goggled at him. Varcaxtan and the dragon just exchanged wan smiles.

Cerven looked at his traveling companions. "I thought you knew."

Ahearn raised an eyebrow. "Didn't exactly spend a lot of time there, lad. Don't suppose you know anything about the ruins just over the river, though?" He had meant it as a means of reminding young Cerven that even a clever youngster like him didn't know everything. But the fellow's face was not so much abashed as uneasy. *Oh, bollocks: he* does *know everything!* "Well, out with it then!"

"It is a very ancient city originally known as Sraisthënu. It is thought to have been one of the greatest regional capitals of Altom-Aila, the domain of Haivor the Fey."

Elweyr frowned. "I know that name."

Varcaxtan supplied the answer. "It was he who brought about the fall of the Uulamantre, and ultimately, the Cataclysm. I am, of course, presuming that the *Costéglan Iavarain* is more fact than fancy."

The dragon looked sideways at his Dunarran friend. "Do you really doubt that?"

Varcaxtan glanced back, studied the avatar's face. "Well, I guess I don't...now."

The dragon looked smugly satisfied at the answer.

"Is it prudent to deem ourselves safe?" asked Umkhira, looking around the group but ending with her eyes on S'ythreni. "Did you not say that your fallen cousins still use that light to bait ships onto the teeth of death?"

The aeosti shrugged. "Maybe, but it's been years since such an incident was reported." Cerven cleared his throat. "Yes?" she said guardedly.

"Alva S'ythreni, just because no such incidents are reported, does it necessarily follow that none have occurred?"

Ahearn nodded. "What's the saying, High Ears? 'Dead men tell no tales'?"

She threw up her hands. "Now you would ask me to prove the absence of a thing that no one may witness? It is not possible for me or anyone else to—"

A long howl arose over the river. Somewhere very close to Kœsdri'yrm. Or possibly within it. It ended on a shrill ululation.

S'ythreni jumped up. "Everyone grab something. We have to leave!"

"Right now?"

"But you said—"

"We leave—now!" she ordered, grabbing as many bits of their best gear as she could before heading directly away from the river and the ruins. "Kick aside the smoking racks!" she tossed over her shoulder.

Umkhira had already done so, her face stolid as

two days' worth of curing fish went into the weeds
and Ahearn sloshed seawater over the coals using the
intact half of a bucket. By the time he was done, the
rest of the group was jogging over the next dune.

An hour later, they all watched as S'ythreni crawled
back up a rise, having waited for the breeze to come
around so that it was in her face. She surveyed the
land behind them.

"Anything?" asked Elweyr after a few seconds.

Ahearn was fairly sure that anyone else asking
that question would have received a snarl instead of
the even-tempered answer she gave. "Hard to see
that far, even for me. But if it *is* Yylm or any of the
breeds they supposedly favor as harriers and guards,
they won't need torches or lanterns. But there may
be movement."

"What kind?" Ahearn asked.

"I can't be sure. It could be silhouettes passing
across the moonlight reflected by the water or the
dunes. Or it could just be changes in the light itself,
shadows of small clouds, or trees and grasses waving."
She was quiet for a long moment as she kept studying
the ground they'd covered since abandoning their
camp. "I was wrong, Master Cerven, and you were
right. That howl was from a *gwybqúsh*; not something
we want to meet without armor."

Ahearn considered. "But is it always the case that
wherever these, eh, *gwibb-koosh* are heard, Yylm are
always nearby? And even if so, I didn't see any intact
bridges over that river."

Varcaxtan shrugged toward Ahearn. "Gwybqúsh
are amphibians."

S'ythreni nodded. "And if there are still Yylmyr in Kœsdri'yrm, they wouldn't use a bridge or boats. They are more likely to use fords or have dug a tunnel under the river."

"That's quite a bit of digging, High Ears!"

"They've had quite a bit of *time*, 'Steel Waver,'" the dragon rebutted. "And from what I know of Yylmyr, they would expend the effort. They are secretive and go to great lengths to remain unseen and un-trackable."

"So," summarized Umkhira, "although we cannot be sure that we are being pursued, we must presume that we are." She looked at the feet of the humans and the aeosti. "And we will be at a disadvantage; there are already cuts on your soles. After a full day of moving, they will be much worse."

"And that's why you call us thinskins, eh, Lightstrider?" Ahearn said with good natured irony that sounded forced even in his own ears. Umkhira just regarded him solemnly. "Well, it's plain that if we meant to try to reach F'Shëssa on foot, we've got enemies in the way and a river none of us know how to cross. And I've read that further from the sea, the land becomes a proper wilderness."

"It is," S'ythreni confirmed. "There's nothing to the northeast until you reach the border of Mirroskye, just outside F'Shëssa."

"And to the east?" Elweyr asked.

Varcaxtan leaned in. "Over two hundred fifty leagues of dead cities and overgrown roads. All lost when the First Consentium retracted. Since then, it's been a lost expanse of tribes, Bent, and predators. There are even reports of feral supragants and, more rarely, cryptigants."

"Sounds like the kind of place we want to avoid."

Varcaxtan nodded somberly. "It's one of the places Outriders almost never go. There's nothing there except for a strong likelihood of never leaving it."

Umkhira folded her arms. "So one direction remains: the south. Of which I know almost nothing, other than it is home to a few backward human realms."

Varcaxtan smiled. "Don't let *them* hear you say that, Lightstrider, but you've got the main of it. Thanks to a few very good deepwater ports and the Consentium roads they work to maintain, they keep up good trade among themselves and are regular stopovers for merchantmen heading west around the southern coast of Ar Navir."

"It sounds as though they're also the best place to seek a ship that could bring us back north to the Medvir Bight and F'Shëssa," Elweyr mused. "Or maybe Eslêntecrë itself."

"They are, but we'll have to show up looking a bit more presentable than this." Varcaxtan indicated his own surf-tattered clothes. "In those four nations, we can find sympathy, fellow-feeling, equipment, and passage—as long as we can pay for all of them. Handsomely."

Ahearn rubbed his chin. "Fortune seekers of my acquaintance who've been there recall them as not being in the habit of embracing folk who simply wander out of the wilds. Consider them barbarians at best and bandits at worst."

"All attitudes inherited from their original, Ballashan founders," pronounced the dragon. "The greatest of their empires, that of Serdarong the Improver, was, even for a human state, obsessed with prestige, social status, and wealth. Any person or nation deemed lacking in one or more of these measures was considered not merely inferior, but irredeemable." He smiled. "And now, they are known as 'backward' to a world-traveling ur zhog." He reclined. "My, how the mighty have fallen. And they always do, you know."

Ahearn sat up. "Well, then let's to practical matters. We need to keep traveling south. And Umkhira's right; we won't get there walking on bloody stumps. So, Elweyr, what about all those potions and philters you, er, acquired, on the border of Kar Krathau? Anything that will help keep our feet from becoming as torn and tattered as our clothes?"

The thaumancer frowned. "No, but there are compounds that can accelerate curing. And perhaps we should sacrifice some of our clothes to wrap and protect our soles."

"Well, then, let's do that." Ahearn was about to move on to the next issue—acquiring adequate gear—but Elweyr was shaking his head. "Problems?"

"I need to mix the right compounds with the right unguents."

"Aye . . . and so?"

"And so it's night. I can't see the labels, much less make accurate measurements."

S'ythreni sighed. "I suppose I can be your eyes, and even your hands. Unless there's alchemy involved."

"There is, but only after the salve's ingredients have been mixed together. At that point, I could do what's necessary with my eyes closed."

Cerven looked like he was about to raise his hand; Ahearn nodded quickly to prevent it. "If yeh have a concern, spit it out!"

"Do we not need to keep Alva S'ythreni's more light-sensitive eyes watching the lands behind us?"

Umkhira tapped her chest. "If what follows us sheds heat as do most animals, then I can take her place."

S'ythreni nodded. "That will suffice."

"Now," Ahearn said with a sigh, "about traveling kit: how do we get any? Which is just a fast way of asking how the divils do we survive a journey of, er... how far is it to these lands to the south?"

Varcaxtan considered his answer for a moment. "The closest is Rettarisha, about sixty leagues."

Ahearn shook his head. "Gods help our feet! Sixty leagues to walk and, sure as shepherds have sheep, no getting shoes or other kit until it's all behind us!"

After a few moments of ominous silence, the dragon rose to an elbow. "What if we could bring the needed 'kit' to us?"

Ahearn smiled. "Sounds like a crafty wyrm-plan in the making, to me."

"A crafty *what*-plan?"

"A crafty *dragon*-plan," Ahearn amended with a roll of his eyes. "Bloody hells, must you be so particular about what you're called?"

"When you are the one doing the calling? Yes, I must," the dragon said with a broad smile, "I really must. Now," he said loudly to the group, "gather around so I need not raise my voice as I tell all of you what to do."

CHAPTER TWENTY-ONE

"Don't fidget," said the dragon.

"I can't help it," Ahearn complained, but managed to snatch his hand away from the rough, irritating collar before actually tugging at it. To the eyes of an alchemist, the parts from which it was fashioned would have been familiar but even more baffling: a pair of distended calipers, joined at their ends by a fine steel chain. Of course it was extremely unlikely that there were any such eyes abroad in a trackless wilderness.

However, the bandits were now close enough that they would surely notice any relaxed exchanges between the two individuals sitting by the smoldering campfire. And for the purposes of the dragon's plan, it was crucial that they not perceive the pair as equals, but master and servant. It was just after dawn and, according to S'ythreni and Umkhira, the half-barbaric band had observed them carefully for most of the night, probably hoping to determine why two poorly equipped individuals would dare camp alone and in the open, particularly in such dangerous country as this.

The scrawniest of the bandits emerged from the tree line ten yards away. The dragon nodded at him. The bandit, probably not quite as old as Cerven, faded back into the underbrush. Less than a minute later, two men—one of whom was immense, thick, and mostly without fat—entered the clearing. They advanced on the campfire with easy confidence.

Ahearn shifted his shoulders inside the sheath armor S'ythreni had loaned him for the occasion, adjusted the bastard sword on his lap, and shifted one leg beneath him so that he could push quickly to his feet.

It seemed that the big fellow was unlikely to stop until he was standing on their toes, so the dragon had to call out, "That's far enough, if you please. At least until we've been properly introduced."

The big bandit responded with a subvocal grunt that sounded a bit like "Huh," and stopping just out of arm's reach, jutted his chin inquiringly at the two of them. "You lost?"

"No," said the dragon, "we are travelers following our intended route."

"To where?"

"A place of considerable interest to us, and quite probably us alone."

"So," the big one said glancing over his shoulder, and paused.

Ahearn managed not to smile. Just as they'd thought, based on S'ythreni's last report; this one wasn't the leader. After sending the most expendable of their number into the brightening clearing to see what the reaction would be, they had now followed up with the muscle. But the brains hadn't shown up yet.

The big one turned back, looked at Ahearn directly.

It was an unmistakable stare of challenge. "You have a sword out," he drawled. "You scared of something?"

Ahearn drawled back. "I have yet to see anything out here that scares me in the least." He returned the big bandit's stare with a small smile.

The fellow bristled, muttered something that sounded like "we'll see about that later," and then nodded in the direction of the wood line.

Another man came out. This one was better dressed than the others. Most of his equipment had been created in a city shop or forge instead of tribal craftsmen and smiths. He was neither smiling nor frowning as he approached. If Ahearn had ever seen a face more devoid of expression, he could not remember it.

The man came to a stop between the other two. "We don't see many travelers out here," he observed. His voice carried easily even though his tone was surprisingly quiet.

"I am not surprised to hear so," the dragon answered. "These lands are less than hospitable."

The smaller of the man's two companions suppressed a chortle. The big one simply frowned uncertainly at the word "hospitable."

"And yet, here you are," the man replied. "All alone."

"Fewer bodies travel faster," the dragon countered, stifling a yawn. "They also hide more easily when need be."

"Maybe you should have hid last night, then," the big one said. The man with the quiet voice turned dead eyes upon him. The big one's jaw snapped closed and he looked away from the others.

"You do seem unusually certain of your safety, however," the man said. "I find that puzzling, because there doesn't seem to be any reason for you to be so confident."

The dragon simply gestured to Ahearn without looking at him. "My bonded armsman is more than sufficient to ensure our safety."

The smaller of the quiet man's companions looked Ahearn up and down, not with disdain, but inspecting him more closely, as if he might have missed something. The big man just glowered.

The soft-voiced man only cocked one eyebrow. "It's unusual to rely so heavily upon a single armsman, even one in Iavan sheath armor," he commented. "He must be a demon in a fight."

The dragon looked up. "He is, actually," he sighed, "but he is not my friend. You see the collar, do you not?"

"So he's your chattel?"

The dragon smiled. Never in his own life had the captain's face appeared so cunning or composed. "Let us say he is bound to my service."

"So you're a wizard, then?"

The dragon couldn't help scowling at the parochial term. "I do not dabble in mancery, but I know those who do. Indeed, one of them sent me on this errand."

"Errand?" the quiet man asked with a bit more interest.

"The strange thing about mantics," the dragon said with another sigh, "is that despite all their power, they are singularly averse to using it in a place where there is any risk to their person. They send others to do that work. And so, here we are."

"In search of what?"

The dragon's smile was broad and predatory. "Why, something of great interest to a powerful thaumancer."

The quiet man folded his arms, but did so using slow, exaggerated movements, nodding at Ahearn to show that he was not reaching toward a weapon.

Ahearn nodded back.

When his arms were crossed, the man said, "It's rare to find good conversation out here in the wilderness. But I confess that I would appreciate a more detailed answer than the one you just gave."

"I appreciate good conversation as well," said the dragon, "but I have yet to encounter any out here in the wilderness. Alas, this one is the best I've had so far." Ahearn wasn't sure how the calm man remained so in the face of such a slight.

But he merely shook his head and repeated his request. "I wish to know what are you searching for. In detail."

"Well," exclaimed the dragon sardonically, "at last: the conversation becomes frank. So I shall be just as frank by sharing the single most important 'detail.'" He leaned toward the man. "It is this: that what I search for is *my* business, not *your* business." He leaned back. "However, if you are interested, I would be amenable to hiring your company as additional protectors for our journey north."

"You're going north? There isn't much there except ruins. Dangerous ones."

"See?" answered the dragon. "You are already familiar with our destination."

"We are," the man answered, "but I don't see how you mean to pay for our services, let alone a bowl of gruel at a seedy tavern."

The dragon considered the state of its fingernails and cuticles. "It is helpful, actually, to appear impoverished in such unpatrolled lands as these. But to allay your doubt in my means..." The captain/dragon produced a sizable emerald: the largest Ahearn and his companions had taken from the Sanslovan assassin they had defeated just days before meeting the dragon.

The three men leaned toward the gem. The quiet man studied it. The large man started to step forward, mesmerized—until he encountered the outthrust arm of his leader. Who nodded at the jewel. "You have satisfied my need for proof of your means. But I am afraid you must now satisfy my need for an advance against our services." He nodded at the emerald. "That would do nicely."

"Far too nicely, I'm afraid," the dragon chuckled. "Besides, payment follows service."

"Does it now?" the leader said. "Where I come from, it is the party on their feet, and with more ready hands on more ready weapons, that usually dictates the terms."

"We shall see," the dragon said airily, glancing at Ahearn.

Who affected a bored sigh before he cocked his head and looked at the calm man. "Must we do this dance?"

The leader frowned—but only for an instant. His expression changed from aggravation to cunning. "Maybe we don't. But that's up to you, armsman."

"How so?"

"Well, what happens if you refuse to obey the one who holds you in thrall?"

Ahearn shrugged. "Not sure, but I assume something similar to the last man I saw wearing this collar."

"Which was?"

"It strangled him . . . before it closed completely and took his head off."

The calm man nodded, considering. "What if I was to tell you I have a charm that could prevent that from occurring?"

Ahearn shrugged. "I'd say I have no way to know if you're telling the truth. Besides, no matter the outcome, it's all the same to you, isn't it?"

"How so?"

"Well, you might have the means to free me. But for your purposes, I'm better dead than alive, so why wouldn't you let the collar do its work? Either way, you have both the gem and your way with him." Ahearn jerked his head toward the dragon.

The leader shook his head, crouched down to look Ahearn in the eye. "You're wrong. A good fighter—so good that this wealthy 'pauper' is willing to travel the wilds with naught but you at his side—is more valuable to my band than that emerald. To add a sword as lethal as yours is the promise of many more gems than just that one. What do you say? Will you rely upon the power of my ancient amulet?" He moved his hand slowly, lifted a rough crystal up from where it hung on a rawhide string about his neck. It was glowing faintly.

"You know," the dragon sighed, "if you try to break the bonding, you'll be the one he kills first. Strictly preemptive, mind you, but he can't be stopped once he begins." He shifted his gaze to the big one. "And you'll be next of course. Tell me, how do you feel about that?"

The massive warrior's eyes widened and he swallowed—before growing very, very calm.

"Enough of this," the quiet man snapped, no longer so calm himself. He glanced at Ahearn and, holding his eyes, ordered, "Do not move." Then, over his shoulder at the large warrior: "Belgur, kill the mouthy little bastard."

Carefully motionless, Ahearn watched as Belgur drew his outsized broadsword. As if fainting from fright, the avatar's eyes rolled back and he slumped over, limp before the threat of the rising blade.

Which slashed down at the calm leader's neck.

As Ahearn had expected, the blow was awkward; the dragon had explained that none of an avatar's skills became his own. The edge bit into the leader's armor halfway along his shoulder.

The third man spun toward the suddenly traitorous Belgur, drawing his own blade to protect his leader and possibly save himself.

But that move fully exposed his left side, which was what Ahearn had been waiting for. Using the leg curled under him, he pushed up into a lunge, driving his bastard sword forward with both hands. The thrust punched through the third man's light leather armor, shoving almost a foot of steel into his left lung, shattering ribs as it continued even deeper.

Ahearn felt the blade snag as the man crumpled; he rolled with the body, pulling hard on the hilt. As it came free, blood sprayed on him, blinding him in one eye as the other saw five more of the bandits emerge from the tree line. Four were charging but the fifth barely stepped beyond the foliage, drawing a bow to his ear.

The instant before he loosed the shaft at Ahearn—who, rolling, was a hard target—a sharp slap sounded

from a thorn-covered hillock at the rear of the clearing. The archer's readied arrow flew wild as he fell
backward, a quarrel protruding from his chest. S'ythreni's ironwood crossbow had once again proven both
accurate and punishing.

Now, if she can load it as quickly as usual, Ahearn
thought, gauging which of the four charging barbarians
would be on him first.

Except, as planned, the two closest slowed dramatically, as if suddenly hip-deep in a swift river, trying
to wade upstream.

The third and fourth bandits were a few steps back,
converging from further points along the tree line, and
quickly swerved to opposite sides of their struggling
fellows. Along with his companions, Ahearn had hoped
that the visual effect of Elweyr's thaumantic construct
would break the morale of the remaining attackers. But
the battle was unfolding and changing so quickly that
their foes' comprehension of the disastrous reversals
was lagging behind events.

The one that had broken from the trees on the
far-left flank began to angle toward the center of
the clearing, but suddenly broke stride, staring wildly
about . . . just as Umkhira seemingly appeared out of
thin air. She had come charging out from a spot just
a few steps further along the tree line, the motion
disrupting the chameleon unguent that had concealed
her. The bandit, apparently hearing the rustle as she
left the undergrowth, had spun so that she was no
longer fully on his flank.

But whereas he had to spot his adversary before
attacking, Umkhira was already leaping in, one of
S'ythreni's shortswords in her right hand, a stout club

in the left. The first weapon cut a bloodred seam down the rear of the bandit's shield arm, followed by a powerful sweep of the club which knocked his hasty axe blow wide. As the fellow stumbled back, Umkhira thrust the shortsword at his sternum; it skittered an inch before the mass and muscle of the Lightstrider forced its point through the leather armor and deep into the flesh behind.

As that bandit yowled and Ahearn rolled to his feet—none too gracefully, but in time—the fourth charging bandit stopped only two yards away from him. Suddenly realizing that the ambush had gone completely awry—underscored when one of his slowly struggling mates suddenly sprouted a quarrel from his head—he turned to flee. Those who had not yet entered the clearing had reached the same tactical conclusion; they were already smashing away through undergrowth, fleeing for the deeper shadows of the forest.

Well, thought Ahearn, *that's an end of it. Now we can just—*

The body that had been Belgur's sprinted past him, big feet thunderous in pursuit of the fourth attacker, broadsword held high and ready.

Ahearn gabbled out, "Hells, Dragon! What're yeh...? *NO, gods damn it!*"

But the shout came too late. The big warrior was surprisingly swift, and although his mighty downcut didn't strike the fourth attacker's head or back, it sliced one of his unarmored buttocks in two and half-trimmed the muscle off the rear of that thigh. Shrieking, the bandit sprawled in the dust, blood gushing out of the gaping wound.

Apparently S'ythreni took that as a cue to continue the attack; another quarrel whistled to a stop in the other fellow who'd been snared in Elweyr's mantic effect, catching him in the side as he laboriously turned to join the retreat. He went over with a grunt and a moan.

"Stop, yeh bloodthirsty idjits!" Ahearn roared above a growing cacophony of men dying in agony. "Are y'all daft?" The dragon looked stunned: whether at his own deeds or Ahearn's rage was unclear. "Who are the 'barbarians' now, hey?" S'ythreni, the chameleon philter disrupted by her movement, flushed slightly where there were gaps in the oily coating.

Elweyr slowly rose from the brambles atop the rise at the back of the clearing; his careful motions didn't fully disrupt the function of his own philter, which continued to partially obscure his outline. Cerven, who'd been detailed to personally guard him, rose to follow as the thaumancer rasped at Ahearn, "Couldn't be sure what to do once the dragon ran after them." He furtively glanced around at the moaning bandits. "So, better safe than sorry."

Cerven, who having been fully concealed was also fully clothed, added: "It was impossible to determine if the battle was still proceeding as planned. There was a great deal of dust, and more movement than we'd counted on."

Ahearn nodded roughly, biting back the reply he wanted to make: *aye, mostly because the dragon wasn't a great killer of men...just a great wounder of 'em.* Resolving to compel the great wyrm to learn how to use a sword in the days to come, Ahearn glared at him, and then the others who had only wounded their opponents. "Show your mercies to the fallen, and quickly. Killing may be needful, but agony never is."

Cerven called to the others from his position just within the tree line. "That's Varcaxtan's birdcall; he is returning."

Ahearn affected an absentminded nod, hoping it would conceal how much that news relieved him. The Dunarran had proven to be a better addition to the group than Ahearn could have imagined. Although experience and skill gave him every right to be its leader, he'd adopted a role situated someplace between mentor and senior counselor. *Probably a role he's filled before,* Ahearn realized. It explained why the "old man" had avoided direct leadership: to help them work better as a group and individually through casual suggestion and silent example.

In fact, that was just how today's plan had begun to take shape. Shortly after the dragon had set forth his basic strategy, Varcaxtan had mused that "it might be helpful" to be selective about whatever unsuspecting raiders or bandits they lured into ambush. An hour later, the group was deep in discussion about creating a scenario in which they could observe the target's numbers, equipment, and behavior before springing their trap. Everything else had flowed naturally from there.

Ironically, as Elweyr stood assessing the unsavory collection of newly harvested gear, he grumbled a complaint which suggested that Varcaxtan's subtle lessons had not made as deep an impress upon him. "This was very expensive. Any one of the three unguents we spent would have paid for this rubbish fifty times over."

"Maybe," called Varcaxtan as he emerged from the tree line, passing Cerven with a pat on his shoulder, "but trade in the wilderness has little in common with trade in a city, Magister."

Elweyr had been ready to scowl, but blinked at the lofty honorific the Dunarran had bestowed upon him. Then he frowned. "I have not earned that standing."

Varcaxtan offered a lopsided smile. "Well, there's no formal guild to assign it, and I've seen far prouder titles affixed to far less capable mantics."

Elweyr didn't like ceding to another point of view any better than Ahearn. So he changed the topic, muttering, "All that aside, this attack proved riskier than we thought." He glanced at the seven bodies. "There were too many to control. The first group we saw, the tribal raiders, were fewer than half a dozen. They would have been a better choice."

"They *would* have been more vulnerable," Cerven agreed politely.

Ahearn shook his head, smiled at him. "It would seem so, wouldn't it, lad? But here's the thing of it: you can't predict what a rabble of wildings like raiders will do. More than half their decisions are based on clan rank and personal honor. But these blaggards?" He nodded meaningfully at the leader's body. "He had this lot in line and could make plans that he knew they'd follow—because even the sorriest bunch of bandits are dependable as long as there's a promise of easy loot.

"And that's what made them predictable—at least enough so that we had a good guess at how they'd react to the little show we put on for them, yeh? Once they settled in to watch the dragon and me overnight, we knew two things about their leader. He was careful, patient, and looking to get whatever he could without a fight. Or to get close enough so, if the two fools in the clearing were more than they seemed, they could be cut down in a trice."

As if determined to sound a sour note in counterpoint, Elweyr held up the blood-spattered crystal the bandit leader had asserted to be a charm. "Even this is worthless. Glow glass."

Umkhira frowned. "It is not a mantic artifact?"

"It is a trick. You keep it against something warm—like your body—and when you take it away, it glows for a few moments." Elweyr sneered at the crystal. "It has one use; to dupe the stupid and the ignorant." He tucked it into his box of alchemical substances, muttering, "Oh, yes, quite a prize. Only cost us three concealing unguents. I'm ecstatic."

"Well, despite your droop-mouthed 'ecstasy,'" Ahearn replied, "not only did we carry the day, but now we have more kit than we can carry!"

"Don't remind me," Elweyr groused, considering the condition and crudity of the "kit."

Umkhira shrugged. "I have traveled and fought using far worse." She inspected the clothes—especially the footwear—before turning to Ahearn. "And what of the three that fled?"

"No need to pursue 'em, my good green lass," Ahearn assured her.

"I haven't worn paint in many years," she corrected irritably, "and the three who survived are oath breakers. They approached a camp with sheathed weapons and conversed peaceably. They all but promised *h'adzok* in so doing. Their violation should not go unanswered."

"Best we let the wilderness have its way with them," counseled Varcaxtan, who was inspecting the compound bow and the arrows; a second missile weapon promised better hunting results. "Who knows? Maybe the young one will be scared into better ways."

Umkhira made a guttural sound resembling a growl. "More likely that he will simply prove more adept at betrayal, come his next opportunity." She sheathed the shortsword, handed it back to S'ythreni. "But I will be guided by our need to move as quickly as possible, and by your charitable nature, Dunarran." She smiled. "I can hardly believe I have now traveled with two Dunarrans who are good companions and honorable, rather than enemies to be avoided or slain."

Ahearn was about to quip that the two of them were strange bedfellows, but before he could, his mind painted a literal picture of them in those circumstances—from which he recoiled. Instead, he set about the task of assessing the rucksacks, satchels, and bags for ruggedness. "Let's be about passing out the kit and getting on the trail."

As the others began discussing who should get what, the dragon remained still, studying its large, hirsute hands.

Ahearn leaned toward him. "You're not above such mundane matters as seeing to a fair share of kit, are yeh?"

"In fact, I am," the dragon murmured, looking up as if awaking from a trance, "but I shall do so, nonetheless."

Ahearn had meant to roll his eyes in response, but the dragon's attention had returned to the body of its avatar. "Takes some getting used to, eh?"

The dragon nodded. "This time, yes." Its voice tapered off for a moment; it had discovered its biceps. They were even larger than Ahearn's, albeit neither as hard nor as sharply defined. "As Varcaxtan can attest, it has been, oh, many centuries now since I entered a body that still has an active mind."

"Hmm . . . sounds like another set of scruples you observe when dealing with us lowly humans, eh?"

The dragon stopped and stared at him. "I find banter—extraordinarily taxing at the moment."

Ahearn frowned, as much at the dragon's tone as its word. "Why so?"

It looked away. "You could not have missed my . . . inexperience with your weapons."

Ahearn swallowed back half a dozen savage jibes and merely nodded. The dragon's ineptitude had been so pronounced that, after putting a grim end to the one it had chased, it then had to return to the still-moaning leader. Despite striking the man a second time, it had *still* failed to dispatch him.

The dragon kept looking into the distance. "I have not fought in this way before. It is . . . very chaotic." It turned back, and the eyes that met Ahearn's were . . . imploring? "I must improve. With your help."

Ahearn almost swallowed his tongue. *That was almost, well . . . polite. After a fashion.* "Then we'll call a truce, yeh?" *And maybe a change of topic won't be amiss either.* "So if you're leery about bein' in a body with a working mind, I confess a bit of curiosity: why this one, and why now?"

The dragon distractedly ran its hands over the cured leather that covered the broad torso it had inherited. "I suspect you and the others presumed

I chose this avatar because of its—er, his—size and prowess."

"Aye, so I thought...at first." Ahearn assessed the eyes of the warrior known as Belgur, which were now as thoughtful and canny as they had been dull and simple. "But the closer we came to putting on our little skit, the more I began to wonder if you made your choice based on his mind more'n his body."

The dragon began walking toward the weapons, all laid in an orderly row. "How so?"

"Well, it stands to reason that if there's still a mind in the brainbox, it's not going to be happy having an uninvited guest, yeh? So, with this big lummox being as dim as he was, I found myself wondering if you chose him because it means less effort in a constant war of wills?" S'ythreni and Cerven had overheard, glanced at the dragon, curious.

The dragon shrugged. "A war of wills? Not with a mind such as this one. Frankly, it cannot even focus on that challenge, and focus is the prerequisite for any act of will. I have constructed the mental equivalent of a maze for him to navigate before he can even touch, let alone understand, my presence in his mind." The dragon paused. "And trust me; this one is not gifted at puzzles."

The others smiled, but Umkhira frowned mightily. "This is all very well, but we have a practical matter to settle." Their combined stares wrested it from her. "Well, it walks as one of us. Are we to continue calling it 'dragon'? That cannot be wise." She turned to the body of the large warrior. "So what shall we call you? Surely you must have a name."

"Surely, I do. But do you really imagine you could pronounce it?"

Cerven rested his chin on his fist. "Is there an approximation?"

"No. Well, one employed by long-dead Uulamantre, but it is far too long. And your beastly truncation of beautiful names into the sobriquets you call 'nicknames' is revolting."

"So what will serve the purpose?" Umkhira asked through a deepening frown.

"Well, we *could* just call it 'Dragon,'" Elweyr suggested as he stood, "so long as we use a language that few understand. A dead language, maybe, or one that is used by a people who would keep the secret safe." He glanced at S'ythreni. "Or maybe both."

The dragon smiled slyly. "Mantic, I am loath to admit it, but I am beginning to find you not just tolerable, but agreeable. So," he said, turning toward the aeosti, "do you feel R'aonsun would be appropriate?"

She frowned. "I'm not sure how many Iavarain will even understand that...unless they are Uulamantre or students of the ancient cants."

"All the better," the dragon said loudly. Standing very straight, Belgur's voice declared, "Then R'aonsun I shall be, for a r'aonsun I am."

Ahearn managed to hide a small smile; *ah, you're halfway back to yer old, insufferable self already!* "Well, whatever you're called, you're still a nasty old wyrm. Aye, that's right: our truce is over! Now get those great ham hocks you call hands around twice your share of the spare gear. You've the brawn and back for the job, and we've still a long way to go to the border of Rettarisha."

JOURNAL Entry Four
Yu'Serda, First City of T'Oridrea

It has been slightly more than four moonphases since
we were shipwrecked near the mouth of the Medvir
Bight, and two days since I found a few sheets on
which to resume this cursed journal. Wouldn't you
know it, but they were folded and secreted in the
back of one of Druadaen's fool books. Did he simply
forget he had a few spare pages there? Or were they
stashed away in case he ran out of a ready supply, like
a drunkard keeps a spare bottle in hiding? Knowing
him, my bet is on the latter.

Unlike him, I use as few words as possible. So
here's all posterity needs to know about our return to
populated lands. Striking south, we ambushed bandits
for new kit (and a new body for the dragon), and then
marched hard for the border of Rettarisha. We only
stopped to hunt. Oh, and twice, we came across a few
standing rocks that I first took to be carved either
by contrary winds or madmen's hands. Possibly both.
S'ythreni and Varcaxtan looked and found carvings
along the bottom, almost wiped away by gods knows
how many years. They had us give them all a wide
berth, convinced they were Yylm shrines. If so, these

fallen Iavarain must worship contorted eels lined with tentacles and a head at either end.

I cannot say exactly when we crossed the border because there was nothing to mark it. However, at a guess, we traveled near twenty leagues before seeing the smoke of a hamlet. Except that when we came closer, it turned out to be naught but a few sturdy-walled farmhouses joined together by a rough palisade. Wheedle as we might, the folk there wouldn't come out and wouldn't let us in. But at least they told us that there was a seaport but a few days' walk to the southwest, one where "real ships" put in. At first I feared they might mean anything bigger than a rowboat, but they explained that some carried passengers as well as cargo to the "great cities" of Rettarisha. By their account, it meant at most half a week's sail, whereas reaching them afoot was the work of a moonphase.

So we headed southwest and discovered that the "seaport" didn't even have so much as a pier, just a beach for careening small ships and an anchorage dotted with old, battered floats. Happily, though, a half-decked bark was riding at anchor when we arrived, freshly returned to the water from the beach, judging from the ruts in the sand. Its captain made his scant pennies hauling small cargos, dragging for fish, and taking on (very infrequent) passengers. He'd only put in to what he called "this cove" to caulk a few leaky seams and replace a split plank; love-taps from canoe-paddling raiders north of the border.

However, inasmuch as he was ready to sail on the morrow and we were obviously not unfamiliar with weapons-play, he offered less than half his usual fee for carrying us to the city that Varcaxtan recommended: Ofthrafarg. The capital and first port of Varda, by his reck, it offered the highest chance of finding a ship willing to take us to Mirroskye at the lowest cost in coin and trouble. So we gladly took the captain's terms, but no sooner had we babbled our eager agreement than we saw a new problem it put before us: getting our hands on ready funds.

Oh, we had more than enough of value from the salvaged box. Besides our best armor, weapons, Elweyr's alchemical kit and books (and Druadaen's as well), we'd included a sturdy wallet of gems, silver, and small gold ingots. A tidy stash and handy, too.

But a stash that is handy can also be a problem. Because when you want a great deal of value in a package of little size and weight, it means you're leaving out the humbler coins used in small trades and small towns.

Now to those who don't travel much, that might not sound like a problem at all; better too rich than too poor, eh? And that's true enough—except who wants to buy a mess of groats with an ingot of gold? So we had to scurry about the "cove" looking for a money changer who could assay the proofe of our coins as well as those less valuable ones he'd give us in fair exchange.

As I wrote the word "proofe," I realized that I've once again run up against one of the thrice-blasted annoyances of keeping this journal: explaining a word sure to be unknown to some readers and probably most of posterity. And while I'm sure any full-blooded Dunarran would have two quibbles for every one word I write about "proofe"... well, they're not here and I don't give gods' damns.

By rights, though, it should *be* a Dunarran explaining proofe, since they were the ones who worked it out back in the First Consentium. Before then, money-changers and merchants could only argue about the worth of the coins they pushed across tables at each other. Alloys, dross, shaving, and sheer stupidity made an agreement on value slightly more rare than a bird with hooves. But the Dunarrans devised a system that, with a sensitive scale the right set of dyes and humours, and a few fine lenses, could quickly muddle through all that and fix the actual value of any coin. And when their First Consentium collapsed (or "retracted": depends who's telling the tale), two things remained in place wherever it had been: its roads and its "proofe."

Happily, one of the local shopkeeps also traded with passing ships. So, having a need, he kept the means to be sure that any coin passing through his hands was proofe.

Once we'd surrendered a few dozen silver for a great many billon marks and copper pence, we asked the fellow which cities had fair markets in which to trade our gems. Learning that we were bound for Varda, he bobbed his head and smiled. "Well, then, ye'll be a-right. But if yeh wander T'Oridrea-way, ye won't be." Why? we asked. The explanation that followed was so tangled that I had to pore over one of Druadaen's books to finally get the gist of his warnings. Jewels are not only measured and poked and ogled more closely in T'Oridrea than any other realm known to man or beast, but the process involves—gods help us!—all manner of arguers-at-law.

Our first days aboard the little bark were as dull

and slow as the wind, which resented having to puff into our sails at all. I'd meant to teach the dragon how to use a sword, but before I could, I was waylaid and held fast in clutches that surprised me more than any I'd known before: two of Druadaen's books! Worse still, I only remembered to tutor the old wyrm in mayhem when the sun was about to fall into the sea.

Two days out from Varda, I had reason to repent that failure: genuine pirates appeared astern and gave chase. We equipped ourselves and stood ready, but the captain made a wise, if hard, choice: to sail according to the wind, not his plot. So we steered whatever course filled our sails best, which in turn filled him with confidence that this time (unlike his run-in with the canoe-paddling raiders), discretion *could* be the better part of valor. The only drawback was that to keep close with the wind, he had to sheer away from the coast and risk open waters long enough to lose the pursuers.

Who, it turned out, were in no mood to allow us to escape. They chased us for the better part of two days before disappearing beneath the horizon during the second night. Our captain brooded over a powerful urge to cut back for the coast right away, but good seamanship and better sense told him that was where the reavers would wait if they'd not sworn off. So he held due south for two more days before edging back toward land.

Which, when it broke above the eastern horizon, turned out to be T'Oridrea. In running before the pirates, we'd overshot Varda. Still, safe harbor was safe harbor, so he made for it gladly. But before the dullest chase and escape I've ever known came to an end, I was resolved to finish the work I'd started. No, not tutoring the dragon—I was a right pillock, there—but scanning the needful bits in Druadaen's bloody book.

Now, mind you: it's not that I *don't* read. I do. When I get the chance. And the spirit moves me. And I don't have something better to do. It's never been a habit, and certainly not a near-religious devotion as with Druadaen. But now, I'm wondering—and fearing for my mind!—that some similar malady has infected me, leaping into my body from right out of the pages of this book! Maybe that's how The Philosopher caught the disease, himself: toiling away his youth in that musty old Archive Esoterica or Exotica or whatever the Dunarrans call that damned mausoleum.

I might have gone through my life, happily immune to this madness, if he'd never packed a handy little tome that natters on about the particulars of the area in which we find ourselves: the Ballashan Littoral.

The Ballash-folk were the first to raise up empires on this coast once the Cataclysm had finished shaking it about. The people here still call themselves "Ballashan," which is wishful thinking, at best; from the start, those empires kept (or were taken by) a long parade of tribute tribes and mercenaries, to say nothing of visits by Dunarra's Consentium and Mihal'j's refugees. And while Ballashan may be the root of the language, it's been bounced around by whatever foreigners have tarried within, or along, the Littoral. The one exception—Taruildor—is also the only inland nation and has separate roots. Seems to prefer it that way, too.

The scribbler responsible for this book claims that the Ballashan empires left their strongest mark upon the habits and traditions that shape the doings of both realms and families. For instance, in all these nations, the final power doesn't ripple out from the throne, but pours out from the doors of those families known for the steady flow of coin and leaders—called *sazhas*—they've loosed upon the country.

Of course, once those who hold power agree amongst themselves that it's their gods-given right to *keep* hold of it, well, that's pretty much the end of any change in that land. Gone is any hope to rise above one's birth or station. And so, it's no different from life under the Ballashan emperors, who are echoed every time some modern sazha explains that their land's happy "stillness" (maybe the correct translation is "paralysis"?) means that there's none of the chop and churn that leads to civil wars, either those that brew up between houses or against kings. To some, such prattle may sound like wisdom, but to my unwashed ear it sounds like a half-truth that can only survive if the other half is strangled. And while I'm the last man to welcome the death and waste of wars, the banning of them has never put an end to the pettiness and greed that *causes* them.

So I was hardly surprised to read that, just as night follows day, the Ballashan became, and have remained, dab hands at plotting assassinations, cajoling lesser houses into trade wars, and bribing faithless bravos to grab or gut the properties of common folk who dare resist. These struggles between the sazhas are a way of life, and those whose skills secure their masters' victories become models for the most sought foot soldiers in these not-wars: liars, toadies, informants, and backstabbers. Small wonder that the appearance of things became more important than their worth, that pageantry and flaunting riches undid any last ties to pointless notions such as oaths and honor.

The most useful pages of the book were those that described the Littoral's five present nations. Among them T'Oridrea makes the best—and loudest—claim to direct Ballashan roots, if for no other reason than the first sazha of the Ballashans was from that land. Whether that's still (or was ever) something to brag about...well, that's another matter. But for good or ill, the last few sazhas have been more than happy to follow in their fathers' ways, some of which are not just blinkered but downright barmy.

Take for instance their belief that there's an eldritch power of prophesy within cats. Yes, cats. From sazha to serf, if your cat shows interest in a guest—whether to rub against their legs or hiss at them from a high shelf—that's held to augur how the outcome of the visit or what may come from it. As if that isn't mad enough, it gave rise to the most daft hanging offense I ever hope to hear of: in T'Oridrea, if a person in a public place is found to be carrying even a small sachet of catnip, it earns them a rope collar.

Another choice bit of strangeness arises from the nobles' need to replace power with prestige. Which means that open battles are replaced with, well, arch snubbery. According to the book, this dates back to one or more early wars that were fought over whose jewels were the most beautiful. Started as a contest between the wives of two sazhas and wound up in battles that left thousands dead, including both husbands and one of the wives. After that, wearing precious stones outside one's abode, or to any gathering, was forbidden. But the sazhas (and probably their wives) weren't willing to give up their contests over who could squander the most coin, so they put their jewels away and began buying land pearls.

Petty cretins that they were, they wasted no time shifting their old jewelry jealousies over to the land pearls and never once saw any irony that they are naught but the waste of rock snails. Didn't matter, of course; one piece of rubbish was as good as the next when it came to jockeying for position. Just as it had been with gems, a slight to the pearl was a slight to the wearer. The same duels and vendettas resulted.

Not to be spared the madness of their social betters, poorer and crafty sazhas learned how to create faithful copies, using a process much like the one by which beads are made. When that was discovered, a special guild arose to test whether what appeared to be land pearl was, in fact, a land pearl. That led to a way of making better fakes, which led to better tests, and round and round until the Great Sazha finally decreed that all the land pearls must go, just like the jewels before them. So, in the end, even the most legendary and precious of these shiny gobs of snail shite disappeared, stored beside the dusty gemstones in the thrice-locked treasuries of all true aristocrats. But the common folk had the last laugh, because the wearing of simple beads had spread widely among them and continues to this very day, whether as signs of rank, marks of allegiance, or merely eye-pleasing ornaments.

Most of the other nations are cut from much the same inherited cloth. By population, the largest is our missed destination of Varda. Originally a poorer cousin to T'Oridrea, it was often a haven for landless peasants, criminals, exiled sazhas or vassals, and other outcasts from the old empire's rigid social order. It became matters of pride that they were always full-ready to reject the bastards who'd rejected them and that displays of wealth were to be met with scorn and savage parody. So it was that, more out of cussedness than conviction, they came to value competence, fairness, and toughness. Despite the social differences that still exist, any grown person—man or woman—may challenge anyone else if a "premagistrate" approves their claim of injury. The matter may be settled by contest or trial, but it seems that most prefer to duel.

Rettarisha, the northernmost of the Littoral lands, has more Torvan in its language and habits than the others. As one would expect of the descendants of those wandering warrior (some say barbarian) tribes, the monarch must answer to the nobles, and it is they who are responsible for upholding the common law. Mostly.

The last of the four nations is not Ballashan and not really part of the Littoral. With the exception of ten miles of mostly useless coastline, Taruildor is an inland nation descended from tribes that the empire invited to live nearby in exchange for their protection. The country's language, customs, and warrior code are a hodgepodge of what the Torvan and Connyl peoples brought with them when they arrived to dwell in and guard the mountain range that shielded T'Oridrea from invasions coming up out of the Shapnapa Desert. Proudly (not to say stubbornly) set in their own ways, they never adopted Ballashan manners or speech, but kept to the hills and stony valleys of the land they'd paid for in blood.

That was the last I read from the book before we

stepped over the little bark's side to set foot on the wharves of Yu'Serda, first city of T'Oridrea. It took a while to get our bearings; these docks are the liveliest and most confusing I have ever seen.

But I cannot deny that, except for the occasional hide-shawled and dour Taruildorean, the noisy, haggling throngs seem perfectly happy with the arrangement. There's a mood on the planks and among the roped-off tables of fare and of chance that if you have business in Yu'Serda, you should be hoarse and sweaty with the doing of it—or you're just not trying hard enough. And so the great, gaudy show remained loud and frantic as the sun sank over the purple horizon of the Great Western Ocean. Newly arrived merchants began replacing those who, business concluded, retired to the rope-pubs and settled back with drinks or pipes or spiced nuts in hand to watch the next act in the continuing drama of shoulder-shoving trade and barter.

And gods be shocked, but before leaving to find lodging, we saw a familiar face in one of the larger bazaars: Captain Firinne of the *Swiftsure*, she who'd provided our first passage from Dunarra to Far Amitryea, now a year and a few odd-moonphases ago. It took us a bit of walking and patience to find a quiet—well, less deafening—spot in the lee of double-stacked crates. We traded news, during which she learned of our long walk from the Medvir Bight and peculiar circumstances. She *tsk*ed mightily upon learning how the ship from Uershael lost its way and foundered, and was so generous as to once again offer us working passage to any place on her route or any short detour to a destination that was beneficial for the *Swiftsure*, as well.

Before any of us could reply, Varcaxtan hastily revealed that we'd already chatted with a few captains, including one who was also owner-aboard on a free merchant out of Menara. He was already heading south around Anatha Damianna, had the berths to give us passage to his home port, or any other on the way there. And although there'd been no promises made, he'd hinted that he might be amenable to accepting a lower fare if we agreed to protect his hull while aboard.

Firinne nodded her understanding, made suggestions for lodgings that were unlikely to prove fatal choices, and wished us very well. We returned her courtesies, careful not to let on that Varcaxtan had, well, if not lied, made it sound like we'd had many discussions about possible passage with many captains. In fact, the only who had free berths was the one who ran the merchantman out of Menara, but who hadn't responded one way or the other when *we* offered to defend the ship in exchange for passage. As Firinne departed, none of us asked why he'd not shared the simple truth with her; that we were bound for Mirroskye. After all, it was now behind her, not before.

As we made our way off the wharves, Varcaxtan in the lead, the rest of us traded occasional glances that confirmed what we all suspected: that each of us was eager to ask him the same question. But we didn't do so until we'd plunked down our belongings in the cheapest place to sleep, a "salt flop": that is, rooms for mariners on a short stay, without meals or even a privy. S'ythreni (always shy and retiring) was the one who started the inquisition, pressing him to explain why he'd lied at all, much less to a fellow Dunarran who'd proven herself our friend on several occasions.

"To protect her," he said miserably.

"How so?" asked Umkhira with a deeper frown than usual.

Elweyr nodded, first to understand. "Because when she makes port anywhere in Dunarra, she'll be honor bound to report her conversation with him."

Varcaxtan nodded. "It's a near certainty she doesn't yet know that my location might be of especial interest to the Consentium. And if some temple's testy orthologe gets wind of her report, they may be able to pressure the Propretoriate to detain her."

"To what end?" asked Cerven.

"Why, to gather a detailed account of her meeting with me, and perhaps, her dealings with Druadaen and his associates." He looked meaningfully around at us. "Besides, if I'd let on we were bound for Mirroskye, she might even have decided to detour there as a favor."

I nodded. "She's done as much before. And gods only know that if she did that and *then* made her report, I doubt the Propretor Princeps himself could have convinced the temples that she'd given us passage innocently."

"It is unfortunate that the powerful temples and mantics of Dunarra cannot be asked for help," Umkhira said, "inasmuch as they are the ones who seem most knowledgeable about the portals that we seek."

Varcaxtan tilted his head slightly. "Well, Lightstrider, it was probably Dunarrans manipulating the portals in question, but Ahearn's ring is right; we'll do best seeking counsel from the Uulamantre. They've deep knowledge of such mancery."

"More than Dunarrans?" Umkhira wondered.

"Much more. We're latecomers to any kind of cosmancy. And even if that wasn't the case, any mention of Druadaen or me will not quicken any helpful hearts in our own land."

S'ythreni's voice was sly. "What about unofficial help?"

Varcaxtan glanced at her, kindly but firm. "Alva S'ythreni, what would you think of me if I were to involve old friends in troubles that invite the scrutiny of both the temples and the state?"

She blinked, lowered her chin slightly, and murmured, "*Veth, Attu'tir* Varcaxtan."

I'd never heard the title *Attu'tir* before, but I waited until all of us were busy with unpacking our kits before drifting over to Elweyr and muttering, "Attu'tir? That's a new one to me."

Elweyr leaned close and whispered, "It is a term reserved for non-Iavarain. It means 'honored.' Few of us earn that title."

Well, I suppose that's what I get, trading one Dunarran for another! With them, it's always lofty titles and loftier chatter as thick as the moss on a tinker's roof. Hopefully all my learned companions will be able to set their blinkin' eloquence aside long enough to mingle with the earthy crowd down by the docks. At least until we've found a ship to Mirroskye.

CHAPTER TWENTY-TWO

Ahearn stared at his oldest friend, who slumped rather than sat at their assigned table. "Yer glum as a starvin' crow, Elweyr."

"I'm fine," he answered, tugging irritably at the truce-bonding on his shortsword. The bell—lashed into the bond-knot to keep it from ringing—clanked as he adjusted the scabbard.

"Yer fine?" Ahearn persisted. "An' when have you—or any mantic, fer that matter—ever been 'fine'? You're a gloomy lot by nature, so spit it out, man: exactly what rat is nibblin' yer toes *now*?"

S'ythreni sat next to Elweyr, shot a knowing glance at him. "He doesn't like the 'rope-pub' rules."

"Well, which one of us does?" Ahearn asked, both hands out, imploring. "Y'think I like having my sword trussed like a hen for roasting?"

The others glanced at the thaumancer. They'd all made their peace with the first and foremost rule of the "rope-houses" that dotted Yu'Serda's wider wharfs. You weren't allowed inside the defining rope—or cable or railing—until your weapons had been "truce-bonded": secured with knots that were not easy to undo and rang when yanked or cut apart. Elweyr just shrugged off their stares.

Ahearn leaned forward, but before he could press further, S'ythreni murmured, "It's not his sword." She rolled her eyes when Ahearn raised a single unenlightened eyebrow. "It's the oath to refrain from mancery."

Ahearn had hardly noticed that part of the rules when they'd been read out. "Ah, well now, that's not so different from us tying off our weapons, is it?"

Elweyr sighed. "That's not what bothers me." Ahearn's steady, questioning stare prompted an expansion. "I don't like lying."

"How have you lied?"

Elweyr glanced at his friend's truce-bonded weapons. "You don't have any choice but to obey. I do."

"Aye . . . and so?"

"And so, they didn't ask if I'm a mantic. And I can use thaumates which they'd never even notice."

The conversation paused as a very fair serving-lad slapped down the drinks that had been the price of their entry. Cerven frowned at his as the fellow departed in a rush. "Does it not seem likely that the proprietors would have some method of detecting active mancery?" Intent on Elweyr's response, he distractedly downed his drink at a gulp.

His eyes widened as he swallowed, then coughed and sputtered.

"What did you *do*, lad?" Varcaxtan asked in alarm.

"I . . . I drank the juice."

"Lad, I can *see* that. Do you really think you're the match of *fire-fruit* juice?"

"Evidently not," Cerven muttered. "I ... I feel strange."

The dragon sighed, sent a long-suffering glance around the table. "Let me guess: this is not simply the juice of something called a fire-fruit?"

Ahearn was finally certain he could speak with a straight face. "Eh. No. Heh, hmm, eh, no. It's made from a mash of roasted fruits. A mash that's well fermented."

"For a very, *very* long time," Varcaxtan added with the solicitous concern that had been half of Ahearn's inspiration to nickname him "Uncle."

"Well," Cerven said, staring at the tabletop. He started to tilt, righted himself. "Well!" he added, still staring.

They'd been seeking passage to Mirroskye for two days with nothing to show for the effort. The trader out of Menara had shown no interest in their services as defenders of his hull and, in the time they'd given him to think it over, had filled his remaining berths. So they were back where they started, but with an added challenge; they'd checked with the captains of almost every vessel in port, so the field of possibilities was far smaller than when they'd started.

"I am less than certain that captains of Davyara-Nadian ships frequent this pub," muttered S'ythreni, "no matter what we've been told."

"Why so?"

"Because it seems like too civilized a place for such boors."

Cerven was staring into his empty cup as if more

fire-fruit juice might have appeared in it while he wasn't looking. "Such hard words are . . . are most unlike you, S'ythre—er, Alva."

"I've got to ask; haven't you *listened* to her these past eight moonphases?" Ahearn's murmur was equal parts wry and wondering.

Which S'ythreni naturally heard and just as naturally ignored. "I think he means hard words *without apparent cause.*" She turned to the bleary-eyed lad. "Any Davyaran who calls himself Davyara-*Nadian* is not to be trusted."

"Wha-wha—I mean, why, Alva S'ythreni?"

"Because the sazha of the Nadia family, which had been exiled generations before, was granted a pardon in exchange for military service against urzhen who'd broken a tribal treaty. The Nadians returned to the capital with trophies from that victory—and slew the entire ruling family of Davyara as they waited to congratulate the victors on the steps of the Sazhale, the palace of the Great Sazha."

Cerven nodded, eyes so fixed on S'ythreni that he didn't realize it when he took her cup instead of his and began draining it.

She sputtered in surprise. Ahearn caught hold of the lad's wrist. "Here now, what do you think yer doin'?"

"Having my drink?" Cerven stated uncertainly, punctuating it with a belch that stunned him more than anyone else.

"Yeh had yer drink. And now half of hers," Ahearn explained, prying his fingers off the cup. "Which is ten times more'n you should have."

"More like twenty times," observed Elweyr with a smile. After which he sat upright abruptly, eyes riveted on the gate. "Is that a—?"

"Davyaran," finished S'ythreni with a nod. "Not wearing any orange, so not a Nadian. Well, maybe we can find a good ship here, after all."

The fellow in question was allowed through the rope "gate" after his curved dagger had been truce-bonded. Ahearn silently congratulated himself and his companions on remaining unobtrusive as they watched the lithe fellow—until Cerven started craning his neck and asking questions in a whisper loud enough to wake zealots from dreams of their creedland. "'Zat him, there? What—is he walking or dancing?"

It's a fair question, Ahearn allowed, smiling at the Davyaran. In the same moment, he hugged Cerven close enough to muffle his mouth in the space between his armpit and the side of his bulging pectoral. The Davyaran moved just as S'ythreni had told them one of their trained warriors might: long, fluid steps, every action flowing seamlessly into the next, the overall visual effect accentuated by his light, loose clothes.

"Mrmph—phrmphh!" Cerven's breathless squall portended suffocation—just before Ahearn released him. "Sorry if yeh couldn't breathe," Ahearn apologized quietly.

The panting lad's pallor seemed more a portent of nausea, however. "I could breathe," Cerven replied with a fearful glance at the big man's sweaty armpit, "but I couldn't bear doing so."

Ahearn resisted the impulse to smother him again for good measure. But the Davyaran had altered course to their table. "Hold yer peace," he muttered out of the corner of his mouth closest to the wobble-eyed Cerven.

But the man dance-walked up to S'ythreni, instead.

He bowed very deeply, and from that position, murmured, "I have no wish to intrude."

"But you deem it necessary. Please be at your ease."

He straightened smoothly, but glanced nervously at Umkhira. "I have no knowledge of how aeosti, my race, Dunarrans, and urzh could travel together, but I must warn you, it invites . . . rudeness, from the folk of this land."

"And by rudeness, you mean—?"

"He means pillorying at the least, vivisection at the worst," the dragon announced before the Davyaran could formulate a more courtly reply. "Is that the gist of what you intended to say, albeit with more euphonious and numerous words?"

The Davyaran gaped at the dragon, his mouth working mutely.

It was that reaction which renewed Ahearn's awareness of just how incongruous a character the dragon had become when in a typical crowd. It wasn't just the sly and almost sardonic expression on the large-featured face, marked by all manner of tribal tattoos. It wasn't even the vague hint of arrogance imparted by the overly straight—and now clean-shaven—ox-neck. No, the truly arresting juxtapositions were the closely trimmed goatee and pencil-thin moustache—oiled and scented—and the vivid colors it had added to its garments wherever possible: oranges, magentas, and bright greens, all hallmarks of Ballashan court-wear. And whereas Ahearn admitted that his own manly pungency might not be pleasing, he could not fathom how any creature furnished with a nose could abide the perfumes in which the dragon apparently bathed. Any one of the many scents—flowers, barks, ambergris—was retch-worthy, but all of them *together*? It was a wonder that the dragon didn't leave a trail of bodies in its broad downwind wake.

Umkhira glanced at the Davyaran, cutting her head toward the dragon. "Our friend R'aonsun is plainspoken," she supplied.

That snapped the courtier-warrior out of his daze. "Plainspoken? Truly. Yet with words that are anything but plain." He smiled at her, but was frowning as he did so. "Thank you for reminding me of my business, er, madam." When she blinked in surprise, he shook his head. "My apologies; I do not know how your people would address you. We used to, in my land, but that died with the treaties."

"The treaties?" she echoed doubtfully.

Understanding widened his eyes. "So—you are not from these lands?"

She shook her head. The others followed her lead, but his raised hand made clear it was unnecessary. "With respects, there was no mistaking the rest of you for anything *but* foreigners. Which is why I intruded, since you seem unaware how much unwanted attention the...the *mix* of your company might attract."

"Due to—?" began Cerven, slurring the words.

"Due to me," Umkhira nodded, frowning.

"I wish it was not true, but it is. Where are you from, if I may be so bold to ask?"

"My people hunt upon the Plains of Hasgar, north of Khassant."

He frowned. "That is quite far. Many hundreds of leagues to the northeast, near the borders of the Consentium."

She shrugged. "As you might measure it, yes."

"And that," added a gruff voice in which Ahearn heard the burr and buzz of a vaguely familiar accent, "is why they've no reck of how the Lady Lightstrider will be seen in these benighted lands."

They looked behind their table.

Sitting mostly concealed by a row of old crates that served as a ramshackle counter for mugs and plates, a grizzled fellow was arranging a hide shawl so that the breeze would pass under as much of it as possible. "Damned hot, this thing," he explained as they stared.

Cerven swayed over to get a better look, almost fell across Ahearn's lap. "He's a...he's from...eh..."

"Taruildor," Ahearn answered, smiling at the man, speaking loud enough for the other to hear him. "Uplander, judging from the kind of hide."

The grizzled man looked up in surprise. "Y' ken me land, stranger?"

"Only by reputation," Ahearn admitted, hastily recalling what Druadaen's book had said of that people. "Your tongue is mostly Torvan and Connyl, if I remember right."

"Well, you've the order of those peoples wrong, but I'll forgive 'ee that." He glanced at Umkhira. "The Davyaran dandy is right enow about how these folk see ye, Lady Lightstrider. They reck no difference between ye and yer kin, I'll wager." When Cerven stared, Varcaxtan supplied, "Down here along the coast, no one knows there are differences among urzhen."

"The unwaller speaks aright, 'e does," the Taruildorean agreed as Umkhira nodded. "Our own flatlanders aren't much keener to the truth than the Ballashan, mind you, but we uplanders know. It's we who fight urzhen in the mountains. And make peace with 'em. And make babes with 'em too, often enow."

He smiled sadly at Umkhira. "O'course, beside your lands, our mountains are but hills and our farms and ranges feed nary a tenth the mouths—which means nay enow food and no deep places to hide. So rather than the great Hordeings of your own kith, urzh here must raid oft and again. And that's why, from yonder sea to my mountains, every town has a wall."

"Which is why,". Varcaxtan said, leaning toward Cerven, "he called me an unwaller."

"Why? D'narra's nothing *but* walls. I look'd atta *map*!" Cerven interjected.

"Those are our wallways, which were built to protect the canals behind them and put a roadway up where enemies can't reach. But because they've never been breached, very few of our towns have walls."

Cerven nodded vigorously. "So, e'en though theys urzh all over—all over th' *world*!—is always differ'nt for 'em, wherever they are."

Umkhira shook her head. "Except for one thing that never changes: wherever we go, we are reviled."

The Davyaran made a faint bow in her direction. "I sorely wish I could contradict you but, Helpers know, I try to live within the currents of truth."

"Aye, well'n it's high time you come by me and we conclude our business, Fancy Man."

The Davyaran smiled. "Coming by you means coming closer to that clan hide you're wearing."

"Aye, an' what's wrong with it?"

"The smell."

"You nervy fop! Ye'd insult me clan's totem, then?"

"Not your totem or your clan; just your irregular

dedication to bathing." He smiled and bowed to the group. "You will forgive me; I must arrange travel home."

"Back to Zodera?" S'ythreni asked quickly.

"Alas, not so far as that, Alva," he answered sadly. "Like you, I am not welcome in the capital. It has been a privilege to meet you all." He walked—almost danced—around the end of their table to join the growling Taruildorean, who, Ahearn finally noticed, only had one arm with which to bear-hug the much younger Davyaran.

No sooner had he moved to the inconspicuous table behind them than a large group of men approached the rope-pub's "gate." Hovering somewhere between boisterous and belligerent, they derided or debated every point of the rules before consenting to them and entering the space with bellows for drink, food, and other services that were, to Ahearn's imperfect knowledge, only offered in establishments with actual walls.

Elweyr scanned the new arrivals. "Can't figure out where they hail from," he mused testily.

"All over, from the look of them," the dragon conjectured as he took a sip of the fire-fruit juice. He made a face, shuddered, set the drink aside.

Ahearn tried not to sound proud, but knew he was failing—miserably—as he launched into his answer. "Actually, there's at least one from every Ballashan nation of the Littoral."

Elweyr raised an eyebrow. Varcaxtan did the same, but with a small smile. Cerven swayed in a small, unsteady circle on his seat and breathed out vapors so densely acrid that Ahearn imagined he could see them. "Really?" the young Amitryean goggled. He gestured at the loud pack. "Which are which...are which?" he asked, confusing himself by the end.

Ahearn resisted the impulse to point. "See all the ones with beads on their clothes, either woven in or on tassels? They're T'Oridreans."

Umkhira's eyebrows rose. "They are beautiful, but I see no other ornaments."

"You won't," Ahearn explained. "Jewels, gold, all the rest were forbidden almost a thousand years ago by royal decree. For a while they were still allowed land pearls but they couldn't keep from insulting each other—and dueling—over 'em. So now it's all just beads."

"Some look very similar," Elweyr said, squinting.

"That's because over the years, certain beads became tokens: of titles, positions, guilds, even royal or noble favor. And the little differences you can see? Those mean greater or lesser ranks within each."

"There's one wearing no beads at all," Umkhira said, pointing to a thin man in rags, moving between the dozen newcomers with a jug of mead.

Ahearn shook his head sadly. "No beads means no rights. None at all."

"So...a slave?"

"Less than that." Ahearn had to unclench his teeth. "A slave is owned—and they've got a particularly rough lot here in T'Oridrea. But they've at least got one gray bead. But that fellow without a bead?" He shook his head. "Anyone can do anything to him at any time."

Cerven was scanning the dozen men uncertainly. "Some are wearing thatches—ehm, sashes."

"From Varda," Ahearn said casually. "The shoulder

drape has small badges that are a record of any challenges they've won."

"You mean, duels?" asked the dragon.

"Could be, but it could be a contest or a legal trial, also. Except for the titles of their toffs, they're a tough lot who've done away with a lot of the Ballashan frippery."

"Is that why their clothes are so dull?" Cerven wondered. Without waiting for an answer, he added, "Almost as dull as the ones with um—wood badges?— on their tunics."

"If you were closer," Ahearn clarified, "you'd see those badges are all in the shape of axes, which marks them as being from Rettarisha."

"The axe was the sign of authority among the ancient Torvan tribes," murmured Elweyr as if remembering a history lesson.

"Who made up over half of Rettarisha's population when the last Ballashan empire fell." Ahearn couldn't help canting his voice a bit lower as if sharing a secret. "Now, if you got close enough, you'd see that each of those axes is carved from a different wood. 'Aromatics,' they're called, and each one of the ancient tribes claimed one as their own. These days some of that wood is still burned in censors in the halls of their rulers. Sometimes it's even set into the hafts of their weapons."

Varcaxtan smiled. "All of which carry 'the smell of nobility,' according to Rettarishan aristocrats." His tone became dark. "Their peasants call it something different, though: the smell of blood."

Ahearn nodded, managing to conceal his chagrin. *Leave it to a damned Outrider to know a detail that* isn't *in Druadaen's blasted book!* On a moment's reflection, however, Ahearn allowed that this particular tidbit of local color sounded too grim to have made its way into a scholarly tome.

"*Ai-hai!*" cried a startled patron in the midst of the new arrivals. "What's happened to this pub? Were one of the ropes cut?"

"Why?" asked a genuinely surprised voice from further back in the pack.

"Why, look what's drinkin' in here with us!" The source of the voice—a man almost as large as Ahearn—stepped forth, pointing with a quivering index finger.

Straight at Umkhira.

A-hey and here we go. Ahearn turned toward her; she noticed his steady gaze an instant before realizing that she had become the object of the other group's attention. Umkhira frowned at her friend but flicked her eyes in assent. They'd foreseen the possibility of just such bigotry and had made plans for dealing with it—mostly by ignoring it as long as possible. A fight—even a fierce dispute—could lead to being detained by authorities who had regard for only two things: beads of high rank or a bribe of high value. And they had neither.

"I thought this was a 'spectable establishment!" the big man said. "But they let Bent in here, now! And a sow, no less!"

Umkhira began to rise. Ahearn's palm pushed down toward the tabletop as the dragon muttered in her direction. "If you mean to continue searching for Druadaen and Indryllis, you must keep your head clear."

"And your weapon truced," added Elweyr from the other side.

"Now you boys, don't hold her back!" shouted her sizable tormentor as a few intervening patrons scattered away from the wharf planks separating the two groups. "Bent-bitch loins are always ready for a bit of masculine entertainment." He guffawed, pawed at himself with one hand and reached out toward her with the other.

CHAPTER TWENTY-THREE

It was S'ythreni who responded, quicker than thought. "Use that hand to entertain yourself—as must be your common practice," she spat at the brute. "That is, if you're up to it." Laughter and hoots met her sally. The big fellow's face became very red.

An especially well-attired man stepped from out of the mass of them, scanning for the source of the retort. His orange sleeves were like flutters of late-sun rays as he gestured toward S'ythreni with both hands and cried, "Ah hah, I thought so! A tree-bugger, as I live and breathe! Oh, there's sport to be had here, men!"

She nodded at his bright sleeves. "What Nadians call sport, most people call murder—you womb-souring beast."

The man turned a surprised gape into a histrionically shocked "Oh, my! Such a mouth on the fairy-eared free-martin! I think she needs a lesson in manners, don't you all agree?" He glanced to either side and started forward. At a nod from the bigger man, the other ten began to fan out to either side.

Ahearn leaned his head close to S'ythreni's, which was jutting forward like a stooping falcon's. He felt her breath fast and hot on his cheek as he whispered, "You land the first blow and there will be a massacre. Of every one of us."

"Can't happen unless they draw weapons," she muttered back. "And if they do that—"

"Oh, this just keeps getting better!" the leader exclaimed, pointing past S'ythreni. She and Ahearn turned to follow the shift in his attention.

The young Davyaran had stood, rising above the crates that had obscured him and his Taruildorean friend. "You shall not lay a hand on the aeosti," he said calmly, walking as if he meant to interpose himself between S'ythreni and the dozen rough men approaching.

Ah, fer the love of gold 'n garters—Ahearn raised his hands, one thrust forward to hold back the mob, the other behind to stop the Davyaran. "Let's all stop right where we are."

"Piss off," said the big man. "You—!"

He was waved to silence by the leader, who spoke with such cool contemptuousness that it actually helped Ahearn check his temper. "Perhaps you are not aware, barbarian, but this is a pub. That's short for '*public house*.' So we walk where we please and say what we like." He continued his approach, the widening rank of his men close behind him. "And as a Loyalist *sozh* in the service of Great Sazha Kohejh of Davyara-Nadia, I am pleased to call the fop hiding behind your skirts a traitor. To both his nation and his kind."

Before the Davyaran could make reply or Ahearn

could intervene, S'ythreni leaned even further forward,
fury seething out along with her retort. "It's said that
Loyalist nobles aspire to be as the Great Sazha. So
I presume that you are as great a liar and murderer
as he is?"

The *sozh*'s big sergeant started forward. "You man-
bitch! I'll tear your—!"

A young, unsteady voice interrupted. "S'rrah! Have
yooo no-shame? Sush deplobba—diplora—debloro...
Sush *terrible* language addressed to a lady!"

"Well, is she a...a *she*, then?" the angry sergeant
roared.

He was stopped by the leader's left hand on his
chest. "By the gods of Serdarong himself," he breathed,
pointing with his right. "That voice, that accent: is
that a young Dunarran? In his cups?"

Cerven swayed upright again. "Jus' one cup. I think."
He shook his head. "But notta Dunar'n."

"You damn well sound like one!" the big man
growled, scanning the group before him as if trying
to choose which he should attack first.

"Thaz nice you to say, but I'm nawtha Dunurn."
Cerven gestured over his shoulder at Varcaxtan. "*He* is."

Ahearn closed his eyes. *Bollocks.*

The leader seemed ready to dance for joy as he
studied Varcaxtan. "My, oh my! We have an actual
*Dooo*narran among us!" He bowed. "So honored. Back
to conquer and ruin us again?"

Ahearn sighed, rose from his chair. *There's the
old Ballashan pride, as thick and wounded as ever.*

Varcaxtan simply stared at the leader's orange sleeves.

The big man stepped toward him. "Ye're a smug,
unwalled coward, you are!"

Varcaxtan shook his head and began moving... away. "Say what you will, you'll have no trouble from me. If I give offense, I shall retire."

"Do that, yeh arrogant bastard of an arrogant race!"

Varcaxtan had reached the smaller gate reserved for those exiting the rope-pub. He lifted the cymbal used to request permission to leave, glanced at Ahearn and the others, and tilted his head toward the double-stranded gate-rope.

Before anyone could move to follow the Dunarran's lead, the sergeant roared, "Oi, you left something behind, lick-spittle!"

Varcaxtan turned, raised an eyebrow.

"See, you've forgotten your young sweet cheeks!" the large man exclaimed, gesturing to Cerven, who was head down on the table. "You wouldn't want to waste all the coin you spent, getting him good and drunk. Betcha can't sleep without at least one go at 'im!"

"Or three!" shouted a Vardan.

From twenty feet away, Ahearn could hear Varcaxtan's teeth grind sharply. But he did not move.

The leader picked up where his sergeant had left off. "What? Not enough excitement for you?" He jutted his chin at Umkhira. "Well, bring the darger bitch with you, then. She's man enough to bugger both of you, I wager!"

Ahearn had to reach out to restrain Umkhira, who yelled defiance at the whole crowd. "I am not 'dark get,' imbecile! I am ur zhog, a Lightstrider." Their answer was laughter and one cry of "Oi! Look! It talks!"

Varcaxtan, however, had taken his hand from the gate-rope. His voice was sharp. "I told you I'd leave. Is that not enough?"

"It'll be enough when you leave the whole sodding world, you amoral bastard!" the leader yelled, his sardonic courtliness stripping away in an eyeblink.

The dragon stood; several of the roughs had to tilt their necks to look up at him. "Amoral," it chuckled. "That's really quite amusing...especially coming from *you*."

Instead of retreating, the leader stepped closer, looked up from the level of the dragon's collarbone. "I don't care how big you are, you prissy barbarian." His smile became savored contempt as he studied the carefully groomed body from head to foot. He ended by poking a finger against the immense chest. "Heh. No amount of cat-house perfume will keep mites from breeding in your dirty fur or crabs away from your putrid bollocks—assuming you have any!"

The dragon stared at the finger jammed against its sternum, then looked the leader full in the face. "Always sexual innuendo with your breed. How banal." It glanced at Ahearn over the man's head. "I forgot to mention that I noticed a strange omission in this establishment's truce rules."

"What's that?"

"Although we were required to forswear weapons, we did not promise to refrain from fighting."

"By damn, you're right!" Ahearn turned to the leader of their antagonists. "Did *you* know that?"

"Know what?"

"That we're allowed to do this." Ahearn's fist—thrown straight from the shoulder—cracked into the man's chin. Senseless, he went backward and crashed to the planks underfoot.

A lot of ducking and punching followed. Unlike

melees with weapons, Ahearn found brawls difficult to keep track of. Too many people, moving too fast, getting too close—and none of the occasional pauses as two opponents with lethal weapons sized each other up for an opening that was optimal for their own weapon and minimized the threat from their opponent's.

The Davyaran was in the fray almost immediately, his distinctive fighting style allowing him to stand off two adversaries—until a third joined in and they mobbed him. With a banshee screech, S'ythreni was on their backs, landing sharp, savage strikes to undefended kidneys. Umkhira cleared the table in a leap, got snagged in midair by the big sergeant, who threw her over his shoulder—or meant to: she hung on and dragged him with her. The two of them sprawling awkwardly across the widest stretch of the rope-pub's planks.

Three attackers clustered around the dragon, which should have been the end of them all. But what little tutoring Ahearn provided him was on how to fight with weapons, not hands and feet. Consequently, R'aonsun usually missed, but when he landed a blow, there was a good chance that the person hit was not getting up soon. If at all.

Using the dragon's body to block his own flank, Elwevr had tucked in behind Varcaxtan. As the Dunarran made his way steadily through defenders—he seemed the best trained for this kind of fight—the thaumancer was clearly doing something to the older man's opponents. Irregularly mistaking each other for the enemy, they only realized their confusion at the last possible instant—which was usually when Varcaxtan landed a heavy blow to one or the other's head.

Ahearn intercepted a man in local garb who, without warning, leaped up from a table toward S'ythreni's back: whether planted there by the leader or simply another bigot with similar hatreds, there was no knowing. And no need to: he didn't see Ahearn angling toward him until the swordsman's fist thudded into his gut. His wind blew out in a single, sharp hoot and he fell aside.

Ahearn turned to help S'ythreni, who was trying to fight off the men who'd flattened the Davyaran. Ahearn closed on one of his intended targets—and watched him topple forward, senseless—revealing the Taruildorean behind him, wielding a small iron mug with a family crest.

The fight was clearly turning in their favor and Ahearn was ready to call for the remaining attackers to yield when the dragon let out a surprised cry and backed up, blood spattering the planks as he retreated. "Knife!" shouted Varcaxtan.

Ahearn, wondering how the Dunarran could see the cause so quickly and surely among the flashing limbs and twisting bodies, swerved toward the rear flank of the dragon's attackers. One of whom heard him coming and swung around, slashing with a short, broad knife as he did. Ahearn leaped back, began to circle—and blinked when an airborne body slammed into his opponent's.

Whether it was the number of the attackers who were down or nursing injuries at that particular moment, or the display of furious urzhen strength that had sent one of them crashing into another, the remaining attackers broke and made for the exit—but discovered it held against them by the rope-pub's staff. And Umkhira was standing nearby, ready to keep them penned in. They dashed for the rope "walls"—but few managed to duck under or leap over them; the feet of patrons tripped them as they ran, and the proprietor's enforcers were on them in a moment. Near the bar, a loud cymbal began crashing; an instant later, a high-pitched clangor of militia bells began answering from every point of the compass that did not border on water.

With the exception of Umkhira, the rest converged on the dragon, who still had a knife stuck in his somewhat heavy midriff. "I appear to be wounded," the big being observed as if he were remarking on a jar of spilled milk.

"I'd say so!" Ahearn exclaimed. Turning to the gathering crowd, he cried, "Is there a physician close at hand? Ship's physicker?"

"Calm yourself," the dragon muttered. "It is not a serious injury."

"No," Elweyr muttered as he pulled away the last of the dragon's shirt and inspected the wounds, "it's *two* serious injuries. One lateral slash and one puncture which is still bleeding heavily. I can't see if the blade broke off in you, or—"

"Allow me to assist," the dragon said, and before anyone foresaw what it meant to do, he yanked out the knife.

Ahearn and his company gasped, as did the crowd beyond them.

"Be still!" it commanded. "It was merely obstructing the ministrations of my half-skilled friend." He grinned down at Elweyr.

Who growled up at him. "Hope you're happy with yourself. Look at the blood pouring out of you now. I'll need to find a way to sew you up."

"Tosh. You are making a ridiculous fuss."

Varcaxtan had come to stand nearby. "Lie down, Dra—er, R'aonsun."

"What? You, too? This is nonsense. I'm perfectly fit as I am."

"No," Ahearn insisted, "you're bleeding like a stuck pig!"

"I am?" The dragon seemed genuinely interested. "Do pigs bleed more rapidly than other farm animals? I never noticed . . . and I've had many opportunities to do so."

"Gods and gophers, will you please shut up?"

"And hold still," muttered Elweyr. "I'm going to have to sear this wound closed."

"You are being ridiculous, all of you. I feel no pain at the point of injury. I am certain it is merely a flesh wound. Accordingly, I shall now—" The dragon's eyes wavered, then rolled back into its head. It fell face first to the planking.

Elweyr sighed. "Will someone—well, will a *few of you* roll him over so I can get that bleeding stopped?"

It ultimately took four people—Ahearn, Varcaxtan, and two large men from the crowd—to get the dragon's avatar on its back so that Elweyr could bring his limited medical skills to bear on the injuries.

Once the deeper wound had been staunched and seared closed, Elweyr leaned back and mopped sweat from his brow.

"So, it seems to have been a bit more than a flesh wound," Ahearn commented drily.

"Well, it was more like a fat wound. Which is why *he* couldn't feel it: still too much blubber on the belly, even since the drag—shite!—since *R'aonsun* changed his habits." Elweyr shook his head, muttered. "And I keep forgetting to call him—"

Ahearn murmured. "I know. We call R'aonsun 'it,' but the rest of the world expects, 'he.' Can't keep that up."

Elweyr nodded. "Remind me never to come anywhere near this cursed part of the world again."

"Hmmph!" snorted S'ythreni. "This general 'part of the world' is where you first met *me*."

Elweyr's glance was baleful. "Do you really think I, or anyone else, would confuse Eslêntecrë with *this* part of the world?" the mantic muttered as he poured a vial of sharp-smelling liquid into the much shallower slash across the dragon's belly.

S'ythreni rolled her eyes. "How wonderfully facile you are. Particularly for a human." She straightened up from her crouch. "Well, this was very diverting, but let's be on our way."

The Taruildorean raised his iron tankard to point at the rope-pub's proprietor, who had wormed his way to the front rank of the crowd surrounding the fallen combatants. "I reck that he wishes words on that matter."

Ahearn turned to face the sharp-eyed pub-keep, discovered that three of his employees—two men and a very heavily built woman—had naked daggers resting against various unprotected parts of Umkhira's body. Including, most significantly, her neck. "Let her go," Ahearn muttered. "She did nothing other than defend herself."

"Might be so, but I saw clear enough who threw the first punch." The man's eyes crinkled in a cruel smile as he kept them on Ahearn's. "Also, it seems that some mancery was at play during the scuffle." He produced a periapt from just below the neckline of his tunic; it was glowing faintly. "Can't say by whom, or what it was, but it surely didn't come from this lot." He jutted his chin at their fallen attackers.

"It was me," Elweyr said loudly, "and it was a means of warding against their attacks, not mounting one of my own." Which was arguably true, but the opposite case could be made also—assuming there was a detailed inquiry into exactly what kind of thaumate he'd brought forth.

The proprietor shook his head. "Can't know it was as you say."

"Can't know it wasn't, either!" S'ythreni objected.

The proprietor's smile became even more predatory. "Yes, but the law is clear. You lot started this brawl, and so I am within my rights to choose to hold you responsible for damages caused by either side."

"I saw it all," called a firm, and familiar, woman's voice, "and the ones still standing did not start the combat." The speaker rose from the other side of the central U-shaped bar, opposite where the attackers had been gathered. It was Captain Firinne of the *Swiftsure*.

"You're blind, you unwall—Dunarran. We all saw it plain as day! This brute of a man hit Nawdgat right in the face."

"On the chin, actually," corrected Ahearn.

Elweyr's swift elbow almost broke a rib. "You're not helping."

"That was not the first threatening contact."

"Eh?" said the proprietor. Almost half of the crowd made similarly confused noises.

Firinne pointed to the still senseless leader. "He was the first to lay a hard hand on another." She pointed at the dragon's chest. "He not only jabbed the big barbarian but did not withdraw his touch. That is a dare, in your laws: the person or side insulted may consider it a challenge. A fitting response is allowed."

Murmurs of surprised assent rose from the crowd.

"Who are you to recite our laws to us?" the owner asked, feigned outrage layered atop obvious worry that her words were influencing the crowd. "You've no place in this debate, you unwal—you Dunarran!"

"Do I not?" Firinne's voice and gaze were very calm.

"You are not of T'Oridrea," said one of the gate guards. "You have no standing."

She shrugged. "Perhaps you should look closer." She turned back the broad lapel of her leather deck-coat. A large sky-blue bead was revealed, surmounted by a smaller one that gleamed like a mixture of cat's-eye and gold.

The crowd fell immediately and completely silent.

"How...how did you get that?" the guard asked as the owner approached.

"Some years back, a Vardan merchantman was run aground by pirates. We happened upon the few remaining survivors, one of whom was from a noble family: a fellow named Marregyel."

The owner looked as though he might vomit as his guard asked in a hushed voice, "Do you mean *Udjho* Marregyel? The youngest son of our Great Sazha?"

"The same," Firinne said with a small nod. "Now, may my words be heard?"

The owner nodded miserably, but pointed at Ahearn. "Your words are heard, but they do not change that he wears no bead! None of them do! They have almost no rights—!"

"Truly?" Firinne interrupted, looking around at the crowd. "Do you assert that half of the people here present—travelers from other lands—also have no rights?"

The proprietor chewed his lip and looked away, clearly angry with himself over the misstep; foreigners enjoyed a set of basic protections while in T'Oridrea, particularly its ports. Whether a product of extreme desperation—or stupidity—he'd made a hasty claim that half his clientele would quickly deduce as being patently false. "Still," he shouted, "who is going to pay for the damage?" He pointed at Ahearn. "That fellow was the first to attack, and he was not provoked!"

"Not so! My friend was, er, insulted and I made a fitting response! Besides, your rules say nothing against fighting. Just truce-bonding our weapons."

"You know what they meant, though!"

"Not so," Elweyr countered loudly. "As you said, we are foreigners here."

"That doesn't mean you have the right to ignore the laws!"

"We didn't. We agreed to and obeyed the ones you read to us. If there are other meanings in them, then how are we to know that?"

"But...the damages!" The proprietor looked around miserably, as if the rope-pub was a smoking ruin. Ahearn couldn't see any damage other than a few chairs and tables. "They must pay!"

"They cannot."

"But they are responsible."

"I am not speaking of whether they are responsible or not. I simply point out that they are not the ones who have the value whereby restitution will be made."

The owner's voice lost the hint of whining, became all business. "So, *you* have coin to replace the losses?"

"I do not need to." Firinne gestured toward Ahearn and the others. "But they *will*, as soon as the matter of the attack is settled." When both the owner and Ahearn fixed hard stares upon her, she waved to the defeated attackers. "By right of triumph—again, your laws—they are entitled to the possessions of the defeated."

That sparked a mix of mutters, where the words "only by challenge" vied with "accused as a traitor" seemed to be neatly mixed.

But the proprietor wasn't satisfied. "Perhaps so, but I wasn't in the fight." He pointed at Ahearn. "He and his lot are the only ones with rights."

Ahearn raised an eyebrow. "Captain, are you suggesting, eh, that we riffle through the pockets of the, uh, challengers we defeated?"

"Well," she said soberly, "judging from their drinks, they seemed well supplied with coin. And their gear is not wanting in value."

Ahearn tilted his head, considering.

The dragon started awake, saw the swordsman. "Where...what is happening?"

"I'm cogitatin', thank you very much." He turned to the owner. "I suspect we could come to a reasonable arrangement if—"

"Do you think I'd haggle with you for a piece of those spoils, taken from my customers?"

"No," Ahearn said slowly, "I'd never think of doing such a thing." He measured the other's response. "I'd never put an honest man such as yerself in such a troublesome position. But I would take it as favor if you would set your lads and lasses about collecting their valuables for us." Ahearn waved at his company. "My lot are weary and nursing wounds." By the time he finished saying it, the job was half done.

In the end, there was a reasonable amount of coin, and several weapons with inlays of silver and semi-precious stones: not a king's ransom, but perhaps the bribe price of a lesser prince.

"Now," said Ahearn as the leader groaned faintly behind him, "I'd be happy to make our rightful gains a gift to you, a means of paying for the damages." Ahearn frowned sadly. "But I suppose, seeing as it all came from your friends—"

The proprietor came forward quickly, reaching for the valuables. "They are customers, not friends."

"Ah, well, but still, inasmuch as they're regular customers of yours, you'd not want to—"

"They're *just customers*. Only been here twice. Trouble both times." He no longer even glanced at Ahearn; his stare of glee and avarice was fixed upon the rich haul. "Still," he muttered as he gathered it upon a wooden salver, "they might be angry that you've emptied their pockets and scabbards. Best you be away before they are fully roused and matters become . . . er, unnecessarily complicated."

"Ah, that's wise, very wise. But before we do—"

The owner turned sharply, his face wary and worried. "Yes?"

"Well, there's also the matter of two others who might have some small claim to a share of those spoils."

The proprietor's neck snapped straight, as if he were a startled badger. "Who?"

"Well, these two behind me." Ahearn indicated the

Davyaran and the Taruildorean, while glancing toward Firinne. Who nodded with a faint smile.

The Davyaran waved a thin palm and did not glance at the wealth. "I only fought to defend the aeosti's honor from boors. Their possessions, as their affairs, are as nothing to me."

The Taruildorean chewed the side of his mouth with obvious regret. "Not as if me an' mine couldn't put that to use, but I want none of their goods. Didn't earn it, and they're like to come after my clan if I touch it."

Firinne walked forward toward them, threading her way through the slowly stirring bigots. "Then allow me to show my appreciation of your role in this affair of honor. You of Davyara, I understand you approached my purser seeking passage earlier today?"

He nodded. "Alas, he informed me that your ship does not take paying passengers, that it is fully upon Consentium business."

"That is true. It does not solicit paying passengers." She smiled. "However, we are pleased to provide berths for friends of our friends." Before he could sputter his thanks, she turned her gaze upon the Taruildorean. "Uplander, what brings you to this port so far away and so different from"—she glanced at his hide shawl—"the tracts of the Murhawen clans?"

He started in surprise, offered a shallow bow. "The Dunarran lady has the reck of a shawl's threads and knots. It will be known among us. I was here to ship cargo to relatives in Uershael. Hoped to work with this young rake"—he poked the smiling Davyaran in the bicep—"to combine coin enow to send him and it on their ways." Seeing Firinne about to speak, he took a short step closer. "But, Lady Captain, I wudno have ye thinking me cargo is a mercy sent to answer family needs. It's aught but goods we mean to sell for profit."

"And it is all the better for you and them if I carry it to Uershael, by way of thanks, is it not?"

He bowed very low. "Lady, ye've a friend among the ridges of the Shyarshaos Uplands, and others will know your name." He leaned closer with a conspiratorial wink. "Doesn't hurt that, of old, ye Dunarrans have Connyl in ye, either. Blood knows blood, eh, Captain?"

"We have always counted Taruildor as a fast friend in this region," Firinne answered warmly, but neither embraced nor acknowledged the fellow's allusion to ancient ethnic overlap. "But unless you all wish to answer yet another challenge, I suggest we leave. Quickly."

"Do!" the proprietor shouted after them as the staff opened the "gate" and, followed by the curious eyes of the crowd, they marched, rather than walked, briskly toward the *Swiftsure*.

"And now," Firinne said, turning to Varcaxtan when their gear was aboard and the great cabin's door was shut behind them, "are you ready to tell me the truth?"

"I'm not sure what you mean," the older Dunarran answered, his face as innocent as his voice was mild.

She crossed her arms. "You may spare both of us the dance of careful words. I'm well aware of your 'situation' back home. I also learned since first meeting you on these docks, that you've been asking up and down them for hulls bound toward Eslêntecrë."

Ahearn leaned in. "He wanted to spare you, er,

complications when next you tie up at a Dunarran wharf."

"Did he, now?" She seemed to lean her head back to release carefully stifled laughter. When Varcaxtan stared at her, she shook her head with a sardonic chuckle. "I appreciate that consideration, Subpretor Varcaxtan, but things back home have moved well past that point." His look changed to one of alarm, even as she glanced at Ahearn. "How soon do you wish to leave?"

"Not to seem hasty, Captain, but yesterday would suit us just fine."

CHAPTER TWENTY-FOUR

As Eslêntecrë hove into sight over the starboard bow, Ahearn turned to Firinne, who'd joined them on the fo'c'sle for a final, private conversation. "We thank the gods for you, Captain. Not sure what would have become of us if you hadn't been in T'Oridrea."

"Oh, you'd have managed," she said lightly, deflecting the gratitude. "You lot always seem to."

Well, there's some truth in that, but... "I know you'll hush me if I say aught about bein' in yer debt. So let's leave it at this: mayhap one day, we'll be able to make our appreciation known by doing you a useful service."

She glanced at him out of the corner of her eyes. "Be careful what you offer, Master Swordsman. Or more importantly, to whom. It's rightly said that it's a mixed blessing, having Dunarrans for companions. Whether we meant to or not, we've made a daunting number of enemies along the way." She frowned. "And these days, it's become just as tricky making friends

385

among Dunarrans themselves. Associating with the wrong one of us can get you in trouble with the temples, the Propretoriate, or—gods forbid!—both."

"Then why did you decide to help us yet again?" Umkhira asked, head canted forward in an ur zhog posture of respect. "Surely by aiding Varcaxtan and those who travel with him, you are making your own position more difficult."

She shrugged. "The temples—or more precisely, the hieroxi of several of the most prominent creeds—have become drunk with delusions of control." She shrugged again. "The Propretoriate evidently feels it necessary to indulge their overreach. I, and others, are not disposed to follow their example."

As Umkhira leaned back in surprise at this explanation, Ahearn leaned in. "But won't those secular superiors of yours hang you by your heels if you don't fall in line?"

Firinne shook her head. "Many above me, all the way up to propretors themselves, have similar feelings about the present state of affairs in the Consentium." She smiled slyly. "About which I know nothing, of course."

"Of course you don't," Elweyr said with a similar smile. "But it sounds as though the secular authorities are not willing to confront the temples about their abuse of power."

It was Varcaxtan who shook his head. "You'd think there'd be clear laws that define the proper domains of both temple and government, that set forth their powers and limits."

Cerven was so surprised that he stammered. "Y-you mean there are none?"

Varcaxtan shrugged; Firinne nodded.

"That was always the Uulamantre's greatest concern regarding Dunarra," the dragon said with a nod.

Firinne shot a curious glance at the immense, hirsute, but oddly eloquent barbarian warrior whom she knew only as R'aonsun. "You, sir, seem unusually well informed on a debate of which most persons are wholly unaware."

It wasn't the first time during their voyage to Mirroskye that the dragon had forgotten the behavior and diction appropriate to its avatar, which sported a good number of expressly tribal tattoos. Therefore, it was also not the first time that he replied with an innocuous generality that could not be probed without seeming rude. "I suppose it comes of traveling with such learned comrades, Captain. Dunarrans and aeosti and young scribes: it seems I am learning a dozen new things every day."

Firinne squinted as she nodded. "I'm sure it has been most enlightening, 'sir,'" she responded in a voice that was not only guarded, but suspicious. As her slight emphasis on "sir" suggested, she had discerned oddities in how he was addressed before the group— and he—had settled on referring to him according to the sex of his avatar. "And now," Firinne said, pushing away from the rail, "I must bid you farewell yet again. I must confer with the pilot on—"

"Captain," Varcaxtan interrupted, "you'll forgive me for saying that you haven't answered Ahearn's question: What happens to you if you're questioned about encountering me? I know you'll keep your oath, so you won't deny you did. And then what keeps you from, as Ahearn put it, being hung by your heels?"

Firinne crossed her arms. "Subpretor Varcaxtan, is it fair to say that, although you are evidently hoping to find your wife, you are also mourning her?"

Varcaxtan frowned. "I suppose I'm doing both, yes."

"Then that is what I shall tell anyone who asks about what you might be doing and why I helped you. That you are mourning your wife and adrift in the world—deny it, if you can!—and sailed to Far Amitryea hoping to find a kindred soul in your adoptive nephew Druadaen. But with him missing as well, you took ship back to Ar Navir without any fixed path before you."

Ahearn stared at her. "Is this something they teach all you Dunarrans in school, then?"

"What?" they asked.

"How to make every word you speak the truth and yet not reveal what yer about?"

They both smiled. "No," Firinne supplied, "we learn that as we grow in age and authority." She frowned. "More so now than in the past, unfortunately." She glanced at Varcaxtan. "So, does that story meet with your approval and calm your worries on my behalf?"

He nodded. "It does. And if I don't return at all, well, they'll be happy enough to think the worst."

"Which is?"

"That I died seeking my darling Indryllis." In the silence that followed, Ahearn could almost hear the unuttered coda, *which might yet prove to be the case.*

Firinne nodded sadly. "That is true, I suppose."

Ahearn shook his head. "It's strange to think of one countryman having that in their heart for another."

The dragon was careful to use a broad accent as he observed, "My tribe holds that temples, even more than states, are likely to justify any means to any end, if they deem that end crucial." The dragon almost winced at every word he uttered which was at odds with his apparent origins, each of which earned another curious glance from Firinne.

Umkhira frowned. "Surely you mean 'that any *deity* deems crucial,' yes?"

S'ythreni saved the dragon the trouble of struggling to find sufficiently simple words. "There's no way to know how much of what sacrists say is the result of divining their deity's wishes . . . or because it's what they *presume* it wishes."

"Y'mean, there's no telling how much they're makin' up as they go along?" Ahearn asked, further simplifying the matter.

Firinne grinned. "So refreshingly forthright. Alas, Master Ahearn, you would make a very poor Dunarran."

"You'll forgive me if I take that as a compliment, ma'am. Now, what about you, Captain? Where are you off to next?"

"Porsyolti, Davyara-Nadia's only major port." She frowned. "I just hope the young patriot we're taking there doesn't get himself strung up."

"He's a rebel, then?"

Firinne glanced at S'ythreni. "I suppose your aeosti friend could explain the circumstances far better than I could. Besides, I must go: we're training a new pilot. This is her first time bringing *Swiftsure* through the shallows." She nodded and started aft, shouting orders to the sailhandlers.

Ahearn turned to his aeosti companion. "So . . . *is* that young Davyaran dandy a rebel?"

She shrugged. "From his point of view—which I

share—he considers the so-called Loyalists in Zodera the traitors, inasmuch as the new Great Sazha murdered the old one."

Ahearn frowned. "Now, High Ears, there must be more to his troubles than that, or the captain herself would have answered. But she pointed at you: why?"

S'ythreni sighed and looked up from under lowered brows. "When that petit noble at the rope-pub returns home, he and his Ballashan lackeys will look for the Davyaran, and not just because we emptied his pockets to pay the pub-keep. It's because the young fool stood up to defend *me*."

Ahearn shook his head. "I still don't see—"

"After the new ruler's men were done putting the whole court to the sword, they went on to kill most of Mirroskye's envoys and their retainers. The survivors fled for home and the regicidal brutes gave chase, following them over the border." Her eyes were as grim as her voice. "Those pursuers never returned. One was a nephew of Kohejh Nadia himself." She shrugged. "So the new rulers—Family Nadia and their sycophants— have a score to settle with us. And inasmuch as the Davyarans were always good neighbors and half their own nobles wound up on the impaler's spike, they feel that we share the same side of a blood feud."

Umkhira's eyes were wide. "Then that young warrior is very mad to return. Or very brave. I can hardly decide which."

"Nor can I," S'ythreni agreed. "Then again, I am hardly in the position of passing judgment on the sanity of others, given that I may soon stand before the Great Pool again." She shook her head at herself and stared beyond the risers that were now battering into the *Swiftsure*'s prow: they had entered the shallows that lay northwest of Eslêntecrë.

Ahearn leaned toward her. "Okay, I'll bite: what's this Great Pool you and Tharêdæath mutter about? I thought it was just another word for Mirroskye."

"No, the Great Pool isn't Mirroskye," S'ythreni confirmed, "but it *is* its heart. Or maybe more akin to its soul."

"Well, that's beautiful poetry, High Ears—but no kind of answer. I'm guessing that this Great Pool is an actual body of water, yeh? A wading pond, at the very least?"

S'ythreni rolled her eyes. "Actually, it's a lake in the shape of a perfect circle, almost ten leagues across, and at the center of the oldest part of Mirroskye. But it's also the name for the council that has always gathered there."

"So, it's the Iavarain capital, then?"

S'ythreni's jaw tightened; but before she could utter a snappish reply, Cerven interceded. "The Great Pool is not a city. It is where the eldest of the Uulamantre meet when they feel the need to confer."

"And they're so fond o' this pool . . . why? For its lovely views? Or because it's a good spot for cogitatin'?"

"No," S'ythreni snapped, "for prophesy. And more. The Pool's surface reveals . . . many things."

Ahearn started. "You can't be serious, High Ears!" He looked around the group. "I mean, don't you all find it a bit tiresome? Every time we turn around, it's another mantic mirror or looking glass or mystic pool." He scoffed. "You'd think that whatever cosmic power is behind the creation of such things would at least have some taste for variety, eh?"

Even the dragon had to suppress a grin at that, before he joined the others at the rail to watch the slender towers and spires of Eslêntecrë push further above the horizon.

Still adjusting to the extreme docility of the mare with which he'd been provided, Ahearn turned to look at the silhouette of the city behind them. "I've never seen a port as strange as that one," he muttered to Elweyr as their horses started forward, bringing up the rear.

"Mm-hmm," the thaumancer agreed absently, his eyes and focus concentrated upon the two riders just ahead of them: Cerven and Varcaxtan.

"Well, don't you agree? Hardly any ships at all, and only that Irrylaish galleoncete was larger than *Swiftsure*. Tidy wharfs, little noise, smaller crowds—be damned, the place looks like a plague emptied it." After a few seconds of silence, Elweyr nodded. Annoyed at his lack of attention, Ahearn continued more loudly. "I don't even know why they bothered to build a city at all. Aye, the towers are impressive—don't see why they don't tip over in a high wind!—but other than that, I ask you: what is it but a collection of warehouses and shops and a handful of inns? Where are the people, man? Where are all the houses? I'm a tinker's bastard if we walked more than one hundred yards before comin' out t'other side of it!"

Elweyr didn't even nod this time; he was too busy measuring the growing distance between them and the two riders ahead.

Thoroughly irked, Ahearn ended by observing, "And what about those naked lads with butterfly wings chasing the long-legged land whales? Now that was a sight."

Elweyr nodded, then shook his head as if a fly was trapped in his ear. "Wha—what did you say?"

"Well, welcome back to the world, you owl-eyed goon! What's got you fixated on the Dunarran and his would-be protégé?"

"Trying to determine if they can still hear us. Now, listen," Elweyr interrupted in a conspiratorial tone, "did you overhear the port recorder when Cerven presented himself?"

"I was too far back to make out much of what was said, particularly when they slipped into Iavarain. Can't follow it."

"Well, they started with the standard, 'What do you here, *eh'hathsha*?'"

"Aye, that's what they called me, too. All of us except Varcaxtan and S'ythreni. What's 'Eh'hathsha'?"

"It's a generic term for any thinking being or entity. But that's not what was important." Elweyr paused. "He answered them in their own language."

"Well, we know he has the knowledge of it."

"Knowledge is one thing. Perfect fluency and accent is another. So much so that one of them apologized and started addressing him as *ur'athsha*."

Ahearn managed not to roll his eyes. "And *that* means . . . ?"

"Something like 'recognized person.'" Seeing Ahearn's widening eyes, Elweyr shook his head. "No, no. It doesn't mean he's Iavarain himself. But it *does* mean they acknowledge that he is 'known' to the Iavarain, that he has 'walked among' them."

"Well, maybe one of his many mentors was aeostun."

Elweyr shook his head. "Learning the language, even from an aeostun mentor, is not enough for them to address him as ur'athsha."

"Well," said Ahearn, trying to change the very dull subject, "while you were picking apart the niceties of a language I don't speak, I almost laughed aloud when R'aonsun approached and gave its name. That fussy high-eared recorder was ready to laugh...until that old wyrm got close and leaned over." Ahearn chuckled. "Then he—or she?—was suddenly as careful and quiet as a mouse among cats. I wonder: is that a bit of Iavan mancery, seeing past appearances?"

"No, not exactly. It's more—damn it, Ahearn, don't change the subject. Did you or didn't you hear any of Cerven's answer when the recorder asked about his background?"

"No: what did I miss? Did he share the titles of the one hundred books he loves best? Seriously, though, that lot waiting in line behind us—the ones from Irrylain—were too loud. I could hardly hear myself think."

"Which is indistinguishable from the silence of the tomb, I'm sure," Elweyr grumbled with dark impatience. "Now shut up and listen to me. Our young companion gave his *full* name: Cerven Ux Reeve." Elweyr uttered those last two words with slow gravity.

Whatever made them portentous was unknown to Ahearn. "Well, based on yer pregnant pause—worthy of triplets, by the way—I gather I'm supposed to know why that name is important. Pity that I don't."

"He's not just Amitryean. His family is *Old* Amitryean."

Ahearn frowned. "I thought they were extinct. Or just legend."

Elweyr shook his head. "I doubt it, given what he said about his mentors."

"So you think one of those mentors *was* aeostun? And that's how he learned Iavarain?"

Elweyr frowned. "If so, I don't think he was just being mentored."

"Why?"

"Because when asked about his family, he only mentioned a sister. No one else."

Ahearn sat straight in the saddle. "You mean . . . yeh think he lost his parents?"

"Sounded like it, given the words he used and his tone of voice."

Ahearn no longer saw the narrow sward of ankle-high grass that passed for a road through the forest. All he could see were his own parents, laughing as they worked a lateen rig, telling him that, when he was ten, he'd have to lend a hand—which was the last thing they ever said to him and the last time he saw them. "Gods, the lad is . . . he's . . ."

"Like you. Late-orphaned."

Ahearn swallowed. "Like Druadaen, too." He glanced at Elweyr, who upon escaping from the Gur Grehar as a teen, had returned to find that his own parents had disappeared without a trace. "And not so very different from yerself, either." Ahearn looked up into the sky, let his puzzlement rise into the vast emptiness: *it's naught but chance, so many of us being stripped of kin . . . but damned if it doesn't* feel *like there's intent in it.*

Without guidance, the mare followed the other horses, unhurried and sure, to wherever their hosts were leading them.

CHAPTER TWENTY-FIVE

Time and distance seemed strangely fluid once the spires of Eslêntecrë were no longer visible, but Ahearn supposed it was a mile further on when a light rain began misting down. Several minutes later, as the path began to rise into a rockier part of the thickening forest, the three aeostu leading them steered their mounts onto a smaller track to the left. Ahearn frowned; *but is it really a "track" when there's not a bit of bare soil in sight? Just a long, winding carpet of grass?*

Whatever its proper label might be, his mare was either familiar with the track or was quite adept anticipating and following the horses ahead. It was nearly walking in their hoofprints as it ambled under the thick boughs that arched overhead. They kept off the rain as well as any tight-woven awning.

Their path soon became perfectly straight, the foliage becoming the walls of a leafy tunnel that smelled like dew on a spring morning. The rain was a soft murmur, the percussive fall of individual drops blending into what sounded vaguely like surf that never ebbed or flowed. Ahearn let out a long sigh, his shoulders and neck less tense than they had been in—how long? He tried to think the last time he felt so relaxed...

He started into wakefulness, roused by a hazy light growing ahead. Looking hastily about, he recognized none of his surroundings. Even the trees had changed; the initial mix of ash and maple had become elm and oak. He wondered how long he'd been drowsing and found out he didn't really care—at least not as much as getting a better view of the clearing into which their guides were leading them.

The grass widened out into a near-perfect circle, with what appeared to be a low, round hump at the center. But as they left the shadow of the forest, Ahearn saw that it was a round berm, the top above the level of his eyes. The horses, obedient either to habit or an undetected command, dutifully began to walk around it. In the course of that stately progress, Ahearn saw that the ring could be entered through smoothly sloped openings, spaced as evenly as the four points of a compass.

When the last of the horses were alongside the outer wall of the berm, the aeostun guides dismounted. They gestured for Ahearn and the others to follow their actions and then their steps, which led through the nearest opening.

The berm proved to be the outer shell of a small amphitheater. Its three broad, grass-covered tiers were wide enough to accommodate a reclining audience. However, the lowest had several stone chairs sprouting up from the ground at the north point of the berm's compass rose. Although rough-hewn, their seats were smooth, with a glassy sheen that was only partly a consequence of the rain that was dwindling to a stop. Their guides waved them away from the risers to stand near the center of the orchestra where they discovered a small, perfectly round pool rimmed by close-set stones.

Ahearn, who'd come to stand between Elweyr and S'ythreni, leaned toward the latter. "Now, this surely isn't the 'Great' Pool."

She sighed. "This is not the time or place for your inane quips, *man*."

Ahearn started; the way she'd said "man" had a generic intonation . . . as if she had said "human." *She's as serious as* that? *Well then, best play along . . .*

As he pushed back against his continuing reflex to diffuse the gravity of the moment with artless gibes, Ahearn saw that two Iavarain had entered the amphitheater through the eastern opening. They were half a head taller than their leaner aeostun guides, who, after exchanging nods with the new pair, exited through the west entry.

Their two new warders were certainly equipped for any eventuality. They both wore Iavan sheath armor, each suit worth a prince's ransom. They had weaponry similar to that which Druadaen preferred, but their single-gripped longswords were a few inches shorter than the Dunarran's hand-and-a-half. Although they had quivers low-slung on their backs, they did not carry bows. Their helmets were so smooth and seamless that it was tempting to imagine that they'd been poured over the heads they protected. They took up positions on the other side of the small pool, flanking it at the same distance and angle from the center. They did not speak and their eyes appeared half closed.

Varcaxtan stiffened slightly, looked deeper into the

forest through the north opening. "Eyes front, now."
Ahearn and Umkhira were the only ones who craned
their necks to see who—or maybe what—might be
approaching.

Two figures emerged from the leafy shadows. Ahearn
recognized one immediately: Tharêdæath. Momentarily
startled to see him here, the swordsman realized anew
just how much time the shipwreck and resulting detour
had cost them. But it was the person with him that
commanded Ahearn's attention.

Very tall and lithe, she—he?—was robed in light
linens that made it impossible to guess at the shape
of the form wearing it. The eyes that looked out of
the almost delicate face were an extremely light gray
that made it difficult to distinguish the pupil from
the whites. It wore a gold necklace, was joined at the
neck by a bright silver link—

Ahearn realized what that "link" actually was when
the sai'niin ring pulsed on his finger: they were identical to each other in size, brightness, and depth of
reflection. The Iavarain's pale eyes met his own and
smiled more than did the thin lips as Ahearn realized:
no, they're both *Uulamantre.*

Their two hosts advanced to the stone chairs at the
center of the northeastern tiers. Without turning, the
two guards in sheath armor stepped back in unison
until they flanked their superiors.

The unknown individual nodded at Tharêdæath who
waved Ahearn and the others forward to a point about
two yards away. "It is good to see you again," he said,
before wryly adding, "and alive, no less."

"That outcome stood in some doubt on more than
one occasion," Ahearn confessed.

"So we heard. You are very welcome here."

Are we? "We are grateful for your help and hospitality." *Austere, though it might be.*

Tharêdæath nodded, turned toward the other Uulamantre without gesturing. "Actually your host is Ilshamësa, child of Enedthræem and ur-Quertheyor."

"What's *ur-* mean?" Ahearn whispered sideways at S'ythreni.

"Slain, not passed," she almost hissed as their host rose slowly. "Now be silent!"

"I welcome you to Mirroskye, travelers and friends of Tharêdæath." Ilshamësa intoned, taking a moment to smile faintly at Varcaxtan before continuing. "And it is well that you are home, S'ythreni." Who did not meet her eyes.

Ilshamësa took in the whole group with a two-handed gesture of inclusion. "I trust you find Eslêntecrë pleasant."

When Varcaxtan did not make polite answer, Ahearn said, "It was a most handsome city." *If small,* he wanted to add, but managed to hold the words frozen behind his smiling teeth.

"'Was' handsome?" The Uulamantre seemed confused. "Why do you speak of it in the past tense, *eh'hathsha?*"

"Well..."—Ahearn struggled to find a way to correct his host's misunderstanding—"it's past tense for *us*, kind Lady, inasmuch as we're not still in it."

Ilshamësa regarded him with a frown. "But you are."

"We're ... what?"

Realization—or perhaps recollection—brightened her expression. "You are still in Eslêntecrë, albeit at its eastern extents. Only upon leaving the buildings, did you enter the city's *Iavarain* precincts." She gestured in the direction of the bay now miles behind them. "Few of the structures in the port were designed or built by us, which exists solely to facilitate exchange with your various species." She shrugged. "After all, it is your world, now." Her falling tone added a sad coda: *more's the pity.*

"All respects and regards, Til-Ilshamësa; in addition to its beautiful lines, it is a very cleverly designed gateway to the world," Cerven murmured. "One must look carefully to see its walls."

As Ilshamësa's eyes widened and she bestowed a surprised and interested smile upon Cerven, Ahearn muttered toward Elweyr, "Did *you* see any walls?"

"Later, Ahearn."

"Yes," Ilshamësa said, turning toward the swordsman, as if awakening to a new fact, "*you* are Ahearn. Tharêdæath has told me of you." From her tone, he couldn't tell if that was good news or bad. "It is you to which the *quelsuur* has affined itself."

Ahearn started. "Eh? What's affined itself to me?" He leaned toward Elweyr. "That's mancery she's speaking of, yeh?"

Instead of sounding annoyed or impatient, Elweyr's tone was focused and even wary. "It might be, but I'm not sure."

Ilshamësa's eyes were suddenly open again. "The *quelsuur* is what your kind have called the Relayer," she said carefully. When Ahearn shook his head in continued perplexity, the Uulamantre jabbed a thin finger at his hand. "You wear the sai'niin link. As a ring. Because it...it chose you."

"Oh!" Ahearn exclaimed with a smile, and just barely

held back a cheeky, *Well, then why didn't you* say *so?*
"Yes, it did. I do," he added lamely. "So I take it that
Tharêdæath has also told you why we traveled here?"

"Yes!" she answered, as if his question had been so
abrupt as to be startling. "At least, in enough detail
to determine our response."

Ahearn exchanged a quick glance with Elweyr, saw
his own reaction in the other's face. *That does* not
sound promising. But it was also a little confusing.
"With all due respect, Lady Ilshamësa, we didn't travel
here with requests, but questions."

"Yes. We are aware."

As pronouns go, her "we" sounded like it represented
a sizeable group, not just Tharêdæath and Ilshamësa.
"So you already know—and have answers for—the
questions we mean to ask and the counsel we seek?"
He felt S'ythreni's urgent eyes on him from the left
and a calmer but steady stare from Varcaxtan on
his right. He looked from one to the other with an
expression which he was sure conveyed his reaction
to theirs: *Well, if ye've something to add, spit it out!*

Ilshamësa reseated herself as if her body had become
quite stiff. "It was not necessary to hear your specific
questions or requests for counsel. They are all quite
predictable."

Umkhira spoke before he could. "Iavarain wisdom
is legendary, but I did not know it included prophesy
that gives foreknowledge of a future conversation!"

Ilshamësa looked at the ur zhog blankly, as if she
had not heard the sarcastic tone behind the words.
"No prophesy is needed. You believe that, in order
to effect the return of your friend, you must locate
a suitable osmotium."

"A what?" Umkhira sputtered.

"A portal between different locations, even worlds," Tharêdæath supplied quietly, with a concerned glance toward Ilshamësa, whose neck was stiff. Its cords were taut, and a pallor was creeping into her face.

"Yes," Ilshamësa agreed almost absently, "a portal. Your friend went through the shimmer tended by the current Lady of the Mirror. You have learned that he may not return by that route. You seek an alternative but do not know where to begin your search. So you come here, hoping we have that knowledge and might offer material aid in your quest." She looked around the group. "Does this not articulate your reasons for coming to Mirroskye?"

As the group exchanged abashed glances, Varcaxtan raised his chin. "It does, Til-Ilshamësa."

She smiled as if surprised at the formal address. "Then we have foreseen your intents correctly."

Ahearn nodded, realizing what that meant. "So you're meeting us here because there's no reason to bring us to your Great Pool. You're not going to help us."

CHAPTER TWENTY-SIX

Before Tharêdæath could intercede, Ilshamësa's long hand rose, fingers erect. "That is not entirely accurate, *eh'hathsha* Ahearn. But what information we do have, and what aid we may render, do not require the time and wakefulness of the Great Pool. So—"

—*"Wakefulness?"*—

"—to answer your most obvious and important question first: no, we have no shimmer within the borders of Mirroskye."

"And no osmotium either," Elweyr added with grim certainty.

"Of course not!" Ilshamësa said, surprised and aghast. Her eyes flashed toward S'ythreni. "Did you not teach these *eh'hathshu* our beliefs, our ways?"

"Til-Ilshamësa," S'ythreni said, lowering her chin, bowing, and keeping her voice low and soft. "I am but an aeosti exile. It is my regret and shame that I know so little of our ways that I could not better educate my *eh'hathsha* companions in them."

Tharêdæath leaned close to Ilshamësa before she could reply. The ancient Uulamantre's face softened, became sad as the other, younger one whispered to her urgently. "Dear child," Ilshamësa resumed, eyes bright, "forgive me. I...I am so filled with memories that, when newly reborn, my mind seems to have little room for anything but what I have seen and heard before. You have done admirably teaching them enough of our courtesies that they give no offense. Well"—she paused to glance at Ahearn—"most of them. Now, magister," she said in a firmer voice as she turned toward Elweyr, "you are correct: there are no osmotia here. They disrupt the flow of the Great Weave and we will not tolerate such phenomena within our borders. But what you require"—she paused to look at each of their faces—"goes beyond that. To reclaim your friend you would need access to the rarest kind of osmotium; a *jaqualq* osmotium."

"*Jaqualq?*" Cerven echoed; the eagerness in his voice told Ahearn that this was a new word for him.

"It means 'breach,' in Uulamantre," S'ythreni said with a slight shiver.

"So you know the term, child?" Ilshamësa said encouragingly.

Again, S'ythreni's eyes lowered. "Only that it signifies more than a mere break or puncture. It is more akin to...to..."

"An aberration or anathema or atrocity," Elweyr said carefully. He shrugged in response to their surprised looks. "The term appears in a few fragments of very old and complex thaumantic sources and codices, usually in relation to apocalyptic events or forces."

Ilshamësa was nodding, eyes more focused. "The

magister speaks with understanding of the word. And an osmotium that connects not merely different places on Arrdanc, but is a gateway to a different world, is labeled thusly."

"But . . . what does it mean, that it is, er, *jaqualq*?"

The Uulamantre looked appraisingly at Ahearn. "Your curiosity is your most redeeming feature, *eh'hathsha*. I wish I could answer that question adequately. But even after millennia of consideration, the nature of *jaqualq* osmotia remains a matter of debate among the Tiri of the Council."

Varcaxtan's eyes opened slightly wider at her explanation, but other than that, his expression was unchanged.

"Suffice it to say that *jaqualq* osmotia are, to use the magister's word, anathema to us."

"Yes, but why them more than others? Because they lead to dangerous places?"

"No, because they wholly violate the natural order."

Ahearn looked at his companions. "'Violate the natural order'! Well, wouldn't Druadaen like to be here to learn that! Start him off on another quest, it would."

"I suspect you are correct, from what I have heard of his investigations. But I grow weary, and we have yet to address the matter which surely brought you here: recommendations for your path going forward. Which means, practically speaking, how to find just such an aberration."

"Well, yes, certainly . . . but I'm sure it wouldn't go amiss if one or two persons with interest in such, er, aberrations, were to join us in our travels. Once we found such a portal, we'd be very much obliged to have the benefit of their knowledge and advice." *Not to mention their skill at arms and mancery—which they've honed longer than I've lived.*

Ilshamësa stiffened. "Mirroskye offers counsel, but we have foresworn interference."

"Interference? In what?"

"In affairs that transpire in the world beyond our borders."

Umkhira spoke even before Ahearn could. "How can you claim this? You have been an active ally of Dunarra for as many years as are recorded in histories."

Tharêdæath's quick reply was clearly to keep Ilshamësa from doing so rashly. "We were indeed 'involved' with Dunarra. But now, its temples have indicated that we are no longer welcome and its Propretoriate chose not to dispute their will in the matter. We have since withdrawn from *all* activities that may require action beyond our own border."

"Also," Ilshamësa added testily, "your present concerns and will to act is driven by individual desires, not a greater duty."

Elweyr frowned. "I would welcome your wisdom, Til-Ilshamësa; what do you mean by 'a greater duty'?"

"Is it not obvious? I refer to actions that arise from the vigilance and deliberations of your councils—or, as you call them, er...tribes?"

"I believe you may mean nations or realms?" Cerven offered quietly.

"Yes, those too." Ilshamësa waved an annoyed hand. "I find the distinctions between your agglomerations difficult to recall, possibly because I find the differences too...too..."

"Complex?" offered Elweyr.

"No; dubious. However, to my point: a 'realm' with

great and unusual powers may not safely exert them simply to satisfy a few individuals. To do so is intemperate and irresponsible. Great power becomes both diluted and untrustworthy when its use becomes too frequent or favors some individuals over others. So, while we share regret over the loss of a friend and a spouse, and have sympathy for many of your goals, we may offer only the most mundane forms of assistance. It is what we would do for any well-meaning travelers fallen into trying circumstances."

Ahearn put out a hand in appeal. "But at least you can tell us where we might find one of these juqwa—jakal—er, violating portals so that we might try to retrieve our friend?"

It was Tharêdæath who answered, shaking his head. "Sadly, that is not so easy as you might think. Time has blurred or wholly erased much of what our distant forebears knew readily. The laws and locations of portals that linked distant places on this world and others has faded from memory."

Cerven's surprise was evident in his tone and face. "And you did not endeavor to restore that knowledge?"

Ilshamësa started violently. "To what end? Understand, young one: great powers never sleep. We always have one eye open when it comes to the unusual abilities of other powers, just as they do concerning ours. A power that does any less does not long remain a great power."

Ahearn was surprised by a torrent of loud, angry words—emerging from his own mouth. But he felt no regret as they poured out. "Then what of us knuckle-dragging mortals who hope to help in our own, small ways? How do you count us as you're movin' beads of power around on your political abacus? As an 'agglomeration' of hapless sheep? As serviceable villeins by which you 'great powers' push and pull at each other without feeling any pain yourselves?"

The Uulamantre were visibly stunned: whether at the volume of Ahearn's speech or its content, he could not tell and did not care. He leaned further forward. "How is it any different from nobles wagering on the ragged curs that they bring to dog-pits? And why do they set those poor beasts to tearing at each other? Why, so those 'great men' can claim a maimed dog's victory as their own, that they're the stronger... while pocketing a few extra billons at a rival's expense." He crossed his heavy arms. "I'm waiting fer yeh to point out the distinctions between that bloody business and the heartless ways of your 'great powers.'"

Tharêdæath nodded, but waited for five full seconds before offering his slow, calm answer. "The differences are these. Firstly, not all great powers use hapless communities and persons as their proxies. Secondly, among those who must do so, some freely share the full truth of what they are doing and why. But beyond those differences, I cannot dispute the parallels you draw."

Umkhira's spine straightened sharply. "'Among those who *must* do so?' How is it that any great power 'must' use those with less power—or none at all—as their catspaws in petty battles?"

Tharêdæath took a moment, considering his reply— but Ilshamësa spoke sharply into that silence. "And let us say you were the chieftain of your tribe, Lightstrider. And let us say that a distantly related and much weaker clan was suffering at the hands of rapacious red urzh from the Under. And let us finally say that those same raiders were certain to come to your own hearth next. Would you fail to help your distant clan-cousins?"

"Of course not! We would attack the raiders!"

"So, in order to spare your weaker kin, you would sally forth *alone*?"

Umkhira frowned. "Well, not alone."

"Or maybe not at all." Seeing Umkhira's eyes widening, Ilshamësa rephrased. "Perhaps *you* would not fail to bring your full strength to the aid of your cousins. But tell me: are there not ur zhog chieftains who would give only limited support to the weaker clan, in the hope that the danger from the red urzh could be averted at a smaller cost in your own hearth's blood? Indeed, would not such chieftains be deemed prudent, wise, even cunning?"

"Perhaps," she fumed, "but never 'heroes'!"

Ilshamësa nodded. "Rightly said, Lightstrider. They are not heroes. And nor are we. To hold a totem or scepter of command means to hold the fate and future of many lives in that same hand. Such a person does not have the *luxury* to be a hero. Their first duty is not to themselves—not even their nobility or honor—but to those whose lives depend upon their prudence, wisdom, and yes, cunning."

"I would reject the fur-robe of such authority! I have no wish to be a chief!"

Ilshamësa smiled. "To be truthful, I never did, either. But if you become renowned among your people—and I foresee that such a thing might happen—it may be that the fur-robe of authority seeks *you*, even if you wish to avoid wearing it."

Ahearn waited patiently through the somber silence

that followed—until he deemed it had gone on entirely too long. "Well, let's leave of worrying over hypothetical futures that may or may not come." Almost everyone stared at him as the word "hypothetical" left his lips. "We came here to determine how to find our friend and bring him home. Whatever help or counsel you can offer, we shall gratefully accept."

Ilshamësa smiled softly. "You love your friend very much, to speak courteous words that cut your throat like glass even as they rise toward your lips." Before Ahearn could find a reply or rub away the sudden heat in his face, she continued. "So frank and heartfelt a request would open the most closed ears—or hearts. We shall confer further. I cannot promise anything to you except this: what we may do, we shall.

"Now, before you take leave of us, I have questions of my own—which may also serve as a form of counsel." She turned toward Varcaxtan. "Other than the *quelsuur*—Relayer—choosing someone besides yourself, why are you not the leader of this group?"

Ahearn started. "Well, now, don't mind that I'm standing here, right in front of yeh! Please: talk of me as if I'm half the world away!"

Ilshamësa's bored sideways glance told Ahearn that, at the moment, that was precisely how she thought of him. "I do not understand how or why you would endure his . . . inexperience. He cannot be a fifth your age."

Varcaxtan's smile proved infectious for Tharêdæath, but not the older Uulamantre as he asked, "Alas, my years show so clearly, then?"

"Only to those who know what to look for," she replied flatly. "Also, you are known to us."

Varcaxtan glanced at Tharêdæath. "Been telling tales on me, have you?"

Til-Ilshamësa found no humor in the situation. "I needed no report from him. We have known of you for decades. You have had increasing responsibilities in the service of the current propretor princeps, and now his grandson. We would be remiss *not* to be aware of you and your capabilities. I ask again; why are you not this group's leader?"

Varcaxtan shrugged. "It had been together for more than a year when I joined. And some have been friends far longer than that. Over that time, it grew its own set of rules and relationships, which is no small feat, given the unusual mix of persons." He shrugged. "Since it works as it is, it hardly seems wise to change it. I have no authority among them, and besides, as you pointed out, the Relayer did not choose me, but Ahearn. No, Til-Ilshamësa, this is best." He allowed himself a small grin and his eyes almost twinkled. "You see, Ti-Alva, choosing *not* to be leader is not only wise, but a great personal relief!"

Ilshamësa tried not to show the thawing effect of Varcaxtan's charm. "Very well. But you might do well to instruct this . . . noble swordsman in the delicate nature of the events in which he now finds himself involved."

"Oh, he understands far better than he lets on." Varcaxtan smiled sideways at Ahearn. "He effects a bumpkin demeanor so that others will underestimate him, and so, come to reveal more of their own thoughts and knowledge."

Ahearn nodded his gratitude, but thought, *Well, thanks for giving away the usefulness of playing the fool, "Uncle Varcaxtan."*

Ilshamësa's response was to let her skeptical gaze drift from one to the other and back again. "Interesting. Let us hope you are right. And you—" she continued, glancing at the dragon.

R'aonsun straightened, bent his thick human neck very slightly. "I attend, Til-Ilshamësa."

"Why do they call you 'R'aonsun'? Do they not know your real name"—she uttered an ear-rending growl-screech—"Osrekheseertheeshrathhuu'aigh?"

"I have not shared it with them."

"Why?"

"Because their tongues would mangle it as surely and as utterly as a wolf mangles a rabbit."

Even Ilshamësa's small smile seemed on the brink of becoming a grin. "I have missed dragon-wit." She pronounced the last word as if it were well established, not an impulsive cognate of its two parts.

His neck bent. "I am gratified."

"And again," Ilshamësa followed quickly, "I must ask: why are *you* not leading this company?"

"Besides having no wish to do so, Til-Ilshamësa?" The big barbarian body shrugged. "For much the same reasons given by this revoltingly cheerful Dunarran I have been cursed to know for—oh, decades now."

"Decades?" Cerven said, leaning over to look at R'aonsun from the other end of the group. "How many?"

"Too many," came the tart reply, before he turned his attention back upon the senior Uulamantre. "I would say it is a pleasure to see you once again, Til-Ilshamësa."

"And why do you not?"

"With respect, *you* have not always been pleased to see *me*."

The Uulamantre's answer had a hint of drollery.

"I have yet to hear of any relationship with a dragon that was anything less than . . . uniquely complicated." Ilshamēsa's face and tone grew serious. "I must imagine that your fellow travelers would agree. It is indeed interesting to see you in company with these beings. It is not something I foresaw."

"Frankly, neither did I."

"Since your . . . 'needs' are well known to us, I cannot help but reflect upon the personal cost you risk in embracing this uncertain path unto its conclusion."

"I am flattered."

"You should not be. I—we—are uncertain about the wisdom of your choice."

"As am I, but I cannot afford uncertainty. Not now."

"If enemies still watch your lair, every further step on this journey is a further temptation to them, or the cruelties of Fate."

The dragon seemed genuinely surprised. "I appreciate and understand your concerns—"

"Well, I don't!" Ahearn exclaimed. "Right now, I'm naught but the bumpkin Varcaxtan says I play, because I haven't the faintest idea what this grave palaver is all about."

Tharêdæath looked quizzically at the dragon. "It was my understanding that you explained to them that your eggs are the means of your own rebirth?"

"I did. But I did not explain what quickens them."

Elweyr frowned. "You told us that you are . . . er, that your species does not mate."

"I'm disappointed in you, 'magister.' Clearly, those two statements are not ineluctably contradictory."

S'ythreni raised an eyebrow of her own. "Then how *do* you quicken your eggs?"

"It is . . . well, a matter of my diet."

Ahearn crossed his arms. "Every time you start answerin' in circles, wyrm, I start getting very, very nervous. Like right now. So be plain: what is it you must eat to quicken an egg?"

The dragon shrugged. "Another being like myself: one that will not die merely from the passage of time."

Umkhira frowned. "So, other cryptigants?"

R'aonsun shook its now close-cropped human head. "Dragons are not cryptigants, but yes, many of those beasts do not die natural deaths any more than we do. But they are not the only creatures with that property and certainly not the easiest to eat."

Elweyr rubbed his hairless chin. "So: other dragons, then?"

"Again, possible but not advisable; a battle between dragons usually ends with one dead and the other dying."

Ahearn's already thin patience ran out. "Then *what*, wyrm?"

"The Fallen." Ilshamësa murmured, leaning back in her chair of stone. "Of our kind."

"You mean, the Yylm?" S'ythreni asked in a gasp that turned into a whisper.

"Yes."

She turned to the dragon. "You *hunted* them?"

"On the contrary, they hunted me." He glanced sideways at the Uulamantre. "But I was unable to establish that to the satisfaction of the Council of Tiri."

Ilshamësa shook her head slowly. "Venerable Dragon, time has revealed what you could not then prove. And which we were loath to believe of our own kin, no matter how distant the relation."

The dragon's barbarian face raised an inquisitive eyebrow.

Tharêdæath explained. "We have since fought many wars against the Yylm." A rare expression of surprise passed over the dragon's face and was gone. "We discovered that, if anything, your descriptions of their treachery and cruelty were not merely measured, but understated."

"They had to be," the dragon explained, "for the very reasons that nestle in your own words: the Yylm are your blood, your kin. What being is willing, let alone eager, to believe the very worst of their own species? So, as you say, I could not be as frank and as brutally honest in my depictions of the Yylm as I would have wished to be."

"Which is why," Ilshamësa said slowly, "we are grateful that you came here, that we might ask your forgiveness, even understanding, for what transpired those many centuries ago."

R'aonsun stared at the Uulamantre. "So you forgive the many deaths I caused among them?"

"As it turns out," Tharêdæath said slowly, "those were not acts that required forgiveness; they warranted thanks. For every two you slew, at least one of us was thereby saved from dying in battle against them."

"*At least* one," Ilshamësa said in a suddenly shaky voice. She stood. She had become deathly pale in the space of a single moment. "I tire. Rebirth becomes more trying." She turned toward S'ythreni. "My child, you seem comfortable with these companions."

S'ythreni looked like she was swallowing nails as she gathered herself to admit aloud, "I am, Til-Ilshamësa."

"Then you mean to travel onward with them. And if

you survive, I suspect you shall not be absent from the glade for so long. To which end: they must know us."

S'ythreni looked as puzzled as she sounded. "Til-Ilshamësa, I do not understand."

"If you return, I feel sure they shall as well. Before they do, and before we may bring them further into any confidences, you must show them our heart and soul."

"How?"

"You mean to travel to that which sustains you, do you not?"

She swallowed. "I can do no less."

"Then you must take them with you to behold what they do not yet understand." She stepped down from the bottom tier. "We shall seek the knowledge you require for your quest. I am weary. Tharêdæath will see you on your way."

CHAPTER TWENTY-SEVEN

Half a dozen Irrylaish gave the group a wide berth as they galloped past, laughing and joking with the three aeosti among them. As they disappeared up the lush path that Ahearn had come to think of a grassway, he leaned over toward Elweyr. "I'll bet they get to see this bloody Great Pool that's apparently the center of t'universe."

"They won't," S'ythreni said as she drew up alongside, moving toward the front where the two guides were now walking their horses. "They're, well, 'pilgrims' for lack of a better translation. They spend several moonphases living with aeostun families that theirs have known for generations. It's an old tradition between Irrylaish borderers and Mirroskye."

"How old?"

"*Very* old. At least as far back as the First Consentium. Possibly long before." She returned a nod from one of their guides. "We're here. Follow me."

The aeostu left the grassway, verging into a similar path that was narrower and more winding. Ahearn and the others trailed after them until they topped a small rise and followed along a curving sweep of granite spur which abruptly fell away, down into a small dell. A rock-strewn creek ambled through it and two stone campfire rings were set just beyond the tightly bunched boughs of thickly needled conifers. Their guides gestured to the larger of the two fire brakes and made for the other.

"Not exactly sociable, are they?" Ahearn wondered aloud as he dismounted.

"It's part of their job *not* to be, when leading groups of *eh'hathsha*," the dragon commented from behind. He was—once again—studying the others as they swung down from their saddles, a feat he had not yet mastered. In general, he still sat a horse rather than rode it and paid the predictable price: sore back and buttocks.

Hiding a smile, Ahearn walked around his own mount, swinging wide as he passed behind.

"You needn't worry about kicking," S'ythreni assured him. "They know not to. Well, unless we ask."

Ahearn nodded, smiled and, hands on his hips, studied the horse. It turned and stared back at him—but with far less interest. "Great Pool or no, it's pleasant traveling in your Mirroskye, High Ea—eh, S'ythreni. Particularly when it comes to the animals and mounts. It's as if every last one of them knows how best to behave."

She glanced at him. "Hmmm. Better than you?"

Ahearn laughed. "Why most *certainly* better than me! Yer lord, or lady, of the Uulamantre made that clear enough. Not that I disagree with her. I possess but one grace of use in a court: sense enough to leave it as soon as I may." He noticed the birds and ground animals about the dell; they'd barely shown interest when the group had descended into it. "But the creatures here, well, there's no contention with or amongst 'em, is there?"

S'ythreni's glance became a surprised stare. "I thought you'd find them too docile."

"Well, maybe a bit. But that's because they also feel like, well, creatures you grew up with." He considered the horse again. "It's better, this way."

Her glance became a frank stare. "Better compared to what?"

"Why, better than the way we find and use animals most everywhere we've sailed. For example, the horses we've engaged throughout our journeys. Living, feeling creatures they are, and yet rented out no different from the cart they might pull." Ahearn shook his head. "I've mixed feelings about travels that take us far from home, including the creatures in our barns or at our hearths. But what's far worse is being pressed into renting replacements for them." He uncinched his saddle's girth strap as he looked around the dell. "But among you Iavarain? Why, from the birds overhead to this horse standing here, all the animals feel as comfy as the ones I knew from me childhood home."

S'ythreni's stare had shaded toward amazement. "At no point or place in our travels did I have the faintest notion that you had such...misgivings."

Ahearn nodded. "Strange: neither did I." He drew in a great lungful of air. "Maybe I didn't. Maybe it only seems so now. Maybe it's a mancery that runs wherever trees in Mirroskye make shadows, eh? If so, it seems to have improving qualities."

S'ythreni's eyes were wide as she turned away. "You'll hear no argument from me."

"Ah, now there's the aeosti I know from long travels together." Ahearn turned and discovered that the two aeostu were gone, but their mounts remained near the smaller firebreak, untethered and grazing.

Glancing after their vanished guides, R'aonsun broke the silence he'd kept since his exchange with Ilshamësa. "They will return in the morning?"

"Yes. When I have done what I must."

"And what is that?" Umkhira asked.

"A visit. One I should have made long ago. We should eat and rest."

"So," asked Cerven, scanning the tree line, "we are alone now?"

"No." In response to their confused stares, she added, "They are still nearby. As are several other aeostu."

"I cannot see them," Umkhira announced.

"They are beyond the deepest shadows. But they are there."

Ahearn squinted, shook his head. "Ah, your kind certainly has eyes for the dark, I'll give you that."

S'ythreni shook her head. "I didn't say I could see them. I can't."

Ahearn frowned. "So you, eh, feel them? Through the Great Weave?" She nodded. "But I thought you had no real sense of direction from it."

She nodded. "Except with Uulamantre, that is usually the case. But our sense of each other and the Great Weave becomes more acute when we are this close to so many *tha'huu*."

"Er . . . ?" began Ahearn.

"The trees that enfold us for rebirth," she translated.

Umkhira was peering peevishly into the darkness. "But why do the other aeostu stay back?" Umkhira wondered.

"They are ... uncomfortable," S'ythreni replied vaguely.

Ahearn *tsk*ed sharply. "Ah, so it's the company you're keeping, eh? More high-and-mighty disgust at the thought of rubbing elbows with barbarous, er, ey-hashas? Well, I've had just about enough of—"

"No," S'ythreni said in a flat tone, "they are uncomfortable with *me*."

Ahearn stared, as did the rest of the group.

"Let us eat and sleep. I must be up before first light."

Elweyr frowned. "And us?"

"You may do as you wish, but for any who might return to Mirroskye in the future, it would be best for you to accompany me." Having finished seeing to the needs of her mount, she walked toward the firebreak.

"Accompany you where?" Ahearn asked after her.

She did not reply.

Elweyr put out a hand that was only partially visible in the predawn glow that filtered through the forest canopy. "We follow S'ythreni at a distance."

Ahearn watched her slender form begin to fade into the dim mists between the trunks. "Why? Mightn't she need our help?"

"She called it a 'visit,' not a fight."

"Hmm ... so do you know what she's about?"

Elweyr resumed walking. "Do I know? No. Do I suspect? Yes."

Ahearn sighed. "Do I have to pull it out of you with tongs, man?"

One of Elweyr's dog-teeth came down on his lower lip. "I'm not sure it's my place to say."

"Well, she did invite us to follow. More or less. So she means us to see what she's up to."

Elweyr considered, then blurted out, "She trusted my family."

"A bit more detail would be welcome."

He sighed. "It happened when I was away studying up in Eld Shire. My parents found her . . . or she found them . . . after she almost killed herself."

Ahearn stopped. "I've never heard of Iavarain taking their own lives."

Elweyr towed him forward. "They don't, but if the one to which they are bound is slain, some have been known to throw themselves at the killers. Without regard to their own survival."

"And S'ythreni did? Because she was, er, bound to someone?"

"As best I can tell, yes and yes."

"'As best yeh can tell?' Gods, mate, how can you be friends with someone and not know for certain? You know her favorite foods, but not *this*?"

Elweyr glanced at Ahearn sharply. "I seem to recall that *you've* tried to get information out of S'ythreni that she didn't want to share."

"A fair point, that. But if she's not shared the tale with you, how do you know any of it?"

"My parents. They mentioned it in the last letter I received in Eld Shire. No names, but they mentioned helping an aeosti who'd been badly wounded in both her body and soul. By the time I got back to Menara, they were gone."

"But she wasn't, eh?"

"Well, she wasn't waiting for me, but a moonphase later, she arrived. She never stayed long, but checked in often enough."

"And did she have any inkling of what happened to your parents?"

"No, but when she was away, she was always looking for some clue as to what had become of them."

"And she never said a word about what had put her in such need of your parents' help, or how she'd met them to begin with?"

Elweyr shook his head, waved Ahearn into a crouch: S'ythreni had stopped before a tree that bore no resemblance to any he'd seen before.

"Well, my friend, you're a damned patient man, not pressing her for those details."

Elweyr shrugged. "You know I'm not *that* patient, but she always avoided the topic and became testy when I tried to speak of it. And inasmuch as she was kind enough to keep coming back and to keep looking for my parents in her travels . . . well, what sort of gratitude would it have been for me to push for details she did not want to share?" He looked toward her; she was kneeling before the strange tree: not in supplication, but as one might beside someone sleeping on a low pallet. "One day, in her own time, I assumed she would begin to reveal the story of what happened. And here we are."

"Meaning what?"

"Meaning, 'shut up—and watch.'"

As they did, she rested her palms against the vine-wreathed trunk. Over the course of several minutes, the pattern of the vines changed. It was as if—slower than an impatient human eye could see—they had entwined themselves around her fingers.

The tree itself was oddly shaped. In Ahearn's experience, most tall trees—this one towered over nearby oaks—had wide, straight trunks that didn't send out branches until they were well off the ground. This one didn't rise more than two yards before it bifurcated, creating a narrow crotch not much wider than the span of Ahearn's shoulders. Following each branch upward—it looked more like twin trunks, actually—they each split again, perhaps thirty feet above the ground. The pattern continued up into its lightless canopy.

After completing his survey, Ahearn glanced back toward the base of the tree, where S'ythreni still knelt. If Elweyr's gaze had wandered at all, there was no sign of it.

Ahearn waited a minute. "Mate, I don't see anything happening." No response. "Do you?" Ahearn counted twenty breaths. "How do we know she's all right? I mean, it's just not natural, the way—"

Elweyr sighed. "Ahearn, have you noticed that everything connected to the Iavarain tends to be subtle, not obvious?"

"Well, yes, but—"

One of Elweyr's eyebrows climbed slightly.

"Oh, all right." Ahearn crossed his arms, tried to find a more comfortable position in which to sit the vigil. "After all, how long can it take to commune with a tree?"

"You do understand that she is *actually* communing with that tree, don't you?"

"Why... What? How is such a thing possible?" He'd thought all the Iavarain references to their connection with the trees was more figurative than literal, but now—"So is that a...a rebirthing tree?"

"A *tha'ha*," Elweyr corrected, "and yes, I believe it is. What else would it be?"

Well, the bloody mancer has a point. "So that's where they—they are made youthful, again?"

Elweyr shook his head but did not take his eyes off S'ythreni. "Much more than that. It's where they change."

"Change?" Ahearn frowned, puzzled—then abruptly felt what he'd dismissed as foggy myth become crisp reality. "So they actually do change sex? In the tree?"

Elweyr shrugged. "They don't speak about it to outsiders, but it explains much."

Ahearn nodded, discovered he was breathing hard. Not at the shock of the discovery, but at the realization of how blind he'd been. "That's why the differences between their sexes are so...so unclear. They have it in them to be both." Questions and uncertainties and contradictions and curiosities ran out from that revelation like rings spreading out from a handful of pebbles cast into a pool of the possible, all intersecting and spawning new rippling patterns. "So all the talk of buggery"—*which was in my own mouth, often enough!*—"is...is..."

"Is ignorant bigotry of the first order," Elweyr finished for him.

"And you *knew*? And you didn't *tell* me?"

"No, I didn't know—but I was pretty sure. And as for telling you"—he turned to glance at his friend— "without proof, you'd have been as stubborn as a mule. And ten times as annoying."

Ahearn would have disagreed had he been able to find a flaw in any of his friend's assertions—but he couldn't. "Well," he said. "Well," he started again, "this changes everything."

"Does it?" Elweyr asked. "S'ythreni is still S'yth-reni, no different than she was before the hammer of truth finally corrected your vision with a blow between the eyes." He glanced over. "It's you who've just changed, Ahearn, which you'll realize as soon as you're no longer stunned."

"I believe you're right," the swordsman muttered, settling down next to his friend again. "I do believe you are right."

Six hours later, S'ythreni edged away from the tree, the vines leaving her hands slowly, almost dragging: as if they were unwilling to do so. She rose, turned and, wordless, strode toward—and then straight past—them.

She remained silent during the entire walk back to the dell. The others rose when she emerged from the tree line. There was still no sign of their guides; their horses had drifted to the other side of the dell.

Varcaxtan approached her. "How long has it been?"

S'ythreni's eyes were suddenly bright, then her face hardened. "Far too long. I do not deserve to be paired to so fine a *tha'ha*. Or to any, for that matter."

Varcaxtan moved so he still looked into her eyes. "And does the *tha'ha* feel so?"

S'ythreni did not meet his eyes. "That is unimportant."

"Oh, no, Alva S'ythreni," Cerven said earnestly, "it is not. You must know that."

S'ythreni wiped at her eyes. "I have no idea what I know...if anything. But I have made what amends I may for my absence, and those who wished to have seen the soul of Iavarain." She glanced almost furtively at Umkhira. "You did not wish to see that?"

"I did not *deserve* to see that," the Lightstrider said, chin high—but quivering. "My people and yours...there is much spilt blood between us. To be made welcome in your lands puts me in a debt I cannot repay."

S'ythreni looked at her more directly. "Yes, you can repay it."

Umkhira stood straight, hand resting firm atop her axe. "I shall. This instant. Name the price."

"Your friendship," S'ythreni whispered, "unmeasured by debts or deaths or past wars between our peoples. All so that, next time, you shall be willing to see what we truly are."

S'ythreni's words seemed to open Umkhira like an eviscerating dagger. "You have it," she said, her jaw out, face rigid, but voice thick and low.

Cerven looked at the older faces surrounding him. "And now?"

"And now," R'aonsun drawled knowingly, "we wait."

"For how long?"

S'ythreni's chin came up; her voice was firm. "For as long as it takes."

PART FOUR
THE GODBARROWS

Journal Entry
Twenty-ninth day on Hystzos

I must make haste to record the events of my journey to Agpetkop, the Sarmese trade station on the far northeast coast of the Sea of Hystzos. It is concluding much sooner than the Vizierate presumed.

Whereas their mariners allot five to eight weeks for this voyage, Lorgan's ship has covered that distance in only two and a half. We did have fine weather, fair winds, and a following sea. Also, Lorgan and his officers proved to be expert navigators and were delighted to learn that I, too, had reasonable proficiency in those skills. But it was that innocent camaraderie among mariners that revealed that I was not merely an outlander; I was an out*worlder*.

On one of our first days a-sea, they noticed me eyeing their instruments, and, unasked, presented them for my inspection. I remarked on their distinct superiority to Sarmese equivalents. In turn, the Tyrmcysan officers remarked on my easy and familiar handling of them. I derived such pleasure from the conversation that arose, and such relief at being freed from the perpetual weighing of words by which I concealed my otherworldly origins, that I eagerly and unthinkingly accepted their offer to join them for that night's triangulation of our position. And in the very next moment, I realized that I had undone all my efforts to obscure my identity.

Because, as I've already recorded but forgot in that moment, the stars on Hystzos are not those of Arrdanc. I have been aware of the difference since the second night; in place of Arrdanc's three moons were two very small ones, so when the stars came out, I was hardly surprised to discover that they were not those beneath which I had been born. And I had already been expecting those differences, not merely because the Shimmer was said to connect different worlds, but because I had noticed the slight difference in the color of Hystzos' sun.

It was probably the lack of surprise and the ready acceptance of my new circumstances that ultimately undid me—that and the distraction of the far more pressing matters with which I had been preoccupied. Learning a local language; finding food and shelter; avoiding other travelers (and remaining innocuous if I did); and finally, wondering at the attack of the purple-robed strangers and their strange equipment and artifacts: I had no want of concerns that demanded my undivided attention. And so, inasmuch as they were not essential to my immediate survival, I paid no further attention to the stars above my head.

Of course, having accepted the Tyrmcysans' congenial offer to shoot the stars that evening, the only plausible excuse to avoid doing so was to plead a sudden illness. But I could hardly claim infirmity every night of our voyage, so that would have only postponed the inevitable. So, when they offered me the astrolabe that night, I demurred, saying it had been so long since I'd actually used one that I was unwilling to embarrass myself in the company of true mariners. They were perplexed but remained undeterred; they made the same offer the very next night. I declined, citing my resolve to redouble my devotion to learning the local languages, which I could only undertake in the evenings. They accepted this explanation, albeit with long and dubious stares.

However, there is no fooling Lorgan or either of his officers, Talac and Rysth. They clearly perceived my excuses as pure fabrications, but by that time, they had almost embraced me as one of their own. In retrospect, sharing their humbler quarters and meals had established me as trustworthy before this incident arose. So my strange demurrals did not make me an object of suspicion, but rather, a mysterious traveler who evidently had some secret to keep.

So after turning north into the Sea of Hystzos and breezing along the coast of Kaande, we began to pass the shores of the Broken Lands: first Bronseca, then Rulam, and finally those that are too small and too many to name, each one less populated than the last. After that, the eastern horizon was simply a wild, rolling coast that had once been cleared for farming but was now almost wholly overgrown. A few fortified trade stations marked our progress, located near, but not on the site of, ruined cities. When I asked why they had not been established where they could make use of the old piers and anchorages, I received a one-word answer: "abominations." As if to underscore the monstrosities' tendency to descend upon points of habitation, one out of every two hamlets we encountered after that were nothing but clusters of weather-savaged shells: not burnt, simply depopulated and abandoned. Further north, the only signs of life were our constant companions the gulls, which often labored to keep up with us.

Their doggedness was probably a product of desperation. From the time the coastline of Rulam disappeared behind us until this very day, we have only seen one ship. It was so large and so far out in the Sea of Hystzos that it was unlikely to be a fisher-boat, and so, unlikely to attract seabirds that follow the smell of bait. And with no storms to cause a bounty of dead fish, and no towns producing scraps, "our" gulls hung on our stern for the scant leavings from our humble galley.

I have wondered if at least some of our extraordinary speed is due to the singular design of the ship, which has an equally singular name: *Fur-Drake's Oath*. In addition to a longer, narrower hull than most high-weather ships, it apparently has a centerboard, although the trunk that houses it down in the bilges is peculiarly wide and shallow. The hull and decks have also been rebuilt so many times, and with so many kinds of wood that every surface bears a faint similarity to a patchwork quilt. This is particularly strange, since captains and shipwrights alike prefer to avoid mixing woods; the innate differences in strength, pliability, and weight can cause problems at those moments when stresses are greatest.

And finally, although it does not impact the performance of *Fur-Drake's Oath*, I would be remiss not to mention the truly bizarre figurehead. In addition to its impressive size and the peculiar detail of the carving, it has large metal eyes, which I imagine to be glaring in defiance of the credo by which any good shipwright lives and works: a hull should not be burdened with unnecessary weight. (Which is why so many shipwrights rail against figureheads to begin with.)

But it is the figurehead's form that is most memorable. It is a large, sinuous combination of a wide-finned eel and a narrow-faced otter, made surprisingly feral by the inclusion of long fangs. Forever frozen in the act of striving forward, it is easy to imagine that it is perpetually determined to detach itself from the prow.

One night, as Lorgan was measuring the height of the brightest object in the sky—the purportedly immense planet of Mag-Orr—I joined him in the bows to ask about that fantastical creature. He smiled and cocked his head. "Well, sure that you are a stranger to the Sea of Hystzos, if you do not know the legends of the fur-drake!" Whereupon he regaled me with fanciful tales of these vanished beasts, which had favored sea-faring peoples but deeply hated those that hunted them—as would be expected. "And it's said some fur-drakes still exist," Lorgan finished with a wink.

"A fine tale," I nodded.

He smiled, patted the head of the fur-drake and left his hand there. While he always wore a ring on that hand, I had not realized until that moment that it too was made in the likeness of a fur-drake, albeit coiled upon itself. I returned his smile. "Asking them for fair seas?" Ever mindful of the sea's pitilessness, almost all mariners leaven their fatalism with just such superstitious rituals.

His smile became thoughtful. "Something like that," he murmured, and said no more.

Perhaps the fur-drakes smiled upon our journey, too.

Something certainly did. In addition to the following seas and the pilot's mastery of always calling for the best set of the sails, we invariably made our best time when ships typically make their worst: during the dark hours of the night. Every morning, I was stunned anew by our progress. In all my years as a Courier I never saw such swift sailing, let alone consistently over the course of two weeks. Having arrived at our destination in less than half the time projected by those who provisioned and readied me in the citadel of the Hazdrabar, I shall investigate this discrepancy when I return to Sarmasid.

As we scudded further north along the eastern boundary of the Sea of Hystzos, conversation among the crew paradoxically turned ever more back to the southern lands from which we sailed. And as the trust that had been so quickly conferred by Lorgan and his lieutenants took hold more gradually among their crew, I learned why they had spent so much time in the Straight Sea, and why their ship was more rigged for blockade-running than trade. They had become peripherally involved in incidents consequent to a recent civil war in Kaande, typically the most stable of all the Lost Lands.

Or had been, until the king, queen, and two of their three children perished under mysterious, and highly questionable, circumstances. The contending factions predictably accused each other, despite the lack of details emerging from the closed capital of Kaande: the fortified port in which the nation's war galleys were berthed. But rather than set aside their ambitions long enough to retake the capital and secure the nation's fleet, the contenders fell to warring with each other, plunging Kaande into a war of succession that spread like wildfire.

The best claim lay with the almost-adult third child: a son who might have been unanimously supported if he was not known for moods that even his supporters described as "extremely erratic." Among various rumored misdeeds, two had been so widely seen or reported that even the royal family had been unable to smother the reports. Specifically, at the age of eleven, he had set fire to his cat, and, mere days after reaching age of majority, he attempted to poison his sister. The throne insisted that the latter had been merely a foolish prank gone spectacularly awry. The people of Kaande merely nodded their heads and remained utterly unconvinced.

The other faction was led, somewhat reluctantly, by the dead king's two younger brothers. They had been passionately importuned by the gentry and commons alike to ensure stable rule at any cost, including violating the laws of succession. There were only two legitimate paths to the throne; the death of the last son, or the declaration that he was insane. But the Mad Princeling was surrounded by bodyguards, and the royal physicians who could legally rule on his competence had (conveniently or otherwise) died along with the royal family.

All of which I found quite interesting, but was at pains to point out to the crew that they had yet to explain how the *Fur-Drake's Oath* had profited from this sad state of affairs. Anticipating a recounting of typical, apolitical wartime profiteering, I was completely unprepared for the extraordinary tale they unfolded, but even more so for the unnerving obliquity with which they told it. As a Courier, I learned that stories become vague when the details are unsafe to share or even know.

As is frequently the case along the coast of the Straight Seas, the opportunity arose from Sarmese scheming, which (as usual) involved plots within plots, which were ultimately undone by the greed and jealousy that prevailed among the Merchant Princes. In this case, the agents of one of those families had approached Lorgan and his crew to reduce Tharn's ability to send galleys along the western, which was to say Kaandean, part of the Straight Sea's northern coast. This stretch—known as Seareach—had not yet been touched by the expanding civil war, but the Sarmese did not want competitors for the profits to be realized when it did.

I remember looking around the faces of the many contributors to the tale. "*Fur-Drake's Oath* must have a reputation for being an extremely formidable ship," I commented. It was the most tactful way to point out that the hull beneath us was barely half as long as a monoreme.

Talac, who was effectively second-in-command, grinned. "Who said anything about *fighting* their ships? 'Removing' them seemed far more prudent."

Rysth saw the uncertainty on my face. "Tharn's a small nation. They've only one good port: the capital at Pasbigt. That's where they keep their galleys. Since becoming allies of Sarma, they don't give much thought to protecting the wharves, as Trawn and Pecthin are too small to try cases with them." Although third-in-command, Rysth was in charge of both boarding and shore parties; as seems common among such officers, it was his habit to speak in short, declarative sentences.

I nodded. "So, you slipped in and, er, removed, a galley."

"Two, actually," corrected Haqtor, a respected sergeant and exiled Tharnan. "Biremes, both. Waited for the right wind, put our prize crews aboard. A few guards later, and we were on our way, as easy as you please. And wouldn't you know, the wind also fanned a mysterious fire that started on the wharf, just moments before we cast off." There were grins all around . . . but then they noticed I wasn't grinning.

"You don't believe us?" asked Marselsar, a Rulami.

"Oh, I believe you," I answered, wondering how to broach a subject that might prove even more touchy. "But I'm not exactly sure how you managed to make all that happen in the order you did."

"Eh?" asked Az-apit, whose name was Sarmese but whose parentage was from all the lands that bordered on the Straight Sea.

"Well, you say you waited for the right wind."

"We did."

"But even under the cover of night, you had to be far enough offshore not to be seen beforehand. Yet you were close enough to arrive in time to make use of that wind. It seems extremely fortunate that the wind didn't turn on you." The winds are notoriously fickle in the Straight Sea, hence the prevalence of lateen-rigged ships that can sail very close-hauled.

Lorgan looked at Talac.

I wasn't done. "But then there's another matter, isn't there? The prize crews. I've seen the biremes in these waters, and a prize crew for the sails and tiller alone would be at least twenty. But you 'removed' two of the galleys, so that means you had to deposit forty able hands on the docks at the very last minute. Again, without attracting the attention of any patrols."

"Ah," put in Woght, the crew's inveterate prankster, "but the *Oath* didn't have to unload us. We were already in the water near the wharves, waiting."

I nodded. "I wondered if that was the case. It makes a great deal of sense, except for this:"—Lorgan and Talac were now smiling at each other; Rysth was frowning—"how did you get in the water around the wharf without being spotted? It must have been a very long swim."

Woght looked like he was about to swallow his tongue, or at least like he wanted to. "It was. Very long indeed."

"Very impressive," I replied with an encouraging nod, "particularly given all the sharks in these waters."

"Oh," Lorgan said with a grin, "the sharks are old friends of ours. Besides, we 'foreigners' taste odd to them."

"I'm sure you do," I grinned back. "But now that you've cleared up all my misconceptions," I added, looking around the faces again, "I am now confused not by the way you 'removed' those two biremes, but that the crew of this ship, let alone its officers, would agree to the single factor upon which success clearly depended."

"Which is?" Talac asked.

"Luck. Absolute, unmitigated, outrageous luck." I pressed on, seeing encouragement rather than discomfiture in the officers' eyes. "After all, you may have waited for the right wind, but you had to trust Dame Luck that it would remain strong and steady long enough for you to approach, crew the biremes, and then make off. Likewise, you had to hope that you'd find the hulls prepared to sail, canvas at the ready, and no anchor watch to object to your presence. Also, however friendly the local sharks might be, you had to hope that none of them would forget, take a quick nibble, and start a feeding frenzy. And finally, you had to trust that the wind would hold steady long enough to fan that mysterious fire on the wharf, which happily made pursuit quite unlikely and damage to other galleys *quite* likely." I let my gaze return to Lorgan as I concluded, "It's almost as though you can make your own luck. Because if you could, then every step of this plan is not only feasible, but logical."

Rysth crossed his arms. "Seems you have a conjecture. Let's hear it."

I shrugged. "The conditions of the ships and the presence of patrols—I *suppose* that could be observed and signaled. But the hinge upon which the plan turns is whether or not the *wind* will turn. From the moment you begin your approach to the time that the Tharnan coast is falling well behind, you must *know* that the wind will remain in your favor.

"That would also allow you to come so close to the wharves that two prize crews could slip over the *Oath*'s extremely crowded side and reach the biremes, without any visit from sharks, friendly or otherwise."

"And most importantly of all, as the *Fur-Drake's Oath* continued to stand off and out of sight, those crews could hoist the sails in the certainty of having enough wind to carry them away from their berths without any rowers. And as for the fire?" I shrugged. "You said it yourself, regardless of the blaze's 'mysterious' origins, you knew there'd be wind enough to turn a broken oil lamp or two into a full-blown conflagration."

Lorgan brought out a bottle, called for everyone's cups. "We are *so* very lucky, indeed," he assured me. "Or"—he winked—"we can bend the wind itself to our will!"

Dour Rysth let out a howl of laughter before he could stop himself.

I smiled back at Lorgan. "You don't rely on luck. But you don't have to control the wind to know how it will blow. Or even have a knack for prophesy."

"Eh?" said Az-apit. It seemed to be his favorite response to almost anything.

Talac pointed at me after taking a sip. "So tell us how that would work."

I shrugged. "I've seen enough wyrdwarding to know that animals can report at great distance to those who are bonded to them. So if I was bonded to birds soaring in circles along the direction from which I was awaiting a stiff breeze, they could alert me when it began blowing past *them* and how long it lasted."

Rysth grunted. "Now a question to you."

"Certainly."

"Sure you're not a wyrdward yourself?" About half of the crew leaned forward to hear my reply.

I shook my head. "No, but I've had the acquaintance of a few. Now a question back at you: How did you turn a profit on this?"

The officers looked at each other. "Would you believe us if I told you we sold the biremes?"

I shook my head again. "Any buyer in the Straight Sea would be marked for revenge by Tharn. Maybe your prize crews were from the Sea of Hystzos, but that kind of exchange would have required more lead time than you've had, if the troubles in Kaande are as recent as you say."

Lorgan winked. "Well, that's a tale for another day, perhaps. And here's supper, just in the nick of time!"

The role of cook rotated aboard the *Oath*, and this day it had fallen to Ertran, who was one of the better ones. Libations were topped off, the table was cleared, and the cook's mate (also the closest thing the ship had to a purser) threw wide a fresh tablecloth. I helped straighten it out, surprised to see that it was gray, and noticed threads of another color in it.

I leaned away sharply before I could stop myself.

Half the compartment had noticed my sudden, backward posture. Talac was closest. "You act as if you'd seen a rat."

"Or worse," Rysth added darkly.

"Worse," I answered, hardly knowing I had because of the question that kept hammering between my ears:

Why does this crew have a tablecloth in the same purple-tinted pattern of the Nightfall cult?

"Peace, now, Druadaen," Lorgan's voice urged calmly. "You seem disturbed by our new 'tablecloth.'"

His emphasis upon the last word sounded facetious, sardonic—but I knew Lorgan might be shrewd enough to effect disregard or disdain that he did not feel. On the other hand, I strongly doubted that I could have wandered into a ship full of Nightfall cultists without having had reservations about at least one of the officers or the crew. So, because all my instincts were to trust them, and because there had been no warnings from either the velene or the sword, I finally answered, "I do not associate that pattern with congenial company."

A moment of silence . . .

Then Rysth emitted an even louder bark of laughter. I felt a wave of relief so great that I would have liked to sit down and rest for a moment. But the rest of the compartment was laughing or chuckling, and Lorgan was shaking his head. "This rag we use to cover our table was one of the prizes from the galleys . . . or aren't you aware of the connections between Tharn and the Nightfall cult?"

My stunned stare elicited an explanation which has given me a great deal of food for thought. In short, the Nightfall cult had long been a poorly organized extremist sect of the larger Temple of Disfa, a god associated with fertility and death rites. However, in the last two generations, it had displaced the more moderate ritualists by producing an increasing number of monks and priests who actually performed miracles and demonstrated other unusual powers. Tharn's monarch had shown interest in this unusual development, if for no other reason than the growing power of the nation's largest temple made it either a more important ally or more worrisome rival.

The Kaandean civil war had been the catalyst for a dramatic shift in that delicate balance. Without seeking the permission of the throne, the Temple of Disfa's recently installed Herald of Heaven (whose demonstrated powers implied a considerable facility with either miracles or mancery) promptly led a popular crusade over Tharn's northern border into Morba.

Morba is not just Tharn's hereditary foe; it is, as Aleasha intimated, Kaande's oldest ally. So while Disfa's

Herald couched his crusade as being religious in nature, it was also blatant national opportunism. Regardless of pretexts, it excited considerable popular support, thereby putting the monarchy on the back foot as it hastened to associate itself with (and contribute to) the campaign. This involved sharing an increasing amount of prerogatives and responsibilities with the temple.

So when Rysth led the prize crews aboard the biremes tied up along Pasbigt's military wharf, they'd run into anchor watches comprised equally of soldiers of the realm and temple guards—whose officers had been garbed in "tablecloths" such as the one just spread out.

They went on to show me some of the other holy garb they'd taken from Disfa's followers. "Useful if we need to walk among 'em," Haqtor muttered with a small, canny smile.

The most unusual item of clothing was a shift of simple cut but striking color: the same purple as that which was woven into the gray of the tablecloth, but far brighter. I asked them why that one was so different from the others. "Because," Rysth explained, "it marks its wearer as one of their berserkers, or *sfadulm.*"

I was able to control my reaction this time. "Sfadulm. Is that how they say 'death-vowed'?"

He nodded. "Why? Do you think you may have run into one?"

"I think one tried to kill me, on my way to Pakobsid."

I had told them about the ambush in general, but now I provided whatever details they asked for. By the time it was over, our supper was only half-done but completely cold.

Talac shook his head. "You had a busy time of it in Sarma, didn't you, Druadaen?"

I agreed that I had and let the conversation drift to other, more casual topics. I was too busy weaving together disparate bits of information into my own, growing pattern.

Specifically, it seemed the twinned threads of the Nightfall cult and the dreaded "sorcerers of the east" had insinuated themselves throughout the greater tapestry of the Last Lands. I wondered if they had agents among the Merchant Princes, pondered the possibility that they might have been behind the massacre of Kaande's royal family, wondered if they were promoting the rise of the abominations. The connections were tentative, but had all been implied in one conversation or another and, if accurate, suggested a plot as invisible, intricate, and yet expansive as a spider web stretched across a lightless passage.

I started this journey hoping to determine why the S'Dyxoi traveled to these remote shores at the northeast end of the Sea of Hystzos. But now, a vague foreboding arises along with my newest question: Are their actions wholly independent (and ignorant) of the web being spun, or have Dunarra's oldest foes imposed their own, otherworldly influences and changes upon it?

CHAPTER TWENTY-EIGHT

Druadaen stood next to the Sarmese trade station. Or rather, what was left of it.

The palisade surmounting the low, rectangular berm was now an uneven row of charred black teeth. In the bailey beyond, the remains of its buildings were little more than scorched outlines and a few crumbling rafters.

Druadaen turned to look back at the small, narrow bay that led to it, fed by a small river to the north. From the post's site on a small rise above the surrounding floodplain, he could make out one of the *Fur-Drake's Oath*'s small boats upon the softly rolling waters. Its crew had tossed an anchor in the shallows, keeping it close to a single, sparless mast poking rakishly above the swells: the resting place of a Sarmese monoreme that had been burned down to her plimsoll line before sinking.

"News," called Lorgan's voice from behind.

Druadaen turned, saw the Tyrmcysan captain clambering up the back of the berm. "From the divers?"

Lorgan nodded as he came down the other side. "Almost all the crew was aboard. Naked, locked to the oars, and burned alive. Az-apit says there's no sign of a fight and there are no goods left aboard."

"So, not an attack. It was a stab in the back." *Certainly in keeping with S'Dyxan tactics.*

Lorgan nodded. "Same with the outpost, from the look of it. Gates were not forced, no one was manning the palisade. Judging from some of the bottles found in the ashes, there may have even been a celebration underway when the abominations came. Every human skeleton down there was naught but bare bones before the fire started."

Druadaen frowned. "I suppose the two attacks could be separate acts of treachery, but I doubt it."

"So do I. The outpost was stripped as carefully as the ship was. And only then was it burned. Some of the guards down fought back, though; more than a few abominate skeletons among the normal ones." At Druadaen's questioning look, he added, "Trust me; you always know the skeleton of an abomination."

"It sounds as if you've seen more than a few."

Lorgan nodded, but instead of revealing how and where he'd come by his experience with them, he gestured to the south.

Krøn, the leader of the crew's small contingent of Ruildine horsemen, was approaching from the sward that fanned out on the landward side of the outpost. His mount kept trying to push its canter into a gallop, eager to stretch out from long weeks aboard ship. "Whoever did this left with a good number of horses," the Ruildine captain reported as he drew up to them, "maybe as many as a dozen. All heading east. All heavily burdened."

"From the trade station or the monoreme, do you think?"

Krøn shrugged. "Can't tell. All their hooves are shod in the southern fashion. A number of abominate tracks flank them for a while, then the monsters began falling off. They spread out singly or in small groups before leaving." He waved his arm from the northeast to the southeast. "They were all heading back to higher ground, from the look of it."

"Such as it is," Lorgan amended, nodding at the flat flood plain before he turned to look squarely at Druadaen. "You're sure this job is worth the risk?"

Druadaen couldn't help smiling. "I wasn't sure when I agreed to it. I'm no more sure now. That's why I asked you to hold my valuables."

Krøn nodded at the ruined trading post. "But that changes things a mite, no? Say you manage to truss up an abomination. Say you even manage to drag it back here alive. Then what? If we've left by then, what shelter will you have? And how will you get it to Sarma?"

Lorgan looked up at the rider. "Well, we might be able to pick him up, if the timing works out. We're putting in at the Luthmaand outpost for a bit. Take on some supplies, give some Ruildines I know some time among their own people."

Krøn's first reflex—a smile—dropped off immediately. He glanced at Druadaen, then back to Lorgan. "All so we can backtrack and take another look here, eh?"

Lorgan's smile was beatific. "Something like that."

Krøn shrugged. "Well, I'll be happy to speak my own tongue for a few days. But it will keep us all from seeing home as soon as we might. And just to discover this place as empty as we left it." He spared Druadaen a sardonic smile. "So be a friend and spare us a pointless trip."

"How?"

"If you die out there, send word, yeh?"

"I will do my very best."

The Ruildine cavalryman laughed, nodded approvingly, and rode off, calling back, "Your horse is off the skiff and your bags and saddle are ashore. I'll have my men see to tacking it."

"Much obliged!" Druadaen replied, using the odd Ruildine idiom for "thanks."

Lorgan didn't speak until Krøn had ridden well beyond earshot. "Now, not that I'm averse to inheriting all your silver, but I have to ask: why are you committing suicide in such an original fashion?"

Druadaen kept his explanation not only shorter, but more vague than the one he'd presented to the viziers of Sarmasid; the fewer details he shared, the less he had to resort to misleading statements. He had no wish to lie to Lorgan, just as he had no wish to flatly rebuff him. But one of the captain's eyebrows crept higher as he concluded with, "So, all in all, by fetching an abomination for the viziers, I may drop two kites with one stone: improve my own circumstances and work against a sworn foe of my people."

Lorgan stared at him for a long moment. "Well," he drawled, "I would have liked to have heard the *full* truth, but a man's business is his own business, as my father used to say."

Abashed, Druadaen could only hope he wasn't blushing, too. "If I could, I'd share the whole of my story, but . . ."

"But?"

"You'd never believe it."

Lorgan's smile was almost a smirk. "Try me."

"Some other time. Besides, I'm not sure that anyone who has the full story is safe from those who'd like to keep it quiet." He paused for emphasis. "I suspect that's why you didn't share the details of what happened after you cut out the galleys in Pasbigt. The less told, the safer the listener."

Lorgan put up his palms in a warding gesture. "Say no more! My curiosity is hereby withdrawn!" He shook his head. "Now, although its long odds that you'll survive long enough to have use of them, here are some words of warning.

"Firstly, if you prize your life—and I'm not convinced you *do*—don't go too far south."

Druadaen frowned. "But that would bring me closer to settled lands, wouldn't it?"

"Yes, and that's the problem. Food is hard to come by out here in the Godbarrows, and it *is* full of hungry stomachs attached to big teeth. So, to survive, some of those stomachs have to travel to where food is more plentiful."

Druadaen nodded. "Settlements. So, they cluster near the frontiers of the Broken Lands?"

"They do, and it's not just abominations, either. It's everything in the Godbarrows that is so hungry that it forgets any fear of us."

Having touched upon the Godbarrows, Lorgan stayed on that topic and reeled off a list of what Druadaen would encounter as he wandered further east. The only humans he was likely to encounter outside walled villages were those few who—for reasons of duty, desperation, or derangement—had no choice to traverse those dangerous lands. He mentioned strange remains of the civilizations that had dwelt there: plains and valleys where magic phenomena still persisted and odd mechanisms of forgotten purpose protruded from the loam. Some claimed these were what remained of the last defenses against the Annihilators and their servile demons. Others insisted the invaders had brought them to help them lay waste to Great Hystzos and all its works. Amidst these strange, or even surreal landscapes, all manner of creatures roamed. Not merely abominations or impossibly large specimens of familiar species, but supragants of legendary size, as well as the ferocious cryptigants which preyed upon them.

"How far do the Godbarrows stretch?" Druadaen asked.

"All the way to the Cloudcap Mountains," Lorgan replied. "And for the rare soul which can find a way through those peaks, they are rewarded by lands that are worse still: the Shuns."

"And what lives there?"

"Everything I've mentioned and more. All lost in the vast reaches of those lands. It's said they stretch halfway around the world. Plains become deserts, which become mountains, which finally flatten back into plains. Again and again and again."

Lorgan, like the best storytellers, partook of the wonder he conveyed with his words. "And there one may come across ruins that precede those in the Godbarrows, of empires that were long fallen when the people of Hystzos were still island-bound fisher-folk who dared not sail behind the sight of their own shores."

"So those ruins are—what? Many thousands of years

old?" Tales of Arrdanc's pre-Cataclysm rose unbidden in Druadaen's mind.

"Maybe older than that," Lorgan sighed. "They are mentioned in all the histories, and in all the legends before those. It's said that they should all be dust by now, but they're not. Some are made of strange stone that no one has been able to assay."

"Why?"

"Because," Lorgan answered, "no known substance can reduce it, not even aqua fortis. There are also strange clockwork devices in the midst of these ruins, their metal tarnished more than rusted—although they should just be so many flakes and flecks if they were simply cast from iron or bronze." When he finished, he kept staring to the east.

Druadaen suspected that for all Lorgan's awe-filled warnings, the captain yearned to see these places for himself. After allowing a few silent moments to pass, he cleared his throat. Lorgan seemed to see him anew. "I know you have no alchemist aboard," Druadaen said apologetically, "but I would ask one last favor of you: can you tell me what these labels say?" He had unslung the wood-framed case he had brought ashore for this purpose.

Lorgan raised an eyebrow at Druadaen's request, leaned over to peer into the sturdy box; three rows of vials stared back at him.

"Where did you get these?"

"From those highwaymen who ambushed me on the road to Pakobsid," Druadaen answered.

Lorgan nodded, squinted to read the labels. A moment later, one eyebrow rose slightly.

It stayed that way for quite some time.

CHAPTER TWENTY-NINE

Well, Druadaen thought as he topped another rise and saw the next stretch of grassland, *at least it's not as flat as the Gur Grehar.*

It was hardly a fair comparison, frankly. Although the north winds upon the Godbarrows became cool with the onset of night, the weather had been fair and he'd been able to supplement his dry rations with small game. And there were signs of habitation, here and there.

But even if Lorgan had failed to warn him against entering them, Druadaen's own instincts inclined him toward wariness. Although the captain had explained that there were normal towns to be found further north and south, in this particular belt of the God-barrows, even the smallest hamlet had walls. Of farms there were none, and of strongly built family steadings, one kind was prevalent: burned shells that stared balefully at him with empty sockets that had once been windows.

The one time he veered within bowshot of one of the larger towns, he discovered two things: that it was more a place of refuge than commerce, and that its denizens did not encourage visitors. In most of his travels, Druadaen had found that the caution natural to such isolated places was usually leavened by curiosity and the possibility of trade. Not here on the Godbarrows. The only reaction to his approach was a slight increase in the number of helmeted figures on the walls and the number of readied bows among them.

At least as striking was the lack of roads into or out of the place. Most of the gates were small and well above the level of the ground. The one that was wide enough for wagons could only be accessed by a drawbridge served by a free-standing ramp of rammed earth.

Right angles and straight lines were rarities along the walls, probably because they hadn't been erected to enclose a core of buildings but mostly plug the gaps between a rough ring of hardened structures that had accrued over time. The lopsided gatehouse before him had clearly begun as two stone barns; they were now joined by indifferent stonework. The central keep—a peculiar, curving, otherworldly structure—had been expanded several times, each addition more slapdash than the last and blocking more useful fields of fire than it added. The spots which boasted an actual curtain wall showed evidence of many breachings and reconstructions. And often as not, lengths of compromised walls had not been rebuilt, but replaced with a squat tower or an earthen rampart studded with abatis. Druadaen wondered how long it took any newcomers to learn their way around the sprawling stronghold.

By the end of the second day, he no longer encountered any of these desperate citadels that purported to be towns, but he did discover how they'd been built without recourse to nearby quarries: they had raided dressed stone from the ruins of the empires that had once held sway here. Druadaen had wondered at the absence of ruins closer to the coast, but now realized that the flattest and most thinly vegetated expanses he'd passed there were just such places, but picked bare of useful material.

Seen from the top of the ridge he'd just ascended, it was clear how the original shape of the land had been altered by the shovels of busy empires. The areas between every south-trailing spine of low hills had been groomed for farming. The winding depression that Druadaen was following had been the roadbed of a wide, paved artery that carried trade in from the coast and produce out toward it. And he wasn't the only one who'd found them useful for swift movement; the S'Dyxoi had as well.

Although Druadaen's tracking skills paled beside career Outriders, they were more than sufficient to show him the numbers and direction of the recently passed packtrain. The tracks were only fragmentary—probably older than two moonphases—but that was offset by the lack of other movement upon the Godbarrows and the S'Dyxoi's utter disregard for leaving a trail. Mere hours after striking inland, Druadaen routinely came across their weather brakes and large cooking fires, usually nestled in low places. This was in stark opposition to what Logan had suggested to Druadaen: that on the Godbarrows, fires were only useful for one thing— attracting trouble. But the S'Dyxoi's puzzling disdain for such caution made tracking them relatively easy, particularly since their horses left deep prints consistent with a steady canter. And if ever Druadaen feared losing the trail of hoofprints, it wasn't long before he'd catch sight of an equally distinctive marker: the occasional bodies they left in their wake.

Most of the corpses had been stripped of gear, clothes, and then flesh, apparently in that order. They were all male and, from what Druadaen could gather, lightly built: probably the ones who broke under the strain of carrying their captors' loads at a brisk pace. On the third day, however, the number of the dead he found around a campsite was much greater and the remains were both human and abominate. However, it took him almost an hour to determine that, since these bodies had not only been picked clean, but pulled apart and strewn over the better part of an acre. Which was how Druadaen, standing at the center of the desiccated carnage, discovered why the fires that Lorgan had decried as great dangers, the S'Dyxoi considered great opportunities.

The broad, deep tracks of five supragants revealed that they had approached the camp on a wide frontage. But their departing prints paralleled those left by the horses of the much diminished group. Once again, the S'Dyxoi had affined with, or dominated, the minds of the great beasts which had obediently traveled on with them. Judging from the depth and space between the prints, they were moving faster than a human could run, and doing so for the entire day. Druadaen wondered how long supragants could endure such a pace, but then remembered that in Sarma, the S'Dyxoi had not scrupled to ride the beasts to death. And here, replacing them might be as simple as building another large fire and waiting for more to arrive.

Druadaen dismounted, considered the distance to the next ridgeline. He would not reach it before dark, so he would have to make camp here. After leading the horse into a small crevice in a rocky spur, he paused before starting to remove its tack. The Godbarrows were becoming so wild and ominous that he had to leave the poor creature ready to ride. So he chose a middle course, and set about unfastening the saddle bags.

As he did so, his thoughts wandered back to the S'Dyxoi. Among all the uncertainties surrounding their intentions and their actions, the one that continued to nag at him was their inexplicable use of time. More narrowly, why had they returned to the watch post half a year after they'd passed through the Shimmer? Perhaps they had come across news, rumors, or legends which indicated the approach of a propitious moment in which to effect a return through it. It seemed unlikely that a highly accomplished S'Dyxan mantic was unaware that the Shimmer only worked in one direction, but then again, Druadaen was not versed in what they did and did not know about it. Perhaps as little as anyone else knew about the strange osmotium they called the Nidus.

Druadaen removed some dried meat and unleavened crackers from his kit and told himself that if he didn't stop pondering such things he would not get the sleep he needed. As he ate, he paid close attention to the tastes and textures of the dull food, hoping that focus on his physical senses would prevent him from pondering his many unanswered questions.

As strategies went, it proved to be a dismal failure.

❖   ❖   ❖

Just before noon the next day, a lone bird soared overhead, wings wide on its southward journey. It was the first sign of movement in three hours. And given the lateness of the season and the increasingly cooler weather, Druadaen allowed that it might be flying before a northern storm. He resolved to stay closer to terrain, even ruins, that offered shelter: cold, wet horses—or riders—rarely acquitted themselves in battle as well as warm, dry ones.

Consequently, when Druadaen spotted the next ruin, he urged his mount to make a closer approach than usual, the structure's strangely smooth west-facing remains shielding whatever might lay behind it. But before reaching the far side, his nose told him at least one thing he would find there: carcasses.

For a moment, he was oblivious to everything except the remains of two supragants, their ribcages reminding him of rafters in the early stages of a barn raising. A veritable cloud of vultures and other, unfamiliar carrion birds rose up at his approach. The vultures were the least skittish; they resettled quickly on the ruin, covering its upper parts in a rustling cloak of black, wing-flicking impatience. A small number of wolves looked up from their sniffing inspection of the second, more distant supragant's blunt-snouted head. They seemed to measure the potential threat of newcomer against the meat's advanced stage of decomposition and decided it was not worth the effort. They loped off, unhurried.

Only then did Druadaen notice the rest of the carcasses: seven horses, at least a dozen humans, and about half that number of abominations. The charred remains of a sizable bonfire predicted what he discovered next: tracks of four new supragants that converged upon the camp. Druadaen glanced up at the ruin, realizing, *This spot was carefully chosen*. Although it was no longer a towering edifice, parts of it were still tall enough to be ideal vantage points from which to keep watch—or to work a mantic effect—in any direction.

But the most significant feature of the killing field was the direction in which the majority of tracks departed from it: due north. And in this group, there was only one kind of print: the deep, loam-churning strides of the four new supragants, traveling in a close and regular formation. The footprints and hoofprints that had arrived at the site did not exit it; clearly, the S'Dyxoi had decided that both their human and equine pack animals were no longer needed.

However, two loose groups of abominations had continued to the east, clearly running—fleeing?— toward the distant, higher hills said to be a haven for their kind.

Druadaen resisted the urge to inspect the readiness of the concoctions the Sarmese had provided for subduing abominations. Not that he was any more likely to need them now than yesterday or the day before. But so long as he'd been traveling in the S'Dyxoi's wake, even at so great a distance, he'd benefited from a measure of safety not unlike that enjoyed by the small fish that swim behind a shark. But now that his eastward path was diverging from theirs, he was truly on his own.

He almost flinched as the vultures rose in a startled mass—and a new, very different bird rushed just over his head: the same bird that he'd seen earlier in the day. The close pass showed it to be much larger than he'd thought, and as it winged eastward, he noted the heavy wings and almost stubby body. Was it an owl? Out here? During the day?

For no logical reason, he scanned the horizon quickly. Nothing. Just the vultures behind him and what might be an owl dwindling toward the hills ahead. Druadaen hunched more closely into his cloak and touched his spurs to the horse, gently prompting it toward the mist-shrouded ridges rippling the horizon.

The number of ruins decreased, but their size burgeoned beyond any proportions to which Druadaen's prior travels had accustomed him. Immense fortifications seemed to rise up from the plains, some towering as high as the hills beyond them. As square and stolid as a citadel built from a child's blocks, some were formed from single slabs of stone over fifty feet high and twice as wide, stacked as if the builders had meant to bump against the sky itself.

However, it was the rounded ruins—agglomerations of curving walls and domes and crumbling galleries—that had evidently given the region its name: they did indeed look like the burial mounds of gods. Instead of climbing toward the clouds, they sprawled across improbable expanses of the plain. Their parapets and revetments were almost as large as the Consentium's wallways, which—until now—had defined Druadaen's concept of truly gargantuan constructions.

The closer he approached, however, the more evident their advanced state of decay and decrepitude became. Their walls and surfaces were riven as if struck by a dying god's battle-axe. The openings in them—shattered gatehouses, casemates, sally ports, even fortified stables—yawned as great black wounds.

And wherever doors or gates were missing, Druadaen observed that the absence was not the result of fires or rams or catapults or even the passage of time; whatever metal had bound those portals together or held them in place was gone. Not reduced to rust, or sundered, or twisted, but methodically and carefully removed.

As the sun continued further along its arc, the winds from the north grew cooler. And when a particularly chilly gust came whistling over the low grasses, Druadaen found himself recalling the miserable and dangerous days he'd spent heading north upon the Gur Grehar. And the parallels did not end there. He'd ventured upon those plains to bring back an urzh from which he might better learn how that race lived and why they emerged as Hordes every ten years or so. Here, too, he was charged with recovering a specimen of an even more mysterious species. And in both places, he'd come to regret pressing onward despite the advice of those who had deemed his mission a sign of madness, suicidal intent, or both. At least all the ground cover on Hystzos seemed to be sweetgrass, rather than the insidious sourgrass which had done in his horse on the Gur Grehar—and just when he'd needed to flee.

Hoping that the Death Lands supposedly scattered about the Godbarrows were nothing more than fearsome rumors, he peered ahead. One, maybe two final lumps rose from the plain between him and his destination. With the threat of foul weather rolling in, he needed shelter, but there was no certainty that either of those dim shapes would provide it. On the other hand, he didn't have any other options.

Drawing the reins slightly in that direction, he urged the horse into a slow canter and hoped for the best.

CHAPTER THIRTY

Druadaen peered down into the pit. Others had sheltered here; several broken weapons, pieces of armor, and smashed overland kit lay at the foot of the rough slope. They ranged from rotting and rusted antiques to recent additions.

Unfortunately, this was no better than the first ruin he'd reached on his day-end push for the hills. That one had bones mixed in with the debris, some of which hadn't been there long enough to be sun bleached. So he'd pressed on in the hope that the second ruin would offer a little more shelter and also appear a little less like a killing ground.

Half of his hopes had been realized; this one offered a great deal more shelter. A tall, saw-toothed remainder of the walls shielded the pit from the west and the north, and where they abutted, supported the remains of two upper stories, creating an overhang. Altogether, it promised a dry night, regardless of the direction or kind of weather. The one drawback was that his horse couldn't fit beneath the overhang.

On the other hand, although this pit contained no bones, it was both larger and richly littered with the mauled remains of equipment. And of course, there might very well be bones hidden beneath the uneven layer of debris that covered the near half of the pit's bottom: shattered masonry, earthenware slivers, rotting timbers, and a pervasive slurry of rain-clotted mud, dust, and ash. A worrisome place to hide, and a worse place to be trapped by anything that might wander past: fighting an uphill foe, even as a defender, was bad enough. Doing so on a slope with treacherous footing was unthinkable.

He glanced east, hoping he had missed some distant silhouette that might signify yet another chance of shelter. But the plain was as level and empty as a tabletop until it ran up against the fog-shrouded hills that were his final destination. And even if he had been able to reach them by pressing on into the early darkness, and even if he was lucky enough to find shelter, there would be no safety there. None at all.

Even rested and in broad daylight, approaching those uplands to find and capture an abomination was as dangerous as anything Druadaen had ever undertaken. With horse in tow, he would have to move stealthily from one screening terrain feature to the next. Then, leaving his mount at a fair distance, he'd have to ascend to a vantage point from which to spot a suitable target, which he would then have to track, capture, and drug. After that, he would have to drag or carry the abomination to (or at least near) the horse, secure his captive, and then ride hard to outpace any pursuit.

So, Druadaen concluded sadly, if he chose to arrive

in those monster-infested hills tired and blind in the
middle of the night, it would only prove that Lorgan
had been right; suicide *was* his actual objective, after
all. Sighing, he peered back down into the pit; *well, if
I'm going to risk sleeping in it, I'd best study it. Closely.*

Judging from the heavy walls and reinforced arches
that framed the depression on all sides except for the
slope down, it had been a basement or sunken court-
yard. As in the rest of the sprawling complex, its walls
had been fashioned from a substance he'd observed
before: an unbreakable mortar or concrete that was as
smooth as slate but had the appearance of a frozen
fluid. Although he'd seen sections of brickwork and
heavy blocks elsewhere, there were none here.

The debris in the pit sloped down from Druadaen's
vantage point toward the back of the pit. It thinned
out and allowed the actual flooring to show through
about halfway to the back wall, which was lined by the
largest of the arched openings. Set atop—or in?—the
exposed floor were the only metal fixtures he'd seen
in this ruin: several pairs of crisscrossing strips that
appeared to be cast from brass. They emerged from
three of the partially obstructed openings in the rear
wall and played across the floor in a pattern that
resembled snakes crawling across each other. Tracing
one of the three twinned curves of brightness back into
the dark openings, Druadaen was abruptly reminded
of the rails used to move ore-carts in mines. These,
however, were far thinner and, despite the elements
and the ages, remained objects of graceful, golden
beauty, made even more so by contrast to the slope
of wreckage and filth leading down to them.

After he'd measured and studied the pit three

times over, Druadaen realized that he was not so much continuing to survey it as he was putting off his inevitable descent. He dismounted, tied off the reins on the stub of a tilting marble column, and began to pick his way down the rough embankment. His first concern was to find a safe path for the horse, and a level spot where it might stand next to the west wall, close to the overhang at the rear. His second, although no less important, job was to search for signs of recent habitation.

The embankment was wetter than it appeared. A small foothold gave way and Druadaen's cautious descent instantly became a fast slide down the black ooze. Covered in the muck, he flung off the gobs coating the hand with which he'd broken his fall and reflected that his misstep had at least one redeeming feature; no one was there to see it.

It took a while to discover a solid path to the point at which the west wall abutted the north, and once there, he began his inspection for signs of recent disturbance or other activity. After examining every inch of the flooring and locating the best spot for his mount, he finally accepted that he'd found everything he could—and that it was all maddeningly inconclusive. Most every piece of junk could have lain there for a few moonphases or as many years. Maybe centuries. However, while he hadn't the time or light to explore all the irregular gaps and holes and half-collapsed openings in the pit's three framing walls, he established that there was no spoor—either scat or kills—near any of them. Only a faint yet pervasive smell that reminded him of pitch, rust, and some of Elweyr's stranger chemicals.

While studying the threshold of one of the doorways

into which the brass rails ran, he made his only unusual discovery: a very small leather pouch. Inside was a pendant of several fused metals and set with an intaglio sigil that resembled no alphabet he had ever seen. Druadaen secured it in his tightly laced purse and leaned closer to examine the rails: the last part of his painstaking survey of the pit.

Even seen from a foot away, the shape of the metal strips was as perfect as their unmarred surfaces. Almost equally miraculous, none of them were buried beneath the debris or muck that adorned the rest of the floor. Druadaen could only suppose that when fortune-seekers sheltered in the pit, they saw the rich golden glints and cleared away the detritus with the intent of removing the metal. If so, none of them had any success. Despite their brass-gold appearance, the narrow rails were at least as hard as Druadaen's steel dagger, and whatever held them in the narrow grooves that accommodated their gracefully intersecting arcs and loops was apparently as invulnerable as they themselves were.

Druadaen had just decided that he had finished his inspection of the pit when he heard a distant, strangely hoarse horn: probably made of wood. Which, according to Lorgan, was typical of abominations; they either lacked the facility or the patience to fashion anything from bone or other materials. Consequently, their horns were typically small, rot-hollowed lengths of tree trunks.

Druadaen tried to gauge the distance and direction of the sound as he considered his options: fight, flight, or hide. Fighting was madness; abominations might lair alone but tended to travel in groups. And any that were large enough to carry a horn fashioned from a log would be extremely dangerous opponents. Flight wasn't promising, either; according to Lorgan and the viziers of Sarma, once an abomination figuratively or literally smelled blood, they would track it relentlessly. And although a horse was faster, they were almost sure to outlast it in a chase.

So the only option was to hide. But that meant getting his mount down into the pit quickly, which was just deep enough to conceal it. Keeping it still and quiet were another issue entirely.

Druadaen scrambled up a rougher part of the slope so as not to erode the narrow path he'd blazed for the horse. He made sure there was no urgency in his actions as he took its reins and led it to the lip of the pit. But whereas Druadaen had merely had some misgivings about his footing, the horse's eyes rolled white in alarm as he started to coax it down the embankment. It shied back twice before he managed to get it to descend in one swift rush. The weight of the animal caused it to sink until the muck was well above its fetlocks. Happily, that put the tops of its ears lower than ground level. Less happily, it also meant that any hope of a speedy escape was now as hopelessly mired as the creature itself.

Using the last bit of dried fruit he'd kept in reserve for moments like this, Druadaen hooded the skittish horse with his cloak, thereby muting the intermittent windings of the horn. Even so, had it not been well trained, Druadaen would not have been able to keep it steady with one hand, sword at the ready in the other, listening for any sounds that might indicate the abominations were coming closer or moving off.

The sun—now a cloud-smothered gray blob—had almost completed its descent to the horizon before Druadaen heard the horn again: more distant and probably slightly further north. Still, if he was close enough to hear their horn, they were too likely to spot him if he left the pit.

He leaned back against the wall, determined to make the best of the night ahead.

After the horn had quieted again, a whisper of thin rain came misting down. Druadaen retreated to the overhang, patting the horse apologetically as he did. Once under that shelf and arranging his gear, he noticed things he'd missed during his faster inspection of it: partially consumed clods of peat and other signs of a comparatively recent fire. There were also a few seared tatters of cloth that, judging from the stains, had been used to wrap wounds. And, in a narrow drainage trench between the floor and the wall, he found broken or discarded bits from the kits of travelers. Most of it had lacing and hides typical of Last Lander artisans, primarily Sarmese and Kaandean. However, as he dug down, he found knives from Absolutia, shreds of Ruildine woolens, and smaller, often unrecognizable bits that could have been, and probably were, from almost every nation of Lorn Hystzos. However, if any of the owners had died here, their bodies or bones had been completely consumed, carried off, or were drowned under the calf-deep slurry just beyond the limit of the brass rails.

As soon as the rain let up, Druadaen exited the low overhang at a crouch; dinner had been cold and dull ever since he'd left the *Fur-Drake's Oath*, but he'd be gods damned if tonight's meal was going to be wet, too. He made his way back to the horse, careful of the slick stone and the increasingly sloppy slurry beyond. He patted it apologetically again. This was the second night he'd had to leave the horse saddled and with some of his bags still upon it; hard on the horse and now, likely to soak his kit. But if a threat drew near, he might be lucky and have enough time to flee—but there'd be no chance of doing so at all if the horse had to be retacked.

The gelding was calm enough as Druadaen began to work at the saddle bag that held his rations, only to discover that the rain had soaked the rawhide ties. Water-swollen, he kept at them with fumbling fingers even as the rain started to return. Eager to finish, he was hurrying when one of the taut loops finally started loosening. He gave it a hasty tug.

The horse flinched, not hard or far, but in doing so, bumped outward from the wall—and straight into Druadaen, who was pulling backward on the tie at that moment. Between the push from the horse's flank, the sudden release of the tie, and the slurry that was running off the hill, he slipped, falling backward as the contents of the saddlebag went flying.

Reaching rearward to break his fall, the backs of Druadaen's arms bumped into the stiff rims of his cuirass's armholes; he pushed harder, trying to get his hands back before he hit the ground.

He landed with a grunt, almost four feet away from the horse. Worrying that it might have been spooked, he took the precaution of scrambling back a few more feet, where he found his footing improved; he was on the open floor of the pit, amidst the rails.

Seeing the contents of his ration bag lying in the

path of the spreading ooze, he pushed to his feet to rescue it, touching one of the rails as he did so.

A noise like grinding metal gears came out of the nearest opening on the north wall.

Food forgotten, Druadaen darted back toward the west wall—before he realized that it was only six feet beyond the closest loop of one of the brass tracks. And if what he heard was connected to those shining rails—

The grinding became a rising screech that rushed out of the opening like the bow wave for the figure that followed. Except, Druadaen realized it was not an actual figure; it was a parody of one:

A head shaped like a sphere, but bisected by a discus. A wasp waist that divided the bipedal form into distinct segments, like the parts of an ant. Legs that ended in wheels that squealed as the metal mannequin flashed, quick as a panther, along the rails. Three similarly segmented arms waved weapons: a long, curving sword; a broad dagger with a narrow point; and a long spear. A fourth appendage mimicked the motions of the others in futility: there was nothing beyond its elbow joint. All of it was made from the same brilliant brass as the rails along which it streaked—

—straight toward Druadaen.

CHAPTER THIRTY-ONE

Druadaen leaped away from the wall. He couldn't tell if the spear could reach his horse, but if it did and the device closed on it...

The metal-man swerved after him, raising its weapons and apparently unaware of the horse. But that split-second of concern for his mount almost cost Druadaen his life. The shining brass automaton jabbed the full length of its spear toward him in one abrupt motion; holding the weapon effortlessly by its butt, it bore down on him.

Training took over. *Just like a charging lancer, and not enough time to draw my sword.*

It was almost upon Druadaen, the sword-arm back for a cut to follow the attack of the lancelike spear.

Wait, wait... now! And as if Druadaen might miss the moment, the velene pulsed—then unfolded explosively off his wrist as he shoulder-rolled—

—toward the automaton.

It wasn't able to drop the spearpoint fast enough,

although it cut a seam along the armor on Druadaen's back. But now its sword was flashing forward, faster than he would have believed a machine could move.

But just as it swung, the blade pulled back—because the automaton had reversed, rotating at the "waist" to keep it facing Druadaen.

Just as the velene flew at its head, a deep hum resonating out of it.

The automaton never stopped moving, but it kept interrupting its own actions, first as its target dove forward and under the lowest angle of its spear. Then again as that target calved off a small metallic ally. The sum effect was that the device's reactions had the appearance of a sudden fit: a flurry of hasty corrections, each abruptly interrupted and reversed by the next.

Druadaen rolled up to his feet already running, drawing his sword as he charged to get beyond the furthest limit of the rails.

A solid *clank*, almost like a muffled bell, sounded behind Druadaen—and the velene went past him, still airborne but not exactly flying. It came out of its aerial tumble as Druadaen realized what had happened: the automaton had swatted it away. Evidently, its attempt to use sound against the device hadn't worked; Druadaen could hear it whirring closer.

But he got beyond the last brass rail and leaped for the slimy slope, hearing the rush of a weapon in the air behind him.

The spearpoint tapped the back of his armor, not quite penetrating it but sending him a few extra feet up the slope ... and safely out of its range.

The velene landed alongside Druadaen as he rolled

over, sword held out in a two-handed guard. *Because if that mad machine can throw the spear...*

But instead, it shot forward to the limit of the rails, spear straining outward...just as its foot-wheels reached the slurry that Druadaen's flight and fall had strewn across the tracks. The automaton jerked and faltered, pebbles snapping. As if pulverized by a foundry hammer, they flashed into sprays of dust as the wheels ground through them, raising a smell as sharp and arresting as the fumes in a stone-cutting mill. It had pushed to the limit of the brass curves; somewhere in its lower body—abdomen?—gears groaned as it struggled to close with its target.

Druadaen rose carefully, still holding his sword before him. The velene crept forward, staying low against the ground.

The gears continued to grind. Its eyes—set wide, far to either side of the crestlike disk that divided the head—were round, lifeless, and maniacally focused on him. Druadaen took a step to the right. They tracked with him. Another step and the whole automaton shifted to remain as close to him as possible. And still, the gears groaned in mechanical frustration.

Druadaen hopped quickly back, then reversed to the prior position.

With a clatter, the brass mannequin shifted back and forth with him, barely lagging the movements it tracked.

The horse started at that sound, its cloaked head rising sharply; it whinnied in an uncertain mix of equine discomfiture and annoyance.

The automaton turned toward it, its gear-whine lessening as it leaned in that direction, clearly ready to switch to a new target. But the horse quieted, and after a moment's pause, it refocused both of its crystal clockwork eyes on Druadaen.

Who had learned what he needed about the device: while unthinkably fast and flexible, it was also somewhat distractable. He glanced toward the other side of the pit, and confirmed what he'd seen on his survey; a particularly rocky mix of the slurry stretched further along that wall, paralleling the rails for a few yards.

But before a plan became clear, the horse shifted again—and the automaton's attention snapped back toward it. One more sound or movement might trigger it to attack—and so, strand Druadaen in the Godbarrows. No time to do anything but—

Druadaen jammed his sword point-down in the muck, and grabbed the nearest semi-intact earthenware bowl to scoop up the muck. Snatching up a stone with his other hand, he rose into a forward step, throwing it at the horse. In that instant, the automaton was already straining toward him again, its weapons vibrating with readiness—

The stone hit; the horse yipped and stamped.

The brass man spun toward it, gear sounds increasing—

Druadaen leapt forward, shifted the broken bowl to his throwing arm and, counting on the automaton's nightmarish speed, threw it at the side of its gleaming head. Which, coming around in a heartbeat, caught the slop-streaming projectile full in its face.

Earthenware fragments flew; the slurry landed with a muddy slap across both its eyes. Leaping into a sprint, Druadaen grabbed his sword as he passed, heading toward the opposite wall while trying to keep the automaton in the corner of his eye.

For a long moment it was motionless. Then it began shaking its head to clear the muck from its eyes—but no, Druadaen realized; its whole head was actually spinning like a top. The black mire sprayed off in a wide arc. Before it had hit the ground, the automaton was after him.

Druadaen sprinted across the clear floor and rails, trading risk for a straight line and solid footing. Although the rails' serpentine and often recursive paths prevented the automaton from coming directly after him, its speed was dizzying as, swerving from side to side, it slipped from one rail intersection to another in a race to cut him off.

Druadaen couldn't even spare a glance as he neared the far limit of the tracks; his head start hadn't been as great as he'd hoped, and to waste even one second looking over his shoulder—he sped over the last rail and leaped.

The jump carried him all the way to the wall and atop the mix of rocks and mire. He turned. The automaton was there. Of course. It was pressed against the farthest rails again, as if straining to break free of them, weapons vibrating faintly. Druadaen moved slightly...

The spear thrust at him, stopping less than a foot away from him. It returned to its vigil.

Drawing a deep breath for the first time since it had emerged, Druadaen glanced up and down the long heap of debris that also defined his margin of safety. It narrowed as it approached the north wall and the openings from which the rails emerged, widened as it rejoined the greater slope. He looked around for the velene—and spotted it lying motionless at the bottom of that pile: waiting.

Clans and Consenters, does it know my plan? Well, let's find out. He began walking slowly along the wall. Predictably, the automaton tracked him. Every step, he stopped and kicked some of the debris at the device, but most of it landed to the side where it had been poised just a moment before. Sometimes it thrust the spear at him; mostly it simply waited for Druadaen to take another step. But before he did, Druadaen always used the point of his sword to build up the part of the slope he'd just kicked down behind his adversary, always making sure it was mostly comprised of pebbles and scree.

By the time Druadaen got to the end of the diminishing margin of stony debris, a good amount of it was scattered in an uneven path behind the metal monster. More had been heaped up along the edge of the pile that had been his safe walkway along the wall. He cleaned the blade—and without any preparation sprinted back the way he had come.

If there was any delay in the automaton's response, he couldn't detect it—but that was less important to him than kicking the newly heaped slurry of grit and scree down upon the prior trail he'd already built in the device's wake. Doing so as he ran made it impossible to stay as close as he had to the wall; the spear jabbed at him repeatedly, once cutting a seam in the topmost spaulder of his cured leather armor.

But the automaton was also beginning to fall behind: not much, but every time its wheels hit a cluster of pebbles that had fallen in the tracks and demolished them in a rapid series of pops, it started and shivered and so, lost a sliver of a second.

Listening for those sounds, Druadaen neared the

juncture where the limb of debris that lined the wall met the slope of rubbish. Ahead, he saw the velene waiting, intently focused on the automaton as it drew closer. One long stride away from the juncture, Druadaen heard what he'd hoped to: a series of larger, ragged snaps as the wheels hit a collection of larger scree that had fallen into the trench that housed the rails. Druadaen spun on his heel and leaped down—to the *rear*.

Directly at the machine.

Its swift motion had become a series of sharp jerks—almost a stagger—as its wheels ground through the scree in a ragged stutter of sharp blasts that made it buck so sharply that it started to tilt.

Its limbs flashed into new positions to rebalance it...

Druadaen leaped inside the range of the spear as the automaton struggled to right itself. The sai'niin sword gleamed like bound lightning as, both hands on the hilt, he brought it back and put all his power into one cut at the steadying device.

The blade hit the thin neck connector with a screech of metal on metal, punctuated by a ragged, hissing squeal: like white-hot steel being quenched in a bucket.

The head lolled and the artifact tipped in the opposite direction, like a top struggling to adapt its spin before recovering from an earlier push.

A silver streak flashed toward the machine: the velene impacted its inverted-triangle thorax with a sharp clang. The metallic dragonette bounced off; the automaton tipped further...

Just as Druadaen's back-cut crashed into it, slamming it even harder in the direction it was falling. With a shriek of shearing metal, it came out of its rails. Druadaen jumped back, recovering to a ready stance: panting, damp with rain and sweat, his nicked and much-dimmed sword held high to either guard or strike.

But the automaton's round, jewellike eyes dimmed and went dark. Sprawled, it was nothing more than a strange, broken travesty of a human form, its discrete sections fallen at impossible angles to each other. He stepped toward it—but as he did, a memory rose up unbidden:

Druadaen was in a different pit, standing over a different slain foe: the mismatched monster that they had narrowly defeated at the Library in Imvish'al. Still furious that Ahearn had dispatched it before he could learn anything from the strange monstrosity, Umkhira had walked up to the body and decapitated it, explaining, "When fighting magical foes, it is best to be sure they will stay slain..."

Druadaen lengthened his step toward his broken adversary, extending into a swifter, harder stride—which gave his double-handed blow just that much more power. The sai'niin blade flashed blue as it severed the already riven neck connector, accompanied by an overpowering foundry smell. A thick black ichor oozed out of the clockwork monster, along with a new odor; it was as if Elweyr's alchemical reagents and compounds had all discharged in one, acrid burst.

Only then did Druadaen realize that, despite the comparative quiet in the wake of the battle, the silence was not absolute: a wooden horn was being winded in the near distance. Faint voices—rough, excited, angry, eager—answered it.

As if emerging from a trance, his horse tossed its

head in alarm. The saddle blanket flew off; its ears were up and trembling, eyes wide and white. Although it had been paralyzed by the sudden, unfamiliar sounds of Druadaen's brief combat with the automaton, it had no difficulty understanding these noises: a bestial hunting party.

Before it could move or nicker, he sprinted across the pit and laid one calming hand on its flank. As soon as he was sure the horse wasn't agitated, he walked briskly to the overhang and opened the small, wood-framed ruck. He studied the marks he'd made on the vials that Lorgan had identified, removed one of the stronger sedatives the Sarmese had provided for use on a captured abomination, and found the tool to deliver it: a short, hollowed awl with remarkably thin walls. Dipping it deep into the thick, almost tarry compound, he walked casually back to the horse, and, resting his hands on the reins, drove the tool into its flank.

The animal turned, startled, but didn't even have time to whinny in fear, pain, or confusion; it slumped toward the wall, nickered groggily, then lowered itself unsteadily to the ground.

As soon as he was sure it was steady, Druadaen returned to the ruck, found several of the other vials that the viziers had provided for his capture and control of abominations: one each of the kind that sent out gouts of smoke, created a flash that dazzled eyes, and produced fumes that made one's vision spin. He left his bow strung and arrows at the ready near the overhang, then moved back to the wall.

As he passed his slumbering mount, he was suddenly glad for the chemical reek in the pit; it was still so overpowering that any pursuers, abominations or otherwise, were not likely to detect the scent of the live horse through it . . .

Or were they? Back home, a snufflecur and certain breeds of dog would probably smell it. And if abominations could have the traits of almost any known animal—

Two minutes later, both Druadaen and his horse were wearing a light coating of the pit's slurry with a few daubs of the automaton's ichor mixed in. The stink was so foul that he wondered if its power as a repellent might be a greater defense than all his weapons and alchemical compounds combined. With his sword slipped beneath the saddle blanket, he took the risk of sliding his body back into one of the small openings in that wall, which was drowned in the shadows left by Hystzos' small moons.

That lightless margin had not moved very far when he heard a group of *somethings* approach the pit. They were not stealthy in the manner of natural predators; their footfalls—because they were clearly bipeds—were audible. And, as they drew close to the edge, even their breathing—labored and uneven—became obvious.

But what they lacked even more than stealth was patience; only a few seconds after they had gathered just beyond the rim over which Druadaen might have seen them—and vice versa—several voices started muttering. The exchange rapidly became a squabble, and as it progressed, he could begin to make out bits of what might have been pidgin—or precursor—Sarmese, including many words borrowed from its Hystzossian overlords. His language amulet, as he'd come to think of it, didn't help, so it took a while to untangle the dialects and crude—crippled?—speech to make out the general gist of the debate.

"I smells bad smells."

"This hole always has."

"It is shun," added another voice. It was tempting to imagine the following silence was one of somber, even fearful reflection.

"Go down look."

"For what?"

"Meat."

A long pause followed. Druadaen tightened his grip on his weapon. Then:

"*You* look. I go safe. Home."

"No. You *look*."

There was no sound or sign of compliance. A few moments later, a meaty thud was answered by a grunt and surly growl.

"You look," repeated the voice that had originally given the order. "Or kill you."

"You kill maybe. But I go down? Mad metal man kill me *sure*."

"Is dead. You see."

"I see one. Maybe more." The voice paused, resumed in a tone of both resignation and defiance. "Hole is shun, death. You want see? *You* go."

The squabbling continued, although after that, it sounded more like annoyed browbeating. In time, Druadaen noticed that it was changing in one other, very welcome fashion: it was growing more distant.

After a few more minutes, it became a dim murmur and was lost in the rush of the rising night wind.

CHAPTER THIRTY-TWO

After a long night in the cold, wet pit, Druadaen climbed up the slimy embankment, pulling and cajoling his mount back over its crest. He led it on a slow walk around the rim, studying the chaos of fresh tracks that had churned its margins until he discovered what he was seeking: two clear and distinctive sets of prints.

One pair of footprints was broader and more spatulate than a human's but otherwise unremarkable except for longer, claw-tipped toes. However, the other pair of prints were like nothing he'd seen before. Or more accurately, they combined parts of tracks with which he was familiar but, in this case, they had been perversely mixed and fused.

Druadaen felt a sudden primal aversion that he couldn't understand at first. It hadn't been caused by counting the eight mismatched human toes that ran halfway around an almost circular sole the size of a newborn elephant's. It wasn't even the heel which ended in a bony spike that left a hard-edged, pristine

hole in the ground. No, it was that the two feet which
had left those prints were only *similar* rather than
identical. Closer study revealed that he was looking at
four, not two prints; either the creature had a bizarre
gait, or its limbs were so asymmetrical that its entire
body moved in a skewed fashion. Whichever it was,
Druadaen could not create a mental picture of it.

He leaned away from the tracks. *And that's what
you're going to go capture and bring back to the
coast.* Druadaen scanned the horizon but was only
half aware of what he was seeing, because his mind's
eye was focused on two diametrically opposed paths.

One led west to the Sea of Hystzos, where he could
probably survive until the *Fur-Drake's Oath* returned
and bore him back to Sarma. There he would report
that he'd given up within a day's ride of his intended
destination, and would return all the equipment they'd
lavished upon him—probably with fees for wear and
interest due.

Or, as his mind's eye settled on the hills to the
east, he could press on. Alone. Just like he had on the
Gur Grehar. Where, by all rights, he should have died.
Granted, the weather here was not lethally cold, and
if the prints of these two abominations were daunting,
the others' tracks agreed with what the viziers had
asserted: that smaller specimens were not uncommon
and probably quite manageable.

Druadaen frowned as he recalled the Sarmese oligarchs' hasty assurances that they meant to keep the
specimen for observation. Vivisection, one had added,
was unthinkable. But the more Druadaen had learned
about the remarkably fluid relationship the Princes
and the viziers had with the truth, the more he'd

begun to wonder if that addition had been a bit too swift, too easy. But there was no way to determine that now, and he was at the point where he had to go forward or turn back.

He rose, patted the flank of his horse, swung up, and stared east. The fog having cleared south with the rain, he could see that horizon clearly now: open woodland that led up into scattered knolls.

Urging his horse in that direction, he reflected that things were better than they might have been. In actuality, last night's danger had become today's good fortune. Because the band of abominations had come so close and left such clear tracks, he no longer had to wander into their hills uncertain of how best to find one, alone and unsuspecting. Now, he simply needed to follow one to its den and take it captive, albeit before being discovered by a much larger number of its kind.

Yes, so very simple.

Ignoring what he knew might be the voice of reason, he eased the horse into a canter that would put the pit—and hopefully, his misgivings—that much further behind.

While the horse drank its fill from a stream chuckling over its rocky bed, Druadaen glanced up from the foot of the knolls, studying their flanks. The midday sun revealed the lower slopes to be grassy, but above that, scant vegetation rapidly gave way to bare rock. Traveling from one point of concealment to the next would become impossible if he had to ascend that far. And the possibility of finding and following tracks in that kind of terrain was low, at best.

He glanced down at the stream's muddy banks. Prints of several abominations were there, notably the one with the round, asymmetrical feet. Midway to the hills, he'd lost the tracks of the group that had passed the pit; the night rains and swards of high, heavy grass had erased or hidden the signs of their passing. But they had kept a steady direction up until that point, so Druadaen had continued on that heading, which had eventually brought him into less thickly thatched meadows which showed fragmentary signs that they had indeed stayed their course. And from the looks of the muddy prints that left the other side of the stream and mounted toward the hills, they would be easy enough to follow for a little longer, at least.

Which meant he could not tarry here as long as he would have liked. Not knowing the habits of the abominations in any detail, he was highly—indeed, overly—dependent upon the tracks they left. It was unknown whether they favored high, open reaches or the more vegetated fringes of the hills, just as it was not a certainty that they tended to lair singly. All of which was made more confounding by the probability that they were as diverse as their strange traits. Logically, then, some were likely to pursue prey while others preferred ambush. Some were likely to have extraordinary senses, others less so. Some were likely to be day-hunters, some night-hunters, and some which did not care.

In short, Druadaen had to be prepared for a wide variety of situations. And because they might arise without warning, he might not have the opportunity to use anything except that which he had ready at hand. And if he had to flee swiftly, he might have to abandon parts of his kit to lighten the horse's load.

In the end, he hid almost all his camp-related kit in the high branches of one of the trees overhanging the stream and surveyed not only the Sarmese compounds, but the ones he'd taken from the bodies of the three men who had tried to ambush him on the road to Pakobsid. In the end, he attached two of their smallest, poison-anointed daggers to his belt. He frowned as he settled them into the small of his back; had his survival not hung in the balance, he would have gladly left them behind. But moments such as these were the only reason he had kept them in the first place.

Mounting his horse and urging it across the stream, he could not dispel one last, nagging uncertainty:

Will I ever cross it again?

The tracks of the abominations ended at a small opening in the side of a rocky spur flanked by fir trees. His horse already tethered halfway down the slope, Druadaen readied his weapons and studied the dark crevice.

Soon after the tracks from the stream had risen up from the scattered copses into the hills, their numbers began to wane. In groups of six or more, they'd begun to split off in different directions. Druadaen had orig-inally planned on following the smallest group with the smallest tracks: that seemed to promise not only the easiest fight, but also a small captive that would be easy to control and even easier to keep sedated.

But Druadaen discovered that while he was able to distinguish all the unique prints, it took a great deal of time. Many looked similar unless one stopped to kneel and study them carefully. Also, with other abominate prints appearing as he climbed higher, it became harder to determine which prints were from the group he had followed, a different one, or had been left by others who had not even been at the pit. Both situations had the same drawback; sorting out the tracks took increasingly more time. And time was in very short supply.

So ultimately, Druadaen decided to follow the group that it was easiest to track: the one which was traveling with the abomination with perverse baby-elephant feet. He could detect those large, unique tracks at a glance and although there were four others with it, their prints were no larger than his and an intermittent spattering of drops told him that the lightest of them was bleeding. A smaller, wound-weakened abomination would be comparatively easy for the horse to carry and for Druadaen to keep sedated.

Two miles into the hills, the group of five split: three who were headed into open woods and two who made for higher ground. The one that was bleeding, as well as the one with the strangely round footprints, were both among those bound for the trees. Druadaen followed carefully; the tracks were getting steadily fresher, so he was traveling faster than they were. And unless he was willing to raise the hills against him, he didn't dare overtake them in the open.

Instead, he had trailed them to the very spot where their prints disappeared into the rocky spur, which he had now been observing for a quarter of an hour. Chief among his concerns was that it might prove to be a side entrance of a much larger warren, teeming with wide-eyed and wide-mawed creatures that wanted nothing more than to gorge on his entrails. But his inspection of the area around the entrance revealed it to be only lightly trafficked and completely unwatched.

Nothing suggested that this was anything other than it appeared; an entry to a den without multiple entries or underground connections to others.

But that was not his only concern. First among the others was the probable lack of light in whatever cavern or tunnels lay beyond. Most abominations lacked traits that conferred superior vision in darkness, but it was not unknown among them. So Druadaen resolved to enter with a pertinent vial in his left hand: one with an alchemical compound that created sudden brightness.

Of almost equal concern was the narrowness of the entrance. If the entire cavern was comprised of similarly constrained spaces, his sai'niin sword would be useless. Although it seemed to intuit his needs at times, it wasn't as if he could simply ask it, "How short can you become?" so he could not risk having it in hand as he entered what might prove to be a labyrinth of tunnels and chambers so small and tight that he could not use it.

He ran a hand over his equipment, made sure it was both secure and handy, carefully adjusting the mallet-backed hatchet he'd kept from his kit. If it proved necessary to subdue his target, he might need the dull side of that tool, and if so, he was likely to need it very quickly.

Druadaen's third concern was the one which had dogged him since he'd arrived within sight of the knolls: time. And all he could do about that was to act.

With the vial in his left hand and shortsword in his right, he courted the rock-spur's shadow as he approached the cleft, crouched next to it, and listened.

Two voices. One was moaning, made faint by distance and occasionally interrupted by words that may have been slurred or simply poorly spoken. The other was muttering in short, annoyed bursts that were not in reference to the other exchanges, or anything else, apparently; it seemed more like a person having, and possibly losing, an argument with themselves. There was almost no echo or muffling to any of the voices or sounds; whatever else the interior might hold, there were probably not any sharp twists or turns just beyond the opening. Probably.

Either way, he knew as much as he was going to; now it was either act, or waste time until he did.

Druadaen shaded his eyes, counted to twenty, took a deep breath, and charged in, shortsword out in a guard position.

The passage was even narrower than the opening, and before Druadaen could throw the vial ahead of him, he almost ran headlong into the abomination that had been muttering to itself. It had apparently stopped and risen in response to the sounds of Druadaen's movement. Startled and squinting into the daylight streaming in around Druadaen, it flung one hand up across its eyes, while grabbing for a club leaning in the passage. Druadaen thrust the shortsword at its chest: the swiftest and easiest attack he could make in tight quarters.

But his wrist scraped against a dark outcropping on the right-hand wall. The bump skewed his thrust to the side and the point went wide, plunging into his opponent's shoulder.

The abomination—which had the face and ears of an urzh—stumbled as the thrust drove it backwards into what was either a chamber or widening passage. It let out a surprisingly shrill cry as it tripped backward into the darkness, using the hand opposite its wounded shoulder to break its fall.

Teeth grinding, Druadaen followed and thrust again.

And again, he did not hit the target as he'd intended. Instead of transfixing the being—for there was nothing beastlike about it—the point caught the side of its neck as it was attempting to roll to the side.

Blood ran freely, the abomination howled, rolled the other direction, and started scrambling to get around Druadaen. Twice wounded and with its weapon arm useless, its initial reflex to fight had become a reflex for flight—particularly now that the attacker's advance into the cave had also unblocked the only exit. Druadaen, still trying to determine the shape of the space he'd entered and recovering to either attack or defend, heard as much as saw his opponent stumbling past him. Which presented an opportunity to use what was, for him, a wholly novel move in combat:

He stuck out his foot.

The abomination, about to complete its first long stride toward the bright opening, hit the unexpected obstacle, tripped, and fell—forehead first—into the side of the passage. With a resounding *crack!* the wiry, urzh-faced creature bounced back from the wall, hit the ground at an angle, and was still.

Victory by prat-fall? Druadaen might have taken another moment to damn his swordsmanship had he not seen a hint of movement at the farthest corner of his vision.

The strange-footed abomination loomed large and swift out of the darkness just a few feet deeper within the narrow cave. There wasn't time to assess: only to react.

Druadaen spun in that direction, shortsword sweeping through a wide arc before the point lightly touched the neck of the tall, heavy creature—and the neck screamed at him, spitting teeth as it did. Startled, Druadaen stumbled backward, barely keeping his feet before remembering the vial in his left hand; he dashed it to the ground at the feet of the new attacker.

The glass shattered and light exploded from it, as bright as a bolt of lightning. Druadaen, forgetting to shield his eyes, blinked hard against it. When he opened his eyes, blue-green spots swirled across everything. He put his shortsword forward in a half-blind guard.

But the creature was wholly sightless and roaring— from a fang-lined vertical mouth that began as a slit at the bottom of its thick, flexible neck and rose all the way to the base of its button-small nose. Lambent fish eyes blinked furiously on either side of its head as one immense arm raised a hand to shield them. The other was wielding a massive club—except, not with a hand. The end of a tentacle was wrapped tight around the cudgel's grip, the sinuous appendage writhing angrily, swatting in a blind fury at the space Druadaen had occupied but a moment before. When it didn't hit anything, the creature reared up, revealing that it had four, rather than two legs. The front pair lashed at the same area, heel-spikes flashing out from their sheathes.

Druadaen shifted tactics; he threw his shortsword against the right wall—hard—and then, in one fluid motion, slipped toward the open space to the left of the creature, reaching for the small of his back as he did.

The abomination—its torso almost as heavy as the one he fought at the hilltop ruins—spun toward the sword's metallic clatter, its front two legs coming back to the ground as the club-wielding tentacle cut an arabesque that first struck the air and then, reaching farther, glanced blows off the wall.

As it turned to do so, Druadaen's side step brought him to the creature's rear flank just as he drew one of his poisoned daggers. He buried it in the closest of the heavy rear legs—which instantly lashed out at him, the heel-spike emerging with a meaty *pop!*

But Druadaen had kept moving, leaving the first blade in the wound, and drawing the next before the creature could recover enough to kick backward. He jammed the second dagger into the plane of muscle just beneath its shoulder, jumped away—and bounced off a bulge in the shadowed wall. Stunned, Druadaen rolled farther back into the irregular cavern, hoping that there wasn't another ready adversary waiting in that direction.

Happily, there wasn't and, in the same moment that he regained his feet, the numb, swaying abomination finally toppled over. It hit the ground with a grunt, exhaled a great sigh, blinked sharply three times, and fell silent. Its eyes seemed to collapse inward, as if they were each housed by sphincters instead of lidded sockets.

A whimper from the darker recesses at the back of the fissure-like cave reminded Druadaen that the third, presumably injured, abomination was still to be confronted. He lit a torch and entered a small, final chamber.

The wounded abomination was half-buried in a pile of blankets that its fellows had not woven and hides they had not tanned. From a few yards away it appeared quite human, if small. But as Druadaen drew closer, he saw that instead of teeth, the mouth housed grinding plates, and in place of lips, a thick ring of fleshy polyps writhed at him.

It moaned and snarled when Druadaen came within touching distance. It tried to rise and bite him, but collapsed with a groan; its left foot was noticeably askew and just below the midpoint of its shin, there was a dark, swollen lump. A few more steps and it would become a compound fracture; if Druadaen was any judge of such things.

He readied the tool he'd used to sedate his horse, put several drops of the least powerful opiate in it, and baiting the abomination to snap at a strip of cloth, found an opening to drive the liquid home. It shrieked in pain, then rage, then its eyes lost focus and it fell back on its squalid nest.

Like any other limp body, it was difficult to handle, and since it was uncertain how long any given opiate would act on any given abomination, Druadaen had to be watchful for its reactions. But once its hands were bound behind it, and its legs tied off—the broken one lashed tight against the other—he was able to drag it to the door. In that process he discovered other features he had not noticed before. Its hands were as webbed as an otter's and it had almost invisible gills behind its ears. Also, its eyes were not the light gray he'd initially assumed, but almost white and strangely round—almost enough to make Druadaen suspect that it may have signified a common family root with the larger one.

He flinched at the memory of attacking it from behind with two poisoned daggers, pushed it away as he went back inside to retrieve the blades. As he did, its fantastically misshapen and mismatched parts brought to mind the strange polyglot monster the group had defeated in the Library of Imvish'al.

He frowned as that image was replaced by one

even more similar, and which made him wonder if
whatever had made this creature had touched his
own world as well. He remembered standing amidst
the dead after defeating a shaman in the Under of
Grehar, staring down at the most fearsome—and
arresting—of all the beings they'd had to vanquish: a
blugner sow. At first, he'd presumed it was a product
of profound inbreeding. But some primal part of him
rejected that, told him that he was not simply looking
at natural breeding gone awry, but the ghastly result
of some fundamental and intentional perversion of the
species' normal form. The creature's unnatural lack
of symmetry seemed like a malign and purposeful
handprint left by some capricious—or vindictive—god.

The same handprint was on the body at his feet,
except many times greater and more arresting. It was
difficult to anticipate what such creatures might be
able to do, what unrevealed traits they might have. At
which another memory rose up, the one that had ultimately led to him removing the head of the automaton
the night before. Wouldn't that be prudent here, too?

He recoiled: that was disabling a machine, but to
remove the head of a being? Whether a creature was
hideous or beautiful was of no count; mutilation was
repellent unless it was clearly necessary. And in this
case it wasn't. Besides, he consoled himself, the neck
was so thick and uneven that he'd have needed a saw
and an hour to get through it. And that was an hour
he didn't have to spare.

Not if he wanted to make it back to the plains of
the Godbarrows before more abominations found him
or his tracks.

CHAPTER THIRTY-THREE

An hour after he'd fed his captive rations laced with opiates, Druadaen crested a ridge several miles west of what he thought of as "The Pit" and reined in. As the first significant high ground since leaving the abominations' den the day before, it was his first opportunity to scan for pursuers. Only once the horse—and its constant jostling—stopped did he detect the almost invisible rabble of abominations well behind him.

There was no mistaking them for any other kind of creature. Even at this range, the differences between their various speeds and gaits were unmistakable. Besides, they were following the precise path by which he'd retreated from their hills to the comparative safety of The Pit. And once they reached it, the scat from his overnight stop would tell them that they were still on the right track.

What was not clear was if these abominations were part of the same group he'd originally tracked. And if so, how had they become aware of his intrusion into their hills? Did they rove about, looking for prey scents or scat? Or did they remain in contact with each other, despite the considerable distances between their lairs? Or was there some other means whereby they knew what had befallen the ones Druadaen had trailed to their narrow cave?

All those were questions which he could not answer, and for which he had no time. He urged his horse over the ridgeline, but not so abruptly as to raise dust. That might attract any horizon-scanning eyes among them, which, once alerted, would not miss his silhouette atop this ridge or the next. And once the abominations could all see their prey, they would no longer need to wait upon those among them with superior senses of smell or tracking abilities. They would simply close the distance as rapidly as they could.

The back side of the ridge was rough, and the horse's irregular gait elicited a comatose grunt from the small abomination across the saddle in front of him. Druadaen tugged the reins slightly, easing the horse into a slower, gentler descent. The longer the abomination was senseless, the better. It had started keening the moment it awakened and continued doing so until the breakfast opiate took effect. And since there was no way of knowing if one of the pursuers had extraordinarily keen hearing...

Druadaen kept his attention on easing his mount down the slope as quickly as he could.

Druadaen mopped his brow, sweaty despite the chill. Riding—or now, marching—across the Godbarrows on only a few hours of rest was not how he'd envisioned the final leg of his mission. The optimist in him admitted it was lucky he was still alive. Unfortunately, the voice of experience whispered that it was becoming less and less certain that he would remain that way.

For the second time in the past hour, Druadaen had heard the hoarse wail of a log horn well to the south. It was cheering that the sound was so distant; it suggested that his pursuers had spent many hours convinced he was still heading west, back toward the Sea of Hystzos. On the other hand, it confirmed that they now realized how he had misled them and were once again on his trail.

He would never have risked the ruse had it not been for the approach of more storm clouds from the north and the serendipity of approaching tracks in which he might conceal his own: those left by the S'Dyxoi when they'd turned north. The ruins where they'd done so had been almost abandoned by vultures, the carcasses stripped clean. However, tracks of various species—some familiar, some not—had accumulated over the past few days: creatures that had stopped by to help remove whatever had been left on the bones.

Druadaen had wasted no time. He left the carefully trussed abomination on a high, flat part of the ruins, and, as soon as it resumed snoring, he remounted and rode his horse hard into the west, the swift gallop leaving deep prints in the loam.

After a half mile, he reached what he'd been looking for: a much smaller, outlying ruin from which the remains of a slightly elevated irrigation system ran hundreds of yards to the south. He rode past it, then backtracked, dismounted, and guided his horse up to the flat stone channel and rode to its end. There, he guided the horse back down to the plain and kept it at a slow walk until he reentered the larger ruin, but from an entirely different point of the compass. He glanced behind; the horse's walking, unburdened hoofprints were fainter—and likely to be washed away if the threatening clouds brought any significant rain.

Putting the startled abomination over the saddle, Druadaen led his horse north. He kept their tracks within the much larger ones left by the S'Dyxoi's gigantic mounts wherever possible. Shortly after the downpour began, he swung around and was relieved to discover that the torrent was already erasing those tracks, rapidly washing and blending them into the much rougher and deeper prints left by the enslaved supragants. After walking another mile, he pushed the abomination further forward on the saddle, remounted and let his horse canter north at a leisurely pace.

Although creating a false extension of his path to the west had consumed considerable time, it paid the dividend he had hoped: they had obviously kept to the tracks which led in the same direction as those they'd been following, and continued to do so until they apparently ended just slightly beyond the smaller ruins and its waist-high aqueduct. By the time Druadaen heard their distant horns as he rode through the storming darkness, the abominations had obviously split into at least two groups, widening their search in an attempt to find the real trail. And because the pounding rain was washing his earlier tracks into rising mud, he was able to sleep despite the wet; his pursuers had little chance of rediscovering his trail before first light.

He was back in the saddle before dawn and, shortly after, heard their hoarse wood horns again. But they

were still far apart, apparently resuming their efforts
to rediscover their quarry's tracks. Indeed, given the
success of Druadaen's ruse, only two things arose to
dampen his spirits as the world started drying out.

Firstly, although the *world* was drying out, his saddle-
blanket was dripping like a freshly dunked mop. Wring-
ing did not make it dry enough to put on his already wet
horse, so he jammed the blanket into his largest sack
and resolved to start the day leading his mount, thereby
giving its coat and the saddle both time to dry out. But
that in turn meant Druadaen couldn't keep his captive
on the saddle in front of him, so the only reasonable
solution was to strap the abomination over the horse.
A workable solution but, for a few hours at least, they
would not be traveling at the speed he'd hoped.

Secondly, after an hour of slow progress north,
Druadaen was startled by a sudden flap of wings,
almost directly overhead; it was the owl he had seen
during his first arrival at the ruins. However, instead
of continuing onward as it had on that occasion, it
banked into a long lazy curve which ultimately became
a wide circle centered on him. He watched it complete
three circuits, his frown deepening with each one.
Owls typically hunted by ambush, descending through
foliage or other concealment until their talons reached
forward to snatch their prey. He'd never heard of—let
alone seen—one flying the way a hawk or vulture did
when it was orienting itself to its target. But even if
it had been such a bird, neither he, nor the horse,
nor even the abomination were small enough for it
to attack, making the pattern of its flight not merely
uncharacteristic but pointless.

Unless it's not choosing how it flies.

Druadaen felt a chill that had nothing to do with his still-damp clothes. What if the S'Dyxoi "priestess" had dominated it as she had numerous supragants? Might she have left it here as a sentinel of sorts, watching for pursuit or anything else of interest? It would certainly explain why it had remained on the plains. Owls typically preferred the cover of woods in which to both hide and hunt. It would also explain why it was flying in a pattern: although useless for its preferred mode of hunting, it was ideal for keeping an eye on him while also indicating his location to a distant observer.

At the end of its third circuit, it veered off to the southeast; not directly toward the abominations, but too close a heading to be comforting, either. Druadaen watched it go: another mystery that was pointless to ponder.

He clicked at the horse to lengthen its strides. Even if the owl was just an owl, it was still prudent to move as quickly as possible. And if it *wasn't* just an owl...

Druadaen tugged at the reins and tried to ignore the distressing fact that he was traveling in the last known direction of the S'Dyxoi.

Three hours later, he decided that the only thing worse than traveling in the direction of the S'Dyxoi was being *chased* in that direction. Because the approaching and converging horns meant that the abominations had found his trail again. It defied explanation how they might be using the owl as a scout, but the fact remained that a few hours after it had spotted—and circled—Druadaen, his pursuers had discovered and corrected their error.

Neither he, nor the saddle, nor the horse were fully

dry yet, but that precaution was now a luxury he could not afford. He led it down to the stream they'd been paralleling for the last half mile. A long drink before galloping wasn't advisable either, but that couldn't be helped. If there was a long chase before them, there might not be time to stop again.

Once his mount began to drink, Druadaen leaned down to pick out a rear hoof—and noticed that its belly seemed to have become larger since breaking camp. He hadn't allowed it to overfeed and he did not know of any parasite—even on Hystzos—that became evident so rapidly. The only logical cause was that over that past few days, it had been feeding on grass that was too soggy or loamy.

Druadaen frowned. He'd kept careful watch over where and upon what it grazed; if his mount went down with colic, he'd go with it. The only exception was the relatively brief interval when he'd tethered it away from the cave of the abominations. But that was too long ago to be the cause; colic almost always appeared within a day and a half of eating bad grass.

Eating bad grass . . . ?

Druadaen's spine straightened. What if, despite Aleasha's assurances and Lorgan's confirmation, Hystzos was not entirely without sourgrass? He'd wondered it before; just as ships and cargo unintentionally carry seeds between continents, could a traveler not do the same when stepping through a portal into another world?

He turned slowly, staring at the Godbarrows' thick green carpet. But in his mind's eye, he saw the sparse growth of the wintry plains of Gur Grehar. There, his inability to distinguish between sweetgrass and sourgrass had fated his horse to receive a final mercy from him. And because of that, he had been seconds away from a similar fate at the far less caring hands of urzh pursuers, had he not been rescued by Crown-Lord Darauf and his Teurond border cavalry.

He shook away the memories and forced himself to focus. He was missing something. Was there any other explanation? Was it credible that two such knowledgeable people as Lorgan and Aleasha—especially her—could be unaware of sourgrass if it existed on Hystzos? The only possibility was that it was extremely rare or no longer present in the settled areas. But Aleasha was *from* the Godbarrows, so surely she would have known of it. But she and Lorgan had also told him of its Death Lands, which legend described as being less hospitable to both man and beast, and not just those that lived there. He'd heard many stories of caravans found abandoned and traveling clans that had sickened and died after passing too close to those places, or after ascending the Cloud-caps to peer over into the Shuns.

Again, his mind froze in mid-thought: *Wait: the Shuns?*

The abominations had used the word "shun" to describe the Pit. But now, Druadaen wondered: when they said "shun," had they meant *the* Shun, or was it their word for any place that was especially dangerous or mysteriously unhealthy?

He backed away from the horse. If it had grazed not only on sourgrass, but a mix, then sourgut might indeed take this long to show up. But once it did, it would not take much longer to kill the poor creature, particularly given the added exertion of carrying the captive.

One way or the other, the horse was not going to

survive. It would not be able to keep a steady pace to remain ahead of the abominations, and if he pushed it into a sustained gallop, it would collapse that much sooner. And he'd die not long after.

Unless . . .

Druadaen started shaping a new plan as he approached the small abomination still strapped over the horse's back. It was futile to carry the being any further. Even though Druadaen no longer had a chance to outrun his pursuers, he still needed time, and burdened with a lamed captive, he'd be swarmed in an hour or two. At most. So he'd failed the Vizierate's contract; time to admit it.

He cut loose the abomination, which emitted a surprised grunt as it hit the ground. As Druadaen lifted the saddle, the grunting behind him became inchoate shouts of rage and hate—which stopped him in mid-motion:

The creature's shouting? Through his gag?

Druadaen turned. The gag had not slipped; it had a hole where the creature's mouth was, the polyps writhing in agitation at the edges of the cloth. A sharp acid smell emerged and a secretion leaked from them; more of the fabric dissolved. Stomach plummeting in both foreboding and revulsion, Druadaen dropped the saddle and moved to the far side of the horse.

A wide, bleeding sore was located where the abomination's head had been hanging. And trailing down from that wound until they ran off its belly were bleached paths left by streams of drool. The acid had not only discolored the horse's chestnut coat and seared away most of the hair, but the flesh beneath had been burned white. In some places, it had been burned through; small red lesions punctuated the white lines that ran toward the ground.

Druadaen stepped back. *How many times can I be wrong or stupid in a single day?* It wasn't sourgrass that was going to kill his horse; it was whatever was dripping from the abomination's polyps. And like many poisons, it probably had a numbing agent so that the horse, and therefore Druadaen, never had any warning that it was under slow, steady, fatal attack. Because even if the toxin couldn't kill such a large animal outright, it had slowed the horse enough so that the pursuers would ultimately chase it down. Which was how they'd rediscovered their trail, too—because the drool dripping off its belly left a distinctive scent, and they'd been depositing it for several hours.

Still prone and now staring up at Druadaen between the horse's legs, the abomination barked out a laugh, tried to speak, but couldn't seem to form words. Whether the inability to do so was the result of mental or physical impediments was uncertain. However, its jeering dwindled when Druadaen began to move and started laughing himself, but silent and mirthless. As he came around the fated horse's haunches, the creature's expression changed to terror. But Druadaen wasn't thinking about his captive. The only thought going through his mind, again and again, was:

All gone to wrack and ruin because of a sodden saddle-blanket.

Since childhood, he'd learned never to drape anything wet across a horse's back. And from the first night in the pit, either rain, sweat, or both had kept the saddle-blanket from ever drying out. Accordingly, when it seemed like they'd lost their pursuers, Druadaen had decided to bag the blanket, lead the horse, and strap the abomination to its back. And in so doing, he'd unwittingly put his captive in just the right spot to do just the kind of damage that the blanket would have prevented or at least slowed.

The greater irony, Druadaen reflected as he drew his shortsword, was that he failed to fully understand the full import of the cautionary advice that the viziers had imparted—and Lorgan had confirmed—about abominations: "even the smallest ones often have unexpected, concealed, or disguised traits that make them difficult to control."

He stood over his captive, which had cowered into as tight a ball as its tightly bound legs allowed. He presented the sword for its consideration, then sliced through one segment of the leather bindings that held its hands.

Stunned, it looked up at him, its misshapen mouth mumbling and mauling words that might have been questions or curses.

Druadaen picked up the now spliced length of rawhide, walked behind it toward his gear—but, as soon as it turned to study its unbound hands, he spun back and looped the thong into its mouth from behind. It spat and uttered what were certainly curses, rather than questions as three turns of the leather strap bound its mouth quite closed.

Druadaen returned to his kit, unbuckled the trail pack from the saddle, and tossed away everything except for his weapons, waterskin, food, unused sandals, and the numerous unusual objects that he had acquired or come across in his journeys. Happily, they were both few and light.

He gently tacked the horse and, after soothing it, swung up into the saddle. It made a sound more like a bleat than a whinny, but it was dramatically less of a reaction than if it had full feeling in its wounds. It was sad to think it could not be saved, but at least he might rely upon it for a last burst of speed, or as a means of leaving yet another false trail. And if he was lucky, maybe both.

Without a backward look at the gagged abomination, Druadaen spurred the horse into a northward canter.

An hour later, Druadaen heard the horns again; slightly fainter but now very close together; the scattered abominations had regathered, but the horse's brisk pace had reopened the distance. However, if he did not come across more ruins soon, neither speed nor guile would save him. His pace on the horse and then his endurance on foot were both likely to dwindle long before his adversaries experienced a reduction in either.

Happily, just as he was considering that unpromising comparison, Druadaen spied what he'd been looking for: one of the many derelict complexes he'd seen at the limit of his vision during his journey from the coast. This set of ruins had been memorable, being particularly low and sprawling as they stretched across acre after acre.

He spurred the horse into a gallop.

Druadaen slowed the horse as he approached the vast stretch of natural and poured rock, much of which was now partially buried, erupting from the plains like flat, gray scabs. The horse had kept to a trot for longer than he had suspected, and in order to preserve its strength for the final part of his plan, he resolved to use the first of the hard expanses so it wouldn't have to carry him any longer than necessary.

He swung his left foot out of its stirrup and slowed the animal to a walk. Standing in the other stirrup, he guided it toward the edge of what appeared to have been a ramp but was now merely an outcropping that never quite rose a yard above the grass. After gathering the minimum gear he'd prepared, he carefully raised his left leg to clear the saddle and he slid off to the right. That foot came down on the low, white, wind-scoured ruin.

The Sarmese had trained the mount well. Feeling the shift in weight, it tried to compensate to assist him. But Druadaen kept a hand pushing against its flank until he had his footing. With a quick step back, he undid his sword's baldric and smacked the scabbarded weapon hard across the horse's flank.

Startled, it leaped away, running a few steps.

Druadaen shouldered his gear and swapped his clean sandals for his dirty and scent-trailing boots. With a last look after the still-trotting horse, he began running along the ramp in the opposite direction, where it touched the edge of a much larger expanse of low ruins, many still joined, some separated by a step or a jump over the wild grasses between them.

With any luck, the horse's continuing tracks would mislead his pursuers one last time.

Druadaen's first startled reaction to the newly risen sun was amazement: he was still alive. His next was remembering, with disbelief, how far he had gone. Indeed, if he could have kept moving he would have; the dangers of traveling in the dark were as nothing compared to the certainty of his fate if caught.

But after two almost sleepless nights and a long, hard push before, he realized that continuing would have been a greater risk than stopping. Between traveling blind and being so groggy that he could not be certain of maintaining a straight line away from the flat ruins, he relented sometime after midnight. He had slept propped up in, and well concealed by, a tooth of rough stone sticking up from the ground. Druadaen rubbed his face, clenched a piece of jerky between his teeth, got his bearings and set out.

From what he'd heard as the prior day came to a close, his ruse of separating from the horse without leaving tracks had been successful. Late in the day, there was a frantic exchange of log-horn hoots: almost certainly, the sign that they had found the hobbled captive. As those who discovered him winded their horns to gather the searchers, he would have no doubt told his fellows—or somehow communicated—that the murderous human had mounted the horse and rode swiftly north: the same direction he'd been traveling ever since abandoning his westward push toward the coast. The frequent hooting afterward ended shortly before the first stars came out; the abominations had regathered and were following the tracks of the horse.

Either through lack of attentiveness or intelligence, it was a near certainty that they missed the point where Druadaen dismounted. Although some of them had keen senses, it did not seem that any of them had any nuanced tracking skills, and so had probably focused on visible tracks and the scent of the horse's dripping wounds. They were also unlikely to have conjectured that the human could have dismounted without stopping the horse, and so, were further misled by the uninterrupted progression of its hoofprints. Otherwise, they would have overtaken him long before.

Instead, the resumption of hootings shortly after the small moons rose almost certainly signified that they had found the horse—dead or alive—and once again had to split their numbers into numerous search parties in order to find the human's trail. Since then, the horns had sent their sonorous messages into the dark at odd intervals. But, particularly when the sun came up, it was only a matter of time before one of them would either notice that he had run on the open rock (unlikely), resumed traveling in grasslands wearing sandals (quite possible), or found where he had pulled on his boots and started leaving clear tracks once again (the most likely by far). But so far they had not found any of those telltale signs. With any luck, Druadaen began to hope that he just might be able to—

An urgent flurry of horns seemed to push the sun fully above the horizon. A bad sign, Druadaen allowed as he increased his pace. The only reason for that kind of exchange would be one of the groups trumpeting their discovery of the human's trail and the others acknowledging that they were beginning to reconverge. At which point they would have no reason to wind their horns, and would refrain from doing so. Even creatures as simple as they would see no reason to reveal their location to elusive prey.

Sure enough, after one of two final hoots, the horns fell silent.

Now, there was nothing left to do but run for as

long as he could, just like the last day upon the Gur Grehar. Except there, he'd had allies.

Here, he was truly alone.

As if things can't get any worse, Druadaen thought as the owl returned, winging in from the north. But instead of orbiting him, it banked and flew rapidly to a point not far off his current heading. Then it flew straight up, as if it meant to bury itself in the low clouds.

Just as Druadaen was ready to wonder what this odd new behavior might portend, the owl leveled off at a great height. It hooted faintly, turned through three fast, tight circles, and then descended sharply to the east.

Druadaen frowned. Those final behaviors weren't just odd; they defied any natural explanation. Nor was it plausible to impute it to careful training, for how would a handler communicate precisely where it wished a creature to go before performing such a complex set of actions? And only after—apparently—attracting the attention of a particular human on the ground. No, his suspicions were confirmed: the only reasonable explanation was mancery. And he knew of only one mantic who was apparently located in the northern reaches of the Godbarrows:

The S'Dyxan "priestess."

But those convincing answers begat another, even more confounding question: Why would the S'Dyxoi send him an indication of where he should go—for that was clearly the message of the owl's strange concluding acrobatics. Logically, they were his arch foes and would want him dead. And if they had observed any part of the life-and-death version of hide-and-seek involving Druadaen and the abominations, they surely knew that it would not end with him alive. So why not let the twisted creatures do their dirty work?

Unless it was more important to their ends to take Druadaen alive. Which, given their reputed abilities, they certainly seemed sure of achieving—just as sure as they were sure of killing him when and if he had served his purpose to their own plans. Still...

He shifted his steps to make for the area the owl had circled.

A moment before it had seemed suicidal, but now it seemed his only chance. Because it was a certainty now that the abominations would make an end of him. He could not outrun them, had no means left to outwit them, and had no way to best them in a fight. So if the S'Dyxoi wanted him alive, that gave him at least a little more time to seek a way out of that new predicament. Besides, it was unlikely that they, any more than anyone else, anticipated how his mere presence defused any attempt at mantic constructs. With that element of surprise, a few fortunate uses of the various compounds and philters in his pack, and an ocean full of luck, he just might live to see another day.

Removing one of his bowstrings from the small ready-pouches on his belt, Druadaen began to run to what might be a place of salvation or death.

Or, conceivably, both.

CHAPTER THIRTY-FOUR

Druadaen drew one of the arrows he'd saved from his encounter with the two wyrdwards—or just as likely, sorcerers—on the road to Pakobsid. He removed the wax tip cover; the point had a viscous shine that told him the poison was still active. He still detested the mere idea of using it, but as it had been every other time, it was likely to mean his life if he didn't.

And of all those times, his present situation was worse—much worse. He'd already spent half the day running from his pursuers: a good effort, but not enough. There were still a dozen of them and they had been gaining steadily. For the last hour, he'd pushed to reach the hillock upon which he now stood, believing it was what the owl had been circling. But either ground mists or the haze of exhaustion had tricked his eyes; there was a longer, lower ridge half a mile further on, directly in line with the hill. From Druadaen's perspective, the two had appeared to be a single terrain feature until he got within a mile.

The moment he discovered his error was also the moment he knew he was doomed; he simply didn't have enough stamina left to reach it, not before the abominations caught up with him.

He turned to survey them as they trotted, loped, waddled, even scuttled toward him. Now within four hundred yards, he was able to confirm what earlier glimpses had suggested; that the largest of them was the same fish-eyed ogre he'd left for dead in the cave. Yet here it was, its mouth now a torn and blood cruciform, its heavy tentacle thrashing in eagerness, fury, or both. Happily, all the other notably large ones had dropped far behind or given up.

The remaining abominations were mostly smaller, several of the swiftest appearing more like insects with only four appendages. Their torsos were low to the ground as they scurried forward on all fours, their flat backs below the reversed knee joints of their legs—all of which were furnished with hands rather than feet.

Two hours earlier, one of them had sprinted ahead of the rest, closing through the intervening half mile in about three minutes. Druadaen had drawn his still-inert sword, planted it point first in the loam, unshouldered his bow and waited until the monstrosity had closed to fifty yards. He'd missed, primarily because he was still drawing ragged breaths. Encouraged by the apparent harmlessness of its adversary, the water-strider man cackled and charged.

Druadaen drew to the ear and released a broad hunting point at less than thirty yards. It sank a quarter of its length into the creature, which flailed backward, kicking and screaming. After dispatching it with his sword, Druadaen started running again but kept an eye on the others' reactions to their still-flailing fellow. Once the rest of the abominations passed the wounded one, two of the smallest furtively broke from the rear and set about devouring it. Chilling, but potentially useful information.

After that, the chase had slowed. The others never drew too far ahead of the large one which, while in no way swift, seemed inexhaustible. Whether its endurance was innate or a product of vengeful rage, it had the same effect on the pursuit; it was slower, but the outcome was no less certain.

Druadaen laid the poisoned arrows out before him, then several of the philters that might prove useful, and drew his sword. He was disappointed to see that the blade was not reacting to his imminent demise. He glanced at the bracer-velene; no reaction there, either.

Some friends you turned out to be, he thought as he chose his targets. The key was the big one. If that one fell dead—or appeared to be—it might give the survivors pause. But as much as he wanted to start on the tentacled monster, Druadaen couldn't afford to; the greater the range, the more likely he might miss, and his only hope was to hit it with almost all but one of his poisoned arrows. He'd spend that shaft in an attempt to immobilize one at longer range and thereby draw in any other abominations that succumbed to their cannibalistic appetites. Only then would he attempt to feather his fish-eyed nemesis. And after that, he could only empty his quiver until they were on him, and then resort to his sword.

At two hundred yards, he drew a field point to his ear and let fly at one of the roughly man-sized

abominations. It barely flinched when the shaft missed
its head by a foot. Druadaen chose a heavier hunting
point, drew again, adjusted and let the shaft fly. Low,
it thudded into the creature's thigh, eliciting a high-
pitched howl as it stumbled and fell. Now that he had
an almost stationary target, Druadaen was willing to
risk one poisoned shaft. He nocked it carefully, ignored
the approach of the others, and loosed it.

The arrow should have missed; an errant breeze
gusted it slightly to the left—but in so doing, it inter-
sected and caught the abomination's flailing arm as
it tried to swing back up to its feet. It howled again,
then grew quiet and motionless, as if puzzled—just
before it fell its length. Several of the smaller ones
tentatively approached . . . but then backed off when
the closest took a few tentative sniffs and swerved
away. Druadaen sighed: most natural creatures cannot
detect poison that has only been in a body for a few
moments, but these obviously could.

So: he had to face all of them at once. *Best start
putting the tainted shafts into the big one before the
rest close with me and . . .*

He flinched as a rush of wind went past his left ear.
By the time he recovered, the cause—the owl—was
already a receding blur. It had almost brushed his
shoulder with its wing. *What now? You've returned
to claw my eyes out?*

And for a moment, it looked as if it might. But the
owl's rapid return was not a prelude to attack; instead,
it turned three tight circles about Druadaen's head.
Then it leveled off and flew back in the direction from
which it had come: straight toward the long ridge
behind him. Druadaen stared after it for a moment he

could not spare—and realized he didn't have enough time to think: only act.

He hastily stripped the wax guard from another of his poisoned arrows, aimed at the body of the fish-eyed ogre—now barely a hundred yards away—and loosed it. He thumbed the cork off a philter, swallowed its contents, scooped up the other arrows, and somehow managed to resist the impulse to see if his arrow had hit and if the poison was at least slowing his enemy. Instead, he focused on the one thing that still mattered:

Running. To the low ridge. As fast as he could.

The philter—a natural compound derived from animal humours—gave him the rush of energy it promised. It also made his senses almost painfully keen, but none of that mattered now as he raced over the crest of the ridge and discovered—

A tangle of scrub and bushes, sheltered in a bowl formed by the back-curving ends of the ridge.

No S'Dyxoi in sight. Not even the owl.

Nothing.

Gritting his teeth, Druadaen plunged down the slope, determined to use his briefly increased vitality to hide and fight as he'd intended before retreating. As he pushed hastily into a likely thicket, he could hardly think through his rising fury at having trusted the owl, only to have it betray him in that last moment. Except . . .

Why would even the most cruel S'Dyxoi waste all the mantic crafting and planning just to bring me here to die? It didn't make any sense.

Which means you're mistaking why it's been done.

As if summoned by that thought, the bushes and scrub around him began to hum.

The abominations topped the rise, following his tracks down into the bowl, the big one standing on the crest, its head turning slightly so that both its eyes could survey what lay below.

The hum around Druadaen became a buzz and the smaller bushes were shaking.

The abominations stopped, glanced around at the sound, one spotting Druadaen as it did. The creature raised a finger in his direction—

—Just as the buzz became a shrill storm of angry insects, erupting out of the bushes as if, against their impulses, they had been held there in readiness until this exact moment.

Druadaen was stunned—but just as swiftly, refocused. *They are not attacking me, only the abominations.* Rising from the thicket into the unfolding opportunity before him, Druadaen stripped the wax tips off all the remaining poisoned shafts and began loosing them in rapid sequence at the fish-eyed ogre less than fifty yards away.

He didn't stop to see their effects. He knew one missed, flying just above its wholly human shoulder and over the crest. But the others feathered its belly, even as the rest of its broad body accumulated a thick coat of biting, stinging insects. It had charged after the first arrow hit, then paused as an angry cloud of wasps and hornets swarmed toward it. A moment later, it stumbled, shaking its head as if trying to clear it.

Arrows kept humming into its sizable flank until Druadaen reached into his quiver and discovered it was empty. Now thoroughly coated by a crawling mass of insects, the abomination slumped to the ground—and three wolves lunged out of the bushes, fangs bared and seeking its throat. Its outline now lost behind their flashing bodies, its limbs continued to flail blindly as it sent up cries of distress that were part the roar of a bull and part the squeal of a pig.

The rest of the brush was alive with separate combats as other wolves and even a bear rushed from where they'd been hiding to attack the scattered abominations...

Wait: a bear? *On the plains?*

Druadaen turned toward the open neck of the bowl and was unsurprised—but greatly relieved—to see Aleasha rise from the bushes there, the two largest wolves flanking her, their eyes roving, alert to threat and hard with menace. She exchanged a quick smile with Druadaen, to which he added a long, grateful nod before cross-drawing his swords and scanning for the place where his blades were needed the most.

A quick glance was not enough to make that determination, because the animals' actions were mostly in response to the abominations' own. Those few that turned and fled back toward the crest of the ridge were ignored. Those that stood their ground uncertainly were threatened, then charged. If they followed the others over the ridge, they too were ignored. But those that stood their ground or sprinted forward to finish their pursuit of Druadaen—or, perhaps, just kill anything they came across—drew the full attention of Aleasha's companions.

Each struggle was distinct, but they all followed a similar pattern. The most aggressive abominations attracted a dense swarm of insects that attacked or buzzed about their heads. Once distracted, two or more wolves sped out of the bush, lunging at and baiting it until one's flashing teeth found their intended mark: the tendon behind the heel. With the enemy hamstrung, hobbling, and unsteady, Druadaen expected the wolves to leap in to finish it off. But instead, they nipped and snapped at it until one of the bears—a second had emerged—rushed into the melee and set about mauling the abomination.

This rarely lasted more than a few seconds. When the abomination was no longer capable of resisting, the bear wandered off to look for a new foe, and the wolves returned to crush the crippled monster's windpipe. All in all, the process was both terribly swift and chillingly efficient.

Only the second largest of the abominations—a large hairless female with serrated pincers instead of hands—had been able to brush off the attacks, largely because she seemed immune, or at least insensate, to the cloud of insects in which she moved and fought. As Druadaen watched, one of her claws flashed at an overly bold wolf and opened a foot-long gash along its flank. He started toward that combat—

—but was stopped by a hand on his arm. Aleasha was just behind him. She shook her head. "No. My friends might misunderstand."

Druadaen glanced back toward the wounded wolf, saw a bear closing in to take its place. "But the animals follow you. As if you were one of them. Their own leader."

She nodded. "Because I smell so to them and act as they expect. But they are still what they are. They are not soldiers, obeying every order with a salute. If I urged them to do something which is not already in their nature, they would be confused. Maybe doubt whether I really *am* their leader."

Druadaen nodded slowly. "Sadly, I never even considered that."

Her reply was wry. "I am glad you said so; I dislike having to tell people that they have been foolish." Her puckish expression became a grin—despite the savage work being completed not twenty yards from where they stood.

She noticed his glances toward the last keening, shrieking abomination; the bear's paws and jaws were busy upon its much-rent body. "You feel pity for them? For the monsters?"

"I am...not unmoved by their suffering."

She glanced sideways at him. "*Taaakh!* Fellow-feeling is not the way of nature when lives are in the balance. You would do well to rid yourself of sentiment, when it comes to them." She flinched when the bear narrowly squirmed away from the dying creature's death blow; a prehensile stinger had whipped out of its abdomen just before it went limp. "The ones who kept attacking even when their own destruction was assured? They have no feelings for others of their kind, or even for themselves, really."

"And the ones who ran?"

She shrugged. "They have enough self-feeling to flee. Some may have feelings for something other than themselves. But most just fear death more than they revel in savagery." She rose, scanned the brush and the concave slopes that hemmed it in. "If these abominations were not so unreachable, or so dangerous to the world, I would not be so hasty to slay them." The only sound in the brush was the whimpering of the wounded wolf. "Nor would I ask my friends or companions to fight them. I do not risk their lives more readily than my own. Often less readily. But this fight concerns us all." She nodded for him to walk with her to where the wolves were gathering around the one that had fallen.

"You believe the abominations are a threat to the whole world?" Druadaen asked.

She nodded. "I am certain of it. They are an affront to the order of all things." She shrugged. "Except for a very few, they live their whole lives as if they were rabid. Their only impulses are to feed and to kill... and not always in that order."

Aleasha's animals parted so that she might kneel next to the wolf. It was a female: light-framed and small-boned. "The wound is grave," she said over her shoulder as she ran a slow hand from the midpoint of its muzzle to the back of its head, smoothing the fur as it licked her hand.

"Can it—can she be saved?" Druadaen asked, trying to remember that when he was with Aleasha, wolves were allies rather than adversaries.

Aleasha shook her head. "Not in time."

"What do you mean?"

"I mean she cannot move yet, and we cannot wait."

Druadaen assessed the animal; it was no bigger than a medium-sized dog. "If you can carry some of my kit, I will bear her across my shoulders. How far have we to go?"

Aleasha turned to stare at him; several of the animals did the same. "Too far. And you already reek of long exhaustion." She sniffed at him. "You might fall over yourself, if you did not have a humour of urgency running in your veins." She smiled. "But your offer is kind and speaks well of you." She turned back to the wolf, soothing it with one hand, as the other scooped a mixture of herbs and half-dried leaves from her shoulder sack. "It is ever thus when one fights for survival. Just like us, some part of them"—she nodded around the circle of patient animal eyes and blood-wet muzzles—"must die to save others of their kind." She crumbled the leaves beneath the wounded wolf's nose. "That is the one kind of human war I understand: to slay an invader before they can destroy your home and your family."

The wolf's eyelids sagged; its breathing became relaxed. Aleasha nodded at it, her eyes gleaming. "I take no pride in killing abominations, and I mourn every friend I lose. But even this gentle creature"—she jutted her chin at the drowsy wolf—"would kill the runt of her own litter if that was the only way for her to save the rest. We do what we must and mourn those we cannot preserve." She frowned. "Although some creatures are more important to preserve than others."

Druadaen shook his head. "In what way?"

"When we flee this place, take note of the dead insects. You will find no bees. Only wasps and hornets." Druadaen nodded to signify his understanding, but she wagged a finger at it. "No, it is not just that bees are the midwives of new flowers. It is because they are cooperative creatures, and also because most do not attack unless provoked. They even share their honey."

Druadaen smiled. "It is true that I have never heard of a 'wasp-keeper.'"

Aleasha tried to smile. "And you never will—which is my point. My arts arise from seeking and creating affinity between living things, regardless of how simple or complex they may be. So, the less capable a species is of affinity"—she shrugged—"the less it matters to the living world if some die. They are necessary to the weave of all things, but inasmuch as the only object of their awareness is their own survival, it is enough that they continue to breed and be present."

"Do all who exercise the, uh, nativist arts share this feeling?"

"To a greater or lesser degree, yes." She drew a small obsidian knife—its napped, midnight blade gleamed—and nodded for the animals to withdraw. She moved it closer to the slumbering wolf's neck.

"Will it wake?" Druadaen asked.

Aleasha's voice was thick. "Yes, but it will be over in a moment."

"It can be over faster than that. Here." He held out a sachet. "It is Sarmese. Given to a large creature in small amounts, it induces sleep." He glanced at the wolf. "In a creature so small, it will not awaken."

Aleasha turned, her eyes grateful behind the tears that almost hid them. She nodded, took the sachet, eased the wolf's jaws slightly wider, poured the white powder onto its tongue.

After a few moments, it released a small sigh, then a much greater one, then was still.

Aleasha rose, wiped her eyes, and nodded at Druadaen. "Thank you. That was a kindness. For both of us." She sighed, and she turned a small shiver into an intentional shake of her upper body, as if dispelling a chill. When she looked up, her cheeks were streaked but her eyes were clear. "Let us go collect what you left on the farther hill and be gone."

❖   ❖   ❖

Druadaen soberly attempted to be happy about how much less his kit would chafe his shoulders, because that was the only happy result of the past two days. He'd consumed almost all his food, had emptied his waterskin as completely as his quiver, and had abandoned other implements in order to improve his speed and endurance while being chased.

However, in his haste to retreat to the ridge, two vials had rolled from the rock where he'd laid them at the ready, and they were too valuable to abandon. Aleasha strolled alongside as he searched for them.

Vials in the weeds like needles in the haystack...

He stopped and straightened. "This must amuse you."

"No," she answered. Her tone suggested it was trying her patience, instead. "Why do you say so?"

"Because here I am looking for two glass ampules I dropped on a few square yards of grassland, but you were able to find me on a whole continent!" He responded to her smile with one of his own. "How did you do it?"

"How did I find you? Why, because I am 'magic'!" she laughed, adding exaggerated emphasis to the quaint term. When he crossed his arms and let his smile become "patient," she added, "My friends told me."

"Your frie—?"

The owl swooped over his shoulder to land on hers. "Yes," she answered almost coyly, "my many, many friends."

"Many friends?" He glanced at the owl, saw her smile widening at his confusion, and then saw her many, many, *many* friends in his memories.

Birds overhead when he trudged north to Pakobsid. Gulls overhead when he sailed to Sarma and then out again. All the way to the western end of the Straight

Sea with Lorgan, and then north along the coast of the Broken Lands. Always there, even when there were no scraps of food to be had nor fish to catch. And then, from the charred remains of the trading station, past the ruins, and finally...

He glanced at the owl. "And finally, one guided me here." Druadaen shook his head, chuckling. "I should have surmised."

"Why?"

"Because I have seen it done on my own world. And because it makes such simple sense that I never conceived of it." He waved a desultory hand at the sky as he returned to his search, asking, "Where can one go where a flock of birds is *not* commonplace? And even if one knows such tracking is possible, how can one live in suspicion of every bird, wondering if they are the eyes of a distant wyldwyrd?"

"Yes," she answered through a faint laugh, "but I suspect there is another reason *you* did not think of it."

"Perhaps because I am stupid *as well* as unobservant?"

"No," she answered seriously, "because from what I saw of your travels, you could not trust those around you. Even on that strange ship, I doubt you told them your true origins."

He nodded solemnly but thought: *So, you can see through their eyes, but not hear through their ears? Or perhaps because they do not understand speech, because it is just scattered sounds, you hear it that way, too?* He smiled as he discovered the simplest explanation of all: *Or maybe it would have been just a bit too obvious if a bird followed me into every room and compartment.*

"You are amused at not being able to trust others on your journey?"

"No," he answered, resuming his search, "but I do not understand how it kept me from speculating that you were watching me!"

"Do you not?" She sounded even more serious than before. "When we have no one to help or stand with us—when safety, maybe survival, rests in our hands alone—we focus on little else. Imagining that we have unseen friends is a pointless, even dangerous, daydream." She smiled. "Particularly if we allow ourselves to think that they are 'magically' watching over us."

He smiled, but gibed, "Well, if you were watching, then why have the owl fetch me from leagues away? Couldn't *you* just come closer?"

She seemed more proficient at poking fun than recognizing when the same was done to her. Smiling through a frown, she very patiently explained, "Because that was the fastest way for us to meet. I, too, had to travel to this place. Which I selected because I knew of the ground hornets in the bowl." Seeing that her explanation was only widening his smile, she risked teasing him back. "You could at least have come the last half mile on your own! Instead, you made me send the owl *again*!"

Druadaen made sure his drollery was exaggerated. "Yes, I thought about that. But there were complications. About a dozen of them. Perhaps you didn't notice."

She looked as though she was about to chuckle, but managed not to. Instead, she put her hands on her hips and huffed, "Just as *you* didn't notice where you put these precious compounds of yours. Have you lost them entirely?"

Druadaen straightened, holding one in either hand. "Apparently not. So now I know *how* you found me, but I still don't know *why* you did it."

"And you're not going to, not standing here! We could be watched ourselves. Besides, we need to find a place to rest before we follow the trail left by the supragants."

"What? Why?"

"To find out where they were going, of course! Must I think of everything? Now, enough: why do you keep distracting me with your foolish questions and even more foolish talk?" She grinned, enjoying the game of blaming her loquacity on him.

"Yes, my apologies; I'm sorry to be such a bother," he smiled back.

"Well, you should be! Now we must hurry, unless you wish to end up as another morsel for whichever scavenger—or predator—first smells the aftermath of a battle."

CHAPTER THIRTY-FIVE

"So," Druadaen asked as he leaned back from a dinner of wild vegetables and truffles, "why *did* you decide to watch me?"

Aleasha stared at him. Had she been a cat, he was sure her ears would have been flattened to either side of her head. "Have you really been waiting to ask that question all this time?"

Druadaen conceived of the last half of the day more in terms of leagues, given that he had spent the first half running for his life. "The question crossed my mind occasionally, yes."

She glowered sideways at him. "That is now the *second* lie you've told me. You were nursing that question even more than you were nursing your blistered feet. Well, you may have your answer.

"I was uncertain what to make of you, even after we had learned some of each other's speech. But what I did not share was that the cult I spoke of was likely to have agents in the area."

"I think I had an unfortunate meeting with them at the camping spot you recommended."

She nodded. "So I learned." In answer to his uncertain frown, she gestured to the owl and other birds. "I did not see that battle, because I did not yet keep you within reach of a bird's eyes. But I saw what remained of those who thought to kill you, and soon after, saw their horses being led north and knew I had found you on your journey to Pakobsid.

"This decided me on several matters. Firstly, that you were so truly ignorant of our world that you could not be from it. That in turn proved that there was no way you could be serving the interests of other powers, not even unwittingly.

"Secondly, you were a far more formidable opponent than I had supposed. And thirdly, having slain the agents of that cult, it was possible that its leaders would endeavor to determine who had done so and visit vengeance upon you. And so, since it was I who sent you that way, and did not give full warning of the dangers you might face, it was upon me to keep eyes upon you and, if possible, intervene if you were put at risk by my failure."

He was about to protest that she had owed him nothing, that in fact he was very much in her debt, when she stopped him with a raised hand. "And," she said, almost smiling, "you were interesting in your own strange way. It is not every day I meet a person from another world, especially one so . . . so imprudent as you!" Then she did smile, slyly. "But what truly decided me was your friend." She glanced at his bracer.

"It is unusual," he allowed.

"It is, but its ability to change form was not what

compelled me; it was its actions. As I told you. Outwardly, it appears to be an artifact created by a master wyrdcrafter—or even a sorcerer—yet it does not act as a servitor, as most such creations are made to do. It is not merely alive; it has intents and goals of its own." She shook her head. "I have never seen its like, nor have I heard of such a creature."

"If it *is* a creature," Druadaen amended.

She raised an eyebrow. "It is strange to hear you doubt that, since you treat it as a being. Which tells me that, even if you do not know it to be one, you suspect it is. That is why you show it respect." She nodded. "That is very important."

He smiled. "So your birds weren't just watching over me; they were also showing you how I acted toward something that might not be alive, but merely a construct. You were determining if I was worthy of your help."

She had begun by nodding at his comments, but ended on an uncomfortable frown. "No, that was not a concern. I know when humans are bad. And if I were somehow to misjudge"—she gestured toward the animals around them—"my friends would not."

He frowned. "Then why did you feel it necessary to measure me, if you did not fear that I was evil?"

She glanced at him then glanced away again. "It was still possible that you might be stupid."

Yet another chastening comment from Aleasha. But his responding smile was genuine, if ironic. "I don't seem to make a very good first impression."

She glanced back but this time left her eyes on him. "It is not that so much. It is just that your entire reason for coming here . . . well, I am sure that many would call it noble. To me, it seems foolhardy."

His smile broadened. "To me, too," he agreed.

Her expression was wiped away by an abrupt, rising chortle. "Then why do it?" she said when they were done laughing.

He shrugged. "It sounds ridiculous, even to me, but when it came time to decide whether I would pass through the Shimmer or not, it seemed as though I *had* to do it. All the questions and quandaries I investigated had gone unanswered or were deflected. But they had this in common: in every case, a supposed rule—or truth—of my world was being violated or suspended by forces that lay beyond it. So, perhaps I had to leave it to discover what those forces were and why they were acting as they did. And since the Mirror had shown my image to the Lady, she surmised that the Shimmer was presenting itself as my portal to such a place. Besides," he added, tapping his bracer and his sword pommel, "these indicated that it was a good idea."

Her brow set in a severe line. "I am still not sure that explanation makes your choice any less foolhardy, but I understand how those would be powerful reasons." She regarded him, raised an eyebrow. "Do you believe that going through the Shimmer was your destiny?"

"You mean, do I believe that there is a special purpose that I had to serve by doing so?" He shook his head. "No, but I acknowledge that sometimes people may come to a place where, although they may choose many different paths, one is clearly more needful than the others."

"Needful to whom?" she persisted.

"I cannot say. Maybe just to me. But if so, then the velene and the sword are very indulgent."

"Unlikely, since they all but pushed you through the Shimmer."

Druadaen simply shrugged and nodded. It would not have supported his easy dismissal of destiny to tell her that his "aunt" had brought the velene to him, or that his uncle, acting on unexplained orders, had put the sword in the care of the dragon decades before Druadaen was born.

Aleasha smiled even as she frowned. "You are not bad for one who comes from under a roof. But I do not trust thinking creatures or their works the way you do. I do not trust kings or countries. I do not trust orders given by gods we cannot see or believe in a fate that seeds our steps before they are taken." She held his eyes. "But sometimes, I trust individual people. And I trust you."

"Enough to finally tell me who those cultists were? I suspect they are what the Sarmese call Nightfall—"

She raised her hand. "Stop. Is that what the Sarmese concluded?"

"They could not agree on what they were. At first they presumed them to be Nightfall cultists because of the robes I found on them. Others feared they might be members of a resurgent order of much-feared sorcerers. They also mentioned a warlord and more mysterious forces, all of which might be using the abominations for one of several purposes. In the end, they didn't agree on very much."

Aleasha nodded. "Their confusion is understandable. It is normal enough to suppose that one's problems are caused by a single enemy. Possibly two, working in concert."

Druadaen heard her tentative tone. "But you believe

there are more than two and they are not allies. Rather, they may be working at crossed purposes."

She nodded back. "You perceive. But the truth is likely to be still more complicated; it is likely that they are not all equally aware of each other. If at all." Noting his raised eyebrow, she expanded: "The sorcerers the Sarmese mentioned are an ancient order known as Pagudon. And I suspect that some of their agents have entered the ranks of Nightfall, claiming their sorcery to be priestly powers."

Druadaen sat straight. "Which is why the Temple of Disfa believes that their deity has awakened. And that in turn has given them the power and authority to exploit the Kaandean war of succession." He smiled bitterly. "With Sarmese backing, no doubt."

Aleasha sighed. "And here you see why I did not name the cult when we first met. It would have meant peeling back all the layers of a rotten onion I had hoped would never concern you." She lifted a powerless palm toward the sky. "Sometimes, I am still an optimist. Even I have failings." They chuckled together.

Druadaen leaned back with a sigh. "It seems a year since I laughed."

She circled her knees with her arms. "Where was it? Back on the ship?" When he nodded, she pressed eagerly, "Were they a merry crew?"

"They were. I have been on many ships. I was happier on that one than most of the others."

"They were so amusing?"

Druadaen shook his head. "No ... well, yes, they were ... but that is not why I was glad to be among them. However different they were—and they were from all the nations of Lorn Hystzos—there was much amity among them."

"As if they were family?"

"Actually," he reflected, "three of them were, I think. The officers and captain—Lorgan—were all from Tyrmcys, at any rate. They claimed to be related, but who can tell?"

Aleasha's face had lost its easy animation. "This captain, Lorgan: you felt you could trust him?"

"I did, in fact."

"Why?" Her tone was surprisingly inquisitive. And serious.

"Well, it began as an impression: that he had nothing to hide." Druadaen frowned. "No, that's not quite right; he made it quite clear he *did* have some things to hide. But that's just it, you see: he said it right out. He was not concealing anything; he openly asserted that there were matters he did not wish to share at that point."

Aleasha shook her head. "The most cunning dissemblers are those who learn how to seem honest about their secrecy. Even you might be deceived by so accomplished a liar."

Druadaen smiled. "Yet, I knew he wasn't."

"How?"

"The way I knew the same about you. And that I could trust you."

She frowned. "I could have misled you about who I am and what I intend, had I wished."

Druadaen grinned. "Perhaps. But your companions could not do so." He gestured at the various members of her furred entourage.

"My companions? And how would they tell you

anything one way or the other about me?" She stopped
when she saw his smile widening, stared in sudden
comprehension, and began smiling back. "Of course;
'One's companions reflect one's character.' It's an axiom
in every language." She nodded, and her tone was
serious when she admitted, "I do not often encounter
wisdom among roof-dwellers."

"It's not my wisdom. I learned it from traveling
with persons far, far more astute than me."

"You were wise enough to listen to them, and that
is a form of wisdom in itself. So, you judged this
Lorgan by his crew."

"Let us say his crew confirmed my instincts. They
were as different as different can be, but had this in
common: I saw no dissemblers, no hypocrites, no factions. Most seemed honest, or at least fair. Still, they
were sailors. I doubt any could be deemed virtuous.
Most of them would probably have deemed that a
slur, not a compliment."

Instead of having grown weary of his description
of the crew, she had remained attentive. "All this is
useful to know."

"Why?"

"I might—" She stopped as if someone had stuck
her with a pin. She rose abruptly. "We must go."

Druadaen rose, grabbed his kit, glanced at the sun.
"Are we to travel in the dark?"

"If need be." She was gathering her many companions, but sent two wolves racing off to the east.

"You have been shown something?"

She glanced at him. "Yes. It concerns you. And
your world. Now hurry."

❖   ❖   ❖

Seen at a distance in the pre-dusk light, their destination was marked by a thin cloud of black smoke, apparently buffeted by fickle winds. But a minute later he realized his eyes had tricked him.

What he'd taken to be smoke was a roiling mass of carrion birds of different kinds, flocking, shifting, some diving, some climbing, but in ever-increasing numbers. Having run almost the entirety of the day, he could not even gasp a question toward Aleasha, who had pulled ahead of him. But after running for almost hour, their destination was finally less than a mile away.

Before reaching it, however, a cacophony of bellows, hoots, roars, and trumpetings dispersed the birds in a startled, complaining mass that rapidly diffused toward every point of the compass.

In response, Aleasha held up a narrow-fingered hand. Her followers stopped. Druadaen staggered up alongside her.

"What is—?" he started.

"We must walk now," she interrupted. "Stay well behind me. My companions will surround you. Stay in their midst. No time for questions; that would slow us even more."

She moved to the front, but whereas she was normally escorted by several of her wolves, this time she was flanked by lately joined antelopes. The wolves arrayed themselves around Druadaen instead, and together, they walked in her wake. After approaching for only a few minutes, the horizon was troubled by low hills.

Moving hills, Druadaen realized a moment later. Which actually meant—

A gathering of supragants. He wondered at them,

not because of their size—he'd seen similar breeds in Dunarra—but because of so large a gathering occurring in the wild. They rarely traveled in groups larger than three, but there were at least four times that number, and they seemed to be circling the same area upon which the now-scolding vultures and ravens had been fixed.

As Aleasha approached the immense creatures, they turned toward her, nostrils and spiracles flaring. One or two took a ground-quaking step forward, then paused, and moved back far enough that she and her loose column of companions had space enough to pass between them.

As he and the wolves entered the gauntlet that remained in her wake, the supragants became more tense, eyes and rows of light-sensitive spots widening. Horns, trunks, tentacles, antennae hovered close, some almost overhead, the various disparate leviathans unified in their readiness to detect any hint of aggression among the predators that moved carefully, cautiously between them.

Emerging from the narrow pass through their ranks, Druadaen saw Aleasha standing very still some yards ahead—and beyond her, what had brought the carrion birds and then the supragants: a small, body-piled battlefield. Or so it appeared, at first, but as the wolves parted to allow him to join her, thereby unveiling the details of the aftermath, he realized that the pattern of the bodies told a different story: almost all the dead had fallen facing away from the center.

This had been a massacre of the unsuspecting, whose flight had been shaped by only one concern: to run in whatever direction they could.

Wordless, he and Aleasha began following the

periphery of the slaughter, she pacing clockwise, he walking the other way.

Druadaen could not distinguish all the species that had met their end in the place. The four supragant corpses were unmistakable, but between and under them were telltale signs of both four- and two-legged bodies, many reduced to skeletons. At least half bore scorch marks or signs of self-inflicted wounds. Many were abominations, easily distinguished by the briefest of glances: mismatched limbs and appendages; asymmetrical torsos; severed extremities on which talons sprouted next to delicate fingers.

However, mixed in among the older remains were ones that were quite recent, possibly no older than two days. These more recent dead had arrived in two different groups: a large party of abominations from the north, and a much smaller group of them from the west. Judging from the way they were arrayed in opposition to each other, it looked as though they had been wrangling over the already present carnage.

Aleasha met Druadaen on the other side of the circle their two paths had traced around the death ground. "Since you do not mention it," she muttered, "I presume you found no bodies of the evil ones from your world."

Druadaen shook his head. "Did you expect to find them?"

She frowned. "No, not initially. But as we approached, a wren showed me—and then I saw—the tracks of the supragants that died here. They are the four the evil ones were riding. So I thought they must have perished, too."

Druadaen was puzzled. "Then what do you think happened here?"

She nodded to herself. "Your path around the bodies

did not show you the other, larger set of prints." She looked up again. "A cryptigant attacked. It came from the north and left heading northeast. It was almost twice as large as the supragants. They had no chance of defeating it." She frowned. "But I am surprised that none of the four made an escape. They died facing away from it, trying to flee."

Druadaen considered the heaped bodies again. "Might the 'priestess' have called the cryptigant?"

Aleasha stared at him. "You mean, *summoned* one? Even in legend, no wyrding can influence them from a distance."

Druadaen reflected. "But once present, could it be controlled?"

Her look suggested she feared for his sanity. "Controlled? Perhaps, but there is only one tale of such, and it was accomplished by a sorcerer of old."

"Is it so difficult?"

"Not difficult: dangerous. All affining requires physical presence, and the more difficult the subject, the closer the one attempting it must be." She shook her head. "The sorcerers have never been brave, and if their wyrding failed, a cryptigant would have slain them instantly. And effortlessly."

Druadaen nodded. "So if the cryptigant couldn't be summoned, then in the tale of the sorcerer who did control one, how did he find it? Even in my world, cryptigants are said to be as reclusive as they are rare."

Aleasha shrugged. "He did it the way you attract any predator: stake out its prey. And wait."

"And what is the preferred prey of cryptigants?"

"Supragants. Anything smaller is not worth their effort."

Druadaen stared at the dead supragants. "Then maybe she finally achieved what she's been working toward since landing near Agpetkop."

"What do you mean?"

"Well, if she learned—or already suspected—that a cryptigant cannot be summoned from afar, what better way to attract one by riding upon four specimens of its favorite prey?"

Aleasha's expression made it quite clear that she no longer doubted Druadaen's sanity; she was quite certain he had lost it. "You are saying it was always her plan to bring a cryptigant to her? But why?"

Druadaen shrugged. "Well, I have also been told that it would take a small army to slay one. And even then—"

"So she wants it as a weapon!" Aleasha's concern was instantly replaced by revelation, and then sharp focus. "But—would she really be so bold? Could she really be so powerful?"

Druadaen shrugged again. "I cannot say. But I saw scorch marks on the dead, and I think I understand them now. They were mostly on the legs of two of the supragants."

"To slow them down?"

He nodded. "And perhaps, while the cryptigant was gorging itself on four supragants, it grew sated, even groggy."

Aleasha smiled; evidently, her insane friend seemed sane again. "And so whatever resistance it had to her affining was lowered." She put her hands on her hips. "And that explains why neither of us saw any signs of her group's gear—which, if the cryptigant devoured them, it would surely have spat out. And this also explains why the great beast departed to the northeast." Druadaen's quizzical look drew an explanation. "That is the direction your enemies have been moving, ever since they left the ruins where my owl first flew past you."

One of the wolves, the oldest female, entered the death ground, edging toward the largest of the supragant carcasses. Aleasha made a nickering noise at it. The animal turned, shook its head with a grumble, looked toward the carcass and whined faintly, pawing the ground.

Aleasha frowned but made a gesture of permission.

The wolf trotted forward beneath the glare of the now inward-staring supragants. Once at the carcass, she picked her way gingerly into what would have been its barrel. The ribs, sagging apart, were mostly open to the sky. Upon reaching the part where the tumbled arcs of bone arose from the spine, she made a sound more like a bark than a howl.

The supragants shifted uneasily. One lifted an immense foot to start forward...

Aleasha stepped toward it, hands raised, singing a strange wordless melody as she crushed a collection of herbs Druadaen had not noticed in her hand. She glanced over her shoulder, met his eyes, and jerked her head in the direction of the wolf.

Druadaen strode toward the female and braced himself, expecting the corpse stench to increase. However, it diminished once he ducked into the collapsing cavity of the behemoth. Everything had been picked clean, right out to the margin of the hide. On reflection, it was not surprising; many carnivores and scavengers consumed viscera before any other parts of a kill.

The wolf pawed at a point where the spine had sunk to the ground, two of the ribs crushed beneath it. Druadaen leaned over, hand still over his nose and mouth.

That was why he did not shout or even gasp in surprise when a voice said, "I'm right here."

Peering under the lower of the two ribs, he found himself staring into two calm, feline eyes looking over the crooked rim of a badly broken human nose.

CHAPTER THIRTY-SIX

Druadaen leaned away. "Aleasha, there is a survivor."

"I thought so. Well, get him out."

"I think it's a her. But I may need your help."

"You will need to find a way to act without it. As long as you are rummaging about inside a corpse of their kin, I must work to reassure the supragants, keep them calm."

"I understand." Druadaen glanced around helplessly. *But what I don't understand is how I'm going to lift those ribs off . . .*

His glance ran across two heavier and wholly bleached ribs that had snapped free of the carcass's spine. So: he had levers. *But on what can I brace them?* Frowning, he leaned down again.

The two feline eyes looked up at him patiently.

"We are working to get you out."

"That would be agreeable."

"I must ask about your other side, the one opposite me. Is it against the supragant's spine?"

"In a manner of speaking. That is what has me pinned here."

"Is there any room between your body and the spine?"

"Up near my armpit, yes. Lower down...none at all."

To Druadaen, that answer sounded like an ominous understatement. "If I were to slide a rib in toward you across your chest, could you snug it in the gap between your armpit and the spine?"

"I shall. I must."

Druadaen nodded agreement. "I will be back soon." The she-wolf stared after him as he moved quietly but quickly out of the cavernous corpse. "Aleasha," he said calmly. Her head turned slightly in his direction. "I need the bear to help me."

She closed her eyes, whether in exhaustion or forbearance, he could not tell. When she opened them, they were on the largest bear, which was sitting at the edge of the circle of death, scratching itself and sniffing uncertainly at the overripe remains. She uttered a low, gargling growl at it, jerking her head toward Druadaen.

The bear looked puzzled for a moment, then shook its massive shoulders and began to pad forward.

She made a warning noise as it was about to clamber over a severed supragant hoof almost as wide as it was.

The bear looked curiously at her, rolled its head, and reared upright to walk around the obstacle. In that instant, Druadaen remembered just how big bears were. This one was at least two feet taller than him.

It dropped to all fours after it cleared the remains and ambled over toward Druadaen, looking up at him with a doglike expression of patient anticipation.

It continued to do so as Druadaen dragged the thicker of the two bleached ribs over to the narrow opening through which he had spoken to the survivor. As Druadaen pushed one end of the rib into the gap, the being labored to guide it over her chest and then down under the carcass's spine. Her grunts were breathless, more the products of pain than effort.

When the bone lever was finally jammed in place, Druadaen checked the nearby ribs that were still attached, found the sturdiest, and drew his sword. Ignoring the stir in the surrounding ring of supragants and Aleasha's singsong efforts to soothe them, he cut a groove in that bone: a channel wide and deep enough to hold and guide the rope he removed from his kit. After a moment's thought, he worked his way down the ribcage to the rear of the beast's barrel; fewer scavengers had ventured that far. The stink made Druadaen retch, but not before he found some partially deliquesced fat, with which he greased the channel and the center of the rope.

He played its two ends out to equal lengths, and angled them so that, when pulled, they would lift the lever up against the underside of the ribs pinning the wounded being. Whether all the parts would hold under the strain was unknowable, but it was the best, and only, plan he had.

After tying a knot in one end of the rope, he laid it to one side and reached around in the bottom of his ruck for the last, and probably most crucial, piece of his plan.

He dusted off the strange handle he'd found in the tower ruins upon arriving in Hystzos. *Well, now we'll find out if you really can adhere to anything.* He fixed it upon the other end of the rope and approached the bear. It stared up at him.

Druadaen opened his mouth, put the handle in it crosswise, and clamped his teeth down upon it. He removed it and held it out toward the bear.

It almost lunged at the unfamiliar object, jaws widening eagerly.

But Druadaen pulled it back, held up a hand, and opened his mouth again.

The bear stared at him. Again.

Proceeding more slowly this time, Druadaen opened his mouth so wide that the joints of his jaw hurt and then, very gradually closed his mouth on the handle.

The bear's head dropped a bit, then raised in growing comprehension. It opened its vast, tooth-filled maw.

Druadaen made soft noises as he laid the handle so that its bar spanned that yawning cavern and then took his hand away.

The bear's mouth closed firmly upon the delicate-looking object—and kept trying to close tighter.

Druadaen felt a flush of dreaded disaster run the length of his body, but it proved unwarranted; the bear's eyes became intense, then annoyed, then angered at a pulse of pain when its teeth ground against the artifact. It spat the object out, eyed it warily where it had landed, still pristine.

Druadaen bent slowly, picked it up, and drawing a deep breath, put it back in his own mouth. Despite the acrid bear drool, he held it there, lips drawn back in a parody of a smile to show that he was holding, not crushing, the handle. He removed it and held it out again.

The bear seemed cross; he'd clearly preferred the

prospect of crushing the object much more than simply holding it. But a well-timed grunt from Aleasha wrenched a doglike sigh out of its chest and it allowed Druadaen to lay the handle across its teeth. Which it clenched there, its own lips pulled far back. It looked sideways at Druadaen, who had the growing impression that this was not emulation; this was annoyed mockery. But he was more than willing to tolerate that if the plan worked.

He tied the other end of the rope securely around the part of the handle that protruded from the bear's mouth, then wrapped the knotted end around his waist. He called down to the trapped being, "We will start in a moment." He raised his voice. "Aleasha?"

"Yes?" She sounded a little less preoccupied.

"Can you get the wolves to understand that they must help pull the survivor out when the collapsed ribs begin to lift?"

"Maybe you'd like them to dance a jig afterward?"

"Please, Aleasha: can you or can't you convey that to them?"

"Yes. Very well. Start pulling. I'll tell them when."

Druadaen looked at the bear. It looked back. He leaned into the rope and cried, "Now!"

The bear started at the loud, sudden word, then puzzled at the straining human beside him, and finally detected movement in the rope. Slow realization, and the promise of exercising its power, got the bear moving—particularly when it began conceiving of the effort as some kind of contest or play.

As soon as the bear's full force began pulling the lever upright, Druadaen put his modest effort into ensuring that the rope remained angled to sustain that pressure while remaining securely within the groove he'd cut.

The only problem with the plan was that only two seconds after the collapsed ribs started lifting, they gave way completely. Tearing away from the spine, they flew up, freeing the survivor—but also releasing the still-overhanging part of the carcass to tip back down.

As the lever flew free, Aleasha bark-yelled. Druadaen fell forward as the rope went slack. The bear charged forward, the handle held high in its jaws. Two wolves leaped into the brief gap that had been opened, just as the unsupported half of the supragant's ribcage began toppling over.

It landed with a sloppy crash—but not before the wolves, teeth locked firmly on the survivor's tunic, dragged her clear of the falling remains.

Once the violent activity was over, the supragants began perceiving Aleasha's followers more as newcomers than intruders, and she was able to leave the periphery of the killing field. She approached Druadaen where he was kneeling beside the survivor. "Why have you not moved her out of this—?"

Druadaen looked up the same moment she saw the survivor clearly—and fell silent.

The feline eyes and otherwise human face were all that Druadaen had been able to see, but once freed from the supragant's ribcage, the survivor's other significant features became apparent: hoofs instead of feet, long limbs and a longer torso, and perfectly formed human hands—except for the retractable claws in place of fingernails.

But more importantly, its pelvis was crushed, flattened where it had been pinned by the dead supragant's spine.

"Is she—?" Aleasha whispered.

But even that soft speech caused the abomination's eyelids to flutter, then open. The slit-irised eyes focused on their faces with difficulty.

"Be at ease," Druadaen said, laying a gentle, restraining hand upon a shoulder that gave beneath it: a shattered breast-bone.

The being tried to keep itself from writhing, but a shudder ran its length, torturing it further. The already ragged remains of the clothing around its hips tore fully apart, revealing that it was both male and female.

"I'm sorry," Druadaen whispered. "I should not have..." He exhaled and started again. "Please tell us where you are injured, so that we may move you without pain."

"Where am I injured?" the being repeated weakly, using the feminine pronoun when referring to herself. "Almost everywhere, I think. Besides, there is no point to moving me." The feline eyes inspected the animal snouts leaning in toward it, then shifted to Aleasha. "You are a wyldwyrd."

"I am. How should we call you? And... how did you learn to speak? Eh, speak so well, I mean?" she hastened to add.

"My name is Neeshu. I speak well because my head has not been touched." She tried to raise her head, winced.

Aleasha moved forward, hand in the satchel she reserved for medicinal herbs. "Here, allow me to—"

"No," Neeshu said with a slow shake of her head. "If you mean to heal me, you cannot. If you mean to ease my pain, I cannot have my wits clouded." She studied the wyldwyrd's face. "Your accent is from the Godbarrows." She turned to study Druadaen. "Yours is not. It is from nowhere I know." She looked from one to the other. "Why are you here?"

Druadaen managed not to avert his eyes. *Well, Neeshu, I came here to take you or those like you captive. To deliver you as a prime specimen into the clutches of a people who named all of yours "abominations." Who told me that your species was incapable of any wit beyond that required to wreak greater and bloodier havoc upon "civilized" realms.* He opened his mouth; too many words clamored to come out, so none did.

Yet again, Aleasha saved him. "We are following marauders who come from afar. They have left a trail of bodies—human, supragant, others—from the Last Lands to this place. And apparently beyond."

Neeshu's head rested back as if part of her pain had lessened. "I am no fool; I do not trust quickly or easily. But I have little time and you called them marauders, so I have no choice but to believe that is your true opinion of them."

"It is," Druadaen and Aleasha chorused.

"Then I must tell you what happened here and plead that you take that message to the only one who might take action against her."

Druadaen nodded toward Aleasha. "'Her.' So this *was* the priestess's work."

"Priestess?" Neeshu echoed. "I would have thought her a sorceress, but no matter. Listen carefully.

"For almost two months now, the ungovernable of my kind have changed their behavior. Usually, they roam wherever they smell prey, but they have begun pressing south more than any other direction, even ignoring promising scents that might lead them elsewhere. This worries the one who cares for us, and sent us to discover the cause of these changes.

"We smelled this death-place and saw the vultures from afar. But when we arrived, we discovered others of our own kind—ungovernables—were already here. But whereas our common scent usually protects us from them, they treated us as if we were just another prey species."

She shook her head, coughed; when she stopped, her lips were bright red. "My first scout was certain it was because they believed we meant to drive them from the meat here, to have it as our own. Before I could calm him, he went ahead to show the ungovernable that it was not our intent.

"Instead, they attacked him and set upon the rest of us, some eating our dead before the fighting was over. I would have perished along with the rest except that a supragant arrived. It showed no interest in me: only them, particularly the ones that pushed in here to come after me.

"But in charging and crushing them beneath its hooves and heavy tail, the supragant broke the skeleton of this carcass. The spine cracked in two, and I have lain here, pinned and crushed beneath it for two days." Neeshu's voice grew weak, distracted. "Or maybe three."

Druadaen leaned toward her. "What is the message you wish us to carry?"

"The sorceress, or priestess: she had the old powers."

"Was she here with the other abomi—ungovernables?"

Neeshu started to shake her head, stopped, hissing

at the pain. "No," she said, refocused, "but I could smell the old powers she had used upon them."

Aleasha frowned. "Those of Pagudon?"

"Perhaps as Pagudon once was...or whatever came before. Her power is so great that I could sense it binding them." Neeshu shook her head at Aleasha's reaction. "No, she cannot see and hear through those she controls. It is not a sharing, not like wyldwyrding. The mark of her will was impressed upon them, driving them when need be."

"They were affined to her," Druadaen muttered.

Neeshu's eyes flicked toward him. "Yes, that is the Old Cant word for it, I think. But much greater than what Pagudon can create, now."

"I'm sorry, but I do not know what or who Pagudon is."

Neeshu forgot the pain that she might cause herself when she turned her head toward him in surprise. "You—*aiii!*—you do not know Pagudon, truly?"

"He will," Aleasha broke in. "I know the name and the threat. I will acquaint him with them. What I do not understand is the presence of the other, older corpses of your species. The sorceress must have killed them herself or allowed the cryptigant to do so."

"Cryptigant?" Neeshu breathed. "Those other tracks that approached—they were not simply from a much larger supragant?"

"It was a cryptigant," Aleasha insisted. "There is no doubt. And I am all but certain that the priestess wished it to come here."

"That is yet more news you must bear. She would only want a cryptigant if she meant—"

"Meant to inflict great destruction. Yes, I know."

Aleasha's voice was sharp, persistently startling Neeshu—just enough to keep her focused. "But again, why would she have had it kill all the other creatures that were with her, were already bent to her will?"

"Possibly because they could not keep pace once she was moving upon a cryptigant."

Aleasha leaned in. "I hear doubt in your voice. There is another reason, one you think more likely."

Neeshu raised and lowered her lids in affirmation. "I, too, saw those earlier bodies. Almost none of their heads had been touched."

Druadaen frowned. "This is the second time you have said that. Why is it important that no one touches your head?"

She closed her eyes. "Listen to my speech: their heads were not *Touched*."

Druadaen heard the emphasis, this time. "You mean that . . . that their heads were symmetrical?"

She nodded and coughed. "Among my kind, one with a misshapen skull shall be, often from birth, ungovernable."

Aleasha nodded, asked softly, "You are one of Ancrushav's, aren't you?"

She started. "I am." The name had focused her the way a cup of water might have focused a man dying of thirst. "I am one of his Children. You know Ancrushav?"

"I know of him, but what I know does not all tell the same story as you."

Neeshu sighed. "It is so. You will meet him and learn. Know that what he most wished was that we gather news of a surprise attack on the Prow. You have heard of it?"

Aleasha nodded. "I have seen it from a safe distance."

But as Neeshu began unfolding the tale of how she'd been sent by Ancrushav to investigate the possible connections between that attack and the changed behavior of the abominations, Druadaen's awareness left the Godbarrows—because the name Ancrushav had put him back among the viziers in Sarma. He once again heard them debating the priestess's arrival in terms of its possible connection to the other malign forces and designs collecting in and around Lorn Hystzos, particularly those of the Nightfall cult:

"You are saying a sorcerer wears the robe of a cultist? Absurd. They can't be working together!"

"Unless they are one and the same, or have been united under the banner of this new warlord, Ancrushav."

He heard Neeshu's voice as she concluded, "Pagudon once again began to gather those of my kind that could be directed at all, mostly to drive them against the Broken and Last Lands. But in the past month, this priestess took absolute control of any she encountered."

"And sent them south?" Aleasha conjectured.

"Eventually, but first she gathered as many as she could for an attack that, it is whispered, destroyed the Prow. We thought this must have required a siege, but could not understand how ungovernables could have suited such an end. They lack the skills or depth of thought for such activities. But if she had a cryptigant to lay the fortress low, and then my kind poured through the broken walls . . . well, it begins to make sense. Particularly if it was the Cryptigant of the Mael."

Aleasha nodded. "That was my thought, too. It is the only known cryptigant in a hundred leagues. And if she is capable of breaking whatever wyrdcraft held it in defense of the Prow and then to turn upon it, then she might very well prevail against its defenders. Besides, it is said that the Prow has fallen into disrepair, that the nations of Lorn Hystzos ignored or forgot their commitments to maintain a watch there. Rumor has it that its parapets are manned only by those who hungered after the modest glory of serving in the most distant wilds of the Godbarrows."

"It was as you say," Neeshu agreed, "until Pagudon did away with the last of those guards and manned the citadel with a few of their own order, mostly to oversee the horde of ungovernables they kept nearby." She had started slurring. "You know all that I do, now. And more. Now, I must go. Quickly. Before my fear becomes too great."

Before Druadaen understood Neeshu's request, Aleasha nodded and a dagger flashed in her hand; it plunged straight through Neeshu's closed eye. She went limp and collapsed.

Druadaen stared down at the abomination that was anything but. "Others, even you, claimed they had no feelings, could hardly speak."

Aleasha did not look at him as she made her slow answer. "I said *most* had no feelings. But I have not encountered one such as this. Ever." She looked up, eyes bright. "This...this complicates many things. And I do not just mean deciding whether we should go to Ancrushav or not." She pronounced the name with the easy facility of someone accustomed to uttering it.

Druadaen nodded. "You mean that we cannot act

as if all abominations are monsters." He stared north along the trail of the S'Dyxoi. "Whereas all too many of our kind are." He looked back at her. She was staring fixedly at a point slightly south of the cryptigant's path. "Is that where Ancrushav is?"

She nodded. "The Armory."

"That sounds ominous."

"It is historical. The Hystzarchs kept a cache of supplies there, near the best pass through the Cloudcap Mountains. It was established to arm multitudes, should some force from the Shun invade by that route."

Druadaen folded his arms. "The Sarmese told me that place is death. One of the old places infested by the most dangerous abominations."

"Shows you what perfumed city fops know. It was dangerous, yes—but because it was rumored to be the last, hidden refuge of Pagudon. Only lately has that rumor changed to warn of it being a lair of abominations." She looked back at Neeshu. "And now I am not even sure what that word means."

Druadaen's eyes followed hers. "Do we have time to...to see to her remains?"

Aleasha shook her head. "If this thrice-damned priestess has such powers of affining that she may bend a cryptigant to her will, and if she wonders why her rabble of 'ungovernables' has not yet returned to her, then she may become curious. If she also is capable of the kind of affining which allows her to see through a creature's eyes, she might send a bird of her own down here. If so, she might find our trail and attack, or follow, us."

"Yes," Druadaen said with a frown, "perhaps."

"You believe she will act differently?"

"Believe is too strong a word," he muttered. "But I do not think she will come seeking us."

"Why? We are vulnerable and we know her plans!"

"Do we?"

Aleasha crossed her arms. "Explain."

"What you project makes perfect sense if she means to make the Prow her seat of power. But I do not think that is what she intends." Aleasha's cocked head was an invitation to explain further. "She did not come here to conquer. She came by mistake and knows that she may be followed. So while she may be seeking a safe haven, I suspect that is simply a temporary expedient."

"While she finds another portal home," Aleasha finished with a nod. "Still, if she has taken the Prow, she has a fortress, for now. And we must report that." She glanced over her shoulder, and the faintest hint of giddiness passed across her dark features. "Besides, I've always wanted to ride a supragant."

"And you mean to do so *now*?"

"Now is when we *must* ride them. We will travel at least five times as fast that way. And if your priestess sends watchful eyes to this place, it is still best that we're long gone before they arrive." She started toward the smallest of the supragants; it resembled one of the aurochs that roamed the steppes of Khazat, back on Arrdanc, but was easily twice as large.

Druadaen checked to make sure that he was carrying what little remained of his original kit and followed her. "So, if you have long wanted to ride one of these creatures, why haven't you?"

"Why do you suppose? Because I do not invite death to come tap my shoulder!"

"And now?"

She frowned, albeit uncertainly. "Besides having a pressing need, these supragants are now joined to us by a common cause. The scent of resolve is upon them. Cryptigants typically lair in harsh climes. For one to appear here and kill four of their kind in a single slaughter? The supragants will band together to stop it—no matter the cost." She looked up into the giant auroch's patient, inscrutable eyes.

"So," Druadaen said, "it is now safe to ride them?"

"Well," she mused, "it is not courting death." She looked up at the auroch's back, which arched high overhead. "Not exactly."

As the sun fell and Druadaen finished his last small slice of cheese, he looked up at the sound of hooves moving off. Half of the supragants were trotting into the gathering dusk.

"Where are they going?"

"A day's ride ahead. We will be much slower, particularly waiting for the wolves." She regarded the last six with a mixture of sadness and worry. Other than the birds perched on the backs of the remaining supragants, they were now her sole companions and exhausted by the travel, lying on their sides, chests heaving. Out of sheer determination, they had kept up with the long-striding supragants who trotted faster than they could sprint . . . and for much, much longer. She sat stroking them with one listless hand while using the other to pluck yard-long auroch hairs off her clothes, arms, and legs.

Druadaen dusted his palms against each other, leaned back on his elbows with a sigh. "When Neeshu mentioned Ancrushav, you knew his name."

She shrugged. "I might have heard it."

He smiled. "And now *you* are almost lying to *me*."

She spared a ghost of a smile, but it was pensive. "I know his name and little else. It is said that he is hard to reach. Until today, I had not heard his name connected with the Armory. But I had heard rumors that he had abominations as followers. Or so it was said."

"You thought he might not?"

"No, I mean that even before today, I suspected that if he did have abominations serving him, that they might be different in some way. For almost ten years, there have been reports of them raiding small communities, but without killing the inhabitants. Or any humans at all. Except, strangely, bandits.

"Now, roof-folk"—she glared at him histrionically— "say that patrols and merchants have been killed by Ancrushav's abominations. And it is true that some of them have been seen not only carrying but using the weapons and goods of just such missing groups." She frowned. "But those who live simple lives beneath roofs become simple themselves."

Druadaen smiled. "And what do *you* suspect?"

"I observe that patrols and merchants have always gone missing, and that there are still bandits aplenty to have killed them."

Druadaen nodded. "And so, when Ancrushav's 'Children' take the goods from dead bandits and are later seen with them, townsfolk presume it was the abominations who killed the original owners."

Aleasha sighed, leaned back against the largest of the male wolves. "It is a pleasure—and a relief—that you are not simple. Even though you were raised beneath a roof."

"Half true. But you never bothered to mention that you are actually from the Godbarrows."

She busied herself removing the supragant hairs. "Well...you never asked."

He smiled. "Hmm. One would have to know it's a question to ask. But more to the point: why did you leave?"

"Because of the troubles in the south."

"You mean the civil war in Kaande?"

Her frown was severe. "I mean what caused it."

"So, whoever killed the royal family?"

"Yes, who also just happened to leave the youngest, cat-burning scion alive. And who still holds the city and has sealed its gates. That is not what coups usually do."

Druadaen nodded. "Quite the opposite. Typically, holding the capital becomes a cornerstone of a faction's claim to the throne. So I agree: the regicide sounds like an attempt to weaken Kaande, not a part of its succession struggles."

She smiled at him wanly. "You have seen this little drama before, then?"

He sighed. "More times than I can quickly count. But I do not understand why you left the Godbarrows to help nations that you say you do not trust and which are the architects of their own troubles."

"And I stand by that. But an innocent babe threatened by war is still an innocent babe, no matter where she was born." She frowned again. "Besides, troubles down there become troubles up here, particularly if Pagudon is involved. For almost forty years, it has been creating more horrific abominations and in greater numbers. And with this priestess bringing them under her influence, they become a singular threat to all around them." She shook her head. "It is said that something very similar was what caused the Annihilators to descend upon us in the first place."

Druadaen started. "The Annihilators were the *enemies* of the abominations?"

"Enemies? The Annihilators came to *exterminate* them." A smile crinkled one corner of her mouth. "You thought the Annihilators brought the abominations with them, didn't you?"

Druadaen shook his head with a rueful grin. "I confess I did."

"Well, you were ignorant, but all of us are in one way or another. And at least you are one of the few willing to smile at it and learn. But on the matter of the Annihilators. When they despaired of eliminating the abominations, they changed their strategy to ensuring that they could never reach their world."

Druadaen nodded. "They resolved to destroy any power that could create or keep control over portals that connected them to Hystzos."

"See? Even if you are ignorant, you are not slow-witted or arrogant. I ask for no more than that in a companion." She huffed at annoying memories. "That's probably why I've had so few." She reached in her larger ruck and pulled out what looked like fluffy, outsized seed cases. "These are tingle pods," she explained, seeing his stare. "They are some of the most useful items made by wyldwyrds." She rose. "If broken and scattered, their dust makes almost any creature sneeze. Without warning." She carried several toward the periphery of their camp. "Almost as good as watch dogs," she called over her shoulder. "Come and see how I place them."

CHAPTER THIRTY-SEVEN

The Armory—a horn of rock that jutted up from a low plateau—was prominent on the horizon when their last set of supragant bearers slowed to a walk. But the gait of those immense creatures was not leisurely but cautious, each step hedged against a possible need to flee in the other direction.

Since Aleasha rarely spoke the obvious, the words with which she broke the long silence struck Druadaen as odd. "We are nearing the end of our journey."

He merely nodded. "Yes."

Her pause was so long that he thought she had fallen fully silent again. "You have been very forthright about your past," she said eventually. "Since our first meeting."

He shrugged. "It is how people come to know each other."

She nodded, frowning. After they had swayed back and forth a few more times in the crude saddle-hammocks that they had woven from the supragant's long hair, her next, sharp words were almost an outburst. "I have been remiss. I have shared very little of my own background."

Druadaen shrugged again. "Each person comes to sharing their past in their own way and in their own time. If they ever do."

She nodded. "I am not hasty in such things."

"I have noticed."

She shot a look at him, saw his smile, and returned it. "Even now I am not eager to do so, but before we meet Ancrushav—if we do—there is something you must know." She sighed the way one might before diving into a very deep, icy pool. "I began learning my art at a young age, apprenticed to a wyldwyrd. That meant roaming these lands with him, for that is what we do. Although our travels are not planned or regular, they are not aimless, either. Those of my craft bring healing to both the animals and hamlets in the further reaches of the Godbarrows, particularly secluded places where there is less danger.

"There is one such place that is almost large enough to be called a town, and we passed through it more frequently than others. It is on a river that runs from highlands all the way down to the Sea of Hystzos. My mentor was much attached to the place. His older brother—also a wyldwyrd—dwelt there. The age difference was actually more than is typical between a father and son, and the deference my mentor showed for the older wyldwyrd made me wonder if he had been apprenticed to him. But that was no more my business than what did or did not occur in that house's one bed. I slept in a hammock or on a pallet, according to my whims.

"The older brother's house was very far outside the town, even for a wyldwyrd. Over the course of our visits, I discovered why, albeit by remaining alert when they thought I was not." She paused. "Five years before, he had sheltered a male child whose mother died even as she birthed him. The infant was malformed and grew very rapidly; surely, an abomination. But the wyldwyrd protected it until he either found it a haven far away from the town that wanted it killed, or it grew aware and old enough to flee for its life.

"I did not learn the child's strange name—Ancrushav—until years later, when I passed through the town with my mentor and we learned that the older wyldwyrd had disappeared. There had been no sign of violence at his hovel, but also, no sign of preparations for a journey. Years later, when I was a wyldwyrd in my own right, it was said that Ancrushav had either fallen or run into the hands of Pagudon." She frowned. "I will know, quickly, whether he is still in the service of that master."

"If he ever was."

"The few reliable persons who shared word of him say that he dwelt among the sorcerers. And that he would be very hard to keep as a prisoner."

Druadaen answered with a small nod. "I will be guided by your assessments."

Aleasha looked at him, quirked a smile. "Not the same thing as following my lead, though, is it?"

Druadaen smiled back. "Not quite, no."

Aleasha laughed. "I have not encountered such polite—and subtle—stubbornness ever before. I have enjoyed our journey together," she finished, sighing through her grin.

"You sound as though our ways might soon part."

"Part? No. But end? All too possible, depending what we might learn upon meeting him."

She peered into the distance, craned her neck and squinted. "Which should occur quite soon, now. It seems we have been noticed. We should ready our gear to go ahead on foot. The supragants will not go much further; they are already catching scents they do not like."

The supragants stamped anxiously behind them as Druadaen and Aleasha entered the rough ground that ran away from the talus-ringed Armory in every direction. From among the rocks and draws of the narrow approach, abominations emerged: always behind them, and from places that Aleasha had not been able to detect in advance. It not only irritated but worried her; half a dozen of her birds were circling overhead and they had given her no warning.

"I don't like this," she muttered.

Druadaen agreed. "Neither do I. That is why I would like to stop and take a sip or two from my skin."

She glared at him. "Are you mad?"

He smiled. "You and others ask that so frequently, I begin to suspect you are right." He stopped and reached for his waterskin.

The half dozen abominations following them started when he reached toward his belt, settled again when they saw what he had produced from it. As they watched him drink, several of them muttered or whispered what sounded like a mantra: "Ancrushav." They kept repeating the name, often struggling to string all the syllables together. Druadaen continued to listen and observe them until he finished drinking and resealed the skin, letting it hang loose over his shoulder.

As they resumed walking, Aleasha muttered, "And what did that accomplish?"

"Well, firstly, they are clearly under orders to not only deliver us intact, but not take us prisoner or exert any undue pressure on us to comply. So they kept their distance. And you no doubt saw what I did; over half of those following us are not Touched."

"All true," she muttered, "but what does it prove?"

"Prove? Nothing. But it suggests that if the Armory still is under Ancrushav's control, he means to speak with us. And that if he has gathered all these 'abominations' to him, none of them seem ungovernable. Rather, they understand, and follow, orders."

"That," a distant voice announced loudly, "is also, 'all true.'"

They looked toward the rocky tooth of the Armory and saw a woman—apparently human—standing alongside a tall, willowy girl who possessed only one distinctly atypical feature visible from where they stood, over a hundred yards away: batlike ears as rough and leathery as her hair was fine and flaxen.

"Approach and fear no harm, unless it is harm you intend. Be brisk; we may not display ourselves so openly for very long."

Aleasha stared at the pair from under lowered brows as she strode forward with Druadaen. "I hope you know what you're doing," she whispered.

"What *I'm* doing?" he whispered back. "This was your idea."

"Don't remind me."

The woman folded her hands before her as they drew

near. She was dressed simply and wore her dark hair long and tied back. It was difficult to read her age from her features; her cheekbones and severe jaw suggested that even as a young girl, she would not have had the rounding facial fat of youth. The woman beside her had very similar features but the complete absence of wrinkles or sun spotting showed her to be significantly younger.

The older woman spoke before either of them could. "What business have you here?"

Aleasha spoke with chin raised. "We bring a message from Neeshu."

"Neeshu delivers her own messages, particularly in this place where she is known and you are not."

Druadaen lowered his head slightly. "When we found her, Neeshu already knew she would not be able to deliver this message. She asked us to do so in her stead."

The older woman looked from one to the other, studying their faces. "I see," she said. "But if she sent you in her stead, clearly she told you something of this place. She declared herself a Sister of Ancrushav, did she not?"

Druadaen heard what sounded like an encouraging tone, heard the trap in that. "No," he answered mildly, "she said she was one of the *Children* of Ancrushav."

The two women—they could be related, Druadaen realized—exchanged glances. "So," said the older, "you did speak to Neeshu, after all. And she trusted you. Follow us."

Only two Untouched trailed behind as they wound through a set of narrow switchbacks that ascended the side of the cuspid-shaped Armory. They were not merely walkways, but grooves cut into its granite flanks, their outward sides forming a low parapet. A third of the way to the top, they stopped before a deep, narrow fault; ten yards into the gloom, Druadaen saw hints of a take-up drum for ropes, akin to the kind he associated with drawbridges. He could not see anything attached to it until the mechanism groaned into activity and drew rope up to them from the chasm below. A narrow bridge, barely five feet wide but at least thirty feet long, emerged from the gloom until it was level with the walkway. Beneath them, they heard the creak of a door or hatch opening, a grunt and then a sharp, stony crack that jarred the bridge itself... which now rested firmly on whatever had been raised from below to brace it.

The woman led the way, followed by her companion, whose ears shifted and rotated upward. Aleasha glanced overhead, nodded at Druadaen: figures that were more shadow than substance moved quietly above them. Some paralleled their motion, others moved only occasionally. Aleasha glanced over her shoulder at the intermittent sounds of the latter. "Are some going back to the start of the ramp, do you think?"

Druadaen shook his head. "I suspect they are archers, changing their positions to keep a clear field of fire upon us as we move."

Aleasha nodded somberly and then flinched as if stung by a bee. She made a small, sharp waving motion, as if shooing just such an insect.

Druadaen frowned. "What is it?" If there was some biting bug hovering around her, he could not detect it.

"You're probably right about those archers," she admitted, "since several just came out from a sally port near the top of the Armory. And they knew exactly where my birds were flying."

"Did they—?"

"None loosed a shaft, but they tracked the birds with obvious intent. I bade them fly off as quickly as they could."

Druadaen nodded. "Must you gesture that way, to send that command?"

She smiled crookedly. "No. It's just a reflex."

They stepped off the reversed drawbridge onto a stone landing. A broad, lightless cave mouth yawned before them. The bat-eared young woman disappeared into the darkness. The older one stood to the side. "The way is smooth, but it is not straight and it leads downward. Do you wish light?"

Druadaen answered before Aleasha's growing anxiety could spark a sarcastic retort. "Yes," he said, "I would appreciate that."

As if summoned by that reply, the young woman emerged from the dark, her black pupils almost the size of her eyes, save a white rim of cornea. As she held out a glass sphere toward Aleasha, her eyes swiftly contracted back to normal proportions. Druadaen stepped back, mindful that if he was too close, any impending mancery might not work. The young woman nodded, murmured. "Reach out to what is within." Her voice was as high and sweet as a four-year-old's.

Aleasha frowned uncertainly "Do you mean—?"

The young woman's eyes contracted further, the pupils becoming pinpoints.

The sphere began to glow a yellow green.

Druadaen stared and suppressed his first, panicked reaction: to shatter it. The color and murkiness of the glow were almost exact matches for the hungry, living lamps that had lit the way down into the depths of the Library of Imvish'al. The older woman's gaze shifted to him, but just for the moment it took him to control his response.

Aleasha had nodded at the young woman and took the globe. As she did, it faded, but a moment later it glowed again. More brightly, it seemed. "Who taught you your wyldwyrding?"

The young woman shrugged, her blonde locks rising and tumbling around the large ears that resembled old, wrinkled leather. "No one. I just ... do it."

Aleasha stared. "I have never heard of such a thing."

"Nor had I," the older woman said with a smile. "But although my mother's gift passed me by, my daughter has it in even greater strength."

"Your daughter?" Druadaen asked, maintaining his distance from the globe.

With Aleasha holding it, they followed the woman into the opening as she answered. "Yes: my daughter. And no, I was not a child bride. This winter will be my thirtieth. It will be her eighth. It is often thus with the Children of Ancrushav."

Aleasha's question held a hint of sharpness. "Is your child not *your* child?"

"Yes, she is. And she could not remain so, anywhere else. He—Ancrushav—cares for them as a father would. So they name themselves his Children."

"Besides," the daughter added, "he really did bring that name on himself."

Druadaen smiled, tried not to be distracted by the mischievous wiggle of her bat ears. "How did he do that?"

"He said we must not call him our leader. Or our king. Or anything else that means we have given the smallest bit of our fate or conscience to another person." They entered a chamber, lit by the same globes. "So one of his first followers—now his steward—spread word that we should all call ourselves his children." As Aleasha let her globe fade out, the young woman laughed; it was as high and simple as a toddler's. "I like telling stories! Even more than hearing them!" She pointed to one of the high cavern's many openings and, taking Aleasha's hand, led the way into it.

Druadaen and the mother followed slightly behind. She stared up at him. "You have questions."

"It is so obvious?"

"Any more so and your eyebrows would spell them out."

"I hardly know where to begin...or what might give offense."

"Then I will help you. 'How,' you wish to ask, 'can you be the mother of a woman who appears to be barely ten years your junior?'"

And how did you come to give birth to an ab— one of the Untouched? But his only reply was a nod.

"It is thus with all the Changed, both Touched and Untouched. The Changing speeds growth."

"And shortens life," the daughter added without any hint of fear or resentment, her ears swiveling backward.

Aleasha's voice was hushed. "Does that not sadden you?" She started by asking the daughter, but at the end, glanced back at the mother.

The daughter shrugged. "Why should it? I hope to live as long a life as possible and end it well before I no longer have control over my actions."

Druadaen nodded. "We should all see our lives so clearly." He glanced sideways at the mother. Her teeth shone in a proud smile but were not quite as bright as the watery glimmer in her pain-pinched eyes.

They left the lit chamber, and all was darkness except for the rekindled globe that led them downward.

CHAPTER THIRTY-EIGHT

The lower levels of the Armory made less use of well-groomed natural caves and passages. Carefully mined tunnels with doglegs led past clusters of rooms; narrow black lines of murder slits marked both the ceiling and walls; empty recesses marked where great doors or small portcullises had been before their wood had crumbled to dust.

Shortly after their path leveled off, they came upon a wide octagonal room with dark tunnels running into every wall, as if the much marred center was sending them out like the rays of a black star.

"What is this place?" murmured Aleasha absently.

"Stores marshalling chamber," Druadaen answered.

She stared at him. "I know what each of those words mean, but I don't understand how this room would serve that need."

"I know, I know!" the young woman almost squealed.

"Yefri," the mother remonstrated gently, "do not interrupt our gues—visitor."

Noting the implicit distinction the mother had just made between him being a "visitor" rather than a "guest," he turned toward Yefri. "Actually, I'd like very much if you'd tell me."

"Yes? Well, then...yes! It's like a mine. There used to be rails on the floor. And, and there were little wagons with wheels that fit over them. And so, when the soldiers had to quickly move something from one place to another, they would put it in the wagons and roll them to where it was needed." She looked eagerly in his face, her eyes level with his, her ears quivering with the sheer joy of telling yet another story to the strangers. "I'm right, aren't I?"

Druadaen nodded. "I certainly think that's how this room was used," he said with a smile. "At least, that's what I've seen in the forts with which I am familiar."

"And where would those forts be, visitor?" asked a very deep and utterly impassive voice from one of the tunnels.

"In a land not known on this side of the Shun." Which was technically true.

An abomination—*no; a Changeling*—as large and broad as the one he'd fought the day he'd emerged from the darkness. The man was perfectly formed— formidably muscled and well over seven feet in height— except for a second, smaller head attached at the juncture of its neck and shoulder. "Your answer is not an answer," the normal, and quite handsome head, declared. "It is an evasion."

"Well, then, have you ever heard of Dunarra? Or Corrovane? Or perhaps Connæar?"

The Changeling—for it was unclear whether he

would be characterized as Touched or Untouched—frowned. "I do not know these names."

"Well, if you know the Godbarrows, you'll know the names I tell you now," Aleasha flared impatiently. "Hudushap, Komkik, Peffem, Srimshyr—"

The big Changeling had been nodding somberly until the last town name; he flung up his hand, palm out to stop her. "You will come with me." He turned and bowed toward the mother. "Thank you, Lamla. And you, Yefri. I shall escort them from here."

They both bowed back and said, almost in unison, "Yes, Steward." Both turned smiles on the two visitors and disappeared back into the tunnel from which they had all emerged.

The big Changeling waited for almost a full minute after their footsteps faded into silence. *Probably familiar with Yefri's acute hearing*, Druadaen guessed as the small head alternatively lolled, blinked, yawned into what seemed like a spasm, and fell quiet. "I am Steward," the normal head announced. "Who are you, how do you know to ask for Ancrushav in this place, and what is your business here?"

Druadaen watched the smaller, wizened head as Aleasha provided Steward with the required information; it rose up when it heard a voice other than that of the normal head, eyes half-lidded as if it were meditating like a Basakayn spiritualist.

"So, you have delivered your message," Steward said after Aleasha had finished. "You may depart in safety. We shall mark you with the scent of Changefriends. Even the ungovernable who roam the Armory's peripheries will not pursue or harm you."

"Neeshu made it plain that we were to speak to Ancrushav directly."

"What can you tell him that you have not already told me?"

"That isn't really the question, is it?" she bristled. "Perhaps it is because he would wish to ask questions that you can't anticipate."

Steward's considerable brow lowered. "Do you suggest I am simple?"

"I suggest that even a trusted Child might not know every thought of its . . . er, parent."

"We do not call him that."

"Steward," Druadaen put in, sensing that the tension between the two was rising rather than easing, "I might be the cause of Neeshu's insistence that we see him. She knew I was not from this side of the Shun. Perhaps she foresaw that would be meaningful to Ancrushav precisely because I come from afar. Even he himself could hardly know what questions he might wish to ask of me until he meets me."

Steward looked suspiciously from one visitor to the other. "It may be as you say. Follow me. Do not fall behind. There are workspawn in this area. They are extremely small but extremely dangerous. They will not accost you so long as you remain within a few feet of me. If you stray further, I cannot answer for what might happen. Let us go."

They followed the tunnel to its apparent end . . . where, at a sign from Steward, a trapdoor opened and a ramp was lowered. What appeared to be the ceiling was apparently a light molding on the back of a wooden walkway. Even as they ascended, the ramp was already being raised back into place. They stood in darkness for a few moments before more yellow-amber lamps began to glow, revealing an extremely well-preserved chamber with many connecting rooms and corridors running off in several directions.

As they made their way to the smallest of the openings, they passed a wide arch that opened into a brightly lit great hall. Half a dozen Untouched were holding bowls near a much larger and hideously deformed Changeling that, despite its perverse amalgam of tentacles and animal limbs and sense organs, was also Untouched. As he watched, two of the attendants with filled bowls withdrew and two new ones—apparently human women—approached to take their place. Druadaen trailed to a stop, trying to make sense of what was obviously some kind of ritual.

"Do not fall behind," Steward warned, just as two cockroach-sized creatures sped out toward them, eye-stalks sweeping from side to side.

Druadaen glanced at the small, intent guardians of whatever was transpiring within. They were an eye-gouging mix of reptile and insect. "I do not understand what is happening in the great hall."

"It is not necessary that you do."

"Still," Druadaen said calmly, "I would greatly appreciate anything you might tell us about it. I did not think that ab—Changelings observed any religious rites."

"We do not." Steward sounded both annoyed and exasperated. "But some insist on gilding mundane activities with divine significance." He sighed; the smaller head wheezed as he did. "What you see therein is the collection rite for creating philters of affinity."

Aleasha glanced over Druadaen's shoulder. "It looks more like they are draining the big one's wounds."

Steward nodded. "The weeping from those sores is the source of the philters."

Druadaen watched as two of the Untouched genuflected before bringing forward broad catch basins of copper to collect what dripped from the large Changeling. By focusing on the details of the gatherers' robes and muttered rites, he managed to ignore feeling queasy.

Aleasha did not seem similarly affected. "It is related to the way we wyldwyrds make our philters. Many of a body's humours are rich in that which shapes the nature of that species...but I have never seen it gathered from wounds."

Steward frowned. "Those are not wounds; they are permanent eruptions that cannot heal." In answer to their curious looks, he explained, "It is common when there are many—and conflicting—differences in a Changeling. A Weeper's body is always at war with itself." He nodded at the lesions on the Untouched's broad, half-scaled back. "Those are the constant battlegrounds between its many natures. Come away. We are expected."

Druadaen had to watch his step to avoid crushing the small guardians underfoot. "And what are these?"

"Those are the workspawn of which I warned you."

Aleasha raised an eyebrow. "And what work do they perform?"

"Anything that their Spawner requires."

"Spawner?"

Steward entered the corridor toward which they'd been heading. "Spawners are akin to Weepers: their changes are many and profound. But their bodies resolve the conflicts between their unharmonious parts by spawning small creatures that conform to one or another of their natures more than the others."

"And they... they understand the instructions of their Spawner?"

As they walked, the corridor's lights glowed to life before them; those behind faded in their wake. "As I understand it—and I don't, really—the Spawner's desires are always known to its spawn. It is akin to the way you make your desires known to the birds that are awaiting your return outside. But it does not require thought; the action of spawn is like a reflex of the Spawner, but at a distance from its body." Steward's voice became a grumble. "And as with the Weepers, the Spawners are called the Holy Accursed of Ancrushav. And he tolerates it, although he hates such terms."

"Why?" asked Druadaen.

"As Yefri may have already implied, Ancrushav takes a dim view of equating physical phenomena with the will or the acts of gods."

"I like him already," Aleasha muttered.

"We shall see."

A light glowed at the end of a long corridor without any doors or chambers communicating with it. Steward's pace did not slow as he warned them, "When you meet Ancrushav, be forthright. If you do not understand what you see, ask."

"What do you mean?" Aleasha almost whispered. "Are his changes very great?"

Steward looked at her. "Ancrushav is not a Changeling."

Druadaen frowned. "What is he then?"

"There are many names for his kind. But we use the term that is said to come from The Maw itself. He is a serratus."

"And what is a serratus?" *And what is The Maw?*

"Again, you shall see. Very soon. You may ask a final question of me."

Aleasha just stared at the well-lit opening ahead.

Druadaen glanced at their guide. "I have not been able to discern if Steward is your title or your name."

"It is both. I am Steward."

"Only that?"

The big Changeling shrugged. "Only that. I need no name other than that which announces what I am and what I do."

Aleasha glanced at him from the other side. "I suspect you are more than a guide for visitors, though."

"You are correct."

"Well, what else do you do?"

"Whatever else Ancrushav requires. In this case, it will be to remember everything that is said in your meeting with him." At those words, the shriveled head seemed to waken, eyes searching the way a blind man's do when his name is called.

"That must be very difficult," Druadaen observed.

"Difficult? I cannot prevent it, even if I wished to."

"You never find it a . . . a great weight upon your mind, having to remember every conversation you hear?"

Steward seemed to reflect for a moment. "No. But sometimes, it is a great weight upon my heart that

I cannot *forget* some of them." He had stopped just beyond the threshold of the lit chamber.

Peering in, Druadaen found it reminiscent of a garrison's ready room. There were hooks on the wall, rough chairs facing inward from the walls, and the smell of oils used upon blade and leather, respectively.

"He is waiting," Steward said. "You are to enter first."

CHAPTER THIRTY-NINE

As Druadaen stepped over the threshold, he discovered that the chamber was much wider than it was deep and that there were matching sets of lightless alcoves to both the left and right. From the one in the center of the far right-hand wall, a voice startled him: "I am here." However, it was not the source of the voice that surprised him, or what it announced, but its sound: almost as deep as a supragant's bellow, but without its rich bass tones. It was as if words were being formed from the stony clashings of a landslide. If this was Ancrushav, he sounded a great deal older than a man in his twenties.

Druadaen approached the alcove, which brightened, revealing a large, cloaked man behind a table. He stood . . . and rose until he was a whole head taller than Druadaen. Proportionally, his shoulders were even broader. He was not aware that Aleasha was standing beside him until the man drew back his hood and she suppressed a gasp.

The face was something out of nightmares or legends of otherworldly fiends. The foundation of the features—broad forehead, straight nose, high cheekbones—was human. It might even have been deemed handsome, but for the night-black ridges that broke through the flesh wherever bone neared the surface. Protrusions like small horns dotted his jaw and sides of his neck, while two much larger ones curved forward from his temples, shining like obsidian. His skin was not like any that Druadaen had ever seen on a living creature: a hairless tan-gray hide. Overlarge incisors pushed out from almost colorless lips, and red-irised eyes regarded him, but they quickly became perplexed; he had no doubt seen many different expressions on newcomers' faces—but not the wondering bafflement that dropped Druadaen's jaw.

Because his eyes had fixed on one other feature: a feature so jarring that his perception of Ancrushav's frankly monstrous face had been little more than peripheral. Instead, he could not look away, laboring to understand how what he was seeing could be possible: Ancrushav's hair was a black-fringed silver-white mane—a match for the one that Druadaen had seen upon Corum Torshaenyx and the other Tualarans he had seen or met.

Ancrushav's stiff black brows rose. "I was told that both of you were accustomed to beings with different forms from your own." He nodded toward Aleasha. "Her behavior agrees with that report. But yours..." He sought and found Druadaen's eyes. "I am accustomed to terror, even revulsion. But your stare is one of surprise. And possibly... recognition?"

Druadaen shook his head, searching for words. "A

bit of both, perhaps." He added a wan wave. "It is easy to imagine strange resemblances when one is weary from long travels."

Ancrushav nodded soberly. "Perhaps. Perhaps we shall speak more of these resemblances later. But, to business: I am told that you bear Neeshu's final words. I would hear those words and how you came to be the bearers of them."

"That last part could prove a very long tale," Druadaen warned him.

"In my experience," Ancrushav replied, "those are the ones that convey the most important information."

Aleasha shrugged and began with the message they'd been enjoined to convey, but then worked back to their respective origins, how they had met, and why their paths had ultimately crossed Neeshu's. They had anticipated being required to provide their own backgrounds, so Aleasha had been chosen to be the initial tale-teller, not only because she was native to the region and its languages, but because it gave Druadaen the opportunity to observe how her story was received.

Ancrushav watched her face intently, but also remained aware of the rest of his surroundings; occasional lapses in his focus signaled the kind of peripheral watching that had been common among senior Outriders. Obversely, Steward's eyes seemed to become empty, as if he were unable to focus ... until Druadaen noticed that the wizened head was now raised, eyes mostly open as it tilted toward whoever was speaking. And, halfway through Aleasha's tale, two of the unnerving workspawn scrambled out of Ancrushav's alcove and drew close, their antennae and eyestalks swaying to and fro in what seemed to be watchfulness.

When she had concluded, Ancrushav murmured thanks and shifted his gaze to Druadaen. "And do you agree that this priestess may have affined with the cryptigant? Do you believe her capable of that?"

Druadaen was impressed at how blithely he'd received the information that one of his visitors was from an entirely different world. "I am quite sure that she can achieve what we project. The viziers in Sarmasid learned that she had done no less in her journey from what they call the Fickle Haze to their own city. And from what I heard of her researches there—both legal and illegal—I suspect she was aware that she would need it to breach the defenses of the Prow. What I do not understand is why she chose that as her destination."

"It is a stronghold," Ancrushav said with a shrug that was not entirely convincing.

"True, and distant from any probable foes. But if she does not mean to remain here, then I suspect she perceives some other value in holding it. Does it guard a ford or pass or some other strategic place, such as this armory does?"

Ancrushav's bloodred eyes bored into his own. "In a manner of speaking."

Aleasha asked—hastily, Druadaen thought—a question of her own before he could pursue his line of inquiry further. "What *I* wish to know is how"—she waved at the walls and the ceiling and the very land upon which the Armory sat—"how this can be. How can you live together this way? Why does the rest of the world not know? How did you come to lead these . . . these people in this—"

Ancrushav held up a hand. "My memory is poor. I cannot remember so many questions."

She stopped, stunned—until she saw the hint of a grin at the corners of his mouth. She smiled. "Allow me to rephrase: How have you managed all of"—she waved again—"this?"

He nodded, gestured to a pair of waiting chairs as he navigated to his own. "It is not so successful or laudable an accomplishment as it might seem."

"How so?" Druadaen asked.

"For every Changeling here"—he gestured beyond the room just as Aleasha had—"there are hundreds who cannot imagine, let alone believe, that such a place exists for them and so will not come. There are thousands more who could not live here at all. They are, as Neeshu told you, ungovernable. And the end is always the same, even for the most Untouched: no matter how long they remain the masters of their own minds, ultimately, their bodies rebel and betray them."

"How do you live with the burden of choosing who may stay and who may not?"

He shrugged. "Happily, I do not need to choose. There are reagents and compounds which indicate how long and to what degree any Changeling is likely to remain stable." He leaned back in his chair with a sigh. "Less than one in a hundred who comes to this place has any hope of mastering themselves."

"And what happens to those who cannot?"

"I do not send them away, but they must live outside the walls of the Armory. Most cannot. Those who can are the ones who arose behind you as you approached, and then shepherded you toward Lamla. Oddly, they are also the ones who insist on calling themselves my Children, so long as they can still form words."

"Why is that?" Druadaen asked.

"I am not sure. Most can barely convey their thoughts."

"Shall I tell you why they call themselves your Children?" Aleasha broke in suddenly, and then answered her own question in the same breath. "Because you brought them as close to the Armory as you could. Because you chose to give them a home rather than forsake them. Because every time they awaken in a protected place, they remember why. And because deep down they know that as long as they can speak, they remain the masters of their own mind. So they keep whispering your name, struggling to remember it as long as they can. They probably repeat it as they go to sleep and then again as soon as they wake. Perhaps even in their dreams."

She leaned forward, as ardent as Druadaen had ever seen her. "Do you not see it? For them, your name is both an anchor and a prayer. It is how they prove to themselves, every day, that they still belong here, that they are still holding their terrible fate at bay. Because I am willing to wager my one black pearl that when their speech goes, their mind follows soon after."

He considered her solemnly. "You have seen little yet understood much, except that you overestimate my role in sustaining this place." Aleasha seemed ready to roll her eyes as he continued. "But you are right about Changelings and speech. First they begin losing words. That is not so bad. But when they no longer have the patience to try *finding* the missing words"— he shook his head—"blind rage soon consumes what remains of their mind."

Druadaen nodded. "And as a serratus, you are not subject to such declines?"

He fixed Druadaen with a stare, then pointed. "No

more than you or she." He reflected. "Or at least, if I do become deranged, it would arise from different causes."

Given the obliquity of Ancrushav's response, Druadaen instinctively changed the topic. "And what of the humans we have seen here? Do they just appear to be unaltered, or are their Changes too subtle to be seen?"

"It is unlikely you saw a Changeling that cannot be detected as such; they are very rare, even here. Lamla and any others you saw—perhaps those who gather the serae required for affinity philters?—are as you: unchanged humans."

"Do they come here with their Changeling children, then?"

Ancrushav nodded. "And with those whose forms are atypical for other reasons."

Druadaen frowned. "I do not understand."

Aleasha blinked, stared at him. "Of course: you would not know."

Druadaen shook his head. "I am not even sure what you are referring to."

Aleasha directed her explanation toward Ancrushav. "In his world, there are no Changelings. So they actually keep blighted infants."

Ancrushav's eyebrows raised. "Truly?"

Druadaen held up a hand. "Wait. Are you saying that children who are born"—he could no longer use the word "malformed"—"with unexpected forms or features are not allowed to live?" As Aleasha nodded, he turned toward Ancrushav. "So the unchanged humans here...that's why they are all women? They are the mothers of Changelings? But I was told—"

"—that Changelings cannot reproduce," Ancrushav finished for him. "In fact, two Changelings cannot reproduce. And it is a further fact that more Changelings are made than are born."

"Made? But . . . how?"

Ancrushav waved the question away. "Too long an explanation, because if the news you bring is accurate, then we have little time."

We? But Druadaen pushed the implications of that pronoun aside. "I mean no disrespect, but then how is it that you survived at all?"

"In one of the towns that Mistress Aleasha has mentioned—"

"Srimshyr," she supplied.

"—my mother's midwife discerned problems soon after she went into labor. She knew that various herbs and philters would be essential if either of us were to survive my birth. I speculate that she also suspected that wyrding might prove necessary. So she sent for a wyldwyrd who lived just outside of that town."

Ancrushav's jaw muscles bunched; his teeth ground like stones. "It was the wyldwyrd who actually brought me into the world. The midwife attempted it, but . . ." He straightened in his chair, face impassive but rigid. "My savior and protector would never share the details of my birth, but I do know this; after that night, the midwife's hands were terribly scarred, and the left one had lost two fingers." He shrugged. "I suppose in the surprise, confusion, and chaos, he was able to spirit me away. For, as I realized the first time I saw my reflection in still water, I was an affront to their notions of purity."

"But I have heard . . ." Aleasha's query dwindled into pensive silence.

Ancrushav nodded at her. "If you have questions about my past, it is best that you ask them. Knowledge of each other will be a strength, whereas ignorance could prove a fatal weakness."

Aleasha straightened. "The few times I have heard your name uttered, it was always as either an agent of Pagudon or as their wayward creation."

He nodded. "At different times, both of those were true. They are not now. Within a year of Pagudon sending me to the Armory, I made a break with those who'd determined I should be its overseer." One corner of his lips sent out creases from the hint of a wintry half-smile. "I did not, however, deem it necessary to inform them of that change."

"But how did you go from a remote town in the north of the Godbarrows to...to wherever Pagudon makes its lair?"

He shrugged. "That touches upon another attribute which may have led to presumptions that I am a Changeling: the speed with which I grew. By the time I was three, I was too restless to remain close to my savior's new and more remote hovel. Curiosity and carelessness brought me to the attention of the townsfolk. I'm sure they had suspected I had survived and lived with him but, to borrow one of their quaint sayings, that was a sleeping bear they had decided not to poke.

"Their reaction showed me that, if I remained near Srimshyr, I would be repaying my savior's kindness by bringing an angry mob to his door. So I left."

Druadaen frowned. "Alone."

"Yes."

"Across the Godbarrows."

"Where else?"

Druadaen saw no deceit in Ancrushav's eyes. *To have survived, he had to be preternaturally swift, strong, and resistant to both the elements and injury. And that was when he was three.* Druadaen nodded; compared to him, he and even Ahearn were rather pitiable weaklings, one barely distinguishable from the other. "How did you know where to go?"

He shrugged. "I only knew I had to go as far away from my savior as I could. And once I began, I suppose I just kept going. One way in which I was not different from a very young human child is that I do not retain many memories from that time. One day was much like the next and I had no one with which to share them.

"But when the agents of Pagudon came upon me, I was glad for the company." He paused. "Well, after their wounds disinclined them from further attacks. They, too, mistook me for an 'abomination,' but upon returning with them, the Pagudon himself inspected me and realized I was serratae."

"Which means what, exactly?" Druadaen tried to affect an offhand tone, but, even to his own ears, failed miserably.

"Outcast, devil, fiend, demon, monster. There are many other variations on that theme."

"I think," Aleasha ventured, "that Druadaen was hoping to learn about where serratae are from, and the ways in which they are different from—or akin to—humans."

Ancrushav nodded. "I myself do not know very much, only what I discovered in dust-coated volumes in the most remote corners of Pagudon's libraries." He shrugged. "In them, serratae are described as savage, deceitful, domineering, and very, very difficult to kill. Some accounts claim we are not natural beings, others assert that we are. Given the opportunity, we eat, sleep, and learn much as humans do, but are far less reliant upon such niceties." He mused for a moment. "I have long wished to learn more about my origins and nature but I would hardly know where to look."

Druadaen glanced at Steward then back at Ancrushav. "The Maw?"

He shrugged. "Whatever that may be. Again, the references are unified only in their disparity. A ghostly domain; a trove of ancient treasures; a place of hellish torment; a lost city or continent: all these have been asserted. None have been proven." His eyes rested on Druadaen. "But given your arrival from an unknown world, I suppose it would be hasty to discount any of those possibilities." He frowned. "In truth, I doubted your stated origin, at first."

"Why?"

"For one who has been here for so short a time, you speak several languages with passable fluency."

"He has much experience doing so," Aleasha put in hastily. "He was what his people called a Courier and an Outrider. They travel to far lands in the service of their empire."

Druadaen was about to correct her by, once again, pointing out that Dunarra was a Consentium, but instead shrugged and drew the unusual torc up over the neck of his tunic. "This has made the process much, much easier."

One of Ancrushav's eyebrows climbed. "I am familiar with that periapt. It was common among the agents of Pagudon." His voice was casual; his eyes were not. Steward roused out of his trance, made a gesture into the room from which they had entered the alcove. Heavy feet thudded closer.

"I am not surprised to learn that," Druadaen answered, "since one of them was how I came by it."

"The agents of Pagudon do not sell those periapts; they are not the possessions of those to whom they are given."

"Happily, money was not an object. When I took it, the owner was in no condition to object. Or do anything else, for that matter."

"Ah," said Ancrushav, who seemed to be trying not to smile. "That is well, then. You may be interested to learn that is not truly wyrdcraft."

Druadaen nodded. "So I have learned. But that is *all* I've learned."

Ancrushav leaned forward, focused and—enthusiastic? "In your travels, have you encountered sages who assert that there are animalcules all around us, but are too small to see?"

Druadaen shrugged. "It is hardly the province of sages to know how diseases are transmitted."

Ancrushav's neck straightened in surprise. He glanced at Aleasha, who shrugged, then back at Druadaen. "And this is . . . common knowledge, on your world?"

Druadaen frowned. "Common in most parts, but there are certain regions where such learning . . . is not held in high regard."

"Well then, Master Druadaen, be warned: if you speak of it here, the best you may hope for is weary tolerance. Laughter or a gibbet is far more likely, and the worst would mean an end of you."

Druadaen nodded, returned the small smile that had risen to Ancrushav's lips as he realized, *He doesn't get to talk about such things. Not so long as he's here, isolated in the most dangerous part of the Godbarrows.*

Ancrushav's face became as animated as his voice. "Within the periapt is a growth not unlike a mold or fungus that deposits some of these invisible animalcules in you through the place where it touches your flesh."

Druadaen nodded. "That is why the skin beneath it appears light, almost sun-bleached."

"Precisely! Once they are within you, the growth that sent them forth is attuned to you, the way fish may detect distant movement by sensing waves and currents in the water. Once it has become familiar with your species, it is able to detect the feeling or general concept in a speaker's mind and convey those sensations to the wearer."

Druadaen continued nodding, but refrained from asking, *all well and good, but...by what mechanism does it know what is in the* speaker's *mind? Because it is a surety that a mold cannot learn words.*

Ancrushav's unbroken stream of words would not have given him the space to ask the question, had he dared do so. "Animalcules of this kind are distant relatives of those in the serae from which we produce the affinity philters with which we may pacify—or if necessary, control—Changelings. They are also present in the compounds from which the Changelings themselves are created."

Aleasha and Druadaen leaned forward at the same moment. She got their shared question out first: "What do you mean when you say that Changelings are *created*?"

Ancrushav straightened, evidently disappointed to leave the original topic. "As I said, most Changelings are not born; they are made." He checked their eyes for comprehension. Finding none, he put his fists on the desk before him. "The serae from which I make philters of affinity may also be worked into substances which cause the Change and govern what manner of alterations are expressed and to what degree."

Aleasha had grown very pale. Druadaen leaned forward and spoke very slowly and carefully. "I understand where the substances come from. But I do not understand what manner of creature receives the infusions."

Ancrushav's fists tightened; it sounded like leather armor being crushed. "The very young. And infants."

Aleasha was half out of her chair. "How—? Who—? What *monster* would be party to such an act? Truly, *they* are the abominations!"

"I agree," sighed Ancrushav. "But is trade in flesh truly surprising in a world where serfdom and slavery are daily realities?"

In his years as a Courier and Outrider, and in the time since, Druadaen had slain enemies, but never had he *desired* to kill any of them. Now, for the first time, he did. "Let me guess," he said, noticing the coldness of his tone and not caring. "Infants who emerge from the womb already 'flawed' are taken aside so the parents do not have to witness them being 'put away.' But if the midwife or an assistant is sufficiently amoral, they pass the newborn to a ghoulish liaison for whatever power wishes to build their own army of 'abominations.'"

Ancrushav straightened to reply, but Druadaen wasn't finished. "Or a sickly child is taken by a temple to be healed. Sadly, it is lost—not to the grave, but to that same set of greedy hands. Or a young child of slaves, whose parents are told that their darling has been sold to a new master but is destined for a far more horrific end. Or the toddlers of struggling serfs, put in the care of distant relatives who truly stain their hands with blood money—their own blood, no less."

Druadaen almost spat instead of concluding. "There are as many ways to steal babes as there are heartless ghouls to plan that crime." He looked at Ancrushav. "And I suspect you know who pays them so that they may raise up such monsters."

The serratus nodded slowly, his face like stone. "I know some names, but they hardly matter. The culprits are legion and all of a type: every wyrdcrafter and alchemist whose humanity has been consumed by their lust for power. To a one, their greatest desire is for a force that knows and hungers for nothing but slaughter, and asks nothing more than the opportunity to slake their unquenchable thirst for it."

"And among all those soulless contenders, I imagine Pagudon creates more Changelings than most?"

"More than all the others combined."

Aleasha's voice was thick. "I feel ill."

Ancrushav's reply was soft, almost solicitous. "It is a terrible thing to learn that fellow beings can commit such atrocities."

"That's not what makes me sick." She looked up. Druadaen had rarely seen eyes lit by such fury. "It is the pain in my gut, the pain I cannot get out."

Ancrushav's concern was palpable. "Pain from what?"

"From the need to kill all those human monsters. Right now."

CHAPTER FORTY

Ancrushav stopped before the wide door that had taken them three concealed passages to reach. "Cover your eyes."

Druadaen was about to do so, noticed that Aleasha was still distracted. He nudged her gently. She flinched, looked up, saw what was required, shielded her face behind her palm.

Ancrushav opened the door and light flooded out, not intense so much as pervasive. He stepped through the yellow-gold rectangle quickly, explaining, "I must pass first."

"There is a trap to be disarmed?" Druadaen wondered, as Aleasha shuffled forward.

"There is a condition to satisfy," Ancrushav amended as he waved them into the room. "If I am not the first to cross the threshold, and if I am not carrying a particular object I do not routinely keep upon my person, the results would be...most unfortunate."

Druadaen hardly heard the serratus's understatement of the consequences of trespassing; he was too busy staring around the unexpectedly vast chamber. Paneled in dark wood, closely spaced sconces held a slightly different variety of the glowing algae; the light was not only brighter and warmer, but it seemed to pulse faintly. Bookcases and scroll racks almost reached the fifteen-foot ceiling, all about two-thirds full. Worktables were clustered in the center, tools of the archivist's trade set in easy reach.

Aleasha looked at him as she lowered her hand. "You must feel right at home, here."

"In fact," Druadaen answered happily, "I do. It has been a . . . a very long time since I have stood in such a place."

"Feeling homesick?"

He thought, then shook his head. "For Arrdanc, yes. But for the Archive? No, I don't think so."

Ancrushav was returning from one of the bookcases with two large tomes. Aleasha looked at them suspiciously. "Are those what you said we must see?"

He nodded, opening and spreading their pages carefully as he gestured them to join him. "You will note the date."

Druadaen shrugged. He read no more than a hundred words of any of the languages of Hystzos and knew nothing of its dating other than the names of the days and months. But Aleasha peered at it in disbelief. "This was written over twenty-five centuries ago?" She frowned. "This must be a copy."

"It is," Ancrushav said with what sounded like suppressed pride.

She looked up at him. "You? Copied this?"

He nodded. "The original is still in one of the libraries of Pagudon."

Druadaen reassessed the size of the collection. "I take those collections are larger than this one?"

He shrugged. "This would barely contain the reading room for the smallest of them." He leaned closer to Aleasha to point out elements of the odd pattern spanning both open pages. "Note the many circles. And the lines joining them, like overlapping spiderwebs."

Druadaen realized what he was looking at. "The Vortex of Worlds," he murmured.

"So you have heard of it. That is good. Then I have relatively little to explain."

"To him, perhaps!" Aleasha exclaimed.

Ancrushav's inclined head was almost a short bow. "My apologies. Where shall I begin?"

"Perhaps by letting me figure out as much as I can on my own!" she retorted.

To which Ancrushav had a singular reaction; he worked—hard—to conceal a small smile. "Of course. Do as you wish."

"Thank you, I will." Her frown changed to one of intense concentration. "Well, I presume these are all different worlds. Or at least different places." She glanced at him.

He nodded but said nothing.

He'd probably lose his fight against that smile, if he spoke, thought Druadaen.

Aleasha pointed. "And I presume the large words underneath each sphere are their names?"

"Yes, but not all are recognizable. Many have probably been forgotten, and not all of the scripts are known, today."

She scanned the arcane array of circles of different sizes. "Well, what's this one say?" It was obvious why she had chosen it; it not only had several names, but had ten times as many lines emanating from it than any other.

"That first word is 'Spindle.' The second is 'Gyre.' I suspect these were the most common names; you will note that others are beneath them in smaller characters. And two are written in a script that I cannot decipher."

"And what of this one?" she asked, pointing to the one that had attracted Druadaen's attention. "It has more names than any other."

He nodded. "That is the strangest part of this map. Or diagram, or whatever it might be. Firstly, several of the labels are just the same word in different languages. The most common is Grinder. Others call it Distaff, but in the explicit and restricted meaning of the shaft upon which a spindle turns. Then there are all these other labels, almost half of which are in forgotten languages. But the ones that I can translate are either Cyclone or Maelstrom."

Druadaen leaned over to study it more closely. "Odd: it has the most names of any object on the two diagrams, yet has the fewest lines connecting it to other circles. But this is what I find particularly interesting." He let his index finger hover above the object before moving it slowly toward the edge of the diagram. "It sends out this line, the only one that does *not* lead to another circle. Instead, it attaches to this strange symbol, here at the margin of the page."

Ancrushav's eyes were steady upon him. "You are a quick study."

Of ancient texts? I ought to be! But Druadaen simply asked, "What does the symbol stand for? Is it . . . mathematical?" It had that look, somehow.

Ancrushav's gaze became a fixed stare. "It is mathematical, but it is not a value. It signifies that whatever value or variable it is affixed to or derived from contains a function which does not end."

"Such as the set of all numbers? Or an irrational number?"

"Yes."

"But here, on the diagram, it stands alone."

"That," Ancrushav said slowly, "signifies both the value and the principle of infinity." He nodded at Druadaen. "You have touched upon the great mystery of this map. If map it is."

"What else would it be?" Aleasha sounded impatient. "And where is Hystzos?"

"If it is on this sheet—and it may not be—I cannot read the label which signifies it. And before you ask, I have found nothing which suggests which one—or *if*—any of these symbols stands for the world of the Annihilators." He crossed his arms. "But even more frustrating are the small sigils which lay along the different connecting lines like notations. They are not from any language or numerical system known on Hystzos. And in all my reading, I have only found them in books like this one."

Aleasha blew a strand of chestnut hair out of her eyes. "And this book is called?"

"The Recursivity of Portals."

A cool, almost cold finger seemed to run slowly down Druadaen's spine; he managed not to shiver. "So these spheres: do they represent different worlds or different portals?"

"That," Ancrushav said with a nod, "is what I have been trying to determine for five years."

Aleasha frowned. "They could be both. And maybe these mysterious chicken scratches next to the lines explain that."

But Druadaen hardly heard her hypotheses. Instead, he seemed to see the Lady's face alongside Ancrushav's, her ghost-voice describing the conclusion of the Hidden Archivist's rescue: the one that had been effected by rerouting portals with what she called her Tower's "Refractorium." That word closely echoed, in both form and concept, the term "Recursivity."

Druadaen did not realize he was speaking aloud until the memory-echo of the Lady's words were chased away by the sound of his own voice. "These notations . . . could they be codes?"

"Codes?" Ancrushav repeated, frowning.

Druadaen found a better comparison. "I mean instructions. Such as the ones used to keep a ship on a course, or change it, by observing the location of known stars at expected times."

Ancrushav's eyebrows rose sharply and his eyes widened; they seemed to grow more red. "Or maybe the formula of a mantic construct?"

Druadaen stared at Ancrushav. "No one on this world has ever used the word 'mantic.'"

The serratus shook his head at his slip. "To be more precise, you have never *heard* anyone use that word."

"The 'Old Arts,'" Druadaen said, nodding as understanding rushed outward from Ancrushav's implied exception. "Pagudon's sorcerous disciplines are not merely similar to those of Arrdanc; they are one and the same." That conclusion spawned another. "And that is why Pagudon is uncertain how to respond to the priestess's actions. And it's why one vizier speculated that the 'sorcerers' might see her as 'a threat, an ally, or a tutor.' Because she is not struggling to piece together some fragmentary 'Old Art'; she is a master practitioner of the complete discipline."

Ancrushav nodded and leaned back from the book. "It doesn't really matter whether this is a map of how to move between worlds, or within them. Either way, it is about portals. Dig deep enough, and you find them at the root of almost every twist and turn of Hystzos' history." He began strolling among the worktables. "Wars. Politics. The Annihilators. Mancery. And now you and the priestess." He gestured to carefully laid out fragments of ancient scrolls, maps, treatises, codices. "Portals are the key to power. They always have been. They probably always will be."

Druadaen followed a step behind, Aleasha lagging further. "So that's why you started talking about 'us' following the priestess. Because that's what the Prow was built to defend: an osmotium."

Ancrushav nodded at the word. "'Osmotium': you do indeed know the cant of the Old Art. And yes, that is what it was built to protect. And it is probably the most important one in this world."

Aleasha had caught up. "Why?"

He glanced at her. "You are familiar with the term 'Annihilation Gate'?"

"Of course. Many legends say that the Annihilators used those portals to reach Hystzos."

Ancrushav shook his head. "That is not legend. That is fact."

"But why is the one near the Prow so important?"

"Because this is not *an* Annihilation Gate; it is *the* Annihilation Gate. The first one they came through."

"First?" Druadaen asked.

"There were others. It remains unclear whether the Annihilators built any themselves, or simply reopened ones that were already here, dormant and forgotten. What little was known and recorded during those times was mostly destroyed later on. Along with everything else."

Aleasha's light brown face might have grown pale. "So...this priestess means to travel to the world of the Annihilators? Is she mad?"

"No, because it is unlikely she means to travel to their world," Druadaen mumbled as pieces of a hypothesis began falling together.

"And how would *you* know?" Aleasha exclaimed.

But Ancrushav was nodding. "If the notes appended to each of the maps'—or diagrams'—connecting lines are codes or mantic referents, then it may be her intent to change the connection of the Annihilation Gate."

Aleasha looked from one to the other. "Is that even possible?"

"I suspect," Druadaen said, "that was part of what she researched in Sarmasid and why she had to break into one of its oldest and most restricted archives."

"You think she learned the...the incantations to change the gate's destination?"

Ancrushav shook his head. "Possibly, and the Sarmese would not realize if she did. If they knew they had such information in their archives, they would certainly have made use of it long before now. I doubt they even know that the Prow guards a portal, let alone the Annihilation Gate." He was quiet for a long moment. "But Pagudon does."

Aleasha nodded. "So: *that's* why you were sent here. To be close enough to watch what might occur there."

"Officially, yes."

Druadaen let one eyebrow rise. "And unofficially?"

"To watch the watchers we already had at the Prow, the command of which had been entrusted to the Pagudon's greatest rival."

Druadaen found a chair and sat. "I fear I am becoming confused."

Aleasha nodded. "Me, too." She sat beside him, but leaned toward Ancrushav. "So you have known about this Annihilation Gate all along?"

"Not as such. For centuries, we only knew it as the Maelstrom; that's what it was called in the epoch of Great Hystzos. But several generations ago, after hundreds of years of poring through the shattered libraries that Pagudon has slowly reclaimed, we learned that the Maelstrom and the Annihilation Gate were one and the same. That transformed Pagudon's plans and ambitions."

"Why?"

"Because it proved that the Annihilators did not build the gate whereby they first arrived. That, in turn, proved that the means of creating and controlling portals was known on Hystzos long before, and that Pagudon might hope to rediscover it."

Druadaen crossed his arms and leaned back. "As a rule, I do not press others for information, but it seems imperative that we have a better understanding of what Pagudon is and what it wants. And to do that, it sounds as if we must understand the Annihilators, first."

Ancrushav shrugged. "Few facts remain, but Pagudon's research has confirmed or uncovered at least this much.

The Annihilators arrived without warning, possessing strange powers as well as artifacts that were reputedly gifts from their gods. They took the Mael—the island complex in which the portal is located—and the Prow within a few hours.

"They swept forth, secured the surrounding lands, and then sent highly disciplined troops marching to various cities of the empire. It is now known, thanks to a few recently discovered diaries, that they sent small detachments to a number of obscure towns and even ruins in remote areas."

Druadaen nodded. "Lending further credence to the theory that they were restoring old portals in those places, rather than creating new ones."

Ancrushav returned his nod. "There is no complete reckoning of the campaign in which the Annihilators toppled the empire. The remaining accounts are fragmentary and mostly refer to persons and places that are no longer known, or at least not by those names. In the course of several decades, the empire was reduced to a number of isolated provinces. In one or two centuries, nothing remained of it, and the Annihilators departed with the same suddenness they had appeared, using the same portals. However, in most cases, they also found a way to destroy those sites shortly after leaving them."

Aleasha frowned. "And how did they do that? Suicidal minions?"

Ancrushav shrugged. "Maybe, but there is another possibility. For centuries, many have searched the Annihilators' old places in hope of uncovering some of their wondrous artifacts." He nodded toward Druàdaen. "At first, they often encountered devices such as you fought in the pit. They are part mechanism, part mancery, and yet no practitioners of either art have ever understood, let alone replicated, them."

Aleasha nodded. "So you presume they were the means whereby the Annihilators sealed the gates behind themselves."

"As well as the collaborators you suggested. Possibly zealots among their own deeply religious ranks who volunteered to remain behind for that purpose. But whatever methods they employed, they either could not—or did not—destroy the Annihilation Gate, at least not completely. However, they did leave it and the surrounding region 'hazardous in the extreme,' as one account puts it. But details of those hazards did not survive the destruction they wrought in their resolve to lay waste to all of Hystzos."

Aleasha leaned forward. "But why lay waste to a world that did not even *know* theirs?"

Ancrushav shook his head. "If that question was asked, no answer was given. Nor could any clues be derived from their actions except that they meant to hunt the Changed to extinction. The only actual communication from them was received just before they departed, when they contacted the King of Sarma with a final ultimatum."

"Which was?" Druadaen asked.

"That if he wished to keep his rather peripheral province from suffering the same oblivion as his armies, he had to reveal whatever he knew of the many sorcerers who had fled Great Hystzos to hide in his lands. In exchange, the Annihilators swore to leave his cities unrazed, thereby ensuring that Sarma would be the greatest remaining power in the known world."

"What a horrible nation to choose," Aleasha observed.

"That was almost certainly their intent," Ancrushav replied. "Witness what the Princes of Sarma have done with that preeminence: squandered it in their endless grasping to have a few coins more than their brothers. And so, Hystzos remains in a state of disarray."

Aleasha steepled her fingers. "So, when Pagudon realized that the Annihilation Gate and the Maelstrom were the same, they went to the Prow and attempted to learn from it, to become masters of the art of creating and controlling portals."

"That was their intent," Ancrushav agreed, "but they have yet to succeed. The Prow was easily secured, but the Mael has proven impossible to control for long. It is infested by Changelings of the most unusual and dangerous sort and there are no maps of its strange tunnels. After many expeditions, Pagudon has only managed to narrow down the number of passages which might lead to the Annihilation Gate."

Aleasha stared over her hands. "And is that yet another reason they sent you? Because your resemblance to Changelings meant that you were more likely to gain their trust?"

"I doubt it. Pagudon knew full well that although the eyes of a distant Changeling might mistake me for kin, their noses will soon tell them a different story. But my mentor did have other reasons, I am sure."

"Did he wish to protect you?" Aleasha's gaze grew shrewd. "Or rather, to cache you in a distant place: an ally kept in reserve beyond the reach of his rivals?"

"I suspect the latter, but also because he, too, had come to fear me. In addition to being harder to kill and accustomed to physical combat, I had skill in their arts."

"So, you were not just an ally; you were a potential threat."

"If so, then he ignored the precautions I took to assure I could not become his rival."

Druadaen leaned forward. "What precautions were those?"

"I avoided training in the Old Art. Had my skill neared that of any of the Senior Order, I would have been too dangerous. They would not have suffered me to live among them, if at all." He stared at his scarred hands. "Besides, even at an early age, I sensed that my gift for the art would entrail a danger to me as well. I had ready access to more power than they did, but I also knew I would pay a greater cost."

"In exhausting yourself?" Druadaen asked, doubting that answer even as he posed the question.

"In *losing* myself." Seeing their looks, Ancrushav shrugged. "Humans, others, must learn to control the source of their effects: what you call *manas*." He shook his head. "I never had to reach out for it. It was in me, waiting, as if it was ready, eager to obey. But by becoming the medium of its release, I sensed that I could also become subject to it."

"You mean, it had—has—a will of its own?"

"I am unsure. But I feared that if I experimented with it to find the answer, I could become ensnared in the process. Or susceptible to direct control through the Pagudon's more nuanced knowledge of the art."

Aleasha's hands were no longer steepled, but extended in an exaggerated gesture of imploring. "We keep hearing that word: Pagudon. But we don't even know who or what it really is. Sometimes it sounds like a place: 'Pagudon.' Other times it sounds like an individual: '*the*

Pagudon.' And sometimes it seems to refer to the whole Order. Which is it?"

Ancrushav almost smiled. "It can be any of those, but the root of it is the title of the head of the Order: *the* Pagudon. He is no longer known by his own name. He is held to have transcended that. It is also a constant reminder to him that he is responsible for the entirety of the group."

"You keep saying 'he' when referring to the Pagudon. Is leadership of the order restricted to males?" Aleasha's voice made her distaste quite plain.

"It goes beyond that; *membership* is restricted to males. At least, that has been the case since the Order went underground and took its current name."

"Which comes from what?" Druadaen asked.

"The library that was the last, hidden refuge of the sorcerers: the only one that was not found when the King of Sarma betrayed them to the Annihilators."

"Because it was so well hidden?"

"That, and because its existence was never shared with anyone outside the Order for that very reason: to protect it from the assured eventuality of betrayal. Since then, the Pagudons have been varied in origins and nature, but all possess one skill in common—and it is the only one that matters to the Order: maintaining power and mastery over others. By any and all means. Experience, social position, family: these are immaterial. In such a collective, there are no complex rules or even debates over how to select or replace or determine the legality or limit of the leader. So long as they can maintain their primacy, by whatever measures, they prove that they are the best: the Pagudon."

Druadaen rubbed his chin. "I could foresee a Pagudon spending all his time simply protecting his position."

Ancrushav nodded. "That is one of the tendencies that has kept the Order so small and insular for so long. Protection is inward looking. But the Order has an axiom: every Pagudon remains such until he is no longer the best one. The logic—specious or not—is that a Pagudon devoted to protecting himself also protects the Order from strife, excesses, and ambitions that it cannot afford. But if new opportunities arose and he failed to capitalize upon them, that shows that he is no longer the best leader and so, he is replaced."

"And is that the kind of leader in charge now? One that has responded to the 'new opportunities' in the Broken and Last Lands?"

"More than that: he has been instrumental in *creating* those opportunities."

Aleasha's smirk was vicious. "So he is the one behind insinuating agents into the Nightfall cult that has been growing in Tharn, passing off powers of the art as priestly miracles."

Ancrushav nodded. "Yes, that sham is his creation. On the surface, it is crafty enough, but I believe it conceals a deeper ploy."

Aleasha looked from him to Druadaen and back again. "With you two, I suspect there will always be a 'deeper ploy.'" She grinned as she said it.

But Ancrushav shook his horned head. "Jests aside, he has used religious crusades—and now, wars among and within nations—to obscure his even more pronounced activities in a direction that had been of no interest to Pagudon for several centuries."

Druadaen nodded. "You mean here in the northern Godbarrows?"

Ancrushav's horns dipped and rose. "Having walked the dark tunnels of the libraries beneath their hidden citadel, I may tell you one thing with certainty; fifteen years ago, there was not one among them who saw any advantage to be gained in the Godbarrows. The communities here do not produce coin or highly desirable goods. Nor do they produce learned youths who might make promising apprentices and eventually journeymen. And whatever old artifacts might once have been here—whether those of the Annihilators or Great Hystzos—they presume to have already been recovered by fortune-seekers.

"But recent documents found during the excavation of newly discovered library sections revealed far more about the creation and control of Changelings."

"In which you were trained," speculated Aleasha.

Ancrushav shrugged. "And which I also helped decipher before being sent here. Not a coincidence, I suspect."

Druadaen smiled. "What was the nature of these new records?"

"Reports from high-ranking imperial commanders about the Changelings. But they were not field officers, and as I read further, I realized that their reports were not so much dedicated to the outcomes of battles as they were on the performance of new breeds of the Touched."

Aleasha sat very straight. "Are you saying that Great Hystzos was using—creating—Changelings as part of their armies?"

"I cannot be sure, but the reports could certainly

be read in that context. Or they could simply have been recounting what occurred when random hordes of Changelings found themselves in combat with the Annihilators. However, the Pagudon doubled the pace of excavation and decreed that further information on the process of Changing was of cardinal importance."

Druadaen heard a hesitation in his conclusion. "And is that another reason you were sent up here: not just because you were more likely to move and survive among the Changelings, but to conduct tests upon them?"

Ancrushav's glance at Aleasha was at once guilty and defiant. "The Pagudon's goal was to learn how to gather existing and new 'abominations' into a controllable horde. My goal was simply to be sent to a place from which I could readily escape the Order. But then I arrived here and found all this." He waved expansively at the shelves of books and beyond, toward his followers. "If Pagudon was to learn what I have about the portals, about the Changelings, and now, about the priestess's skill"—he shook his head—"I do not know what force might be able to stop the Order, once it is armed with all that knowledge."

Aleasha stood. "Then it is upon us to prevent that from happening." Her chin came up. "I am very tired. I am also very hungry."

Ancrushav stood as well. "Then you shall have a good meal and a clean bed."

"Make it a pallet," she corrected. "Then, in the morning, I shall contemplate how best to save this wretched world of ours."

CHAPTER FORTY-ONE

Aleasha pushed aside the plate which had held her now vanished breakfast and demanded, "What do you think this priestess is doing, Druadaen?"

"Yes," Ancrushav added, making sure his own plate did not come to rest on the map of portals—or worlds—spread out on the table, "and let us assume she knows everything that we know."

Druadaen surprised them by calmly, unhurriedly finishing his citrus-infused water. "I thought you might ask that," he said with a smile.

It had hardly required great leaps of foresight. While the road ahead was strewn with unknowns, the greatest danger at the end of it—the priestess—was from his world. Her people had fought against his, and her mancery was related to the kinds he had witnessed. So it was natural for them to presume him to be the authority on her intents and powers. *Which would be comical, if we weren't contemplating a course of action that seems sure to get us killed.*

But at least he was well prepared. "Once the priestess realized that she could not return through the Fickle Haze, she likely resolved to find some portal that could take her back to where she started: the Nidus."

"That's the island with many gates," Aleasha said with a nod, "and near her homeland."

"Correct. So she decided to find the best collection of either present or historical accounts that might point to another active portal on this world. And whoever might know even more about them."

Ancrushav nodded. "So she broke into the Principiate Repository."

Druadaen nodded. "Yes, but while she was there, I suspect she saw something which has been missed by centuries of Sarmese researchers. But she would notice immediately."

"You mean something other than the Prow and the Maelstrom being the Annihilation Gate?"

"Yes, although it's related. Now, this is conjecture, because there's no way to be certain without reading all the books she did. But as you pointed out yesterday, Ancrushav, she is practicing an intact and complete art, whereas even the most accomplished sorcerers of Pagudon know but a smattering of fragments from it."

Ancrushav set his immense fists upon the table. "And would that have determined the actions she has taken since coming through what you call the Shimmer?"

Druadaen shrugged. "Well, if she has any familiarity with the discipline called cosmancery, she will almost surely have much greater knowledge of portals than anyone on this world. That might not only include having cognates to control and change them, but greater knowledge of the Vortex of Worlds." He leaned forward, pointed to the map. "We're not even sure what all the symbols on this diagram mean. But what if *she* did? Or just knew half of them?

"At the very least, she'd know that this was a world with other portals which might ultimately lead to a way home. At the best, she might take one look at this and know exactly where she has to go to return to the Nidus."

"Or, failing that, just head here." Aleasha's finger rested on the symbol that sent out so many crisscrossing connecting lines that it resembled a spider web.

Which stopped Druadaen for a moment: *A spider web? Or maybe a spider nest: which is to say, a nidus. Possibly the Nidus? Is that a connection or a coincidence? Not enough information, and not enough time, to consider that now.*

"She might do that," Druadaen agreed, pointing at the same jumbled intersection of lines. "In fact, even if all she knows is that such a multiple crossroads exists, she would be likely to make it her next destination. And from the moment she left Sarmasid, she was heading as directly and quickly as she could to the Maelstrom. So yes, she almost certainly knows it is the Annihilation Gate and the references to it may have made her confident that it is the kind of osmotium with which she is familiar: that of the Old Art. In which she is a master."

Aleasha was staring at the diagram in something like dread. "So, if she *is* a...a cosmancer, is it possible that she's heard of Hystzos before? That she might have been here? Or, by other means, might know who and what the Annihilators were?"

The profundity of her simple, clear-sighted question

struck Druadaen dumb. Because if any of those free-wheeling possibilities touched on the truth, it had immense ramifications for Arrdanc as well as Hystzos. "There is no way to know that. I do not know much about my world's cosmancers. They are figures as little spoken about as were portals during your world's epoch of Great Hystzos; they are known to exist but little more. However, perhaps something she read about the Annihilation Gate suggested a parallel or shared property with the Nidus."

"Such as their ability to withstand attempts to destroy them?" Ancrushav offered.

Druadaen nodded. "I hadn't thought of that, but yes, that might certainly fix her attention upon the Maelstrom: a portal that is likely to still exist and is known to work in both directions. Which means it is either located on, or at least one step closer to, this"—Druadaen gestured toward the diagram on the table—"the Vortex of Worlds."

"Where she can try to find her way to the big crossroads," Aleasha added, pointing to the spiderweb.

"Or find lore which would reveal a portal that has, at some point, been connected to the Nidus," Ancrushav amended. He leaned back. "Very well. There seems no other logical course of action for her *if* she means to return to your world as swiftly as possible." He squinted at the map. "And you feel sure she presumes that people from your world are trying to catch her?"

"I wouldn't say that, but she can hardly assume they *won't*. So, to the extent she fears pursuit, she will be in a hurry to get out of this world. And perhaps the next as well."

"And where would such flight end?"

Druadaen shook his head. "That is an excellent and troubling question. Logically, every world she enters is one more to which, and *through* which, pursuers must track her. But logically speed cannot be her *only* concern. Everywhere she travels, she must stop and converse long enough to learn about any gates there, always mindful of any hints which suggest that one of them is, or could be, connected to the Nidus. So she will have to strike a balance between fleeing swiftly, yet conducting that research as quietly as she may."

"She did a poor job of that here," Aleasha snorted.

Druadaen shrugged. "In some ways, but she managed to gather what she needed before disappearing into a remote area beyond the reach of any nation and from which rumors, let alone news, rarely come. And I suspect she has learned many lessons here which will prove very valuable in every new world she might enter."

Aleasha crossed her arms. "Well, I am resolved to pursue her. And to stop her, even if the odds seem impossible. Which they do, insofar as none of us have powerful allies that we might ask to join us in such a quest. But still, to plan in ignorance of your enemy is to ensure that they will defeat you. So Druadaen, tell us: what powers might this cosmancer bring to bear against us?"

Druadaen frowned, rubbed his chin. "Firstly, I doubt she *is* a cosmancer, at least not primarily. But that question is far faster in the asking than the answering, and we can discuss it just as well once we are underway."

Ancrushav nodded. "Which should be no later than tomorrow."

"Really?" Aleasha's voice was playfully facetious. "Why not today?"

Ancrushav's tone and face remained akin to granite. "If I thought we could, I would press for that. But it will take that long for us to prepare. I am told that the supragants which bore you here have not left. Will they bear us to the Prow?"

Aleasha nodded slowly. "I believe that is why they have stayed. They sense we share mortal enemies."

"Excellent. You shall equip yourselves as you wish."

"Equip ourselves?" Druadaen echoed. Since arriving, he'd seen very little that would answer to such a description, despite the place being named the Armory.

Ancrushav waved an unconcerned hand. "I have much equipment from caravans that did not successfully cross the Godbarrows. Most of it does not fit any of the Changelings, so you may take whatever you find in the storerooms."

Aleasha looked up from under beetled brows. "Speaking of Changelings; do you mean to take any of them with us?"

"It would not be right. It would also be unwise. Should we fail and they be captured, what resides in their mind may ultimately come to be in our adversary's mind. And that could be the end of all we hope to achieve. I cannot risk that."

Her gaze was curious, not accusatory. "But we, too, have seen much."

"Yes, but as yet, understand little. And you have not seen what the priestess would most want to."

She gestured at the shelves surrounding them. "Certain of these books, I imagine?"

"Yes, but more importantly, any hint of my discoveries

concerning the animalcules of Change. My old Pagudon masters congratulated themselves on having the greatest knowledge of the compounds which effect it, but they were merely following recipes. They had no real insight into the ingredients."

"And you do?"

"I believe I might. If so, much of what I have discovered must never come to light. It would enable the unscrupulous to propagate even greater and more dangerous Changes."

Druadaen frowned. "Why not destroy the knowledge, then?"

"Because the same knowledge holds the key to *preventing* Changes. Now, we are agreed that there is much to do before we may depart. And while haste is a friend to no plan, time is against us."

"So, we should make haste slowly," Druadaen offered with a grin.

Ancrushav stopped, stared. "That could be an aphorism."

Aleasha scowled. "That contradictory bit of nonsense? Never. Let's be about our tasks. Tomorrow will be here sooner than we wish."

"And our journey harder than we'd like," Ancrushav added.

Nodding, Druadaen kept his final caveat silent: *And peril our only certain companion.*

PART FIVE
REPOSITORIES

CHAPTER FORTY-TWO

Ahearn wondered if anything ever changed in what he'd come to think of as the council glade. It wasn't just that both Tharêdæath and Ilshamësa were sitting in the same fur-softened seats. The same guards were there as well, standing in the same place and in the same posture. The only discernible difference was that Ilshamësa looked less frail and drawn than last time. However, she was still markedly thin and any physical exertion brought on a slight pallor.

She was the first to speak once the scant formalities were over. "We trust your stay in Mirroskye has been restful and restoring."

Ahearn did not have to dissemble when he responded that it certainly had been. "However," he added, "the need to find our friend Druadaen—and Varcaxtan's wife—keeps our feet restless, no matter how pleasant the place where we put them up for a spell."

"So I perceive. We shall dispense with pleasantries." She turned to Tharêdæath.

Who nodded and said, "We regret the delay, but the information you seek is not collected in one place or as a whole. Rather, it is akin to building a mosaic: finding the needed tiles in many places. But a picture has taken shape.

"The first and simplest part was provided by the Last Hidden Archivist of Tlu'Lanthu. He confirms that it was your wife, Guide Indryllis, who redirected the Nidus' osmotium and held it fixed so that he could escape. Our current skrying confirmed that she remains alive."

Varcaxtan's eyes closed momentarily. When they opened, they were clear and focused. "Where?"

Tharêdæath shook his head. "Farseeing could not show us the place."

"But it is on this world?"

Tharêdæath paused. "Even that is not clear."

"But how could that be? I've always been told that it is far simpler to determine if a thing still exists—a simple yes or no—than it is to fix its location."

Ilshamësa glanced at them. "And yet, that is what the patterns of the Great Weave revealed; that she is both on this world and not on this world." Seeing Ahearn's worried frustration, she held up a stilling hand. "Do not be alarmed, Master Swordsman. The pattern in which your group moves continues to gather many unfinished event-strands which time has yet to weave together."

Ahearn leaned forward. "But by which osmotium shall we reach her? Or Druadaen?"

Tharêdæath steepled his fingers. "It is as yet impossible to tell. And more powerful means of skrying would likely attract the attention of the greater powers we mentioned last time. If that occurred, it would be costly to us. And deadly to you."

"However," R'aonsun mused, "if that was the limit of useful information you had to share, I suspect you would have already said so."

Tharêdæath nodded. "You are correct. But be warned: the path to the eventual destination might prove... quite circuitous."

"When has it ever been otherwise?" Elweyr muttered, obviously loud enough for the Uulamantre to hear. "Although it makes me wonder; if the Relayer—erm, *quelsuur*—is like a lodestone, pointing toward the best place to recover Druadaen, then why would it lead us to you?"

Tharêdæath seemed to suppress a smile. "It may be that until you have our counsel, the *quelsuur* would remain uncertain as to the best path. Furthermore, we discovered—"

"The threads of your path needed to twine with ours in order to become more reified within the Great Skein," Ilshamësa interrupted abruptly, then winced... apparently at her own impatience.

Ahearn shook his head. "Once again, I find m'self not feigning the part of an ignorant bumpkin, but being one. So yer saying the que—quas—Relayer *doesn't* know the best path?"

"Yes, but knowing the best path to a thing is not the same as knowing that thing's location," Tharêdæath replied. "Sometimes, the best path means seeking those who can help you narrow your search. And so it led you to Mirroskye." He glanced at the ring on Ahearn's hand. "Tell me, has it prompted you in any direction since you arrived here?"

Ahearn shrugged. "Hasn't prompted me at all. Thought it might be having misgivings about choosing a lummox such as meself."

Ilshamësa's sudden laugh seemed to surprise even her.

Tharêdæath merely smiled. "The reason it is not prompting you to the final destination, Ahearn, is because it is not yet final."

"Those words seem to undo each other," Umkhira muttered with a frown.

The younger of the Uulamantre nodded. "They would seem to, but consider: what makes a path 'best'?"

"Well, the shortest distance..." Umkhira stopped, obviously rethinking her first, reflexive answer. "No: the matter of a 'best' path is more complex."

Ilshamësa nodded. "Yes, Lightstrider; you see it a-right. No path is fixed. All paths are shaped by our own actions. So, even if you—or we—knew the location of all osmotia, that would not necessarily establish the best path by which to reach it. You would still not know which osmotia are *jaqualqu*—the 'breaches' that connect to other worlds—and which are not. Also, the one that is most direct might require you to fight through an impregnable stronghold held by thousands of foes. Other suitable osmotia might remain active and be closer but, after the Cataclysm, now lie deep under the ground or in the crushing depths of the oceans."

S'ythreni nodded. "So, decisions we have yet to make are likely to change the osmotium to which the *quelsuur* would ultimately guide us."

Tharêdæath smiled and nodded in return. "In this, the behavior of all sai'niin objects aligns with our understanding of the Great Weave: although it embodies the existence and interaction of all things, no outcomes are preordained. It does not simply obey the known laws of the physical world. Rather, the unfolding of the Great Weave is also shaped by the cascading influences of the actors within it."

"Well," drawled Ahearn facetiously, "if it's as simple as all that, why didn't you say so at the outset? But now that the air is clear of such long and mighty words, it still comes down to this: we've no way to make any one choice over t'other."

"That," Ilshamësa intoned, "is where the memories and knowledge of the Great Pool have suggested a way forward."

Ahearn idly wondered if, in this case, the Great Pool referred to the living Council that bore its name, or the mystic puddle itself. "So, it's shown a way for us to find choices that the Relayer can use?"

"The Council has. It seems your first step is not to find any given osmotium, but many of them."

"Truly, a modest requirement." R'aonsun's sarcasm was offset by his wry tone.

"It might not be so daunting a task as you project, Osrekheseertheeshrathhuu'aigh," Ilshamësa broke in.

"You may recall," Tharêdæath continued calmly, "that after you dispatched the guardian of the lost library at Imvish'al, I had my crew commence removing items of particular interest."

Elweyr nodded, frowning. "Right up until we sailed for Saqqaru." He leaned forward. "What else did you find?"

"Something we have not encountered in a very, very long time." He nodded to the closest of the two guards, who handed him a shining metal plaque. "Do you know what this is?"

Elweyr glanced furtively toward Varcaxtan, who was already looking at him . . . but it was Cerven who spoke first, "Is that a moonfall plaque?"

Tharêdæath's straight eyebrows became high arches. "Tell us what you know of them, Cerven Ux Reeve."

"Very little, Tir-Tharêdæath." Cerven's voice became faintly monotone and his eyes seemed to lose focus. "They are commonly called moon plates. They cannot be deciphered. They are unusually heavy. They are indestructible. Because they cannot be damaged, they cannot be sampled for assay. They are only mentioned in the oldest records. They are incised with cyphered messages." Sense came back to his eyes. "That is all I have learned of them." His speech, too, reverted to its usual cadence and tone.

Ahearn frowned at the Uulamantre. "So, since you say our path is circuitous, I'm guessing that we won't find the answers on that shiny slab, but that it's the key to where we *can* find 'em."

"Astute, Master Swordsman!" Ilshamësa almost shouted before calming herself. "When the plaque from Imvish'al was first brought to the Great Pool, we could not decipher it. But prompted by your inquiry, and with the return of the Last Hidden Archivist, it was finally accomplished." Her rigid cheeks fought against the emergence of a brittle smile. "As is often the case with great mysteries, the flaw that frustrated our earlier attempts was in first assumptions. Our loremasters could not initially decipher it because they presumed its contents to be a report, like all other known moon plates. But this one was not; it was a code."

"And the Hidden Archivist was able to decipher it?" Varcaxtan's voice was eager.

Tharêdæath leaned toward the group. "You misunderstand. All moonfall plaques' contents are written in a cypher. But not this one; *this* is the key to that cypher."

Ahearn wondered why the Uulamantre seemed enamored of always saying things in the most complicated way possible. "So, you're sayin' it's a code book."

Tharêdæath nodded. "A very complicated one, since its sigils cannot simply be transposed into letters and numbers."

Umkhira's voice was relieved. "Still, with this cypher-of-cyphers in hand, all that remains is to find the moon plate that lists the portals."

"Yes, although in order to read the cyphers at all, one must be able to attain a state of mind that transcends physical perception."

Umkhira's frown was swift and annoyed. "That sounds like still more mancery."

"Not necessarily," Ilshamësa murmured. "There are other ways to achieve the consciousness required. But it is uncommon in minds that have been shaped by physical existence. A reader can only understand the arrangement and interaction of the cypher's sigils if they are capable of perceiving principles that undergird our existence, but are not evident in its worldly manifestations."

While Ahearn and the others were still struggling to parse what they had just heard, the dragon's avatar asked in a droll tone, "And these principles are...?"

"Formulae which are means of representing realities that lie beyond our senses, and so, have no referents in common speech."

R'aonsun frowned. "You are speaking of mathematical relationships."

"You perceive. Excellent."

"I perceive the concept; I do not comprehend how it would be used."

"And again," sighed Ahearn, "I must ask: what are you lofty beings on about?"

R'aonsun looked only moderately irritated. "I shall use the simplest example. Imagine that you must measure and perfectly recall every square inch of a tower. You walk around it, then ascend ladders along all of its walls, committing every square inch to memory. Then you do the same with its interior, including the battlements, roof, and basement."

"Aye. And?"

"Did you see all of the tower?"

Ahearn frowned. "Obviously so."

The dragon smiled. "Now, can you see all of it *at once*?"

Ahearn frowned. "Well, no. A body only sees a thing from one place at a time."

"Precisely. But the complete reality of the tower is defined by all those properties existing *at the same time*. No one glance can show you more than a small part of them."

"So?"

"So," Cerven said excitedly, apparently unaware that he was interrupting the dragon, "there are ways to use numbers so that they represent all the tower's properties, all at once." He didn't even notice the dragon's approving nod. "In fact, there are ways to represent measurements that go beyond mere height, width, and—"

Tharêdæath held up his hand. "You have made your point, Master Cerven—most adequately." He turned to the others. "The ability to apprehend reality in this fashion—which is called *fullsee*—is the rarest of perceptive talents. Unfortunately, none of the Council's current proleptants possess it."

"Then how do they skry?" wondered Umkhira.

"That is a different ability. We call that *farsee*, which is a learned skill exercised in the presence of the Great Pool or its lesser equivalents. *Fullsee* is the ability to perceive a thing in its totality at any given moment."

Varcaxtan frowned. "Then how did your folk decipher *any* of the moon plates?"

"Two of our proleptants are accomplished thaumantics. They effected a cognate which grants perception akin to *fullsee*, but only briefly and at a very great cost." He smiled at Elweyr. "As your own thaumancer has no doubt surmised."

Elweyr shrugged. "The only references I have seen to such a thaumate were in the codices from Imvish'al. All I know is that it is complicated, cumbersome, and requires a great deal of *manas*."

Varcaxtan looked back to Tharêdæath. "In the space of a minute, I've heard that *fullsee* is mancery, but that some persons possess it innately. But how can that be, since no one is born a mantic?"

Tharêdæath shook his head. "It is the other way around. True and constant *fullsee* is a rare *natural* ability. Thaumancers and cosmancers only have ways of approximating it."

"So, if I understand the sum of all this," Ahearn said, eyes closed against a mounting headache, "we need someone who can *fullsee and* understand this, er, double cypher, if we're to suss out what's been carved into other moon dishes."

"Moon plates. Or more properly, moonfall plaques. But otherwise, you are correct."

Ahearn sighed. "Still, until we find a plate that shows the location of a useful osmotium, we're no better off than we started. As you said, the Relayer won't point in a direction until we have some sense of what we're looking for." He crossed his arms. "So it seems that all this learned jaw-wagging isn't worth a tinker's damn."

Tharêdæath raised an eyebrow. "Patience and peace, *eh'hathsha.* Did I not say at the outset that the Council had identified a way forward?"

Then yeh might have started *there, eh?* But Ahearn only said, "Aye, and I'll be sorely relieved to hear it."

"Once we deciphered the moonfall plaque from Imvish'al, we were finally able to read others that we have had in our possession for—well, for a very long time. Most were primarily of historical interest, but one was a very detailed list. Specifically, it was a master list." Seeing uncertainty on Ahearn's and several other faces, Tharêdæath added, "It is the list of all other lists, each of which are identified both by title and a unique number."

Elweyr frowned. "Like the index of a library's various sections?"

Tharêdæath nodded. "Yes, except it also indicates the places where the lists were kept."

Elweyr sat straight. "So, it gives the names and locations of all the moon-plate repositories?"

Tharêdæath smiled. "Yes. And among the many

lists it refers to is the one that you require: an index of all—"

"All known osmotia!" finished Cerven excitedly. "And logically, there would be a copy of that index in each of the moonfall plaque repositories!"

"But how many of these repositories still exist?" Elweyr muttered suspiciously.

Tharêdæath shook his fine-boned head. "We cannot be sure. Even the one we do know about—the Hidden Archive beneath Tlu'Lanthu—may not be complete, and the Last Hidden Archivist remains oath-bound not to disclose its contents.

"Most of the other listed repositories are not known to us. Some are not even identified by names, only a string of sigils, so there is no way to be certain which of those—if any—still exist. Furthermore, regardless of the identifier used, many will have had different names than the ones by which they are known today. Many of the names we recognize only because they appear in ancient histories which mention their destruction: by the Cataclysm, wars, or centuries of pilfering.

"However, besides Tlu'Lanthu and Imvish'al, three of the names are still familiar and still exist. One is Shadowmere, although it is called by an ancient name that has come down to us: Averroës. However, if that repository still exists, it is assuredly buried deep in the many layers of the city's preceding incarnations. Whether it is intact is beyond speculation."

"The status of the second repository cannot even be conjectured due to the absolute secrecy and stiff defenses surrounding it. I believe it is pointless to include it in your deliberations."

"Still, where is it?" Cerven asked.

"In Shulthektes, the capital of S'Dyxia."

Merely hearing that name gave Ahearn a sensation like a shadow passing overhead. "And the third?" the swordsman prompted.

"It is on Mihal'j. In a city known as Zatsakkaz."

For the first time in Ahearn's knowledge of him, Varcaxtan sounded impatient. "I've never heard of that place, and I've traveled to most every realm on Mihal'j."

"That is because Zatsakkaz is not part of any modern nation," Tharêdæath explained. "It is said to have disappeared during or shortly after the Cataclysm, presumably destroyed by invaders. However, in the First Consentium, rumors of its existence began surfacing. Every few decades, its name rises anew: a whisper among grave robbers and treasure seekers. Recently, it has done so again."

"Perhaps you have already heard of it," Ilshamësa speculated, "given your group's original livelihood." Her voice was frank, rather than disapproving.

Ahearn muttered an abashed correction: "Our *intended* livelihood."

"Ah, for the good old days," Elweyr drawled sardonically.

Ahearn ignored him, remained focused upon Tharêdæath. "And you heard this from, er, fortune seekers?"

"No, but it is attributed to them."

"Ah. But it was reported by people you trust?"

Tharêdæath nodded. "Word came from one of the bands of aeosti who still dwell on Mihal'j."

"And they heard the name muttered among fortune-seekers, eh?"

"Not exactly. A lone fortune-seeker whispered it as his final, dying word."

"My," breathed the dragon, "doesn't *that* sound auspicious?"

Elweyr was frowning. "So, if we find our way to Zatsakkaz, we *might* find the repository. Once inside, we *could* find the moon plate with the list, if it's still there. But even if it is, and even *if* I can read it, how will we know which osmotium to choose?"

Ahearn smiled, held up his hand; the sai'niin ring shone upon it. "I suspect that's when this doodad might start showing our way again, eh?"

Elweyr only frowned more deeply. "Will it, even if I can't read the list? I don't have the *fullsee* thaumate. And even if I did, I'd have to master it. If not, I suspect the Relayer would just point us back here."

Tharêdæath shook his head. "I do not think it would. We have exhausted all sources and skills that might help you find your way along this path. Besides, your company already has a resource that will allow you to understand the moonfall plaque."

Ahearn frowned. "And what resource is that?"

Ilshamësa pointed at Cerven. "Him. Unless I am much mistaken, he has true *fullsee*. That is typical among those chosen to be trained as what the Old Amitryeans called a scriverant. He is one such."

Ahearn and the others turned questioning eyes upon Cerven. His response was a nervous and very audible gulp.

"Do not fault him for being secretive," Ilshamësa told them sharply. "He will have been enjoined by oath to conceal it, in order to protect his people."

"His people—?" Ahearn began, confused yet again.

But Elweyr's spine had become straight as a ruler. "Of course. His speech, when you asked him about the moon plate: he was using a recall-trance."

Tharêdæath nodded. "So you know of scriverants?"

"Only through some brief passages in old books. Very, very old books."

Umkhira was shaking her head. "But what *are* they?"

Elweyr waved a vague hand. "They are... It's hard to explain."

The voice that took up the definition was the dragon's. "You may think of scriverants this way; as alchemists are to different substances, scriverants are to letters and words. And numbers and calculations."

"You mean," asked Ahearn uncertainly, "a scriverant is some kind of... of ill-savant?" He looked at Cerven who did not strike him at all like the one or two ill-savants he'd encountered.

Tharêdæath shook his head. "An ill-savant's mind is not reliable. It is both a gift and a curse. It has a natural mastery of perceiving and manipulating quantities, but it is mostly—often wholly—unable to grasp anything else. Scriverants are very capable persons who can attain a similar level of perception, but only by acquiring the mental discipline that allows it to work alongside the ordinary part of their mind."

Ahearn stared at Cerven; *poor lad, sounds a sad way to grow up.* "So the training—endless hours of schooling, eh?"

"Much more than that," Ilshamësa broke in. "It is a discipline that borders on the spiritual. You heard the way he recounted what he knew of the moon-fall plaques. As the magister perceived, he entered a recall-trance to summon knowledge he imprinted upon a dormant part of his mind. By entering a similar trance, he is able to order his thought and blend greater memory, induction, deduction, and perception—and so, achieve *fullsee*." She looked at Cerven. "Am I correct?"

The young man nodded.

Tharêdæath leaned forward. "Scriverants also excel at remaining calm in extremely trying and chaotic situations. Without the training and temperament to do so, they would not be able to exercise their skills when under duress."

Umkhira crossed her arms. "Yes. I have observed that he *is* extremely calm."

"When he's not drinking," Ahearn whispered sideways toward Elweyr.

"My hearing is quite good"—Ilshamësa's ears trembled slightly as she said it—"but I could not understand your words."

Ahearn spoke more forcefully, as if the louder words might overtake and bury his muttered quip. "I was merely observing that the lad is full of interesting surprises. Now, on the matter of the aid you show to travelers fallen on hard times. As you can see, we've naught but what we saved from the wreck off Kœsdri'yrm. That, and the odds and ends we've picked up since then . . ."

Tharêdæath waved a reassuring palm at the problem. "On returning to Eslêntecrë, you shall be guided to a storehouse filled with equipment that is . . . no longer required by its original owners." If his words were vague, his eyes and tone were not.

Ahearn's eyebrows raised. "A whole storehouse, you say?" Visions of fast dockside sales on the long voyage to Mihal'j danced in his head—just as S'ythreni jammed an elbow into his right ribs. Elweyr did the same to his left. "Must be quite a nuisance," Ahearn finished morosely.

Ilshamësa shrugged. "It is merely space in a building we would not otherwise use. Take what you need. But only that."

"Of course . . . but why keep it at all, if you've no use for it?"

"Because there may be heirlooms among the common items."

"That's"—Ahearn struggled to find words—"very considerate of you."

The ancient Uulamantre's eyes seemed to focus on something very far in the distance. "We understand the value of heirlooms. And keepsakes."

"I wonder if you understand them as well as we do," Umkhira asserted boldly, "whose entire lives are but an afternoon in your own."

Ilshamësa's smile was wan. "Those words are half-wise, Lightstrider. They do remind me of what I often forget: how many pass so quickly in your lands. By comparison, death is infrequent among Iavarain. But for the living, those losses accrue not just year to year but century to century, each a new hole in our heart. Eventually, it is a single void, as wide and as deep as the full measure of time we spent with them." Ilshamësa stopped, the trembling glitter in her eyes marking unshed tears. "That is why we cherish keepsakes, Lightstrider. They sustain our memories of the hundreds we have loved and lost: memories by which we hope to find, and join, with them after the passing of all things."

Tharêdæath's eyes had shifted to S'ythreni as the older Uulamantre finished. "I have a related matter to discuss with you, Alva S'ythreni. Your guides informed me that you requested they bear away the sheath armor you discovered in the Library of Imvish'al."

She bent her neck. "*Veth*, Tir-Tharêdæath. I asked them not to disturb you with that matter."

"They are sworn to make full report, so they acted as their oaths demanded. But they were unable to tell me why you so ardently pressed them to take the armor from you."

S'ythreni kept her chin and eyes down. "I hoped it might be restored to the family of the fallen. Her armor should have been conveyed to them along with her remains. I have no claim on it, I have done nothing to deserve it, and I dishonor it every time I wear it. Since they lacked the authority to respond to my request, I plead with you, Tir-Tharêdæath, to take the armor from my hands: to give it to those that deserve it, by dint of blood and deed."

"I cannot do so."

She glanced up. "You *cannot* do so? Who may challenge your will in this matter?"

"The very family to which you wish the armor returned. I informed them of your petition. They, in response, asked that you do one of two things with the sheath-suit: wear it or destroy it."

S'ythreni rarely looked surprised, but this was one of those times. "Destroy it?"

Tharêdæath shrugged. "Only a few remain alive who remember the loss of the armor and its wearer. You brought home the remains of their fallen kin; they rightly say their remembrance is thus made whole.

So, they mean you to have the armor, both out of gratitude and for the honor you would bring to it."

"But . . . did you not tell them of my *dis*honor?"

"They have long known of the events which you *assert* soiled your honor. Like me, they ardently disagree with that assertion. Rather, they hope that you will not be so selfish—or stubborn—as to reject your obvious duty: to honor the wearer's sacrifice and the crafter's labor by restoring the armor to its purpose." He paused for a long moment. "To carry it forward into worthy deeds befitting the Iavarain."

S'ythreni bowed very low. As she did, Ahearn saw a shining droplet run off her cheek and vanish into the grass. "Instruct me, Tir-Tharêdæath, who knows my regrets and misgivings better than any alive: how may I demur without further injuring them . . . and dishonoring myself?"

Tharêdæath seemed to be preparing an answer when Ilshamësa snapped, "It is unseemly to even ask such a thing." Her voice softened. "I understand your grief; I have felt no less. I also understand your guilt, but it is pride and self-indulgence to nurse it so fiercely, so jealously." Her voice faded to a whisper. "Give it to the wind, child. That is where it belongs, now."

"I shall strive to do as you counsel. But I have a final amend to make when next I return."

Tharêdæath nodded. "I understand. The matter of the armor is settled. Wear it in remembrance and resolve." Ahearn saw that S'ythreni's back was quivering. "You have our leave to seek solace in solitude."

She nodded and turned sharply, keeping her face averted as she strode away.

Ahearn let out a long sigh. "Ever since you refused

to take the armor after we sailed from Imvish'al, she's dwelt on it. Didn't say why she felt unworthy, but it was as clear as if she'd shouted it from the foretop."

Tharêdæath shook his head sadly as he watched S'ythreni exit the amphitheater. "In time, I hope she shall take you and the others into her confidence and share the events that haunt her so. Even among the few—the *very* few—who felt she bore any fault, no judgment was ever so harsh and unyielding as her own." He stood. "I contacted Captain Firinne at Eslêntecrë. She awaits you there."

"But she was going on to Porsyolti," Varcaxtan protested.

"And so she did, and has now returned. It is best that you gather your belongings without delay; your guides are waiting. They bear gifts for you all, and shall escort you to the edge of the forest where it overlooks the bay. We wish you fair weather and swift travels to Mihal'j."

JOURNAL Entry Five
Ruins of Zatsakkaz, South of Pawnkam

So here I sit, trying to keep my body between the wind and this damned journal, half-blind as I scribble in the double moonshadow of the great gate of Zatsakkaz...or at least, what's left of it. Having finally found a way into the ancient, sand-buried city, we are trying to get what sleep we can before starting our descent tomorrow.

Yes, we're set to plumb the depths of yet another forlorn ruin buried by time. It's enough to make a fellow think that the universe lacks imagination—or novelty, when you come right down to it.

But if I were fool enough to complain aloud, Elweyr would heckle me like a fishwife. "No pleasing you, is there, Ahearn?" he's crowed on a few occasions now. "Before we met Druadaen, you couldn't wait to get into lost ruins and find all the treasure there." And then he gets my goat by doing the one thing he knows I just can't stand: he snickers. I'd mind a full belly laugh a great deal less. I could live with one loud guffaw at my hopes. But a measly, weaselly snicker? It's almost a way of saying, "mind, I'm not done yet; I'll be back to turn the knife again...you eejit."

Not that I don't deserve it. Ruins sound a great deal more profitable—and tidy—than the grimy Unders in which I've both fought and fled the Bent. But in the end, whether the walls are rough or smooth, one dark, dank maze is pretty much like any other.

But as Tharêdæath saw us off from the wharf at Eslêntecrë, I smiled—fool that I am—at the prospect of riches and that familiar rush of hope and greed: the two cornerstones of all treasure hunting. Just before boarding, our Uulamantre friend had stood us a meal and a drink and shared what he knew of Zatsakkaz, as well as a few signs to watch for as we sought its long-lost repository of moon plates. *Surely,* I thought as we waved goodbye, *if any of the little metal slabs remain unpilfered, other more profitable items will be there as well.* And I suppose that may yet prove to be the case, but it will have to be quite a grand treasure to be fair recompense for all the nuisance and danger we've already faced just getting here.

Our voyage started out well enough. It is always a pleasure to be reunited with Captain Firinne. She seems to have adopted us as her own, probably because she and Varcaxtan knew each other from times before. Or maybe it was just that they knew *of* each other. However, given the way she glances at him sometimes, I wouldn't at all be surprised if she knew a good deal more about him than he did about her—at least until he became a blissfully married man. But if the good captain still carries a torch for our favorite Dunarran uncle, she remains the good captain in every measure of the word; she gives no sign of having any feelings other than those that would be right and proper for any two Dunarrans who share a devotion to both homeland and duty.

The cruise to the southern tip of Ar Navir was not graced by fair winds or weather. But being aboard the *Swiftsure*, we were unworried. If anyone could get us through, it would be Captain Firinne. And if she couldn't, well, that's no fault of hers. Fate holds the highest card of every suit and can trump any trick you might hope to play in this chancy and fickle game of life.

During one particularly fierce blow, the good captain ran for the land-sheltered bay at Bajeos, second city of Anatha Damianna. With the weather sitting slow and surly offshore, she decided to lay over and take on supplies for the much longer part of our journey: all the way to the eastern coast of Mihal'j. We were inspired by her prudence and so, when we went ashore in Bajeos, it was always in the company of her crew and with a firm resolve to keep both our coin in our purses and trouble at arm's length. For once, we succeeded at both.

Anatha Damianna is different from the other Ballashan realms in that it is freewheeling and openhanded where the others are aloof and closed-fisted. Half the nation's blood came from waves of Othaericæn refugees, a sea-people driven from their islands by Lajantpurn conquerors. Hardly a surprise, then, that in Bajeos' wide and bustling markets, the most oft-told tales are not of warriors or rulers but of daring captains who sailed in search of new markets, brought home new goods, or died trying. However, since a "Dami" presumes (and expects) a trader to be an adventurer, it is a hard snub if one refers to a merchant as a mere "shopkeeper."

From Bajeos it was a long, sun-punished sail—almost

a quarter of Arrdanc's girth—to our destination: the free port of Pawnkam. Pinched between Obdapur to the north and Shaddishir to the south, it was the closest to our destination and had harbor masters who didn't care a whit if there happened to be a Dunarran hull riding at anchor in their moorings. It's a bit puzzling why so many of the nations of Mihal'j have such hard opinions of Dunarra and its allies. I'm sure they can cite grievances against the old Empire—well, *Consentium*—but it was their own rulers who had—and still have—a taste for massacring their enemies. So in the case of Dunarra, I suspect that their ill temper isn't quickened so much by remembered offenses as it is by sour grapes. As Elweyr and Druadaen and other overeducated people tell me, in the years after the Cataclysm, Mihal'j was home to the greatest powers, some of which became empires in their own right. But for reasons that are equally unknown and uninteresting to me, they went the way of all things: blown away by the winds of time, just like the sands of the desert that dominates the north half of this bloody continent.

Pawnkam proved itself a riot of different goods, different peoples, and different languages. Happily, the local dialect is naught but a mix of Mihal'j's two most common tongues. Less happily, only Elweyr could make heads or tails of that jabber. His (still missing) mother was only a wee tot when her family fled Lajantpur (or parts thereabout) when yet another religious war boiled over and sent a new flood of refugees streaming north to Ar Navir.

Still, despite having his mother's complexion and a smattering of her native tongue, Elweyr was known for a foreigner even before he opened his mouth.

Not that it mattered, at first. There were smiles and
friendly jostles and patted hands aplenty in the suqs
of Pawnkam. No merchant approached us to ask what
we sought without a great many wishes for our continued good health and assurances of assistance. Oddly,
Elweyr's was the only glum face among us. I poked
fun at his sour response to the friendly greetings, but
he only shook his head and muttered, "just you wait."

As we kitted ourselves for desert travel, we asked
about the best path to Zatsakkaz. The most common
response was a blank stare, but a few knew of it. Once
a capital of Mihal'j's most storied empire, it was built
to be just that and *only* that: a seat of power in a
place where no faction or family held sway. Naught
but sand now, it was founded with water in mind.
It was a backwater region but at the headwaters of
the river that runs south to Gamalaj: a once thriving
port on an inlet further down the coast. So Zatsakkaz boasted a direct route to the sea, yet was distant
enough to be spared the disasters—both of weather
and invaders—that might come from it.

However, even though the merchants' tales of those
bygone days had fewer parts in common than a spider
and a sparrow, they all came to the same grisly end as
Tharêdæath's account. Zatsakkaz was sacked and razed
not only before and during the fall of the empire, but
twice after. The desert pushed further south and filled
the first ten miles of the river. The water struggled back
to the surface downstream, but as a marshy maze of
shallow streams and rills. The road that had run north
alongside its old course disappeared from want of traffic
as much as the sands that blanketed it.

When we asked how to reach Zatsakkaz now, we

received as many opinions as there were old, snaggle-toothed vendors to offer them. But each long-winded explanation ended with the same caveat: "Of course, that city has been nothing but sand-covered ruins for five centuries. Wait: no, ten centuries. Or maybe more. I am unsure. But I fear there are no paths to the place nor guides who know the way."

The last old vendor did drop a useful crumb despite himself. Insofar as Zatsakkaz had been built into the side of a rocky hill, he thought it might still be used as a landmark by the only persons who still crossed the wastes: the men who worked for Jossgob, ostler for the forces of the Mayor-General of Pawnkam and purveyor of transport for those foolish—or desperate—enough to journey into the desert. But Jossgob's *kraal* and *keddah* was almost an hour's walk beyond the port's mud-brick outskirts, so we settled on an early start the next morning.

The matter of whether or not we should bring our kit with us stirred up some testy wrangling among the group. But we knew that Captain Firinne was itching to sail south to a friendlier port where Dunarra had a trading station. Not only could she be provisioned there, but the exchange of reports and advice pouches would be an ample excuse for having wandered so far beyond her normal ports of call.

None of us wanted to be more beholden to her than we already were, so the matter was decided: at first light, we'd head for Jossgob's in full kit so she could be on her way. But as we topped the ridge that kept the sand from drifting into Pawnkam's streets, we saw the *Swiftsure* slip under the horizon ... and with her, the only persons we could trust.

Once we'd passed the tilting shacks that marked the limits of the city, we entered a surrounding belt of *mastabas*: low buildings in which desert-dwellers place their dead. Not long after we started seeking the shortest path through that graveyard jumble, S'ythreni caught up to me and muttered, "We have an escort."

"Aye? So someone has decided to watch us leave their fair city?"

"No. I think that almost a score of some*ones* are quite happy that we've left it behind—along with any potential witnesses."

"Ah. So, we've been followed out by thieves, then."

She nodded. "Or spotted by bandits who hide out here."

The two of us began to lollygag, letting the others pass ahead. As they did, we mentioned the blaggards trailing us. There was nary a raised voice or betraying glance at the squat crypts around us. Not even Cerven revealed that we knew ourselves to be stalked like so many sheep.

When the attack finally came, it was really quite a sad business. Perhaps the glare of the sun kept our enemies from seeing the full measure of our weapons and armor. Or maybe they thought we didn't know how to use them. Or that foreigners like us would soon be dizzy with heatstroke. Whatever the reason, an occasional glance from the corner of our eyes showed a small group of them—archers, we reasoned—trotting alongside us to the left. They clearly meant to ambush us from that side, and so, drive us toward the larger group we could hear pacing us on the right.

We waited until the bunch on the left slipped behind a row of large *mastabas*. Their intent was as plain as the trunk on an elephant's face: use the lumpy buildings and mounds to screen them as they moved into positions from which they'd let loose at us. I almost pitied the poor bastards; the moment the *mastabas* blocked their view, we reversed and trotted over to the rearmost of the sunbaked buildings. We peeked around its corner; we were directly behind them. And with a clear line of sight.

Between S'ythreni's ironpith crossbow and Varcaxtan's compound bow, half of them were down or wounded in a trice. Cerven may have feathered one as well. Charging along with R'aonsun and Umkhira, I was too busy to notice. The two still standing drew their self-bows but loosed too quickly; the shafts went wide and high. One of them fled a moment after the other: too late to escape the edge of our green lass's axe. The sole survivor went yowling off toward the larger bunch waiting on the right flank. As he did, we set up in the very position from which the archers had meant to ambush us.

I don't know why the rest of that sorry lot charged through the same open ground where they'd hoped to catch us, but that's just what they did. Maybe they paid no mind to the warnings of the last archer. Or maybe he was too addled to offer any. But whatever the reason, they came straight into the rain of our arrows and bolts, which didn't let up until the rest of us jumped out of the shadows and countercharged.

The half dozen blaggards who'd made it that far didn't handle their weapons any better than they'd set their ambush. Which told me straight away that they weren't bandits, but must have both those skills to come away with their lives, let alone any loot. So that made this bunch naught but a pack of thieves who'd decided that an odd lot of newcomers would be easy pickings. "Not so easy after all," I muttered as we all stood panting over their bodies on the hard-packed sand. But how'd they'd come to know of us and our plans so quickly—or at all—was still a puzzlement.

Until, that is, Elweyr left off watching the last four flee back to the city and shot a hard stare at me. "*This* is what I meant when I said 'just you wait.'"

Which I understood right enough. Back in Menara, he and I had often relied upon folk whose keen eyes and loose lips were well worth the coppers we put in their grasping palms. So it stood to reason that, among the fawning hawkers in the suqs, there were a few that padded their profits by selling word of what they saw or heard.

Ironically, we were the ones who profited from their treachery. In addition to billon coins and waterskins, our attackers donated a few poisoned weapons to our kits. However, their ham-handed ambush brought a new annoyance: the chance of trouble with Pawnkam's authorities. Not because of the bodies we left in the shadows of the *mastabas*; there's little doubt that they and their deeds are already well known to the militia. But, as travelers from afar, we are easy targets for all manner of petty officials who could make our waking hours nightmares. Either we'd endure their countless inquiries and hearings and all manner of official folderol and lose both time and coin as we waited for it to end, or we could grease their palms and be on our way. For a group like ours, that choice was no choice at all, and they'd know it the moment they laid eyes on us. And with an aeosti and a Dunarran in the mix, they might become especially greedy. So we knew that our choice was between striking out directly into the dunes or being held ransom by a crew of quill-necked leeches who made their living by extracting legal *bakshish*.

It took us the better part of that day to reach Jossgob's. By the time we had reached an agreement for guides and camels, the bright desert stars were out and it was either sleep on the sand or pay a fistful of silver to snuggle together one stall over from the goats. I wasn't the only one who got more sleep the next morning—atop a camel, no less.

Our guides proved as stingy with words as we were with coin, but they brought us safe across seventy leagues of sand. They had us travel in the cool of the night, with only a few glances at the stars to keep us moving true. Along the way, small winged snakes followed us more closely than our own shadows, small jaws snapping like skeleton fingers. The guides chortled when we put our hands on our hilts, and one actually spared a few words to explain that the odd beasts weren't hungry for our flesh, but for the flies that trailed us and swarmed in clouds around camels.

But I was still powerfully annoyed at the flapping pests and was about to shoo one away when our oldest guide grabbed my arm. Seems the annoying airborne asps are just that: testy little buggers that, when angered, spit deadly venom. Had we had more time, the guide explained, they would have tried to capture as many as they could. Their powerful poison gets good coin and they do not breed in captivity. Indeed, the thieves' weapons had been painted with their venom. So after that, we sat as still as statues whenever they swooped close in pursuit of an especially juicy horsefly.

A day ago, we finished our journey alone and on foot. The guides would not go closer to Zatsakkaz for fear of ghosts and walking skeletons and monsters they called "dry-men." They seemed ready to wet their *galabijas* when nattering about the last, but not a one of their tales agreed on who or what these marauders actually were. I suspect that's because they're no more real than the specters or ghouls the guides presume to be stalking around the ruins. Which, so far as we can tell, are empty and lifeless as the well-baked rocks that throw back the sun's heat with the same force as furnace doors swung wide. The only pleasant thing about the ruins? We're quit of those damn flying snakes: *hsitsé*, they're called.

I should be sleeping, or at least staring at the desert-bright stars, but I couldn't put off writing in this blasted journal any longer. Besides, I'm twitchy with the thought of going underground again. You'd think that after crawling and skulking in the Under of Gur Grehar I'd shrug off another plunge into the bowels of the earth as naught but a trifle, particularly with so formidable a group as ours. We carry fine weapons and armor, as well as various charms and amulets bestowed upon us by Tharêdæath and even Ilshamësa: ones that bring luck, give warnings, point toward water, or calm a given species.

But for all that kit—every bit of it better than what we had before the shipwreck—there's a final cost and travail that no amount of money, equipment, or planning can reduce:

Time.

It's been better than a dozen moonphases since Druadaen disappeared on his fool errand into the beyond—which might yet prove to be oblivion. Gods know why I worry about him as if he were my brother. Well, my half-brother. Or maybe a second cousin. Ah, bollocks: he's grown on me and that's all there is to it.

But having spent all these days crisscrossing the whole bleedin' world in search of a hint on how best to find him, we're hardly closer to an answer than when we started. And here we are, about to dive blind into yet another perilous ruin, all on the hope—the mere *hope*, mind you!—that we'll stumble onto a long-lost trove of little metal plaques that were already old when the Cataclysm began.

If it wasn't for this "relayer" I'm wearing—this *quelsuur*—we wouldn't even have known how to start. And all we can do is trust that it will always point us toward Druadaen (and maybe its cousin metals), much the way a lodestone points to the pole. And with all the gods to witness, I've often wondered if the others might have left off if it wasn't for that bloody ring.

I'd thought—well, I'd *hoped*—it would have all sorts of wondrous powers, but so far, the only help it's given is to lead me to those who needed saving after the wreck. But even then, I have to wonder: did the ring do that for *our* good? Or is it because we are the only means to its own end: finding Druadaen. And perhaps the sai'niin bits with him. Or maybe they've become one and the same. These damn wizardly mysteries make my skin crawl.

But damned if it doesn't make its wants known when it comes time for us to choose our next direction. Its pulses may not be powerful, but they're as clear as the looks of a moody spouse: not a word spoken, but you know right enough which way to step if you don't want to sleep in the barn.

Back in the early days of our travels with Druadaen—when we thought him naught but a means to hobnobbing with the wealthy and powerful—there'd have been grumbling aplenty at all the moonphases we've spent accomplishing damn-all. But now, even High Ears just sighs and shakes her fine-boned head when we bump our noses into yet another delay or detour. That said, it's a right soothing salve to keep company with an ancient dragon and an august Dunarran warrior as we rove about. And naught but a fool would whine about having the ear and the blessings of the Great Pool of Mirroskye. Having such acquaintances makes it a near surety that you'll not die in the gutter. Well, at least not because of an empty purse or empty belly.

But it's not their generosity with goods and graces that keep us on this mad course; it's the time and attention they devote to it and to us. Sure but they'd not trouble themselves if finding Druadaen was of no more moment than to see him safely home. Something greater than our lot, or even those lofty folk themselves, is at stake. But I'll be a turtle's twig if I can suss out just what that might be. My old self would dun me for want of a brain if I tried to make a case for a journey with no clear path to profit—or to anything else.

And yet, I'll be damned if I'm not dogged by an odd presentiment: that having kept to this path may prove to be a greater wealth than gold when it's time to shrug off this mortal coil. I've seen silver come and silver go (it's no mistake that the demigod of coin is also the deity of caprice), but to be part of something greater than oneself? Of a purpose so steeped in mystery and consequence that it may echo down through later ages? Most folk only hear of such adventures 'round campfires and laugh them off as hogwash. But we are living it, and there's a powerful pull in that ... whatever it might cost in wealth, well-being, or both.

But having set down all these reasons, I now see them for what they truly are: high-sounding excuses to avoid admitting why I'm making yet another of the stupid decisions that have kept me on the edge of paupery my whole life long: the kind where I follow my fool heart. Because, damn it, I know that Dunarran bookworm would do no less for me. And, truth be told (though I'll *never* admit it beyond these pages), I miss having him as a true brother-in-arms.

But in the very act of scribbling that confession, I see a deeper reason. Yes, I miss Druadaen, but more than that, I *need* him. Not for my sake, but for me little tad. Two years ago, I rested sure in knowing what was needed to make her safe: an ample and steady flow of coin. But now? The world around me looks the same, even the parts I regarded with a knowing wink; after all, I knew better than most that appearances can be deceiving. But traveling with that blasted Dunarran opened my eyes wider still: it's not just that appearances *can* be deceiving; they mostly *are* deceiving. And the more power that's at stake, the more deceiving the appearances.

I'm no one's fool, and gods know I'm not afraid to fight the shadowy threats that have loomed up before us, but that's not the same thing as knowing where to *look* for them. And I fear—every day—that I'll never learn how.

Mind you, I don't lose a wink of sleep worrying over what may become of me because of what I don't see approaching. It's a fool of a man who chooses to live by the sword if he can't also live with the near certainty that he'll die by one, too. But my tad! How do I keep her safe from what I can't see? Hovering near to protect her is the worst answer, since any shadow following me would then be sure to fall across her, as well.

That leaves only one option: to take the war to what threatens her rather than waiting for it to slouch toward that moss-roofed cottage outside Menara. It's an ancient and ever-green truth that if we don't go out to hunt the beasts that mean to devour us, they will breed like rats and, in time, swarm over our walls and thresholds.

But *how* do I do that if I don't know where to seek them, don't recognize the subtle tracks they leave in the loam of human events? That's why I miss—*I need*—Druadaen: to point out the threats I might miss. Or to teach me how to see them for myself.

Ever since he stepped through a door into nowhere, each day has become a little more worrisome than the last. I seem to hear great leathery wings flying above the black clouds of every storm.

And they always sound like they're heading toward a cottage on the outskirts of Menara.

CHAPTER FORTY-THREE

"Ahearn," asked Umkhira in a low mutter, "what will it take for you to believe me?"

"With all respect fer yer roots," he muttered back as they re-formed after entering yet another empty chamber, "I've had more time in tunnels than you have, Lady Lightstrider."

"Yes," she agreed, "you have. But tell me: have you seen any of the signs—or spoor—that the Bent would leave in such a place?"

Ahearn paused; it was strange hearing her speak of "the Bent," inasmuch as her own people were typically included in that unflattering label. But it was the only term that included all the denizens of the Under, whether or not they were a species of urzhen. His other reason for pausing was his reluctance to concede her point. "No, there's no hint that any underkin dwell here at all. But that's no reason not to treat every room and every corner as if we expect it to be held against us."

"I can think of one," R'aonsun observed unhelpfully.

"Well, don't wait for me to coax it out of yeh."

The dragon's avatar yawned expansively. "Boredom. There are only so many times that we can gird our loins—a more meaningful phrase now that I have loins to gird—before it becomes dull rote, rather than poised readiness."

Ahearn bit his lip, because he had felt no less. "What do you propose, then?" he finished with a glance toward Varcaxtan.

The Dunarran shrugged. "S'ythreni and Umkhira have the eyes for this place. They could take turns walking ten yards ahead, relieving each other every ten minutes or so. Or perhaps Elweyr would be so good to affine with the next rat we encounter."

Ahearn frowned at both suggestions. "I'm loath to ask Elweyr to expend any *manas* before it is absolutely needed. Nor am I one to ask others to take on the danger of leading us at a distance if I don't as well."

Elweyr shook his head. "I have a philter for the affining. I wouldn't need to draw upon *manas*."

"But it will cost us a precious resource!"

S'ythreni leaned toward him. "Ahearn, you're not scrabbling after every bit of kit that might help you escape the Under anymore. It's been three years."

"And I should become a spendthrift, instead?" But even as he said it, Ahearn felt the truth of the aeosti's observation settling in his gut. Survival no longer depended upon hanging on to every rusty scrap.

"Is it profligacy to expend supplies to ensure that a band of warriors remains alert? Would that not be the mark of capable leadership, instead?" R'aonsun asked mildly.

Ahearn shook his head. At himself. "It's a fair point. All of 'em are, in fact." He looked up. "Of Uncle Varcaxtan's two suggestions, we'll use the philter." He tried to make his tone light-hearted. "Easier to replace a bit of mancery than a few comrades, I suppose." But the words came out as sardonic drollery that just barely cloaked the surge of worry beneath it. Ahearn had never been with any group for so long, nor risked mates on such an uncertain journey. The thought of losing any of them was, well, unthinkable.

Varcaxtan answered with a serious nod. "No shame in erring to the side of caution where the safety of your followers is concerned."

Ye're calling this lot my followers? Are yeh daft, Uncle? But all he said was, "Elweyr, where's the last place you saw or heard rats?"

Elweyr was peering toward the chamber's far wall. "There's at least one right over there."

"Just like old times. Be about making friends with it, then. Then join us for a quick sit, sip, and bite." Ahearn leaned toward Varcaxtan. "So, you agree with Umkhira? No Bent hereabouts?"

Varcaxtan shrugged, staring into the darkness as they all sat in an outward-facing circle. "I suspect you and she have more experience detecting them than I do. But it's true that they're not common on Mihal'j, particularly in the desert."

"Well, *nothing* is particularly common in the desert, is it?"

The Dunarran smiled. "I'll rephrase: they find it especially difficult to survive in *this* desert."

"Because it's the hottest? Driest?"

"No: it's because there's almost no workable metal."

He answered the group's puzzled stares with a question. "You all inspected the weapons and tools in Pawnkam's suqs, yes?"

Ahearn frowned, thinking. "Anything iron was very dear, copper and bronze not far behind. Most were made from what looked like horn. From a supragant of some kind, if I remember a-right."

He nodded. "It's called an *ishart*. Treating its hide is a closely held secret amongst the guild masters who handle it."

Cerven nodded. "The mountains in this part of the continent have very few veins of ore."

Ahearn nodded, trying to remember casual remarks he'd heard about that. "Comes back to me now. Not so much absent as all mined out, if I recall."

"That's the guess," Varcaxtan agreed, "but Couriers who've seen those tunnels say it's as if the metal just vanished. They tell of open creases where there had once been pure veins. What started as mixed formations looked moth-eaten, as if the metal had evaporated right out of the stone."

Ahearn stared at him. "Any idea how that came about, because it certainly doesn't sound like mining."

"It surely doesn't. But the only other explanation I've ever heard is that it's the work of tiny insects called iron mites."

"Y'mean they *ate* the metal? That's daft!"

Cerven cleared his throat deferentially. "And yet, there are precedents."

"Such as?"

"In Tvedraand, it is said that mining is, in part, carried out by the action of what translate roughly as lithophages. It is unclear whether they are fauna or flora, but they reduce rock, leaving metal behind. The description of iron mites suggests that they are simply a reverse of those creatures: consumers of metal, instead of rock."

Ahearn nodded at the rough walls around them. "And it's a certainty that a pickaxe made of hardened hide wouldn't last an hour at tunneling in this rock. Weapons wouldn't be much better for long use."

Varcaxtan nodded. "That's why the eastern desert has so few walled towns: almost no Bent. And they never go a-Hordeing. Besides, the local *jahi*—leaders—frown on fortifications of any kind. Well, except ones built by those of their own class."

Elweyr returned, a rat scrabbling devotedly behind him. "Let's go," he said. "The affining doesn't last for more than an hour."

"According to what S'ythreni just described," whispered R'aonsun, "she and Umkhira saw a dry-man."

Ahearn wished he'd caught a glimpse himself. "You've actually met them?"

The dragon-avatar nodded. "One or two." As if anticipating the flood of questions that might cause, he added, "That was several millennia ago. What our two scouts describe is somewhat different. And no, I have no useful knowledge of the species. They have little use for other races and their aims were just as unknown as their origins."

Umkhira nodded. "I had thought them nothing more than myths with which to scare the young." She lowered her voice to a whisper and looked meaningfully over her shoulder. "And if I recall correctly, they were said to have hearing almost as keen as Iavarain."

S'ythreni scowled, but gestured them to fall back around a farther corner, putting them over thirty yards from the dry-man who'd been guarding another opening that led into the chamber they'd seen. "Legend also says their eyes are more sensitive to light than humans'." She took a periapt from around her neck—a personal gift from Tharêdæath—and, removing one gauntlet, held it in the palm of that hand. As if warmed by her touch, it glowed faintly: just enough to see nearby faces or read if held over each successive word. Elweyr nodded, uncovered the much dimmer glow-glass crystal that they had taken from the leader of the bandits they'd ambushed three days south of Kœsdri'yrm.

Varcaxtan nodded back toward the intersection from which they'd withdrawn. "How certain are you that there was another entrance on the far wall?"

The aeosti shrugged. "It was either that or a very deep alcove. I did hear echoes of other, similar voices, but they were more distant."

"Do you think they were from behind the guard or elsewhere in the chamber?"

"The chamber. The echoes weren't the kind that come out of a tunnel. They were the kind that echo up high in a big cavern, which goes with what we saw: those slowly curving walls went up beyond where we could see."

Elweyr appeared disgusted. "Anybody else recall a situation very like this one?"

Umkhira grunted. "The first intersection of tunnels we came upon in the Undergloom of Gur Grehar. That was a fearful moment."

"Aye," Ahearn agreed, rubbing his chin, "but we

had a good plan, didn't we?" Assenting murmurs arose. "Maybe something similar might work here."

Umkhira nodded hesitantly. "Here, as there, the sentry is almost certainly guarding the limit of a tribal territory. So the great balance of their forces are probably well back from his position."

Ahearn nodded. "And if these dry-men are anything like the Bent, these sentries are just trip wires: a challenge that says, 'just try and come at us, yeh bastards!'"

"Yes, and if anyone does," pointed out Elweyr, "those guards will surely summon any reinforcements that might be lurking around the corner behind them."

Cerven glanced at Ahearn. "Is that typical?"

The swordsman shrugged. "It can go either way. Sometimes the guards are but a nervy bluff, but sometimes, there's a dozen more just a few feet behind 'em, ready and eager to charge into a scrap."

But Elweyr was shaking his head. "Back in the Under, we knew that because it's what we experienced there. And the last time, we had a guide: Kaakhag. He knew roughly where we were, what tribes were in the area, and—most important—which of the tunnels led to our destination." He shook his head. "Here, we have no way to know how our enemy will react, or if any of those openings aren't just dead ends."

"We have not found any other path into the deeper rock, where the repository is said to be," Umkhira countered.

R'aonsun shrugged. "Which could mean that we must go through, not around, these dry-men. That requires a plan that is focused on attack, not avoidance, of their forces."

S'ythreni's tone was sour. "Fight them? What if

the whole dry-man nation lies between us and what lies beyond?"

Ahearn shook his head. "Fight doesn't mean bulling our way through them, High Ears. If it's a whole nation we must face, then we draw their warriors after us, back toward the surface. And as we whittle away at them, we stay alert for a way to take a prisoner who might be persuaded to tell us the way down. Or if they've lost so many that they're spread thin in the tunnels, *that's* when we might find a way to slip through."

"All that assumes there *is* a way down," Elweyr sighed.

Ahearn pushed back at him. "Look: we know that not long ago, fortune-hunters made it beyond this point and returned to tell of it. We've tried every other tunnel branch and still haven't found any way down. So if we can go forward, we will, and if we can't, we'll go back. But here's one other thing of which I'm absolutely certain: every moment we stand here wagging our jaws about what to do is another moment that more enemies might show up, either to the front or the rear of us."

"And *that*," Varcaxtan followed promptly, "is why we talk tactics. Now." He turned to Umkhira. "The sentry: how close was he hanging on the tunnel he was guarding?"

She shrugged; her light leather jack emitted a creaking rustle where it bunched against the fine mail she wore beneath it. "Never more than a yard into the chamber, never more than three back from it. And there could have been two; there was no way to be certain whether it was one guard moving back and forth, or two trading places."

Ahearn sucked his teeth in frustration. "So no hope of making quick work with a single bowshot, then." He thought. "Do *they* have bows?"

S'ythreni shrugged. "I don't think so. Not at the ready, at least."

"Not much use, perhaps, if their eyes aren't much better than ours."

"Perhaps, but that is only a guess, and I'd rather not discover otherwise by suddenly sprouting arrows."

Varcaxtan waved away the discussion of bows. "If we are forced to attack around the corner, it is unlikely we shall be able to silence both of them as swiftly as we must. It is likely that they will have time enough to raise an alarm, or that the combat will be loud enough to bring reinforcements." He looked around the group. "We must find a way to bring the two guards out so we may take them silently."

Elweyr almost groaned. "As I said: just like Gur Grehar."

But Cerven was frowning slowly as he asked, "And how did guards in the Under react if they heard unfamiliar sounds?"

"Such as?" Ahearn asked.

"Such as, say, a few rats."

Umkhira matched the young man's frown. "A few rats they would ignore. Anything else? It would depend on the nature of the sound. Or the numbers it suggested."

"So . . . if they heard a *lot* of rats?"

Umkhira shrugged. "I suspect they would send at least one guard out to determine if it was any cause for alarm."

Cerven nodded meaningfully at her, and then glanced at Ahearn.

Who smiled, understanding. "I think we have the beginnings of a plan."

Huddling close against the wall of the tunnel that led into the chamber, Ahearn patted Varcaxtan on the shoulder. The Dunarran swallowed the philter he'd uncorked and, standing behind the kneeling S'ythreni, used that hand to pull a waiting shaft from his quiver. As he drew the bow held fast in his other hand, the arrowhead caught the faint glow of S'ythreni's periapt, now held by Cerven. Poison glistened on the tip.

Ahearn glanced behind. Elweyr was tucked into a cleft on the same side of the tunnel, repeating the syllables that kept one construct active in his mind, and another poised on the cusp of completion. Behind the thaumantic, Umkhira kept a hand on Cerven's shoulder; he had the light, but she had the eyes that could see far ahead without it.

At the rear of the group, R'aonsun sighed and hissed, "And what, exactly, are we waiting for?"

Around the corner they were all watching, the dim torchlight darkened briefly. "That," Ahearn answered. The guard that had checked around both corners within the past minute was walking farther back into the tunnel, momentarily blocking the unsteady yellow glow. "Elweyr—"

But the mantic had seen it, too. The affined rat scuttled from alongside his boot, its claws scratching the stone floor as it approached the tunnel mouth. The thaumancer's face relaxed slightly, and his syllables rose to a climax.

S'ythreni lifted her crossbow, sighted along it as

the faint sounds of the sentry's booted feet reversed. The torchlight failed again as he began to return ...

Just as the rat scuttled past the tunnel opening, and Elweyr completed the second thaumate with a relieved sigh. Ahead of the rat that was now racing toward the other opening they'd spotted, sounds of dozens more arose.

A wiry shadow pushed out beyond the mouth of the tunnel; it was a dry-man, its *isharti* scale mail rattling dully as it leaned out, its head pitched forward as if squinting after the rat.

As soon as the silhouette's back was fully exposed, S'ythreni discharged her ironpith crossbow. Ahearn gripped his hand-and-a-half and leaned forward on the balls of his feet, ready to charge.

The figure fell forward, limp; the tremendous power of the crossbow had killed the dry-man outright, before the poison could take effect. As the scraping and scratching of hundreds of nonexistent rats receded toward the farther opening, another set of footsteps approached. Hearing that, Varcaxtan stepped away from the wall, aiming at the tunnel's corner.

Another silhouette—shaped like the first—leaned out, but stopped suddenly: he'd probably just seen the body of his comrade—and then the fins of S'ythreni's quarrel protruding from its spine. The form started to draw back in haste.

Varcaxtan's composite compound bow sang. Despite the power of the Dunarran weapon and the skill of the wielder, the shaft barely caught the adversary before he successfully ducked behind the corner; it had lodged in his forearm, eliciting a curse.

Which Ahearn barely heard as he charged forward

to finish the work, trusting that the inconstant torch-light wouldn't erode his aim overmuch.

But even as he swept around the corner, he saw that he'd only need to deliver a coup de grace—a mercy, given the spasms wracking the narrow, almost haggard warrior before him. Ahearn's two-handed cut hit at the juncture of the neck and shoulder. His enemy's isharti scale resisted the blow...which sent it skittering straight into the dry-man's jugular, and clean through his throat and spine.

Ahearn jumped for the torch, preparing to dash it from its crude cresset—but froze.

A third dry-man was hunched against the wall, bound and blindfolded—and, significantly, utterly silent.

Behind Ahearn, footfalls thudded across the tunnel's entry. "What are you doing?" Umkhira hissed, weapon in one hand, Cerven's shoulder in the other. He was holding the periapt aloft as she steered him toward the same patch of darkness where the sound of rats had been but a moment earlier. The hasty steps of the others followed close behind them.

Except for one more measured tread which closed on Ahearn as he dragged the dry-man up to his feet. "Taking him is a risk," Varcaxtan observed over his shoulder.

"Isn't everything?" Ahearn countered, and removed the dry-man's blindfold. Orange-hazel eyes glared out of wrinkled, leathery sockets. "We go down," Ahearn said in Commerce; there was no response. *And as there's not any time to try other tongues*—Ahearn jabbed his finger repeatedly at the floor.

The dry-man's eyes narrowed, then he nodded and held out his tied hands.

Ahearn drew one of the curved knives they'd taken from the thieves outside Pawnkam, used the base of the blade to slice through the rawhide wraps, and then held it up so the point was directly between their eyes. Its tip had a syrupy sheen. "Obey or die."

Either the man understood those words or knew a poisoned blade when he saw one; he nodded again and led them around the corner, following after the others. As they plunged into the darkness, the periapt bobbing ahead of them like a firefly drawing them into an abyss, the dry-man motioned toward the head of the group. Ahearn locked one hand on his captive's arrestingly thin arm and hustled him forward until he was alongside Umkhira.

She looked over as they fled downward, eyes wide in fear, loathing, or both. "We are to trust him?"

"For now, yes." Dim voices and running feet echoed down from the chamber behind them. "He could betray us."

"Or he may need to run away from his folk even more than we do. We'll find out which soon enough."

CHAPTER FORTY-FOUR

Ahearn whispered in S'ythreni's direction. "Can you still hear 'em, High Ears? Are they following us?"

"Hear them? Yes. Following us? I don't know."

Ahearn nodded. "As soon as you do, give a sign." He walked away from her post near one of the five openings in a much smaller, low-ceilinged chamber. Originally a cavern, its floor had been made level by occasional pick work and centuries of use. Still, he almost stubbed a toe as he crossed the room to an opening where the others were gathered. "So, are we having a nice, cozy chat yet?"

Umkhira's response was guttural and tight. "It has barely been a minute and this dry-man is not cooperative." She settled herself in front of their captive and spoke in Undercant. "Do you speak this language?" The dry-man continued to stare at the opposite wall, his posture haughty rather than bowed. Umkhira frowned, tried a harsher tongue that Ahearn had never heard before.

The dry-man, however, was quite familiar with it. He snapped an irritated reply at the Lightstrider, looking down his withered nose as he did.

Umkhira's head snapped back as she uttered a surprised growl.

"What language was that?" Cerven wondered.

"Deepcant," R'aonsun answered, folding his arms.

"And what did he say?" Elweyr pressed.

"I said," answered the dry-man in passable Commerce, "that I understand both Deepcant *and* Undercant, but that I won't lower myself to speak to a *pekt*."

Ahearn flinched at the last word; it had been a long time since he had heard that slur for urzhen. He put a hand on Umkhira's rage-quaking shoulder. "I'm sure you'd like to teach our guest how to keep a civil tongue in his head"—*before ripping it clean out*—"but for now, he seems more willing to talk to us thinskins."

"Barely," the dry-man sneered. "There's little to choose between your waterfat breeds."

Ahearn held his tongue—and sword—in check just long enough for R'aonsun to interpose himself. "Perhaps," he mused, eyes on the dry-man, "you would prefer conversing with me?"

The dry-man looked the dragon-avatar's immense human body up and down. "Your size does not frighten me."

"I'm sure it doesn't," R'aonsun smiled, nodding, welcoming his opponent's angry glare.

The dry-man started. His face went through an arrestingly swift sequence of expressions: surprise was succeeded by hatred, then terror, then despair, and finally, a vacant stare.

"Now," said R'aonsun, "I believe we may converse in a more congenial fashion." He smiled. "Well, congenial for us, at any rate."

The dry-man's eyes remained blank, but seemed to quiver in their sockets.

R'aonsun stepped aside. "You may ask your questions, now."

Ahearn glanced at the dragon. "Seems like you'd have some questions, too, no?"

The hulking avatar shrugged. "None that are pressing. Besides, when I am in another body, it is difficult to do anything that requires either intense or long concentration. I shall exert my influence to ensure that he answers truthfully."

"And the sooner, the better," added S'ythreni in a loud whisper from the edge of the tunnel that had brought them to the present chamber. "I don't know if they are following our trail, but they are certainly getting louder."

Ahearn leaned toward the dry-man. "The intersection where we found you: is that a crossroads? Between rival tribes?"

The dry-man's speech was slow, halting, as if each word was a piece of broken glass that he was trying to keep from scarring his throat as it rose up. "Firstly, we are not tribes, not barbarians. We are . . . are *Izi*: 'lineages of repute.' Secondly, the chamber from which we fled is not a crossroad, but a meeting place."

"Are those not the same?" Umkhira asked.

His corpselike lips curled in derision before the answer came out of them. "Idiot *pekt*. A crossroad is a hub of travel. The place you violated is the *Qōqazkep*, the 'meeting ground' of Great Lineages.' It is above common use; travelers may *not* move through it and nothing may obstruct it. It belongs to all equally. It is where parleys, exchanges, and contests are conducted."

Ahearn was about to ask how to flee lower, and if he had heard of Zatsakkaz when Varcaxtan crossed his arms and asked, "Why were you bound and blindfolded?"

"Because I am not *Iz*. You would say mine is a family without a name or honor. At least, we are now. We were *Iz* until stripped of our surname generations ago."

"And that makes you a criminal?" Cerven wondered.

"It does if one refuses to recognize the preeminence of the *Iz*. So, too, if one refuses to forsake the name of one's dishonored family. The penalty for either is death."

"So," Ahearn quipped as he raised an eyebrow, "you were to be killed twice, then."

"Yes."

Ahearn stared at the dry-man's flat, unironic confirmation, glanced at R'aonsun, who shrugged. Their captive had not misspoken. *Well, how the hells——?* "Where I come from, a fellow's first execution tends to be his last."

"Killed is a legal term, when used by the *Huzhkepbar Iz*, the Tribunal of the Lineages. It refers to an execution effected by no fewer than three, and no more than five, blows, cuts, or thrusts. All trials are observed by representatives of rival *Izi*, and every strike is made at the explicit direction of an *Izroj*— Lord—whose *Iz* is party to the proceedings. Members of rival *Qōqaz*, the greatest families, are included in the tribunal to ensure that no judgment or punishment becomes too harsh or too lenient."

"How . . . compassionate," Elweyr muttered. "So you were to be killed by, er, six to ten 'strikes'?"

"Yes."

"But to come back to my point," Varcaxtan asked sharply, "what were you doing there? Waiting?"

"Yes. Waiting. The representatives of the other *Izrojagi*—Great Lords—who judged my case had not arrived yet. It is not uncommon that one *Izrojag* keeps another waiting. This is common among those who are most eager to assert their status."

Ahearn shook his head. *No matter how far you travel, some things don't change.* "It sounds as though they'll be mighty determined to find yer sorry self."

"That is correct. The power—and so, the authority—of the *Izrojagi* will be questioned if they fail to settle affronts. And in this case, they must address two of them. First, they must determine whether or not my disappearance was the work of, or arranged by, one or more rival *Qōqaz*. Second, they must ensure that their judgment is carried out, or the law, and they themselves, will be deemed to be without force."

Cerven leaned toward him. "Then it seems most prudent for you to travel with us." The dry-man did not disagree, but he might have spit if R'aonsun had allowed it. "So that we may not offend, by what name does your kind refer to itself. And also, to you?"

R'aonsun was incapable of keeping the disdain out of their captive's voice. "Being a prisoner of the *Huzhkepbar Iz* does not mean I am a traitor to my race. Our name—and our purposes—are our own, wetgut. The same goes for mine."

Varcaxtan leaned toward him, arms taut. "So, you want us to call you 'dry-man,' then?"

The prisoner considered, then smiled. "You may call me Izroj, if you must call me at all."

Umkhira stepped toward him, hand on axe. "I will be gutted before I call you 'lord,' you vermin!"

The dry-man looked at her calmly. "Nothing would give me greater pleasure than to see that oath fulfilled, if I only had the means and freedom to do so."

Ahearn shook his head and smiled. "Ah, now see? That's just the sort of nastiness that makes it hard to trust even such a fine person as yerself." Ahearn stared at the dry-man. "You've got him tight in yer clutches, yeh, R'aonsun?"

"What do you mean to do?"

"Why, I mean to improve his mood!" Ahearn walked behind the dry-man, studied the light shift that was his only garment. "After all, we'll be moving soon again, and no end in sight to that, eh? So every bit of weight makes a body weary. And weariness is, in turn, a great weight upon one's temper."

Ahearn continued his circuit around the increasingly anxious dry-man, drawing his own, longer dagger as he did. "But there's only so much to be done, hey? Can't do without shoes—which is a right pity, seein' as they've such thick soles. But without those, he'd be slowing us down. So I suppose, this is the only way we lighten the poor sod's burden—" And with two quick slashes, the rough-sewn shift fell free, pooling around the dry-man's knees.

Only R'aonsun seemed unsurprised by what was revealed; a body so tight-skinned that it seemed to be little more than a withered sack in which to keep the wiry muscles close against the bones they served. Ahearn was too surprised to notice the total lack of hair at first; instead the torso's expansive constellation of mauve, gray, and mustard mottles compelled, and then repelled, the entire group's eyes.

Ahearn swallowed, resolved to keep up his bluff demeanor. "So, then, if you're very polite to my friend the Lady Lightstrider, you might get a stitch or two back . . . should you care."

"I've endured worse. Much worse."

"Well then, I guess we can just dispose of this." Ahearn tossed the slashed shift aside. "Now, if you don't want us to leave you trussed up for the coursers sent by your *Izroji*, you'll—"

"They're coming," S'ythreni hissed.

"How long?" Varcaxtan insisted.

"Can't say. Could be fifteen minutes; could be five. But they're following our trail, now. I'm sure of it."

Ahearn stepped so close to the dry-man that their noses nearly touched. "Answers. Quickly. Will all your lot have metal weapons like the guards near your parley chamber?"

"Yes. And isharti armor."

Ahearn managed to control his expression and his stomach; the dry-man's breath was almost unbearable. It had a sharp, alchemical reek that Ahearn had only smelled among the starving, or people who'd been living on a diet of meat. "Attack animals?"

"Rats, large ones. Not well trained, but they know to look for an open flank."

"Alchemy?"

"Not much. Except poison. Made from *hsitsé*, just like on your weapons. Wait: some *Qōqaz* have elders who can combine it with other compounds. When thrown, it bursts into fire and the smoke is poisonous."

Well, bugger me! "And mancery?"

The dry-man licked his lips with a leathery tongue. "Not as you mean."

Elweyr leaned in. "Every legend says that mantics are plentiful among your kind."

He struggled to explain. "Maybe more than among you, but still not many. And it is not akin to yours; it is not taught as special disciplines."

"Why?"

"Because our knowledge of it is incomplete and the *Qōqaz* guard it jealously. As do lone mantics without families. Each knows only a few, unrelated pieces of the whole."

R'aonsun muttered, eyes closed in concentration. "It has ever been thus. They do not seem capable of the trust required to pool their knowledge in any orderly fashion. But whereas their individual mantics lack sophistication and control, they often compensate with surprising power."

Ahearn glanced at Elweyr. "Is that enough for you to work with?"

The other nodded, producing the sealed light sphere he hadn't used since Gur Grehar. "I have a few ideas."

"As do I," Varcaxtan added. "I'll need everyone's spare lamp oil."

Ahearn suspected the Dunarran had been mulling over a defense of the chamber since they'd entered it. "Then let's hear your plans—and quickly, if we're to use them at all."

CHAPTER FORTY-FIVE

Although uneven, the increasing play of torchlight on the target tunnel's walls outlined its opening. And as the flickering grew brighter, it sparked red glints from eyes that were approaching about a foot above the floor: big rats, or something similar.

Ahearn leaned back into his ready position halfway across the chamber; if he could see them, they could see him, black cloak notwithstanding. Sword at the ready, he pressed his left foot against the stone floor. With a sound like a crystal whisper, the sole of his boot crushed the small ampule Elweyr had given him. The resulting smell added a second, even more intense carrion stink to the scent they'd already put out around the entrance. Ahearn had never heard, or even thought, of using a sudden, intense odor as both bait and a ready signal for defenders. And if Elweyr had conceived of it before now, he'd not shared it.

Although Ahearn was no longer in a position where he could see the torch-lit eyes, his ears told him everything he needed to know about the creatures' reactions. Frenzied skitterings vied with voices shouting commands that reminded him of handlers trying to bring dogs to heel—and then the urgent orders were drowned out by eager squealing and a scrabbling rush toward the chamber: toward the redoubled, irresistible smell of rotting meat.

Ahearn couldn't make out individual silhouettes among the roiling clutter of shadows that burst through the entrance. But instead of continuing deeper, the creatures stopped just beyond the threshold. Outlines of questing noses rose frantically above that dark, turbulent mass. The smell—the delicious smell that had swept aside whatever training they had—was all around them.

Or, more accurately, was beneath them.

In the other half of the room, and similarly offset from the entrance, a brief flicker picked out the lines of Elweyr's own cloak, leaning down—but there was nothing visible within it. As the flame touched the floor, a heavy smear of oil lit just beyond the fringe of the garment, which then fell, suddenly empty. As it did, three narrower trails of oil flared and raced toward the door like a trident of fire.

One of the tines sputtered and died, but the other two reached the spot where the monstrous rodents were suddenly silent and alert, the threat of fire having taken a moment to push through their frustrated feeding frenzy. Three yards from the door, the carrion-scented oil ignited with a sound like the breathy flap of a ripped sail. The five calf-high creatures, having crawled through the oil, did not merely catch fire; they exploded into writhing, squealing balls of flame.

One ran beyond the edge of the blaze, sparks trailing behind as bits of its wiry hair burned off. It ran in a mad serpentine as it realized enemies were all around it and finally darted into one of the other tunnel openings. The light of its flaming fur faded even more rapidly than its infantlike screams.

Another's eyes were seared in the first instant, and, bumping into others that had followed it in, succumbed to the flames and fell, twitching and shrieking.

But the last three knew to turn tail and sped back down the tunnel like a brace of frantic meteors—and as they went, they illuminated startled dry-men who pressed themselves to the walls as the monstrous rodents swept past them. Darkness drew across the dozen or so warriors again, but with their numbers revealed, they would attack as soon as they adjusted their plans for the rout of their rats.

Well, Ahearn allowed, they weren't rats, actually. They were some cave-bred version of *hodpaqt*—swamp cavies—with wide, bulbous eyes and brittle fur that burnt like dry hay. But most importantly, they were even more distracted by a carrion scent than their surface-dwelling cousins.

But Ahearn and his lot had their own, unexpected reaction to the scent; they were all gagging on the thick, putrid smoke now spreading through the chamber. The esters Elweyr had mixed into the oil doubled the intensity of the smell and its appeal to the "cave cavies" but each breath now prompted retching. And as the flames died down, less of the greasy residue was burned away, becoming heat-vaporized smoke, instead.

Well, Ahearn allowed, *one can't think of everything.* And at least the surprise to the dry-men had been much, much greater. As their questions and commands filled the tunnel with the sounds of the dry-men's harsh, unfamiliar language, Ahearn leaned back toward their wrist-bound captive. "Can you make that out?"

"They are discussing mancery," the prisoner whispered in Commerce.

"Ours or theirs?"

"Theirs. They mean to still the fire. Then charge in. If they suspect you used—or even have—mancery, they did not mention it."

More or less what Elweyr expected. Ahearn swallowed back a wave of vomit before he could speak again. "Well, the better for us and the worse for them. You stay still, now, or I'll have to—"

Without any current of cooling air or other evident change, the flames in front of the entrance died down swiftly. It was as if they were being smothered by a blanket, but the effect was too uniform to be natural.

Ahearn drew his cloak closer, black side facing out, and knelt closer to the makeshift apparatus that Elweyr had set up, angled toward the tunnel mouth. A few stealthy sounds came out of that dark opening, then silence. Ahearn poised a finger above the most crucial part of the apparatus: the small metal light sphere, reflecting dim spindles from the guttering flames sheltered beneath the mass of the burning cave cavy. Ahearn held his breath. Nothing but silence, then more silence—and then an abrupt thunder of charging feet.

Making sure his movement wouldn't topple the shield they'd propped up behind Elweyr's light sphere, Ahearn tapped the small device on the side facing the entrance. As it had in Gur Grehar, the little ball sprouted legs with a snap and its top snicked open, revealing the blinding white light of a *manas* crystal. But this time, only two of the eight slivers of its cover opened, sending a narrow, sharp-edged beam of light toward the entrance—just as the first two dry-men charged into the room.

They came in with their two-handed swords held in a close high guard, the point of the blade aiming straight out in front of them, just above the line of the shoulder. Their prisoner had told them to expect that stance; given the awkward length of their hereditary weapons, they felt it was the only way for two men to enter abreast while ready to attack or defend. But with a sudden light shone in their faces—?

Unable to see whatever opponents, or pits, or traps might be before them, both reflexively threw up a hand, trying to orient themselves as they stumbled through the smoking oil.

Off in the dark, S'ythreni's ironpith crossbow snapped. The leader of the two—judging from his necklaces and strings of withered trophies—took the bolt in the center of his chest. He staggered and fell forward at the very instant that the softer slap of two bows—Varcaxtan's and Cerven's—sent a pair of shafts at the one beside him.

Varcaxtan's long arrow caught that intruder in the belly, but his isharti armor kept it from penetrating deeply. But, in the space of a heartbeat, he began convulsing; the arrowhead's *hsitsé* poison had begun its grim work. And although Cerven's shaft went just low and wide of the same mark, it punched into the kirtle of yet another dry-man coming in right behind him. It inflicted little more than a flesh wound on the thigh beneath the lighter armor, but that was enough for the shaft's venom-painted point to induce similar spasms.

The other attacker in the second rank stepped to the side as he entered, angling for the darkness as one hand came away from his heavy weapon's hilt to shield his eyes. As he squinted into the shadows, looking for the source of the arrows and bolts, he took a second long step—and ran directly into Umkhira's axe.

Hiding flush against the wall and just a yard beyond the edge of the darkness, the Lightstrider's ambush gave her the rare opportunity to employ precision in lieu of strength. Her first cut almost took off the hand he'd raised to his eyes; it looked and flopped like a gutted fish before he could get it back to the hilt. Umkhira stepped in as she muscled the axe through a back cut which found his neck. Before he'd fallen, she'd stepped back into the dark—but not to the same spot.

Yet another attacker charged in to replace the dry-man that Cerven's arrow had dropped, quaking, to the ground. He, too, entered at an angle and dodged sideways, trying to slip into the shadows on that side and get his back against the wall. But R'aonsun was there, waiting in ambush just as Umkhira had been on the other side. Armed with an even larger greatsword than his opponent, what he lacked in skill at weapons was amply offset by his size and brute force. Starting from a high guard, he brought his blade down on the still-blinded intruder's shoulder. The actual wound was diminished by the isharti armor, but did little to lessen the sheer impact; the sound of the dry-man's shattering collarbone foretold his fate a full second before the dragon's neck-level back cut dispatched him. And, following the plan and Umkhira's example, he leaped back into the shadows. Across the light's cone of brightness, Ahearn could not tell if R'aonsun had remembered to change his position as he fell back.

Low swift muttering resumed in the tunnel. "What are they saying?" Ahearn asked.

The prisoner sounded as though he might gag on every word. "They speak about alchemy. About mancery."

"Theirs, again?"

"Yes. But they are cautious. They assume you have resources they do not know."

Ahearn nodded, leaned in the direction he'd last seen Elweyr—or rather, the cloak that had hidden his invisible body. "Hsst! Elweyr! Word from our captive."

Ahearn started when Elweyr's voice whispered from only a few feet away. "I heard."

"Blast it! What are you doing here?"

"Moving to a new position. And keep your voice down."

"And what's wrong with your first—?"

"I acted from the first position. Could have been seen. We certainly saw *their* numbers."

Ahearn nodded. "They'll play their high card now or not at all. Not enough of 'em left for anything else." The muttering in the passage fell silent.

"Any moment, now," Elweyr predicted. "I've already given the sign for Umkhira and R'aonsun to stand farther back. And Ahearn, remember: you don't go closer than this."

"But if you're—!"

"We talked about this. You agreed."

Without liking it a bit, damn you. Ahearn nodded. "Be where yeh must." He had no way of knowing when Elweyr drifted off; the unguent worked like a chameleon's skin, so long as one didn't move too abruptly. And, since the thaumancer was unclothed, there was no rustling of cloth or tapping of boots on stone.

Ahearn heard the murmuring resume...then abruptly realized it was too singsong to be speech. It was more akin to what he'd heard some austere monks do...

"Wetgut, that drone: that is *mantichant*."

"It's what?"

The captive's voice was impatient. "Our mantics achieve focus through repetition and voice, not writings."

Ahearn nodded, moved farther out of the passage's line of sight, considered switching to his bow...but never got a chance to finish the thought. The mantichant increased tempo a moment before two stealthy steps came closer to the entrance—out of which a vial flew, tumbling end over end. It smashed just beyond the limit of the oil. In the instant that it did, the droning abruptly ceased and a flame-flecked explosion spewed vapor in every direction. And then seemed to explode a *second* time.

But no, that wasn't what happened; it was more like the force of the blast doubled in the first instant of its expansion. As a result, it produced twice the flame, twice the noise, and although not twice the smoke, the fumes expanded so quickly that a full-sized cloud appeared in the blink of an eye.

The greasy reek of the carrion was no longer the only scent in the chamber; a sharp new smell, like acid and rancid almonds, cut through the stink. The odor was vaguely familiar—from working with *hsitsé*, Ahearn realized. He didn't even think of running, but barely kept himself from leaning into a first, sprinting step away from what he knew—*knew*—were lethal fumes.

As abrupt as the burst of smoke, a sharp, icy crackle echoed out of the passage, as if the air in it had frozen and broken. A brief wave of intense cold radiated from the entrance—but was gone in the same instant that Ahearn felt it. Instead, a stiff, outgushing gust pulled the deadly cloud to a stop and then back out into the passage itself.

Ahearn almost cried out in surprise as he realized what had happened; Elweyr had cast some strange thaumate into the passage, one that caused such a sharp drop in temperature that the difference in pressure was sucking the hot, poisonous cloud straight back at the dry-men who'd created it. Their panicked shouts confirmed their realization that, if they stood their ground, they would become the victims of their own attack.

As the sharp, dangerous smell rapidly diminished in the chamber, Elweyr's cloak was snatched into midair. The next moment, his readied kit was yanked off the ground and came bobbing toward Ahearn. The motion caused the thaumancer to become partly visible; a vague gray figure that became more solid the faster he moved.

Varcaxtan had been the first to see Elweyr's gear seemingly float into the air. He let loose one sharp, shrill whistle: time to go. As if answering that sound, the dry-men unleashed a final, verbal attack: hissed imprecations that had the cadence of profanities and which faded into the distance along with their footfalls.

Ahearn, bow drawn and ready to make reply to any unexpected movement from the other passages, fought a powerful instinct to abandon his post and press the advantage, to attack the enemy while they were still on their back foot. But in the very moment he struggled with that impulse, Varcaxtan approached with a knowing smile, repeating the words he'd muttered to Ahearn as they'd prepared their ambush: "We're fighting so we can escape. We only take risks that we must."

He patted Ahearn on the shoulder and led the others into the passage that their captive had deemed most likely to take them deeper. Ahearn stared after the Dunarran, annoyed. The dry-men might try to return as soon as the fumes subsided, and yes, Ahearn might be able to step out from the corner and put a shaft into a survivor or two, and yes, that might kill them or at least set them fleeing even faster.

But the other possibility was that they'd left behind some manner of trap, or, instead of charging back into the chamber, would wait for someone to pop around the corner and either put a hole in his gut, or send him to the Great Tract. And then, because Ahearn's friends wouldn't abandon him, *he'd* likely be the death of them all.

Meaning that the amiably insufferable old Dunarran had just proven himself that much more insufferable by being right yet again. So Ahearn stood rearguard as Elweyr sent his affined rat down one of the other passages, swaddled in their sanitary rags and carrying a smoking ember in its teeth. But rather than run after the others, Elweyr—marked by his floating gear—remained motionless.

"What are you waiting for?" Ahearn hissed at him.

"The longer the rat runs down that tunnel, the more

likely he is to continue doing so when I release the thaumate. Which I will do ... now." The cape and kit started jouncing forward to follow the others. Ahearn was right behind, shouldering his bow and snatching up his shield.

But only fifty feet in, the cloak dropped to the ground. Elweyr's swift hands—ghostly as his motion increased—rummaged in his pack and produced two smooth, onyx disks. He put one on either side of the passage, both snugged behind a small outcropping in the rough walls.

"What are you—?"

"Shhh," whispered Elweyr, whose hands moved far apart, reaching across the width of the tunnel. He extended his index fingers, one hovering over each of the stones, then tapped them both at the same instant.

Ahearn stared. "What in blazes are those?"

"*Velitæ.*" Elweyr translated when Ahearn shook his head. "Watch-stones. For a few hours, I'll know if something moves across the line between them. Or touches either one." The floating kit raised and the straps shifted—first one, then the other—to accommodate unseen arms.

"Well, that's new!" Ahearn sputtered as they hurried after the distant light of the bobbing Uulamantrene periapt.

Elweyr's voice suggested a smile. "Our sea voyages afforded me a lot of time for study ... and the manufacture of a few simple artifacts. Now, give me the light sphere; I need to adjust it, make it less bright. We don't want to attract unwanted attention."

CHAPTER FORTY-SIX

"We are safe now," their prisoner muttered, leaning against the smooth wall of the room they'd just entered.

And it was, indeed, a room. Every surface was well graded, carved out of the native rock with a degree of precision that Ahearn associated with official buildings of the Consentium. Well, more accurately, ruins of them: he'd never actually been under any roof raised by present-day Dunarrans.

Umkhira was also staring around at the perfectly flat surfaces and plumb-trued lines. "Would your people's warriors have chased us, had we not taken you?"

He considered. "Probably, but not with such determination. Particularly when they realized you meant to go to a place they fear."

S'ythreni looked up from where she was sitting against a wall. "And what place is that?"

"This." He gestured at their surroundings. "The uppermost reaches of the old city from before the Great Dying."

R'aonsun yawned. "*Which* 'Great Dying'?" When the dry-man stared at him, he sighed. "There have been several."

Their prisoner answered with a long, sideways glance. "Legend says that in this part of Mihal'j, where there is sand, there were once plains. And what are now plains were once jungles."

Ahearn frowned. "So, you mean the Cataclysm?"

"I have heard that word in my travels." The dry-man shrugged. "That may be one and the same as the Great Dying."

"I believe this construction dates from a later time," R'aonsun muttered. "The millennium after the Cataclysm was not quiescent. Other shocks—and 'Great Dyings'—followed. Not all arose from natural causes."

"Such as the one that may have caused Saqqaru to rise up out of the sea?"

Ahearn sighed. "I confess, I thought Druadaen more than half mad when first he spoke of that." He shook his head, glanced at the dry-man. "So you've heard of the Cataclysm and speak passable Commerce. You seem to have traveled a bit."

Another shrug. "I have. Including your own lands." He allowed himself a small, wintry smile in response to their stares and spoke in Midlander. "You see, I am *very* acquainted with Ar Navir."

Umkhira started. "Truly? And your presence there did not cause panic, or . . . or . . . ?"

"Or loathing?" he finished for her. "With care, it is quite easy to pass among your breeds. I traveled well cloaked. On those occasions when my body was seen—usually my arms—I was not attacked, merely shunned. We have learned that to all but those few who have actual knowledge of us, we appear to be afflicted with an especially grievous case of one of your wasting diseases. 'Leper,' is what I was most frequently called, even though the mottling of my skin hardly resembles the sores of that malady."

Cerven patted the perfectly straight wall. "So, are we now in the upper reaches of Zatsakkaz?" he asked.

"That is the word humans use for this place, now. But that is only the more recent name, for the more recent parts of it."

S'ythreni stood, frowning. "What do you mean by 'more recent parts'?"

"Just what I said, aeosti. This room was once at the top of an earlier tower around which Zatsakkaz was built."

Of all of Ahearn's companions, only the dragon seemed unsurprised.

Cerven spoke through a puzzled frown. "We were told that Zatsakkaz was built in an unpopulated area, in a place where there was no prior construction at all."

Their captive looked bored. "Your breeds have such short memories that I am not surprised the truth has fallen from memory."

Varcaxtan's voice was uncommonly sharp. "Then educate us about this earlier city. Who built it and what was it called?"

"Firstly, its name was Loësnum—"

"That's Old Amitryean," Cerven said with a frown.

"It may be. I do not know, and I do not care." The dry-man glanced at Varcaxtan. "Just as you don't seem to—even when it comes to matters of your own history."

Varcaxtan frowned. "I've no interest in your riddles. If you've something to say, say it."

"Remember," the other smiled, "I do so at your

request. I did not say that Loësnum was a city; you *presumed* that. I told you quite plainly that it was a *tower*."

Elweyr looked dubious. "So Zatsakkaz was built *long* after the tower?"

The captive glanced at him, lip curled. "Reportedly, human mantics are famed for their intelligence. That is apparently an exaggeration. Attend, fools: the tower began as a watch post for a larger structure that the ages buried. By the time your sand-crawling cousins decided to build Zatsakkaz, the tower was so weathered that they were able to convince others that it had been the first construction on the site."

"Because that way," Varcaxtan grunted, "they kept the secret—and value—of what was buried beneath for themselves."

"Obviously."

Ahearn crossed his arms. "And so what is this valuable buried secret, this Loësnum?"

"Oldest memory says it was a citadel of some kind."

"You mean, a fastness?"

The dry-man shrugged. "That, too, I suspect."

"Well, if that's but a small part of the tale, what is Loësnum *mostly* known for?"

A greater shrug accompanied his answer: "Wonders."

"Just that?"

He pointed at Elweyr and, more cautiously, R'aonsun. "You travel with mantics." His tone became derisive. "Surely *they* must know more than I do about such things."

"Mayhap they do," Ahearn asked, stepping very close to the dry-man. "But I'm asking *you*."

The prisoner swallowed—a sound like a cheese grater—and shook his head. "If I knew I'd tell you."

"So you're saying we just go down the stairs I see across the room, and we're at the top of this Loësnum?"

"Well...you would have been, in earlier times."

"Eh?"

"The ruins of Zatsakkaz are just beneath us, in a cavern."

"How is that possible?" Cerven asked. "We were told it was built on the surface!"

The dry-man nodded. "It was. But it was in a sheltering cleft, and once it was abandoned, sand filled it in. Later, the mountain against which it was built collapsed. Some say it was toppled to ensure that Zatsakkaz could not be rebuilt. Whichever it was, the city was buried, but the sand kept it from being crushed. However, whatever caused the mountain to fall upon it opened seams in the bedrock. They widened into crevasses and, over time, most of the sand drained into them."

R'aonsun's face brightened. "So you are telling us that, not far beneath our feet, there is a city sealed in a...a bubble within the rock?"

"I am."

"And that the tower of which this room was the pinnacle was broken? And that the section in which we stand is embedded in the roof of that bubble, whereas the tower's bottom still stands in the city below?"

The dry-man just nodded, wide-eyed at the dragon's inexplicable excitement and jollity.

Ahearn wasn't much less confused. "Eh, R'aonsun, why are yeh acting as if you're going to a spring revel?"

The avatar snorted. "I have no interest in spring revels—except possibly for scaring the crowds witless. Easy to accomplish, given how little wit they start with. But this? *This?* What a fabulous novelty!" When he realized they were all staring at him, he glanced at the dry-man and continued in a more guarded tone. "Bear in mind how much—living I've seen. How many unusual places. Eventually, it all becomes, well, repetitive. Mere variations upon a theme. And eventually, the variations themselves become familiar." His eyes widened, brightened. "But what this being describes? I've never seen its like. I've never imagined it! So by all means, let us not tarry here, but find a way down to this anomaly!"

The dry-man seemed unable to decide if the dragon-avatar's outré exclamations were the greatest sign of the group's insanity, or that none of its companions seemed terribly surprised by them.

"I agree," Elweyr said in a tone that had a hint of placation in it, "but before we resume our journey, I want two things."

"Which are?" S'ythreni asked, one corner of her mouth suggesting a smile.

"First, I want to sit, eat, and close my eyes for a few moments. And second"—Elweyr rounded on the captive—"I want to know why your people so fear Loësnum."

"That is not what they fear."

"Then what kept them from following you?"

He nodded at the space beneath their feet.

"Do you mean the ruins of the city or the way down to it?"

"Both. My people tell stories of great guardian beasts, warriors made all of metal, and demon ghosts who lure the unsuspecting into a garden of death."

Elweyr frowned. "And you believe these things exist?"

"Again, I did not say that. I said my people tell tales of foes that the ages should long since have turned to dust. Many believe those tales to be fact."

Ahearn crossed his arms. "Aye, and maybe you do, as well. I notice you haven't yet said that you believe the way before us is safe."

The dry-man nodded. "I do not say that because I cannot know it. Deep caverns are often the domain of creatures of great size, strangeness, and ferocity. So it would be unwise to deem them free of hazard. But like you, I have no choice but to see for myself."

"Is that the only way for you to escape the, eh, *Izrojagi* who wish to execute you?"

Their captive shrugged. "It is the only path that is said to offer another route to the surface. I would not survive an attempt to slip back through the caverns of the *Huzhkepbar Iz*. There are too many patrols, and they will all be watching for me."

Varcaxtan came to stand next to Ahearn. "Tell us about this other route to the surface."

"I know very little about it. It is said to rise up in the mountains to the south."

Cerven seemed to be visualizing the maps they'd studied aboard the *Swiftsure*. "That is a very long journey."

The dry-man nodded. "And dangerous, not the least because I do not know the way until I begin rising up through the tunnels beneath those mountains. But at least I will not have to worry about the *Huzhkepbar Iz*'s executioners."

R'aonsun approached him slowly, eyes unblinking. "And do you know the way down to the citadel itself?"

Despite himself, their captive shrank back. "I know

the approximate area." He paused. "For a skin of your water and a sack of your rations, I might be able to share some additional details."

The towering avatar let a slow smile spread across his face; there was no humor in it. "You're hardly in a position to negotiate."

The other failed to suppress a rasping gulp. "You can hardly afford to have your only guide's wits dulled by thirst or hunger."

"He has a point," Ahearn grumbled, tossing the dry-man paper-wrapped rations and a spare waterskin. "Now, start talking—and plainly, or this will be your last meal."

As they descended the stairs, a greenish-yellow glow grew beneath them. Before long, they realized what it was: the hole that marked where the top of the tower had broken off from the bottom. Nearing that jagged limit, they began to make out shapes in the dim light below: buildings, some intact, some ruined. But before they could pick out particular details, the stairs ended; at least two stories of risers had fallen, along with whatever had held them to the interior walls. They found only one way to continue; at the stairway's last landing, a crude tunnel had been hewn through the tower's wall into the same mass of rock that held it aloft.

The tunnel was short, coming out on a ledge that had been widened, enough to make Ahearn think of it as a gallery. Although he was comfortable with heights, his first look over the edge was accompanied by a moment of vertigo—and then, it was forgotten in the rush of wonder inspired by the scene far, far below.

Graceful towers stretched up toward him. Stately

buildings—some fronted by columns, others by immense arches—lined wide boulevards. In several places, ziggurats poked up over the tops of smaller houses of stone, the latter's glazed terra-cotta and polished slate shingles blurring into a busy mosaic. Glowing mosses covered the cavern's sides, which curved upward and toward each other until they met almost directly overhead in a peaked ceiling which ran the length of the valley-cavern. The soft light from that growth lay upon the scene as a yellowish twilight which hid flaws and smoothed any of the ravages that time might have wrought.

But closer inspection pierced that flattering haze. The many triumphant arches that sat astride the great ways, and the narrow, curving flyovers of alabaster, were all topped by dead moss and the rocky debris from the roof of this self-contained world. Several of the tallest towers, built in the form of narrowing spirals, had been battered by falling stalactites. In some cases, those stone icicles had come to hang so far down from the ceiling that they had touched and ultimately fused with the pinnacles of those towers. Ahearn marveled at the strange image; it was as if a mudflow had frozen upon touching the top of a narwhal horn.

The city beneath was no better. Alongside the broad avenues, medians that had once housed plantings were straggling graveyards of slender shoots that they'd sent across the streets, as fine and brittle as varicose veins. Stretches that had once been parks or parade grounds or other public places were now ruffled thatchworks of trees and bushes that had grown together in wild confusion before falling apart in desiccated decay. And at the far edges of Ahearn's vision, out beyond the proud

stone and brick building of the city's center, he could
just barely descry the fate of the less stoutly constructed
homes and shops of its outskirts: a great midden heap
of wood, mortar, and adobe so reduced by age that it
was nothing more than irregular gray piles that faded
into the darkness at the far reaches of the cavern.

"The architecture looks a bit like Tlulanxu," Varcaxtan murmured. "Especially those flyover walkways."

S'ythreni nodded. "Maybe that's why it reminded
me of old Uulamantre ruins." She expanded when
Umkhira tilted her head questioningly. "Dunarra's
capital—Tlulanxu—was originally Tlu'Lanthu, the only
great city that survived both the *Costéglan Iavarain*
and the Cataclysm."

Cerven's eyes, which had been scanning the entire
vista as if committing all of it to memory, shifted
his gaze to the decapitated remains of the tower just
beneath them. What was left of it stuck up like a hollow spike, the top ragged, the debris of the shattered
middle section surrounding its base like the waste pile
of a quarry. He aimed an index finger down at a point
just beyond its ruined skirts. "Is that a...a garden?"

Ahearn and the others craned their necks to follow
the implied trajectory. There was indeed an oasis in
that rough margin of broken stone. Spared from the
devastation as if by miracle, they could make out
trees and even a still, clear pond within its sharply
delimited borders.

"You've good eyes," S'ythreni breathed appreciatively.
"For a human." She and Cerven exchanged smiles.
"Interesting location, that garden."

"Better that we get to it than look at it," Ahearn
muttered. "Let's keep going."

CHAPTER FORTY-SEVEN

After the ledge bored back into the side of the cavern, it seemed to take them farther away from the city. Cerven offered a somewhat consoling explanation: Since they were just beneath the high spine of the long cavern, any tunnel would necessarily have to track outward to stay within the widening curvature of the walls until it came out level with the ruins of Zatsakkaz. So even though they seemed to be getting farther from their destination, they were probably on the shortest path to it. Cold comfort given that it meant more hours of walking in darkness.

Or, rather, near darkness: the cavern's ubiquitous glowing moss had sent colonies into connecting tunnels. Infrequent at first, they eventually became a sufficiently reliable source of light that the group no longer needed torches: arguably the surest way to warn potential adversaries of their approach.

Attempts to get more information from their captive proved even more frustrating than the long march.

He did reveal that his people gleaned most of their arms and armor, that their two-handed swords were both heirlooms and the minimum sign of wealth that a named family was expected to display, and that going much lower than the chamber in which they had fought was considered a deed of great daring. However, those deep places were also the only reliable source of old tools and weapons that were reworked to serve the needs of the dry-men. How they fed themselves in such a comparative barren underground, and how that might limit their population, were topics he managed to deflect, often by hastening their descent. Whether his exhortations to do so were a means of keeping them so active that there was no breath to be spared on more questions, or because he was genuinely convinced that they'd be hotly pursued was impossible to discern.

About an hour after the group had been able to douse their torches, the tunnel leveled off and, two turns later, opened into a true cave, the ceiling and walls verging away from them. At the end of it, there was the faintest hint of the same glow that had illuminated the ruins of Zatsakkaz.

Their prisoner breathed a deep sigh, pointed to the distant light. "There. We have arrived. I have done as you asked."

"You will have, once we get to that light," Ahearn answered. "Assuming the ruins are just beyond. Besides, doesn't your path lie with ours for a little longer, yet?"

"I cannot be sure. I only know that none of the tales associated with the passage to the south mentions going through the ruins. So I may need to go back to one of the fissures we passed during the past few hours."

"They're hardly wide enough to fit a man going sideways!"

"True, but that does not mean they do not lead to where I must go." He paused. "When we part, I ask that you return what is left of my garment."

Ahearn felt a momentary prick of regret. The dry-man was arrogant, rude, and a right bastard, but that didn't warrant sending him into the unknown without even a stitch of cloth to cover himself. The swordsman rustled around in this ready-sack, held out the sliced shift. "Here. No reason not to have it now." The dry-man bowed his thanks and began arranging the torn garment into a makeshift kirtle. As he did, Ahearn stepped closer to Varcaxtan. "I'm thinking our boy might have earned the right to walk along with us," he whispered, "rather than out in front like a staked goat."

Varcaxtan shrugged. "I suppose so."

Ahearn stared at the older Dunarran's utterly emotionless tone. "Yer mighty hard on this fellow."

Varcaxtan returned his stare. "He and his kind have been mighty hard to our kind, over the years."

Ahearn raised an eyebrow and stepped back to their captive, who was starting to move toward the front of the group as they prepared for what they hoped was the final leg of the march. "No need to blaze the trail, from here. Stay in the middle rank."

The dry-man's surprise was evident as he nodded. Perhaps with a hint of gratitude, Ahearn thought. *Or perhaps I'm just seein' what I'd like to, rather than what's there. Tract knows, it wouldn't be the first time.*

He took the lead with Umkhira; the dragon and S'ythreni were the rearguard. The mosses and bright end of the cavern made it easier to assess the way forward, but the light was so diffuse that it tended to obscure details. So later, when Umkhira signaled for a halt, she could not immediately be sure what she was seeing ahead.

She stepped closer to a wide depression that stretched across the width of the cavern.

"An obstacle?" Cerven asked from the middle rank.

"That remains to be seen," the Lightstrider answered.

Ahearn joined her and realized why her reply had been so cryptic.

The depression was littered with bones. Not just picked clean, but bleached. His time in the Under having given him a practiced eye for such remains, Ahearn knew them to be a mix of four-legged and two-legged creatures. But there was one typical detail that was strangely absent: no damage to the bones themselves. No teeth marks. No weapon cuts or scrapes. No splintering. It was almost as if they'd been swallowed whole, just like . . .

He spun. "Circle! Weapons pointing out!"

But there was already motion in the group. The dry-man had managed to drift backward out of the middle rank, was slipping between the momentarily distracted R'aonsun and S'ythreni. Moving past them, his eyes remained fixed on the kill pit to the front, wide with terror.

Which is why he did not see what Ahearn glimpsed over the captive's shoulder: the floor rising up soundlessly behind him as he turned to flee.

"The rear!" Ahearn shouted as he ran in that direction, sword out, eyes catching sight of a strange glistening streak on the wall. It started someplace among the rough angles and protuberances of the ceiling and ended at the point where the floor was still rising, even as the now sprinting dry-man turned toward it—and gasped.

With terrible abruptness, the chameleon color of the creature bled away, revealing its true color—a mottling of mauve and gray—and its true form. Almost four feet high and at least twenty long, it had the shape of an elongated pancake that tapered to less than half its height around its margins. There, stubby tentacles—or polyps?—were unfolding from its sluglike skirt, and just above them, small black dots—primitive eyes—ringed the creature's body. Which slid forward.

"Stay here!" Ahearn shouted as he passed Elweyr. His friend's unguent had become inert hours ago, and while the thaumancer was no slouch as a swordsman, that was not likely to be the role in which he might make his decisive contribution.

The dry-man turned to run to the front, eyes backcast at the horror—and bounced off the dragon-avatar's broad back. Even as he scrambled to his feet, the creature humped its back forward until that gathering mass erupted upward. It unfolded into a thick, tentacular stalk—the end of which opened to reveal an enormous eye. The dry-man's attempt to flee had frozen in midstep, his two eyes locked upon that of the creature.

Ahearn pushed Cerven hard to the side, yelling, "Flanks, flanks!" as he grabbed the still-recovering R'aonsun and tugged him out of the creature's path. And as he maneuvered around it—

The cyclopean eye began flashing like a watchtower's signal fire. Multiple layered irises opened and closed, glowing and then fading as they did, each a different color, faster and faster, until—

All at once, they went still—and collapsed inward, all the light appearing to rush down into a black pinprick—that instantly burgeoned to become the whole eye.

The dry-man spasmed hard, his joints cracking—and then fell lifeless.

Ahearn looked over as he got round the monstrosity's flank, saw the cyclopean protrusion shiver through a long, ecstatic blink—as if that was how it swallowed. "Flanks!" he yelled again. "Rear! Don't look into its eye!" He hacked at the polyps that reached out toward him, but a hand-and-a-half sword was awkward at such close quarters.

R'aonsun had reached the rear and delivered a two-handed cut from a high guard; it slashed a shallow seam in the rubbery flesh. S'ythreni had fallen further back and to the side of the cavern, from where she fired her ironpith crossbow. The quarrel—tipped with venom—disappeared into the flexible mass of the creature, which merely rippled like impossibly thick mud.

Varcaxtan had gone to the other flank with Umkhira who, following his lead, did not attack the body of the creature but hacked at the polyps; half a dozen had been sheared away, spraying ichor as they squirmed, but too many remained.

Ahearn had less room—the creature was closer to his side of the tunnel—but was busy cutting back the ones that were close enough to attempt to enfold him in their thick, writhing mass. And Elweyr—

Elweyr had just handed two vials to Cerven, who darted to the side. Averting his eyes and still five yards from the creature, he shouted, "Dragon?"

R'aonsun hacked again and shouted back. "Yes?"

"When it turns, show me."

"What do you mean?" The dragon stepped back: whether in surprise or to give himself enough room to comply with Elweyr's mad-sounding request, Ahearn could not tell. Not as if the polyps were giving him much chance to puzzle it out.

"You know of this beast, mantic?" R'aonsun roared, taking another step back.

"I think so. Stay to the side and show me what you see."

"You want me to—?"

But the creature, sensing attacks from all directions but the front, twisted the heavy tentacle around until it resembled a half-screw, the deadly eye sweeping across its rear. If it really *had* a rear; without changing facing, it flowed in that direction, swiftly orienting on the attackers there, the closest being the dragon.

R'aonsun's two surrogate eyes met the widening one of the creature. "I shall master it," he announced calmly.

"No!" Elweyr yelled. "Don't look straight into its eye! Just show me from the side!" But the dragon and the creature were motionless, staring at each other. Elweyr groaned, holding his head. "No, it will—"

"Do not fear; I shall not show you the last moment," the dragon shouted as the massive eye-extrusion reared back like a comically stubby cobra. The eye started spinning, glowing.

Gods, they're both *mad!* Ahearn hacked wildly at the polyps, but they were either insensate or of no individual consequence to the beast. The swordsman swung as fast and hard as he ever had, sometimes severing two at a blow, but it was like trying to cut through a waving thicket of rubbery worms, always stretching and retracting.

The monster's eye was a flashing pinwheel of bright colors—which plummeted to black.

But instead of that lightless pinprick expanding, the eye shuddered and blinked repeatedly, as if it had been hit with a dusting of salt.

The dragon staggered back, fell to a knee, steadied himself with one hand. The eye snapped open again—streaked with pulsing yellow-green veins—and slid toward him, raising its front skirt in an attempt to flow over the stunned avatar. The edges rippled upward and a nostril-biting smell filled the air as its underside was revealed: a fleshy sphincter dripping acid, lined by smaller, hooked polyps—all seeking blindly, hungrily. Varcaxtan leaped forward toward the dragon in a desperate running tackle to pull him aside—

A thunder clap—so loud it seemed to be a physical blow—brought everyone to a halt. Except Varcaxtan who, in that instant, managed to knock the dragon out of the path of the suddenly motionless creature.

Except, that is, for the eye, which turned back to the front, its multiple irises already starting to brighten, to spin.

Varcaxtan hauled the dragon to his feet, ran him over against the wall, moved to take his place at the rear of the creature, mowing down the polyps.

Ahearn glanced desperately at the Dunarran's progress—*not fast enough*—before swiveling his head back toward the front.

Elweyr, who had not moved, was half wreathed in smoke and lowering his arm. He'd thrown a vial of storm fluid just a few feet in front of him;

unfortunately its flash and thunderclap lacked any electric discharge. But Ahearn's friend obviously hadn't intended to wound the creature; he'd intended to get its attention. As the mist of the discharge began wafting away from his face, the thaumantic's eyes were hard on the monster's own.

Elweyr! No! was the thought behind Ahearn's wordless roar of warning. He sprang forward in an attempt to get on the creature's back, hew at the thick protrusion that held the eye aloft...but before his feet cleared its skirt, they were clutched by more than a dozen of the polyps. He fell on his elbows, only half on the top of the beast, unable to help as he watched his oldest and dearest friend face its utterly annihilating gaze.

But Elweyr was smiling and...counting? As the speed of the eye's flashing cycles reached its peak, the thaumancer's arms traced a great circle in the air before him, and with a sigh and a shimmer, a mirror appeared there: an utterly, impossibly, perfect mirror. From the side, Ahearn saw it reflect the creature's eye as it imploded to a single dark point—which instantly exploded into absolute blackness.

The eye, staring into itself, quaked like jelly. A spasm surged through the monster's body, throwing Ahearn clear. As it did, a noise that was partly the hoarse roar of an alligator and partly the squeal of a gored pig rose up from beneath it. The eye blinked, was suddenly still—and then burst. The entire creature collapsed, flattening into a low heap of viscous meat that began to stink and fume as if its acids were slowly consuming it from within.

As Ahearn scrambled back to the floor of the

cavern, he heard the unflappable "Uncle Varcaxtan" roar—actually *roar*—"You killed it? How?"

"*I* didn't kill it," Elweyr muttered. "*It* killed it."

"What?"

"For lack of a better explanation, I believe it just ate itself."

"Well, its own *anima*," Cerven added.

"You know what this is?" S'ythreni asked, impressed but also a little bit aghast.

"I believe we both do," he replied, glancing at Elweyr.

The thaumantic nodded. "There are stories of cryptigants created to suck the life out of thinking beings. And there are as many speculations about how they did that as tales of them." He looked at their already deliquescing attacker. "Frankly, I never believed a word of those tales. After all, how could such a thing be possible?" He smiled. "Now I've got something else to figure out. Unless, you can shed some light on it," he added, glancing at the dragon.

R'aonsun shook his head. "I cannot. At least, not yet. That was yet another, er, unique experience. I did not master the beast, but nor could it reach my mind. Or as young Master Cerven says, my *anima*. Mind you, I always considered that term—and concept—highly suspect. But now? Well, as with our thaumantic, I may have to revisit that conclusion. Not as enjoyable as the prospect of walking out into that city ahead of us, but stimulating, nonetheless."

Umkhira looked around the group. "So, do you think the dry-man meant to lead us here? He mentioned a soul-eating monster. Maybe this was his way to free—or even avenge—himself?"

Varcaxtan frowned, chin in hand. "We'll never know for sure, Lightstrider, but he was drifting back in the ranks even before you realized what was in that kill pit. And even before Ahearn here knew that we'd be facing anything but a typical denizen of the Unders."

"The bones were the giveaway," Ahearn nodded. "No way to be that clean without kerf- or teeth-marks. Like some of the horrors that dwelt beneath the Underblack." He turned on Elweyr. "But you! Where in all the hells did you learn to do *that*?" He imitated the circling motion with which his friend had summoned the perfectly reflective surface.

"Like I said earlier," the thaumancer replied with a sly, sideways smile, "long sea voyages give me a lot of time for study."

"Well, we have traveled on the ocean before," Umkhira pointed out, "but it has never resulted in such a change."

He nodded. "This is the first time I've had copies of the books from Imvish'al. They've shown me things I've never seen in any other codices...*couldn't* have seen in any other codices."

"'Couldn't'?" Ahearn echoed.

The dragon folded his tree-trunk arms. "Unless I am much mistaken, our increasingly formidable thaumantic has discovered parts of his art that were as long lost as the library itself."

Elweyr nodded. "Sometimes I find whole thaumates I've never even read about in the most obscure tracts...and believe me, I've read a lot of obscure tracts. But just as often, I find the missing pieces of constructs that did not come down through history intact. There's a whole class of these—called Lost Thaumates—which I've been completing. And then there are the theoretical and experimental treatises of the thaumancers of the pre-Cataclysm: books that are just names or are completely unknown, now." He shook his head. "It's been—well, I don't really have a word for it."

S'ythreni smiled. "Sounds like you're in the middle of discoveries as sweeping—and important—as Druadaen's."

"Aye, which got him disappeared to the great beyond, I'll remind yeh all!" Ahearn was only partly jesting. He wasn't about to lose any more mates to the problems that arose when folk uncovered what had been forgotten—or hidden—and was supposed to stay that way. "So don't you go flinging off these new, eh, thaumates right and left, now! Yer likely to attract all the wrong sorts of attention that way."

Elweyr's answering smile was crooked. "No worries, there, old friend. I may understand these new thaumantic constructs, but that doesn't mean I can keep them active for very long."

Varcaxtan nodded. "Your knowledge has proceeded beyond your *manas*. At least, I think that's the mantic axiom."

Elweyr nodded. "It is. And that's one reason why you won't see me use most of this knowledge frequently, not for a very long time."

"Ah, so you have to grow into your sorcerous britches, then!" Ahearn was able to sound lighthearted enough to conceal the relief behind it. Or so he hoped. "Well, there's no point standing around here watching as that mystic death slug—"

"It's an Eye of Oblivion, I believe," Cerven interrupted softly.

"—as that Eye of Oblivion finishes turning into a pool of malodorous goo. I'd much rather visit that garden we saw from on high. Who's with me?"

CHAPTER FORTY-EIGHT

They stood at the edge of the grass, silent and solemn. The only sound was a distant fountain chuckling softly, its basin angled so that the water fed the pond that fanned out from it.

Ahearn glanced at his feet; dust and dead moss clung to his boots. That mixture filled the ghostly streets of Zatsakkaz. The yellow light that had been so helpful to movement in the tunnels had become disquieting, even oppressive, as if it encouraged the decay of everything except for the moss and its jaundiced glow.

But within the perfectly circular world of the garden, there wasn't a hint of that bilious haze. It was a perfect half-sphere of clear, bright light which cast shadows that shifted with the slow progress of the unseen sun. None of the cavern's detritus spoiled its cool green lawn or had crushed its irises and lilies. Butterflies flitted back and forth between the flowers and the willows that seemed to lean toward the surface of the pond, as if mesmerized by their own reflections there.

"It's not real," Ahearn announced firmly.

S'ythreni stared sidelong at him. "Of course not."

Impatience got the better of him. "Well, if yer so eager to sound like a schoolmaster, teach us a bit then, hey? What's behind this? How could it be here after all this time?"

S'ythreni frowned, grumbled. "I'm no mantic, but maybe it's not so complex as it looks."

"No," Elweyr corrected gently. "It's *more* complex than it looks."

Umkhira frowned. "Explain, please."

Cerven was nodding as Elweyr replied. "Firstly, Ahearn's wonder at it being here at all is quite apt. This is a mantic effect. That means it is effected by a constant influx of *manas*. I know of no construct, not even from the cosmantic codices, that could sustain so great a flow for so long a time. And its design is not static."

Umkhira's sigh was slightly impatient. "Please, friend; I do not speak the language of wizards. Do you mean that because it moves, it is a more intricate creation?"

"An image that has no movement within it is a 'still' construct, the simplest kind," Cerven offered when Elweyr did not. "A 'static' construct moves, but only in a set pattern that continues until the effect is discontinued. But this? Watch the butterflies."

"I have been doing just that."

"In all the time you have, have you seen their movements repeat? In the slightest particular?"

Umkhira's brow rose. "No. It is as if they are alive, each beat of their wings different from the last."

Elweyr, tired by the day's many mantic exertions, gratefully nodded for Cerven to complete the explanation, who did so in the same patient tone with which he'd begun. "Designing a mantic construct to vary as much as life itself, and indefinitely, is very, very complex."

"Frankly," Elweyr added, "I have never even heard of a static design that followed a pattern a tenth as long as the time we've been observing this one. And it has yet to repeat in any particular." He shrugged; at the end, his shoulders drooped lower than usual. "When this day began, I'd have told you it was impossible. Yet here it is."

"Which delights me no end," the dragon murmured in an unusually reflective tone. "After having spent decades watching the same tiresome parade of events, I have seen three wholly novel things in a single day: this city, the Eye of Oblivion, and now a garden that is as ageless as I am." When he spoke again, it almost sounded as if he was speaking to himself. "For this alone, I am glad to have joined you, come what may."

Ahearn took it upon himself to break the silence that followed. "Well, having picked our way through the rubble surrounding this tower"—he glanced up at what was left of it—"and finding no way in, it seems that the way down to this Loësnum must be through this garden. But I've misgivings about what happens if, by stepping into it, we pop this mantic bubble."

Varcaxtan nodded. "You're not alone in that." He squinted into the pastoral scene. "I'm no mantic, but what I've seen suggests that a trespasser would disrupt the pattern. So given all the effort that was involved, it stands to reason that it must also have a way to repel intruders."

"That," Elweyr said, "is my fear, as well. But without knowing anything more about its creation or creator—"

"Perhaps," Cerven said quietly, "this might help." He was pointing at the ground just outside the faintly curved limit of perpetual perfection. "I saw an irregular shape through the dust." He toed a spot he'd cleared with his boot. "There is a legend here, written in an ancient forerunner of the modern language of northern Mihal'j. But it does not make any sense to me."

"What does it say?" asked S'ythreni, leaning over to look at the strangely whorled script.

"'Where we met.' There was another, similar phrase, but the last word was pulverized, probably by falling debris. What's left reads 'Where time...'"

"'Where time ended.'" Elweyr finished in a haunted voice. "I know this place. My mother"—he had to pause before continuing—"my mother told me fairy tales about a garden where a great wizard and a wise princess met, married, and ultimately watched the world end." He stared at the garden, eyes wide. "Is this just coincidence? I mean, can small, ancient events really live on through so many ages as...as a fairy tale?"

"They can," R'aonsun answered with finality. "The details are lost, but your species holds on to lives and deeds that embody your essential values." His voice became a mumble. "It is one of your redeeming features."

Ahearn wondered if the dragon had hit his head at some point, or if his face-to-face bout with the Eye of Oblivion had damaged his sarcastic wit. But perhaps it was also a consequence of dwelling in human form for so long. *Harder to taunt a folk when it's one of their faces you see in the mirror every day.* He shook off that notion and squared his shoulders. "Right. Well, unless the fairytale says anything about how to enter the garden, there's really only one way to find out." He started undoing the buckle of his baldric; if the 'construct' somehow had a mind of its own, then any weapon might be seen as ill intent. At any rate, Ahearn suspected it would be useless once he stepped over the boundary. But before he could finish removing his gear, he felt a hand on his shoulder; he turned.

Varcaxtan's smile wasn't just one of a fond uncle, but a husband torn between despairing grief and desperate hope. "No, lad: this is for me to do. And save the objections you're readying. I'm the one to make this appeal, or to suffer the consequences for trying."

Before Ahearn could object, the Dunarran had handed his weapons off to the dragon and moved to the edge of the garden. He advanced a finger over the boundary...

The sunlight darkened, taking on an orange tint. Not the color of a setting sun, but of fire, as if the garden and the city around it was on the verge of bursting into flame.

Varcaxtan paused until the change had finished, then eased his whole hand in.

The orange light roiled, as if beams of the unseen sun were being riven by the liquid wavering of heat mirages. As red flecks appeared in it, one of the nearby butterflies abruptly became jet black and approached his hand. It did not alight on his finger—the one with his vow-band—but hovered, though the wings were beating too slowly to have kept a real insect aloft. For several long moments it remained there...

Its former colors flooded back into it and it flew off, even as the unseen sun's light became less agitated and angry. It mellowed but never quite returned to the bright, clear hue they had seen as they approached. The faint tint of orange left Ahearn with a purely subjective impression that conveyed a wary warning, but not an actual threat.

Very slowly, Varcaxtan stepped across the threshold. The orange deepened, but faded again when he did not advance any further. He hung his head as he started. "I would that I had never needed to see this place, friend. That I never had to come here to disturb it, to trouble the memory you left here. Not for posterity but as a testament to each other, a love you meant to defy mortality and time itself: to say, 'this one I loved beyond all else. Beyond wealth, beyond works, even beyond words.'"

Varcaxtan lifted his head. "I do not belong here. I want to turn about and leave your garden untroubled, leave this place where both your worlds became one. And ended as one. There's nothing I wish more than that . . . except to save my own love.

"I wish I knew your love's name. Mine is named Indryllis. She's my heart and my all. They say she's alive, but by now, she may be dead or, worse yet, adrift in some Limbo. All I know is that I will find her or die trying."

He put out his arms in supplication. "I don't know if there's something here, listening to my voice, or not. And if there is, whether you can understand my words, or feel my feelings, or simply know whether I mean harm or not. I only ask this: whatever or whoever you are—or were—I hope you feel a kindred spirit in me, not a despoiler, and so, shall let me pass."

For a moment, the only sound was the distant

burble of the fountain. But then the leaves rustled; a faint breeze went through them with a soft rush. Which built into a wind that bent the branches as the sunlight darkened into a sullen orange.

"It's going to kill him," Elweyr muttered, hands raising into a pattern that drew a thaumate from his memory, complete and ready for creation. Umkhira had her axe out. Ahearn drew his sword and he brought the point up. *For all the good it'll do.*

But R'aonsun stepped between them and the limit of the garden. "No."

In the moment he stayed them in place, the orange light darkened into an apocalyptic red. Dark shadows of absent clouds scudded across the tableau as the rising wind bent the tips of the willows to dab at the frothing surface of the pond. The shadows and the red light merged, burgeoned, filled the garden so that there was nothing in it but a tempest of light and shadow... and the solitary form of Varcaxtan.

"Damn you, wyrm, he'll be—!"

"Hold, I say." R'aonsun's voice was strangely calm.

The gathering storm did not rush over Varcaxtan, but broke, swirling around its own core, stretching upward. As it breached the top of the garden's limit, it coalesced into a vague figure of sable and scarlet, roaring like an approaching tornado. The outline of a head emerged from that ominous shape, in which two blazes of white light existed long enough to register as eyes, angry and sorrowing...

Before the image folded in upon itself and faded, as if made of dust motes blown asunder by an unfelt breeze.

Varcaxtan stood, head bent. The garden was gone.

In its place was what, obviously, had been there all along; a barren circle made of a single, smooth expanse of stone—or possibly, a cement so fine that it rivaled the kind found in a few Consentium ruins.

Directly across from them, a metal gate hung askew in the side of the tower. Beyond it was a darkness that seemed to bend down and away from the pervasive yellow glow.

"I suspect," the dragon said quietly, "that is the way to Loësnum."

As Ahearn stood, arms akimbo, surveying the long, precisely cut stone receptacles of the moon-plate repository, he could not help but be impressed. Given how long they had traveled and sought this archive, it and the final descent had proven quite anticlimactic.

The moment they pushed beyond the hanging gate, it was clear that if any explorers or creatures had reached this place since the creation of the garden, they had left no trace of themselves. Even the dust and debris of Zatsakkaz had not managed to find its way to this precisely constructed but austere interior, where a staircase—a match for the one they'd descended earlier—led down into blackness. Periapt out, torches in one hand and weapons in the other, they readied themselves for whatever might lie ahead. Yet, despite their prodigious and dire imaginings of what that might be, none of them foresaw the true strangeness of what they discovered:

Absolutely nothing. From the first step, they encoun-. tered no sign of trespass or habitation, only a patina of dust. No debris from above, no remains, not even any signs of leakage. And if the extraordinary regularity of the steps made them easy to descend in the near dark, they also became dreadfully monotonous. After four hundred, Ahearn stopped counting.

Much later, they arrived at a landing in the shape of a hexagon. One side accommodated the end of the staircase, the other five presented wide, identical doors, one of which was ajar. The sai'niin ring pulsed in its direction, so they rearranged themselves to enter.

It was a worrisome maneuver, insofar as the opening was barely wide enough for them to slip through sideways, and the door itself could not be moved. It was, if Ahearn recalled the correct term, a pocket door: one which slid in and out of a reservoir, or "pocket," built into the wall. But whereas they were usually reserved for lighter constructions, this door was a heavy slab fashioned from more of the smooth stone used throughout the tower. Because they could not widen the aperture, even a small number of indifferently trained and equipped defenders could make it a deadly business, indeed.

But the tense, whispered debate Ahearn and the others had over the best way to enter proved extraneous. There were no mysterious guardians, no metal soldiers, no traps. Just row after row of the chest-high stone sarcophagi, filled with moon plates. Even those weren't protected or locked; the metal plaques were arrayed vertically in slots carved into the brutishly plain rectangular boxes. Elweyr muttered that it looked like a library's worth of basalt shelves had been tipped over on their backs. But to Ahearn, the Repository of Loësnum resembled nothing so much as a painfully austere mausoleum.

Cerven immediately discovered that the work of

finding the desired moon plate would prove much easier than feared. Unlike other archives and libraries—even those still in use, and with attentive staffs—the plates themselves were organized not by subject or scholar or even date. Rather, each had a different code incised on its top: a string of numbers that matched those which Mirroskye's loremasters had conjectured to be a filing system. And, because the repository had not been rifled by fortune-seekers, or gnawed by vermin, or ruined by damp or heat, the plaques were not only completely legible, but still arrayed in numerical order.

Cerven located the master list of osmotia within five minutes, called for steady light, and dropped into the trance that was a near approximation of *fullsee*. After ten minutes, he leaned back.

"What did you learn?" asked Elweyr eagerly.

The Amitryean frowned. "Many names, but not many details. But enough to discern which additional plaques we might want." He yawned, looked around at the dimly lit walls. "Such a pity that there's no way for us to carry more than a few out."

Ahearn raised an eyebrow. "I'm sweating at the mere thought of us each carrying one. Like bars of gold, they are."

"No more than a quarter that weight," the young man replied with a puzzled frown.

"Yer a scholar," Ahearn replied through a sigh, "so I'm supposing you're acquainted with the phrase, 'a figure of speech,' yeh?"

Cerven may have blushed; it was hard to tell in the faint light. "Apologies." He waved at the moon plate he'd been hovering over. "Sometimes it takes a while to return to a . . . a regular state of mind." He rose.

"I'll set about finding those plaques I mentioned." As soon as he was out of earshot, most of the others turned a brief glare or frown toward Ahearn.

He stared back. "What?"

"Boor," S'ythreni hissed as she stalked off.

"What? Lad is too precious to take a joke?" he whispered after the aeosti.

As the dragon turned his back on the exchange, his chin and nose a bit higher than usual, Elweyr slipped an arm around his friend's much wider shoulders. "Give it up, Ahearn. You lost that debate before it started. You were only a little bit of a turd, but *he's* a lovable innocent."

"I'm lovable!" It didn't sound that convincing, but had he claimed to be "innocent," Ahearn knew it would have elicited barks of laughter.

Elweyr only chuckled. "Oh, yes. Certainly. Lovable as a puppy, you are. Now, down to business: what's the watch rota? It's been a long day. Besides, you need extra sleep."

"Me? Why?"

Elweyr's grin was very wide and slightly malicious. "To keep the lovable, boyish twinkle in your eye."

Ahearn stalked off. A few minutes later, the rota was set. Cerven was not included when it became obvious that either the day's physical demands, his fixed focus upon the plaques, or both had exhausted him. As soon as he'd finished half a ration, he wrapped himself in his sleeping roll and was asleep in seconds.

The positions from which any pair on watch could best protect the five that were asleep were at either end of the repository. Because the opening was so narrow, a skilled fighter was stationed near the half-open door. The other person on that watch was selected for their ability to attack at distance, and so, was perched upon one of the receptacles at the far end of the chamber, ready to force any intruders to duck back and reconsider. By then, hopefully, the fighter watching the opening would have roused the rest of the company with kicks, curses, or anything else that might make them scramble to their feet.

Ahearn relieved Umkhira as the door guard at the start of the second watch, heard some hushed conversation at the far end, where Varcaxtan was relieving S'ythreni. Gesturing for Umkhira to stay alert a minute longer, he moved back to the post at the other end of the chamber. But instead of finding either of them watching the door from the top of the last receptacle, they were both standing in front of the rear wall. "What gives?" he muttered.

S'ythreni pointed at the wide slab of stone. "Something's in there, scratching."

"Beneath us, too." Varcaxtan added. "I think."

Ahearn listened. "Too soft for me to hear, I suppose."

The aeosti shook her head. "It was just a moment, when I hopped down from the receptacle and moved close to the wall. But nothing since then."

Ahearn frowned. On the one hand, it was just some vague scratching. On the other hand, they hadn't encountered so much as a cockroach since descending from the illusionary garden. "I don't like it."

Varcaxtan's frown was a match for his own. "Nor do I, but there's no way to learn more about it, not without having the means to pull apart the walls or floor."

Ahearn nodded. "Aye, but at the first hint of more scratching—"

"I'll sound the alarm."

But the watch passed without the faintest sound or disturbance. At its end, Ahearn jostled R'aonsun to replace him, and then Elweyr to replace Varcaxtan. He unfurled his sleeping roll and had just slipped his feet back into it when Elweyr shouted from the rear wall—not words, but a cry of alarm.

Words were hardly necessary, though. Even at the other end of the room, Ahearn could hear the groan from the back wall, which was almost immediately joined by a vibration that ran the length of the room. He was already on his feet, sword in hand, when the sound became motion, as well.

The entirety of the back wall was lowering into the floor, rasping as it went.

"Uncle," the swordsman shouted over his shoulder, sprinting for the rear, "defend the door with the dragon. The rest: with me!"

He ran past Elweyr—whose hands were alive with the motions of calling a thaumate to mind—and stopped at the edge of the new opening, sword in a high guard as the wall finished sinking into the floor. The others gathered to his flanks, ready to attack, lights aiming at the widening gap.

They showed a broad ramp, large enough for a small wagon, leading upward at a gentle angle. As in the tower itself, there was no sign of any creatures, their spoor, or their remains. And if there was a bit more dust, there was still no sign of leakage.

They waited for any further hint of sound or movement. There was none, except for a gentle inward breath of air; it was slightly warmer in the space that had been revealed.

After a full minute of waiting, S'ythreni muttered, "And now what?"

"Good question." Ahearn considered the options. So long as the damned door had been in place, they'd no need to worry about attack from that direction. Now, in a trice, they were exposed at either end. *On the other hand—*

As if awakened by the mere thought of the word "hand," the sai'niin ring pulsed toward the opening.

Ahearn nodded. "We go up."

"What?" asked half of the others in a ragged chorus.

Ahearn held up the hand with the ring. "Apparently, this is the best path toward Druadaen. Besides, it's that or try to finish sleeping with an opening to front and rear. Frankly, even without the ring's say-so, I'd have been ready to give this ramp a try. It's the only way we've seen to leave these damned caverns without going through the dry-men again. Or has someone seen a better way back up to the surface?"

The group was silent; most shook their heads.

"Well, then: half a sip, weapons out, and then a morsel as we move. Let's see where this ramp leads. And who knows? Maybe this lazy ring will show us the fastest way to the *Swiftsure!*"

CHAPTER FORTY-NINE

Captain Firinne waited until her master-at-arms had closed the door to the great cabin before scanning the faces crowded around the tables she'd had brought in. Her eyes stopped their slow circuit when they came to Ahearn's. "Well, it's about time."

"You've been as patient as a monk," the swordsman said in genuine appreciation. "But this is the very soonest we could tell our tale."

She folded her arms and leaned back in her chair. "Why?"

"Well, as mad as it might sound, it wasn't until yestereve we actually knew how it would end."

She frowned. "The only reason I don't dismiss that as pure rubbish is because you obviously understand that's just what it sounds like. And because the rest of the long faces around you look like those of mourners, not swindlers."

"Well," Ahearn allowed, "you're right that we have reason enough to grieve."

"Grieve who? You're all here, so none of your company has died."

"Yet," added Varcaxtan with a sigh.

She stared at him in frank surprise, after mastering a brief look of worry. "So is it you who has the story to tell?"

"The story," Umkhira said respectfully, "is ours, all equally. As is the path before us."

The captain studied their faces again. "I've waited two weeks. You've spent most of them closeted away, muttering among yourselves. And you must have observed that I'm not one to pick up passengers—no matter how well known or liked—without having a full report of what kind of cargo, or trouble, is coming aboard with them." She turned back to Ahearn. "Convince me that I haven't been a sorry fool for setting aside a rule that's stood me in such good stead for so many years."

Ahearn nodded, sighed. "What did Tharêdæath tell you about why we were journeying to Mihal'j?"

"Not a gods damned thing. And I could tell that asking wouldn't get any answers. Besides, I trusted you lot."

Ahearn winced at the past tense: *trusted*. "Fair enough. And no surprise he didn't tell you aught of our purposes."

"Were they...unsavory?"

As Ahearn fought against a grin at her prim tone, Varcaxtan answered. "They were of a delicate nature."

Firinne stared at him in renewed surprise. From the look they exchanged, it was clear that this was almost a professional code for a matter which the Consentium would deem both important and sensitive. "Indeed," she said.

Varcaxtan merely nodded.

She turned back to Ahearn. "And how did you become involved in such a venture?"

He shrugged. "Trying to find Druadaen."

She nodded. "I see," she said, but her tone made it sound more like "Of course." Firinne leaned forward, steepling her hands. "Given where we picked you up, I presume things did not go well?"

"Oh, they went well enough, just not the way we planned. But knowing when you were due back in Pawnkam, we also knew when and where to watch for *Swiftsure*'s sails. We'd only been waiting on the coast a few days before you hove into view."

"Why there?"

"Well, it wouldn't have done for you to go to Pawnkam itself."

She almost smiled. "Don't you mean it wouldn't have done for *you* to go to Pawnkam, again?"

Umkhira leaned forward. "We did nothing wrong. We were ambushed, well outside the city. But there was reason to suspect that we would be held without cause and required to pay fees we did not owe and acquire pardons we did not need." She sat back. "Pawnkam's officials are without honor. More so than in most human cities."

"I see," Firinne murmured. "But I still haven't heard anything about this 'delicate matter.'" Her eyes flicked toward Varcaxtan for a moment.

Ahearn drew a breath: *now or never.* "Well, we were set on grabbing a special moon plate from the ruins of a forgotten city named Zatsakkaz."

Firinne jerked upright as if she'd been stuck by a pin. "What do you know of such things?" Her eyes went sideways toward Varcaxtan again, but this time, in alarm.

Varcaxtan extended a calming hand. "They recovered some moonfall plaques while shipmates with the Uulamantre." When the captain's eyebrow rose, he expanded, "They were sailing to assist in the rescue of the Hidden Archivist."

She looked away from her countryman and surveyed the group as if through new eyes. "Well, that explains much," she murmured. "But I must ask, Varcaxtan: should you—or any of your group—be talking to me about these . . . these objects?"

"You mean the 'objects' for which you have explicit special orders?" He smiled at her widened eyes. "I've traveled on too many Courier ships, or those with similar remits, not to know that their captains *have* to know of them. Because you are tasked to always be on the watch for them."

"So you will also know that I can't speak to the accuracy or inaccuracy of those assertions."

"Of course not. But we can speak hypothetically, can't we? As if my words *were* accurate?"

Firinne looked very much like she was about to squirm in her seat, but to her credit, she didn't. "I am not aware of any order which would preclude such a conversation. Particularly if it allows me to gather what the propretors might consider useful information."

It was Ahearn's turn to straighten in his chair. "Wait: you mean to report us . . . er, this conversation? To your superiors?"

Firinne's look made it quite clear that she had significant doubts whether, at that particular moment, Ahearn's intelligence exceeded that of a flounder. A very stupid flounder. "I am not required to report hypothetical conversations about hypothetical topics."

"Ah," Ahearn said. "Right. Well, then, I reck you'd like a quick sketch of what we ran into once we found Zatsakkaz?"

"No. I want the full story."

That unleashed a reasonably complete recounting of their underground journey. Except for a few points where she asked for details that were most properly Cerven's province, Ahearn and the others told the tale up to the point where they started their return to the surface. "After we made our way across a bone-dry catch basin for runoff, the ramp began to show itself worse for wear. Sand had found its way in and there were cracks starting in every surface. Two were passable fissures: fortunate, since at the next catch basin, the shaft was filled in with sand. But the wettest of the fissures brought us up into some low hills halfway to the coast." He did not include that the sai'niin ring's meaningful pulses had dispelled any doubt about the fissure's safety, nor that it had aimed them at a particular point on that coast. "We made that trek over three days and settled in to wait for you."

"You are lucky you did not die of thirst."

S'ythreni shrugged. "We filled our skins with water in the fissure, husbanded it carefully, found a small oasis just a league inland from the point where we signaled you with Elweyr's light sphere."

"And in code no less," Firinne added. She looked at Varcaxtan. "You, of course?"

He smiled. "I'm old, not senile. Yet."

She smiled back—and Ahearn saw her feeling for the Dunarran light her eyes for the briefest instant… before she abruptly extinguished it. "So, why did you not tell me all this when we took you aboard? Why the mystery and silence?"

Cerven leaned forward with a glance at Ahearn, who nodded. "Captain, as Ahearn said, the last, crucial part of our story was not yet settled. Specifically, we knew that the outcome, and our next destination, would both be dependent upon what we learned in the process of deciphering the list of osmotia. However, between trips to the oasis for water, lying in wait for game, fishing as best we could, and keeping watch for the *Swiftsure*'s sails, I did not make much progress prior to your arrival. And once I had the time to examine them more closely—"

"You are a scriverant?" she asked, her surprise supplanted by a settled nod even as the word left her lips.

"I am, Captain, but as my age surely indicates, I am but a journeyman in my abilities."

"His skills proved far beyond his years," the dragon said in a tone that established he would brook no debate.

Cerven may have blushed slightly before he rushed on. "The moonfall plaque presented unforeseen challenges. We had anticipated that many of the names would be unknown to us, but the reality was much more difficult. With only a few exceptions, the named locations are either completely unreachable now, or completely forgotten.

"But more troublesome still, the great majority of the entries were identified only by a code: three long numerical strings for which we had no key. However, after a certain amount of trial and error, we ultimately recognized them as positional coordinates."

"*He* ultimately recognized them as coordinates,"

S'ythreni corrected with a small grin. "The rest of us just stared like dazed cows. But it's what he did next that was truly inspired."

Cerven, flustered, was unable to rebut her praise or continue the story before Varcaxtan took up the tale. "It seems our scriverant is highly accomplished in the high mathematics of three-dimensional objects."

It took Firinne a moment to process that. "You mean, the ones from which our navigation charts were originally derived?"

Varcaxtan nodded at Firinne. "He knows those arcane formulae—and can calculate them without picking up chalk or abacus. In this case, while the rest of us were still trying to grasp what he'd explained to us, he scanned the list for place names we still know, plotted their coordinates, and compared those positions to their actual locations in the here and now." He snapped his fingers. "Exact matches, every one of them."

Firinne glanced from him to Cerven to Ahearn. "That's why you asked to make tracings of my navigation charts. You made an overlay to confirm that it was a coordinate system for the entirety of Arrdanc's surface." She stared at Cerven as if he had transformed into a rare creature out of legend. "Such a detailed system was rumored to exist before the Cataclysm, but attempts to rebuild it, even by the greatest scholars of the First Consentium—came to naught. The amount of measurement required . . ." She shook her head. "What you have discovered—and reconstructed—could be extremely useful."

If Cerven heard the awe behind her words, he gave no sign of it. "Perhaps, but in their kindness, my friends have neglected to tell you where my efforts faltered. As I mentioned, there were *three* numerical strings for each entry. But positional coordinates only use two values. I have been unable to solve the mystery of the third."

"Could it be elevation?" Firinne wondered aloud.

Cerven nodded. "That was my first thought also, but after much trial and error, I cannot find any way to make it successfully function as such. Besides, there is a fundamental impediment to checking any such conjectures."

"Which is?"

"All coordinate systems must have a zero value. On the sphere, deriving that from the coordinates of the known locations was fairly simple—"

Umkhira and S'ythreni both rolled their eyes at his dismissal of that feat. The dragon just smiled.

"—but if the third numerical string is indeed a third axis value whereby elevation, volume, or curvature can be measured—"

Ahearn rubbed his eyes, fearing the onset of another of the headaches brought on by Cerven's explanations.

"—it does not conform to the distance scale of the first two coordinates."

"Wait; what?" Firinne said.

Elweyr sighed. "You'll see what he means. Eventually."

Firinne nodded. "So...so, you arrived at a distance scale by plotting the known locations on the maps, and comparing the separation between those coordinates to the physical distances between them."

Cerven nodded encouragingly. "Yes, but it made no sense when applied to the third coordinate set. None at all. In fact, some of the third set of values were negative."

"So...a subterranean location, perhaps?"

"Again, that was my first thought, but more problems intruded. Firstly, the two dimensional coordinates that I plotted on the globe follow the convention of all such calculations: they presume a perfect sphere. However, if one *adds* a third axis, what would the zero value be?"

"The level of the sea?" Firinne postulated.

"I thought that, too. So I calculated the elevation based on that assumption, and using the same distance scale. That is where I encountered impossible results. There was so little variation among those third axis values that no change in elevation was greater than four hundred yards: a mere fraction of the height of most mountains." He frowned mightily. "No. I am missing something, and we should not proceed until I have determined what it is."

Firinne leaned forward. "But does that third string of numbers truly matter? The first two have shown where all of the osmotia are located."

Elweyr raised a finger. "Cerven's concern is not unwarranted." Firinne's gaze invited explication. "I'm the source of his worry. It's a mantic matter that is either one of the most confounding—or well-guarded—secrets of all the arts."

"And it is—?"

"Changing connections between osmotia, or any other kinds of portal."

Firinne looked around the circle of faces. "I wasn't aware there *are* other kinds of portals. And I never imagined they could be, er, changed."

Elweyr nodded. "It is not undertaken lightly."

"It must consume a great deal of . . . what do you call it? *Manas?*"

The thaumantic tilted his head. "That is more a problem with *creating* a portal. Changing one requires great knowledge and precision . . . and the price of failure can be considerable."

"And how does this relate to the mysterious third string of numbers?"

Elweyr leaned forward. "Most portals have very precise properties. The most delicate of them indicates how they are situated in both the physical world and those which may lay beyond. The few mantic constructs designed to change their connection by altering those properties. They are also the most elaborate of constructs, requiring centuries or millennia of research, followed by exhaustive testing by trial and error. Which is often fatal. So is learning to use them, even once a construct has been proven to work and remain stable.

"Much of the danger lies in our imperfect knowledge of the cosmos and how its various domains interact with each other. But it is possible—likely, even—that when all these osmotia were created, knowledge of their properties was more complete." He shrugged. "So it's possible that the third string of numbers may refer to factors that are not restricted to the physical world, or may not refer to it at all."

"Well." Firinne's frown had deepened. "What else *could* it be?"

Elweyr sighed. "I suspect it's actually a . . . a compressed record of the properties of each gate, properties one would need to know in order to manipulate them." Elweyr paused, raised his hands as if seeking an answer from above. "If so, trying to change them without that information might be impossible . . . or worse."

Firinne frowned. "Wait: you do not mean to merely

use the osmotia, but *change* them? I mean no disrespect magister, but are you . . . adequately prepared for such a task?"

"No, and that's what worries me, because from what I have read, these older osmotia seem to be more complicated than the ones crafted with today's cognates. That's likely to make them much more dangerous."

Firinne nodded, re-steepled her fingers. "So, I hear two reasons why you feel the list has not given you a clear path forward. Firstly, all of them have a third set of values which could mean that they are not exactly where the first two coordinates indicate. And secondly, you cannot determine if it is safe to attempt to manipulate any of them without understanding exactly what that third set of values refers to."

Ahearn leaned forward. "That's the main of it."

"So why did you plead for me to set a northerly heading? Happily, I was already bound that way, but it was unsettling when you wouldn't tell me why you were making that request. Or why you couldn't tell me 'for a week or two.' If it was anyone but you lot who'd asked me to take it all on faith, I'd have surely said no. And maybe put you overboard."

She paused, then glanced at Varcaxtan, even though her voice remained pitched toward the whole group. "But you knew I would trust you."

He nodded. "I did not know, but I hoped."

"More to the point," Ahearn added, "from the very start of our hopping from continent to continent and back again, you've always been a fast friend to us. Even when we didn't ask. Even when it meant altering your route to help us on our way to find Druadaen, which must have earned a few frowns from the high and mighty back in Tlulanxu. Bloody hells, how could we *not* trust you?"

"Fair enough," she replied, "but answer me now: why northward?"

Ahearn shrugged. "Because we've but one person who might be able to solve some of the mysteries before us: Shaananca." *And because the damn bloody ring is pushing in that direction.*

Firinne's eyes had widened at Shaananca's name. "Well, from what I know of her, if she cannot answer your questions, I doubt anyone can." The captain frowned. "But I do not know how you plan to contact her. Surely you do not mean to go ashore, given your association with Druadaen."

"Or my own extended absence," Varcaxtan added with a rueful grin.

"If you've no orders, there's no law against it," Firinne objected in a tone of finely honed irony.

"Yet," he amended.

She nodded as her eyes moved slowly around the faces ringing her. They stared back quietly. "Well," she muttered after a long moment, "don't keep me waiting."

"For what?"

"For the other shoe to fall." Her smile was genuine if weary. "So now I know that you came aboard unwilling to tell your tale because until you finished deciphering the moonfall plaque, you wouldn't know how it ended. Then you let slip that you're mourning your own sorry selves in advance." She shook her head. "There's something missing. So the moonfall plaque has stymied you and you have to see if you can get that untangled in Tlulanxu. Hardly a surprise, but more important, hardly any reason to be mourning ourselves. You'd be fools for sure to walk right up to the Archive Recondite in broad daylight, but it wouldn't be the death of you. So I ask again: what thing is so mournfully grim that you couldn't reveal until now? Where's the other shoe?" She settled back, arms crossed. "Let it fall; I haven't all day."

Ahearn nodded. "Fairly said. Here's as fair an answer as we have. As you say, in the last two days, we've had to accept we've naught but questions about the list on the plaque. Common sense tells us we'd be fools to still cling to the simple hope with which we started: that it will simply show us which one portal will lead us straight to Druadaen and Indryllis. Fact is, there's every reason to doubt such a thing is possible.

"But as we felt ourselves drawing closer to that conclusion, we began asking, 'if there's nothing useful on the plaque, then what?'"

Firinne's glance flitted toward Varcaxtan for a moment, too briefly for their eyes to meet. Never had Ahearn seen the bluff, redoubtable captain appear so tentative, let alone anxious. "There is a point," she began carefully, "at which one must consider the possibility that the failure to find a way forward is because there isn't one to be found." She paused, resumed as if trying to step around snares. "It can be difficult to mark that moment when one's dogged search for a solution is only a way to avoid accepting that all reasonable hope is gone."

"Well, as it happens, there may be a new solution," Varcaxtan replied.

"Which," Ahearn added, "has been right in front of us, unnoticed, from the very start." Firinne folded her arms, waiting for him to make his cryptic words more plain. "When we sailed from Shadowmere, we were set on finding folk who could educate and advise us in the matter of portals. Just the day before, Druadaen had traipsed through one, and Varcaxtan brought news that Indryllis had been left behind in the Nidus: home to the most lively of all osmotia—as well as a damned undesirable spot to be stranded."

Firinne held up a hand as she glanced at Varcaxtan. "What happened there?" she murmured, her voice barely raising above the sound of the sea on the sides of the ship.

Varcaxtan would not meet her eyes as he shrugged. "Don't know, really. Some of them got behind us. Don't know how they did that, either. The Nidus is . . . well, there seem to be more ways into and out of it than it has doors. So it may have more than just one osmotium in it. But to make a sad story brutally short, a few of those with us—the Guides and the mantics—were very familiar with osmotia. And since I didn't know that, I had less than no idea that they'd been sent along as a special reserve to ensure that we got the Hidden Archivist back home."

"Then why didn't everyone come back through the osmotium?"

Another shrug. "That's another thing I don't know. And there's been no great sharing of information regarding what happened elsewhere during the rescue. What I do know is that Indryllis and her group were deep in the Nidus when the rest of us were told to withdraw, that the Hidden Archivist had been rescued. When we emerged, we looked around, expecting those who'd reached him to be on the boats pulling us off the island. No sign of 'em. Not then nor later. But by the time we'd sailed back to Tlulanxu—and you know how fast *that* flotilla was—the Hidden Archivist had already returned."

Ahearn nodded at the end of the tale. "It wasn't until we finally reached Mirroskye—thanks to you—that we learned Indryllis was still alive. Unfortunately, the Iavarain puddle-gazers were confounded when it came to *locating* her: according to them, she was both on Arrdanc and not on Arrdanc. A puzzling bit of magical mummery, that. But we also learned why she'd been left in the Nidus: if the rescuers couldn't bring out the Hidden Archivist through the front door, they'd sneak him out the back—by changing the connection of the Nidus' portal."

"So why didn't she just run through the portal with the others who escaped?"

Elweyr folded his hands. "When we learned about what happened at the Nidus, I knew a great deal less about osmotia than I do now. But since then, I've seen hints that it's also possible to change the connection briefly. Any osmotium's parameters are a bit like gutta-percha: if you apply the right adjustment, you can stretch it to take a different shape, a different connection. But as soon as you let go, it snaps back to its original shape."

Firinne frowned, stared at Varcaxtan. "I find it hard to believe that Indryllis wouldn't have told you about being part of such a plan, given how much was at stake."

Varcaxtan sighed. "It's a sad truth that when we married, we had to promise our superiors that one of us would often be told—or do—things that couldn't be shared with the other. Usually, that meant her. On rare occasions, that secrecy ran the other way . . .

such as when I delivered a very special sword to this old wyrm." He poked R'aonsun, who rolled his eyes. "But when it came to osmotia...well, no information is more closely guarded. I didn't even know she had such capabilities, which was probably for the best."

He shrugged. "It certainly wouldn't have done anyone any good if I had—not that day. What I know about mancery would fit in the palm of a snake's hand. I was there as a soldier. So if one of us didn't come back, it was to be me." Varcaxtan's eyes became hollow. "It *should* have been me."

Firinne waited, looked from face to face, frowning. "So what is this new solution that's been in front of you all along?"

Ahearn shifted, hated to be the one to say it, but it was his job. "Well, at the end of the day, we still know where to find one portal that can be changed safely." When Firinne just frowned in greater perplexity, he sighed. "Maybe more than one, truth be told."

Her perplexity became more intense—and then transformed into horror and shock. "The Nidus? Are you mad?" As if appealing to the collective sanity of the others, she looked around at them...and saw the same graveyard faces. "You *are* mad. All of you."

The dragon regarded his fingernails critically. "I prefer the term, 'uncommonly resolute.'"

But S'ythreni was shaking her head. "Actually, Captain, I agree with you. Completely. We're mad. But me most of all, since I can see the lunacy quite clearly, and I'm *still* going to the Nidus, if that's our only option."

"An 'option,' you call it? It's a certainty—of suicide."

Varcaxtan tapped his finger on the table: a slow,

steady metronome. "Actually, we did it once. The return of the Hidden Archivist is proof of that."

"You call it a success when you lost as many as you did—and left your wife behind?" She blanched. "I'm sorry. I . . . I didn't mean it as it sounded. I meant—"

"You were speaking in the context of the mission, the cost," Varcaxtan said quietly. "Not my personal culpability. I understand that. However, we would have advantages that our rescue mission did not."

"Such as?"

"They were expected," Umkhira countered firmly. "Indeed, it may well be that they were being baited." She crossed her arms. "But now, it has been over a year, and there has been no sign that the Consentium is returning. We will be entirely unexpected."

"And I know the interior," Varcaxtan added. "And given that labyrinth, that will be a huge help."

"Also," murmured Elweyr, "we have a great deal of experience working in that kind of—irregular area. Forces trained for predictable engagements on a plain battlefield often do not fare so well."

Firinne sighed. "And when you get to Tlulanxu, you're in the best place to ask questions about the moonfall plaque and the Nidus." She looked around the group. "And I suppose you'll want a ship to get to that infernal pit," she muttered.

"It would be very kind of you," Cerven replied.

She nodded. "I just hope you know what you're doing."

Ahearn nodded back. "After a chat with Shaananca, I'm sure we will," he replied, then glanced at the sai'niin ring: *And if we don't, you'd better damn well let us know . . . and right away!*

CHAPTER FIFTY

Ahearn made sure he was on the fo'c'sle when, shortly after dawn, the *Swiftsure* began tacking up the long, twisting bay that ended at the Dunarran port of Trianthia. It was unusual among Consentium seaports in that it was not walled, but given steep coastal hills and sheer cliffs through which the waterway wound, it had proven unnecessary. Overlooking forts and ramparts were a constant reminder how utterly exposed a ship's deck was.

Footsteps mounting the stairs from the weather deck turned him around; Firinne waved away his quickly straightened posture. "Enjoying the view?"

"That I am," Ahearn replied. "The port just now peeked out around that rocky point. Pretty as a picture." He looked at her from the corner of his eyes. "But I still wonder just how *safe* it is."

She smiled. "You know, that's one of the reasons you're the leader of your lot."

"I don't follow you, Captain."

Firinne laughed lightly. "You're always worrying, and not just about your own hide. But to put you at ease yet again, we've nothing to worry from officials here. As I told you, all the suspicious and military folk are back there." She waved at the bay's defenses. "And while Trianthia sees a steady stream of hulls, most of the big cargos go the extra fifty leagues across the channel to Tlulanxu." She glanced at him. "What I can't figure is why you and yours insisted that we go here in the first place, since none of you knew much about it. Even Varcaxtan hadn't been here in a decade. But here you are, at the admirably calm port that you chose, and you're all nervous."

Ahearn laughed . . . convincingly, he hoped. "Ah, we're just jumpy, is all. Returning to Dunarra and all that. Not exactly friendly to our cause, if you take my meaning."

"I most certainly do, but then why didn't you choose one of the smaller port towns I suggested?"

Ahearn paused before beginning his rehearsed explanation. "Well, it's as you said when you pointed out those little cove towns. They were far less likely to have nosey officials, but a ship like *Swiftsure* was far more likely to attract attention." He closed his right hand more tightly around the rail, thereby hiding the real reason for their insistence upon porting at Trianthia: the sai'niin ring. Less than a week out from Dunarran waters, it had awakened and made it very clear that this was the best path. Though gods only knew why.

But still, the proximity to the larger, more developed, and more vigilant northern part of Dunarra made him nervous. "So, Captain, are you saying that the local authorities here won't bother to report our presence at all?"

She shook her head. "In every port, no matter how small, there's a harbormaster. And it's his or her duty to record all the traffic that arrives and leaves from their docks and anchorages. And inasmuch as *Swiftsure* is not a private vessel, but dedicated to Consentium business, it would be their position and reputation were they to miss recording it.

"But this is not a port favored by black marketeers or other suspicious craft, so Trianthia simply forwards its reports in due course. That usually means a delay of a week, maybe two, before the papers get across the channel to the people who would ask questions. And even if we put in at Tlulanxu, at the biggest, busiest, most scrutinizing port in Dunarra, it would still take a few days for the reports to be read." She shrugged. "Things being as they are, I suspect agents of the temples would see and remark on us first, but it would still take them a few days to learn what ship this is and who might be on it."

"So," she finished, "you've no reason to second-guess your choice of Trianthia. It's as calm a port as you can find, where nothing unusual ever ha—" Firinne blinked, snapped upright. "I may have spoken too soon."

"Why? What?" asked Ahearn, scanning the docks that had come into full view around the rocky drop that shielded them. He saw nothing "unusual."

Firinne pointed. "That's a very strange ship to see here."

Ahearn followed her finger. It was a three-master, high-sided for high seas. Just above the foretop crow's nest, a large pennant fluttered in the mostly land-blocked breeze: a white eagle on a black field with three silver stripes at the end of it. "It looks familiar, although I—"

But the captain was already heading down to the weather deck two steps at a time. "That hull's out of Teurodn. And those stripes means there's an heir to the throne on board."

"And that worries us . . . how?"

"Don't know if it does, but I mean to find out. Get below. Keep your lot there. I'll send word when I've words to send."

Ahearn led the others into Firinne's great cabin, minus Varcaxtan. Three men—in armor and clothes consistent with the regions near Teurodn and the far north of Ar Navir—were in stances of patient readiness: a posture quite common among experienced soldiers: the kind who never completely relax.

"I thought," Firinne said, standing in the now-open center of her quarters, "that they should be present for introductions. And for the news you bring."

The youngest of the three men stepped forward. "Our business here is—"

The tallest man touched the fellow's shoulder. "I shall be my own voice here," he said. "We are among friends—or so I mean and hope." He stepped forward, removing his hand from his subordinate's shoulder and offering it to Firinne. "I am Crown-Lord Darauf of the line of Teurodn, grandson of King Tandric V, and a sworn friend of your people, Captain Firinne."

"This I know," she acknowledged with a smile as bemused as his own became. There were a few more words exchanged between them—formal and formulaic—but Ahearn didn't hear them.

Because he knew the Teurond's name; Darauf had rescued Druadaen upon the north steppe of the Gur Grehar—the Graveyard—just a few moonphases before they first met in Menara.

The Crown-Lord's smile was wide and genial. "Your patience with the bothersome rituals of presentation is much appreciated."

Her smile became wry. "These are as an eyeblink compared to the recitations of lineage and position in some lands, Crown-Lord Darauf."

"Please, just 'Darauf.'" His younger aide stirred but managed to hold his tongue.

Darauf smiled as if he'd seen the fellow's reaction, gestured toward the older man. "May I present my aides, Osanric of the line of Aulenreur—"

A large man, Osanric bowed casually, with a smile almost as amused as his superior.

"—and Sut-Uldred of the line of Koronark. We bear greetings from the court at Teurhark and dossiers of new appointees to our embassy and secure correspondence for the Propretor Princeps, the esteemed Alcuin II."

Ahearn discovered his lungs were still working and was glad for it; the names that were being bandied about were of persons so elevated that he marveled he could breathe among such high political peaks.

Firinne nodded her gratitude. "You are very welcome aboard the *Swiftsure*. The Couriers would consider it a great honor and pleasure to provide any assistance or service you might find helpful. And my given name is Merrua." When they'd exchanged their last obligatory bows, the captain went straight to the question on Ahearn's mind—and no doubt, his friends' as well. "It is a singular privilege to meet you in these waters, Darauf—but also, most unexpected." She stopped shy of asking any questions.

Ahearn suppressed a grin. *Aye, yer a shrewd one, cap'n, You start the match, but he must make the first move. Well played.*

But evidently, Darauf had not come to play games. "Indeed, Trianthia is not my final destination within the Consentium, Captain."

"Oh? May I ask where that is?"

"Tlulanxu. I have sent our other ship—a swift packet—ahead with our bona fides and letters of greeting." He shook his head at Ahearn's and his companions' best, and apparently unsuccessful, attempts to render their faces expressionless. "Be at peace. I am well aware you have no reason to journey there." He smiled. "And probably, every reason not to." He waited. "Given what you seek."

Before Firinne could say anything, Ahearn stepped forward. "And what is it you suppose we might be seeking?"

"Well, it wouldn't surprise me if you were in search of a missing friend." Darauf scanned the group. "And perhaps his uncle, too."

Firinne stepped between them. "All respects to your king and your line, sir, but I'd be glad to hear why you'd make such a strange—supposition."

He sighed. "I've never had much patience for dancing—of any kind—Merrua, so here's my best attempt to make a very long answer very, very short. My sires are friends—in some cases, *close* friends—of your Consentium's Alcuin II and IV. Who of course are well known to Shaananca. Who was a guardian and mentor to Druadaen. Who I encountered out upon the Gur Grehar—the part we call the Graveyard."

Ahearn scratched his ear. "Well, that's as good an answer as could have been had—and with an hour's less talking."

Darauf smiled at him. "A man after my own heart, I see. But I wonder, is Varcaxtan about? I was led to believe it was likely."

Firinne raised a hand before anyone else could respond. "That's a fair question. But here's a consideration, before you press me to answer it. Let us suppose that you learned Varcaxtan's whereabouts, wherever they might be. And then let us say you were asked—well, 'leading questions' about him when you put ashore at Tlulanxu. Asked by persons you could not easily turn aside with a meaningless platitude. Let's say hieroxi of one of the Helper deities that are prominent in your own land." She paused, held his eyes. "If you prevaricated, would it not potentially compromise your honor, and potentially be detected as deceit, even as you accept the hospitality of Dunarra?"

Darauf's frown was clearly directed inward. "My question was rash. I withdraw it . . . and thank you for being a better guardian of my honor than I was."

Firinne offered a slight bow. "It is always easier to perceive such things from the outside. Besides, I suspect the reasons for your visit here would be equally inadvisable to share with anyone who might be in contact with Consentium authorities within the next, oh, two weeks or so."

He stared at her. "You might be right. And I take it you have no plans for contacting those authorities?"

"No plans whatsoever," she answered.

"Even less than that," Ahearn added.

That raised a smile from Darauf and lightened the mood all around. "Very well. I'm sure you've already deduced most of it and shall not be surprised by the rest. As far back as a year ago, I planned to visit the Consentium, but my father requested that I wait. He lifted that constraint several moonphases ago. I am not sure of the causes, but the change came from higher up the family tree. Much higher. It came with instructions that, in addition to visiting the Archive Recondite, I was to present my credentials to the propretors who caretake our alliance with Dunarra."

"Of course," S'ythreni nodded, her voice smooth and shrewd. "Just what a scion in the line of succession would be expected to do. Probably overdue, in fact." She smiled. "So: what is your *real* reason they sent you to Tlulanxu?"

Darauf's answering smile was genuine, but pinched. "Mine is a delicate mission. As most of you are probably aware, there has been a change among the temples in Dunarra. Historically, they have strictly refrained from intruding into secular affairs, more so than any other nation on the face of Arrdanc.

"But recently, that has reversed. They have not only become more insistent upon having information about, and a role in, the doings of the Propretoriate, but are increasingly removing themselves from any sort of concourse with temples from outside the Helper pantheon. And even from some of those within it.

"This is a deep concern to the king, but he is extremely reluctant to give unasked advice or even send a private delegation to address these concerns.

On the other hand, he can no longer remain a mere spectator. Word has come to the court in Teurhark that hieroxi of Helper creeds common to both our lands have been communicating more frequently—and less openly."

"Not a promising sign," R'aonsun muttered.

"Indeed not. So I am here much like bait trailed in the water. I am to make myself accessible to any and all leaders, secular and sacred. Merely seeing which ones contact me and which do not may tell us something. And any who actually invite me to visit them—well, official pleasantries often are shaped by political aims."

"Not for a thousand coins of gold," Ahearn said with a shake of his head, "would I want to be on such a visit as lies before you." He smiled. "You're sure to wear out all yer shoes."

Darauf smiled through a puzzled frown. "Wear out all my shoes?"

"Aye, from doing all that dancing you love *so* much."

The crown-lord chuckled, stepping forward and offering his hand. "You must be Ahearn, late of Menara. Now of the whole world, from the sound of it."

Ahearn shook the firm hand—almost as big as his own—while controlling the full measure of his surprise. "And how is it that you know aught of me?"

Darauf's squint might have been his version of a wink. "I did say my family knows Shaananca, did I not?"

"Yeh did . . . and yet, you just happen to be waiting for us?"

Darauf's smile widened. "Well, if I were to guess . . . she let my grandfather know that useful people would be bound for these waters."

"Oh, she did, did she?" *Nosy old magistra! But I'm glad she's on our side...whichever that is.*

But Darauf hadn't waited on his reply; he was already working his way around the rest of the group, shaking hands as he went. The crown-lord's youngest aide followed with a frown, the older one moderately amused at his discomfiture.

Darauf's steady progress halted when he turned toward R'aonsun. The Teurond started. The dragon-avatar raised an eyebrow in response. "I believe," the crown-lord said without a trace of banter, "that Mentor Sha'ananca is awaiting your contact."

R'aonsun's eyebrow raised slightly higher. "Indeed?"

Darauf simply nodded, continuing around until he reached Umkhira.

Who crossed her arms against his proffered hand. "I know your name. And your deeds."

The crown-lord lowered his hand, nodding solemnly. "I regret that spilled blood cannot be unspilt, Mistress Lightstrider."

Now it was her eyebrows that rose. "I had expected an insult, such as *'pekt'*—not respectful address."

He frowned, but not at her. "I have never used that word nor contemned your people—by which I mean the ur zhog known as Lightstriders."

"No: you just slew them—and thousands of our cousins!"

The group was very still. The younger aide's hand moved toward his hilt: noiselessly.

Darauf turned his head slightly, his eyes suddenly hard and disapproving. Behind him, the aide swallowed and recovered his hand to his belt. Darauf faced Umkhira again. "I do not even contemn those urzhen who dwell in the Under and come a-Hordeing among my people. But I do call them enemies. As they no doubt consider us."

"Yet some of my people have been among those hosts, and you killed them with the same readiness—and absence of quarter—as you did our urzhen cousins!"

The Teurond closed his eyes. "I would it were not so, but I know it has happened." He opened his eyes. "But since they were among your kin from the Under, I can only ask this: when your lands are invaded and your people killed, do you—*could* you—stop to sort out the raiders by their origins? Or do you fight—and kill—those raiders based on the deeds of the whole host?"

Umkhira did not unfold her arms, but her brow was not quite so furrowed as it had been.

"But," Darauf continued, "I know that you, the ur zhog of the plains, have been hunted—bountied— on your own lands. I swear—on my family and my honor—that such orders were never issued by the present king of Tar-Teurodn, my grandfather. I also know that simply refusing to order killing is in no way the same as issuing a decree *prohibiting* it. I further know that while many castle-holders and mayors forbade the bountying of Lightstriders, the power of those bans decreased as the distance from those authorities increased."

Ahearn inspected the crown-lord with a sidelong glance. *The setting of those bans: that's yerself yer talkin' about, or I'm a feathered fish.*

Darauf nodded solemnly. "For all those failures, and the deaths they caused, I apologize, Mistress Lightstrider." He drew his shortsword slowly and extended it, hilt-first, in her direction. "This was my great-grand-uncle's. It has been in our family for at least six generations; the earlier provenance of the blade has been lost." Umkhira's frown deepened again. "Material things have no value when compared to lives wrongly taken. This is but a means of marking, for all time, the apology I make today."

Umkhira did not touch the shortsword. "This apology: do you make it on behalf of your king or yourself?"

"I am not empowered to speak for my king. This is my apology to you. As one individual to another. I would be lying to say or suggest it has more scope than that."

Umkhira looked at the sword again, then looked away. "Keep your blade. Your words—and your eyes as you speak them—tell me what I need to know about you. And here is my answer to your apology; your own actions will decide whether I accept it."

"You speak as if you will be there to watch them."

She shrugged. "Unless I am very wrong, I will be." She held his gaze. "That, too, was in your eyes."

Darauf nodded somberly and re-sheathed the short-sword, oblivious to the stunned expressions on his aides' faces. He squared his shoulders. "Master Ahearn, she of the Lightstriders is quite correct; I am here to assist you."

"In what way?"

"In all ways that I may."

"That's a...a kind, but very broad, offer, Crown-Lo... er, Darauf."

"It is simply 'unconstrained.' Come, let's sit." The younger aide started forward; his lord stopped him with a slight rise of his hand. "There will be no ceremony here. Happily, in this place, we've no need of it. But ashore in Tlulanxu, I am a great-grand-nephew of the king, a high officer in the forces of Dunarra's closest ally, and known to be a modest scholar in my own right. And so, there will be ceremony." His smile at Ahearn was sly. "And all too much dancing. So if I'm to hop about as custom demands, let's put our heads together and see if there's a way to make good use of it!"

CHAPTER FIFTY-ONE

The dragon-avatar seated itself, assessed its comfort. "I am ready," it said. "No, not yet." The large body shifted minutely. "There. It is imperative that I have as few distracting sensations as possible."

Elweyr frowned. "Will being in contact with Shaananca be so much harder, this time?"

The dragon nodded. "I expect that to be the case."

Ahearn crossed his arms. "Even though this body is as healthy and strong as a prize bull?"

"Do not refer to herd animals; it makes me hungry. And yes, even despite the condition of this body. The difficulty is caused by the activity of the mind within it."

S'ythreni couldn't help smiling. "You mean the mind that you said 'compares unfavorably to a mollusk's'?"

R'aonsun's glare was histrionic... mostly. "You are Iavarain. I thought your people *invented* figurative language. Or is it hyperbole? Suffice it to say that my avatar's mind does not have to be particularly

758

perspicacious for it to complicate the process of contacting another. If it wasn't for my prior contacts with Shaananca, I doubt I could maintain my end of that thought-bridge for more than a minute, maybe two."

Ahearn *tsk*ed. "Ah, well, given the plan we've come to, it's a pity that *fullsee* isn't one of your dragon-tricks. It would make this much, much easier."

"How so?"

"Well, if Shaananca can see out of your eyes, and you can see out of hers..."

"I see your intent; we would not need to insinuate Cerven into the Archive as part of Darauf's retinue."

The Teurond crown-lord looked from one to the other. "That would make it unnecessary to perpetrate a ruse. Success—and safety from discovery—would be far more likely." He looked at the avatar cautiously. "I notice, R'aonsun, that you did not answer Ahearn's question in the negative. So I ask it, as well: Is there any chance that you might possess the gift of *fullsee*? Has a dragon ever attempted it?"

The avatar closed his eyes, spoke after a long moment. "That question stirs a memory I have had no reason to recall in...well, several millennia." R'aonsun shook his head in answer to the hopeful stares that were suddenly fixed upon him. "I never had a desire to learn it in my early years. And I certainly lacked opportunity in more recent ones. But now that I think back..."

"Yes?" prompted Elweyr.

"I saw two different moon plates in ages past, but on neither occasion was I allowed to study them."

"Why?" Ahearn asked, surprised.

"Among many likely reasons, I now suspect there was one that loomed over all the others," R'aonsun mused. "Perhaps it was known that dragons *could* read them, despite the deep-cyphers."

Cerven's voice was hushed. "You mean, that dragons might have innate *fullsee*?"

The round, heavy shoulders of the dragon's barbarian-avatar shrugged. "Would it be so surprising?"

"And just *when* were you going to mention that you might have the very skill we most require?" Ahearn almost sputtered.

"Possibly never," it answered somberly. "Understand: your varied species have often inquired after dragon abilities. It is how we discovered many powers we did not even know we possessed. Nor did we foresee that using them—either for your nations or for ourselves—might embroil us in your own struggles and, in the end, be blamed for causing them." His neck stiffened. "I have no desire to become the catalyst for a new round of demonizations. So I have no wish to determine if I have an innate talent for *fullsee*."

"What are you leaving out of your story?" asked Cerven suddenly.

R'aonsun stared at him. "What do you mean?"

"I observe speakers. I recall their voices, gestures, expressions in the context of what they were communicating when they spoke."

"Careful, now..." muttered R'aonsun sharply.

Cerven's voice became oddly flat...even menacing. Ahearn discovered that the hair on the back of his neck rose as the young man replied, very coolly, "Are you threatening me...Osrekheseertheeshrathhuu'aigh?" He pronounced the dragon's full name with the same sure fluidity as the ancient Uulamantre had.

The dragon-avatar narrowed his eyes. "No, I was not

threatening you, Cerven Ux Reeve. I do not threaten my *friends.*" His eyes softened, became almost vacant. "But it is so easy to lose friends . . . as time has taught dragons over and over again."

Cerven's voice was no longer icy and detached, but emphatic, almost beseeching. "I . . . we would never forsake you."

"You cannot make promises about what you do not know. And no, the problem does not lie in what you don't know about dragons; it lies in what you don't know about yourselves. About how fearsome knowledge and endless foreboding can change what you perceive in other species."

"And particularly in dragons?"

"Yes." The wyrm's voice was both sad and sly. "Even the most able and high-minded of you communal beings had uneasy relationships with my breed. Not that I blame you, given what so many of us became." He sighed. "You see, there is a legend that one of us *was* trained in *fullsee.* As the story goes, the skill did not prove to be innate, but once shown the way of it, mastery came easy to the dragon-mind."

"And what became of that dragon?"

"Nothing."

"Nothing?"

"Allow me to amend that; nothing*ness.*" When they stared at him, the avatar's face darkened with impatience. "Do you not understand? The outcome of that episode was utter oblivion: for the dragon and for thousands of your species.

"It had to be slain. It had too much power, too much control." In answer to their disbelieving stares, R'aonsun sighed and asked, "Can you not see the compounded implications? My breed can exert control over and read your minds—well, most of them. In combination with our ability to inhabit those with rudimentary intellect, that means we possess the ability to see and hear things in distant places, become the assassins or advisors of kings—possibly both.

"Now, endue that mind with a form of perception that effortlessly unveils the complete reality and shape of all things. It becomes a mind that can often look backward from effects to discover their likely causes. Or, by reversing that process, may hope to project probable outcomes from present conditions."

The avatar shook its heavy-boned head. "Legend says that particular dragon was chosen among all others not because of its power, or its cleverness, but because of its *virtue*. But amplified by that terrible power, its impulse to do good became like a roaring in its ears, shouting ever more loudly that it alone could set the world aright. Ultimately, it drowned out the most important virtue of all: humility. And so the dread legend of dragons as embodiments of annihilation was graven into memory; the most virtuous one started by wishing to make the world a paradise, but between the innate arrogance of our breed and the unthinkable power that was wed to it, its path led not to perfection, but delusion, derangement, and near-total destruction. In the end, it was either its survival, or ours."

Darauf frowned, puzzled. "By 'our survival,' do you refer to the species of your avatar: we humans?"

"No. I am not referring just to human survival. No matter the being, the danger was the same: dragons or humans, philosophers or farmers, there was no difference. Any being beside itself would eventually have proven to be nothing more than an impediment to its realization of a universal ideal. Which is to say, a universe empty of everything but itself."

He frowned and resettled himself, as if shaking off a bad memory. "This is a very dull conversation. I shall contact Shaananca now."

Darauf leaned away slightly as Shaananca's words reached out to them through the deep voice of the dragon's avatar. "I can feel that this is a struggle for Osrekheseertheeshrathhuu'aigh." She pronounced its formal name well, but with nowhere near the facility of Cerven. "So we must be swift. My welcome to all and I shall presume you would respond in kind. Now, to business. I am aware that you will need information from, but also about, the contents of several moonfall plaques. Most pertinently, the master list of osmotia. The repository here is the most complete known, and I have begun to identify resources I believe you will desire, but the process is much slower now. Much, much slower."

"Interference from the temples?" wondered Ahearn.

"No, Swordsman. They haven't the run of the Archive—yet. The problem is that without the Hidden Archivist, and since I cannot involve anyone else in this matter, all such sorting must go through my already full hands. Before we leave the topic, do you foresee any other needs?"

Ahearn discovered that all the eyes in the room were on him. "Any information on the Nidus would be most useful, Shaananca."

The dragon was silent. Darauf's eyes widened slightly,

the other two Teuronds grew pale. *Well, we could hardly keep* that *cat in the bag any longer.*

The avatar finally emitted a long sigh. "I was afraid of that. I presume it is the osmotium of last recourse?"

"It is. Perhaps Elweyr could explain why we—"

"No need. Osrekheseerthee—er, R'aonsun—has reprised the discoveries and discussions that led you to consider it. Do not mistake my tone as disapproving; it is worried. I hope another path presents itself. Now, I am told that a young Amitryean by the name of Cerven is with you at the moment."

Ahearn shook his head. *Damn it all, why do you even bother with Couriers when you know everybody's business faster than ships can carry word of it?*

Cerven had leaned forward. "I am here, Magistra."

"I am Shaananca, young scriverant. It is a great shame that the Hidden Archivist is not here for you to meet him."

"Er, but, if he was there, wouldn't he have to remain . . . well, hidden?"

The avatar guffawed; Ahearn imagined he could hear Shaananca's soft chortle behind it. "I suspect he would have made an exception in your case. Not many have perused half as many moonfall plaques as you have now. And soon, you will have deciphered some that have remained unreadable for many, many millennia. You understand that you will have to work swiftly?"

He nodded, then realized that Shaananca wouldn't know he had; the dragon's eyes were closed. "I do, Magi—eh, Shaananca. I just hope there is a way for me to slip into the Archive."

"Be at your ease, young scriverant. I believe we shall solve that very matter in the next few minutes."

"Before we do," began S'ythreni, "I wish to ask a question."

"Please, do so without preamble, Alva S'ythreni."

The aeosti's query was, for her, unusually measured. "Would it not be possible to avoid the complexity of bringing Cerven into the Archive if there was already someone there who was capable of *fullsee*?"

Shaananca's light laugh came out of the dragon-avatar like a rumble of distant thunder. "That question is as delightfully oblique as its true intent is obvious. No, S'ythreni, I am not a scriverant. Few mantics are, and even fewer sacrists." She frowned. "Possibly none, now that I think on it.

"Besides," Shaananca continued without pausing, "I suspect Elweyr already knows why the *fullseeing* we require cannot be provided by mantic constructs or miracles."

Elweyr turned toward the group. "Mantic *fullsee* would take far too much time and *manas*. The cognates that emulate it are so short that it would take several weeks just to distinguish the moonfall plaques we need from those that are useless to us. That's why Cerven's skill is the only way to achieve this. It lasts as long as he can concentrate and does not require frequent rest between applications of *manas*."

"Which brings us back to the challenge of slipping him into the Archive," Ahearn muttered.

Firinne shook her head. "We have problems to address before that one. *Swiftsure* may not enter Tlulanxu's bay, let alone tie up at the docks. This ship—and all of this lot—must remain hidden and their presence unsuspected."

The dragon's seemingly sleeping head nodded. "You

are more right than you know. These days, even I am watched, and it is entirely likely that if any of you are recognized, you would be followed—by temple devotees, if not the militia. And if you attempted to enter any but the most common, public spaces, I suspect they would petition to have you approached for questioning."

"Would such observation apply even to Darauf? Even when he's inside the Archive?"

"If you mean to determine if he might have 'escorts' who would learn of his interest in osmotia and moonfall plaques, you are quite right. And even if the temples' interest did not become overt—for fear of causing a diplomatic incident—the mere news of what he was researching is likely to spark swift and accurate speculation."

S'ythreni nodded. "Because Indryllis disappeared in the Nidus. So if anyone—*anyone*—enters the Archive seeking information on ancient portals *and* accounts about the Nidus, they'd be fools not to connect the two."

Ahearn sighed. "Aye, we'd be lucky to get to sea again before the Consentium's troops and ships were both hanging on our heels—or putting manacles on our wrists."

"Correct. So, as Captain Firinne has aptly asserted, the *Swiftsure* may not enter the waters near Tlulanxu, nor may those now aboard walk its streets. If you did, your mission would be over before it started."

Darauf folded his arms as he thought. "Would there be any way for me, or my aides, to remove the needed sources from the Archive, given my lineage and the millennia-long alliance between our nations?"

"No, because all the sources you require are housed in the Hidden Archive, from which no holdings may be removed. Under any circumstances."

Cerven had, quite independently, adopted an identical posture for his ruminations. "The moonfall plaques are incised. A rubbing could be made quite easily. That could be brought out."

"It could, but the Archive is closely policed, now. All objects leaving the premises are subject to inspection, including personal items."

"That is madness," muttered S'ythreni.

"It was also inevitable, given the increasing distrust the temples have for anything secular. And because we take steps to frustrate their intrusive actions, their distrust grows."

Darauf shook his head. "I fail to see a way forward. We will not be allowed to remove anything from the Archive. Nor can I access the sources within the Archive, since we must presume that I will be followed into it."

"Yes, but we can be certain that those watchers will also follow you *out* of it."

"And how does that help us—?" began the younger aide. Darauf raised a stilling hand.

Shaananca explained. "Since we must indeed presume that you will be watched, and whatever you touch examined, the actual quandary is no longer 'How may you remove sources from the Archive?' It becomes, 'How can your researches be conducted without being observed?'"

"With respect, Magistra, if this is not a riddle, then it is doing a most excellent job masquerading as one."

The dragon's avatar smiled, although its eyes remained

closed. "Riddles are often another way of saying, 'Seek the solution that is hiding in plain sight.' So, let us start with a certainty: the temples or the Propretoriate—or both—will provide you with assistants and scribes when you enter the Archive. These persons will no doubt offer to take any notes you might wish, as well as to copy passages from sources and like tasks. And there will be one or more accomplished observers and spies among them."

"But what would occur if your plans changed? Suppose—for sake of argument"—her tone had become ironic—"that upon debarking, you sent word that your visit would regrettably be much shorter than anticipated. Tell me: what manner of response do you anticipate this would cause among the officials in Tlulanxu?"

The older aide laughed. "They'd be running around like wet hens, each scratching to get their hour or two with an heir to the throne of Tar-Teurodn."

"I agree," Shaananca answered. "So it would be apt and useful if a large, collective event were hastily arranged so that all the officials who wished to meet with you still might—including those from the temples who have sent spies to walk in your shadow."

The younger aide folded his arms. "How would this be arranged?"

"Simplicity itself. Since—as your colleague observed—there will be more temples and propretors looking to meet the crown-lord than he has hours in Tlulanxu, it would be a masterstroke of convenience and cooperation if the Propretor Princeps were to ask for one of the many august institutions in the city to host a gathering. This would allow your lord Darauf to present his credentials to all major parties at once.

"It would, of course, require a sizeable structure with large open areas for such an affair. Which would give any temples vying to host this meeting an advantage. And those who most suspect the motives for his visit would undoubtedly be the ones who'd most enjoy vouchsafing the prestige of the event—as well as the profound convenience of observing him from within their own halls. And through their own spyholes."

You shrewd old bird! Ahearn mused appreciatively—before he realized he'd actually muttered it aloud. "Er, I—apologies, Magistra!" was his very late and very lame attempt to lessen the insult.

He couldn't tell if it was the dragon grinning or Shaananca doing so through him. "It is very kind of you to think so highly of my abilities," was her wry reply. "Now, let us assume that—by *sheerest* coincidence—this event falls on the same day that you have reserved for your researches at the Archive. So, you will have to leave it earlier than planned.

"Of course, you shall be detained that morning, and thus arrive late with your scribe and an assistant, having even less time to gather the sources you wished. When you lose track of the passing hours, it will be your escorts—assuredly the ones from the temple which is now hosting the event—who will endeavor, within the limits of diplomatic courtesy, to shoo you on your way. And so you shall leave, with them urging you on and functioning as your entourage and bodyguards, even as you are instructing your scribe's assistant how to finish a few last transcriptions."

She paused. "Now, do you really think that any of those temple or Propretoriate escorts will, in their distraction to ensure your timely arrival, give a single thought to monitoring the actions of a lowly scribe's apprentice? Would they even be able to justify it, since none of his patron's researches have been provocative in any fashion?"

Darauf was smiling, as was everyone else in the great cabin. "Of course they won't watch the young fellow. And if they were thoughtful enough to wonder if maybe they should, they'd also realize that doing so would also bring suspicion upon *them*—and those who pull their strings."

"So, young Cerven," Shaananca resumed, "you shall be apprenticed to the crown-lord's staff: an aspiring scribe soon to be a journeyman."

Cerven frowned. "I am not sure I will be able to affect a believable Teurond accent, Magis—Shaananca."

"You will not need to. Your credentials—if any ask for them—will indicate that you are finishing your apprenticeship under the auspices of Talshane of the Outrider Expeditionary Cohort. It is he who has arranged your final test: to serve under an heir to the throne of an allied state. And inasmuch as you were headed to Dunarra, he also elected to use you as a confidential courier for an advice packet to authorized parties in Tlulanxu."

"But . . . but," stammered Cerven, "that's a lie."

"In fact, it is not. It was he who sent you with this motley band, was it not? And I have received such a packet from Talshane two moonphases ago. The accompanying letter indicated that he commended you to foreign service, and named Tar-Teurodn as one of three excellent places you might gain that experience. And note my careful wording regarding his packet, which I shall remit to you upon your arrival: Talshane 'elected to use you as a confidential courier for an advice pouch sent to *authorized parties* in Tlulanxu.' There is no mention of their identity or the nature of their 'authorization.'"

Elweyr rarely grinned widely, but he did now. "That is as masterful a fusion of truth and misdirection as I have ever heard or read." While Ahearn felt a slow smile coming on—a match for S'ythreni's own—he watched the puzzled frowns on both Umkhira's and Cerven's faces. "There is no lie in that statement," he explained, "but it is easy to misread."

Umkhira frowned. "Those words may not contain a lie, but they are crafted to create misunderstanding in those who read them."

Ahearn shook his head. "No, Green Lass: only those who should *not* be reading them." When she looked unconvinced, he added, "So you're saying you've never left a false trail to confound enemies that might be following you?"

Umkhira muttered darkly, but nodded her acceptance—however grudging it might be.

Firinne was nodding in frank admiration of the ploy. "There's one last piece of the plan that must be set in place: Darauf's arrival."

The crown-lord's older aide, Osanric, shook his head. "That's been seen to, Captain. You may recall we had a second boat with us, an advice packet that we sent ahead to Tlulanxu, bearing word of the impending visit. We proposed no itinerary nor identified any particular interests, which gives us much flexibility now. It's enough that they know he's coming, that he's traveling with his staff, and under the graces of the king. And so we have ample room to adapt to this—or any other—plan that might have made use of our presence and the crown-lord's position."

"All considerations have been addressed, then," Shaananca said. Even through the avatar, her weariness was audible. "All know their roles in this. Darauf, how soon do you plan to sail?"

"Yesterday, Shaananca!" The crown-lord's smile was broad and winning, the very picture of a worthy scion who still retained a bit of boyish charm. "But I suppose I'll have to settle for this afternoon. If tides are with us and seas are following, we should see you in three days."

EPILOGUE

THRESHOLD

OFF TRIANTHIA

The great-room was brighter this time, the rising sun streaming in through the wide gallery window in the *Swiftsure*'s stern. They'd spotted the *Schkretlich*'s running lanterns just after midnight, but since meetings at sea could even prove tricky in broad daylight and good weather, she'd stood off at about a mile to wait out the dark. The tall Teurond ship had closed to a hundred yards by the time they'd awakened, had their boats in the water by the time they'd breakfasted, and now Darauf and Cerven were finally coming aboard. More than a week of waiting, uncertain of whether the plan had succeeded, had not improved anyone's temper.

However, even as the door to the great-cabin opened, Ahearn knew the substance of the news they brought. One glimpse of Darauf's face and he knew what the two had learned. "So, none of the osmotia on the list will work for us, eh?"

Darauf shook his head, sat wearily at the twinned

tables that Firinne had returned to the center of the cabin. "Rather a disappointment," he muttered, "given how smartly the plan came off. Presented my credentials, was feted, and in the course of watching which sacrists were most eager to play the part of the doting host, even learned which temples are the ones most suspicious of the secular leadership. Successful and informative in every way—except the reason we went to Tlulanxu in the first place."

Cerven had slipped into the chair next to him. "I failed to find what we needed."

"Or it was not there to begin with," the dragon corrected. The others looked at him. "While I was in contact with Shaananca, she shared some of her misgivings across our mind-bridge."

Varcaxtan crossed his arms irritably. "And you only think to share that now, you beastly wyrm?"

R'aonsun glared at him. "I would have done so gladly. It was Shaananca who prevailed upon me to desist. I don't recall the specifics, but it involved some typically human, weak-minded mewling about it being best for you to hear and ponder the results as a group. Now, to resume: Shaananca had come to fear that even the most complete repository—the one upon which the Hidden Archive was founded—is not so encyclopedic as we, and no small number of scholars, had hoped."

Elweyr nodded bitterly. "No detailed explanations or expansions of how the osmotia were made or how they should be altered—if, that is, they can be."

Cerven nodded his morose confirmation of Elweyr's synopsis. "Now that more have been deciphered, it seems that repositories are not expansive archives, but rather, vaults in which to store a narrowly focused collection of reports, lists, and even correspondence. Furthermore, some are written in other languages, only one of which I recognized. There are also words in those languages I *can* translate that are utterly meaningless. I saw hints of etymological roots and what might have been abbreviations, but I would have needed weeks, maybe months, to have formulated any guesses at their meaning."

Varcaxtan stared at the dragon. "Did Shaananca foresee those difficulties, as well?"

It was Darauf who replied. "I think she did. When I arrived, she used words and tones which suggested that, in the process of collecting the sources you asked for, she'd become less rather than more hopeful about the outcome of Cerven's work." He smiled. "Also, it is a pleasure to finally meet you... Varcaxtan, is it not?"

"It is, and the honor is mine, Crown-Lord."

"Have your friends not told you that here, I go by Darauf?"

"Yes, but it would have been disrespectful to do so without your leave."

"As if I would stand on ceremony with a friend of my father. Who sent his greetings, on the hope that our paths would cross."

"And please bear my regards back to him."

Darauf smiled. "He foresaw that reply. This is his answer to it: 'Come bring your regards yourself!' He may have said something about not using me as your errand boy..."

Ahearn continued to smile at the indirect reunion of friends, but realized, *Hey-oh, so Shaananca seems*

*to know the Teurodn king, and Uncle Varcaxtan cer-
tainly knows the king's son.* So maybe it *might* have
been intention rather than chance that put Darauf out
on the Graveyard to rescue Druadaen. *Aye, just as it*
might *be true that bunnies crave carrots.*

Cerven had resumed sharing the list of disap-
pointments. "And what I found most aggravating was
that what the coordinates actually signify was utterly
beyond my ability to discover."

"You mean they are yet another form of code?"

"No, the opposite. Apparently, their use was so
routine and their referents such common knowledge
that what they actually stand for was not explained
anywhere. But inasmuch as the first two coordinates
match the locations that persist today, it is only the
third coordinate that remains a mystery. But this was
our last hope for gaining any additional insight into it."

Elweyr sighed. "So as far as we know, the third
string might not contain any properties of the osmotia
at all. And even if it does, we have no better idea of
the nature of that information, how to extract it from
the numbers, or how it should be used. Assuming I
had the thaumates and the skills to do so."

Darauf signaled for and was handed a book by
his junior aide. "This may start you on the path of
gaining those needed talents, Elweyr." He passed the
narrow tome to the thaumantic. "Shaananca copied
it herself, immediately after R'aonsun allowed us to
converse with her, the last time we were in this very
room—er, compartment."

Elweyr took it carefully. "I presume the topic is
osmotia?"

"Yes, but rather focused, if I understood her

correctly. Cerven understands more and will explain when we discuss the choice before us."

"Ah, now we're upon it," Ahearn sighed. "The choice that means we're out of choices: the Nidus. Must say I'm still puzzled why a portal so troublesome as that one wasn't on the list."

"In fact," Cerven admitted with a sigh, "it was."

"But—why didn't yeh plot it, then?"

Cerven's voice was flat and bitter. "Because I didn't know it was the Nidus. It wasn't one of the few that had names. In fact, it was the entry for which all three coordinates were not fixed values, but ranges of them."

While Ahearn was still musing on the strange irony of that coincidence—*or is it?*—Varcaxtan, S'ythreni, and Elweyr began peppering the hapless scriverant with questions:

"Could that be a sign that it *does* have more than one osmotia?"

"Or that it only has one, but it changes its connection of its own accord?"

"Or that the osmotium changes both its location within the Nidus *and* its connections to other worlds?"

"Or perhaps that coordinate range is where it has been known to exist? That perhaps it has even been out upon the ocean?"

"Or maybe there was land in that place before the Cataclysm?"

"You mean," Ahearn said, exasperated, "the opposite of how Saqqaru just popped up from the waves? Except most of the Nidus' island sank beneath 'em?"

Cerven nodded at Ahearn. "As good an explanation as any, I suppose. It certainly has a very, very long history. As I remarked, some entries were written in an old language with which I am familiar. Many of the notes on the Nidus were written in one of the two precursors of that language: a very ancient tongue called Mrelnorasi."

The dragon perked up. "I know of that speech, but I never learned it. Even in my earliest years, it was barely spoken except as a secret language."

Umkhira nodded at Cerven. "And what language is it that claims roots in Mrelnorasi?"

"It is now mostly a scholarly language, rarely spoken today: Tsostzasos."

"That word sounds familiar," muttered Varcaxtan, head lowered as he searched his memories.

"That is logical," Cerven agreed, "it sounds very much like a word in the language that evolved out of Tsostzasos. The term can mean either 'scribe' or 'observer.'"

"What modern dialect is that?" Varcaxtan asked, frowning.

Cerven blinked, clearly having expected the Dunarran to have already made the connection. "Why, S'Dyxan, of course."

The table grew very quiet. "Of course," Ahearn echoed, his stomach knotting.

S'ythreni's query sounded like it had to fight up out of her throat. "Are you telling us that those *dsejtoq* S'Dyxan bastards made these moon plates?"

Cerven shook his head vigorously. "Of course not! The Mrelnorasi lived long before the Cataclysm, possibly alongside the Uulamantre. Very little is known of those epochs, but there is nothing to suggest that there are any parallels between the extinct Mrelnorasi and the present-day S'Dyxoi."

The dragon's voice was casual, even cool. "These Mrelnorasi addenda to the listing of the Nidus: could you discern what they referred to?"

Cerven frowned. "I cannot be sure, but I believe it was an ordinal ranking of conditional alternatives."

"A what?" asked Osanric, with a bemused smile.

"Erm, a sequence of preference among different options. So, it seemed to be a list that set forth something akin to: 'if not x, then y; if not y, then z,' and so forth."

Varcaxtan leaned forward, hands folded but so tense that the veins stood up from them more than usual. "You also gathered accounts about the Nidus, reports, did you not?"

"I did." Cerven stared. "But I presumed you would be the least interested in them."

"Why?"

"Well . . ." The scriverant's pause was agonizing. "Well, you've actually *been* there."

Varcaxtan shook his head. "That doesn't matter. Specifically, I'm interested in any sources that have been added since the rescue of the Hidden Archivist, and any from over a year before."

"The most recent you must already know; they were the basis of the information given to you and the rest of the rescuers. Two have been added since. But those from long before: why are you interested in them?"

"Because what I saw when I was there, I should not—cannot—expect to see again. As I said, the Nidus changes."

"In what way?"

"Before we shipped, I'd scrounged about to find other accounts, some kept as heirlooms in families

I knew. It might be more fancy than fact, but over time, many have claimed that its exterior has been altered, but there are never any signs of construction. And the interior? I fought through tunnels not so different than those we saw on the way down to Zatsakkaz. But some write that in the Nidus, they fought through passages that were more like an oversized rat warren, or a nest built by insane ants, or the inside of a supragant's guts—or made up from parts of each and more besides. All the hells, no one is even sure that the osmotium itself has always been in the same place."

Cerven nodded. "That is consistent with the accounts and reports I brought back. Some also mention messages scrawled on or carved into the sides of the passages, written in languages that have not been spoken on Arrdanc in tens of thousands of years. Or ever.

"The two recent reports were, I am happy to say, terribly misfiled: Shaananca's way of keeping them away from unauthorized or unfriendly eyes. They mostly concerned what the Hidden Archivist had seen and committed to memory while a prisoner there. Never before had so skilled an observer had so long an opportunity to study the details of that place.

"It appears that the Nidus is no longer, or never was in its entirety, a S'Dyxan stronghold. More recent conjecture suggested that it was not so much a place where their ward-pacters recruited infernal allies, but some kind of truce zone between them and whatever was on the other side of the portal. What the Hidden Archivist was able to discern was that there was an ebb and flow in the various beings which came through the osmotium, both in terms of their numbers and tractability. In his final assessment, he felt that S'Dyxan control of the Nidus was not simply complicated by that unpredictability but that there seemed to be an increasing trend toward conflict rather than cooperation and that the S'Dyxoi were losing what control they had."

"That may be the first good news we have had," Umkhira said with a sharp nod of her head. "A divided foe is a foe half-conquered."

Elweyr shook his head. "Still, we don't have the strength to press through a bear pit like that."

The dragon folded his arms. "No, perhaps not. Yet Shaananca was of the opinion that a few more companions might bring you to the point where your chance of success is optimal."

"A few more?" repeated Sut-Uldred. "I'd say a few hundred more!"

The dragon raised an eyebrow. "Shaananca projected—and I agreed with her—that if our numbers were much greater than they are now, our odds of success would be lower, not higher."

Darauf leaned forward, curious. "Why?"

Varcaxtan was staring at the tabletop, his voice unfolding the logic of those limited numbers. "If we are too few, then even a small enemy force could undo us. But if we are too many and attract greater attention, a larger force will come—and again, undo us."

The dragon nodded at its human friend. "Exactly her reasoning. And mine."

Ahearn nodded, turned to Cerven. "I was too much of a pillock to see what Corum and Talshane meant when they said you'd be the best possible help to our company. I don't profess to know or understand what clockwork contraption is always whirring between those ears of yours, but it has helped us puzzle our way through more unusual twists and find more hidden clues than I'd ever bargained on encountering. In a whole lifetime." Ahearn smiled, genuinely sad for what he had to say next. "We'll miss you in the Nidus, Master Cerven."

"But—"

"Sorry, lad, but this is not a debate—"

"But nor is it what Shaananca advised," Darauf pointed out.

Ahearn turned to stare at him. "Is that a fact, now?"

R'aonsun spoke softly, but also carefully. "She made the same quite clear to me, as well."

Damn your magic auntie, Druadaen! I'll not let her put this young fellow out as Fate-bait just to save your sorry self! But before he could frame a riposte, Darauf spoke again.

"Shaananca also anticipated that you—and possibly others—might be reluctant to take him into such peril. For peril it surely is. But, consistent with keeping faith with the role he played in the Archive Recondite, he now is truly my aide. And so, my charge. You need not carry the decision for this upon your shoulders." Darauf's gaze slid to Cerven. "That is how we may proceed, but only if it is met with your will, also."

Cerven acknowledged the Teurond with a long, respectful nod, but said, "If it is all the same to you, Crown-Lord Darauf, for now, I should like to remain with my captain, Ahearn." He looked at the stunned swordsman. "That is, if he will continue to have me in spite of his reservations."

Ahearn looked at Cerven's hopeful, trusting eyes—and

suddenly saw only those of his tad. And in that instant, one sympathetic thought pushed all others out of the way: *Keep this boy away from the Nidus and whatever hell-gate it houses!*

But then he became aware of the face around Cerven's eyes: the mature jaw-line, the resolute set of the chin, the toned arms. And Ahearn heard the same voice needling, *And so, are you sure it's really this lad you're roiled about? Or are you trying to save him because you know what it's like to be an orphan that doesn't get saved, hey? But this lad had mentors, learning, and a full stomach: not the life you lived. Besides, both his body and his brains are part of why we've come this far, so whatever we're fighting for or against, it's his fight, too. And at nineteen, either he grabs that nettle or should realize he never will.*

"Aye," Ahearn muttered, looking away, "I'll have yeh. Now, Captain, what about you?"

"What about me? You know I'm coming."

"I do, and I am more grateful than I've words to say. But the Nidus isn't the risk I'm thinking about. It's what might come after. First there's the nuisance of your being gone for a long sail halfway around the world—again! And secondly, it's a surety that there are tongues among your crew which will wag for want of care—or want of coin—upon yer return. Their tales could have you sailing back to Tlulanxu, but in the brig rather than on the bridge."

Firinne smiled at him. "You are kind to worry on my behalf, Ahearn . . . but it's an insult to my abilities. See here: I've foreseen and handled all these concerns, and a dozen more you'd never think of.

"Firstly, this ship is secure because its crew are

true sons and daughters of the sea. I haven't needed to replace a one of them in a year and a half. Which is fortunate, because I've spent a good part of that time sailing outside my circuit. If they were wanting release to shore, they know they need only ask—but none have. And they already have more than an inkling of what's going on, and that you—our almost permanent, unpaying passengers—are somehow at the center of it. Your half-known secrets are as safe with them as they are with me."

"Well, what about the ones who are, well, are more interested in the opinions of their creeds than they are of the Consentium?"

Firinne raised a vaguely amused eyebrow. "It's funny how few of those actually stay with this ship for very long. But I'm told they get very good promotions when they leave."

"That sounds like the work of higher connections. Theirs?"

Firinne leaned back. "Here's my answer to that question: what you don't know, and even what *I* don't know, can't hurt the people who help us from afar. Such as people who can move a potentially troublesome crewman to another ship before any trouble starts—and leave him happy with a bonus for his trouble. People who are both subtle and sitting on such lofty slopes that not even the sacrists can reach them."

Varcaxtan raised an eyebrow, glanced at Darauf before asking, "Young Alcuin himself?"

"Maybe," Firinne answered with a smile. "And maybe others beyond him. But that's all baseless speculation." Her smile said that it was anything but. "And so far as our unusual destinations are concerned, I'll continue to relay plausible, even likely, reasons why *Swiftsure* strayed outside her normal circuit."

"Such as?" Darauf asked with a frown. "My knowledge of things nautical is sorely lacking."

"Well, take our 'detour' to Trianthia. In the advice pouch that will make its way to Tlulanxu come the morrow, there will be a report that on our way to Tlulanxu, we found water spoilage and headed to the nearest deep-draught port that was sure to be able to replenish it."

"But," Cerven said hesitantly, "is that not a lie?"

Firinne smiled. "It is not, strictly speaking. I had my quartermaster inventory our water casks. One was found to have the kind of mold that can progress swiftly to rot." Her smile became an almost evil grin. "I grant you, it required a fish-lens to see it, but it was there.

"Next: Master Cerven, unless I am much mistaken, there's a sealed message for me in the pouch you brought back, is there not?"

Cerven frowned. "How did you kno—? Yes, there is."

"I'll continue to amaze you with my powers of prophesy," Firinne assured him. "Go ahead and open it. It will say, more or less, that *Swiftsure* is instructed to convey two other sealed letters to the Orex Islands. I am empowered to sail under my own authority to ensure secure delivery, even at the expense of speed."

Umkhira's eyes opened in surprise. "I have not heard of the Orex Islands. Are they Dunarran territory?"

It was R'aonsun who answered. "The Orexils are well to the east of us. They are not often mentioned. Which is quite strange."

"Why? Are they important?"

Firinne laughed. "You tell me! They are one of

Dunarra's three administrative regions and the second most populous. They are also the original home of the Connyl seafarers who migrated to Ar Navir."

"It's odd they don't figure more in our mercantile or diplomatic exchanges," Sut-Uldred muttered, chin cradled in his hand.

"That may be intentional," Osanric drawled. "Everything in the Orexils is far out of sight, and so, conveniently out of mind." His eyes seemed to twinkle. "Makes you wonder what might be there, eh?" His tone suggested that his question was purely, even ironically, rhetorical.

Cerven looked up from scanning Firinne's orders. "These instructions are just as you predicted, Captain. However, they specify where the two letters are to be delivered: Crysmaran and Nrulessë." Firinne smiled, nodded as if she had expected that detail. Cerven raised an eyebrow. "Why are these ports significant?"

"Because they have no Helper temples in them," she answered. "Which is all part of the actual objective underlying those orders: that our actions—and especially our *absence*—are the result of unremarkable, and very dull, duties. Those temples won't think twice about the *Swiftsure* not porting in their cities and won't have any chance to know you're aboard, since we'll fulfill those duties only after I bring you to the Nidus. Which gives you an advantage over almost every other piece on whatever game board you've now either stumbled, or been placed, upon."

Elweyr nodded. "No one even knows we're *on* the board."

"And that is how it must stay."

"Aye, but it comes at a price," Ahearn objected,

folding his arms. "Keeping our heads down means we've not been able to peer about for likely allies to swell our ranks."

Firinne nodded. "And those ranks may be thinner than you've reason to hope."

It was S'ythreni's turn to fold her arms. "By which you mean...what?"

"By which I mean that the *Swiftsure* cannot be jeopardized."

"Or involved."

Firinne's nod was pained. "They're the same thing, so far as the Consentium would be concerned, and I will not and cannot put your cause above my country and my oath. The most I can do is put you down in a boat, but only if you do not tell me what you plan to do, or where, or why."

Ahearn shrugged. "Well, seems to me it's a little late to claim that, even now. You've been in on our plans from the moment we mentioned the moon plates. Putting us down in a boat off the Nidus is the same as knowing we've put those plans in motion."

"In fact, insofar as mancery can determine, there *is* a difference. If I put you down in open water to comply with your unexplained request, and then return to that spot two days later, I can honestly say I have no knowledge of what you meant to do, or did, once I sailed away. Neither my crew, nor my orders, will bear upon anything you did. I am simply the ship that dropped off some passengers who may have had clandestine business of their own to conduct nearby. That is the only way to be certain that no examination of my actions, mantic or mundane, will show them to be at the pleasure or behest of the Consentium."

"So," Ahearn muttered, "whatever we might have to do at the Nidus, you can have no part of it. At a guess, you'll not join us in our planning, anymore, either?" When she shook her head regretfully, he nodded. "So, we'll be alone, come what may."

"Not entirely alone," Darauf said.

Osanric leaned forward sharply. "Let me go, my lord. The line of Teurodn cannot afford to lose so promising an heir."

Darauf smiled. "Who is also a very *distant* heir. And redundant: if anything were to happen to me, there are half a dozen more to step forward. But here, *here* I can make a difference."

Sut-Uldred's voice was shrewd as he observed, "And in so doing, advance your standing at court."

The older one looked at him sharply but had to nod. "I can't say he's wrong, my lord, once such deeds become known."

"*If* such deeds become known," Darauf corrected.

"As you say, my lord, *if* such deeds become known. But there are many who'd welcome knowing that a possible future king is capable of doing those deeds for honor, good friends, and a world with less evil in it."

Darauf grinned, almost amused. "Those are wonderful words that I'm hoping no one ever has to hear."

"Officially no one will," the younger one said, "but my lord, you know how rumors start in barracks, and how they can spread to—"

"Not in this case," said Darauf sharply. "It is *not* upon you to spread flattering rumors about me. It is upon you to make sure that such rumors are never spread, let alone conceived." He laid his hand flat upon the table with a soft, but quite intentionally conclusive thump. "We go without fanfare and, gods willing, return as quietly as we left." He let his eyes touch all the faces that ringed the table. "Our only pride shall reside in the new friends we make on the journey."

Ahearn, leaning back in his chair, met Darauf's gaze. "I'll not lie; I'm powerfully glad for the company. But I admit, naught you said before told me that you were comin' along fer sure."

The crown-lord answered with a lazy smile. "I thought it was obvious."

"Only thing obvious to any of us in this life," Ahearn answered, stretching, "is that one day we won't be in it. But there's no reason to rush that day along, eh?"

Growing grins were doused by the entrance of the most trusted members of Darauf's retinue. They were led by his armsman, who went by the single name of Wulfget. "My lord?"

"Be at your ease. What news?"

"All our cargo and gear is aboard and fit to the lay of the dunnage."

He rose. "Then let us wave our farewells to the *Schkretlich*. It's best if she were underway before the sun sinks further." He smiled at Ahearn and the others and was out the door, his aides and Firinne behind him.

After watching him go, S'ythreni leaned against the nearest bulkhead, chortling. "I'm on a ship of the mad—and me more than any!"

Cerven frowned in perplexity. "Why do you say so?"

She smiled. "How apt that it should be you who asks me."

"I do not understand."

"Truly? Look at us; misfits and mismatched from the moment any of our stars began to steer together. And all the more so, the more who join us." She gestured as she pointed from one to another. "A dragon who's decided to travel with humans. Then a master of ancient languages who is barely ready to grow a beard. And just now, the high and mighty of Tar-Teurodn make ready to travel in concert with a Lightstrider. All bound for a doom-mouth that the Uulamantre tell us is both in and yet *not in* this world." S'ythreni emitted a silvery laugh. "Is there any limit to the strangeness of our path?"

Glancing after Darauf, Umkhira's rejoinder was gruff and dyspeptic. "Apparently not. I'm hungry. Let's eat."

NEAR THE MAELSTROM

Sitting within a collapsible frame affixed to the first supragant's back, Druadaen turned to stare over its immense, rolling haunches. As he had seen many times since leaving the Armory a week before, Ancrushav was facing that direction, even though the tip of that granite horn had long since dipped below the horizon.

Druadaen cleared his throat. "I have seen that look on other faces. Many times."

"What faces?" Ancrushav asked absently.

"Leaders who'd been forced to make the hardest choice of all."

"What leaders were these?" Ancrushav asked, interest creeping into his tone. "And what choices?"

Druadaen shrugged. "Senior Outriders racing to leave a foreign land who had no way to take the bodies of the fallen with them. Ship captains who had to weigh anchor and sail out of hostile waters, some of their crew still missing on dangerous coasts or in unfriendly ports."

Ancrushav nodded but did not take his eyes away from the notional location of the Armory. "I swore a silent oath that I would never leave them, the Children and the others, not so long as they needed me. Yet here I am, far away and without surety of when—or even if—I shall return."

"You left to save them," Aleasha added, shifting so that she, too, was looking back along their wake of flattened grass.

"I did not adequately prepare for this, for being either slain or absent." His voice lowered in anger. "I made many mistakes, the worst of which I did not even realize until this day: that I did not make myself replaceable. In that way, they would have been better off without me."

Aleasha huffed in disdain. "That is a half-lie founded upon a full-lie."

Ancrushav turned toward her, his eyes wide at her flippant insult.

"The half-lie," she explained blithely, "is your claim of having made 'many mistakes.'"

"I made more than I can count."

"And for every one of those, you made a thousand decisions that were right, many of which, to my mind, border on brilliant. To ignore those is to tell us—but more importantly, yourself—an untruth about what you accomplished.

"Which brings us to your full-lie: that the Armory would have been better off without you. Steward is an excellent lieutenant, but *you* had the vision and the will to build what you did. And the part of you that knows the truth of what I say, of what you accomplished, will naturally insist otherwise." •

"I do not labor under the onus of false humility," Ancrushav muttered, eyes still wide to the point of distension.

"Oh, no, not false humility," Aleasha agreed archly. "Nothing so noble as that! You will insist that you are not a worthy architect of that unique refuge so that you will not be consumed by guilt for leaving it. Or by the grief of parting from those you know there." She stared back into his wide eyes. "I *would* say 'those you love there' but then I would have to hear you insist that as a serratus, you are incapable of such feelings—and I have neither the interest nor the patience to debate with someone who makes a steady habit of telling lies to avoid facing the truth."

Ancrushav's eyes opened even wider—much wider than was possible for a human; they looked more like those of a great cat ready to pounce. "I . . . How do you know this? I know you are a wyldwyrd, but—"

Aleasha shook her head. "Those arts did not give me these insights. *Tosh*, they haven't the power to do so! Shall I tell you the only reason it is so simple for me to see this so clearly?" She leaned so far forward that her nose almost touched his. "I see it easily because I am not *you*."

He leaned back slightly, his formal demeanor forgotten. "I do not understand what you mean by that."

"I mean that because you refuse to make yourself a king among those who wish you to be *exactly* that, and because you counsel against their adulation and worship, you cannot allow yourself to realize that without you, they would all have slipped into the abyss of madness and savagery just that much faster."

He looked away. "That is not...I have no such—"

Druadaen tilted toward him. "I suspect you prefer a hard truth to a pleasant lie?"

His eyes flashed at Druadaen. "Of course!"

"Then do not deny the hard truths spoken by Aleasha. It is a lie to deny what you are to them. Or that you are the reason the Armory became a place of refuge, of hope. Since the moment we arrived, we saw signs of your care and canniness at every turn. No, it is not perfect, but it is a miracle that it exists at all. And your part in it may be the hardest truth you will ever have to accept: that you are worthy of the honor they do you."

Ancrushav looked from one to the other, his eyes appearing human again. "Whether or not I agree with you, I shall admit this much: you are a most congenial pair. I am...unaccustomed to conversation of this type. But understand: though you both perceive much, you do not understand that my battle with pride is far greater than any you have known."

Aleasha cocked her head. "Why?"

Ancrushav shrugged. "I am serratae. It is in our nature to be extremely—*dangerously*—prideful."

Druadaen shook his head. "Then here is another hard truth. If the only way one can temper their pride is by insisting that they have no valid reason to feel any pride *at all*...well, then your fear of pride is still controlling you, isn't it?"

Ancrushav's red eyes narrowed. "Young warrior, I find it disturbing when you sound like an old sage." He almost smiled. "Useful, perhaps...but still disturbing."

"Yes," Aleasha put in with a crooked smile, "he gets like that, sometimes. Now, these supragants are starting to get lazy." She thumped the back of the one they were riding. "Without regular reminders, they begin dragging their feet, and we still have a way to go."

Once the supragants had been settled and the wolves set out from the camp ring at three points of a triangle, Aleasha approached Druadaen with the bag of tingle pods that she set out every night and then collected every morning.

"You are good to travel with," she started without preamble. "You have always taken on more than your share of every task. So I am puzzled why, of all activities, you have not offered to help me with these." She lifted the bag of tingle pods.

He shrugged. "When you first showed them to me, you spoke of them as being one of the ways that your wyldwyrding could protect us at night."

She frowned. "If I said that—or if it is what you believe you heard—then your fears have been unfounded." She raised an eyebrow. "But even if you believed that somehow I have altered them with wyrding before or after harvesting them, why would you avoid merely handling them?"

"Surely you have noticed I always stand at a distance when you are readying an effect of wyldwyrding?"

Her frown deepened. "Now that you mention it, yes, I have. But why?"

Druadaen synopsized what he knew of the strange way in which his mere presence could prevent a mantic construct from completing or even disrupt an active one. "I suspected this was the case here, as well. It seemed to disrupt the efforts of the sorcerers who attempted to waylay me. It may also have frustrated the Vizierate's attempt to determine if I was telling them the truth. But there are other instances when I have been less certain that it functions here exactly as it does on Arrdanc."

Aleasha stared at him. "And you never thought to tell me?"

Druadaen shook his head. "I presumed you knew. When we first met, you recall what occurred when you attempted to reach out to my mind? You said you could not 'reach' me. As the first mantic—well, wyrd—that I met here, I had not yet considered that such powers could differ so greatly from world to world. So, I presumed that you would understand what that signified, and that I had to stand back when you were creating your effects."

Aleasha's frown had grown deeper. He could not tell if it was at him or herself. Or, most likely, both. "Well," she grumbled, "I see it well enough, now." She blinked, looked up at him in surprise. "But you—you haven't realized how early others *clearly* knew that about you."

"What do you mean?"

"The animals that destroyed your childhood home, that orphaned you: whoever sent them *knew*."

Druadaen's stomach plummeted as vertigo threatened to rise up . . . but he refused to let it show in his face.

Lost in her own unfolding of those horrible events, Aleasha pushed on. "The attackers didn't use the animals simply because it allowed them to remain anonymous. It was also because, if they came too close to you, they would be rendered powerless. So they had to addle the wits of those creatures that were beyond the reach of whatever disruption you project."

Druadaen swallowed, light-headedness giving way to his focused recollection of those events. "That's why they had to kill Shoulders and Grip."

"What? Who?"

"Our horse and our dog." He nodded. "It's as you said just after saving me from the Touched: if you press an animal to act against its own intents or instincts, that weakens your ability to influence them. So if the assassins had come closer, the animals who loved us best would have been free to fight alongside us. And if they were too far away, maybe that's why their control wasn't complete. That would explain why Shoulders threw himself off the river-cliff: so he couldn't be forced to harm us. And it's why Grip moved as if every limb was weighted: because he was still determined to protect us."

Aleasha was looking into his face with almost doe-like eyes. "I am sorry. I should have thought..." She turned away. "I made you relive that terrible day."

Druadaen grasped her hand. "But you also helped me understand it. For which I am very, very grateful. I only wish I had some way to show how much I—" *Come to think of it, I do have a way.* He dug down into his rucksack, produced a handful of vials, and held them out toward her. "I have not thought of these since leaving the *Fur-Drake's Oath*, when I presumed that they would not be useful to a wyldwyrd. I should have remembered and given them to you sooner."

Aleasha frowned as she took them. "You have a strange way of reacting to those who cause you to relive grief."

He smiled. The pain of recollection was ebbing. In its place, his new understanding of that day seemed to be dissolving a measure of the helplessness that had persisted in its aftermath. He'd come to accept his inability to stop the attack—he was too young—but he'd continued to wrestle with the gnawing mystery of why it had occurred at all—a mystery he might now be able to solve. Assuming he ever returned.

"It's not such a grand gift," he told her, gesturing toward the vials. "Some, or maybe all, of them would be useless around me."

"I am aware of that," she murmured inspecting the labels. "But many of these have . . . considerable value." She looked at him questioningly. "In coin, I mean."

Druadaen scanned the horizon. "I do not see any likely purchasers nearby."

Her smile told him she knew that he would have done no different had they been surrounded by crowds clamoring to buy them. "And these were all spoils from defeating the three agents of Pagudon?" When he nodded, she studied the vials again and raised appreciative eyebrows. Noticing his attention, she lowered them into a frown of disappointment. "And these are *all* you have to give me? There are no more?" she complained.

Druadaen happily played along. "In fact, there are more. But I had to leave the rest behind when I came ashore at Agpetkop, including a considerable mass of tomes, papers, and maps of places of which I have no knowledge. Although they seem useless at the moment, perhaps they shall prove to have some value later on."

Aleasha stared at him in wonder. "And where is all this hidden?"

"It is not hidden but in storage, under the care

of captain Lorgan R'Mura of the *Fur-Drake's Oath.*"

Aleasha gaped, then cried out, "It exists?"

Druadaen recoiled from her sudden outburst. "What do you mean? The ship? Is there word that it sank?"

Ancrushav had evidently overheard; he'd approached and was now studying Druadaen with the practiced gaze of a person who assesses sane people for signs of impending madness. "The ship you name—Aleasha apparently harbors hope that it is the one out of legend."

"What do you mean?"

"Are my words unclear? There is a legend of a ship by that name. It was the hull of heroes and carried them on many great deeds, journeys, and quests." He shook his head. "But it is just a legend."

"And how do *you* know that?" Aleasha retorted, almost poking her finger into Ancrushav's massive and strangely angular chest. "Were you there? And besides"—she rotated so that her finger was now aimed at Druadaen—"legend or not, if the present owner of the *Fur-Drake's Oath* is *not* a liar, I will take the time—and risk—of seeking him out." She frowned. "I knew you liked him and felt he was honorable... but I did not know you had put so much of your fortune—and future—in his hands. It sounds like you would trust him with your life."

"I would. Without question. But why are you so determined to meet him?"

She sent a fierce glare southward. "Because if he's not a liar, that means that he *was* the one who destroyed Tharn's fleet, eliminated Kaande's mad prince, and slowed the civil war in that land. And so, he might have deeper knowledge about how and why the Temple of Disfa, the mad death-vowed *sfadulm* of its Nightfall cult, the throne of Tharn, and Pagudon are coordinating apparently separate efforts to crush the Shield of Morba."

She stored the vials in her own rucksack and caught up the bag with which she'd approached him in the first place. "Now, help me with the rest of these tingle pods; they won't place themselves!"

Druadaen stared at the fire, wondered if he should add another brick of peat: the Godbarrows' answer to wood. He'd need it—for light, if not warmth—if he meant to complete his journal entry.

But tonight, for whatever reason, the words that usually flowed so swiftly from his pen—or here, a graphite stylus—were dripping as slowly as syrup in winter. He had the early watch, and for the first night since setting out for the Mael, he welcomed the fire's glow as well as its warmth. No amount of assurance quelled his concern about attracting predators with the light, even though Aleasha offered a very convincing report from her wolves. In short, the closer they came to their destination, the less wildlife they encountered. Which was to be expected, Druadaen mused, since wild animals are too smart to remain near the lairs of murderous monsters. *That is the sole province of we "intelligent" species.*

But the wolves' noses and eyes had not misled them yet, and judging from the past two nights, the lands about them were as still and silent as a tomb. Again, not a particularly reassuring image, so Druadaen elected to review what he'd written. Perhaps that would decide him on whether there was reason enough to struggle to commit more unwilling words to the page.

He read:

I am mindful that this may be my final entry. Thinking back, I cannot recall if I have ever written that sentence before. The journal of my travels on Arrdanc was left with those who remain there. And who I dearly miss.

As we journey to confront a scourge that my world unwittingly sent to this one, I find myself contemplating threads that seem to join the two. Elements in each that initially seemed unconnected are beginning to weave together into an elusive pattern, a shared tapestry. Or perhaps it is not a tapestry, but a noose that—while certainly sufficient for my neck—could still prove large enough to encompass this whole world. And maybe others as well.

But just as there is a vague, linked menace winding through much of what I have encountered here, I also reflect on the many mysteries that seem not merely benign, but possibly revealing. For instance, I wonder what the Lady would say about the serendipity(?) of my meeting both Lorgan and Ancrushav: two clear connections between our worlds through the medium of the Tualarans. And so I must wonder: is it chance that Corum, her lieutenant (if that's what he is), is also a Tualaran? Is the echo of that people on Hystzos an indicator that they have an understanding of portals that is even greater than—

A loud snort and a louder sneeze erupted well beyond the camp circle. Druadaen dropped his journal, grabbed his sword, kicked waiting dirt onto the peat, and swerved after the youngest of the wolves. It had already disappeared into the tall grass; the rest were hard behind it.

As Druadaen followed their swift, ghostly shadows into the brush, growls and snarls rose along with a deep roar. Dim in the light of the tiny moons, a patch of the otherwise motionless sward surged and thrashed with violent movement. Druadaen angled toward it, sword in one hand, the other out to recover balance in the event of rough footing he wouldn't discover until he was about to fall.

As he reached the edge of the waving grasses, a startled yip became the rapid, desperate cries of a badly wounded canine—and he almost tumbled over the young wolf. It was dragging itself away from the scene of combat, but making little progress; its front left paw was missing and the bone protruding from that leg was splintered and glistening in pulses. A severed artery was coating it in blood, again and again.

Druadaen heard the grunting and roaring sound rotating away from him. Having dispatched the wolf, the enemy was turning toward the others. Meaning that the last thing it would expect is—

Druadaen bounded forward, bringing his sword into a high guard, looking for any moving shadow that wasn't a wolf. He glimpsed a broad, squat shape, and using the momentum of his charge, drove his sword into it, and quickly sprang to the side.

Which very possibly saved his life. The creature, although heavy, had breathtakingly swift reactions. The jaws—part frog, part baby hippo, but not truly either—snapped down just behind his leg. He took another step, turned to face it—but never got the chance. His thrust had inflicted a deep, gushing wound of putrid ichor, and the wolves wasted no time seizing the advantage. By dodging in, wrenching at its six legs, and then getting clear before the slowing creature could fully turn on them, they reduced it to a stumbling ruin of wounds. By the time Druadaen could be sure of not striking one by mistake, his blade was no longer essential.

The reason for their withdrawal became evident a moment later; Aleasha appeared, waving them off. She studied the creature for a moment, then, with surprising speed, drew her slender sword and drove it into one of its lambent eyes. It shuddered, snapped once at the air and collapsed. She turned, released the wolves with a gesture. Growling and snarling, they leaped back to ensure that if there was any life left in the monster, they'd pull it out with their teeth.

Only one followed her to the dying wolf. She kneeled beside it, held its head. It roused, licked at her hands, whimpered once, sighed, and did not breathe again.

When Aleasha looked up, her eyes were pools of moonlit tears that did not run down her cheeks as she glanced over at the charnel heap the wolves had left behind. "This beast is not a product of Change. It is otherworldly. It's smell is . . . very wrong. Too wrong to have come from the breeds of Hystzos. I presume you do not recognize it either?"

Druadaen resisted the urge to hold his nose against the growing stench. "I do not. And I have never seen anything do that." He pointed; a vapor was rising up from its savaged gut. It wasn't simply moisture or a release of gases and fluids; it was already beginning to deliquesce, and doing so with extraordinary speed.

Aleasha stood as Ancrushav appeared. "I have the supragants in hand," he reported. "There are no other attackers nearby." He looked at the now fuming remains of the monster. "What is that?"

"I was hoping you might know," Aleasha said.

He shook his head. "I do not. But I suspect I know who does."

They followed his eyes toward the northern horizon. A dim red glow limned a small stretch of it. It was so faint that Druadaen could easily have thought he was imagining, rather than seeing it. He wondered if, had they not had the peat fire, they would have seen it before the attack.

"The Mael," Aleasha whispered, announcing what he had already deduced. "We were closer than we knew."

"Or we can see it from afar because it is fully aflame," Ancrushav countered. He glanced at Druadaen. "Either way, we must assume that the priestess might have been looking through its eyes, or at least, will know that this creature is no more."

"If so," Druadaen wondered, "would she not have withdrawn it rather than send it to attack? This way, she has shown us she knows of our approach."

Ancrushav shrugged. "I agree that would be her likely course of action, which in turn suggests that she had only the faintest of mantic ties to this creature, if any. But we cannot afford to *presume* either is true."

Druadaen nodded, sheathed his sword. "How many leagues to the Maelstrom, would you guess?"

The serratus's irises changed shape slightly. "No more than seven. Perhaps as few as four. It is impossible to be more precise without knowing the size of that fire. Either way, we should get as much sleep as we may."

Aleasha nodded. "Agreed. There is nothing nearby. The wolves have already ranged far and found neither tracks nor spoor. This creature is the first living thing to pass this way in a week." She looked over her shoulder at the glow. "And it's simple enough to understand why."

She turned and walked back to the camp circle, where the supragants were lowing anxiously.

As Druadaen watched her go, the velene pulsed. He expected it to spring up, but it remained in the shape of a bracer. "What?" he muttered. "Are you that eager to get there?"

When it did not respond in any way, he turned back toward the red glow on the horizon. For an instant, he perceived it as a bloody, mostly lidded eye, staring up out of the Vortex of Worlds behind it.

Aware of how ludicrous and pointless it was to return that imaginary stare, Druadaen did so nonetheless. *And tomorrow,* he thought, *we'll cut straight down into you.*

As far as we can go.

AT THE NEXUS OF TIME AND SPACE

The human spoke. "What? Are you that eager to get there?"

The *velene*-object gauged the human's resolve and that of its companions.

Satisfied, it reached out to the *quelsuur*-object:

✧   ✧   ✧

Those with whom I travel approach the decoherence point.

> As do those with
> whom I travel.

*

Is the timing propitious?

*

> My assessment lacks
> the clarity of yours.

*

Explain.

*

> This group's selected decoherence point
> not only violates the law of balance; it
> exerts a further, unfamiliar violation.
>
> Take my perceptions for your own.

*

*I perceive. That group's
decoherence point also
violates the laws of
sequence and consequence.*

I must embody the timing.

✿

> *You must embody
> the timing.*

✿

✿

> We are in concord,
> they harmonized.

Poised at the cusp of resynchrony, they awaited
the proper moment.

At the End of the Journey   HC: 978-1-9821-2522-6 • $25.00
Six mismatched teenagers and their crusty British captain
were out at sea when the world ended. Now, they must step
up to leadership or face disaster.

THE VORTEX OF WORLDS SERIES
This Broken World   HC: 978-1-9821-2571-4 • $25.00
PB: 978-1-9821-9232-7 • $9.99
Fate has plans for Druadaen, a young man destined to
become a military leader when he begins to question every-
thing about the world as he knows it . . .

Into the Vortex   HC: 978-1-9821-9247-1 • $26.00
Druadaen remains determined to uncover "the truth of the
world"—which might only be gained by travelling beyond
it. But powers on Arrdanc don't want him to succeed. In
fact, they'd rather Druadaen doesn't return at all.

OTHER TITLES
Mission Critical   TPB: 978-1-9821-9260-0 • $18.00
(with Griffin Barber, Chris Kennedy, and Mike Massa)
Major Rodger Y. Murphy should have died when his heli-
copter crashed off the coast of Mogadishu in 1993. Instead,
he woke up in 2125, 152 light-years from home . . .

GREGORY FROST

"Gregory Frost brings real magic to *RHYMER!* The novel is a mystical blend of ancient folklore, new ideas, dynamic action, and real surprises. Very highly recommended!"
—Jonathan Maberry, *NY Times* best-selling author

RHYMER
HC: 978-1-9821-9266-2 • $25.00

He's known by many names over time—Tam Lin, Robin Hood, and numerous other incarnations reaching into the present—but at his heart he is still True Thomas, one man doing all he can to save us all from a powerful foe.

Rhymer reimagines Thomas the Rhymer, legendary twelfth-century figure of traditional Scottish balladry, as a champion who must battle the alien race thought to be elves and faeries—hell-bent on conquering our world. This saga pits Thomas against the near-immortal elves, first with only his wits, then with powers of his own that enable him to take on these evil creatures throughout the centuries.

RHYMER: HOODE
HC: 978-1-9821-2541-7
COMING JULY 2024

It's been nearly a century since Thomas Rimor last battled Yvag knights. In that time his wife and daughter have grown old and died, and he has discovered that he ages not at all. The elven world believes him long dead. In his grief, he has retreated to the depths of Sherwood and Barnsdale Forests and became a hermit, lost in his memories, his grief.

But when a dying outlaw arrives on his doorstep with items stolen from an Yvag skinwalker, it sets in motion events that thrust Thomas back into the world. To keep his true identity hidden from the Yvags, he creates an alter-ego named Robyn Hoode, whose exploits, unbeknown to Thomas, are about to become the stuff of legend.

HOWARD ANDREW JONES

Lord of a Shattered Land
TPB: 978-1-9821-9347-8 • Coming June 2024

The Dervan Empire has at last triumphed over Volanus, putting the great city to the torch, its treasures looted, temples defiled, and fields sown with salt. But hope is not lost. Hanuvar, last and greatest general of Volanus, still lives and, driven by a singular purpose, will find what remains of his people who were carried into slavery across the empire, and free them from subjugation by any means necessary.

The City of Marble and Blood
HC: 978-1-9821-9294-5 • $26.00 US/$34.00 CAN

Hanuvar had pledged to find the remnants of his people, scattered into slavery across the whole of the peninsula. This time he had no army to help him. Arrayed against them were the mighty legions, the sorcerous Revenants, and the wily Metellus of the Praetorian guard, ever alert to seize advantage. Worst of all, a magical attack had left Hanuvar with a lingering curse that might change him forever . . . or lead him to an early grave.

Shadow of the Smoking Mountain
Coming October 2024!

THE ECCENTRICS

Powered by science and steam, the Eccentrics travel the world in their airship, but something new threatens the Gestalt, a timeline of the future that never was. Will John and Knight Watch be able to navigate a world of clockwork and science to save the day?

TPB: 978-1-9821-9339-3 • $18.00 US / $25.00 CAN

THE SPIRITBINDER SAGA
WRAITHBOUND

Rae Kelthannis has always dreamed of being a stormbinder like his father, with an air elemental stitched into the fabric of his soul and the winds of heaven at his command. Those dreams died when his father fell into disgrace and was banned by the justicars of the Iron Council. When Rae's attempt to stitch an air elemental to his and he instead binds himself to a mysterious wraith, things get complicated and the world starts to fall apart around him. Literally.

"Tim Akers' *Wraithbound* is everything you want in an epic fantasy: engaging characters, intricate worldbuilding, plenty of action and adventure. You can't go wrong with this book."
—Charlaine Harris, #1 *NY* Times best-selling author of
The Southern Vampire Mysteries

"This heart-pounding series opener from Akers (*Wraithbound*) launches young Rae Kelthannis on a career as a spiritbinder . . . Akers slowly reveals the secrets of this world while leaving plenty to be explored in future volumes. Epic fantasy fans of all ages will look forward to Rae and Lalette's next adventure."
—Publishers Weekly